LITANY

OF THE

LONG SUN

LITANY
OF THE
LONG SUN

NIGHTSIDE THE LONG SUN

LAKE OF THE LONG SUN

GENE WOLFE

GuildAmerica
Books

Published by arrangement with
Tor Books
Tom Doherty Associates, Inc.
175 Fifth Avenue
New York, NY 10010

Tor® is a registered trademark
of Tom Doherty Associates, Inc.

ISBN 1-56865-096-5

Printed in the United States of America

CONTENTS

CONTENTS

NIGHTSIDE
THE
LONG
SUN

This book is dedicated to Joe Mayhew
for at least a dozen reasons.

CHAPTER 1

THE MANTEION
ON SUN STREET

Enlightenment came to Patera Silk on the ball court; nothing could ever be the same after that. When he talked about it afterward, whispering to himself in the silent hours of the night as was his custom—and once when he told Maytera Marble, who was also Maytera Rose—he said that it was as though someone who had always been behind him and standing (as it were) at both his shoulders had, after so many years of pregnant silence, begun to whisper into both his ears. The bigger boys had scored again, Patera Silk recalled, and Horn was reaching for an easy catch when those voices began and all that had been hidden was displayed.

Few of these hidden things made sense, nor did they wait upon one another. He, young Patera Silk (that absurd clockwork figure), watched outside a clockwork show whose works had stopped—tall Horn reaching for the ball, his flashing grin frozen in forever.

—dead Patera Pike mumbling prayers as he slit the throat of a speckled rabbit he himself had bought.

—a dead woman in an alley off Silver Street, and the people of the quarter.

—lights beneath everyone's feet, like cities low in the night sky. (And, oh, the rabbit's warm blood drenching Patera Pike's cold hands.)

—proud houses on the Palatine.

—Maytera Marble playing with the girls, and Maytera Mint wishing she dared. (Old Maytera Rose praying alone, praying to Scalding Scylla in her palace under Lake Limna.)

—Feather falling, not so lightly as his name implied, shoved aside by Horn, not yet quite prone on the crumbling shiprock blocks, though shiprock was supposed to last until the end of the whorl.

—Viron and the lake, crops withering in the fields, the dying fig and the open, empty sky. All this and much else besides, lovely and appalling, blood red and living green, yellow, blue, white, and velvet black, with minglings of other colors and of colors he had never known.

* * *

Yet all these were as nothing. It was the voices that mattered, only the paired voices (though there were more, he felt sure, if only he had ears for them) and all the rest an empty show, shown to him so that he might know it for what it was, spread for him so that he might know how precious it was, though its shining clockwork had gone some trifle awry and must be set right by him; for this he had been born.

He forgot the rest at times, though at others all these things would reoccur to him, rough truths cloaked in a new certainty; but he never forgot the voices that were in fact but one voice, and what they (who were one) had said; never forgot the bitter lesson, though once or twice he tried to push it away, those fell words heard as Feather fell, poor little Feather, as the rabbit's hot blood spilled from the altar, as the First Settlers took up the homes prepared for them in this familiar Viron, as the dead woman seemed to stir, rags fluttering in the hot wind born halfway 'round the whorl, a wind that blew ever stronger and wilder as clockwork that had never really stopped began to turn again.

"I will not fail," he told the voices, and felt he lied, yet felt the approbation, too.

And then.

And then . . .

His left hand moved, snatching the ball from Horn's very fingers.

Patera Silk spun about. The black ball flew like a black bird, straight through the ring at the opposite end of the ball court. It struck the hellstone with a satisfying thump and an irruption of blue sparks, and threaded the ring a second time as it bounced back.

Horn tried to stop him, but Patera Silk knocked him sprawling, caught the ball again, and smoked it in for a second double. The monitor's chimes sang their three-note paean, and its raddled gray face appeared to announce the final score: thirteen to twelve.

Thirteen to twelve was not a bad score, Patera Silk reflected as he took the ball from Feather and stuffed it into a trousers pocket. The bigger boys would not be too downcast, while the smaller boys would be ecstatic.

This last, at least, was already quite apparent. He repressed the impulse to hush them and lifted two of the most diminutive onto his shoulders. "Back to class," he announced. "Class for all of you. A little arithmetic will do you good. Feather, throw Villus my towel, please."

Feather, one of the larger small boys, obliged; Villus, the boy perched upon Silk's right shoulder, managed to catch it, though not deftly.

"Patera," Feather ventured, "you always say there's a lesson in everything."

Silk nodded, mopping his face and rubbing his already disheveled yellow hair. He had been touched by a god! By the Outsider; and although the Outsider was not one of the Nine, he was an undoubted god nevertheless. This, *this* was enlightenment!

"Patera?"

"I'm listening, Feather. What is it you want to ask?" But enlightenment was for theodidacts, and he was no holy theodidact—no gaudily painted gold-crowned figure in the Writings. How could he tell these children that in the middle of their game—

"Then what's the lesson in our winning, Patera?"

"That you must endure to the end," Silk replied, his mind still upon the Outsider's teaching. One of the hinges of the ball-court gate was broken; two boys had to lift the gate to swing it, creaking, backward. The remaining hinge would surely break too, and soon, unless he did something. Many theodidacts never told, or so he had been taught in the schola. Others told only on their deathbeds; for the first time he felt he understood that.

"*We* endured to the end," Horn reminded him, "but we lost just the same. You're bigger than I am. Bigger than any of us."

Silk nodded and smiled. "I did not say that the only object was to win."

Horn opened his mouth to speak, then shut it again, his eyes thoughtful. Silk took Goldcrest and Villus from his shoulders at the gate and dried his torso, then reclaimed his black tunic from the nail on which he had hung it. Sun Street ran parallel to the sun, as its name indicated, and as usual at this hour it was blazing hot. Regretfully, he pulled his tunic over his head, smelling his own sweat.

"You lost," he remarked to Villus once the stifling tunic was in place, "when Horn got the ball away from you. But you won when everyone on our team did. What have you learned from that?"

When little Villus said nothing, Feather answered, "That winning and losing aren't everything."

The loose black robe followed the tunic, seeming to close about him. "Good enough," he told Feather.

As five boys shut the court gate behind them, the faint and much-diffused shadow of a Flier raced down Sun Street. The boys glared up at him, and a few of the smallest reached for stones, though the Flier was three or four times higher than the loftiest tower in Viron.

Silk halted, raising his head to stare upward with a long-felt envy he struggled to suppress. Had he been shown the Fliers, among his myriad, leaping visions? He felt he had—but he had been shown so much!

The disproportionate, gauzy wings were nearly invisible in the glare of the unshaded sun, so that it seemed that the Flier flew without them, arms outstretched, feet together, an uncanny figure black against the burning gold.

"If the Fliers are human," Silk admonished his charges, "it would surely be evil to stone them. If they are not, you must consider that they may be higher than we are in the spiritual whorl, just as they are in the temporal." As an afterthought he added, "Even if they *are* spying on us, which I doubt."

Had they, too, achieved enlightenment, and was that why they flew? Did some god or goddess—it would be Hierax, perhaps, or his father, sky-ruling Pas—teach those he favored the art of flight?

The palaestra's warped and weathered door would not open until Horn had wrestled manfully with its latch. As always, Silk delivered the smaller boys to Maytera Marble first. "We won a glorious victory," he told her.

She shook her head in mock dismay, her smooth oval face, polished bright by countless dustings, catching the sunlight from the window. "My poor girls were beaten, alas, Patera. It seems to me that Maytera Mint's big girls grow quicker and stronger with each week that passes. Wouldn't you think our Merciful Molpe would make my smaller ones quicker, too? Yet it doesn't seem she does it."

"By the time they're quicker, they'll be the big girls, perhaps."

"That must be it, Patera. While I'm only a small girl myself, snatching at every chance to put off the minuends and subtrahends for as long as possible, always willing to talk, never willing to work." Maytera Marble paused, her work-worn steel fingers flexing the cubit stick while she studied Silk. "You be careful this afternoon, Patera. You must be tired already, after scrambling around up there all morning and playing with the boys. Don't fall off that roof."

He grinned. "I'm finished with my repairs for today, Maytera. I'm going to sacrifice after manteion—a private sacrifice."

The old sib tilted her gleaming head to one side, thus lifting an eyebrow. "Then I regret that my class will not participate. Will your lamb be more pleasing to the Nine, do you think, without us?"

For an instant Silk was tempted to tell her everything there and then. He drew a deep breath instead, smiled, and closed the door.

Most of the larger boys had already gone into Maytera Rose's room.

Silk dismissed the rest with a glance, but Horn lingered. "May I speak with you, Patera? It'll just take a minute."

"If it *is* only a minute." When the boy said nothing, Silk added, "Go ahead, Horn. Did I foul you? If I did, I apologize—it certainly wasn't intentional."

"Is it . . ." Horn let the question trail away, staring at the splintering floorboards.

"Speak up, please. Or ask your question when I come back. That would be better."

The tall boy's gaze moved to the whitewashed mud-brick walls. "Patera, is it true that they're going to tear down our palaestra and your manteion? That you're going to have to go someplace else, or noplace? My father heard that yesterday. Is it true?"

"No."

Horn looked up with new hope, though the flat negative had left him speechless.

"Our palaestra and our manteion will be here next year, and the year after that, and the year after *that* as well." Suddenly conscious of his posture, Silk stood straighter, squaring his shoulders. "Does that put your mind at rest? They may become larger and better known, and I hope that they will. Perhaps some god or goddess may speak to us through our Sacred Window again, as Pas once did when Patera Pike was young—I don't know, though I pray for it every day. But when I'm as old as Patera Pike, the people of this quarter will still have a manteion and a palaestra. Never doubt it."

"I was going to say . . ."

Silk nodded. "Your eyes have said it for you already. Thank you, Horn. Thank you. I know that whenever I'm in need I can call on you, and that you'll do all that you can without counting the cost. But, Horn—"

"Yes, Patera?"

"I knew all that before."

The tall boy's head bobbed. "And all the other sprats, too, Patera. There are a couple of dozen that I know we can trust. Maybe more."

Horn was standing as straight as a Guardsman on parade now. With a slight shock of insight, Silk realized that this unaccustomed perpendicularity was in imitation of his own, and that Horn's clear, dark eyes were very nearly level with his.

"And after that," Horn continued, "there will be others, new boys. And men."

Silk nodded again, gravely reflecting that Horn was already a grown

man in every way that mattered, and a man far better educated than
most.

"And I don't want you to think I'm mad about it—knocking me over
like that, Patera. You hit me hard, but that's the fun of the game."

Silk shook his head. "That's merely how the game is played. The fun
comes when someone small knocks down someone larger."

"You were their best player, Patera. It wouldn't have been fair to them
if you hadn't played as well as you can." Horn glanced over his shoulder
at Maytera Rose's open door. "I have to go now. Thanks, Patera."

There was a line in the Writings that applied to the game and its
lessons—lessons more important, Silk felt, than any Maytera Rose might
teach; but Horn was already almost to the doorway. To his back, Silk
murmured, " 'Men build scales, but the gods blow upon the lighter
pan.' "

He sighed at the final word, knowing that the quotation had come a
second too late, and that Horn, too, had been too late; that Horn would
tell Maytera Rose that he, Patera Silk, had detained him, and that
Maytera Rose would punish him nevertheless without bothering to find
out whether it was true.

Silk turned away. There was no point in remaining to listen, and Horn
would fare that much worse if he tried to intervene. How could the
Outsider have chosen such a bungler? Was it possible that the very gods
were ignorant of his weakness and stupidity?

Some of them?

The manteion's rusty cash box was bare, he knew; yet he must have a
victim, and a fine one. The parents of one of the students might lend him
five or even ten bits, and the humiliation of having to beg such poor
people for a loan would certainly be beneficial. For as long as it took him
to close the unwilling door of the palaestra and start for the market, his
resolution held; then the only-too-well-imagined tears of small children
deprived of their accustomed supper of milk and stale bread washed it
away. No. The sellers would have to extend him credit.

The sellers must. When had he ever offered a single sacrifice, however
small, to the Outsider? Never! Not one in his entire life. Yet the Outsider
had extended infinite credit to him, for Patera Pike's sake. That was one
way of looking at it, at least. And perhaps that was the best way. Certainly he would never be able to repay the Outsider for the knowledge
and the honor, no matter how hard or how long he tried. Small wonder,
then . . .

As Silk's thoughts raced, his long legs flashed faster and faster.

The sellers never extended a single bit's credit, true. They gave credit to no augur; and certainly they would not extend it to an augur whose manteion stood in the poorest quarter of the city. Yet the Outsider could not be denied, so they would have to. He would have to be firm with them, extremely firm. Remind them that the Outsider was known to esteem them last among men already—that according to the Writings he had once (having possessed and enlightened a fortunate man) beaten them severely in person. And though the Nine could rightly boast . . .

A black civilian floater was roaring down Sun Street, scattering men and women on foot and dodging ramshackle carts and patient gray donkeys, its blowers raising a choking cloud of hot yellow dust. Like everyone else, Silk turned his face away, covering his nose and mouth with the edge of his robe.

"You there! Augur!"

The floater had stopped, its roar fading to a plaintive whine as it settled onto the rutted street. A big, beefy, prosperous-looking man standing in its passenger compartment flourished a walking stick.

Silk called, "I take it you are addressing me, sir. Is that correct?"

The prosperous-looking man gestured impatiently. "Come over here."

"I intend to," Silk told him. A dead dog rotting in the gutter required a long stride that roused a cloud of fat blue-backed flies. "*Patera* would be better mannered, sir; but I'll overlook it. You may call me 'augur' if you like. I have need of you, you see. Great need. A god has sent you to me."

The prosperous-looking man looked at least as surprised as Horn had when Silk had knocked him down.

"I require two—no, three cards," Silk continued. "Three cards or more. I require them at once, for a sacred purpose. You can provide them easily, and the gods will smile on you. Please do so."

The prosperous-looking man mopped his streaming brow with a large peach-colored handkerchief that sent a cloying fragrance to war with the stenches of the street. "I didn't think that the Chapter let you augurs do this sort of thing, Patera."

"Beg? Why, no. You're perfectly correct, sir. It's absolutely forbidden. But there's a beggar on every corner—you must know the kinds of things they say, and that's not what I'm telling you at all. I'm not hungry, and I have no starving children. I don't want your money for myself, but for a god, for the Outsider. It's a major error to restrict one's worship to the Nine, as I— Never mind. The Outsider must have a suitable offering from me before shadedown. It's absolutely imperative. You'll be certain to gain his favor by supplying it."

"I wanted—" the prosperous-looking man began.

Silk raised his hand. "No! The money—three cards at least, at once. I've offered you a splendid opportunity to gain his favor. You've lost that now, but you may still escape his displeasure, if only you'll act without further delay. For your own sake, give me three cards immediately!" Silk stepped closer, scrutinizing the prosperous-looking man's ruddy, perspiring face. "Terrible things may befall you. Horrible things!"

Reaching for the card case at his waist, the prosperous-looking man said, "A respectable citizen shouldn't even stop his floater in this quarter. I simply—"

"If you own this floater, you can afford three cards easily. And I'll offer a prayer for you—many prayers that you may eventually attain to . . ." Silk shivered.

The driver rasped, "Shut your shaggy mouth and let Blood talk, you butcher." Then to Blood, "You want me to bring him along, Jefe?"

Blood shook his head. He had counted out three cards, and now held them in a fan; half a dozen ragged men stopped to gawk at the gleaming gold. "Three cards you say you want, Patera. Here they are. Enlightenment? Was that what you were going to ask the gods to give me? You augurs are always squeaking about it. Well, I don't care about that. I want a little information instead. Tell me everything I want to know, and I'll hand over all three. See 'em? Then you can offer this wonderful sacrifice for yourself if you want to, or do whatever you want with the money. How about it?"

"You don't know what you're risking. If you did—"

Blood snorted. "I know that no god's come to any Window in this city since I was a young man, Patera, no matter how you butchers howl. And that's all I need to know. There's a manteion on this street, isn't there? Where Silver Street meets it at an angle? I've never been in that part of this quarter, but I asked, and that's what I was told."

Silk nodded. "I'm augur there."

"The old cull's dead, then?"

"Patera Pike?" Silk traced the sign of addition in the air. "Yes. Patera Pike has been with the gods for almost a year. Did you know him?"

Ignoring the question, Blood nodded to himself. "Gone to Mainframe, eh? All right, Patera. I'm not a religious man, and I don't pretend to be. But I promised my—well, I promised a certain person—that I'd go to this manteion of yours and say a few prayers for her. I'm going to make an offering, too, understand? Because I know she'll ask if I did. That's besides these cards here. So is there somebody there who'll let me in?"

Silk nodded again. "Maytera Marble or Maytera Mint would be delighted to, I'm sure. You'll find them both in the palaestra, on the other side of our ball court." Silk paused, thinking. "Maytera Mint's rather shy, though she's wonderful with the children. Perhaps you'd better ask for Maytera Marble, in the first room to your right. She could leave one of the older girls in charge of her class for an hour or so, I would think."

Blood closed his fan of cards as if about to hand them over to Silk. "I'm not too crazy about chemical people, Patera. Somebody told me you've got a Maytera Rose. Maybe I could get her, or isn't she there any more?"

"Oh, yes." Silk hoped his voice did not reflect the dismay he felt whenever he thought of Maytera Rose. "But she's quite elderly, sir, and we try to spare her poor legs whenever we can. I feel sure that Maytera Marble would prove completely satisfactory."

"No doubt she will." Blood counted his cards again, his lips moving, his fat, beringed fingers reluctant to part from each wafer-thin, shining rectangle. "You were going to tell me about enlightenment a minute ago, Patera. You said you'd pray for me."

"Yes," Silk confirmed eagerly, "and I meant it. I will."

Blood laughed. "Don't bother. But I'm curious, and I've never had such a good chance to ask one of you about it before. Isn't enlightenment really pretty much the same as possession?"

"Not exactly, sir." Silk gnawed his lower lip. "You know, sir, at the schola they taught us simple, satisfying answers to all of these questions. We had to recite them to pass the examination, and I'm tempted to recite them again for you now. But the actualities—enlightenment, I mean, and possession—aren't really simple things at all. Or at least enlightenment isn't. I don't know a great deal about possession, and some of the most respected hierologists are of the opinion that it exists potentially but not actually."

"A god's supposed to pull on a man just like a tunic—that's what they say. Well, some people can, so why not a god?" Watching Silk's expression, Blood laughed again. "You don't believe me, do you, Patera?"

Silk said, "I've never heard of such people, sir. I won't say they don't exist, since you assert that they do, although it seems impossible."

"You're young yet, Patera. If you want to dodge a lot of mistakes, don't you forget that." Blood glanced sidelong at his driver. "Get on these putts, Grison. Make them keep their paws off my floater."

"Enlightenment . . ." Silk stroked his cheek, remembering.

"That ought to be easy, it seems to me. Don't you just know a lot of things you didn't know before?" Blood paused, his eyes upon Silk's face. "Things that you can't explain, or aren't allowed to?"

A patrol of Guardsmen passed, their slug guns slung and their left hands resting on the hilts of their swords. One touched the bill of his jaunty green cap to Blood.

"It's difficult to explain," Silk said. "In possession there's always some teaching, for good or ill. Or at any rate that's what we're taught, though I don't believe— In enlightenment, there's much more. As much as the theodidact can bear, I would say."

"It happened to you," Blood said softly. "Lots of you say it did, but from you it's lily. You were enlightened, or you think you were. You think it's real."

Silk took a step backward, bumping against one of the onlookers. "I didn't call myself enlightened, sir."

"You didn't have to. I've been listening to you. Now you listen to me. I'm not giving you these cards, not for your holy sacrifice or for anything else. I'm paying you to answer my questions, and this is the last one. I want you to tell me—right now—what enlightenment is, when you got it, and why you got it. Here they are." He held them up again. "Tell me, Patera, and they're yours."

Silk considered, then plucked them from Blood's hand. "As you say. Enlightenment means understanding everything as the god who gives it understands it. Who you are and who everyone else is, really. Everything you used to think you understood, you see with complete clarity in that instant, and know that you didn't really understand it at all."

The onlookers murmured, each to his neighbor. Several pointed toward Silk. One waved over the drawer of a passing handcart.

"Only for an instant," Blood said.

"Yes, only for an instant. But the memory remains, so that you know that you knew." The three cards were still in Silk's hand; suddenly afraid that they would be snatched away by one of the ragged throng around him, he slipped them into his pocket.

"And when did this happen to you? Last week? Last year?"

Silk shook his head, glancing up at the sun. The thin black line of the shade touched it as he watched. "Today. Not an hour ago. A ball—I was playing a game with the boys . . ."

Blood waved the game away.

"And it happened. Everything seemed to stand still. I really can't say whether it was for an instant, or a day, or a year, or any other period of time—and I seriously doubt that any such period could be correct. Perhaps that's why we call him the Outsider: because he stands outside of time, all the time."

"Uh-huh." Blood favored Silk with a grudging smile. "I'm sure it's all smoke. Just some sort of daydream. But I've got to admit it's interesting smoke, the way you tell it. I've never heard of anything like this before."

"It's not exactly what they teach you in the schola," Silk conceded, "but I feel in my heart that it's the truth." He hesitated. "By which I mean that it's what I was shown by him—or rather, that it's one of an endless panorama of things. Somehow he's outside our whorl in every way, and inside it with us at the same time. The other gods are only inside, I think, however great they may appear inside."

Blood shrugged, his eyes wandering toward the ragged listeners. "Well, they believe you, anyhow. But as long as we're in here too, it doesn't make a bad bit's difference to us, does it, Patera?"

"Perhaps it does, or may in the future. I don't know, really. I haven't even begun to think about that yet." Silk glanced up again; the sun's golden road across the sky was markedly narrower already. "Perhaps it will make all the difference in the whorl," he said. "I think it will."

"I don't see how."

"You'll have to wait and see, my son—and so shall I." Silk shivered, as he had before. "You wanted to know why I received this blessing, didn't you? That was your last question: why something as tremendous as this should happen to someone as insignificant as I am. Wasn't that it?"

"Yes, if this god of yours will let you tell anybody."

Blood grinned, showing crooked, discolored teeth; and Silk, suddenly and without in the least willing it, saw more vividly than he had ever seen the man before him the hungry, frightened, scheming youth who had been Blood a generation before.

"And if you don't gibbe yourself, Patera."

"Gibbe?"

"If you've got no objections. Don't feel like you're stepping over his line."

"I see." Silk cleared his throat. "I've no objection, but no very satisfactory answer for you, either. That's why I snatched my three cards from your hand, and it's why I need them, too—or a part of it. It may be only that he has a task for me. He does, I know, and I hope that that's all it is. Or, as I've thought since, perhaps it's because he means to destroy me, and felt he owed this to me before he struck. I don't know."

Blood dropped to his seat in the passenger compartment, mopping his face and neck with his scented handkerchief, as he had before. "Thanks, Patera. We're quits. You're going to the market?"

"Yes, to buy him a fine victim with these cards you've given me."

"Paid you. I'll have left your manteion before you get back, Patera. Or anyhow I hope I will." Blood dropped into the floater's velvet seat. "Get the canopy up, Grison."

Silk called, "Wait!"

Blood stood again, surprised. "What is it, Patera? No hard feelings, I hope."

"I lied to you, my son—misled you at least, although I didn't intend to. He—the Outsider—told me why, and I remembered it a few minutes ago when I was talking with a boy named Horn, a student at our palaestra." Silk stepped closer, until he was peering at Blood over the edge of the half-raised canopy. "It was because of the augur who had our manteion when I came, Patera Pike. A very good and very holy man."

"He's dead, you said."

"Yes. Yes, he is. But before he died, he prayed—prayed to the Outsider, for some reason. And he was heard. His prayer was granted. All this was explained to me, and now I owe it to you, because it was part of our bargain."

"Then I may as well have it explained to me, too. But make it as quick as you can."

"He prayed for help." Silk ran his fingers through his careless thatch of straw-colored hair. "When we—when you pray for his help, to the Outsider, he sends it."

"Nice of him."

"But not always—no, not often—of the sort we want or expect. Patera Pike, that good old man, prayed devoutly. And I'm the help—"

"Let's go, Grison."

The blowers roared back to life. Blood's black floater heaved uneasily, rising stern first and rocking alarmingly.

"—the Outsider sent to him, to save the manteion and its palaestra," Silk concluded. He stepped back, coughing in the billowing dust. Half to himself and half to the shabby crowd kneeling around him, he added. "I am to expect no help from him. I *am* help."

If any of them understood, it was not apparent. Still coughing, he traced the sign of addition and muttered a brief formula of blessing, begun with the Most Sacred Name of Pas, Father of the Gods, and concluded with that of his eldest child, Scylla, Patroness of this, Our Holy City of Viron.

As he neared the market, Silk reflected on his chance encounter with the prosperous-looking man in the floater. Blood, his driver had called him. Three cards was far, far too much to pay for answers to a few simple questions, and in any case one did not pay augurs for their answers; one made a donation, perhaps, if one was particularly grateful. Three full cards, but were they still there?

He thrust a hand into his pocket; the smooth, elastic surface of the ball met his fingers. He pulled it out, and one of the cards came with it, flashing in the sunlight as it fell at his feet.

As swiftly as he had snatched the ball from Horn, he scooped it up. This was a bad quarter, he reminded himself, though there were so many good people in it. Without law, even good people stole: their own property vanished, and their only recourse was to steal in turn from someone else. What would his mother have thought, if she had lived to learn where the Chapter had assigned him? She had died during his final year at the schola, still believing that he would be sent to one of the rich manteions on the Palatine and someday become Prolocutor.

"You're so good-looking," she had said, raising herself upon her toes to smooth his rebellious hair. "So tall! Oh, Silk, my son! My dear, dear son!"

(And he had stooped to let her kiss him.)

My son was what he had been taught to call laymen, even those three times his own age, unless they were very highly placed indeed; then there was generally some title that could be gracefully employed instead, Colonel or Commissioner, or even Councillor, although he had never met any of the three and in this quarter never would—though here was a poster with the handsome features of Councillor Loris, the secretary of the Ayuntamiento: features somewhat scarred now by the knife of some vandal, who had slashed his poster once and stabbed it several times. Silk felt suddenly glad that he was in the Chapter and not in politics, though politics had been his mother's first choice for him. No one would slash or stab the pictured face of His Cognizance the Prolocutor, surely.

He tossed the ball into his right hand and thrust his left into his pocket. The cards were still there: one, two, three. Many men in this quarter who worked from shadeup to dark—carrying bricks or stacking boxes, slaughtering, hauling like oxen or trotting beneath the weighty litters of the rich, sweeping and mopping—would be fortunate to make three cards a year. His mother had received six, enough for a woman and a child to live decently, from some fund at the fisc that she had never explained, a fund that had vanished with her life. She would be unhappy now to see him in this quarter, walking its streets as poor as many of its people. She had never been a happy woman in any case, her large dark eyes so often bright with tears from sources more mysterious than the fisc, her tiny body shaken with sobs that he could do nothing to alleviate. ("Oh, Silk! My poor boy! My son!")

He had at first called Blood *sir,* and afterward, *my son,* himself scarcely conscious of the change. But why? *Sir* because Blood had been riding in a floater, of course; only the richest of men could afford to own floaters. *My son* afterward. "The old cull's dead, then? . . . It doesn't make a bad bit's difference to us, does it, Patera? . . . Nice of him." Blood's choice of word and phrase, and his almost open contempt for the gods, had not accorded with the floater; he had spoken better—far better—than most people in this quarter; but not at all like the privileged, well-bred man whom Silk would have expected to find riding in a private floater.

He shrugged, and extracted the three cards from his pocket.

There was always a good chance that a card (still more, a cardbit) would be false. There was even a chance, as Silk admitted to himself, that the prosperous-looking man in the floater—that this odd man Blood—kept false cards in a special location in his card case. Nevertheless all three of these appeared completely genuine, sharp-edged rectangles two thumbs by three, their complex labyrinths of gold encysted in some remarkable substance that was almost indestructible, yet nearly invisible. It was said that when two of the intricate golden patterns were exactly alike, one at least was false. Silk paused to compare them, then shook his head and hurried off again in the direction of the market. If these cards were good enough to fool the sellers of animals, that was all that mattered, though he would be a thief. A prayer, in that case, to Tenebrous Tartaros, Pas's elder son, the terrifying god of night and thieves.

Maytera Marble sat watching, at the back of her class. There had been a time, long ago, when she would have stood, just as there had been a time when her students had labored over keyboards instead of slates. Today, now—in whatever year this might be . . . Might be . . .

Her chronological function could not be called; she tried to remember when it had happened before.

Maytera Marble could call a list of her nonfunctioning or defective components whenever she chose, though it had been five years or fifty since she had so chosen. What was the use? Why should she—why ever should anyone—make herself more miserable than the gods had chosen to make her? Weren't the gods cruel enough, deaf to her prayers through so many years, so many decades and days and languid, half-stopped hours? Pas, Great Pas, was god of mechanisms, as of so much else. Perhaps he was too busy to notice.

She pictured him as he stood in the manteion, as tall as a talus, his smooth limbs carved of some white stone finer grained than shiprock—his grave, unseeing eyes, his noble brows. Have pity on me, Pas, she prayed. Have pity on me, a mortal maid who calls upon you now, but will soon stop forever.

Her right leg had been getting stiffer and stiffer for years, and at times it seemed that even when she sat so still—

A boy to a girl: *"She's asleep!"*

—that when she sat as still as she was sitting here, watching the children take nineteen from twenty-nine and get nine, add seven and seventeen and arrive at twenty-three—that when she sat so still as this, her vision no longer as acute as it once had been, although she could still see the straying, chalky numerals on their slates when the children wrote large, and all children their age wrote large, though their eyes were better than her own.

It seemed to her that she was always on the point of overheating any more, in hot weather anyway. Pas, Great Pas, God of Sky and Sun and Storm, bring the snow! Bring the cold wind!

This endless summer, without snow, with no autumn rains and the season for them practically past now, the season for snow nearly upon us, and no snow. Heat and dust and clouds that were all empty, yellow haze. What could Pas, Lord Pas, Husband of Grain-bearing Echidna and Father of the Seven, be thinking of?

A girl: *"Look—she's asleep!"*

Another: *"I didn't think they slept."*

A knock at the Sun Street door of the palaestra.

"I'll get it!" That was Asphodella's voice.

This was Ratel's. *"No, I will!"*

Fragrant white blossoms and sharp white teeth. Maytera Marble meditated upon names. Flowers—or plants of some kind, at least—for bio girls; animals or animal products for bio boys. Metals or stones for us.

Both together: *"Let me!"*

Her old name had been—

Her old name had been . . .

A crash, as a chair fell. Maytera Marble rose stiffly, one hand gripping the windowsill. "Stop that this instant!"

She could bring up a list of her nonfunctioning and defective parts whenever she chose. She had not chosen to do so for close to a century; but from time to time, most often when the cenoby lay on the night side of the long sun, that list came up of itself.

"Aquifolia! Separate those two before I lose my temper."

Maytera Marble could remember the short sun, a disk of orange fire; and it seemed to her that the chief virtue of that old sun had been that no list, no menu, ever appeared unbidden beneath its rays.

Both together: *"Sib, I wanted—"*

"Well, neither of you are going to," Maytera Marble told them.

Another knock, too loud for knuckles of bone and skin. She must hurry or Maytera Rose might go, might answer that knock herself, an occasion for complaint that would outlast the snow. If the snow ever arrived.

"I am going to go myself. Teasel, you're in charge of the class until I return. Keep them at their work, every one of them." To give her final words more weight, Maytera Marble paused as long as she dared. "I shall expect you to name those who misbehaved."

A good step toward the door. There was an actuator in her right leg that occasionally jammed when it had been idle for an hour or so, but it appeared to be functioning almost acceptably. Another step, and another. Good, good! Praise to you, Great Pas.

She stopped just beyond the doorway, to listen for an immediate disturbance, then limped down the corridor to the door.

A beefy, prosperous-looking man nearly as tall as Patera Silk had been pounding the panels with the carved handle of his walking stick.

"May every god favor you this morning," Maytera Marble said. "How may I serve you?"

"My name's Blood," he announced. "I'm looking at the property. I've already seen the garden and so on, but the other buildings are locked. I'd like you to take me through them, and show me this one."

"I couldn't possibly admit you to our cenoby," Maytera Marble said firmly. "Nor could I permit you to enter the manse alone. I'll be happy to show you through our manteion and this palaestra—provided that you have a valid reason for wishing to see them."

Blood's red face became redder still. "I'm checking the condition of the buildings. All of them need a lot of work, from what I've seen outside."

Maytera Marble nodded. "That's quite true, I'm afraid, although we do everything that we can. Patera Silk's been repairing the roof of the manteion. That was most urgent. Is it true—"

Blood interrupted her. "The cenoby—is that the little house on Silver Street?"

She nodded.

"The manse is the one where Silver Street and Sun come together? The little three-cornered house at the west end of the garden?"

"That's correct. Is it true, then, that this entire property is to be sold? That's what some of the children have been saying."

Blood eyed her quizzically. "Has Maytera Rose heard about it?"

"I suppose she's heard the rumor, if that's what you mean. I haven't discussed it with her."

Blood nodded, a minute inclination of his head that probably escaped his own notice. "I didn't tell that tow-headed butcher of yours. He looked like the sort to make trouble. But you tell Maytera Rose that the rumor's true, you hear me? Tell her it's been sold already, sib. Sold to me."

We'll be gone before the snow flies, Maytera Marble thought, hearing her future and all their futures in Blood's tone. Gone before winter and living somewhere else, where Sun Street will be just a memory.

Blessed snow to cool her thighs; she pictured herself sitting at peace, with her lap full of new-fallen snow.

Blood added, "Tell her my name."

CHAPTER 2
THE SACRIFICE

As it was every day except Scylsday, "from noon until the sun can be no thinner," the market was thronged. Here all the produce of Viron's fields and gardens was displayed for sale or barter: yams, arrowroot, and hill-country potatoes; onions, scallions, and leeks; squashes yellow, orange, red, and white; sun-starved asparagus; beans black as night or spotted like hounds; dripping watercresses from the shrinking rivulets that fed Lake Limna; lettuces and succulent greens of a hundred sorts; and fiery peppers; wheat, millet, rice, and barley; maize yellower than its name, and white, blue, and red as well, spilling, leaking, and overflowing from baskets, bags, and earthenware pots—this though Patera Silk noted with dismay that prices were higher than he had ever seen them, and many of the stunted ears were missing grains.

Here still despite the drought were dates and grapes, oranges and citrons, pears, papayas, pomegranates and little red bananas; angelica, hyssop, licorice, cicely, cardamom, anise, basil, mandrake, borage, marjoram, mullein, parsley, saxifrage, and scores of other herbs.

Here perfumers waved lofty plumes of dyed pampas grass to strew the overheated air with fragrances matched to every conceivable feminine name; and here those fragrances warred against the savory aromas of roasting meats and bubbling stews, the stinks of beast and men and of the excrements of both. Sides of beef and whole carcasses of pork hung here from cruel-looking hooks of hammered iron; and here (as Silk turned left in search of those who dealt in live beasts and birds) was the rich harvest of the lake: gap-mouthed fish with silver sides and starting eyes, mussels, writhing eels, fretful black crawfish with claws like pliers, eyes like rubies, and fat tails longer than a man's hand; sober gray geese, and ducks richly dressed in brown, green, black, and that odd blue so seldom seen elsewhere that it is called teal. Folding tables and thick polychrome blankets spread on the trampled, uneven soil held bracelets and ornamental pins, flashing rings and cascading necklaces, graceful swords and straight-bladed, double-edged knives with grips of rare hardwoods or colored leathers, and hammers, axes, froes, and scutches.

Swiftly though he shouldered his way through the crowd, greatly aided by his height, his considerable strength, and his sacred office, Silk lingered to watch as a nervous green monkey picked fortunes for a cardbit, and to see a weaver of eight or nine tie the ten thousandth knot in a carpet, her hands working, as it seemed, without reference to her idle, empty little face.

And at all times, whether he stood watching or pushed through the crowd, Silk looked deep into the eyes of those who had come to buy or sell, and tried to look into their hearts, too, reminding himself (whenever such prompts were needed) that each was treasured by Pas. Great Pas, with an understanding far beyond that of mere men, accounted this faded housewife with her basket on her arm more precious than any figurine carved from ivory; this sullen, pockmarked boy (so Silk thought of him, though the youth was only a year or two the younger), standing ready to snatch a brass earring or an egg, worth more than all the goods that all such boys might ever hope to steal. Pas had built the whorl for Men, and not made men, or women, or children, for the whorl.

"Caught today!" shouted half a dozen voices, by the goodwill of Melodious Molpe or the accident of innumerable repetitions for once practically synchronized. Following the sound, Silk found himself among the sellers he sought. Hobbled deer reared and plunged, their soft brown eyes wild with fright; a huge snake lifted its flat, malevolent head, hissing like a kettle on the stove; live salmon gasped and splashed in murky, glass-fronted tanks; pigs grunted, lambs baaed, chickens squawked, and milling goats eyed passersby with curiosity and sharp suspicion. Which of these, if any, would make a suitable gift of thanks to the Outsider? To that lone nebulous god, mysterious, beneficent, and severe, whose companion he had been for a time that had seemed less than an instant and longer than centuries? Motionless at the edge of the seething crowd, one leg pressed against the unpeeled poles that confined the goats, Silk ransacked the whole store of dusty knowledge he had acquired with so much labor during eight years at the schola; and found nothing.

On the other side of the goat pen, a well-marked young donkey trotted in a circle, reversing direction each time its owner clapped, bowing (a foreleg stretched forward, its wide forehead in the dust) when he whistled. Such a trained animal, Silk reflected, would make a superb sacrifice to any god; but the donkey's price would be nearer thirty cards than three.

A fatted ox recalled the prosperous-looking man called Blood, and Blood's three cards might well obtain it after a session of hard bargaining. Many augurs chose such victims whenever they could, and what remained after the sacrifice would supply the palaestra's kitchen for at least a week, and feed Maytera Rose, Maytera Mint, and himself like so many commissioners as well; but Silk could not believe that a mutilated and stall-fed beast, however sumptuous, would be relished by a god, nor did he himself often indulge in meats of any kind.

Lambs, unrelieved black for Stygian Tartaros, Deathly Hierax, and Grim Phaea, purest white for the remainder of the Nine, were the sacrifices most frequently mentioned in the Chrasmologic Writings; but he had offered several such lambs already without attracting a divine presence to the Sacred Window. What sort of thanks would such a lamb—or even an entire flock of such lambs, for Blood's cards put a sizable flock within his reach—be now to the veiled god who had, unbribed, so greatly favored him today?

This dog-headed ape, trained to light its master's way with cresset or lantern, and (according to a badly lettered placard) to defend him from footpads and assassins, would cost at least as much as the donkey. Shaking his head, Silk walked on.

A Flier—perhaps the same Flier—sailed serenely overhead, his widespread, gauzy wings visible now, his body a dark cross against the darkening streak of the sun. The burly, bearded man beside Silk shook his fist, and several persons muttered maledictions.

"Don't nobody ever want it to rain," the nearest of the sellers of beasts remarked philosophically, "but everybody wants to go on eatin'."

Silk nodded his agreement. "The gods smile on us, my son, or so it is written. It's a wonder they don't laugh aloud."

"Do you think they're really spyin' on us, Patera, the way the Ayuntamiento keeps tellin' us? Or do they bring on rain? Rain and storms, that's what my old father used to say, and his before him. I've noticed myself that it's true pretty often. Lord Pas must know that we could use some these days."

"I really don't know," Silk confessed. "I saw one around noon today, and it hasn't rained yet. As for spying upon Viron, what could a Flier see here that any foreign traveler couldn't?"

"Nothin' I know about." The seller spat. "That's supposed to bring on rain, too, Patera. Let's hope it works this time. Lookin' for a good sacrifice, are you?"

Silk's face must have betrayed his surprise, because the seller grinned, revealing a broken front tooth. "I know you, Patera—that old manteion on Sun Street. Only you went right on past the sheepfold today. Guess they haven't been workin' out for you."

Silk endeavored to appear indifferent. "I'll recognize the beast I want when I see it."

" 'Course you will—so let me show you mine." The seller raised a soiled finger. "No, wait a bit. Let me ask you one question first. I'm just an ignorant man, Patera, but isn't a child the best sacrifice of all? The very best gift that a man or even a whole city can make to the gods? The greatest and the highest?"

Silk shrugged. "So it's written, though no such victim has been offered here within living memory. I don't believe that I could do it myself, and it's against the law in any case."

"Exactly what I'm gettin' at!" Like a conspirator, the seller glanced warily from side to side. "So what's nearest to a child, eh? Only on the right side of the law? What is it, I ask you, Patera—you and me bein' flash grown men and not no sprats—that half those high-bred females up on the Palatine is givin' suck to on the side? A catachrest, isn't that it?"

With a showman's flourish, the seller reached beneath the stained red cloth that draped his table and produced a small wire cage containing an orange-and-white catachrest. Silk was no judge of these animals, but to him it appeared hardly more than a kitten.

The seller leaned forward, and his voice dropped to a hoarse whisper. "Stolen, Patera. Stolen, or I couldn't possibly sell it, even to you, for—." He licked his lips, his restless gaze taking in Silk's faded black robe and lingering on his face. "For just six little cards. It talks. It walks on its hind legs sometimes, too, and it picks up things to eat with its little paws. It's exactly like a real child. You'll see."

Looking into the animal's melting blue eyes (the long, nycterent pupils were rapidly narrowing in the sunlight) Silk could almost believe him.

The seller tested the point of a long-bladed knife with his finger. "You recollect this, don't you, Tick? Then you better talk when I tell you to, and not try to get away, neither, when I let you out."

Silk shook his head.

If he had seen the motion, the seller ignored it. "Say *shop*. Talk for the rev'rend augur, Tick. Say *shop!*" He prodded the unhappy little catachrest with the point of his knife. *"Shop!* Say it!"

"Never mind," Silk told the seller wearily. "I'm not going to buy him."

"It'd make you a fine sacrifice, Patera—the finest you could have, inside of the law. What was it I told you? Seven cards, was that it? Tell you what. I'll make it six, but only for today. Just six cards, because I've heard good things about you and hope to do more business with you in the future."

Silk shook his head again.

"Told you Tick was boilin', didn't I? I knew it, and believe me I put crimp on the lad that did it, or I wouldn't have got Tick here half so cheap. Talked about rollin' him over to Hoppy and all that."

"It doesn't matter," Silk said.

"So now I'm goin' to let you steal him off me. Five cards, Patera. You can—talk, you little faker, say somethin'—you can go through the whole market, if you like, and if you can find a nice catachrest like this any cheaper, bring me there and I'll match the price. Five cards, we'll say. You won't be able to touch one half this good for five cards. I promise you that, and I'm a man of my word. Ask anybody."

"No, my son."

"I need the money bad, Patera. I guess I shouldn't say that, but I do. A man has to have some money to buy animals so he's got somethin' to sell, see?" His voice fell again, so low this time that it was scarcely audible. "I put mine into a few cold 'uns. You take my meanin', Patera? Only they warmed up an' went bad on me 'fore I could move 'em. So here's what I say—five cards, with one of 'em chalked. How's that? Four down, see, right now. And a card next time I see you, which I will on Molpsday after this comin' Scylsday, Patera, I hope."

"No," Silk repeated.

"Word," the little catachrest said distinctly. "Shoe word, who add pan."

"Don't you call me a bad man." Sliding the slender blade between the wires, the seller prodded the catachrest's minute pink nose with the point of his knife. "The rev'rend augur's not interested in seein' any cully bird, you flea-bit little pap-sucker." He glanced up hopefully at Silk. "Are you, Patera? It *is* a talkin' bird at that. Naturally it doesn't look exactly like a child. It's a good talker, though—a valuable animal."

Silk hesitated.

"Berry add word," the catachrest told him spitefully, gripping the wire mesh of his cage. "Pack!" He shook it, minute black claws sharper than pins visible at the tips of his fuzzy white toes. "Add word!" he repeated. "Add speak!"

No god had spoken through the Sacred Window of the old manteion on Sun Street since long before Silk had been born, and this was an omen beyond question: one of those oracular phrases that the gods, by means no mere human being could ever hope to understand, insert at times into the most banal speech. As calmly as he could manage, Silk said, "Go ahead and show me your talking bird. I'm here, so I might just as well have a look at it." He glanced up at the narrowing sun as if on the point of leaving. "But I've got to get back soon."

"It's a night chough, Patera," the seller told him. "Only night chough I've had this year."

This cage as well appeared from under the table. The bird crowded into it was large and glossy black, with bright red legs and a tuft of scarlet feathers at its throat; the "add speak" of the catachrest's omen was a sullen crimson, long and sharp.

"It talks?" Silk asked, though he was determined to buy it whether it could or not.

"They all do, Patera," the seller assured him, "all of these here night choughs. They learn from each other, don't you see, down there in the swamps around Palustria. I've had a few before, and this 'un's a better talker than most, from what I've heard it say."

Silk studied the bird with some care. It had seemed quite plausible that the little orange-and-white catachrest should speak: it was in fact very like a child, despite its fur. There was nothing about this downhearted fowl to suggest anything of the kind. It might almost have been a large crow.

"Somebody learned the first 'un back in the short sun time, Patera," the seller explained. "That's the story they tell about 'em, anyhow. I s'pose he got sick of hearin' it jabber an' let it go—or maybe it give him the air, 'cause they're dimber hands for that—then that 'un went home an' learned all the rest. I bought this 'un off of a limer that come up from down south. Last Phaesday, just a week ago it was. I give him a card for it."

Silk grinned. "You've a fine manner for lying, my son, but your matter gives you away. You paid ten bits or less. Isn't that what you mean?"

Sensing a sale, the seller's eyes brightened. "Why, I couldn't let it go for anything under a full card, don't you see, Patera? I'd be losing on it, an' just when I need gelt so bad. You look at this bird, now. Young an' fit as you could ask for, an' wild bred. An' then brought here clean from Palustria. A bird that'd cost you a card—every bit of one an' maybe some over—in the big market there. Why this cage here, by itself, would cost you twenty or thirty bits."

"Ah!" Silk exclaimed, rubbing his hands. "Then the cage is included in the price?"

The clack of the night chough's bill was louder than its muttered, "No, no."

"There, Patera!" The seller seemed ready to jump for joy. "Hear it? Knows everythin' we're sayin'! Knows why you want him! A card, Patera. A full card, and I won't come down by one single bit, I can't afford to. But you give me back what I paid the limer and this bird's yours, as fine a sacrifice as the Prolocutor himself might make, and for one little card."

Silk feigned to consider, glancing up at the sun once more, then around him at the dusty, teeming market. Green-shirted Guardsmen were plying the butts of their slug guns as they threaded the crowd, no doubt in pursuit of the lounging youth he had noticed earlier.

"This bird's stolen property, too, isn't he?" Silk said. "Otherwise you wouldn't have been keeping him under your table with the catachrest. You talked of threatening the poor wretch who sold you that. Roll him over to Hoppy, isn't that what you said, my son?"

The seller would not meet Silk's eyes.

"I'm no flash cull, but I've learned a little cant since I've been at my manteion. It means you threatened to inform on him to the Guard, doesn't it? Suppose that I were to threaten you in the same way now. That would be no more than just, surely."

The seller leaned closer to Silk, as he had before, his head turned to one side as if he himself were a bird, though possibly he was merely conscious of the garlic that freighted his breath. "It's just to make 'em think they're gettin' a bargain, Patera, I swear. Which you are."

The hour for the palaestra's assembly was striking when Silk returned with the night chough. A hurried sacrifice, he decided, might be worse than none, and the live bird would be a ruinous distraction. The manse had doors on Sun and Silver Streets, but he kept them bolted, as Patera Pike had. He let himself in by the garden gate, and trotted down the graveled path between the west wall of the manteion and the sickly fig tree, swung left between the grape arbor and Maytera Marble's herb garden, and took the manse's disintegrating steps two at a time. Opening the kitchen door, he set the birdcage on the shaky wooden table, pumped vigorously until the water gushed forth clear and cold, and left a full cup within easy reach of the big bird's crimson beak. By then he could hear the students trooping into the manteion. Smoothing his hair with a damp hand, he darted off to address them at the conclusion of their day.

The low door at the rear of the manteion stood open for ventilation. Silk strode through it, up a short stair whose treads had been sloped and hollowed by the hastening feet of generations of augurs, and into the dim sanctum behind the Sacred Window. Still thinking of the market and the morose black bird he had left in the kitchen of the manse, fumbling mentally for something of real significance that he might say to seventy-three students whose ages ranged from eight to almost sixteen, he verified power and scanned the Sacred Window's registers. All were empty. Had Great Pas actually come to this very Window? Had any god, ever? Had Great Pas, as Patera Pike had averred so often, once congratulated and encouraged him, urging him to prepare, to stand ready for the hour (soon to come, or so Pas had appeared to intimate) when this present whorl would vanish, would be left behind?

Such things seemed impossible. Testing connections with an angled arm of the voided cross he wore, Silk prayed for faith; and then—stepping carefully across a meandering primary cable whose insulation was no longer to be relied upon—drew a deep breath, stepped from behind the Window, and took his place at the chipped ambion that through so many such assemblies had been Patera Pike's.

Where slept Pike now, that good old man, that faithful old servant who had slept so badly, who had nodded off for a moment or two—only a moment or two—at each meal they had shared? Who had both resented and loved the tall young acolyte who had been thrust upon him after so many years, so many slow decades of waiting alone, who had loved him as no one had except his mother?

Where was he now, old Patera Pike? Where did he sleep, and did he sleep well there at last? Or did he wake as he always had, stirring in the long bedroom next to Silk's own, his old bed creaking, creaking? Praying at midnight or past midnight, at shadeup with the skylands fading, praying as Viron extinguished its bonfires and its lanterns, its many-branched candelabras, praying as they were forfeited to the revealed sun. Praying as day's uncertain shadows reappeared and resumed their accustomed places, as the morning glories flared and the long, white trumpets of the night silently folded themselves upon themselves.

Sleeping beside the gods, did old Patera Pike waken no longer to recall the gods to their duties?

Erect at Patera Pike's ambion, beside the luminous gray vacuity of the Sacred Window, Silk took a moment to observe the students before he began. All were poor, he knew; and for more than a few the noon meal that half a dozen mothers had prepared in the palaestra's kitchen had been the first of the day. Yet most were almost clean; and all—under the sharp gaze of Maytera Rose, Maytera Marble, and Maytera Mint—were well behaved.

When the new year had begun, he had taken the older boys from Maytera Mint and given them to Maytera Rose: the reverse of the arrangement Patera Pike had instituted. As he ran his eyes over them now, Silk decided it had been unwise. The older boys had, for the most part, obeyed timid Maytera Mint out of an odd, half-formed chivalry, enforced when necessary by leaders like Horn; they had no such regard for Maytera Rose, and she herself imposed an inflexible and merciless order that might very well be the worst possible example to give the older boys, young men who would so soon (so very, very quickly) be maintaining order in families of their own.

Silk turned from the students to contemplate the images of Pas and his consort, Echidna: Twice-Headed Pas with his lightnings, Echidna with her serpents. It was effective; the murmur of young voices faded, dying away to an expectant hush. At the back of the manteion, Maytera Marble's eyes gleamed like violet sparks beneath her coif, and Silk knew that those eyes were on him; however much she might approve of him, Maytera Marble did not yet trust him to speak from the ambion without making a fool of himself.

"There will be no sacrifice today, at this assembly," he began, "though all of us know that there should be." He smiled, seeing that he had their interest. "This month began the first year for eleven of you. Even so, you probably know by now that we rarely have a victim for our assembly.

"Perhaps some of you are wondering why I've mentioned it today. It's because the situation on this particular day is somewhat different—there will be a sacrifice, here in this manteion, after you have gone home. All of you, I feel quite certain, recall the lambs."

About half nodded.

"I bought those, as I think you know, using money I had saved while I was at the schola—money that my mother had sent to me—and with money I had saved here from the salary I receive from the Chapter. Do all of you realize that our manteion operates at a loss?"

The older ones did, as was plain from their expressions.

"It does," Silk continued. "The gifts we receive on Scylsday, and at other times, aren't enough to offset the very small salaries paid to our sibyls and me. Our taxes are in arrears—that means we owe money to the Juzgado, and we have various other debts. Occasionally animals are presented by benefactors, people who hope for the favor of the merciful gods. Perhaps your own parents are among them, and if they are we are very grateful to them. When no such victims are presented, our sibyls and I pool our salaries to buy a victim for Scylsday, generally a pigeon.

"But the lambs, as I said, I bought myself. Why do you think I did that, Addax?"

Addax, as old as Horn and with coloring nearly as light as Silk's own, stood. "To foretell the future, Patera."

Silk nodded as Addax resumed his seat. "Yes, to know the future of our manteion. The entrails of those lambs told me that it is bright, as you know. But mostly because I sought the favor of various gods and hoped to win it by gifts." Silk glanced at the Sacred Window behind him. "I offered the first lamb to Pas and the second to Scylla, the patroness of our city. Those, so I thought, were all that I had funds for—a single white lamb for All-powerful Pas, and another for Scylla. And I asked, as I should tell you, for a particular favor—I asked that they appear to us again, as they did of old. I longed for assurances of their love, not thinking how needless they would be when ample assurances are found throughout the Chrasmologic Writings." He tapped the worn book before him on the ambion.

"Late one evening, as I read the Writings, I came to understand that. I'd read them from boyhood—and never learned in all that time how much the gods love us, though they had told me over and over. Of what use was it, in that case, for me to have a copy of my own? I sold it, but the twenty bits it brought would not have bought another white lamb, or even a black lamb for Phaea, whose day this is. I bought a gray lamb instead, and offered it to all the gods, and the entrails of the gray lamb held the same messages of hope that I had read in the white lambs. Then I should have known, though I did not, that it was not one of the Nine who was speaking to us through the lambs. Today I learned the identity of that god, but I won't tell you that today; there is still too much I have not understood." Silk picked up the Writings and stared at the binding for a moment before he spoke again.

"This is the manteion's copy. It's the one that I read now, and it's a better one—a better printed copy, with more extensive notes—than my old one, the one I sold so that I might make a gift to all the gods. There are lessons there, and I hope that every one of you will master them. Wrestle with them a while, if they seem too difficult for you at first, and never forget that it was to teach you these wrestlings that our palaestra was founded long ago.

"Yes, Kit? What is it?"

"Patera, is a god really going to come."

Some of the older students laughed. Silk waited until they were quiet again before he replied. "Yes, Kit. A god will come to our Sacred Window, though we may have to wait a very long time. But we need not wait —we have their love and their wisdom here. Open these Writings at any point, Kit, and you'll find a passage applicable to your present condition —to the problems you have today, or to the ones you'll have to deal with tomorrow. How is this possible? Who will tell me?" Silk studied the blank faces before him before calling on one of the girls who had laughed loudest. "Answer, Ginger."

She rose reluctantly, smoothing her skirt. "Because everything's connected to everything else, Patera?" It was one of his own favorite sayings.

"Don't you know, Ginger?"

"Because everything's connected."

Silk shook his head. "That everything in the whorl is dependent on every other thing is unquestionably true. But if that were the answer to my question, we ought to find any passage from any book as appropriate to our condition as one from the Chrasmologic Writings. You need only look into any other book at random to prove that it isn't so. But," he tapped the shabby cover again, "when I open *this* book, what will we find?"

He did so, dramatically, and read the line at the top of the page aloud: " 'Are ten birds to be had for a song?' "

The clarity of this reference to his recent transaction in the market stunned him, afrighting his thoughts like so many birds. He swallowed and continued. " 'You have daubed Oreb the raven, but can you make him sing?'

"I'll interpret that for you in a moment," he promised. "First I wish to explain to you that the authors of these Writings knew not only the state of the whorl in their time—and what it had been—but what was yet to come. I'm referring," he paused, his eyes lingering on every face, "to the Plan of Pas. Everyone who understands the Plan of Pas understands the future. Am I making myself plain? The plan of Pas *is* the future, and to understand it and follow it is the principal duty of every man, and of every woman and each child.

"Knowing the Plan of Pas, as I said, the Chrasmatists knew what would best serve us each time this book would be opened—what would most firmly set your feet and mine upon the Aureate Path."

Silk paused again to study the youthful faces before him; there was a flicker of interest here and there, but no more than a flicker. He sighed. "Now we return to the lines themselves. The first, 'Are ten birds to be had for a song?' bears three meanings at least. As you grow older and learn to think more deeply, you'll learn that every line of the Writings bears two meanings or more. One of the meanings here applies to me personally. I'll explain that meaning in a moment. The other two have application to all of us, and I'm going to deal with them first.

"To begin, we must assume that the birds referred to are of the singing kind. Notice that in the next line, when the singing kind isn't intended, that is made plain. What then, is signified by these ten singing birds? Children in class—that is to say yourselves—provide an obvious interpretation, surely. You're called upon to recite for the good sibyls who are your teachers, and your voices are high, like the twitterings of songbirds. To buy something for a song is to buy it cheaply. The meaning, as we see, is: *is this multitude of young scholars to be sold cheaply?* And the answer is clearly, no. Remember, children, how much Great Pas values, and tells us over and over again that he values, every living creature in the whorl, every color and kind of berry and butterfly—and human beings above all. No, birds are not to be sold for a song; birds are precious to Pas. We don't sacrifice birds and other animals to the immortal gods because they are of no value, do we? That would be insulting to the very gods.

" 'Are ten birds to be had for a song?' No. No, you children are not to be sold cheaply."

He had their interest now. Everyone was awake, and many were leaning forward in their seats. "For the second, we must consider the second line as well. Notice that ten singing birds might easily produce, not ten, but tens of thousands of songs." For a moment the picture filled his mind as it had once, perhaps, filled that of the long-dead Chrasmologic author: a patio garden with a fountain and many flowers, its top covered with netting—bulbuls, thrushes, larks, and goldfinches, their voices weaving a rich fabric of melody that would stretch unbroken through decades and perhaps through a century, until the netting rotted and the birds flew free at last.

And even then, might they not return at times? Would they not surely return, darting through rents in the ruined netting to drink at that tinkling fountain and nest in the safety of the patio garden, their long concerto ended yet continued beyond its end, as the orchestra plays when the audience is leaving a theater? Playing on and on for the joy of the music, when the last theater-goer has gone home, when the yawning ushers are snuffing the candles and the guttering footlights, when the actors and actresses have washed away their makeup and changed back into the clothing they ordinarily wear, the plain brown skirts and trousers, drab blouses and tunics and coats worn to the theater, worn to work as so many other drab brown garments, as plain as the bulbuls' brown feathers, were worn to work?

"But if the birds are sold," Silk continued (actors and actresses, the-ater and audience, garden, fountain, net, and songbirds all banished from his consciousness), "how are songs to be had? We, who were so rich in songs, are now left poor. It will not help us, as the foreknowing authors point out in the next line, to daub a raven, smearing a black bird with the delicate beauties of the lark or the decent brown of the bulbul. Not enough, even, to gild it like a goldfinch. It is still a raven."

He drew a deep breath. "Any ignorant man, you see, my children, may find himself in a position of veneration and authority. Suppose, for exam-ple, that some uneducated man—let us say an upright and an honorable man, one of you boys in Maytera Marble's class taken from her class and brought up with no further education—were by some chance to be thrust into the office of His Cognizance the Prolocutor. You would eat and sleep in His Cognizance's big palace on the Palatine. You would hold the baculus and wear the jeweled robes, and all the rest of us would kneel for your blessing. But you could not provide us with the wisdom that it would be your duty to supply. You would be a croaking raven daubed with paint, with gaudy colors."

While he counted silently to three, Silk stared up at the manteion's dusty rafters, giving the image time to sink into the minds of his audi-ence. "I hope that you understand, from what I've said, why your educa-tion must continue. And I hope, too, that you also understand that though I took my example from the Chapter, I might just as easily have taken it from common life, speaking of a trader or a merchant, of a chief clerk or a commissioner. You have need of learning, children, in order that the whorl will someday have need of you."

Silk paused once more, both hands braced upon the old, cracked stone ambion. The tarnished sunlight that streamed through the lofty window above the wide Sun Street door was perceptibly less brilliant now. "Thus the Writings have made it abundantly clear that your palaestra *will not* be sold—not for taxes, or any other reason. I've heard that there is a rumor that it will be, and that many of you believe it. I repeat, that is not the case."

For a moment he basked in their smiles.

"Now I'll tell you about the meaning that this passage holds for me. It was I who opened the Writings, you see, and so there was a message for me as well as for all of us here. Today, while you were studying, I went to market. There I purchased a fine speaking bird, a night chough, for a private sacrifice—one that I shall make when you have gone home.

"I've already told you how, when I bought the lambs you enjoyed so much, I hoped that a god, pleased with us, would come to this Window, as gods appeared here in the past. And I tried to show you how foolish that was. Another gift, a far greater gift, was given me instead—a gift that all the lambs in the market could not buy. I've said that I'm not going to tell you about it today, but I will tell you that it wasn't because of my prayers, or the sacrifices, or any other good work of mine that I received it. But receive it I did."

Old Maytera Rose coughed, a dry, sceptical sound from the mechanism that had replaced her larynx before Silk had spoken his first word.

"I knew that I, and I alone, must offer a sacrifice of thanks for that, though I had already spent all of the money that I had on the lambs. I would like very much to explain to you now that I had some wise plan for dealing with my dilemma—with my problem—but I didn't. Knowing only that a victim was necessary, I dashed off to the market, trusting in the merciful gods. Nor did they fail me. On the way I met a stranger who provided me with the price of an excellent victim, the speaking night chough I told you about earlier, a bird very like a raven.

"I found out, you see, that birds are not sold for a song. And I was given a sign—such is the generosity of the gracious gods to those who petition them—that a god will indeed come to this Sacred Window when I have made my sacrifice. It may be a long time, as I told Kit, so we must not be impatient. We must have faith, and remember always that the gods have other ways of speaking to us, and that if our Windows have fallen silent, these others have not. In omens and dreams and visions, the gods speak to us as they did when our parents and grandparents were young. Whenever we are willing to provide a victim, they speak to us plainly through augury, and the Writings are always here for us, to be consulted in a moment whenever we have need of them. We should be ashamed to say, as some people sometimes do, that in this age we are like boats without rudders."

Thunder rumbled through the windows, louder even than the bawlings of the beggars and vendors on Sun Street; the children stirred uneasily at the sound. After leading them in a brief prayer, Silk dismissed them.

Already the first hot, heavy drops of the storm were turning the yellow dust to mud beyond the manteion's doors. Children scurried off up or down Sun Street, none lingering this afternoon, as they sometimes did, to gossip or play.

The three sibyls had remained inside to assist at his sacrifice. Silk jogged from the manteion back to the manse, pulled on leather sacrificial gauntlets, and took the night chough from its cage. It struck at his eyes like an adder, its long, crimson beak missing by a finger's width.

He caught its head in one gauntleted hand, reminding himself grimly that many an augur had been killed by the victim he had intended to sacrifice, that scarcely a year passed without some unlucky augur, somewhere in the city, being gored by a bull or a stag.

"Don't try that again, you bad bird." He spoke half to himself. "Don't you know you'll be accursed forever if you harm me? You'll be stoned to death, and your spirit handed over to devils."

The night chough's bill clacked; its wings beat vainly until he trapped its struggling body beneath his left arm.

Back in the dim and airless heat of the manteion, the sibyls had kindled the sacrificial fire on the altar. When Silk entered, a solemn procession of one down the central aisle, they began their slow dance, their wide black skirts flapping, their tuneless voices lifted in an eerie, ritual wail that was as old as the whorl itself.

The fire was a small one, and its fragrant split cedar was already burning fast; Silk told himself that he would have to act quickly if his sacrifice were not to take place when the flames were dying, always a bad omen.

Passing the bird quickly over the fire, he pronounced the shortest invocation and gave his instructions in a rush of uncadenced words: "Bird, you must speak to every god and goddess you encounter, telling them of our faith and of our great love and loyalty. Say too how grateful I am for the immense and undeserved condescension accorded me, and tell them how earnestly we desire their divine presence at this, our Sacred Window.

"Bird, you must speak thus to Great Pas, the Father of the Gods.

"Bird, you must speak thus also to Sinuous Echidna, Great Pas's consort. You must speak so to Scalding Scylla, to Marvelous Molpe, to Black Tartaros, to Mute Hierax, to Enchanting Thelxiepeia, to Ever-feasting Phaea, to Desert Sphigx, and to any other god that you may encounter in Mainframe—but particularly to the Outsider, who has greatly favored me, saying that for the remainder of my days I will do his will. That I abase myself before him."

"No, no," the night chough muttered, as it had in the market. And then, "Please, no."

Silk pronounced the final words: "Have no speech with devils, bird. Neither are you to linger in any place where devils are."

Grasping the frantic night chough firmly by the neck, he extended his gauntleted right hand to Maytera Rose, the senior among the sibyls. Into it she laid the bone-hilted knife of sacrifice that Patera Pike had inherited from his own predecessor. Its long, oddly crooked blade was dull with years and the ineradicable stains of blood, but both edges were bright and keen.

The night chough's beak gaped. It struggled furiously. A last strangled half-human cry echoed from the distempered walls of the manteion, and the wretched night chough went limp in Silk's grasp. Interrupting the ritual, he held the flaccid body to his ear, then brushed open one blood-red eye with his thumb.

"It's dead," he told the wailing women. For a moment he was at a loss for words. Helplessly he muttered, "I've never had this happen before. Dead already, before I could sacrifice it."

They halted their shuffling dance. Maytera Marble said diplomatically, "No doubt it has already carried your thanks to the gods, Patera."

Maytera Rose sniffed loudly and reclaimed the sacrificial knife.

Little Maytera Mint inquired timidly, "Aren't you going to burn it, Patera?"

Silk shook his head. "Mishaps of this kind are covered in the rubrics, Maytera, although I admit I never thought I'd have to apply those particular strictures. They state unequivocally that unless another victim can be produced without delay, the sacrifice must not proceed. In other words, we can't just throw this dead bird into the sacred fire. This could just as well be something that one of the children picked up in the street."

He wanted to rid himself of it as he spoke—to fling it among the benches or drop it down the chute into which Maytera Marble and Maytera Mint would eventually shovel the still-sacred ashes of the altar fire. Controlling himself with an effort, he added, "All of you have seen more of life than I. Haven't you ever assisted at a profaned sacrifice before?"

Maytera Rose sniffed again. Like her earlier sniff, it reeked of condemnation; what had happened was unquestionably Patera Silk's fault, and his alone. It had been he and none other (as the sniff made exquisitely plain), who had chosen this contemptible bird. If only he had been a little more careful, a little more knowledgeable, and above all a great deal more pious—in short, much, much more like poor dear Patera Pike —nothing of this shameful kind could possibly have occurred.

Maytera Marble said, "No, Patera, never. May I speak with you when we're through here, on another topic? In my room in the palaestra, perhaps?"

Silk nodded. "I'll meet you there as soon as I've disposed of this, Maytera." The temptation to berate himself proved too strong. "I ought to have known better. The Writings warned me; but they left me foolish enough to suppose that my sacrifice might yet be acceptable, even if our Sacred Window remained empty. This will be a salutary lesson for me, Maytera. At least I certainly hope it will be, and it had better be. Thank Phaea that the children weren't here to see it."

By this time Maytera Mint had nerved herself to speak. "No one can ever know the mind of the Outsider, Patera. He isn't like the other gods, who take counsel with one another in Mainframe."

"But when the gods have spoken so clearly—" Realizing that what he was saying was not to the point, Silk left the thought incomplete. "You're right, of course, Maytera. His desires have been made plain to me, and this sacrifice was not included among them. In the future I'll try to confine myself to doing what he's told me to do. I know I can rely upon all of you to assist me in that, as in everything."

Maytera Rose did not sniff a third time, mercifully contenting herself with scratching her nose instead. Her nose, her mouth, and her right eye were the most presentable parts of her face; and though they had been molded of some tough polymer, they appeared almost normal. Her left eye, with which she had been born, seemed at once mad and blind, bleared and festering.

While trying to avoid that eye, and wishing (as he so often had since coming to the manteion) that replacements were still available, Silk shifted the night chough from his left hand to his right. "Thank you, Maytera Rose, Maytera Marble, Maytera Mint. Thank you. We'll do much better next time, I feel certain." He had slipped off his sacrificial gauntlets; the hated bird felt warm and somehow dusty in his perspiring hands. "In the palaestra, in five minutes or so, Maytera Marble."

CHAPTER

3   TWILIGHT

"In here, Patera!"

Silk halted abruptly, nearly slipping as the wet gravel rolled beneath his shoes.

"In the arbor," Maytera Marble added. She waved, her black-clad arm and gleaming hand just visible through the screening grape leaves.

The first fury of the storm had passed off quickly, but it was still raining, a gentle pattering that settled like a benediction upon her struggling beds of kitchen herbs.

We meet like lovers, Silk thought as he regained his balance and pushed aside the dripping foliage, and wondered for an instant whether she did not think the same.

No. As lovers, he admitted to himself. For he loved her as he had loved his mother, as he might have loved the older sister he had never had, striving to draw forth the shy smile she achieved by an inclination of her head—to win her approval, the approbation of an old sibyl, of a worn-out chem at whom nobody, when he had been small and there had been a lot more chems around, would ever have troubled to glance twice, whom no one but the youngest children ever thought interesting. How lonely he would have been in the midst of the brawling congestion of this quarter, if it had not been for her!

She rose as he entered the arbor and sat again as he sat. He said, "You really don't have to do that when we're alone, sib. I've told you."

Maytera Marble tilted her head in such a way that her rigid, metal face appeared contrite. "Sometimes I forget. I apologize, Patera."

"And I forget that I should never correct you, because I always find out, as soon as it's too late, that you were right after all. What is it you want to talk to me about, Maytera?"

"You don't mind the rain?" Maytera Marble looked up at the overarching thatch of vines.

"Of course not. But you must. If you don't feel like walking all the way to the palaestra, we could go into the manteion. I want to see if the roof still leaks, anyway."

She shook her head. "Maytera Rose would be upset. She knows that it's perfectly innocent, but she doesn't want us meeting in the palaestra, with no one else present. People might talk, you know—the kind of people who never attend sacrifices anyway, and are looking for an excuse. And she didn't want to come herself, and Maytera Mint's watching the fire. So I thought out here. It's not quite so private—Maytera can see us through the windows of the cenoby—and we still have a bit of shelter from the rain."

Silk nodded. "I understand."

"You said the rain must make me uncomfortable. That was very kind of you, but I don't feel it and my clothes will dry. I've had no trouble drying the wash lately, but it takes a great deal of pumping to get enough water to do it in. Is the manse's well still good?"

"Yes, of course." Seeing her expression, Silk shook his head. "No, not of course. It's comforting to believe as children do that Pas won't resist his daughter's pleas in our behalf much longer, and that he'll always provide for us. But one never knows, really; we can only hope. If we must have new wells dug, the Church will have to lend us the money, that's all. If we can't keep this manteion going without new wells, it will have to."

Maytera Marble said nothing, but sat with head bowed as though unable to meet his eyes.

"Does it worry you so much, Maytera? Listen, and I'll tell you a secret. The Outsider has enlightened me."

Motionless, she might have been a time-smoothed statue, decked for some eccentric commemorative purpose in a sibyl's black robe.

"It's true, Maytera! Don't you believe me?"

Looking up she said, "I believe that you believe you've been enlightened, Patera. I know you well, or at least I think I do, and you wouldn't lie about a thing like that."

"And he told me why—to save our manteion. That's my task." Silk stumbled after words. "You can't imagine how good it feels to be given a task by a god, Maytera. It's wonderful! You know it's what you were made for, and your whole heart points toward that one thing."

He rose, unable to sit still any longer. "If I'm to save our manteion, doesn't that tell us something? I ask you."

"I don't know, Patera. Does it?"

"Yes! Yes, it does. We can apply logic even to the instructions of the gods, can't we? To their acts and to their words, and we can certainly apply logic to this. It tells us two things, both of major importance. First, that the manteion's in danger. He wouldn't have ordered me to save it if it weren't, would he? So there's a threat of some sort, and that's vital for us to know." Silk strode out into the warm rain to stare east toward Mainframe, the home of the gods.

"The second is even more important, Maytera. It's that our manteion can be saved. It's endangered, not doomed, in other words. He wouldn't have ordered me to save it if that couldn't be done, would he?"

"Please come in and sit down, Patera," Maytera Marble pleaded. "I don't want you to catch cold."

Silk re-entered the arbor, and she stood.

"You don't have—" he began, then grinned sheepishly. "Forgive me, Maytera. Forgive me, please. I grow older, learning nothing at all."

She swung her head from side to side, her silent laugh. "You're not old, Patera. I watched you play a while today, and none of the boys are as quick as you are."

"That's only because I've been playing longer," he said, and they sat down together.

Smiling she clasped his hand in hers, surprising him. The soft skin had worn from the tips of her fingers long ago, leaving bare steel darkened like her thoughts by time, and polished by unending toil. "You and the children are the only things at this manteion that aren't old. You don't belong here, neither of you."

"Maytera Mint's not old. Not really, Maytera, though I know she's a good deal older than I am."

Maytera Marble sighed, a soft *hish* like the weary sweep of a mop across a terrazzo floor. "Poor Maytera Mint was born old, I fear. Or taught to be old before she could talk, perhaps. However that may be, she has always belonged here. As you never have, Patera."

"You believe it's going to be torn down, too, don't you? No matter what the Outsider may have told me."

Reluctantly, Maytera Marble nodded. "Yes, I do. Or as I ought to say, the buildings themselves may remain, although even that appears to be in doubt. But your manteion will no longer bring the gods to the people of this quarter, and our palaestra will no longer teach their children."

Silk snapped, "What chance would these sprats have—without your palaestra?"

"What chance do children of their class have now?"

He shook his head angrily, and would have liked to paw the ground.

"Such things have happened before, Patera. The Chapter will find new manteions for us. Better manteions, I think, because it would be difficult to find worse ones. I'll go on teaching and assisting, and you'll go on sacrificing and shriving. It will be all right."

"I received enlightenment today," Silk said. "I've told no one except a man I met in the street on my way to the market and you, and neither of you have believed me."

"Patera—"

"So it's clear that I'm not telling it very well, isn't it? Let me see if I can't do better." He was silent for a moment, rubbing his cheek.

"I'd been praying and praying for help. Praying mostly to the Nine, of course, but praying to every god and goddess in the Writings at one time or another; and about noon today my prayers were answered by the Outsider, as I've told you. Maytera, do you . . ." His voice quavered, and he found that he could not control it. "Do you know what he said to me, Maytera? What he told me?"

Her hands closed upon his until their grip was actually painful. "Only that he has instructed you to preserve our manteion. Please tell me the rest, if you can."

"You're right, Maytera. It isn't easy. I had always thought enlightenment would be a voice out of the sun, or in my own head, a voice that spoke in words. But it's not like that at all. He whispers to you in so many voices, and the words are living things that show you. Not just seeing, the way you might see another person in a glass, but hearing and smelling— and touch and pain, too, but all of them wrapped together so they become the same, parts of that one thing.

"And you understand. When I say he showed me, or that he told me something, that's what I mean."

Maytera Marble nodded encouragingly.

"He showed me all the prayers that have ever been said to any god for this manteion. I saw all the children at prayer from the time it was first built, their mothers and fathers too, and people who just came in to pray, or came to one of our sacrifices because they hoped to get a piece of meat, and prayed while they were here.

"And I saw the prayers of all you sibyls, from the very beginning. I don't ask you to believe this, Maytera, but I've seen every prayer you've ever said for our manteion, or for Maytera Rose and Maytera Mint, or for Patera Pike and me, and—well, for everyone in this whole quarter, thousands and thousands of prayers. Prayers on your knees and prayers standing up, and prayers you said while you were cooking and scrubbing floors. There used to be a Maytera Milkwort here, and I saw her praying,

and a Maytera Betel, a big dark woman with sleepy eyes." Silk paused for
breath. "Most of all, I saw Patera Pike."

"This is wonderful!" Maytera Marble exclaimed. "It must have been
marvelous, Patera." Silk knew it was impossible, that it was only their
crystalline lenses catching the light, but it seemed to him that her eyes
shone.

"And the Outsider decided to grant all those prayers. He told Patera
Pike, and Patera Pike was so happy! Do you remember the day I came
here from the schola, Maytera?"

Maytera Marble nodded again.

"That was the day. The Outsider granted Patera Pike enlightenment
that day, and he said—he said, here's the help that I'm—that I'm . . ."

Silk had begun to weep, and was suddenly ashamed. It was raining
harder now, as if encouraged by the tears that streaked his cheeks and
chin. Maytera Marble pulled a big, clean, white handkerchief out of her
sleeve and gave it to him.

She's always so practical, he thought, wiping his eyes and nose. A
handkerchief for the little ones; she must have a child sobbing in her
class every day. The record of her days is written in tears, and today I'm
that sobbing child. He managed to say, "Your children can't often be as
old as I am, Maytera."

"In class, you mean, Patera? They're never as old. Oh, you must mean
the grown men and women who were mine when they were boys and
girls. Many of them are older than you are. The oldest must be sixty, or
about that. I was—didn't teach until then." She called her memorandum
file, chiding herself as she always did for not calling it more often.
"Which reminds me. Do you know Auk, Patera?"

Silk shook his head. "Does he live in this quarter?"

"Yes, and comes on Scylsday, sometimes. You must have seen him.
The large, rough-looking man who sits in back?"

"With the big jaw? His clothes are clean, but he looks as if he hasn't
shaved. He wears a hanger—or perhaps it's a hunting sword—and he's
always alone. Was he one of your boys?"

Maytera Marble nodded sadly. "He's a criminal now, Patera. He
breaks into houses."

"I'm sorry to hear that," Silk said. For an instant he had a mental
picture of the hulking man from the back of the manteion surprised by a
householder and whirling clumsily but very quickly to confront him, like
a baited bear.

"I'm sorry, too, Patera, and I've been wanting to talk to you about him.

Patera Pike shrove him last year. You were here, but I don't think you knew about it."

"If I did, I've forgotten." To quiet the hiss of the wide blade as it cleared the scabbard, Silk shook his head. "But you're right, Maytera. I doubt that I knew."

"I didn't learn about it from Patera myself. Maytera Mint told me. Auk still likes her, and they have a little talk now and then."

Blowing his nose in his own handkerchief, Silk relaxed a trifle. This, he felt certain, was what she had wanted to speak to him about.

"Patera was able to get Auk to promise not to rob poor people any more. He'd done that, he said. He'd done it quite often, but he wouldn't any more. He promised Patera, Maytera says, and he promised her, too. You're going to lecture me now, Patera, because the promise of a man like that—a criminal's promise—can't be trusted."

"No man's promise can be trusted absolutely," Silk said slowly, "since no man is, or can ever be, entirely free from evil. I include myself in that, certainly."

Maytera Marble pushed her handkerchief back into her sleeve. "I think Auk's promise, freely given, can be relied on as much as anybody's, Patera. As much as yours, and I don't intend to be insulting. That was the way he was as a boy, and it's the way he is as a man, too, as well as I can judge. He never had a mother or a father, not really. He—but I'd better not go on, or I'll let slip things that Maytera's made me promise not to repeat, and then I'll feel terrible, and I'll have to tell both of them that I broke my word."

"Do you really believe that I may be able to help this man, Maytera? I'm surely no older than he is, and probably younger. He's not going to respect me the way he respected Patera Pike, remember."

Rain dripping from the sparkling leaves dotted Maytera Marble's skirt; she brushed at the spots absently. "That may be true, Patera, but you'll understand him better than Patera Pike could, I think. You're young, and as strong as he is, or almost. And he'll respect you as an augur. You needn't be afraid of him. Have I ever asked a favor of you, Patera? A real favor?"

"You asked me to intercede with Maytera Rose once, and I tried. I think I probably did more harm than good, so we won't count that. But you could ask a hundred favors if you wanted to, Maytera. You've earned that many and more."

"Then talk with Auk, Patera, some Scylsday. Shrive him if he asks you to."

"That isn't a favor," Silk said. "I'd do that much for anyone; but of course you want me to make a special effort for this Auk, to speak to him and take him aside, and so on; and I will."

"Thank you, Patera. Patera, you've known me for over a year now. Am I lacking in faith?"

The question caught Silk by surprise. "You, Maytera? Why—why I've never thought so. You've always seemed, I mean to me at least—"

"Yet I haven't had the faith in you, and the god who enlightened you, that I should've had. I just realized it. I've been trusting in merely human words and appearances, like any petty trader. You were saying that the god had promised Patera Pike help, I think. Could you tell me more about that? I was only listening with care before. This time I'll listen with faith, or try to."

"There's more than I could ever tell." Silk stroked his check. He had himself in check now. "Patera Pike was enlightened, as I said; and I was shown his enlightenment. He was told that all those prayers he had said over so many years were to be granted that day—that the help he had asked for, for himself and for this manteion and the whole quarter, would be sent to him at once."

Silk discovered that his fists were clenched. He made himself relax. "I was shown all that; then I saw that help arrive, alight as if with Pas's fire from the sun. And it was me. That was all it was, just me."

"Then you cannot fail," Maytera Marble told him softly.

Silk shook his head. "I wish it were that easy. I can fail, Maytera. I dare not."

She looked grave, as she often did. "But you didn't know this until today? At noon, in the ball court? That's what you said."

"No, I didn't. He told me something else, you see—that the time has come to act."

Maytera Marble sighed again. "I have some information for you, Patera. Discouraging information, I'm afraid. But first I want very much to ask you just one thing more, and tell you something, perhaps. It was the Outsider who spoke to you, you say?"

"Yes, I don't know a great deal about him, however, even now. He's one of the sixty-three gods mentioned in the Writings, but I haven't had a chance to look him up since it happened, and as I remember there isn't a great deal about him anyway. He told me about himself, things that aren't in the Writings unless I've forgotten them; but I haven't really had much time to think about them."

"When we were outside like him, living in the Short Sun Whorl before this one was finished and peopled, we worshipped him. No doubt you knew that already, Patera."

"I'd forgotten it," Silk admitted, "but you're right. It's in the tenth book, or the twelfth."

"We chems didn't share in sacrifices in the Short Sun Whorl." Maytera Marble fell silent for a moment, scanning old files. "It wasn't called manteion, either. Something else. If only I could find that, I could remember more, I think."

Without understanding what she meant, Silk nodded.

"There have been many changes since then, but it used to be taught that he was infinite. Not merely great, but truly without limit. There are expressions like that—I mean in arithmetic. Although we never get to them in my class."

"He showed me."

"They say that even the whorl ends someplace," Maytera Marble continued, "immense though it is. He doesn't. If you were to divide him among all the things in it, each part of him would still be limitless. Didn't you feel awfully small, Patera, when he was showing you all these things?"

Silk considered his answer. "No, I don't think I did. No, I didn't. I felt —well, great. I felt that way even though he was immeasurably greater, as you say. Imagine, Maytera, that His Cognizance the Prolocutor were to speak to me in person, assigning me some special duty. I'd feel, of course, that he was a far greater man than I, and a far, far greater man than I could ever be; but I'd feel that I too had become a person of significance." Silk paused, ruminating. "Now suppose a Prolocutor incalculably great."

"I understand. That answers several questions that I've had for a long while. Thank you, Patera. My news—I want to tell you why I asked you to meet me."

"It's bad news, I assume." Silk drew a deep breath. "Knowing that the manteion's at risk, I've been expecting some."

"It would appear to indicate—mistakenly, I feel sure, Patera—that you've failed already. You see, a big, red-faced man came to the palaestra while you were away. He said that he'd just bought it, bought the entire property from the city." Maytera Marble's voice fell. "From the Ayuntamiento, Patera. That's what he told me. He was here to look at our buildings. I showed him the palaestra and the manteion. I'm quite sure he didn't get into the cenoby or the manse, but he looked at everything from the outside."

"He said the sale was complete?"

She nodded.

"You're right, Maytera. This sounds very bad."

"He'd come in a floater, with a man to operate it for him. I saw it when we were going from the palaestra to the manteion. We went out the front, and along Sun Street past the ball court. He said he'd talked to you before he came here, but he hadn't told you he'd bought it. He said he'd thought you'd make trouble."

Silk nodded slowly. "I'd have hauled him out of his floater and broken his neck, I think, Maytera. Or at least I would have tried to."

She touched his knee. "That would have been wrong, Patera. You'd go to the Alambrera, and into the pits."

"Which wouldn't matter," Silk said. "His name's Blood, perhaps he told you."

"Possibly he did." Maytera Marble's rapid scan seldom functioned now; she fell silent as she searched past files, then said, "It's not a common name at all, you know. People think it's unlucky. I don't believe I've ever had a single boy called Blood."

Silk stroked his cheek, his eyes thoughtful. "Have you heard of him, Maytera? I haven't, but he must be a wealthy man to have a private floater."

"I don't think so. If the sale is complete, Patera, what can you do?"

"I don't know." Silk rose as he had before. A step carried him out of the arbor. A few drops of rain still fell through sunshine that seemed bright, though the shade had more than half covered the sun. "The market will be closing soon," he said.

"Yes." Maytera Marble joined him.

The skylands, which had been nearly invisible earlier, could be seen distinctly as dawn spread across them: distant forests, said to be enchanted, and distant cities, said to be haunted—subtle influences for good or ill, governing the lives of those below. "He's not a foreigner," Silk said, "or at least he doesn't talk like any foreigner I've ever met. He sounded as though he might have come from this quarter, actually."

Maytera Marble nodded. "I noticed that myself."

"There aren't many ways for our people here to become rich, are there, Maytera? I wouldn't think so, at least."

"I'm not sure I follow you."

"It doesn't matter. You wanted me to speak with this man Auk. On a Scylsday, you said; but there are always a dozen people waiting to talk to me then. Where do you think I might find Auk today?"

"Why, I have no idea. Could you go and see him this evening, Patera? That would be wonderful! Maytera Mint might know."

Silk nodded. "You said that she was in the manteion, waiting for the fire to die. Go in and ask her, please, while you're helping her purify the altar. I'll speak with you again in a few minutes."

Watching them from a window of the cenoby, Maytera Rose grunted with satisfaction when they separated. There was danger there, no matter how Maytera and Patera might deceive themselves—filthy things she could do for him, and worse that he might do to her. Undefiled Echidna hated everything of that kind, blinding those who fell as she had blinded her. At times Maytera Rose, kneeling before her daughter's image, felt that she herself was Echidna, Mother of Gods and Empress of the Whorl.

Strike, Echidna. Oh, strike!

It was dark enough already for the bang of the door to kindle the bleared light in one corner of Silk's bedroom, the room over the kitchen, the old storeroom that old Patera Pike had helped clean out when he arrived. (For Silk had never been able to make himself move his possessions into Pike's larger room, to throw out or burn the faded portraits of the old man's parents or his threadbare, too-small clothing.) By that uncertain glow, Silk changed into his second-best robe. Collar and cuffs were detachable in order that they might be more easily, and thus more frequently, laundered. He removed them and laid them in the drawer beside his only spare set.

What else? He glanced in the mirror; some covering for his untidy yellow hair, certainly. There was the wide straw hat he had worn that morning while laying new shingles on the roof, and the blue-trimmed black calotte that Patera Pike had worn on the coldest days. Silk decided upon both; the wide straw would cast a strong shadow on his face, but might blow off. The calotte fit nicely beneath it, and would supply a certain concealment still. Was this how men like this man Auk felt? Was it how they planned?

As reported by Maytera Marble, Maytera Mint had named half a dozen places in which he might come across Auk; all were in the Orilla, the worst section of the quarter. He might be robbed, might be murdered even though he offered no resistance. If Blood would not see him . . .

Silk shrugged. Blood's house would be somewhere on the Palatine; Silk could scarcely conceive of anyone who rode in a privately owned floater living anywhere else. There would be Civil Guardsmen everywhere on the Palatine after dark, Guardsmen on foot, on horseback, and in armed floaters. One could not just kick down a door, as scores of housebreakers did in this quarter every night. The thing was impossible.

Yet something must be done, and done tonight; and he could not think of anything else to do.

He fingered his beads, then dropped them back into his pocket, removed the silver chain and voided cross of Pas and laid them reverently before the triptych, folded two fresh sheets of paper, put them into the battered little pen case he had used at the schola, and slipped it into the big inner pocket of his robe. He might need a weapon; he would almost certainly need some sort of tool.

He went downstairs to the kitchen. There was a faint stirring from the smelly waste bin in the corner: a rat, no doubt. As he had often before, Silk reminded himself to have Horn catch him a snake that might be tamed.

Through the creaking kitchen door, he stepped out into the garden again. It was almost dark, and would be fully dark by the time he reached the Orilla, eight streets away. The afternoon's rain had laid the dust, and the air, cooler than it had been in months, was fresh and clean; perhaps autumn was on the way at last. He should be tired, Silk told himself, yet he did not feel tired as he unlocked the side door of the manteion. Was this, in sober fact, what the Outsider wanted? This rush to battle? If so, his service was a joy indeed!

The altar fire was out, the interior of the manteion lit only by the silver sheen of the Sacred Window and the hidden flame of the fat, blue-glass lamp between Echidna's feet—Maytera Rose's lamp, burning some costly scented oil whose fragrance stirred his memory.

He clapped his hands to kindle the few lights still in working order, then fumbled among the shadows for the long-hafted, narrow-bladed hatchet with which he split shingles and drove roofing nails. Finding it, he tested its edge (so painstakingly sharpened that very morning) before slipping its handle into his waistband.

That, he decided after walking up and down and twice pretending to sit, would not do. There was a rusty saw in the palaestra's supply closet; it would be simple to shorten the handle, but the hatchet would be a less useful tool, and a much less serviceable weapon, afterward.

Stooping again, he found the rope that had prevented his bundle of shingles from sliding off the roof, a thin braided cord of black horsehair, old and pliant but still strong. Laying aside robe and tunic, he wound it about his waist, tied the ends, and slid the handle of the hatchet through several of the coils.

Dressed again, he emerged once more into the garden, where a vagrant breeze sported with the delectable odor of cooking from the cenoby, reminding him that he ought to be preparing his own supper at this very moment. He shrugged, promising himself a celebratory one when he returned. The tomatoes that had dropped green from his vines were still not ripe, but he would slice them and fry them in a little oil. There was bread, too, he reminded himself, and the hot oil might be poured over it afterward to flavor and soften it. His mouth watered. He would scrape out the grounds he had reused so long, scrub the pot, and brew fresh coffee. Finish with an apple and the last of the cheese. A feast! He wiped his lips on his sleeve, ashamed of his greed.

After closing and carefully locking the side door of the manteion, he made a wary study of the cenoby windows. It would probably not matter if Maytera Marble or Maytera Mint saw him leave, but Maytera Rose would not hesitate to subject him to a searching cross-examination.

The rain had ended, there could be no doubt of that; there had been an hour of rain at most, when the farmers needed whole days of it. As he hurried along Sun Street once more, east this time and thus away from the market, Silk studied the sky.

The thinnest possible threads of gold still shone here and there among scudding clouds, threads snapped already by the rising margin of the ink-black shade. While he watched, the threads winked out; and the skylands, which had hovered behind the long sun like so many ghosts, shone forth in all their beauty and wonder: flashing pools and rolling forests, checkered fields and gleaming cities.

Lamp Street brought him to the Orilla, where the lake waters had begun when Viron was young. This crumbling wall half buried in hovels had been a busy quay, these dark and hulking old buildings, warehouses. No doubt there had been salting sheds, too, and rope walks, and many other things; but all such lightly built structures had disappeared before the last caldé, rotted, tumbled, and at last cannibalized for firewood. The very weeds that had sprouted from their sites had withered, and the cellar of every shiprock ruin left standing was occupied by a tavern.

Listening to the angry voices that issued from the one he approached, Silk wondered why anyone went there. What sorts of lives could they be to which fifty or a hundred men and women preferred this? It was a terrifying thought.

He paused at the head of the stair to puzzle out the drawing chalked on the grimy wall beside it, a fierce bird with outstretched wings. An eagle? Not with those spurs. A gamecock, surely; and the Cock had been one of the places suggested by Maytera Mint, a tavern (so Maytera Marble had said) she recalled Auk's mentioning.

The steep and broken stairs stank of urine; Silk held his breath as he groped down them, not much helped by the faint yellow radiance from the open door. Stepping to one side just beyond the doorway, he stood with his back to the wall and surveyed the low room. No one appeared to pay the least attention to him.

It was larger than he had expected, and less furnished. Mismatched deal tables stood here and there, isolated, but surrounded by chairs, stools, and benches equally heterodox on which a few silent figures lounged. Odious candles fumed and dribbled a sooty wax upon some (though by no means all) of these tables, and a green and orange lampion with a torn shade swung in the center of the room, seeming to tremble at the high-pitched anger of the voices below it. The backs of jostling onlookers obscured what was taking place there.

"Hornbus, you whore!" a woman shrieked.

A man's voice, slurred by beer yet hissing swift with the ocher powder called rust, suggested, "Stick it out your skirt, sweetheart, an' maybe she will." There was a roar of laughter. Someone kicked over a table, its thud accompanied by the crash of breaking glass.

"Here! Here now!" Quickly but without the appearance of haste, a big man with a hideously scarred face pushed through the crowd, an old skittlepin in one hand. "OUTside now! OUTside with this!" The onlookers parted to let two women with dirty gowns and disheveled hair through.

"Outside with *her!*" One woman pointed.

"OUTside with both." The big man caught the speaker expertly by the collar, tapped her head almost gently with the skittlepin, and shoved her toward the door.

One of the watching men stepped forward, held up his hand, and gestured in the direction of the other woman, who seemed to Silk almost too drunk to stand.

"Her, too," the big man with the skittlepin told her advocate firmly. He shook his head.

"Her too! And you!" The big man loomed above him, a head the taller. "OUTside!"

Steel gleamed and the skittlepin flashed down. For the first time in his life, Silk heard the sickening crepitation of breaking bone; it was followed at once by the high, sharp report of a needler, a sound like the crack of a child's toy whip. A needler (momentarily, Silk thought it the needler that had fired) flew into the air, and one of the onlookers pitched forward.

Silk was on his knees beside him before he himself knew what he had done, his beads swinging half their length in sign after sign of addition. "I convey to you, my son, the forgiveness of all the gods. Recall now the words of Pas—"

"He's not dead, cully. You an augur?" It was the big man with the scarred face. His right arm was bleeding, dark blood oozing through a soiled rag he pressed tightly against the cut.

"In the name of all the gods you are forgiven forever, my son. I speak here for Great Pas, for Divine Echidna, for Scalding Scylla, for—"

"Get him out of here," someone snapped; Silk could not tell whether he meant the dead man or himself. The dead man was bleeding less than the big man, a steady, unspectacular welling from his right temple. Yet he was surely dead; as Silk chanted the Final Formula and swung his beads, his left hand sought a pulse, finding none.

"His friends'll take care of him, Patera. He'll be all right."

Two of the dead man's friends had already picked up his feet.

". . . and for Strong Sphigx. Also for all lesser gods." Silk hesitated; it had no place in the Formula, but would these people know? Or care? Before rising, he finished in a whisper: "The Outsider likewise forgives you, my son, no matter what evil you did in life."

The tavern was nearly empty. The man who had been hit with the skittlepin groaned and stirred. The drunken woman was kneeling beside him just as Silk had knelt beside the dead man, swaying even on her knees, one hand braced on the filthy floor. There was no sign of the needler that had flown into the air, nor of the knife that the injured man had drawn.

"You want a red ribbon, Patera?"

Silk shook his head.

"Sure you do. On me, for what you done." The big man wound the rag about his arm, knotted it dexterously with his left hand, and pulled the knot tight with his left hand and his teeth.

"I need to know something," Silk said, returning his beads to his pocket, "and I'd much rather learn it than get a free drink. I'm looking for a man called Auk. Was he in here? Can you tell me where I might find him?"

The big man grinned, the gap left by two missing teeth a little cavern in his mirth. "Auk, you say, Patera? Auk? There's quite a few with that name. Owe him money? How'd you know I'm not Auk myself?"

"Because I know him, my son. Know him by sight, I should have said. He's nearly as tall as you are, with small eyes, a heavy jaw, and large ears. I would guess he's five or six years younger than you are. He attends our Scylsday sacrifices regularly."

"Does he now." The big man appeared to be staring off into the dimness of the darkest corner of the room; abruptly he said, "Why, Auk's still here, Patera. Didn't you tell me you'd seen him go?"

"No," Silk began. "I—"

"Over there." The big man pointed toward the corner, where a solitary figure sat at a table not much larger than his chair.

"Thank you, my son," Silk called. He crossed the room, detouring around a long and dirty table. "Auk? I'm Patera Silk, from the manteion on Sun Street."

"Thanks for what?" the man called Auk inquired.

"For agreeing to talk with me. You signaled to him somehow—waved or something, I suppose. I didn't see it, but it's obvious you must have."

"Sit down, Patera."

There was no other chair. Silk brought a stool from the long table and sat.

"Somebody send you?"

Silk nodded. "Maytera Mint, my son. But I don't wish to give you the wrong impression. I haven't come as a favor to her, or as a favor to you, either. Maytera was doing me a favor by telling me where to find you, and I've come to ask you for another one, shriving."

"Figure I need it, Patera?" There was no trace of humor in Auk's voice.

"I have no way of knowing, my son. Do you?"

Auk appeared to consider. "Maybe so. Maybe not."

Silk nodded—understandingly, he hoped. He found it unnerving to talk with this burly ruffian in the gloom, unable to see his expression.

The big man with the wounded arm set an astonishingly delicate glass before Silk. "The best we got, Patera." He backed away.

"Thank you, my son." Turning on his stool, Silk looked behind him; the injured man and the drunken woman were no longer beneath the lampion, though he had not heard them go.

"Maytera Mint likes you, Patera," Auk remarked. "She tells me things about you sometimes. Like the time you got the cats' meat woman mad at you."

"You mean Scleroderma?" Silk felt himself flush, and was suddenly glad that Auk could not see him better. "She's a fine woman—a kind and quite genuinely religious woman. I was hasty and tactless, I'm afraid."

"She really empty her bucket over you?"

Silk nodded ruefully. "The odd thing was that I found a scrap of—of cats' meat, I suppose you'd call it, down my neck afterward. It stank."

Auk laughed softly, a deep, pleasant laugh that made Silk like him.

"I thought it an awful humiliation at the time," Silk continued. "It happened on a Thelxday, and I thanked her on my knees that my poor mother wasn't alive to hear about it. I thought, you know, that she would have been terribly hurt, just as I was myself at the time. Now I realize that she would only have teased me about it." He sipped from the graceful little glass before him; it was probably brandy, he decided, and good brandy, too. "I'd let Scleroderma paint me blue and drag me the whole length of the Alameda, if it would bring my mother back."

"Maytera Mint was the nearest to a real mother I ever had," Auk said. "I used to call her that—she let me—when we were alone. For a couple of years I pretended like that. She tell you?"

Silk shook his head, then added, "Maytera Marble said something of the sort. I'm afraid I didn't pay a great deal of attention to it."

"The Old One brought up us boys, and he raised us hard. It's the best way. I've seen a lot that didn't get it, and I know."

"I'm sure you do."

"Every so often I tell myself I ought to stick my knife in her, just to get her and her talk out of my head. Know what I mean?"

Silk nodded, although he could not be certain that the burly man across the table could see it. "Better than you do yourself, I think. I also know that you'll never actually harm her. Or if you do, it won't be for that reason. I'm not half as old as Patera Pike was, and not a tenth as wise; but I do know that."

"I wouldn't take the long end of that bet."

Silk said nothing, his eyes upon the pale blur that was Auk's face, where for a moment it seemed to him that he had glimpsed the shadow of a muzzle, as though the unseen face were that of a wolf or bear.

Surely, he thought, this man can't have been called Auk from birth. Surely "Auk" is a name he's assumed.

He pictured Maytera Mint leading the boy Auk into class on a chain, then Maytera Mint warned by Maytera Rose that Auk would turn on her when he was grown. He sipped again to rid himself of the fancy. Auk's mother had presumably named him; the small auks of Lake Limna were flightless, thus it was a name given by mothers who hoped their sons would never leave them. But Auk's mother must have died while he was still very young.

"But not here." Auk's fist struck the table, nearly upsetting it. "I'll come Scylsday, day after tomorrow, and you can shrive me then. All right?"

"No, my son," Silk said. "It must be tonight."

"Don't you trust—"

"I'm afraid I haven't made myself entirely clear," Silk interposed. "I haven't come here to shrive you, though I'd be delighted to do it if you wish, and I'm certain it would make Maytera Mint very happy when I told her I had. But you must shrive me, Auk, and you must do it tonight. That is what I've come for. Not here, however, as you say. In some more private place."

"I can't do that!"

"You can, my son," Silk insisted softly. "And I hope you will. Maytera Mint taught you, and she must have taught you that anyone who is himself free of deep stain can bring the pardon of the gods to one who is in immediate danger of death."

"If you think I'm going to kill you, Patera, or Gib over there—"

Silk shook his head. "I'll explain everything to you in that more private place."

"Patera Pike shrove me one time. Maytera got after me about it, so I finally said all right. I told him a lot of things I shouldn't have."

"And now you're wondering whether he told me something of what you told him," Silk said, "and you think that I'm afraid you'll kill me when I tell you that I told someone else. No, Auk. Patera told me nothing about it, not even that it took place. I learned that from Maytera Marble, who learned it from Maytera Mint, who learned of it from you."

Silk tasted his brandy again, finding it difficult to continue. "Tonight I intend to commit a major crime, or try to. I may be killed, in fact I rather expect it. Maytera Marble or Maytera Mint could have shriven me, of course; but I didn't want either of them to know. Then Maytera Marble mentioned you, and I realized you'd be perfect. Will you shrive me, Auk? I beg it."

Slowly, Auk relaxed; after a moment he laid his right hand on the table again. "You don't go the nose, Patera, do you?"

Silk shook his head.

"If this's a shave, it's a close one."

"It's not a shave. I mean exactly what I say."

Auk nodded and stood. "Then we'd better go somewhere else, like you want. Too bad, I was hoping to do a little business tonight."

He led Silk to the back of the dim cellar room, and up a ladder into a cavernous night varied here and there by pyramids of barrels and bales; and at last, when they had followed an alley paved with refuse for several streets, into the back of what appeared to be an empty shop. The sound of their feet summoned a weak green glow from one corner of the overlong room. Silk saw a cot with rumpled, soiled sheets; a chamber pot; a table that might have come from the tavern they had left; two plain wooden chairs; and, on the opposite wall, what appeared to be a still-summonable glass. Planks had been nailed across the windows on either side of the street door; a cheap colored picture of Scylla, eight-armed and smiling, was tacked to the planks. "Is this where you live?" he asked.

"I don't exactly live anywhere, Patera. I've got a lot of places, and this is the closest. Have a seat. You still want me to shrive you?"

Silk nodded.

"Then you're going to have to shrive me first so I can do it right. I guess you knew that. I'll try to think of everything."

Silk nodded again. "Do, please."

With speed and economy of motion surprising in so large a man, Auk knelt beside him. "Cleanse me, Patera, for I have given offense to Pas and to other gods."

His gaze upon the smiling picture of Scylla—and so well away from Auk's heavy, brutal face—Silk murmured, as the ritual required, "Tell me, my son, and I will bring you his forgiveness from the well of his boundless mercy."

"I killed a man tonight, Patera. You saw it. Kalan's his name. Gurnard was set to stick Gib, but he got him . . . ."

"With his skittlepin," Silk prompted softly.

"That's lily, Patera. That's when Kalan come out with his needler, only I had mine out."

"He intended to shoot Gib, didn't he?"

"I think so, Patera. He works with Gurnard off and on. Or anyway he used to."

"Then there was no guilt in what you did, Auk."

"Thanks, Patera."

After that, Auk remained silent for a long time. Silk prayed silently while he waited, listening with half an ear to angry voices in the street and the thunderous wheels of a passing cart, his thoughts flitting from and returning to the calm, amused and somehow melancholy voices he had heard in the ball court as he had reached for the ball he carried in a pocket still, and to the innumerable things the owner of those voices had sought to teach him.

"I robbed a few houses up on the Palatine. I was trying to remember how many. Twenty I can think of for sure. Maybe more. And I beat a woman, a girl called—"

"You needn't tell me her name, Auk."

"Pretty bad, too. She was trying to get more out of me after I'd already given her a real nice brooch. I'd had too much, and I hit her. Cut her mouth. She yelled, and I hit her again and floored her. She couldn't work for a week, she says. I shouldn't have done that, Patera."

"No," Silk agreed.

"She's better than most, and high, wide and handsome, too. Know what I mean, Patera? That's why I gave her the brooch. When she wanted more . . ."

"I understand."

"I was going to kick her. I didn't, but if I had I'd probably have killed her. I kicked a man to death, once. That was part of what I told Patera Pike."

Silk nodded, forcing his eyes away from Auk's boots. "If Patera brought you pardon, you need not repeat that to me; and if you refrained from kicking the unfortunate woman, you have earned the favor of the gods—of Scylla and her sisters particularly—by your self-restraint."

Auk sighed. "Then that's all I've done, Patera, since last time. Solved those houses and beat on Chenille. And I wouldn't have, Patera, if I hadn't of seen she wanted it for rust. Or anyhow I don't think I would have."

"You understand that it's wrong to break into houses, Auk. You must, or you wouldn't have told me about it. It is wrong, and when you enter a house to rob it, you might easily be killed, in which case you would die with the guilt upon you. That would be very bad. I want you to promise me that you will look for some better way to live. Will you do that, Auk? Will you give me your word?"

"Yes, Patera, I swear I will. I've already been doing it. You know, buying things and selling them. Like that."

Silk decided it would be wiser not to ask what sorts of things these were, or how the sellers had gotten them. "The woman you beat, Auk. You said she used rust. Am I to take it that she was an immoral woman?"

"She's not any worse than a lot of others, Patera. She's at Orchid's place."

Silk nodded to himself. "Is that the sort of place I imagine?"

"No, Patera, it's about the best. They don't allow any fighting or any-thing like that, and everything's real clean. Some of Orchid's girls have even gone uphill."

"Nevertheless, Auk, you shouldn't go to places of that kind. You're not bad looking, you're strong, and you have some education. You'd have no difficulty finding a decent girl, and a decent girl might do you a great deal of good."

Auk stirred, and Silk sensed that the kneeling man was looking at him, although he did not permit his own eyes to leave the picture of Scylla. "You mean the kind that has you shrive her, Patera? You wouldn't want one of them to take up with somebody like me. You'd tell her she de-served somebody better. Shag yes, you would!"

For a moment it seemed to Silk that the weight of the whole whorl's folly and witless wrong had descended on his shoulders. "Believe me, Auk, many of those girls will marry men far, far worse than you." He drew a deep breath. "As penance for the evil you have done, Auk, you are to perform three meritorious acts before this time tomorrow. Shall I explain to you the nature of meritorious acts?"

"No, Patera. I remember, and I'll do them."

"That's well. Then I bring to you, Auk, the pardon of all the gods. In the name of Great Pas, you are forgiven. In the name of Echidna, you are forgiven. In the name of Scylla, you are forgiven . . ." Soon the moment would come. "And in the name of the Outsider and all lesser gods, you are forgiven, by the power entrusted to me."

There was no objection from Auk. Silk traced the sign of addition in the air above his head.

"Now it's my turn, Auk. Will you shrive me, as I shrove you?"

The two men changed places.

Silk said, "Cleanse me, friend, for I am in sore danger of death, and I may give offense to Pas and to other gods."

Auk's hand touched his shoulder. "I've never did this before, Patera. I hope I get it right."

"Tell me . . ." Silk prompted.

"Yeah. Tell me, Patera, so that I can bring you the forgiveness of Pas from the well of bottomless mercy."

"I may have to break into a house tonight, Auk. I hope that I won't have to; but if the owner won't see me, or won't do what a certain god—the Outsider, Auk, you may know of him—wishes him to do, then I'll try to compel him."

"Whose—"

"If he sees me alone, I intend to threaten his life unless he does as the god requires. But to be honest, I doubt that he'll see me at all."

"Who is this, Patera? Who're you going to threaten?"

"Are you looking at me, Auk? You're not supposed to."

"All right, now I'm looking away. Who is this, Patera? Whose house is it?"

"There's no need for me to tell you that, Auk. Forgive me my intent, please."

"I'm afraid I can't, my son," Auk said, getting into the spirit of his role. "I got to know who this is, and why you're going to do it. Maybe you won't be running as big of a risk as you think you are, see? I'm the one that has to judge that, ain't I?"

"Yes," Silk admitted.

"And I see why you looked for me, 'cause I can do it better than anybody. Only I got to know, 'cause if this's just some candy, I got to tell you to go to a real augur after you scrape out, and forget about me. There's houses and then there's Houses. So who is it and where is it, Patera?"

"His name is Blood," Silk said, and felt Auk's hand tighten on his shoulder. "I assume that he lives somewhere on the Palatine. He has a private floater, at any rate, and employs a driver for it."

Auk grunted.

"I think that he must be dangerous," Silk continued. "I sense it."

"You win, Patera. I got to shrive you. Only you got to tell me all about it, too. I need to know what's going on here."

"The Ayuntamiento has sold this man our manteion."

Silk heard Auk's exhalation.

"It was bringing in practically nothing, you realize. The income from the manteion is supposed to balance the loss from the palaestra; tutorage doesn't cover our costs, and most of the parents are behind anyway. Ideally there should be enough left over for Juzgado's taxes, but our Window's been empty now for a very long while."

"Must be others doing better," Auk suggested.

"Yes. Considerably better in some cases, though it's been many years since a god has visited any Window in the city."

"Then they—the augurs there—could give you a little something, Patera."

Silk nodded, remembering his mendicant expeditions to those solvent manteions. "They have indeed helped at times, Auk. I'm afraid that the

Chapter has decided to put an end to that. It's turned our manteion over to the Juzgado in lieu of our unpaid taxes, and the Ayuntamiento has sold the property to this man Blood. That's how things appear, at least."

"We all got to pay the counterman come shadeup," Auk muttered diplomatically.

"The people need us, Auk. The whole quarter does. I was hoping that if you—never mind. I intend to steal our manteion back tonight, if I can, and you must shrive me for that."

The seated man was silent for a moment. At length he said, "The city keeps records on houses and so on, Patera. You go to the Juzgado and slip one of those clerks a little something, and they call up the lot number on their glass. I've done it. The monitor gives you the name of the buyer, or anyhow whoever's fronting for him."

"So that I could verify the sale, you mean."

"That's it, Patera. Make sure you're right about all this before you get yourself killed."

Silk felt an uncontrollable flood of relief. "I'll do as you suggest, provided that the Juzgado's still open."

"They wouldn't be, Patera. They close there about the same time as the market."

It was hard for him to force himself to speak. "Then I must proceed. I must act tonight." He hesitated while some frightened portion of his mind battered the ivory walls that confined it. "Of course this may not be the Blood you know, Auk. There must be a great many people of that name. Could Blood—the Blood you know—buy our manteion? It must be worth twenty thousand cards or more."

"Ten," Auk muttered. "Twelve, maybe, only he probably got it for the taxes. What's he look like, Patera?"

"A tall, heavy man. Angry looking, I'd say, although it may only have been that his face was flushed. There are wide bones under his plump cheeks, or so I'd guess."

"Lots of rings?"

Silk struggled to recall the prosperous-looking man's fat, smooth hands. "Yes," he said. "Several, at least."

"Could you smell him?"

"Are you asking whether he smelled bad? No, certainly not. In fact—"

Auk grunted. "What was it?"

"I have no idea, but it reminded me of the scented oil—no doubt you've noticed it—in the lamp before Scylla, in our manteion. A sweet, heavy odor, not quite so pungent as incense."

"He calls it musk rose," Auk said dryly. "Musk's a buck that works for him."

"It is the Blood you know, then."

"Yeah, it is. Now be quiet a minute, Patera. I got to remember the words." Auk rocked back and forth. There was a faint noise like the grating of sand on a shiprock floor as he rubbed his massive jaw. "As a penance for the evil that you're getting ready to do, Patera, you got to perform two or three meritorious acts I'll tell you about tonight."

"That is too light a penance," Silk protested.

"Don't weigh feathers with me, Patera, 'cause you don't know what they are yet. You're going to do 'em, ain't you?"

"Yes, Auk," Silk said humbly.

"That's good. Don't forget. All right, then I bring to you, Patera, the pardons of all the gods. In the name of Great Pas, you're forgiven. In the name of Echidna, you're forgiven. In the name of Scylla, of Molpe, of Tartaros, of Hierax, of Thelxiepeia, of Phaea, of Sphigx, and of all the lesser gods, you're forgiven, Patera, by the powers trusted to me."

Silk traced the sign of addition, hoping that the big man was doing the same over his head.

The big man cleared his throat. "Was that all right?"

"Yes," Silk said, rising. "It was very good indeed, for a layman."

"Thanks. Now about Blood. You say you're going to solve his place, but you don't even know where it is."

"I can ask directions when I reach the Palatine." Silk was dusting his knees. "Blood isn't a particular friend of yours, I hope."

Auk shook his head. "It ain't there. I been there a time or two, and that gets us to one of those meritorious acts that you just now promised me about. You got to let me take you there."

"If it isn't inconvenient—"

"It's shaggy—excuse me, Patera. Yeah, it's going to put me out by a dog's right, only you got to let me do it anyhow, if you really go to Blood's. If you don't, you'll get lost sure trying to find it. Or somebody'll know you, and that'll be worse. But first you're going to give Blood a whistle on my glass over there, see? Maybe he'll talk to you, or if he wants to see you he might even send somebody."

Auk strode across the room and clapped his hands; the monitor's colorless face rose from the depths of the glass.

"I want Blood," Auk told it. "That's the buck that's got the big place off the old Palustria Road." He turned to Silk. "Come over here, Patera. You stand in front of it. I don't want 'em to see me."

Silk did as he was told. He had talked through glasses before (there had been one in the Prelate's chambers at the schola), though not often. Now he discovered that his mouth was dry. He licked his lips.

"Blood is not available, sir," the monitor told him imperturbably. "Would someone else do?"

"Musk, perhaps," Silk said, recalling the name Auk had mentioned.

"It will be a few minutes, I fear, sir."

"I'll wait for him," Silk said. The glass faded to an opalescent gray.

"You want to sit, Patera?" Auk was pushing a chair against the backs of his calves.

Silk sat down, murmuring his thanks.

"I don't think that was too smart, asking for Musk. Maybe you know what you're doing."

Still watching the glass, Silk shook his head. "You had said he worked for Blood, that's all."

"Don't tell him you're with me. All right?"

"I won't."

Auk did not speak again, and the silence wrapped itself about them. Like the silence of the Windows, Silk thought, the silence of the gods: pendant, waiting. This glass of Auk's was rather like a Window; all glasses were, although they were so much smaller. Like the Windows, glasses were miraculous creations of the Short-Sun days, after all. What was it Maytera Marble had said about them?

Maytera herself, the countless quiescent soldiers that the Outsider had revealed, and in fact all similar persons—all chems of whatever kind— were directly or otherwise marvels of the inconceivably inspired Short-Sun Whorl, and in time (soon, perhaps) would be gone. Their women rarely conceived children, and in Maytera's case it was quite . . . .

Silk shook his shoulders, reminding himself severely that in all likelihood Maytera Marble would long outlive him—that he might be dead before shadeup, unless he chose to ignore the Outsider's instructions.

The monitor reappeared. "Would you like me to provide a few suggestions while you're waiting, sir?"

"No, thank you."

"I might straighten your nose just a trifle, sir, and do something regarding a coiffeur. You would find that of interest, I believe."

"No," Silk said again; and added, as much to himself as to the monitor, "I must think."

Swiftly the monitor's gray face darkened. The entire glass seemed to fall away. Black, oily-looking hair curled above flashing eyes from which Silk tore his own in horror.

As a swimmer bursts from a wave and discovers himself staring at an object he has not chosen—at the summer sun, perhaps, or a cloud or the top of a tree—Silk found that he was looking at Musk's mouth, lips as feverishly red and fully as delicate as any girl's.

To damp his fear, he told himself that he was waiting for Musk to speak; and when Musk did not, he forced himself to speak instead. "My name is Patera Silk, my son." His chin was trembling; before he spoke again, he clenched his teeth. "Mine is the Sun Street manteion. Or I should say it isn't, which is what I must see Blood about."

The handsome boy in the glass said nothing and gave no sign of having heard. In order that he might not be snared by that bright and savage stare again, Silk inventoried the room in which Musk stood. He could glimpse a tapestry and a painting, a table covered with bottles, and two elaborately inlaid chairs with padded crimson backs and contorted legs.

"Blood has purchased our manteion," he found himself explaining to one of the chairs. "By that I mean he's paid the taxes, I suppose, and they have turned the deed over to him. It will be very hard on the children. On all of us, to be sure, but particularly on the children, unless some other arrangement can be made. I have several suggestions to offer, and I'd like—"

A trooper in silvered conflict armor had appeared at the edge of the glass. As he spoke to Musk, Silk realized with a slight shock that Musk hardly reached the trooper's shoulder. "A new bunch at the gate," the trooper said.

Hurriedly, Silk began, "I'm certain for your sake—or for Blood's, I mean—that an accommodation of some sort is still possible. A god, you see—"

The handsome boy in the glass laughed and snapped his fingers, and the glass went dark.

CHAPTER 4   NIGHTSIDE

It had been late already when they had left the city. Beyond the black streak of the shade, the skylands had been as clear and as bright as Silk (who normally retired early and rose at shadeup) had ever seen them; he stared at them as he rode, his thoughts drowned in wonder. Here were nameless mountains filling inviolate valleys to the rim with their vast, black shadows. Here were savannah and steppe, and a coastal plain ringing a lake that he judged must certainly be larger than Lake Limna—all these doming the gloomy sky of night while they themselves were bathed in sunlight.

As they had walked the dirty and dangerous streets of the Orilla, Auk had remarked, "There's strange things happen nightside, Patera. I don't suppose you know it, but that's the lily word anyhow."

"I do know," Silk had assured him. "I shrive, don't forget, so I hear about them. Or at least I've heard a few very strange stories that I can't relate. You must have seen the things as they occurred, and that must be stranger still."

"What I was going to say," Auk had continued, "was that I never heard about any that was any stranger than this, what you're going to do, or try to do. Or seen anything stranger, either."

Silk had sighed. "May I speak as an augur, Auk? I realize that a great many people are offended by that, and Our Gracious Phaea knows I don't want to offend you. But this once may I speak?"

"If you're going to say something you wouldn't want anybody to hear, why, I wouldn't."

"Quite the contrary," Silk had declared, perhaps a bit too fervently. "It's something that I wish I could tell the whole city."

"Keep your voice down, Patera, or you will."

"I told you a god had spoken to me. Do you remember that?"

Auk had nodded.

"I've been thinking about it as we walked along. To tell the truth, it's not easy to think about anything else. Before I spoke to—to that unfortunate Musk. Well, before I spoke to him, for example, I ought to have been thinking over everything that I wanted to say to him. But I wasn't, or not very much. Mostly I was thinking about the Outsider; not so much what he had said to me as what it had been like to have him speaking to me at all, and how it had felt."

"You did fine, Patera." Auk had, to Silk's surprise, laid a hand on his shoulder. "You did all right."

"I don't agree, though I won't argue with you now. What I wanted to say was that there is really nothing strange at all about what I'm doing, or about your helping me to do it. Does the sun ever go out, Auk? Does it ever wink out as you or I might snuff out a lamp?"

"I don't know, Patera. I never thought about it. Does it?"

Silk had not replied, continuing in silence down the muddy street, matching Auk stride for stride.

"I guess it don't. You couldn't see them skylands up there nightside, if it did."

"So it is with the gods, Auk. They speak to us all the time, exactly as the sun shines all the time. When the dark cloud that we call the shade gets between us and the sun, we say it's night, or nightside, a term I never heard until I came to Sun Street."

"It don't really mean night, Patera. Not exactly. It means . . . All right, look at it like this. There's a day way of doing, see? That's the regular way. And then there's the other way, and nightside's when you do this other way—when everything's on the night side of the shade."

"We're on the night side of the shade for only half the day," Silk had told him. "But we are on the night side of whatever it is that bars us from the gods almost constantly, throughout our whole lives. And we really shouldn't be. We weren't meant to be. I got that one small ray of sunshine, you see, and it shouldn't be strange at all. It should be the most ordinary thing in the whorl."

He had expected Auk to laugh, and was surprised and pleased when he did not.

They had rented donkeys from a man Auk knew, a big gray for Auk and a smaller black for Silk. "Because I'll have to lead him back," Auk had said. "We got to get that straight right now. He don't stay with you."

Silk had nodded.

"You're going to get caught, like I told you, Patera. You'll talk to Blood, maybe, like you want. But it'll be after they get you. I don't like it, but there it is. So you're not going to need him to ride back on, and I'm not going to lose what I'm giving this donkey man to hold, which is double what he'd cost in the market."

"I understand," Silk had assured him.

Now, as they trotted along a narrow track that to him at least was largely invisible, with the toes of his only decent shoes intermittently intimidated by the stony soil, Auk's words returned to trouble him. Tearing his eyes from the skylands, he called, "You warned me that Blood was going to catch me, back there in the city while you were renting these donkeys for us. What do you think he'll do to me if he does?"

Auk twisted about to look at him, his face a pale blur in the shadow of the crowding trees. "I don't know, Patera. But you're not going to like it."

"You may not know," Silk said, "but you can guess much better than I can. You know Blood better than I do. You've been in his house, and I'm sure you must know several people who know him well. You've done business with him."

"Tried to, Patera."

"All right, tried to. Still you know what kind of man he is. Would he kill me, for breaking into his house? Or for threatening him? I fully intend to threaten his life if he won't return our manteion to the Chapter, assuming that I get that far."

"I hope not, Patera."

Unbidden and unwanted, Musk's features rose from Silk's memory, perfect—yet corrupt, like the face of a devil. So softly that he was surprised that Auk heard it, Silk said, "I have been wondering whether I shouldn't take my own life if I am caught. If I am, I say, although I hope not to be, and am determined not to be. It's seriously wrong to take one's own life, and yet—"

A chain or more ahead, Auk chuckled. "Kill yourself, Patera? Yeah, it could be a good idea. Keep it in mind, depending. You won't tell Blood about me?"

"I've sworn," Silk reminded him. "I would never break that oath."

"Good." Auk turned away again, his posture intent as his eyes sought to penetrate the shadows.

Clearly Auk had been less than impressed by his mention of suicide, and for a moment Silk resented it. But Auk was right. How could he serve any god if he set out determined to resign his task if it became too difficult? Auk had been correct to laugh; he was no better than a child, sallying forth with a wooden sword to conquor the whorl—something that he had in fact done not too many years ago.

Yet it was easy for Auk to remain calm, easy for Auk to mock his fears. Auk, who had no doubt broken into scores of these country villas, was not going to break into this one, or even to assist him in doing it. And yet, Silk reminded himself, Auk's own position was by no means impregnable.

"I would never violate my solemn oath, sworn to all the gods," Silk said aloud. "And besides, if Blood were to find out about you and have you killed—he didn't strike me as the type who kill men themselves—there would be no one to help me escape him."

Auk cleared his throat and spat, the sound unnaturally loud in the airless stillness of the forest. "I'm not going to do a shaggy thing for you, Patera. You can forget about that. You're working for the gods, right? Let them get you out."

Almost whispering, because he was saddened by the knowledge, Silk said, "Yes, you will, Auk."

"Sneeze it!"

"Because you couldn't ever be certain that I wouldn't tell, eventually. I won't, but you don't trust me. Or at least not that much."

Auk snorted.

"And since you're a better man than you pretend to be, the knowledge that I—not I particularly perhaps, but an augur who had been a companion of sorts, if only for this one night—required your help would devour you, even if you denied it a hundred times or more, as you very probably would. Thus you'll help me if you can, Auk, eventually and possibly quite quickly. I know you will. And because you will, it will go much better for me if Blood doesn't know about you."

"I'd crawl a long way in for a while, maybe, but that's all. Maybe go see Palustria for a year or three till Blood was gone or he'd forgotten about me. People ain't like you think, Patera. Maybe you studied a long time, but there's a lot that you don't know."

Which was true enough, Silk admitted to himself. For whatever inscrutable reasons, the gods thrust bios into the whorl knowing nothing of it; and if they waited until they were so wise as to make no mistakes before they acted, they waited forever. With sudden poignancy Silk wished that he might indeed wait forever, as some men did.

And yet he felt certain that he was right about Auk, and Auk wrong about himself. Auk still returned at times to talk with little Maytera Mint; and Auk had killed a man that evening—a serious matter even to a criminal, since the dead man had friends—because that man had been about to kill the big man called Gib. Auk might be a thief and even a murderer; but he had no real talent for murder, no innate bent toward evil. Not even Blood had such a bent, perhaps. He, Silk, had seen someone who did in Blood's glass, and he promised himself now that he would never again mistake mere dishonesty or desperation for it again.

"But I know you, Auk," he said softly. He shifted his weight in the vain hope of finding a more comfortable spot on the crude saddle. "I may be too trusting of people in general, as you say; but I'm right about you. You'll help me when you think that I require it."

Auk made a quick, impatient gesture, barely visible in the gloom. "Be quiet there, Patera. We're getting pretty close."

If there had ever been a real path, they were leaving it. With seeing feet, the donkeys picked their way up a rock-strewn hillside, often unavoidably bathed in the eerie skylight. At the top, Auk reined up and dismounted; Silk followed his example. Here the faintest of night breezes stirred, as stealthy as a thief itself, making away with the mingled scents of post oak and mulberry, of grass and fern withered almost to powder, of a passing fox, and the very essence of the night. The donkeys raised their long muzzles to catch it, and Silk fanned himself with his wide straw hat.

"See them lights, Patera?" Auk pointed toward a faint golden glimmer beyond the treetops. "That's Blood's place. What we did was circle around behind it, see? That's what we been doing ever since we got off the main road. On the other side, there's a big gate of steel bars, and a grassway for floaters that goes up to the front. Can you see that black line, kind of wavy, between us and the house?"

Silk squinted and stared, but could not.

"That's a stone wall about as high as that little tree down there. It's got big spikes on top, which I'd say is mostly for show. Could be if you threw your rope up there and caught one, you could climb up the wall—I don't know that anybody's ever tried it. Only Blood's got protection, understand? Guards, and a big talus that I know about for sure. I don't know what else. You ever done anything like this before, Patera?"

Silk shook his head.

"I didn't think so. All right, here's all that's going to happen, probably. You're going to try to get over that wall, with your rope or whatever, only you're not going to make it. Along about shadeup, you're going to start hiking back to the city, feeling worse than shit in the street and thinking that I'm going to laugh myself sick at you. Only I'm not. I'm going to sacrifice 'cause you came back alive, understand? A black ram to

Tartaros, see? A good big one, at your manteion the day after tomorrow, you got my word on that."

Auk paused for breath.

"And after my sacrifice is over, I'm going to make you swear you'll never try anything this stupid ever again. You think you can make Blood swear to give back your manteion, which you can't. And you think he'll stick with whatever he swore to afterward, which he wouldn't, not for every god in Mainframe. But I can make you swear, Patera, and I'm going to—see if I don't. And I know you'll stick. You're the kind that does."

Silk said gratefully, "This is really very good of you, Auk. I don't deserve it."

"If I was really good I wouldn't have hired us these donkeys, Patera. I'd have hiked out here with you and let you tire yourself—that way you'd come back that much quicker."

Troubled, Auk paused, running his fingers through his hair. "Only if you do get inside, it'd be all queer if you was tired. You don't work when you're fagged out, not in my trade, only when you're cold up and full of jump. Only I've done a hundred or more, and I wouldn't try to solve this one for a thousand goldboys. Good-bye, Patera. Phaea smile on you."

"Wait a moment." Silk took him by the sleeve. "Haven't you been inside that house? You said you had."

"A couple of times on business, Patera. I don't know anything much about it."

"You said that I was certain to be caught, and I'll concede that you may very well be correct. Nevertheless, I don't intend to be caught; and if I am, I will have failed the Outsider, the god who has sent me, just as I will have failed him if I don't make the attempt tonight. Can't you see that? Haven't you ever been caught yourself, Auk? You must have been."

Auk nodded reluctantly. "Once, Patera, when I was just a sprat. He winnowed me out. By Phaea's sow, I thought he was going to kill me. And when he was through, he kicked me out into the street. That was right in our quarter. I'll show you the house sometime."

He tried to pull free, but Silk retained his grip on his sleeve. "How were you caught, Auk? What was it that you did wrong? Tell me, please, so I won't make the same mistake."

"You done it already, Patera." Auk sounded apologetic. "Look here. I'd solved a few places, and I got pretty hot on myself and thought I couldn't get caught. I had some picks, know what I mean? And I showed 'em off and called myself a master of the art, thinking Tartaros himself would pull his hat off to me. Got to where I never troubled to look things over the way a flash buck ought to."

Auk fell silent, and Silk asked, "What was the detail you overlooked?"

"Debt, Patera." Auk chuckled. "That don't go with Blood, 'cause it's not him you got to worry about."

"Tell me anyway," Silk insisted.

"Well, Patera, this bucko that had the house had a good lay, see? Taking care of all the shoes and such like up at Ermine's. You know about Ermine's? A goldboy or maybe two for supper. Gilt places like that deal on Scylsday, 'cause Sphigxday's their plum night, see? So I gleaned once he'd got off he'd put down a few and snoodge like a soldier. If I was to flush his fussock—rouse up his wife, Patera—she'd stave her broom getting him off straw, and I'd beat the hoof to my own tune. Only he owed 'em, you see? Up to Ermine's. They're holding his lowre back on him, so he was straight up, or nearly. So he napped me and I owed it."

Silk nodded.

"Now you tonight, Patera, you're doing the same thing. You're not flash. You don't know who's there or who ain't, or how big the rooms might be, or what kind of windows. Not a pip of the scavy you got to have right in your hand."

"You must be able to tell me something," Silk said.

Auk adjusted the heavy hanger he wore. "The house's a tidy stone place with a wing to each side. Three floors in 'em, and the middle's two. When you come in the front like I did, there's a big front room, and that's the farthest I got. Him that told me about floors says there's a capital cellar and another underneath. There's guards. You saw one of that quality in my glass. And there's a tall ass, begging your pardon, Patera. Like what I told you already."

"Have you any idea where Blood sleeps?"

Auk shook his head, the motion scarcely visible. "But he don't sleep a hour, nightside. The flash never do, see? His business'll keep him out of bed till shadeup." Sensing Silk's incomprehension, Auk elaborated. "People coming to talk to him like I did, or the ones that work for him with their hats off so he can tell where they come from and where they're going, Patera."

"I see."

Auk took the reins of the smaller donkey and mounted his own. "You got four, maybe five hours to shadeup. Then you got to get back. I wouldn't be too close to that wall then if I was you, Patera. There might come a guard walking the top. I've known 'em to do that."

"All right." Silk nodded, reflecting that he had some ground to cover before he was near the wall at all. "Thank you again. I won't betray you, whatever you may think; and I won't get caught if I can help it."

As he watched Auk ride away, Silk wondered what he had really been like as a schoolboy, and what Maytera Mint had found to say to that much younger Auk that had left so deep an impression. For Auk believed, despite his hard looks and thieves' cant; and unlike many superficially better men, his faith was more than superstition. Scylla's smiling picture on the wall of that dismal, barren room had not come to its place by accident. Its presence there had revealed more to Silk than Auk's glass: deep within his being, Auk's spirit knelt in adoration.

Inspired by the thought, Silk knelt himself, though the sharp flints of the hilltop gouged his knees. The Outsider had warned him that he would receive no aid—still, it was licit, surely, to ask help of other gods; and dark Tartaros was the patron of all who acted outside the law.

"A black lamb to you alone, kindly Tartaros, as quickly as I can afford another. Be mindful of me, who come in the service of a minor god."

But Blood, too, acted outside the law, dealing in rust and women and even smuggled goods, or so Auk had indicated; it was more than possible that Tartaros would favor Blood.

Sighing, Silk stood, dusted off the legs of his oldest trousers, and began to pick his way down the rocky hillside. Things would be as they would be, and he had no choice but to proceed, whether with the aid of the dark god or without it. Pas the Twice-Seeing might side with him, or Scalding Scylla, who wielded more influence here than her brother. Surely Scylla would not wish the city that most honored her to lose a manteion! Encouraged, Silk scrambled along.

The faint golden lights of Blood's house soon vanished behind the treetops, and the breeze with them. Below the hill, the air lay hot and close again, stale, and overripe with a summer protracted beyond reason.

Or perhaps not. As Silk groped among close-set trunks, with leaves crackling and twigs popping beneath his feet, he reflected that if the year had been a more normal one, this forest might now lie deep in snow, and what he was doing would be next to impossible. Could it be that this parched, overheated, and seemingly immutable season had in actuality been prolonged for his benefit?

For a few seconds the thought halted him between step and step. All this heat and sweat, for him? Poor Maytera Marble's daily sufferings, the children's angry rashes, the withered crops and shrinking streams?

No sooner had he had the thought than he came close to falling into the gully of one, catching hold by purest luck to a branch he could not see. Cautiously he clambered down the uneven bank, then knelt on the water-smoothed stones of the streambed to seek water with his fingers, finding none. There might be pools higher or lower, but here at least what had been a stream could be no drier.

With head cocked, he listened for the familiar music of fast-flowing water over stones. Far away a nightjar called; the harsh sound died away, and the stillness of the forest closed in once more, the hushed expectancy of the thirsting trees.

This forest had been planted in the days of the caldé (or so one of his teachers at the schola had informed him) in order that its watershed might fill the city's wells; and though the Ayuntamiento now permitted men of wealth to build within its borders, it remained vast, stretching more than fifty leagues toward Palustria. If its streams were this dry now, how long could Viron live? Would it be necessary to build a new city, if only a temporary one, on the lakeshore?

Wishing for light as well as water, Silk climbed the opposite bank, and after a hundred strides saw through the bare, close-ranked trees the welcome gleam of skylight on dressed and polished stone.

The wall surrounding Blood's villa loomed higher and higher as he drew nearer. Auk had indicated a height of ten cubits or so; to Silk, standing before its massive base and peering up at the fugitive glints of skylight on the points of its ominous spikes, that estimate appeared unnecessarily conservative. Somewhat discouraged already, he uncoiled the thin horsehair rope he had worn about his waist, thrust the hatchet into his waistband, tied a running noose in one end of the rope as Auk had suggested, and hurled it up at those towering points.

For a moment that seemed at least a minute, the rope hung over him like a miracle, jet black against the shining skylands, lost in blind dark where it crossed the boundless, sooty smear of the shade. A moment more, and it lay limp at his feet.

Biting his lips, he gathered it, reopened the noose, and hurled it again. Unlooked-for, the last words of the dying stableman to whom he had carried the forgiveness of the gods a week earlier returned, the summation of fifty years of toil: "I tried, Patera. I tried." With them, the broiling heat of the four-flight bedroom, the torn and faded horsecloths on the bed, the earthenware jug of water, and the hard end of bread (bread that some man of substance had no doubt intended for his mount) that the stableman could no longer chew.

Another throw. The ragged, amateurish sketch of the wife who had left when the stableman could no longer feed her and her children . . .

One last throw, and then he would return to the old manse on Sun Street—where he belonged—and go to bed, forgetting this absurd scheme of rescue with the brown lice that had crept across the faded blue horsecloths.

A final throw. "I tried, Patera. I tried."

Descriptions of three children that their father had not seen since before he, Silk, had been born. All right, he thought, just one more attempt.

With this, his sixth cast, he snared a spike, and by this time he could only wonder whether someone in the house had not already seen his noose rising above the wall and falling back. He heaved hard on the rope and felt the noose tighten, wiped his sweating hands on his robe, planted his feet against the dressed stone of the wall, and started up. He had reached twice his own considerable height when the noose parted and he fell.

"Pas!" He spoke more loudly than he had intended. For three minutes or more after that exclamation he cowered in silence beside the base of the wall, rubbing his bruises and listening. At length he muttered, "Scylla, Tartaros, Great Pas, remember your servant. Don't treat him so." And stood to gather and examine his rope.

The noose had been sliced through, almost cleanly, at the place where it must have held the spike. Those spikes were sharp-edged, clearly, like the blades of swords, as he ought to have guessed.

Retreating into the forest, he groped among branches he could scarcely see for a forked one of the right size. The first half-blind blow from his hatchet sounded louder than the boom of a slug gun. He waited, listening again, certain that he would soon hear cries of alarm and hurrying feet.

Even the crickets were silent.

His fingertips explored the inconsiderable notch in the branch that his hatchet had made. He shifted his free hand to a safe position and struck hard at the branch again, then stood motionless to listen, as before.

Briefly and distantly (as he had long ago, a child and feverish, heard through a tightly closed window with drawn curtains, from three streets away, the faint yet melodious tinklings of the barrel organ that announces the gray beggar monkey) he caught a few bars of music, buoyant and inviting. Quickly it vanished, leaving behind only the monotonous song of the nightjar.

When he felt certain it would not return, he swung his hatchet again and again at the unseen wood, until the branch was free and he could brace it against its parent trunk for trimming. That done, he carried the rough fork out of the darkness of the trees and into the skylit clearing next to the wall, and knotted his rope securely at the point where the splayed arms met. A single hard throw sent the forked limb arching above the spikes; it held solidly against them when he drew it back.

He was breathless, his tunic and trousers soaked with sweat, by the time he pulled himself up onto the slanting capstone, where for several minutes he stretched panting between the spikes and the sheer drop.

He had been seen, beyond doubt—or if he had not, he would inevitably be seen as soon as he stood up. It would be utter folly to stand. As he sought to catch his breath, he assured himself that only such a fool as he would so much as consider it.

When he did stand up at last, fully expecting a shouted challenge or the report of a slug gun, he had to call upon every scrap of self-discipline to keep from looking down.

The top of the wall was a full cubit wider than he had expected, however—as wide as the garden walk. Stepping across the spikes (which his fingers had told him boasted serrated edges), he crouched to study the distant villa and its grounds, straightening his low-crowned hat and drawing his black robe across the lower half of his face.

The nearer wing was a good hundred cubits, he estimated, from his vantage point. The grassway Auk had mentioned was largely out of sight at the front of the villa, but a white roadway of what appeared to be crushed shiprock ran from the back of the nearer wing to the wall, striking it a hundred strides to his left. Half a dozen sheds, large and small, stood along this roadway, the biggest of them apparently a shelter for vehicles, another (noticeably high and narrow, with what seemed to be narrow wirecovered vents high in an otherwise blank wall) some sort of provision for fowls.

What concerned Silk more was the second in size of the sheds, whose back opened onto an extensive yard surrounded by a palisade and covered with netting. The poles of the palisade were sharpened at the top, perhaps partly to hold the netting in place; and though it was difficult to judge by the glimmering skylight, it seemed that the area enclosed was of bare soil dotted with an occasional weed. That was a pen for dangerous animals, surely.

He scanned the rest of the grounds. There appeared to be a courtyard or terrace behind the original villa; though it was largely hidden by the wing, he glimpsed flagstones, and a flowering tree in a ceramic tub.

Other trees were scattered over the rolling lawns with studied carelessness, and there were hedges as well. Blood had built this wall and hired guards, but he did not really fear intrusion. There was too much foliage for that.

Although if his watchdogs liked to lie in the shadows, an intruder who sought to use Blood's plantings to mask his approach could be in for an ugly surprise; in which case an uncomplicated dash for the villa might be best. What would an experienced and resolute housebreaker like Auk have done in his place?

Silk quickly regretted the thought; Auk would have gone home or found an easier house to rob. He had said as much. This Blood was no common magnate, no rich trader or graft-swollen commissioner. He was a clever criminal himself, and one who (why?) appeared more anxious than might be expected about his own security. A criminal with secrets, then, or with enemies who were themselves outside the law—so it appeared. Certainly Auk had not been his friend.

At the age of twelve, Silk had once, with several other boys, broken into an empty house. He remembered that now, the fear and the shame of it, the echoing, uninhabited rooms with their furniture swathed in dirty white dustcovers. How hurt and dismayed his mother had been when she had found out what they had done! She had refused to punish him, saying that the nature of his punishment would be left to the owner of the house he had violated.

That punishment (the mere thought of it made him stir uneasily on top of the wall) had never arrived, although he had spent weeks and months in dread of it.

Or possibly had arrived only now. That deserted house, after all, had loomed large in the back of his mind when he had gathered up his horsehair rope and his hatchet and gone out looking for Auk, then only a vague figure recalled from Scylsdays past. And if it had not been for Auk and Maytera Mint, if it had not been for the repairs he had been making on the roof of the manteion, but most of all if it had not been for that well-remembered house whose rear window he had helped to force—if it had not been for all those things together, he would never have undertaken to break into this villa of Blood's. Or rather, into an imagined house on the Palatine belonging to Blood. On the Palatine where, as he realized now, the respectable rich would never have allowed such a man as Blood to live. Instead of this preposterous, utterly juvenile escapade, he would have . . .

Would have what? Have penned another appeal to Patera Remora, the coadjutor of the Chapter, perhaps, although the Chapter had, as seemed clear, already made its decision. Or have sought an interview with His Cognizance the Prolocutor—the interview that he had tried and failed to get weeks before, when it had at last become apparent to him (or so he had thought at the time) exactly how serious the manteion's financial situation was. His hands clenched as he recalled the expression of His Cognizance's sly little prothonotary, his long wait, ended only when he had been informed that His Cognizance had retired for the night. His Cognizance was quite elderly, the prothonotary had explained (as though he, Patera Silk, had been a foreigner). His Cognizance tired very easily these days.

And with that, the prothonotary had grinned his oh-so-knowing, vile grin; and Silk had wanted to strike him.

All right then, those possibilities had been explored already, both of them. Yet surely there was something else he might have done, something sensible, effectual, and most significantly, legal.

He was still considering the matter when the talus Auk had mentioned glided ponderously around a corner of the more remote wing, appearing briefly only to vanish and reappear as its motion carried it from skylight into shadow and from shadow into bright skylight again.

Silk's first thought was that it had heard him, but it was moving too slowly for that. No, this was no more than a routine patrol, one more among the thousands of circuits of Blood's high, crenelated villa it must have made since Blood engaged its services. Nervously, Silk wondered how good the big machine's vision was, and whether it routinely scanned the top of the wall. Maytera Marble had told him once that hers was less acute than his own, though he had worn glasses for reading since turning twelve. Yet that might be no more than the effect of her great age; the talus would be younger, although cruder as well. Certainly movement was more apt to betray him than immobility.

And yet he found immobility more and more difficult to maintain as the talus drew nearer. It appeared to wear a helmet, a polished brazen dome more capacious than many a respectable tomb. From beneath that helmet glared the face of an ogre worked in black metal: a wide and flattened nose, bulging red eyes, great flat cheeks like slabs of slate, and a gaping mouth drawn back in a savage grin. The sharp white tusks that thrust beyond its crimson lips were presumably mere bluster, but the slender barrel of a buzz gun flanked each tusk.

Far below that threatening head, the talus's armored, wagon-like body rolled upon dark belts that carried it in perfect silence over the close-sheared grass. No needler, no sword, and certainly no hatchet like the one he grasped could do more than scratch the talus's finish. Met upon its own terms, it would be more than a match for a whole platoon of armored Guardsmen. He resolved—fervently—never to meet it on its own terms, and never to meet it at all if he could manage it.

As it neared the pale swath that was the white stone roadway, it halted. Slowly and silently, its huge, frowning head revolved, examining the back of the villa, then each of the outbuildings in turn, then staring down the roadway, and at last looking at the wall itself, tracing its whole visible length (as it appeared) twice. Silk felt certain that his heart had stopped, frozen with fear. A moment more and he would lose consciousness and fall forward. The talus would roll toward him, no doubt, would dismember him with brutal steel hands bigger than the largest shovels; but that would not matter, because he would already be dead.

At length it seemed to see him. For a long moment its head ceased to move, its fierce eyes staring straight at him. As smoothly as a cloud, as inexorably as an avalanche, it glided toward him. Slowly, so slowly that he would not at first permit himself to believe it, its path inclined to the left, its staring eyes left him, and he was able to make out against its rounded sides the ladders of bent rod that would permit troopers to ride into battle on board its flattened back.

He did not move until it had vanished around the corner of the nearer wing; then he stepped across the spikes again, pulled his rope and the forked limb free, and jumped after them. Although he struck the drought-hardened ground with bent knees and rolled forward, putting back into practice the lessons of boyhood, the drop stung the soles of his feet and left him sprawled breathless.

The rear gate, to which the white roadway ran, was a grill of bars, narrow and recessed. A bellpull beside it might (or might not, Silk reflected) summon a human servant from within the house. Suddenly reckless, he tugged it, watching through the four-finger interstices to see who might appear, while the bell clanged balefully over his head. No dog barked at the sound. For a moment only, it seemed to him that he caught the flash of eyes in the shadow of a big willow halfway between the wall and the house; but the image had been too brief to be trusted, and the eyes (if eyes they had been) at a height of seven cubits or more.

The talus itself threw open the gate, roaring, *"Who are you!"* It seemed to lean forward as it trained its buzz guns at him.

Silk tugged his wide-brimmed straw hat lower. "Someone with a message for Blood, your master," he announced. "Get out of my way." Quickly, he stepped under the gate, so that it could not be dropped again without crushing him. He had never been so close to a talus before, and there seemed no harm in satisfying his curiosity now; he reached out and touched the angled plate that was the huge machine's chest. To his surprise he found it faintly warm.

"Who are you!" the talus roared again.

"Do you wish my name or the tessera I was given?" Silk replied. "I have both."

Though it had not appeared to move at all, the talus was nearer now, so near that its chest plate actually nudged his robe. *"Stand back!"*

Without warning, Silk found himself a child once more, a child confronting an adult, an uncaring, shouting giant. In a story his mother had read to him, some bold boy had darted between a giant's legs. It would be perfectly possible now; the seamless black strips on which the talus stood lifted its steel body three cubits at least above the grass.

Could he outrun a talus? He licked his lips. Not if they were as fast as floaters. But were they? If this one chose to shoot, it would not matter.

Its chest plate shoved him backward, so that he reeled and nearly fell. *"Get out!"*

"Tell Blood I was here." He would surely be reported; it might be best if he appeared to wish it. "Tell him that I have information."

"Who are you?"

"Rust," Silk whispered. "Now let me in."

Suddenly the talus was rolling smoothly back. The gate crashed down, a hand's breadth in front of his face. Quite possibly there was a tessera— a word or a sign that would command instant admittance. But *rust* certainly was not it.

He left the gate, discovering with some surprise that his legs were trembling. Would the talus answer the front gate also? Very probably; but there was no harm in finding out, and the back of the villa seemed unpromising indeed.

As he set off upon the lengthy walk along the wall that would take him to the front gate, he reflected that Auk (and so by implication others of his trade) would have attempted the rear; a foresighted planner might well have anticipated that and taken extra precautions there.

A moment later he rebuked himself for the thought. Auk would not

have dared the front gate, true; but neither would Auk have been terrified of the talus, as he had been. He pictured Auk's coarse and frowning
face, its narrowed eyes, jutting ears, and massive, badly shaved jaw. Auk
would be careful, certainly. But never fearful. What was still more important, Auk believed in the goodness of the gods, in their benign personal
care—something that he, whose own trade it was to profess it, could only
struggle to believe.

Shaking his head, he pulled his beads from his trousers pocket, his
fingers reassured by their glassy polish and the swinging mass of the
voided cross. Nine decades, one with which to praise and petition each
major divinity, with an additional, unspecified decade from which the
voided cross was suspended. For the first time it occurred to him that
there were ten beads in each decade as well. Had the Nine been the Ten,
once? He pushed the heretical thought aside.

First the cross. "To you, Great Pas . . ."

There was a secret in the empty, X-shaped space, or so one of his
teachers had confided, a mystery far beyond that of the detachable arms
he showed the smallest boys and girls at the palaestra and used (as every
other augur did) to test and tighten sacred connections. Unfortunately,
his teacher had not seen fit to confide the secret as well, and probably
had not known it himself—if any such secret actually existed. Silk
shrugged aside the memory, ceased fingering the enigmatic emptiness of
the voided cross, and clasped it to his chest.

"To you, Great Pas, I present my poor heart and my whole spirit, my
mind and all my belief . . ."

The grass thinned and vanished, replaced by odd little plants like mul-
tilayered, greenish umbrellas that appeared healthy and flourishing, yet
crumbled to mere puffs of dust when Silk stepped on them.

Blood's front gate was less promising than the other, if anything, for an
eye in a black metal box gleamed above the top of its arch. Should he
ring here, Musk or someone like him inside would not only see him, but
interrogate him, no doubt, speaking through a mouth in the same box.

For five minutes or more, sitting on a convenient stone while he
rubbed his feet, Silk considered the advisability of submitting himself to
the scrutiny of that eye, and thus of the unknown inquisitor who would
examine him through it. He knew himself to be a less than competent
liar; and when he tried to concoct a tale that might get him into Blood's
presence, he was dismayed at how feeble and unconvincing even the best
of his fabrications sounded. Eventually he was driven to conclude, with a

distinct sense of relief, that the prospect was hopeless; he would have to get into the villa by stealth, if he got into it at all.

Retying his shoes, he rose, advanced another hundred paces along the wall, and once more heaved the forked limb over its spikes.

As Auk had indicated, there was a central building of two stories, with wings whose rows of windows showed them to be three, although the original structure was nearly as tall as they. Both the original structure and its wings appeared to be of the same smooth, grayish stone as the wall, and all three were so high that throwing the limb onto the roof of any appeared quite impossible. To enter them directly, he would have to discover an unbolted door or force one of the ground-floor casements, exactly as he and the other boys had broken into the deserted house a few years before he left home to attend the schola. He winced at the thought.

On the farther end of the wing on the right, however (the structure most remote from his old vantage point), was a more modest addition whose decorative merlons appeared to stand no more than a scant ten cubits above the lawn; the size and close spacing of its numerous windows suggested that it might be a conservatory. Silk noted it for future use and turned his attention to the grounds.

The broad grassway that curved so gracefully up to the pillared portico of Blood's villa was bordered with bright flower beds. Some distance in front of that entrance, a fine porcelain Scylla writhed palely among the sprays of an ostentatious fountain, spewing water alike from her woman's mouth and her upraised tentacles.

Scented water, in fact; sniffing the almost motionless air like a hound, Silk caught the fragrance of tea roses. Postponing judgement on Blood's taste, he nodded approvingly at this tangible evidence of pious civic feeling. Perhaps Blood was not really such a bad man after all, no matter what Auk thought. Blood had provided three cards for a sacrifice; it might well be that if Blood were approached in the right way he would be amenable to reason. Possibly the Outsider's errand would come to no more than that, in the end. Giving rein to this pleasing line of thought for a second or two, Silk imagined himself comfortably seated in some luxurious chamber of the villa before him, laughing heartily over his own adventures with the prosperous-looking man with whom he had spoken in Sun Street. Why, even a contribution toward necessary repairs might not be entirely out of the question.

On the farther side of the grassway . . .

The distant roar of an approaching floater made him look around.

With running lights blazing through its own dust, it was hurtling along the public road in the direction of the main gate. Quickly he stretched himself flat behind the row of spikes.

As the floater braked, two figures in silvered conflict armor shot away from the portico on highriders. At the same moment, the talus rounded the conservatory (if that was what it was) at full tilt, dodging trees and shrubs as it rolled across the lawn nearly as fast as the highriders; after it bounded half a dozen sinuous, seemingly tailless beasts with bearded faces and horned heads.

While Silk watched fascinated, the thick metal arms of the talus stretched like telescopes, twenty cubits or more to catch hold of a ring high in the wall near the gate. For a second they paused. An unseen chain rattled and creaked. They shrank, drawing the ring and its chain with them, and the gate rose.

The shadow of a drifting cloud from the east veiled the pillars of the portico, then the steps at their bases; Silk murmured a frantic appeal to Tartaros and tried to judge its speed.

There was a faint and strangely lonely whine from the blowers as the floater glided under the gate's rounded arch. One of the horned beasts sprang onto its transparent canopy, appearing to crouch upon empty air until it was driven off snarling by the armored men, who cursed and brandished their short-tubed slug guns as if to strike it. The drifting shadow had reached Scylla's fountain by the time the horned beast sprang away.

The talus let the heavy gate fall again as the floater swept proudly up the darkening grassway, escorted by the highriders and accompanied by all six horned beasts, which rose upon their hind legs again and again to peer inside. It halted and settled onto the grass before the wide stone steps of the villa, and the talus called the horned beasts from it with a shrill shuddering wail that could have issued from no human throat.

As the brilliantly dressed passengers disembarked, Silk leaped from the wall and dashed across the lawn toward the conservatory, with a desperate effort flung the forked limb over its ornamental battlement, and swarmed up the horsehair rope, over the battlement, and onto the roof.

CHAPTER
5   THE WHITE-HEADED ONE

For what seemed to him the greater part of an hour, Silk lay behind the battlement trying to catch his breath. Had he been seen? If the talus or one of the armored men had seen him, they would have come at once, he felt certain; but if one of Blood's guests had, it might easily be ten minutes or even longer before he decided that he should report what he had seen, and reached the appropriate person; it might be that he would not so much as try until prompted by another guest to whom he mentioned the incident.

Overhead the skylands sailed serenely among broad bars of sterile cloud, displaying countless now-sunlit cities in which nobody at all knew or cared that one Patera Silk, an augur of faraway Viron, was frightened almost to death and might soon die.

The limb, too, might have given him away. He was sure that he, on the ground, had heard it thump down on the warm, tarred surface of the roof; and anyone in the conservatory below must have heard it very distinctly. As he sought to slow the pounding of his heart by an effort of will, and to force himself to breathe through his nose, it seemed to him that anyone who had heard that thump would realize at once that it had been made by an intruder who had climbed onto the roof. As the thunder of his own pulse faded away, he listened intently.

The music he had heard so faintly from the wall was louder now. Through it, over it, and below it, he heard the murmur of voices—the voices of men, mostly, he decided, with a few women among them. That piercing laugh had been a woman's, unless he was greatly mistaken. Glass shattered, not loudly, followed by a moment of silence, then a shout of laughter.

His black rope was still hanging over the battlement. He felt that it was almost miraculous that it had not been seen. Without rising from his back, he hauled it in hand over hand. It would be necessary, in another minute or two, to throw the limb again, this time onto the roof of the wing proper. He was not at all sure he could do it.

An owl floated silently overhead, then veered away to settle on a convenient branch at the edge of the forest. Watching it, Silk (who had never considered the lives of Echidna's pets before) suddenly realized that the building of Blood's wall, with the cleared strip on its forest side and the closely trimmed lawn on the other, had irrevocably altered the lives of innumerable birds and small animals, changing the way in which wood-mice foraged for food and hawks and owls hunted them. To such creatures, Blood and his hired workmen must have seemed the very forces of nature, pitiless and implacable. Silk pitied those animals now, all the while wondering whether they did not have as much right, and more reason, to pity him.

The Outsider, he reflected, had swooped upon him much as the owl would stoop for a mouse; the Outsider had assured him that his regard for him was eternal and perfect, never to be changed by any act of his, no matter how iniquitous or how meritorious. The Outsider had then told him to act, and had withdrawn while in some fashion remaining. The memory, and the wonder of the Outsider's love and of his own new, clean pride in the Outsider's regard, would make the rest of his life both more meaningful and more painful. Yet what could he do, beyond what he was doing?

"Thank you," he whispered. "Thank you anyway, even if you never speak to me again. You have given me the courage to die."

The owl hooted from its high branch above the wall, and the orchestra in Blood's ballroom struck up a new tune, one Silk recognized as "Know I'll Never Leave You." Could that be an omen? The Outsider had indeed warned him to expect no help, but had never (as well as Silk could remember, at any rate) actually told him that he would never be vouch-safed omens.

Shaking himself, his self-possession recovered and his sweat dried, he lifted his knees and rolled into a crouch behind one of the merlons, peering through the crenel on its left. There was no one on that part of the grounds visible to him. He readjusted the long handle of the hatchet while changing position slightly in order to look out through the crenel on the right. Half the grassway was visible from that angle, and with it the gate; but there was no floater on that section of the grassway, and the talus and the horned beasts that had come at its call had gone elsewhere. The skylands were brightening as the trailing edge of the cloud that had favored him left Viron for the west; he could make out the iron ring the talus had pulled to raise the gate, to the left of the arch.

He stood then and looked about him. There was nothing threatening or even extraordinary about the roof of Blood's conservatory. It was level or nearly so, a featureless dark surface surrounding an abatjour for the illumination of the conservatory, itself enclosed on three sides by chest-high battlements. The fourth was defined by the south wall of the wing from which the conservatory extended; the sills of its second-story windows were three cubits or a trifle less above the conservatory roof.

Silk felt a thrill of triumph as he studied the windows. Their casements were shut, and the rooms that they lighted, dark; yet he felt an undeniable pride in them that was not unrelated to that of ownership. Auk had predicted that he would get roughly this far before being captured by Blood's guards—and now he had gotten this far, doing nothing more than Auk, who clearly knew a great deal about such things, had expected. The manteion had not been saved, or even made appreciably safer. And yet . . .

Boldly, he leaned over the nearest battlement, his head and shoulders thrust beyond the merlons. One of the horned beasts was standing at the base of the conservatory wall, directly below him. For an instant he was acutely conscious of its amber stare; it snarled, and cat-like padded away.

Could those fantastic animals climb onto the roof? He decided that though possible it was unlikely—the walls of the villa were of dressed stone, after all. He leaned out farther still, his hands braced on the bottom of the crenel, to reassure himself about the construction of the wall.

As he did, the talus rolled into view. He froze until it had passed. There was a chance, of course, that it had concealed, upward- or rearward-directed eyes; Maytera Marble had once mentioned such features in connection with Maytera Rose. But that, too, seemed less than probable.

Leaving his limb and horsehair rope where they lay, he walked gingerly across the roof to the abatjour and crouched to peer through one of its scores of clear panes.

The conservatory below apparently housed large bushes of some sort, or possibly dwarfed trees. Silk found that he had unconsciously assumed that it had supplied the low-growing flowers that bordered the grassway. That had been an error, now revealed; while examining the plants below, he cautioned himself against making any further unconsidered assumptions about this villa of Blood's.

The panes themselves were set in lead. Silk scraped the lead with the edge of his hatchet, finding it as soft as he could wish. With half an hour's skillful work, it should be possible, he decided, to remove two panes without breaking them, after which he could let himself down among the lush, shining leaves and intertwined trunks below—perhaps with an undesirable amount of noise, but perhaps also, unheard.

Nodding thoughtfully to himself, he rose and walked quietly across the conservatory roof to examine the dark windows of the wing overlooking it.

The first two he tested were locked in some fashion. As he tugged at each, he was tempted to wedge the blade of his hatchet between the stile and casing to pry them open. The latch or bolt would certainly break with a snap, however, if it gave at all; and it seemed only too likely that the glass would break instead. He decided that he would try to throw the limb onto the roof two stories above him (diminished by a third, that throw no longer appeared nearly as difficult as it had when he had reconnoitered the villa from the top of its surrounding wall) and explore that roof as well before attempting anything quite so audacious. Circuitous though it seemed, removing panes from the abatjour might actually be a more prudent approach.

The third casement he tried gave slightly in response to his tentative pull. He pushed it back, wiped his perspiring palms on his robe and tugged harder. This time the casing moved a trifle farther; it was only jammed, apparently, not locked. A quick wrench of the hatchet forced it open enough for him to swing it back with only the slightest of protests from the neglected hinges. Vaulting with one hand upon the sill, he slid headfirst into the lightless room beyond.

The gritty wooden floor was innocent of carpet. Silk explored it with his fingertips, in ever-wider arcs, while he knelt, motionless, alert for any sound from within the room. His fingers touched something the size of a pigeon's egg, something spherical, hard, and dry. He picked it up—it yielded slightly when squeezed. Suspicious, he lifted it to his nostrils and sniffed.

Excrement.

He dropped it and wiped his fingers on the floor. Some animal was penned in this room and might be present now, as frightened of him as he was of it—if it was not already stalking him. Not one of the horned cats, surely; they were apparently freed to roam the grounds at night. Something worse, then. Something more dangerous.

Or nothing. If there was an animal in the room, it was a silent one indeed. Even a serpent would have hissed by now, surely.

Silk got to his feet as quietly as he could and inched along the wall, his right hand grasping his hatchet, the fingers of his left groping what might have been splintered paneling.

A corner, as empty as the whole room seemed to be. He took a step, then another. If there were pictures, or even furniture, he had thus far failed to encounter them.

Another step; pull up the right foot to the left now. Pausing to listen, he could detect only his own whistling breath and the faint tinklings of the distant orchestra.

His mouth felt dry, and his knees seemed ready to give way beneath him; twice he was forced to halt, bracing his trembling hands against the wall. He reminded himself that he was actually in Blood's villa, and that it had not been as difficult as he had feared. The task to follow would be much harder: he would have to locate Blood without being discovered himself, and speak with him for some time in a place where they could talk without interruption. Only now was he willing to admit that it might prove impossible.

A second corner.

This vertical molding was surely the frame of a door; the pale rectangle of the window he had opened was on the opposite side of the room. His hand sought and found the latch. He pushed it down; it moved freely, with a slight rattle; but the door would not open.

"Have you been bad?"

He jerked the hatchet up, about to strike with deadly force at whatever might come from the darkness—about to kill, he told himself a moment later, some innocent sleeper whose bedchamber he had entered by force.

"Have you?" The question had a spectral quality; he could not have said whether it proceeded from a point within arm's reach or wafted through the open casement.

"Yes." To his own ears, the lone syllable sounded high and frightened, almost tremulous. He forced himself to pause and clear his throat. "I've been bad many times, I'm afraid. I regret them all."

"You're a boy. I can tell."

Silk nodded solemnly. "I used to be a boy, not so long ago. No doubt Maytera R—No doubt some of my friends would tell you that I'm a boy still in many respects, and they may well be right."

His eyes were adjusting to the darker darkness of the room, so that the skylight that played across the roof of the conservatory and the grounds in the distance, mottled though it was by the diffused shadows of broken clouds, made them appear almost sunlit. The light spilling through the open window showed clearly now the precise rectangle of flooring on which he had knelt, and dimly the empty, unclean room to either side. Yet he could not locate the speaker.

"Are you going to hurt me with that?"

It was a young woman's voice, almost beyond question. Again Silk wondered whether she was actually present. "No," he said, as firmly as he could. He lowered the hatchet. "I will do you no violence, I swear." Blood dealt in women, so Auk had said; now Silk felt that he had a clearer idea of what such dealings might entail. "Are you being kept here against your will?"

"I go whenever I want. I travel. Usually I'm not here at all."

"I see," Silk said, though he did not, in either sense. He pushed down the latchbar again; it moved as readily as it had before, and the door remained as stubborn.

"I go very far, sometimes. I fly out the window, and no one sees me."

Silk nodded again. "I don't see you now."

"I know."

"Sometimes you must go out through this door, though. Don't you?"

"No."

Her flat negative bore in its train the illusion that she was standing beside him, her lips almost brushing his ear. He groped for her, but his hand found only empty air. "Where are you now? You can see me, you say. I'd like to see you."

"I'll have to get back in."

"Get back in through the window?"

There was no reply. He crossed the room to the window and looked out, leaning on the sill, there was no one on the roof of the conservatory, no one but the talus in sight on the grounds beyond. His rope and limb lay where he had left them. Devils (according to legends no one at the schola had really credited) could pass unseen, for devils were spirits of the lower air, presumably personifications of destructive winds. "Where are you now?" he asked again. "Please come out. I'd like to see you."

Nothing. Thelxiepeia provided the best protection from devils, according to the Writings, but this was Phaea's day, not hers. Silk petitioned Phaea, Thelxiepeia, and for good measure Scylla, in quick succession before saying, "I take it you don't want to talk to me, but I need to talk to you. I need your help, whoever you are."

In Blood's ballroom, the orchestra had struck up "Brave Guards of the Third Brigade." Silk had the feeling that no one was dancing, that few if any of Blood's guests were even listening. Outside, the talus waited at the gate, its steel arms unnaturally lengthened, both its hands upon the ring.

Turning his back on the window, Silk scanned the room. A shapeless mass in a corner (one that he had not traversed when he had felt his way along the walls to the door) might conceivably have been a huddled woman. With no very great confidence he said, "I see you."

"To fourteen more my sword I pledged," sang the violins with desperate gaiety. Beardless lieutenants in brilliant green dress uniforms, twirling smiling beauties with plumes in their hair—but they were not there, Silk felt certain, no more than the mysterious young woman whom he himself was trying to address was here.

He crossed to the dark shape in the corner and nudged it with the toe of his shoe, then crouched, put aside his hatchet, and explored it with both hands—a ragged blanket and a thin, foul-smelling mattress. Picking up his hatchet again, he rose and faced the empty room. "I'd like to see you," he repeated. "But if you won't let me—if you won't even talk to me any more—I'm going to leave." As soon as he had spoken, he reflected that he had probably told her precisely what she wanted to hear.

He stepped to the window. "If you require my help, you must say so now." He waited, silently reciting a formula of blessing, then traced the sign of addition in the darkness before him. "Good-bye, then."

Before he could turn to go, she rose before him like smoke, naked and thinner than the most miserable beggar. Although she was a head shorter, he would have backed away from her if he could; his right heel thumped the wall below the window.

"Here I am. Can you see me now?" In the dim skylight from the window her starved and bloodless face seemed almost a skull. "My name's Mucor."

Silk nodded and swallowed, half afraid to give his own, not liking to lie. "Mine's Silk." Whether he succeeded or was apprehended, Blood would learn his identity. "Patera Silk. I'm an augur, you see." He might die, perhaps; but if he did his identity would no longer matter.

"Do you really have to talk with me, Silk? That's what you said."

He nodded. "I need to ask you how to open that door. It doesn't seem to be locked, but it won't open."

When she did not reply, he added. "I have to get into the house. Into the rest of it, I mean."

"What's an augur? I thought you were a boy."

"One who attempts to learn the will of the gods through sacrifice, in order that he may—"

"I know! With the knife and the black robe. Lots of blood. Should I come with you, Silk? I can send forth my spirit. I'll fly beside you, wherever you go."

"Call me Patera, please. That's the proper way. You can send forth your body, too, Mucor, if you want."

"I'm saving myself for the man I'll marry." It was said with perfect (too perfect) seriousness.

"That's certainly the correct attitude, Mucor. But all I meant was that you don't have to stay here if you don't wish to. You could climb out of this window very easily and wait out there on the roof. When I've finished my business with Blood, we could both leave this villa, and I could take you to someone in the city who would feed you properly and—and take care of you."

The skull grinned at him. "They'd find out that my window opens, Silk. I wouldn't be able to send my spirit any more."

"You wouldn't be here. You'd be in some safe place in the city. There you could send out your spirit whenever you wanted, and a physician—"

"Not if my window was locked again. When my window is locked, I can't do it, Silk. They think it's locked now." She giggled, a high, mirthless tittering that stroked Silk's spine like an icy finger.

"I see," he said. "I was about to say that someone in the city might even be able to make you well. You may not care about that, but I do. Will you at least let me out of your room? Open your door for me?"

"Not from this side. I can't."

He sighed. "I didn't really think you could. I don't suppose you know where Blood sleeps?"

"On the other side. Of the house."

"In the other wing?"

"His room used to be right under mine, but he didn't like hearing me. Sometimes I was bad. The north addition. This one's the south addition."

"Thank you," Silk stroked his cheek. "That's certainly worth knowing. He'll have a big room on the ground floor, I suppose."

"He's my father."

"Blood is?" Silk caught himself on the point of saying that she did not resemble him. "Well, well. That may be worth knowing, too. I don't plan to hurt him, Mucor, though I rather regret that now. He has a very nice daughter; he should come and see her more often, I think. I'll mention it forcefully, if I get to talk with him."

Silk turned to leave, then glanced back at her. "You really don't have to stay here, Mucor."

"I know. I don't."

"You don't want to come with me when I leave? Or leave now yourself?"

"Not the way you mean, walking like you do."

"Then there's nothing I can do for you except give you my blessing, which I've done already. You're one of Molpe's children, I think. May she care for you and favor you, this night and every night."

"Thank you, Silk." It was the tone of the little girl she had once been. Five years ago, perhaps, he decided; or perhaps three, or less than three. He swung his right leg over the windowsill.

"Watch out for my lynxes."

Silk berated himself for not having questioned her more. "What are those?"

"My children. Do you want to see one?"

"Yes," he said. "Yes, I do, if you want to show him to me."

"Watch."

Mucor was looking out the window, and Silk followed her gaze. For half a minute he waited beside her, listening to the faint sounds of the night; Blood's orchestra seemed to have fallen silent. Ghost-like, a floater glided beneath the arch, its blowers scarcely audible; the talus let down the gate smoothly behind it, and even the distant rattle of the chain reached them.

A section of abatjour pivoted upward, and a horned head with topaz eyes emerged from beneath it, followed by a big, soft-looking paw.

Mucor said, "That's Lion. He's my oldest son. Isn't he handsome?"

Silk managed to smile. "Yes, he certainly is. But I didn't know you meant the horned cats."

"Those are their ears. But they jump through windows, and they have long teeth and claws that can hurt worse than a bull's horns."

"I imagine so." Silk made himself relax. "Lynxes? Is that what you call them? I've never heard of the name, and I'm supposed to know something about animals."

The lynx emerged from the abatjour and trotted over to stand beneath the window, looking up at them quizzically. If he had bent, Silk could have touched its great, bearded head; he took a step backward instead. "Don't let him come up here, please."

"You said you wanted to see them, Silk."

"This is close enough."

As if it had understood, the lynx wheeled. A single bound carried it to the top of the battlement surrounding the conservatory roof, from which it dived as though into a pool.

"Isn't he pretty?"

Silk nodded reluctantly. "I found him terrifying, but you're right. I've

never seen a lovelier animal, though all Sabered Sphigx's cats are beautiful. She must be very proud of him."

"So am I. I told him not to hurt you." Mucor squatted on her heels,
folding like a carpenter's rule.

"By standing beside me and talking to me, you mean." Gratefully, Silk
seated himself on the windowsill. "I've known dogs that intelligent. But a
—lynx? Is that the singular? It's an odd word."

"It means they hunt in the daytime," Mucor explained. "They would,
too, if my father'd let them. Their eyes are sharper than almost any other
animal's. But their ears are good, too. And they can see in the dark, just
like regular cats."

Silk shuddered.

"My father traded for them. When he got them they were just little
chips of ice inside a big box that was little on the inside. The chips are
just like little seeds. Do you know about that, Silk?"

"I've heard of it," he said. For an instant he thought that he felt the
hot yellow gaze of the lynx behind him; he looked quickly, but the roof
was bare. "It's supposed to be against the law, though I don't think that's
very strictly enforced. One could be placed inside a female animal of the
correct sort, a large cat I'd imagine, in this case—"

"He put them inside a girl." Mucor's eerie titter came again. "It was
me."

"In you!"

"He didn't know what they were." Mucor's teeth flashed in the darkness. "But I did, a long while before they were born. Then Musk told me
their name and gave me a book. He likes birds, but I like them and they
like me."

"Then come with me," Silk said, "and the lynxes won't hurt either of
us."

The skull nodded, still grinning. "I'll fly beside you, Silk. Can you bribe
the talus?"

"I don't think so."

"It takes a lot of money."

There was a soft scraping from the back of the room, followed by a
muffled thump. Before the door swung open, Silk realized that what he
had heard was a bar being lifted from it and laid aside. Nearly falling, he
slid over the sill, and crouched as Mucor's window shut silently above his
head.

For as long as it took him to run mentally through the formal praises
of Sphigx, whose day was about to dawn (or so at least he felt), he waited,

listening. No sound of voices reached him from the room above, though once he heard what might have been a blow. When he stood at last and peeped cautiously through the glass, he could see no one.

The panes that Lion had raised with his head yielded easily to Silk's fingers; as they rose, a moist and fragrant exhalation from the conservatory below invaded the dry heat of the rooftop. He reflected that it would be simple now—much easier than he had thought—to enter the conservatory from above, and the trees there had clearly supported Lion's considerable weight without damage.

Silk's fingertips described slow circles on his cheek as he considered it. The difficulty was that Blood slept in the other wing, if Mucor was to be believed. Entering here, he would have to traverse the length of the villa from south to north, finding his way though unfamiliar rooms. There would be bright lights and the armored guards he had seen in Auk's glass and on the highriders, Blood's staff and Blood's guests.

Regretfully Silk let down the movable section of the abatjour, retrieved his horsehair rope, and untied the rough limb that had served him so well. The merlons crowning the roof of the south annex would not have cutting edges, and a noose would make no dangerous noise. Three throws missed before the fourth snared a merlon. He tugged experimentally at the rope; the merlon seemed as solid as a post; drying his hands on his robe, he started up.

He had reached the roof of the wing and was removing his noose from the merlon when Mucor's spectral voice spoke, seemingly in his ear. There were words he could not quite hear, then, ". . . birds. Watch out for the white-headed one."

"Mucor?"

There was no reply. Silk looked over the battlement just in time to see the window close.

Although it was twenty times larger, this roof had no abatjour, and was in fact no more than a broad and extremely long expanse of slightly sloping tar. Beyond the parapet at its northern end, the lofty stone chimneys of the original structure stood like so many pallid sentries in the glimmering skylight. Silk had enjoyed several lively conversations with chimney sweeps since arriving at the manteion on Sun Street, and had learned (with many other things) that the chimneys of great houses were frequently wide enough to admit the sweep employed to clean and repair them, and that some had interior steps for his use.

Walking softly and keeping near the center so that he could not be seen from the ground, Silk walked the length of the roof. When he was

near enough to look down on it, he saw that the more steeply pitched
roof of the original structure was tiled rather than tarred. Its tall chimneys were clearly visible now; there were five, of which four appeared to
be identical. The fifth, however—the chimney farthest but one from him
—boasted a chimney pot twice the height of the rest, a tall and somewhat
shapeless pot with a pale finial. For a moment, Silk wondered uneasily
whether it could be the "white-headed one" Mucor had warned him
against, and resolved to examine it only if he could not gain entry to any
of the others.

Then another, more significant, detail caught his eye. The corner of
some low projection, dark and distinct, could be seen beyond the third
chimney, its angular outline in sharp contrast to the rounded contours of
the tiles, and its top a cubit or so higher than theirs. He moved a few
steps to his left to see it better.

It was, beyond question, a trapdoor; and Silk murmured a prayer of
thanks to whatever god had arranged a generation ago that it should be
included in the plan of the roof for his use.

Looping his rope around a merlon, he scrambled easily down onto the
tiles and pulled the rope down after him. The Outsider had indeed
warned him to expect no help; yet some other god was certainly siding
with him. For a moment Silk speculated happily on which it might be.
Scylla, perhaps, who would not wish her city to lose a manteion. Or grim
and gluttonous Phaea, the ruler of the day. Or Molpe, since— No,
Tartaros, of course. Tartaros was the patron of thieves of every kind, and
he had prayed fervently to Tartaros (as he now remembered) while still
outside Blood's wall. Moreover, black was Tartaros's color; all augurs and
sibyls wore it in order that they might, figuratively if not literally, steal
unobserved among the gods to overhear their deliberations. Not only was
he himself clothed entirely in black, but the tarred roofs he had just left
behind had been black as well.

"Terrible Tartaros, be thanked and praised most highly by me forever.
Now let it be unlocked, Tartaros! But locked or not, the black lamb I
pledged shall be yours." Recalling the tavern in which he had met Auk,
he added in a final burst of extravagance, "And a black cock, too."

And yet, he told himself, it was only logical that the trapdoor should be
precisely where it was. Tiles must break at times—must be broken fairly
frequently by the violent hailstorms that had ushered in every winter for
the past few years; and each such broken tile would have to be replaced.
A trapdoor giving access to the roof from the attic of the villa would be
much more convenient (as well as much safer) than a seventy-cubit lad-

der. A ladder of that size would very likely require a whole crew of workmen just to get it into place.

He tried to hurry across the intervening tiles to the trapdoor, but their glazed, convex, and unstable surfaces hindered him, quite literally at every stride. Twice tiles cracked beneath his impatient feet; and when he had nearly reached the trapdoor, he slipped unexpectedly and fell, and saved himself from rolling down the roof only by clutching at the rough masonry of the third chimney.

It was reassuring to note that this roof, like those of the wings and the conservatory, was walled with ornamental battlements. He would have had a bad time of it if it had not been for the chimney; he was glad he had escaped it. He would have been shaken and bruised, and he might well have made enough noise to attract the attention of someone inside the villa. But at the end of that ignominious fall he would not have dropped from the edge of the roof to his death. Those blessed battlements (which had been of so much help to him ever since he had dashed from the wall across the grounds) were, now that he came to think of it, one of the recognized symbols in art of Sphigx, the lion-goddess of war; and *Lion* had been the name of Mucor's horned cat—of the animal she called her lynx, which had not harmed him. Taking all that into account, who could deny that Fierce Sphigx favored him also?

Silk caught his breath, made sure of his footing, and let go of the chimney. Here, not a hand's breadth from the toe of his right shoe, was the thing that he had slipped on—this blotch on the earthen-red surface of the roof. He stooped and picked it up.

It was a scrap of raw skin, an irregular patch about as large as a handkerchief from the pelt of some animal, still covered with coarse hair on one side and slimy with rotting flesh and rancid fat on the other, reeking with decay. He flung it aside with a snort of disgust.

The trapdoor lifted easily; below it was a steep and tightly spiraled iron stair. A more conventional stairway, clearly leading to the upper floor of the original villa, began a few steps from the bottom of the iron one. Briefly he paused, looking down at it, to savor his triumph.

He had been carrying his horsehair rope in an untidy coil, and had dropped it when he slipped. He retrieved it and wound it around his waist beneath his robe, as he had when he had set out from the manteion that evening. It was always possible, he reminded himself, that he would need it again. Yet he felt as he had during his last year at the schola, when he had realized that final year would actually be easier than the one before it—that his instructors no more wished him to fail after he had studied so long than he himself did, and that he would not be permitted to fail unless he curtailed his efforts to an almost criminal degree. The whole villa lay open before him, and he knew, roughly if not precisely, where Blood's bedchamber was located. In order to succeed, he had only to find it and conceal himself there before Blood retired. Then, he told himself with a pleasant sensation of virtue, he would employ reason, if reason would serve; if it would not . . .

It would not, and the fault would be Blood's, not his. Those who opposed the will of a god, even a minor god like the Outsider, were bound to suffer.

Silk was pushing the long handle of his hatchet through the rope around his waist when he heard a soft thump behind him. Dropping the trapdoor, he whirled. Leaping so that it appeared taller than many men, a huge bird flapped misshapen wings, shrieked like a dozen devils, and struck at his eyes with its hooked bill.

Instinctively, he threw himself backward onto the top of the trapdoor and kicked. His left foot caught the white-headed bird full in the body without slowing its attack in the least. Vast wings thundering, it lunged after him as he rolled away.

By some prodigy of good luck he caught it by its downy neck; but the carpels of its wings were as hard as any man's knuckles, and were driven by muscles more powerful than the strongest's. They battered him mercilessly as both tumbled.

The edge of the crenel between two merlons was like a wedge driven into his back. Still struggling to keep the bird's cruel, hooked beak from his face and eyes, he jerked the hatchet free; a carpal struck his forearm like a hammer, and the hatchet fell to the stone pavement of the terrace below.

The white-headed one's other carpal struck his temple, and the illusory nature of the world of the senses was made manifest; it narrowed to a miniature, artificially bright, which Silk endeavored to push away until it winked out.

CHAPTER 6   NEW WEAPONS

A whole whorl swam beneath Silk's flying, beclouded eyes—highland and tableland, jungle and dry scrub, savannah and pampa. The plaything of a hundred idle winds, buffeted yet at peace, he sailed over them all, dizzy with his own height and speed, his shoulder nudged by storm cloud, the solitary Flier three score leagues below him a darting dragonfly with wings of lace.

A black dragonfly that vanished into blacker cloud, into distant voices and the odor of carrion . . .

Silk choked on his own spew and spat; terror rose from the wheeling scene to foot him like a falcon, its icy talons in his vitals. He had blinked, and in that single blink the whorl had rolled over like a wind-tumbled basket or a wave-tossed barrel. The drifting skylands were *up* and the uneven, unyielding surface on which he lay, *down*. His head throbbed and spun, and an arm and both legs burned.

He sat up.

His mouth was wet with slime, his black robe discolored and stinking. He wiped them clumsily with numbed hands, then wiped his hand on his robe and spat again. The gray stone of the battlement had been crowding his left shoulder. The bird he had fought, the "white-headed one" of Mucor's warning, was nowhere to be seen.

Or perhaps, he thought, he had only dreamed of a terrible bird. He stood, staggered, and fell to his knees.

His eyes closed of themselves. He had dreamed it all, his tortured mind writhing among nightmares—the horrible bird, the horned beasts with their incandescent stares, the miserable mad girl, his dark rope reaching blindly again and again for new heights, the silent forest, the burly burglar with his hired donkeys, and the dead man sprawled beneath the swinging, hanging lamp. But he was awake now, awake at last, and the night was spent—awake and kneeling beside his own bed in the manse on Sun Street. It was shadeup and today was Sphigxday; already he should be chanting Stabbing Sphigx's morning prayer.

"O divine lady of the swords, of the gathering armies, of the swords . . ."

He fell forward, retching, his hands on the still-warm, rounded tiles.

The second time he was wiser, not attempting to stand until he was confident that he could do so without falling. Before he gained his feet, while he lay trembling beside the battlement, dawn faded and winked out. It was night again, Phaesday night once more—an endless night that had not yet ended and might never end. Rain, he thought, might wash him clean and clear his head, and so he prayed for rain, mostly to Phaea and Pas, but to Scylla as well, remembering all the while how many men (men better than himself) were imploring the gods as he did, and for better reasons: how long had they been praying, offering such small sacrifices as they could, washing Great Pas's images in orchards of dying trees and in fields of stunted corn?

It did not rain, or even thunder.

Excited voices drifted to him from somewhere far away; he caught the name Hierax repeated over and over. Someone or something had died.

"Hierax," Feather had replied at the palaestra a week or two before, fumbling after some fact associated with the familiar name of the God of Death. "Hierax is right in the middle."

"In the middle of Pas and Echidna's sons, Feather? Or of all their children?"

"Of their whole family, Patera, There's only the two boys in it." Feather, also, was one of a pair of brothers. "Hierax and Tartaros."

Feather had waited fearfully for correction, but he, Patera Silk, had smiled and nodded.

"Tartaros is the oldest and Hierax is the youngest," Feather had continued, encouraged.

Maytera's cubit stick tapped her lectern. "The older, Feather. And the younger. You said yourself that there were only two."

"Hierax . . ." said someone far below the other side of the battlement.

Silk stood up. He head still throbbed, and his legs were stiff; but he did not feel as though he were about to gag again. The chimneys (they all looked the same now) and the beckoning trapdoor seemed an impossible distance away. Still reeling and dizzy, he embraced a merlon with both arms and peered over the battlement. As if it belonged to someone else, he noted that his right forearm was oozing blood onto the gray stones.

Forty cubits and more below, three men and two women were standing in a rough circle on the terrace, all of them looking down at something.

For a slow half minute at least, Silk could not be certain what it was. A third woman pushed one of the others aside, then turned away as if in disgust. There was more talk until one of the armored guards arrived with a lamp.

The bird, Mucor's white-headed one, lay dead upon the flagstones, appearing smaller than Silk could have imagined, its unequal wings half spread, its long white neck bent back at an unnatural angle. He had killed it. Or rather, it had killed itself.

One of the men around the dead bird glanced upward, saw Silk watching him, pointed, and shouted something Silk could not understand. Rather too late (or so he feared), he waved as though he were a member of the household and retreated up the steep slope of the roof.

The trapdoor opened upon the dim and lofty attic he had glimpsed earlier, a cobwebbed cavern more than half filled with musty furniture and splintering crates. Feeble lights kindled at the muted clank of his foot upon the first iron step; he had hardly descended to the second when one winked out. It was a promising place in which to conceal himself, but it would no doubt be the first to be searched should the man on the terrace raise the alarm. Silk had rejected it by the time he reached the bottom of the spiraling steps, and with a pang of regret hurried straight to the wider wooden stair and ran down them to the upper floor of the original villa.

Here a narrow, tapestry-covered door opened onto a wide and luxuriously furnished corridor not far from a balustraded staircase up which cultured voices floated. A fat, formally dressed man sat in an elaborate red velvet and gilt armchair a few steps from the top of the staircase. His arms rested on a rosewood table, and his head upon his folded arms; he snored softly as Silk passed, jerked to wakefulness, stared uncomprehendingly at Silk's black robe, and lowered his head to his arms again.

The stair was thickly carpeted, its steps broad, and its slant gentle. It terminated in a palatial reception hall, in which five men dressed much like the sleeper stood deep in conversation. Several were holding tumblers, and none seemed alarmed. Some distance beyond them, the reception hall ended with wide double doors—doors that stood open at present, so that the soft autumn night itself appeared as a species of skylit hanging in Blood's hall. Beyond any question, Silk decided, those doors represented the principal entrance to the villa; the portico he had studied from the wall would be on the other side; and indeed when he had surveyed the scene below him for a moment—not leaning across the balustrade as he had so unwisely leaned across the battlement to stare down at the flaccid form of the white-headed one, but from the opposite side of the corridor, with his back against the nude, half again life-sized statue of some minor goddess—he could just make out the ghostly outlines of the pillars.

Unbidden, the manteion's familiar, fire-crowned altar rose before him as he stared at the open doors: the altar, the manse, the palaestra, and the shady arbor where he had sometimes chatted too long with Maytera Marble. Suppose that he were to walk down this staircase quite normally? Stroll through that hall, nodding and smiling to anyone who glanced toward him. Would any of them stop him, or call for guards? It seemed unlikely.

His own hot blood trickling down his right arm wet his fingers and dripped onto Blood's costly carpet. Shaking his head, Silk strode swiftly past the stair and seated himself in the matching red armchair on the other side. As long as his arm bled, he could be tracked by his blood: down the spiral stair from the roof, down the attic stair, and along this corridor.

Parting his robe, he started a tear above the hem of his tunic with his teeth and ripped away a strip.

Could not the blood trail be turned to his advantage? Silk rose and walked rapidly along the corridor, flexing his wrist and clenching his right hand to increase the bleeding, and entered the south wing by a short flight of steps; there he halted for a moment to wind the strip about his wound and knot it with his teeth just as Gib, the big man in the Cock, had. When he had satisfied himself that it would remain in place, he retraced his steps, passing the chair in which he had sat, the stairhead, the sleeper, and the narrow tapestry-covered door leading to the attic. Here, beyond paired icons of the minor deities Ganymedia and Catamitus, wide and widely spaced doors alternated with elaborately framed mirrors and amphorae overfilled with hothouse roses.

As Silk approached the entrance to the north wing, an officer in the uniform of the Guard emerged from an archway at the end of the corridor. The door nearest Silk stood half open; he stepped inside and shut it softly behind him.

He found himself facing a windowless pentagonal drawing room furnished in magnificent chryselephantine. For a moment he waited with his back to the corridor door, listening as he had listened so often that night. When he heard nothing, he crossed the thick carpet and opened one of the drawing room's ivory-encrusted doors.

This was a boudoir, larger and even more oddly shaped. There were wardrobes, two chairs, a rather tawdry shrine of Kypris whose smoldering thurible filled the room with the sweetness of frankincense, and a white dressing table before a glass whose pearlescent glow appeared to intensify as he entered. When he shut the door behind him, a swirl of colors danced across the glass. He fell to his knees.

"Sir?"

Looking up, Silk saw that the glass held only the gray face of a monitor. He traced the sign of addition. "Wasn't there a god? I saw . . ."

"I am no god, sir, merely the monitor of this terminal. What may I do to serve you, sir? Would you care to critique your digitally enhanced image?"

Disconcerted, Silk stood. "No. I—No, thank you." He struggled to recall how Auk had addressed the monitor in his glass. "I'd like to speak to a friend, if it isn't too much trouble, my son." That had not been it, surely.

The floating face appeared to nod. "The friend's name, please? I will attempt it."

"Auk."

"And this Auk lives where?"

"In the Orilla. Do you know where that is?"

"Indeed I do, sir. However, there are . . . fifty-four Auks resident there. Can you supply the street?"

"No, I'm afraid I have no idea." Suddenly weary, Silk drew out the dressing table's somewhat soiled little stool and sat down. "I'm sorry to have put you to so much trouble. But if you're—"

"There is an Auk in the Orilla with whom my master has spoken several times," the monitor interrupted. "No doubt he is the Auk you want. I will attempt to locate him for you."

"No," Silk said. "This Auk lives in what used to be a shop. So it must be on a shopping street, I suppose, with a lot of other stores and so on. Or at least on a street that used to have them." Remembering it, he recalled the thunder of the cartwheels. "A street paved with cobblestones. Does that help?"

"Yes. That is the Auk with whom my master speaks, sir. Let us see whether he is at home."

The monitor's face faded, replaced by Auk's disordered bed and jar of slops. Soon the image swelled and distorted, becoming oddly rounded. Silk saw the heavy wooden chair from which he had shriven Auk and beside which he had knelt when Auk shrived him. He found it heartening, somehow, to know that the chair was still there.

"I fear that Auk is unavailable, sir. May I leave a message with my similitude?"

"I—yes." Silk stroked his cheek. "Ask him, please, to tell Auk that I appreciate his help very, very much, and that if nothing happens to me it will be my great pleasure to tell Maytera Mint how kind he was. Tell him, too, that he's specified only one meritorious act thus far, while the penance he laid upon me called for two or three—for two at least. Ask him to let me know what the others should be." Too late, it occurred to Silk that Auk had asked that his name not be mentioned to the handsome boy who had spoken through Blood's glass. "Now then, my son. You referred to your master. Who is that?"

"Blood, sir. Your host."

"I see. Am I, by any chance, in Blood's private quarters now?"

"No, sir. These are my mistress's chambers."

"Will you tell Blood about the message I left for—for that man who lives in the Orilla?"

The monitor nodded gravely. "Certainly, sir, if he inquires."

"I see." A sickening sense of failure decended upon Silk. "Then please tell Auk, also, where I was when I tried to speak to him, and warn him to be careful."

"I shall, sir. Will that be all?"

Silk's head was in his hands. "Yes. And thank you. No." He straightened up. "I need a place to hide, a good place, and weapons."

"If I may say so, sir," remarked the monitor, "you require a proper dressing more than either. With respect, sir, you are dripping on our carpet."

Lifting his right arm, Silk saw that it was true; blood had already soaked through the strip of black cloth he had torn from his tunic a few minutes earlier. Crimson rivulets trickled toward his elbow.

"You will observe, sir, that this room has two doors, in addition to that through which you entered. The one to your left opens upon the balneum. My mistress's medicinal supplies are there, I believe. As to—"

Silk had risen so rapidly that he had knocked over the stool. Darting through the left-hand door, he heard nothing more.

The balneum was larger than he had anticipated, with a jade tub more than big enough for the naked goddess at the head of the staircase and a separate water closet. A sizable cabinet held a startling array of apothecary bottles, an olla of violet salve that Silk recognized as a popular aseptic, a roll of gauze, and gauze pads of various sizes. A small pair of scissors cut away the blood-soaked strip; he smeared the ragged wound that the white-headed one's beak had left in his forearm with the violet salve, and at the second try managed to bandage it effectively. As he ruefully took stock of his ruined tunic, he discovered that the bird's talons had raked his chest and abdomen. It was almost a relief to wash and salve the long, bloody scratches, on which he could employ both his hands.

Yellowish encrustations were forming on his robe where he had wiped away his spew. He took it off and washed it as thoroughly as he could in the lavabo, wrung it out, smoothed it as well as he could, pressed it between two dry towels, and put it back on. Inspecting his appearance in a mirror, he decided that he might well pass a casual examination in a dim light.

Returning to the boudoir, he strewed what he took to be face powder over the clotted blood on the carpet.

The monitor watched him, unperturbed. "That is most interesting, sir."

"Thank you." Silk shut the powder box and returned it to the dressing table.

"Does the powder possess cleansing properties? I was unaware of it."

Silk shook his head. "Not that I know of. I'm only masking these, so visitors won't be unsettled."

"Very shrewd, sir."

Silk shrugged. "If I could think of something better, I'd do it. When I came in, you said that you weren't a god. I knew you weren't. We had a glass in the—in a palaestra I attended."

"Would you like to speak to someone there, sir?"

"Not now. But I was privileged to use that glass once, and it struck me then—I suppose it struck all of us, and I remember some of us talking about it one evening—that the glass looked a great deal like a Sacred Window. Except for its size, of course; all Sacred Windows are eight cubits by eight. Are you familiar with them?"

"No, sir."

Silk righted the stool and sat down. "There's another difference, too. Sacred Windows don't have monitors."

"That is unfortunate, sir."

"Indeed." Silk stroked his cheek with two fingers. "I should tell you, then, that the immortal gods appear at times in the Sacred Windows."

"Ah!"

"Yes, my son. I've never seen one, and most people—those who aren't augurs or sibyls, particularly—can't see the gods at all. Although they frequently hear the voice of the god, they see only a swirl of color."

The monitor's face flushed brick red. "Like this, sir?"

"No. Not at all like that. I was going to say that as I understand it, those people who can see the gods first see the swirling colors as well. When the theophany begins, the colors are seen. Then the god appears. And then the colors reappear briefly as the god vanishes. All this was set down in circumstantial detail by the Devoted Caddis, nearly two centuries ago. In the course of a long life, he'd witnessed the theophanies of Echidna, Tartaros, and Scylla, and finally that of Pas. He called the colors he'd seen the Holy Hues."

"Fascinating, sir. I fear, however, that it has little to do with me. May I show you what it is I do, sir? What I do most frequently, I should say. Observe."

The monitor's floating face vanished, replaced by the image of a remarkably handsome man in black. Although the tunic of the man in the glass was torn and white gauze showed beneath it, Silk did not recognize this man as himself until he moved and saw the image move with him.

"Is that . . . ?" He leaned closer. "No. But . . ."

"Thank you, sir," his image said, and bowed. "Only a first attempt, although I think it a rather successful one. I shall do better next time."

"Take it away, please. I am already too much given to vanity, believe me."

"As you wish, sir," his image replied. "I intended no disrespect. I merely desired to demonstrate to you the way in which I most frequently serve my mistress. Would you care to see her in place of yourself? I can easily display an old likeness."

Silk shook his head. "An old unlikeness, you mean. Please return to your normal appearance."

"As you wish, sir." In the glass, Silk's face lost its blue eyes and brown cheeks, its neck and shoulders vanished, and its features became flatter and coarser.

"We were speaking of the gods. No doubt I told you a good deal that you already knew."

"No, sir. I know very little about gods, sir. I would advise you to consult an augur."

"Then let's talk about monitors, my son. You must know more than most about monitors. You're a monitor yourself."

"My task is my joy, sir."

"We're fortunate, then, both of us. When I was at—in the house of a certain man I know, a man who has a glass like this one, he clapped his hands to summon the monitor. Is that the usual method?"

"Clapping the hands or tapping on the glass, sir. All of us much prefer the former, if I may be excused for saying it."

"I see." Silk nodded to himself. "Aren't there any other methods?"

"We actually appear in response to any loud sound, sir, to determine whether there is something amiss. Should a fire be in progress, for example, I would notify my master or his steward, and warn his guests."

"And from time to time," Silk said, "you must look into this room although no one has called you, even when there has been no loud sound. Isn't that so?"

"No, sir."

"You don't simply look in to make certain everything's all right?"

"No, sir. My mistress would consider that an invasion of her privacy, I'm sure."

"When I entered this room," Silk continued, "I did not make any sound that could be called loud—or at least none that I'm aware of. Certainly I didn't clap my hands or tap on this glass; yet you appeared. There was a swirl of color, then your face appeared in the glass. Shortly afterward you told me you weren't a god."

"You closed the door, sir."

"Very gently," Silk said. "I didn't want to disturb your mistress."

"Most considerate, sir."

"Yet the sound of my shutting that door summoned you? I would think that in that case almost any sound would do, however slight."

"I really cannot say what summoned me, sir."

"That's a suggestive choice of words, my son."

"I concede that it may be, sir." The monitor's face appeared to nod. "Such being the case, perhaps I may proffer an additional suggestion? It is that you abandon this line of inquiry. It will not reward your persistence, sir. Prior to entering the balneum, you inquired about weapons, sir, and places of concealment. One of our wardrobes might do."

"Thank you." Silk looked into the nearest, but it was filled almost to bursting with coats and gowns.

"As to weapons, sir," the monitor continued, "you may discover a useful one in my lowest left drawer, beneath the stockings."

"More useful than this, I hope." Silk closed the wardrobe.

"I am very sorry, sir. There appear to have been many purchases of late of which I have not been apprised."

Silk hardly heard him—there were angry and excited voices in the corridor. He opened the door to the drawing room and listened until they faded away, his hand upon the glass latchbar of the boudoir door, acutely conscious of the thudding of his heart.

"Are you leaving, sir?"

"The left drawer, I think you said."

"Yes, sir. The lowest of the drawers to your left. I can guarantee nothing, however, sir. My mistress keeps a small needler there, or perhaps I should say she did so not long ago. It may, however . . ."

Silk had already jerked out the drawer. Groping under what seemed to be at least a hundred pairs of women's hose, his fingers discovered not one but two metal objects.

"My mistress is sometimes careless regarding the safety catch, sir. It may be well to exercise due caution until you have ascertained its condition."

"I don't even know what that is," Silk muttered as he gingerly extracted the first.

It was a needler so small that it lay easily in the palm of his hand, elaborately engraved and gold plated; the thumb-sized ivory grips were inlaid with golden hyacinths, and a minute heron scanned a golden pool for fish at the base of the rear sight. For a moment, Silk too knew peace, lost in the flawless craftsmanship that had been lavished upon every surface. No venerated object in his manteion was half so fine.

"Should that discharge, it could destroy my glass, sir."

Silk nodded absently. "I've seen needlers—I saw two tonight, in fact—that could eat this one."

"You have informed me that you are unfamiliar with the safety catch, sir. Upon either side of the needler you hold, you will observe a small movable convexity. Raised, it will prevent the needler from discharging."

"This," Silk said. Like the grips, each tiny boss was marked with a hyacinth, though these were so small that their minute, perfect florets were almost microscopic. He pushed one of the bosses down, and the other moved with it. "Will it fire now?"

"I believe so, sir. Please do not direct it toward my glass. Glasses are now irreplaceable, sir, the art of their manufacture having been left behind when—"

"I'm greatly tempted nevertheless."

"In the event of the destruction of this glass I should be unable to deliver your message to Auk, sir."

"In which case there'd be no need of it. This smooth bar inside the ring is the trigger, I suppose."

"I believe that is correct, sir."

Silk pointed the needler at the wardrobe and pressed the trigger. There was a sharp snap, like the cracking of a child's whip. "It doesn't seem to have done anything," he said.

"My mistress's wardrobe is not a living creature, sir."

"I never thought it was, my son." Silk bent to examine the wardrobe's door; a hole not much thicker than a hair had appeared in one of its polished panels. He opened the door again. Some, though not all, of the gowns in line with the hole showed ragged tears, as if they had been stabbed with a dull blade a little narrower than his index finger.

"I should use this on you, you know, my son," he told the monitor, "for Auk's sake. You're just a machine, like the scorer in our ball court."

"I am a machine, but not *just* a machine, sir."

Nodding mostly to himself, Silk pushed up the safety catch and dropped the little needler into his pocket.

The other object hidden under the stockings was shaped like the letter *T*. The stem was cylindrical and oddly rough, with a single, smooth protuberance below the crossbar; the crossbar itself seemed polished and slightly curved, and had upturned ends. The entire object felt unnaturally cold, as reptiles often do. Silk extracted it from the stockings with some difficulty and examined it curiously.

"Would it be convenient for me to withdraw, sir?" the monitor asked.

Silk shook his head. "What is this?"

"I don't know, sir."

He regarded the monitor narrowly. "Can you lie, under extreme provocation, my son? Tell an untruth? I know a chem quite well; and she can, or so she says."

"No, sir."

"Which leaves me not a whit the wiser." Silk seated himself on the stool again.

"I suppose not, sir."

"I think I know what this is, you see." Silk held the T-shaped object up for the monitor's inspection; it gleamed like polished silver. "I'd appreciate confirmation, and some instructions on how to operate it."

"I am afraid I cannot assist you, sir, although I would be glad to receive your own opinion."

"I think it's an azoth. I've never actually seen one, but we used to talk about them when I was a boy. One summer all of us made wooden swords, and sometimes we pretended they were azoths."

"Charming, sir."

"Not really," Silk muttered, scrutinizing the flashing gem in the pommel of the azoth. "We were as bloodthirsty as so many little tigers, and what's charming about that? But anyway, an azoth is supposed to be controlled by something called a demon. If you don't know about azoths, you don't know anything about that, I suppose."

"No, sir." The monitor's floating face swung from side to side, revealing that there was no head behind it. "If you wish to conceal yourself, sir, should you not do so at once? My master's steward and some of our guards are searching the suites on this floor."

"How do you know that?" Silk asked sharply.

"I have been observing them. I have glasses in some of the other suites, sir."

"They began at the north end of the corridor?"

"Yes, sir. Quite correct."

Silk rose. "Then I must hide in here well enough to escape them, and get into the north wing after they've left."

"You haven't examined the other wardrobe, sir."

"And I don't intend to. How many unsearched suites are there between us?"

"Three, sir."

"Then I've still got a little time." Silk studied the azoth. "When I made my sword, I left a nail sticking out, and bent it. That was my demon. When I twisted it toward me, the blade wasn't there any more. When I twisted it away from me, I had one."

"I doubt, sir—"

"Don't be too sure, my son. That may have been based on something supposedly true that I'd heard. Or I may have been imitating some other boy who'd gotten hold of a useful fact. I mean a fact that would be useful to me now."

The roughened stem of the T was the grip, obviously; and the crossbar was there to prevent the user's hand from contacting the blade. Silk tried to revolve the gem in the pommel, but its setting kept it securely in place.

The bent-nail demon of his toy sword had been one of those that had held the crosspiece; he felt certain of that. There was an unfacetted crimson gem (he vaguely remembered having heard a similar gem called a bloodstone) in the grip, just behind one of the smooth, tapering arms of the guard. It was too flat and much too highly polished to turn. He gripped the azoth as he had his wooden sword and pressed the crimson gem with his thumb.

Reality separated. Something else appeared between the halves, as a current divides a quiet pool. Plaster from the wall across the room fell smoking onto the carpet, revealing laths that themselves exploded in a shower of splinters with the next movement of his arm.

Involuntarily, he released the demon, and the azoth's blade vanished.

"Please be more careful with that, sir."

"I will." Silk pushed the azoth into the coiled rope about his waist.

"If it should be activated by chance, sir, the result might well be disastrous for you as well as others."

"You have to press the demon below the level of the grip, I think," Silk said. "It should be difficult for that to happen accidentally."

"I profoundly hope so, sir."

"You don't know where your mistress got such a weapon?"

"I did not even know she possessed it, sir."

"It must be worth as much as this whole villa. More, perhaps. I doubt that there are ten of them in the city." Silk turned toward the wardrobe and selected a blue winter gown of soft wool.

"They have left the suite they were searching earlier, sir. They are proceeding to the next."

"Thank you. Will you leave when I tell you to go?"

"Certainly, sir."

"I ought to destroy your glass." For a second, Silk stared at the monitor. "I'm tempted to do it. But if a god really visited it when I arrived . . ." He shrugged. "So I'm going to tell you to go instead, and cover your glass with a gown. Perhaps they won't notice it. Did they question the glasses in the other suites?"

"Yes, sir. Our steward summoned me to each glass. He is directing the searchers in person, sir."

"While you were here talking to me? I didn't know you could do that."

"I can, sir. One strives to best utilize lulls in the conversation, pauses, and the like. It is largely a matter of allocation, sir."

"But you didn't tell them where I was. You can't have. Why not?"

"He did not inquire, sir. As they entered each suite, he asked whether there was a stranger present."

"And you told them there wasn't?"

"No, sir. I was forced to explain that I could not be certain, since I am not perpetually present."

"Blood's steward—is that the young man called Musk?"

"Yes, sir. His instructions take precedence over all others, except my master's own."

"I see. Musk doesn't understand you much better than I do, apparently."

"Less well, perhaps, sir."

Silk nodded to himself. "I may remain in this suite after you've gone. On the other hand, I may leave, too, as soon as you're no longer here to watch what I'm doing. Do you understand what I've just told you?"

"Yes, sir," the monitor said. "Your future whereabouts will be problematical."

"Good. Now vanish at once. Go wherever it is that you go." Silk draped the glass, covering it completely in a way that he hoped would seem merely careless, and opened the door to his right.

For the space of a heartbeat, he thought the spacious, twilit bedchamber unoccupied; a faint moan from the enormous bed at its center revealed his mistake.

The woman in the bed writhed and keened aloud from the depths of her need. As he bent over her, something within him reached out to her; and though he had not touched her, he felt the thrill of touch. Her hair was as black as the night chough's wings, and as glossy. Her features, as well as he could judge in the uncertain glow, exquisite. She groaned softly, as though she knew he was looking down on her, and rolling her head upon her pillow, kissed it without waking.

Beyond the boudoir, the drawing room door opened.

He tore off his black robe and straw hat, ducked out of his torn tunic, kicked all three far under the big bed, and scrambled in, shoes and all. He was drawing up the gold-embroidered oversheet when he heard the door through which he had entered the boudoir open.

Someone said distinctly, "Nothing in here."

By then his thumb had found the safety catch. He sat up, leveling the needler, as the searchers entered.

"Stop!" he shouted, and fired. By the greatest good luck, the needle shattered a tall vase to the right of the door. The report brought the bedchamber's lights to their brightest.

The first armored guard halted, his slug gun not quite pointing at Silk; and the black-haired woman sat up abruptly, her slightly tilted eyes wide.

Without looking at her, Silk grated, "Go back to sleep, Hyacinth. This doesn't concern you." Faintly perfumed, her breath caressed his bare shoulder, deliciously warm.

"Sorry, Commissioner," the guard began, uncertainly. "I mean Patera—"

Too late, Silk realized that he was still wearing the old, blue-trimmed calotte that had once been Patera Pike's. He snatched it off. "This is unforgivable. Unforgivable! I shall inform Blood. Get out!" His voice was far too high, and mounting toward hysteria; surely the guard must sense how frightened he was. In desperation, he brandished the tiny needler.

"We didn't know—" The guard lowered his slug gun and took a step backward, bumping into the delicate-looking Musk, who had stepped through the boudoir behind him. "We thought everybody had— Well, just about everybody's already gone."

Silk cut him off. "Out! You've never seen me."

It had been (as he decided as soon as he had said it) the worst thing he could possibly have said, since Musk had certainly seen him only a few hours earlier. For an instant he felt certain that Musk would pounce upon it.

Musk did not. Silencing the sputtering guard with a shove, Musk said, "The outside door should've been locked. Take your time." He turned on his heel, and the guard shut the boudoir door quietly behind them.

Trembling, Silk waited until he heard the corridor door close as well before he kicked away the luxurious coverings and got out of the bed. His mouth was parched, and his knees without strength.

"What about me?" the woman asked. As she spoke, she pushed aside the oversheet and the red silk sheet, revealing remarkably rounded breasts and a small waist.

Silk caught his breath and looked away. "All right, what about you? Do you want me to shoot you?"

She smiled and threw her arms wide. "If it's the only thing you can do, why, yes." When Silk did not reply, she added, "I'll keep my eyes open, if that's all right with you. I like to see it coming." The smile became a grin. "Make it fast, but make it last. And make it good."

Both had spoken softly, and the lights were no longer glaring; Silk kicked the bed to re-energize them. "You have been given a philtre of some sort, I think. You'll feel very differently in the morning." Pushing up the safety catch, he dropped her needler back into his pocket.

"I was *given* nothing." The woman in the bed licked her lips, watching for his reaction. "I took what you're calling a philtre before the first ones got here."

"Rust?" Silk was on his knees beside the bed, groping for the clothing he had kicked beneath it. Fear was draining from him, and he felt immensely grateful for it. Lion-hearted Sphigx still favored him—nothing could be more certain.

"No." She was scornful. "Rust doesn't do this. Don't you know anything? On rust I'd have itched to kill them all, and I might've done it, too. Beggar's root's what they call it, and it turns a terrible bore into a real pleasure."

"I see." Wincing, Silk pulled out his ruined tunic and his second-best robe.

"Want me to give you some? I've got a lot more, and it only takes a pinch." She swung amazingly long legs over the side of the bed. "It's a lot more expensive than rust, and a lot harder to find, but I'm in a generous mood. I usually am—you'll see." She favored Silk with a sidelong smile that made his heart leap.

He stood up and backed away.

"They call it beggar's root because it makes you beg. I'm begging now, just listen to me. Come on. You'll like it."

Silk shook his head.

"Come sit next to me." She patted the rumpled sheet. "That's all I'm asking for—right now, anyway. You were here in bed with me a minute ago."

He tried to pull his tunic over his head and failed, discovering in the process that even the slightest movement of his right arm was painful.

"You're the one that they were looking for, aren't you? Aren't you glad that I didn't tell them anything? You really ought to be, Musk can be awfully mean. Don't you want me to help you with that?"

"Don't try." He retreated another step.

Sliding off the bed, she picked up his robe. She was completely naked; he closed his eyes and turned away.

She giggled, and he was suddenly reminded of Mucor, the mad girl. "You really are an augur. He called you Patera—I'd forgotten. Do you want your little hat back? I stuck it under my pillow."

The uses to which Patera Pike's calotte might be put if it remained with her flashed through Silk's mind. "Yes," he said. "Please, may I have it back?"

"Sure, I'll trade you."

He shook his head.

"Didn't you come here to see me? You don't act like it, but you knew my name."

"No. I came to find Blood."

"You won't like him, Patera." Hyacinth grinned again. "Even Musk doesn't like him, not really. Nobody does."

"He has my sympathy." Silk tried to raise the tunic again, and was deterred by a flash of pain. "I've come to show him how he can be better liked, and even loved."

"Well, Patera, I'm Hyacinth, just like you said. And I'm famous. Everybody likes me, except you."

"I do like you," Silk told her. "That is one of the reasons I won't do what you want. It's a rather minor one, actually, but a real reason nonetheless."

"You stole my azoth, though, didn't you, Patera? I can see the end of it poking out of that rope."

Silk nodded. "I intend to return it. But you're quite right, I took it without your permission, and that's theft. I'm sorry, but I felt I'd better have it. What I'm doing is extremely important." He paused and waited for remonstrances that did not come. "I'll see that it's returned to you, and your needler as well, if I get home safely."

"You were afraid of the guards, weren't you? There in my bed. You were afraid of that one with Musk. Afraid that he'd kill you."

"Yes," Silk admitted. "I was terrified, if you want the truth; and now I'm just as terrified of you, afraid that I'll give in to you, disgrace my calling, and lose the favor of the immortal gods."

She laughed.

"You're right." Silk tried to put on his tunic again, but his right forearm burned and throbbed. "I'm certainly not brave. But at least I'm brave enough to admit it."

"Wait just a minute," she said. "Wait right here. I'm going to get you something."

He glimpsed the balneum through the door she opened. As she closed it behind her, it occurred to him that Patera Pike's calotte was still in the bed, under her pillow; moved by that weak impulse which turns back travelers to retrieve trifles, he rescued it and put it on.

She emerged from the balneum, naked still, holding out a gold cup scarcely larger than a thimble, half filled with brick-colored powder. "Here, Patera. You put it into your lip."

"No. I realize that you mean well, but I'd rather be afraid."

She shrugged and pulled forward her own lower lip. For a moment it made her ugly, and Silk felt a surge of relief. After emptying the little cup into the hollow between lip and gum, she grinned at him. "This is the best money can buy, and it works fast. Sure you don't want some? I've got a lot."

"No," he repeated. "I should go. I should have gone before now, in fact."

"All right." She was looking at the gem in the hilt of the azoth again. "It's mine, you know. A very important man gave it to me. If you're going to steal it, I ought to at least get to help you. Are you sure you're a real augur?"

Silk sighed. "It seems that I may not be much longer. If you're serious about wanting to help me, Hyacinth, tell me where you think Blood is likely to be at this hour. Will he have retired for the night?"

She shook her head, her eyes flashing. "He's probably downstairs saying good-bye to the last of them. They've been coming all night, commissioners and commissioners' flunkies. Every once in a while he sends a really important one up here for me. I lost count, but there must have been six or seven of them."

"I know." Silk tried to push the hilt of the azoth more deeply into the coil of rope. "I've lain between your sheets."

"You think I ought to change them? I didn't think men cared."

Silk knelt to fish his broad-brimmed straw hat from beneath the bed. "I doubt that those men do."

"I can call a servant."

"They're busy looking for me, I imagine." Silk tossed the hat onto the bed and readied himself for one last try at his tunic.

"Not the maids." She took his tunic from him. "You know, your eyes want to look at me. You ought to let them do it."

"Hundreds of men must have told you how beautiful you are. Would you displease the gods to hear it once more? I wouldn't. I'm still young, and I hope to see a god before I die." He was tempted to add that he might well have missed one by a second or less when he entered her chambers, but he did not.

"You've never had a woman, have you?"

Silk shook his head, unwilling to speak.

"Well, let me help you get this on, anyway." She held his tunic as high as she could stretch while he worked both arms into the sleeves, then snatched her azoth from the rope coiled around his waist and sprang toward the bed.

He gaped at her, stunned. Her thumb was upon the demon, the blade slot pointed at his heart. Backing away, he raised both hands in the gesture of surrender.

She posed like a duelist. "They say the girls fight like troopers in Trivigaunte." She parried awkwardly twice, and skewered and slashed an imaginary opponent.

By that time he had recovered at least a fraction of his composure. "Aren't you going to call the guards?"

"Don't think so." She lunged and recovered. "Wouldn't I make a fine swordsman, Patera? Look at these legs."

"No, I don't think so."

She pouted. "Why not?"

"Because one must study swordsmanship, and practice day after day. There is a great deal to learn, or so I've been told. To speak frankly, I'd back a shorter, less attractive woman against you, assuming that she was less attracted to admiration and those bottles in your balneum, too."

Hyacinth gave no sign of having heard. "If you really can't do what I want—if you won't, I mean—couldn't you use this azoth instead? And kiss me, and pretend? I'd show you where I want you to put the big jewel, and after a while you might change your mind."

"Isn't there an antidote?" To prevent her from seeing his expression, he crossed the room to the window and parted the drapes. There was no one around the dead bird on the terrace now. "You have all those herbs. Surely you must have the antidote, if there is one."

"I don't want the antidote, Patera. I want you." Her hand was on his shoulder; her lips brushed his ear. "And if you go out there like you're thinking, the cats'll tear you to pieces."

The blade of the azoth shot past his ear, fifty cubits down to the terrace to slice the dead bird in two and leave a long, smoking scar across the flagstones. Silk flinched from it. "For Pas's love be careful!"

Hyacinth whirled off like a dancer as she pressed the demon again. Shimmering through the bedchamber like summer heat, the azoth's illimited discontinuity hummed of death, parting the universe, slitting the drapes like a razor and dropping a long section slabbed from wall and window frame at Silk's feet.

"Now you have to," she told him, and came at him with a sweeping cut that scarred half the room. "Say you will, and I'll give it back."

As he dove through the window, the azoth's humming blade divided the stone sill behind him; but all the fear he ought to have felt was drowned in the knowledge that he was leaving her.

Had he struck the flagstones head first, he would have been spared a great deal of pain. As it was, he turned head over heels in midair. There was only a moment of darkness, like that a bruiser knows when he is knocked to his knees. For what might have been seconds or minutes, he lay near the divided body of the white-headed one, hearing her voice call to him from the window without comprehending anything it said.

When at last he tried to stand, he found that he could not. He had dragged himself to within ten paces of the wall, and shot two of the horned cats Mucor called lynxes, when a guard in silvered armor took the needler from his hand.

After what seemed a very long time, unarmored servants joined him; these carried torches with which they kept the snarling lynxes at bay. Supervised by a fussy little man with a pointed, iron-gray beard, they rolled Silk onto a blanket and carried him back to the villa.

CHAPTER 7 THE BARGAIN

"It isn't much," the fussy little man said, "but it's mine for as long as he lets me have it."

"It" was a moderately large and very cluttered room in the north wing of Blood's villa, and the fussy little man was rummaging in a drawer as he spoke. He snapped a flask under the barrel of a clumsy-looking gun, pushed its muzzle through one of the rents in Silk's tunic, and fired.

Silk felt a sharp pain, as though he had been stung by a bee.

"This stuff kills a lot of people," the fussy little man informed him, "so that's to see if you're one of them. If you don't die in a minute or two, I'll give you some more. Having any trouble breathing?"

Clenching his teeth against the pain in his ankle, Silk drew a deep breath and shook his head.

"Good. Actually, that was a minimal dose. It won't kill you even if you're sensitive to it, but it'll take care of those deep scratches and make you sick enough to tell me I mustn't give you any more." The fussy little man bent to stare into Silk's eyes. "Take another deep breath and let it out."

Silk did so. "What's your name, Doctor?"

"We don't use them much here. You're fine. Hold out that arm."

Silk raised it, and the bee stung again.

"Stops pain and fights infection." The fussy little man squatted, pushed up Silk's trousers leg, and put the muzzle of his odd-looking gun against Silk's calf.

"It didn't operate that time," Silk told him.

"Yes, it did. You didn't feel it, that's all. Now we can take that shoe off."

"My own name is Patera Silk."

The fussy little man glanced up at him. "Doctor Crane, Silk. Have a good laugh. You're really an augur? Musk said you were."

Silk nodded.

"And you jumped out of that second-floor window? Don't do that again." Doctor Crane untied the laces and removed the shoe. "My mother hoped I'd be tall, you see. She was tall herself, and she liked tall men. My father was short."

Silk said, "I understand."

"I doubt it." Doctor Crane bent over Silk's foot, his pinkish scalp visible through his gray hair. "I'm going to cut away this stocking. If I pull it off, it might do more damage." He produced shiny scissors exactly like those Silk had found in Hyacinth's balneum. "She's dead now, and so's he, so I guess it doesn't matter." The ruined stocking fell away. "Want to see what he looked like?"

The absence of pain was intoxicating; Silk felt giddy with happiness. "I'd love to." He managed to add, "If you care to show me."

"I can't help it. You're seeing him now, since I look exactly like him. It's our genes, not our names, that make us whatever we are."

"It's the will of the gods." Silk's eyes told him that the little physician was probing his swollen right ankle with his fingers, but he could feel nothing. "Your mother was tall; and if you were tall as well, you would say that it was because she had been."

"I'm not hurting you?"

Silk shook his head. "I don't resemble my own mother in the least; she was small and dark. I have no idea what my father looked like, but I know that I am the man that a certain god wished me to be before I was born."

"She's dead?"

Silk nodded. "She left us for Mainframe a month before I was designated."

"You've got blue eyes. You're only the second—no, the third person I've ever seen with them. It's a shame you don't know who your father was. I'd like to have a look at him. See if you can stand up."

Silk could and did.

"Fine. Let me take your arm. I want you up there on that table. It's a nice clean break, or anyway that's what it looks like, and I'm going to pin it and put a cast on it."

They were not planning to kill him. Silk savored the thought. They were not planning to kill him, and so there might still be a chance to save the manteion.

Blood was slightly drunk. Silk envied him that almost as much as his possession of the manteion. As though Blood had read his thoughts, he said, "Hasn't anybody brought you anything, Patera? Musk, get somebody to bring him a drink."

The handsome young man nodded and slipped out of the room, at which Silk felt somewhat better.

"We've got other stuff, Patera. I don't suppose you use them?"

Silk said, "Your physician's already given me a drug to ease the pain. I doubt that it would be wise to mix it with something else." He was very conscious of that pain, which was returning; but he had no intention of letting Blood see that.

"Right you are." Blood leaned forward in his big red leather chair, and for a moment Silk thought that he might actually fall out of it. "The light touch with everything—that's my motto. Always has been. Even with that enlightenment of yours, a light touch's best."

Silk shook his head. "In spite of what has happened to me, I cannot agree."

"What's this!" Grinning broadly, Blood pretended to be outraged. "Did enlightenment tell you to come out here and break into my house? No, no, Patera. Don't try to tell me that. That was greed, the same as you'd slang me for. Your tin sibyl told you I'd bought your place—which I have, and everything completely legal—so you figured I'd have things worth taking. Don't tell me. I'm an old hand myself."

"I came here to steal our manteion back from you," Silk said. "That's worth taking, certainly. You took it legally, and I intended to take it from you, if I could, in any way I could."

Blood spat, looked around for his drink, and finding the tumbler empty dropped it on the carpet. "What did you think you could do, nick the shaggy deed out of my papers? It wouldn't mean a shaggy thing. Musk's the buyer of record, and all he'd have to do is pay a couple of cards for a new copy."

"I was going to make you sign it over to me," Silk told him. "I intended to hide in your bedroom until you came, and threaten to kill you unless you did exactly as I ordered."

The door opened. Musk entered, followed by a liveried footman with a tray. The footman set the tray on an inlaid table at Silk's elbow. "Will that be all, sir?"

Silk took the squat, water-white drink from the tray and sipped. "Yes, thank you. Thank you very much, Musk."

The servant departed; Musk smiled bitterly.

"This's getting interesting." Blood leaned forward, his wide, red face redder than ever. "Would you really have killed me, Patera?"

Silk, who would not have, felt certain he would not be believed. "I hoped that it wouldn't be necessary."

"I see. I see. And it never crossed your mind that I'd yell for some friends in the City Guard the minute you left? That I wouldn't even have had to use my own people on you, because the Guard would do their work instead?" Blood laughed, and Musk concealed his smile behind his hand.

Silk sipped again, wondering briefly whether the drink was drugged. If they wanted to drug him, he reflected, they would have no need of subterfuge. Whatever it was, the drink was very strong, certainly. Drugged or undrugged, it might dull the pain in his ankle. He ventured a cautious swallow. He had drunk brandy already tonight, the brandy Gib had given him; it seemed a very long time ago. Surely Blood would make no charge for this drink, whatever else he might do. (Not once in a month did Silk drink anything stronger than water.)

"Well, didn't you?" Blood snorted in disgust. "You know, I've got a few people working for me that don't think any better than you do, Patera."

Silk returned his drink to the tray. "I was going to make you sign a confession. It was the only thing I could think of, so it was what I planned."

"Me? Confess to what?"

"It didn't matter." Fatigue had enfolded Silk like a cloak. He had never known that a chair could be as comfortable as this one, a chair in which he could sleep for days. "A conspiracy to overthrow the Ayuntamiento, perhaps. Something like that." Recalling certain classroom embarrassments, he forced himself to breathe deeply so that he would not yawn; the faint throbbing in his foot seemed very far away, driven beyond the fringes of the most remote Vironese lands by the kindly sorcery of the squat tumbler. "I would have given it to one of my—to another augur, one I know well. I was going to seal it, and make him promise to deliver it to the Juzgado if anything happened to me. Something like that."

"Not too bad." Blood took Hyacinth's little needler from his waistband, thumbed off its safety catch, and aimed it carefully at Silk's chest.

Musk frowned and touched Blood's arm.

Blood chuckled. "Oh, don't worry. I only wanted to see how he'd behave in my place. It doesn't seem to bother him much." The needler's tiny, malevolent eye twitched to the right and spat, and the squat tumbler exploded, showering Silk with shards and pungent liquor.

He brushed himself with his fingers. "What would you like me to sign over to you? I'll be happy to oblige. Give me the paper."

"I don't know." Blood dropped Hyacinth's gold-plated needler on the stand that had held his drink. "What have you got, Patera?"

"Two drawers of clothing and three books. No, two; I sold my personal copy of the Writings. My beads—I've got those here, and I'll give them to you now if you like. My old pen case, but it's still in my robe up in that woman's room. You could have somebody bring it, and I'll confess to climbing onto your roof and entering your house without your permission, and give you the pen case, too."

Blood shook his head. "I don't need your confession, Patera. I have you."

"As you like." Silk visualized his bedroom, over the kitchen in the manse. "Pas's gammadion. That's steel, of course, but the chain's silver and should be worth something. I also have an old portable shrine that belonged to Patera Pike. I've set it up on my dresser, so I suppose you could say it's mine now. There's a rather attractive triptych, a small polychrome lamp, an offertory cloth, and so on, with a teak case to carry them in. Do you want that? I had hoped—foolishly no doubt—to pass it on to my successor."

Blood waved the triptych aside. "How'd you get through the gate?"

"I didn't. I cut a limb in the forest and tied it to this rope." Silk pointed to his waist. "I threw the limb over the spikes on your wall and climbed the rope."

"We'll have to do something about that." Blood glanced significantly at Musk. "You say you were up on the roof, so it was you that killed Hierax."

Silk sat up straight, feeling as if he had been wakened from sleep. "You gave him the name of the god?"

"Musk did. Why not?"

Musk said softly, "He was a griffon vulture, a mountain bird. Beautiful. I thought I might be able to teach him to kill for himself."

"But it was no go," Blood continued. "Musk got angry with him and was going to knife him. Musk has the mews out back."

Silk nodded politely. Patera Pike had once remarked to him that you could never tell from a man's appearance what might give him pleasure; studying Musk, Silk decided that he had never accorded Patera Pike's sagacity as much respect as it had deserved.

"So I said that if he didn't want him, he could give him to me," Blood continued, "and I put him up there on the roof for a pet."

"I see." Silk paused. "You clipped his wings."

"I had one of Musk's helpers do it," Blood explained, "so he wouldn't fly off. He wouldn't hunt anyhow."

Silk nodded, mostly to himself. "But he attacked me, I suppose because I picked up that scrap of hide. We were next to the battlement, and in the excitement of the moment he—I will not call him Hierax, Hierax is a sacred name—forgot that he could no longer fly."

Blood reached for the needler. "You're saying I killed him. That's a shaggy lie! You did it."

Silk nodded. "He died by misadventure while fighting with me; but you may say that I killed him if you like. I was certainly trying to."

"And you stole this needler from Hyacinth before she drove you through the window with her azoth—must be about a thirty-cubit drop. Why didn't you shoot her?"

"Would you have," Silk inquired, "if you had been in my place?"

Blood chuckled. "And fed her to Musk's birds."

"What I have done to you already is surely much worse than anything that Hyacinth did to me; I say nothing of what I intended to do to you. Are you going to shoot me?" If he lunged, Silk decided, he might be able to wrestle the little needler from Blood in spite of his injured leg; and with the muzzle to Blood's head, he might be able to force them to let him go. He readied himself, calculating the distance as he edged forward in his chair.

"I might. I might at that, Patera." Blood toyed with the needler, palming it, flipping it over, and weighing it in his hand; he seemed nearly sober now. "You understand—or I hope you do, anyway—that we haven't committed any kind of a crime, not a one of us. Not me, not Musk here, not any of my people."

Silk started to speak, then decided against it.

"You think you know about something? All right, I'll guess. Tell me if I'm wrong. You've been talking with Hy, and so you think she's a whore. One of our guests tonight gave her that azoth. Quite a little present, plenty good enough for a councillor. Maybe she bragged on some of her other presents, too. Have I hit the target?"

Silk nodded guardedly, his eyes on the needler. "She'd had several . . . Visitors."

Blood chuckled. "He's blushing, Musk. Take a look at him. Yes, Patera, I know. Only they didn't pay, and that's what matters to the law. They were my guests, and Hy's one of my houseguests. So if she wants to show somebody a good time, that's her business and mine, but none of yours. You came out here to get back your manteion, you tell me. Well, we didn't take it away from you." Blood emphasized his point with the needler, jabbing at Silk's face. "If we're going to talk about what's not legal, we've got to talk about what's legal, too. And legally you never did own it. It belonged to the Chapter, according to the deed I've got. Isn't that right?"

Silk nodded.

"And the city took it from the Chapter for taxes owed. Not from you, because you never had it. Back last week that was, I think. Everything was done properly, I'm sure. The Chapter was notified and so on. They didn't tell you?"

"No." Silk sighed, and forced himself to relax. "I knew that it might happen, and in fact I warned the Chapter about it. I was never informed that it had happened."

"Then they ought to tell you they're sorry, Patera, and I hope they will. But that's got nothing to do with Musk and me. Musk bought your manteion from the city, and there was nothing irregular about it. He was acting for me, with my money, but there's nothing illegal about that either, it's just a business matter between him and me. Thirteen thousand cards we paid, plus the fees. We didn't steal anything, did we? And we haven't hurt you—or anybody—have we?"

"It will hurt the entire quarter, several thousand poor families, if you close the manteion."

"They can go somewhere else if they want to, and that's up to the Chapter anyhow, I'd say." Blood gestured toward the welts on Silk's chest with the needler. "You got hurt some, and nobody's arguing about that. But you got banged up fighting my pet bird and jumping out a window. Hy was just defending herself with that azoth, something she's got every right in the whorl to do. You aren't planning to peep about her, are you?"

"Peep?"

"Go crying to the froggies."

"I see. No, of course not."

"That's good. I'm happy to hear you being reasonable. Just look at it. You broke into my house hoping to take my property—it's Musk's, but you didn't know that. You've admitted that to Musk and me, and we're ready to swear to it in front of a judge if we have to."

Silk smiled; it seemed to him a very long time since he had last smiled. "You aren't really going to have me killed, are you, Blood? You're not willing to take the risk."

Blood's finger found the trigger of the needler. "Keep on talking like that and I might, Patera."

"I don't believe so. You'd have someone else do it, probably Musk. You're not even going to do that, however. You're trying to frighten me before you let me go."

Blood glanced at Musk, who nodded and circled behind Silk's chair. Silk felt the tips of Musk's fingers brush his ears.

"If you go on talking to me like you have been, Patera, you're going to get hurt. It won't leave any marks, but you won't like it at all. Musk has done it before. He's good at it."

"Not to an augur. Those who harm an augur in any way suffer the displeasure of all the gods."

The pain was as sudden as a blow, and so sharp it left Silk breathless, an explosion of agony; he felt as though his head had been crushed.

"There's places behind your ears," Blood explained. "Musk pushes them in with his knuckles."

Gasping for air, his hands to his mastoids, Silk could not even nod.

"We can do that again and again if we have to," Blood continued. "And if we finally give up and go to bed, we can start over in the morning."

A red mist had blotted out Silk's vision, but it was clearing. He managed, "You don't have to explain my situation to me."

"Maybe not. I'll do it whenever I want to, just the same. So to get on with this—you're right, we'd just as soon not kill you if we don't have to. There's three or four different reasons for that, all of them pretty good. You're an augur, to start with. If the gods ever paid any attention to Viron, they quit a long time ago. Myself, I don't think there was ever anything in it except a way for people like you to get everything they wanted without working. But the Chapter looks after you, and if it ever got out that we did for you—I mean just talk, because they'd never be able to prove anything—it would get people stirred up and be bad for business."

Silk said, "Then I would not have died for nothing," and felt Musk's fingers behind his ears again.

Blood shook his head, and the contingent agony halted, poised at the edge of possibility. "Then too, we just bought your place so that might make some people think of us. Did you tell anybody you were coming?"

Here it was. Silk was prepared to lie if he must, but preferred to dodge if he could. He said, "You mean one of our sibyls? No, nothing like that."

Blood nodded, and the danger was past. "It could get somebody's attention anyway, and I can't be sure who's seen you. Hy has, and talked with you and so on. Probably even knows your name."

Silk could not remember, but he said, "Yes, she does. Can't you trust her? She's your wife."

Musk tittered behind him. Blood roared, his free hand slapping his thigh.

Silk shrugged. "One of your servants referred to her as his mistress. He thought that I was one of your guests, of course."

Blood wiped his eyes. "I like her, Patera, and she's the best-looking whore in Viron, which makes her a valuable commodity. But as for that—" Blood waved the topic aside. "What I was going to say is I'd rather have you as a friend." Seeing Silk's expression, he laughed again.

Silk strove to sound casual. "My friendship's easily gained." This was the conversation he had imagined when he had spied on the villa from the top of the wall; frantically he searched for the smooth phrases he had rehearsed. "Return my manteion to the Chapter, and I'll bless you for the rest of my life." A drop of sweat trickled from his forehead into his eyes. Fearing that Musk might think he was reaching for a weapon if he got out his handkerchief, he wiped his face on his sleeve.

"That wouldn't be what I'd call easy for me, Patera. Thirteen thousand I've laid out for your place, and I'd never see a card of it again. But I've thought of a way we can be friends that will put money in my pocket, and I always like that. You're a common thief. You've admitted it. Well, so am I." Blood rose from his chair, stretched, and seemed to admire the rich furnishings of the room. "Why should we, two of a kind, circle around like a couple of tomcats, trying to knife each other?"

Musk stroked Silk's hair; it made him feel unclean, and he said, "Stop that!"

Musk did.

"You're a brave man, Patera, as well as a resourceful one." Blood strode across the room to study a gray and gold painting of Pas condemning the lost spirits, one head livid with rage while the other pronounced their doom. "If I had been sitting where you are, I wouldn't have tried that with Musk, but you tried it and got away with it. You're young, you're strong, and you've got a couple of advantages besides that the rest of us haven't. Nobody ever suspects an augur, and you've had a pretty fair education—a better education than mine, I don't deny that. Tell me now, as one thief to another, didn't you know down in the cracks of your guts that it was wrong to try to steal my property?"

"Yes, of course." Silk paused to gather his thoughts. "There are times, however, when one must choose among evils. You're a wealthy man; stripped of my manteion, you would be a wealthy man still. Without my manteion, hundreds of families in our quarter—people who are already very poor—would be a great deal poorer. I found that a compelling argument." He waited for the crushing pain of Musk's knuckles. When it did not come he added, "You suggested that we speak as one thief to another, and I assumed that you intended for us to speak freely. To speak frankly, I find it just as compelling now."

Blood turned to face him again. "Sure you do, Patera. I'm surprised you couldn't come up with just as good a reason for shooting Hy. These gods of yours did worse pretty often, didn't they?"

Silk nodded. "Worse superficially, yes. But the gods are our superiors and may act toward us as they see fit, just as you could clip your pet's wings without guilt. I am not Hyacinth's superior."

Blood chuckled. "You're the only man alive who doesn't think so, Patera. Well, I'll leave morality to you. That's your business after all. Business is mine, and what we have here is a very simple little business problem. I paid the city thirteen thousand for your manteion. What do you think it's really worth?"

Silk recalled the fresh young faces of the children in the palaestra, and the tired, happy smiles of their mothers; the sweet smoke of sacrifice rising from the altar through the god-gate in the roof. "In money? It is beyond price."

"Exactly." Blood glanced at the needler he still held and dropped it into the pocket of his embroidered trousers. "That's how you feel, and that's why you came out here, even though you must have known there was a good chance you'd get killed. You're not the first who's tried to break in here, by the way, but you're the first who got inside the house."

"That is some consolation."

"So I admire you, and I think we might be able to do a little business. On the open market, Patera, your place is worth exactly thirteen thousand cards, and not one miserable cardbit more or less. We know that, because it was on the market just a few days ago, and thirteen thousand's what it brought. So that's the businessman's price. You understand what I'm telling you?"

Silk nodded.

"I've got plans for it, sure. Profitable plans. But it's not the only possible site, so here's my proposition. You say it's priceless. That's a lot of money, priceless." Blood licked his lips, his eyes narrowed, their gaze fixed on Silk's face. "So as a man that takes a lily profit wherever he can find one but never gouges anybody, I say we split the difference. You pay me twice what I paid, and I'll sell it to you."

Silk started to speak, but Blood raised a hand. "Let's pin it down like a couple of dimber thieves ought to. I'll sell it to you for twenty-six thousand flat, and I'll pay all costs. No tricks, and no splitting up the property. You'll get everything that I got."

Silk's hopes, which had mounted higher with every word, collapsed. Did Blood really imagine that he was rich? There were laymen, he knew, who thought all augurs rich. He said, "I've told you what I have; altogether, it wouldn't bring two hundred cards. My mother's entire estate amounted to a great deal less than twenty-six thousand cards, and it went to the Chapter irrevocably when I took my vows."

Blood smiled. "I'm flash, Patera. Maybe you'd like another drink?"

Silk shook his head.

"Well, I would."

When Musk had gone, Blood resumed his seat. "I know you haven't got twenty-six thousand, or anything close to it. Not that I'm swallowing everything you told me, but if you had even a few thousand you wouldn't be there on Sun Street. Well, who says that just because you're poor you've got to stay poor? You wouldn't think so to look at me, but I was poor once myself."

"I believe you," Silk said.

Blood's smile vanished. "And you look down on me for it. Maybe that made it easier."

"No," Silk told him. "It made it a great deal harder. You never come to the sacrifices at our manteion—quite a few thieves do, actually—but I was setting out to rob one of our own, and in my heart of hearts I knew that and hated it."

Blood's chuckle promised neither humor nor friendship. "You did it just the same."

"As you've seen."

"I see more than you think, Patera. I see a lot more than you do. I see that you were willing to rob me, and that you nearly brought it off. A minute ago you told me how rich you think I am, so rich I wouldn't miss four old buildings on Sun Street. Do you think I'm the richest man in Viron?"

"No," Silk said.

"No what?"

Silk shrugged. "Even when we spoke in the street, I never supposed that you were the wealthiest man in the city, although I have no idea who the wealthiest might be. I only thought that you were wealthy, as you obviously are."

"Well, I'm not the richest," Blood declared, "and I'm not the crookedest either. There are richer men than I am, and crookeder men than I am, lots of them. And, Patera, most of them aren't anywhere near as close to the Ayuntamiento as I am. That's something to keep in mind, whether you think so or not."

Silk did not reply, or even indicate by any alteration of his expression that he had heard.

"So if you want your manteion back, why shouldn't you get it from them? The price is twenty-six thousand, like I told you. That's all it means to me, so they've got it just as much as I have, and they'll be easier, most of them. Are you listening to me, Patera?"

Reluctantly, Silk nodded.

Musk opened the door as he had before and preceded the footman into the room. This time there were two tumblers on the footman's tray. Blood accepted one, and the footman bowed to Silk. "Patera Silk?"

Everyone in the household must know of his capture by now, Silk reflected; apparently everyone knew who he was as well. "Yes," he said; it would be pointless to deny it.

With something in his expression Silk could not fathom, the footman bowed deeply and held out his tray. "I took the liberty, Patera. Musk said I might. If you would accept it as a favor to me . . . . ?"

Silk took the drink, smiled, and said, "Thank you, my son. That was extremely kind of you." For an instant the footman looked radiant.

"If you're grabbed," Blood continued when the footman had gone, "I don't know you. I've never laid eyes on you, and I'd never suggest anything like this to anybody. That's the way it's got to be."

"Of course. But now, tonight, you're suggesting that I steal enough money to buy my manteion from you. That I, an augur, enter these other men's houses to steal, as I entered yours."

Blood sipped his drink. "I'm saying that if you want your manteion back, I'll sell it to you, and that's all I'm saying. How you get the money is up to you. You think the city asked where I got the price?"

"It is a workable solution," Silk admitted, "and it's the only one that has been proposed so far."

Musk grinned at him.

"Your resident physician tells me that my right ankle is broken," Silk continued. "It will be quite some time, I'm afraid, before it heals."

Blood looked up from his drink. "I can't allow you a whole lot of time, Patera. A little time, enough for a few jobs. But that's all."

"I see." Silk stroked his cheek. "But you'll allow me some—you'll have to. During the time you *will* allow, what will become of my manteion?"

"It's my manteion, Patera. You run it just like you did before, how's that? Only you tell anybody that wants to know that I own the property. It's mine, and you tell them so."

"I could say you've paid our taxes," Silk suggested, "as you have. And that you're letting us continue to serve the gods as an act of piety." It was a lie he hoped might eventually become the truth.

"That's good. But anything you take in over expenses is mine, and anytime I want to see the books, you've got to bring them out here. Otherwise it's no deal. How much time do you want?"

Silk considered, uncertain that he could bring himself to conduct the robberies Blood was demanding. "A year," he ventured. A great deal could happen in a year.

"Very funny. I bet they roar when you've got a ram for Scylsday. Three weeks—oh, shag, make it a month. That's the top, though. Will your ankle be all right in a month?"

"I don't know." Silk tried to move his foot and found as he had before that the cast immobilized it. "I wouldn't think it very likely."

Blood snorted. "Musk, get Crane in here."

As the door closed behind Musk, Silk inquired, "Do you always have a physician on the premises?"

"I try to." Blood set aside his tumbler. "I had a man for a year who didn't work out, then a brain surgeon who only stayed a couple of months. After that I had to look around quite a while before I found Crane. He's been with me . . ." Blood paused, calculating, "pretty close to four years now. He looks after my people here, naturally, and goes into the city three times a week to see about the girls there. It's handier, and saves a little money."

Silk said, "I'm surprised that a skillful physician—"

"Would work for me, taking care of my whores?" Blood yawned. "Suppose you'd seen a doctor in the city for that ankle, Patera. Would you have paid him?"

"As soon as I could, yes."

"Which would have been never, most likely. Working for me, he gets a regular salary. He doesn't have to take charity cases, and sometimes the girls'll tip him if they're flush."

The fussy little man arrived a moment later, ushered in by Musk. Silk had seen a picture of a bird of the crane kind not long before, and though he could not recall where it had been, he remembered it now, and with it Crane's self-mockery. The diminutive doctor no more resembled the tall bird than he himself did the shimmering fabric from which his mother had taken his name.

Blood gestured toward Silk. "You fixed him up. How long before he's well?"

The little physician stroked his beard. "What do you mean by well, sir? Well enough to walk without crutches?"

Blood considered. "Let's say well enough to run fast. How long for that?"

"It's difficult to say. It depends a good deal on his heredity—I doubt that he knows anything useful about that—and on his physical condition. He's young at least, so it could be worse." Doctor Crane turned to Silk. "Sit up straight for a moment, young man. I want to listen to you again, now that you've had a chance to calm down."

He lifted Silk's torn tunic, put his ear against Silk's chest, and thumped his back. With the third thump, Silk felt something hard and cold slide into his waistband beneath the horsehair rope.

"Should've brought my instruments. Cough, please."

Already frantic with curiosity, Silk coughed and was rewarded with another thump.

"Good. Again, please, and deeper this time. Make it go deep."

Silk coughed as deeply as he could.

"Excellent." Doctor Crane straightened up, letting Silk's tunic fall back into place. "Truly excellent. You're a fine specimen, young man, a credit to Viron." The timbre of his voice altered almost imperceptibly. "Somebody up there likes you." He pointed jocularly toward the elaborately figured ceiling, where a painted Molpe vied with Phaea at bagatelle. "Some infatuated goddess, I should imagine."

Silk leaned back in his chair, although the hard object behind his spine made actual comfort impossible. "If that means I get less time from your employer, I would hardly call it evidence of favor, my son."

Doctor Crane smiled. "In that case, perhaps not."

"How long?" Blood banged his tumbler down on the stand beside his chair. "How long before it's as good as it was before he broke it?"

"Five to seven weeks, I'd say. He could run a little sooner than that, with his ankle correctly taped. All this assumes proper rest and medical treatment in the interim—sonic stimulation of the broken bone and so forth."

Silk cleared his throat. "I cannot afford elaborate treatment, Doctor. All I'll be able to do is hobble about and pray that it heals."

"Well, you can't come here," Blood told him angrily. "Was that what you were hinting at?"

Doctor Crane began, "Possibly, sir, you might retain a specialist in the city—"

Blood sniffed. "We should've shot him and gotten it over with. By Phaea's sow, I wish the fall had killed him. No specialist. You'll see himself whenever you're in that part of the city. When is it? Sphigxday and Hieraxday?"

"That's right, and tomorrow's Sphigxday." Doctor Crane glanced toward an ornate clock on the opposite side of the room. "I should be in bed already."

"You'll see him then," Blood said. "Now get out of here."

Silk told Crane, "I sincerely regret the inconvenience, Doctor. If your employer will only give me a bit more time, it wouldn't be necessary."

At the door Crane turned and appeared, almost, to wink.

Blood said, "We'll compromise, Patera. Pay attention, because it's as far as I'm willing to go. Aren't you going to drink that?"

Feeling Musk's knuckles behind his ears, Silk took a dutiful sip.

"In a month—one month from today—you'll bring me a substantial sum. You hear that? I'll decide when I see it whether it's substantial enough. If it is, I'll apply it to the twenty-six thousand, and let you know how long you've got to come up with the rest. But if it isn't, you and that tin sibyl will have to clear out." Blood paused, his mouth ugly, swirling his drink in his hand. "Have you got anybody else living there? Maybe another augur?"

"There are two more sibyls," Silk told him. "Maytera Rose and Maytera Mint. You've met Maytera Marble, I believe. I am our only augur."

Blood grunted. "Your sibyls will want to come out here and lecture me. Tell them they won't get past the gate."

"I will."

"They're healthy? Crane could have a look at them when he comes to see you, if they need doctoring."

Silk warmed to the man. "That's exceedingly kind of you." There was always some good to be found in everyone, he reminded himself, the unnoted yet unfailing gift of ever-generous Pas. "Maytera Mint's quite well, as far as I know. Maytera Rose is as well as could be expected, and is largely prosthetic now in any case, I'm afraid."

"Digital arms and legs? That sort of thing?" Blood leaned forward, interested. "There aren't too many of those around any more."

"She got them some years ago; before I was born, really. There was some disease requiring amputations." It occurred to Silk that he should know more about Maytera Rose's history—about the histories of all three sibyls—than he did. "They were still easily found then, from what she says."

"How old is she?"

"I'm not sure." Silk berated himself mentally again; this was something he should know. "I suppose it's in our records. I could look it up for you, and I would be happy to do so."

"Just being polite," Blood told him. "She must be—oh, ninety, if she's got a lot of tin parts. How old would you say I am, Patera?"

"Older than you look, I suppose," Silk ventured. What guess would flatter Blood? It would not do to say something ridiculous. "Forty-five, possibly?"

"I'm forty-nine." Blood raised his tumbler in a mock toast. "Nearly fifty." Musk's fingers had twitched as Blood spoke, and Silk knew with an absolute certainty he could not have defended that Blood was lying: that he was at least five years older. "And not a part in my body that isn't my own, except for a couple teeth."

"You don't look it."

"Listen, Patera, I could tell you—" Blood waved the topic aside. "Never mind. It's late. How much did I say? In a month? Five thousand?"

"You said a substantial sum," Silk reminded him. "I was to bring you as much as I could acquire, and you would decide whether it was enough. Am I to bring it here?"

"That's right. Tell the eye at my gate who you are, and somebody will go out and get you. Musk, have a driver come around out front."

"For me?" Silk asked. "Thank you. I was afraid I'd have to walk—that is, I couldn't have walked, with my leg like this. I would have had to beg rides on farm carts, I'm afraid."

Blood grinned. "You're a thirteen thousand card profit to me, Patera. I've got to see you're taken care of. Listen now. You know how I said those sibyls of yours weren't to come out here and bother me? Well, that still goes, but tell that one—the old one, what's her name?"

"Maytera Rose," Silk supplied.

"Her. You tell Maytera Rose that if she's interested in getting another leg or something, and can raise the gelt, I might be able to help her out.

Or if she's got something like that she'd like to sell, maybe to help you out. She won't get a better price anywhere."

"My thanks are becoming monotonous, I'm afraid," Silk said. "But I must thank you again, on Maytera's behalf and in my own."

"Forget it. There's getting to be quite a market for those parts now, even the used ones, and I've got a man who knows how to recondition them."

Musk's sleek head appeared in the doorway. "Floater's ready."

Blood stood, swaying slightly. "Can you walk, Patera? No, naturally you can't, not good. Musk, fetch him one of my sticks, will you? Not one of the high-priced ones. Grab on, Patera."

Blood was offering his hand. Silk took it, finding it soft and surprisingly cold, and struggled to his feet, acutely conscious of the object Crane had put into his waistband and of the fact that he was accepting help from the man he had set out to rob. "Thank you yet again," he said, and clenched his teeth against a sharp flash of pain.

As his host, Blood would want to show him out; and if Blood were in back of him, Blood might well see the object under his tunic. Wishing mightily for the robe he had left behind in Hyacinth's bedchamber, half incapacitated by guilt and pain, Silk managed, "May I lean on your arm? I shouldn't have had so much to drink."

Side by side they staggered into the reception hall. Its wide double doors still let in the night; but it was a night (or so Silk fancied) soon to be gray with shadeup. A floater waited on the grassway, its canopy open, a liveried driver at its controls. The most eventful night of his life was nearly over.

Musk rattled the cast on Silk's ankle with a battered walking stick, smiled at his wince, and put the stick into his free hand. Silk discovered that he still detested Musk, though he had come, almost, to like Musk's master.

". . . floater'll take you back there, Patera," Blood was saying. "If you tell anyone about our little agreement, it's cancelled, and don't you forget it. A high stack next month, and I don't mean a few hundred."

The liveried driver had left the floater to help. In a moment more, Silk was safely settled on the broad, cushioned seat behind the driver's, with Doctor Crane's chilly, angular mystery again gouging at his back. "Thank you," he repeated to Blood. "Thank you both." (He hoped that Blood would take his phrase to include Musk as well as Blood himself, though he actually intended Blood and the driver.) "I do appreciate it very much. You mentioned our agreement however. And—and I would be exceedingly grateful . . ." Tentatively, he put out his hand, palm up.

"What is it now, for Phaea's sake?"

"My needler, please. I hate to ask, after all you've done, but it's in your pocket. If you're not still afraid I might shoot you, may I have it back?"

Blood stared at him.

"You want me to bring you several thousand cards—I presume that's what you mean when you speak of a substantial sum. Several thousand cards, when I can scarcely walk. The least you can do is return my weapon, so that I've something to work with."

Blood giggled, coughed, then laughed loudly. Perhaps only because Silk heard it in the open air for the first time that night, Blood's laughter seemed to him almost the sound that sometimes rose, on quiet evenings, from the pits of the Alambrera. He was forced to remind himself again that this man, too, was loved by Pas.

"What a buck! He might do it, Musk. I really think he might do it." Blood fumbled Hyacinth's little needler out of his pocket and pushed its release; a score of silver needles leaped from its breach to shower like rain upon the closely cropped grass.

Musk leaned toward Blood, and Silk heard him whisper, "Lamp Street."

Blood's eyebrows shot up. "Excellent. You're right. You always are." He tossed the golden needler into Silk's lap. "Here you go, Patera. Use it in good health—yours, I mean. We're going to make a slight charge for it, though. Meet us about one o'clock at the yellow house on Lamp Street. Will you do that?"

"I must, I suppose," Silk said. "Yes, of course, if you wish me to."

"It's called Orchid's." Blood leaned over the door of the floater. "And it's across from the pastry cook's. You know exorcism? Know how it's done?"

Silk ventured a guarded nod.

"Good. Bring whatever you'll need. There've been, ah, problems there all summer. An enlightened augur may be just what we need. We'll see you there tomorrow."

"Good-bye," Silk said.

The canopy slid soundlessly out of the floater's sides as Blood and Musk backed away. When it latched, there was a muffled roar from the engine.

It felt, Silk thought, as if they were indeed floating; as if a flood had rushed invisibly to lift them and bear them off along the greenway, as if they were always about to spin away in the current, although they never actually spun.

Trees and hedges and brilliant flower beds reeled past. Here came Blood's magnificent fountain, with Soaking Scylla reveling among the crystal jets; at once it was gone and the main gate before them, the gate rising as the long, shining arms of the talus shrank. A dip and a wiggle and the floater was through, blown down the highway like a sere leaf, sailing through an eerie nightscape turned to liquid, leaving behind it a proud plume of swirling, yellow-gray dust.

The skylands still shone overhead, cut in two by the black bow of the shade. Far above even the skylands, hidden but present nonetheless, shone the myriad pinpricks of fire the Outsider had revealed; they, too, held lands unknowable in some incomprehensible fashion. Silk found himself more conscious of them now than he had been since that lifetime outside time in the ball court—colored spheres of flame, infinitely far.

The ball was still in his pocket, the only ball they had. He must remember not to leave it here in Blood's floater, or the boys would have no ball tomorrow. No, not tomorrow; tomorrow was Sphigxday. No palaestra. The day to prepare for the big sacrifice on Scylsday, if there was anything to sacrifice.

He slapped his pockets until he found Blood's two cards in the one that held the ball. He took them out to look at, then replaced them. They had been below the ball when he had been searched, and the ball had saved them. For what?

Hyacinth's needler had fallen to the floater's carpeted floor. He retrieved it and put it into his pocket with the cards, then sat squeezing the ball between his fingers. It was said to strengthen the hands. Minute lights he could not see burned on, burning beyond the skylands, burning beneath his feet, unwinking and remote, illuminating something bigger than the whorl.

Doctor Crane's mystery gouged his back. He leaned forward. "What time is it, driver?"

"Quarter past three, Patera."

He had done what the Outsider had wanted. Or at least he had tried—perhaps he had failed. As though a hand had drawn aside a veil, he realized that his manteion would live for another month now—a month at least, because anything might happen in a month. Was it possible that he had in fact accomplished what the Outsider had desired? His mind filled with a rollicking joy.

The floater leaned to the left as it rounded a bend in the road. Here were farms and fields and houses, all liquid, all swirling past as they breasted the phantom current. A hill rose in a great, brown-green wave, already breaking into a skylit froth of fence rails and fruit trees. The floater plunged down the other side and shot across a ford.

Musk adjusted the shutter of his dark lantern until the eight-sided spot of light remaining was smaller than its wick and oddly misshapen. His key turned softly in the well-oiled padlock; the door opened with a nearly inaudible creak.

The tiercel nearest the door stirred upon its perch, turning its hooded head to look at the intruder it could not see. On the farther side of a partition of cotton netting, the merlin that had been Musk's first hawk, unhooded, blinked and roused. There was a tinkle of tiny bells—gold bells that Blood had given Musk to mark some now-forgotten occasion three years ago. Beyond the merlin, the gray-blue peregrine might have been a painted carving.

The end of the mews was walled off with netting. The big bird sat its roweled perch there, immobile as the falcon, still immature but showing in every line a strength that made the falcon seem a toy.

Musk untied the netting and stepped in. He could not have said how he knew that the big bird was awake, and yet he did. Softly he said, "Ha, hawk."

The big bird lifted its hooded head, its grotesque crown of scarlet plumes swaying with the motion.

"Ha, hawk," Musk repeated as he stroked it with a turkey feather.

CHAPTER 8

THE BOARDER

ON THE LARDER

As they sped across a field of stubble the driver inquired, "Ever ridden in one of these before, Patera?"

Drowsily, Silk shook his head before he realized that the driver could not see him. He yawned and attempted to stretch, brought up sharply by pain from his right arm and the gouged flesh of his chest and belly. "No, never. But I rode in a boat once. Out on the lake, you know, fishing all day with a friend and his father. This reminds me of that. This machine of yours is about as wide as the boat was, and only a little bit shorter."

"I like it better—boats rock too much for me. Where are we going, Patera?"

"You mean . . . ?" The road (or perhaps another road) had appeared again. Seeming to gather its strength like a horse, the floater soared over the wall of dry-laid stones that had barred them from it.

"Where should I drop you? Musk said to take you back to the city."

Silk edged forward on the seat, knowing himself stupid with fatigue and struggling against it. "They didn't tell you?"

"No, Patera."

Where was it he wanted to go? He recalled his mother's house, and the wide, deep windows of his bedroom, with borage growing just beyond the sills. "At my manteion, please. On Sun Street. Do you know where it is?"

"I know where Sun Street is, Patera. I'll find it."

Here was a cartload of firewood bound for the market. The floater dipped and swerved, and it was behind them. The man on the cart would be first at the market, Silk thought; but what was the point of being first at the market with a load of firewood? Surely there would be wood there already, wood that had not sold the day before. Perhaps the man on the cart wanted to do a little buying of his own when he had disposed of his cargo.

"Going to be another hot one, Patera."

That was it, of course. The man on the cart—Silk turned to look back at him, but he was gone already; there was only a boy leading a mule, a laden mule and a small boy whom he had never noticed at all. The man on the cart had wanted to avoid the heat. He would sell what he had brought and sit drinking till twilight in the Cock or someplace like it. In the coolest tavern he could find, no doubt, and spend most of the money his wood had brought him, sleep on the seat of his cart as it made its slow way home. What if he, Silk, slept now on this capacious seat, which was so tantalizingly soft? Would not the driver, would not this old half-magical floater take him where he wanted to go in any event? Would the driver rob him while he slept, find Blood's two cards, Hyacinth's golden needler, and the thing that he still did not dare to look at, the thing—he felt he had guessed its identity while he still sat in that jewel box of a room to one side of Blood's reception hall. Would he not be robbed? Had the man upstairs, the man asleep in the chair near the stair ever gotten home, and had he gotten home safely? Many men must have slept in this floater, men who had drunk too heavily.

Silk felt that he himself had drunk too heavily; he had sipped from both drinks.

Blood was certainly a thief; he had admitted as much himself. But would Blood employ a driver who would rob his guests? It seemed unlikely. He, Silk, could sleep here—sleep now in safety, if he wished. But he was very hungry.

"All right," he said.

"Patera?"

"Go to Sun Street. I'll direct you from there. I know the way."

The driver glanced over his shoulder, a burly young man whose beard was beginning to show. "Where it crosses Trade. Will that be all right, Patera?"

"Yes." Silk felt his own chin, rough as the driver's looked. "Fine." He settled back in the soft seat, almost oblivious of the object beneath his tunic but determined not to sleep until he had washed, eaten, and wrung any advantage that might be gained from his present position. The driver had not been told he was Blood's prisoner; that was clear from everything he said, and it presented an opportunity that might not come again.

But in point of fact he was a prisoner no longer. He had been freed, though no fuss had been made about it, when Blood and Musk had taken him to this floater. Now, whether he liked it or not, he was a sort of factor of Blood's—an agent through whom Blood would obtain money. Silk weighed the term in his mind and decided it was the correct one. He had given himself wholly to the gods, with a holy oath; now his allegiance was inescapably divided, whether he liked it or not. He would give the twenty-six thousand cards he got (if indeed he got them) not to the gods but to Blood, though he would be acting in the gods' behalf. Certainly he would be Blood's factor in the eyes of the Chapter and the whorl, should either the Chapter or the whorl learn of whatever he would do.

Blood had made him his factor, creating this situation for his own profit. (Thoughtfully, Silk stroked his cheek, feeling the roughness of his newly grown beard again.) For Blood's own personal profit, as was only to be expected; but their relationship bound them both, like all relationships. He was Blood's factor whether he liked it or not, but also Blood's factor whether Blood liked it or not. He had made good use of the relationship already when he had demanded the return of Hyacinth's needler. Indeed, Blood had acknowledged it still earlier when he had told Doctor Crane to look in at the manteion.

Further use might be made of it as well.

A factor, but not a trusted factor to be sure; Blood might conceivably plan to kill him once he had turned over the entire twenty-six thousand, if he could find no further use for him; thus it would be wise to employ this temporary relationship to gain some sort of hold on Blood before it was ended. That was something more to keep in mind.

And the driver, who no doubt knew so many things that might be of value, did not know that.

"Driver," Silk called, "are you familiar with a certain house on Lamp Street? It's yellow, I believe, and there's a pastry cook's across the street."

"Sure am, Patera."

"Could we go past it, please? I don't think it will be very much out of our way."

The floater slowed for a trader with a string of pack mules. "I can't wait, Patera, if you're going to be inside very long."

"I'm not even going to get out," Silk assured him. "I merely wish to see it."

Still watching the broadening road, the driver nodded his satisfaction. "Then I'll be happy to oblige you, Patera. No trouble."

The countryside seemed to flow past. No wonder, Silk thought, that the rich rode in floaters when distances were too great for their litters. Why, on donkeys this had taken hours!

"Have a good time, Patera? You stayed awfully late."

"No," Silk said, then reconsidered. "In a way I did, I suppose. It was certainly very different from everything I'm accustomed to."

The driver chuckled politely.

"I did have a good time, in a sense," Silk decided. "I enjoyed certain parts of my visit enormously, and I ought to be honest enough to admit it."

The driver nodded again. "Only not everything. Yeah, I know just what you mean."

"My view is colored, no doubt, by the fact that I fell and injured my ankle. It was really quite painful, and it's still something of a discomfort. A Doctor Crane very kindly set the bone for me and applied this cast, free of charge. I imagine you must know him. Your master told me that Doctor Crane has been with him for the past four years."

"Do I! The old pill-pounder and me have floated over a whorl of ground together. Don't make much sense sometimes, but he'll talk you deaf if you don't watch out, and ask more questions than the hoppies."

Silk nodded, conscious again of the object Crane had slipped into his waistband. "I found him friendly."

"I bet you did. You didn't ride out with me, did you, Patera?"

Blood had several floaters, obviously, just as he had implied. Silk said, "No, not with you. I came with another man, but he left before I did."

"I didn't think so. See, I tell them about Doc Crane on the way out. Sometimes they get worried about the girls and boys. Know what I mean, Patera?"

"I think so."

"So I tell them forget it. We got a doctor right there to check everybody over, and if they got some kind of little problem of their own . . . I'm talking about the older bucks, Patera, you know? Why, maybe he could help them out. It's good for Doc, because sometimes they give him something. And it's good for me, too. I've had quite a few of them thank me for telling them, after the party."

"I fear I have nothing to give you, my son," Silk said stiffly. It was perfectly true, he assured himself; the two cards in his pocket were already spent, or as good as spent. They would buy a fine victim for Scylsday, less than two days off.

"That's all right, Patera. I didn't figure you did. It's a gift to the Chapter. That's how I look at it."

"I can give you my blessing, however, when we separate. And I will."

"That's all right, Patera," the driver said. "I'm not much for sacrifice and all that."

"All the more reason you may require it, my son," Silk told him, and could not keep from smiling at the sepulchral tones of his own voice. It was a good thing the driver could not see him! With Blood's villa far behind them, the burglar was fading and the augur returning; he had sounded exactly like Patera Pike.

Which was he, really? He pushed aside the thought.

"Now this here, this feels just like a boat, and no mistake. Don't it, Patera?"

Their floater was rolling like a barrel as it dodged pedestrians and rattling, mule-drawn wagons. The road had become a street in which narrow houses vied for space.

Silk found it necessary to grasp the leather-covered bar on the back of the driver's seat, a contrivance he had previously assumed was intended only to facilitate boarding and departure. "How high will these go?" he asked. "I've always wondered."

"Four cubits empty, Patera. Or that's what this one'll do, anyhow. That's how you test them—run them up as high as they'll go and measure. The higher she floats, the better shape everything's in."

Silk nodded to himself. "You couldn't go over one of these wagons, then, instead of around it?"

"No, Patera. We got to have ground underneath to push against, see? And we'd be getting too far away from it. You remember that wall we cleared when I took the shortcut?"

"Certainly." Silk tightened his grip on the bar. "It must have been three cubits at least."

"Not quite, Patera. It's a little lower than that at the place where I went over. But what I was going to say was we couldn't have done it if we'd been full of passengers like we were coming out. We'd have had to stay on the road then."

"I understand. Or at any rate, I think I do."

"But look up ahead, Patera." The floater slowed. "See him lying in the road?"

Silk sat up straight to peer over the driver's liveried shoulder. "I do now. By Phaea's fair face, I hope he's not dead."

"Drunk more likely. Watch now, and we'll float right across him. You won't even feel him, Patera. Not no more than he'll feel you."

Silk clenched his teeth, but as promised felt nothing. When the prostrate man was behind them, he said, "I've seen floaters go over children like that. Children playing in the street. Once a child was hit in the forehead by the cowling, right in front of our palaestra."

"I'd never do that, Patera," the driver assured Silk virtuously. "A child might hold up his arm and get it in the blowers."

Silk hardly heard him. He attempted to stand, bumped his head painfully against the floater's transparent canopy, and compromised on a crouch. "Wait! Not so fast, please. Do you see that man with the two donkeys? Stop for a moment and let me out. I want a word with him."

"I'll just put down the canopy, Patera. That'll be a little safer."

Auk glanced sourly at the floater when it settled onto the roadway beside him. His eyes widened when he saw Silk.

"May every god bless you tonight," Silk began. "I want to remind you of what you promised in the tavern."

Auk opened his mouth to speak, but thought better of it.

"You gave me your word that you'd come to manteion next Scylsday, remember? I want to make certain you'll keep that promise, not only for your sake but for mine. I must talk to you again."

"Yeah. Sure." Auk nodded. "Maybe tomorrow if I'm not too busy. Scylsday for sure. Did you . . . ?"

"It went precisely as you had predicted," Silk told him. "However, our manteion's safe for the time being, I believe. Good night, and Phaea bless you. Knock at the manse if you don't find me in the manteion."

Auk said something more; but the driver had overheard Silk's farewell, and the transparent dome of the canopy had risen between them; it latched, and Auk's voice was drowned by the roar of the blowers.

"You better watch your step, talking to characters like that, Patera," the driver remarked with a shake of his head. "That sword's just for show, and there's a needler underneath that dirty tunic. Want to bet?"

"You would win such a bet, I'm certain," Silk admitted, "but no needler can turn a good man to evil. Not even devils can do that."

"That why you want to see Orchid's place, Patera? I kind of wondered."

"I'm afraid I don't understand you." Crane's mystery had just given Silk a particularly painful job. He wiggled it into a new position as he spoke. Deciding that it would be harmless to reveal plans Blood knew of already, he added, "I'm to meet your master there tomorrow afternoon, and I want to be certain I go to the correct house. That's the yellow house, isn't it? Orchid's? I believe he mentioned a woman named Orchid."

"That's right, Patera. She owns it. Only he owns it, really, or maybe he owns her. You know what I mean?"

"I think so. Yes, of course." Silk recalled that it was Musk, not Blood,

whose name appeared on the deed to his manteion. "Possibly Blood
holds a mortgage upon this house, which is in arrears." Clearly Blood
would have to protect his interest in some fashion against the death of
the owner of record.

"I guess so, Patera. Anyhow, you talked about devils, so I thought
maybe that was it."

The hair at the back of Silk's neck prickled. It was ridiculous (as if I
were a dog, he said to himself later) but there it was; he tried to smooth
it with one hand. "It might be useful if you would tell me whatever you
know about this business, my son—useful to your master, as well as to
me." How sternly his instructors at the schola had enjoined him, and all
the acolytes, never to laugh when someone mentioned ghosts (he had
anticipated the usual wide-eyed accounts of phantom footsteps and
shrouded figures after Blood's mention of exorcism) or devils. Perhaps it
was only because he was so very tired, but he discovered that there was
not the least danger of his laughing now.

"I never seen anything myself," the driver admitted. "I hardly ever
been inside. You hear this and that. Know what I mean, Patera?"

"Of course."

"Things get messed up. Like, a girl will go to get her best dress, only
the sleeves are torn off and it's all ripped down the front. Sometimes
people just, like, go crazy. You know? Then it goes away."

"Intermittent possession," Silk said.

"I guess so, Patera. Anyhow, you'll get to see it in a minute. We're
almost there."

"Fine. Thank you, my son." Silk studied the back of the driver's head.
Since the driver thought he had been a guest at Blood's, it would probably do no harm if he saw the object Crane had conveyed to him; but
there was a chance, if only a slight one, that someone would question the
driver when he returned to Blood's villa. Satisfied that he was too busy
working the floater through the thickening stream of men and wagons to
glance behind him, Silk took it out.

As he had suspected, it was an azoth. He whistled on a small footlight
he had noticed earlier, holding the azoth low enough to keep the driver
from seeing it, should he look over his shoulder.

The demon was an unfacetted red gem, so it was probably safe to
assume it was the azoth he had taken from Hyacinth's drawer and she
had snatched out of the coiled rope around his waist. It occurred to Silk
as he examined the azoth that its demon should have been a blue gem, a
hyacinth. Clearly the azoth had not been embellished in a style intended

to flatter Hyacinth, as the needler in his pocket had been. It was even possible that it was not actually hers.

Rocking almost imperceptibly, the floater slowed, then settled onto the roadway. "Here's Orchid's place, Patera."

"On the right there? Thank you, my son." Silk slid the azoth into the top of the stocking on his good foot and pulled his trousers leg down over it; it was a considerable relief to be able to lean back comfortably.

"Quite a place, they tell me, Patera. Like I said, I've only been inside a couple times."

Silk murmured, "I very much appreciate your going out of your way for me."

Orchid's house seemed typical of the older, larger city houses, a hulking cube of shiprock with a painted façade, its canary arches and fluted pillars the phantasmagoria of some dead artist's brush. There would be a courtyard, very likely with a dry fishpond at its center, ringed by shady galleries.

"It's only one story in back, Patera. You can get in that way, too, off of Music Street. That might be closer for you."

"No," Silk said absently. It would not do to arrive at the rear entrance like a tradesman.

He was studying the house and the street, visualizing them as they would appear by day. That shop with the white shutters would be the pastry cook's, presumably. In an hour or two there would be chairs and tables for customers who wished to consume their purchases on the spot, the mingled smells of maté and strong coffee, and cakes and muffins in the windows. A shutter swung back as Silk watched.

"In there," the driver jerked his thumb at the yellow house, "they'll be getting set to turn in now. They'll sleep till noon, most likely." He stretched, yawning. "So will I, if I can."

Silk nodded weary agreement. "What is it they do in there?"

"At Orchid's?" The driver turned to look back at him. "Everybody knows about Orchid's, Patera."

"I don't, my son. That was why I asked."

"It's a—you know, Patera. There's thirty girls, I guess, or about that. They put on shows, you know, and like that, and they have a lot of parties. Have them for other people, I mean. The people pay them to do it."

Silk sighed. "I suppose it's a pleasant life."

"It could be worse, Patera. Only—"

Someone screamed inside the yellow house. The scream was followed at once by the crash of breaking glass.

The engine sprang to life, shaking the whole floater as a dog shakes a rat. Before Silk could protest, the floater shot into the air and sped up Lamp Street, scattering men and women on foot and grazing a donkey cart with a clang so loud that Silk thought for a moment it had been wrecked.

"Wait!" he called.

The floater turned almost upon its side as they rounded a corner, losing so much height that its cowling plowed the dust.

"That might be a—whatever the trouble is." Silk was holding on desperately with both hands, pain and the damage the white-headed one had done to his arm forgotten. "Go back and let me out."

Wagons blocked the street. The floater slowed, then forced its way between the wall of a tailor shop and a pair of plunging horses.

"Patera, they can take care of it. It's happened there before, like I told you."

Silk began, "I'm supposed—"

The driver cut him off. "You got a real bad leg and a bad arm. Besides, what if somebody saw you going in there—a place like that—at night? Tomorrow afternoon will be bad enough."

Silk released the leather-covered bar. "Did you really float away so quickly out of concern for my reputation? I find that difficult to believe."

"I'm not going to go back there, Patera," the driver said stubbornly, "and I don't think you could walk back if you tried. Which way from here? To get to your manteion, I mean." The floater slowed, hovered.

This was Sun Street; it could not have been half an hour since they had floated past the talus and out Blood's gate. Silk tried to fix the Guard post and soiled statue of Councillor Tarsier in his memory. "Left," he said absently. And then, "I should have Horn—he's quite artistic—and some of the older students paint the front of our manteion. No, the palaestra first, then the manteion."

"What's that, Patera?"

"I'm afraid I was talking to myself, my son." They had almost certainly been painted originally; it might even be possible to find a record of the original designs among the clutter of papers in the attic of the manse. If money could be found for paint and brushes as well—

"Is it far, Patera?"

"Another six blocks perhaps."

He would be getting out in a moment. When he had left Blood's reception hall, he had imagined that the night was already gray with the coming of shadeup. Imagination was no longer required; the night was virtually over, and he had not been to bed. He would be getting out of the floater soon—perhaps he should have napped upon this soft seat after all, when he had the opportunity. Perhaps there was time for two or three hours sleep in the manse, though no more than two or three hours.

A man hauling bricks in a handcart shouted something at them and fell to his knees, but whatever he had shouted could not be heard. It reminded Silk that he had promised to bless the driver when they parted. Should he leave this walking stick in the floater? It was Blood's stick, after all. Blood had intended for him to keep it, but did he want to keep anything that belonged to Blood? Yes, the manteion, but only because the manteion was really his, not Blood's, no matter what the law, or even the Chapter, might say. Patera Pike had owned the manteion, morally at least, and Patera Pike had left him in charge of it, had made him responsible for it until he, too, died.

The floater was slowing again as the driver studied the buildings they passed.

Silk decided that he would keep the manteion and the stick, too—at least until he got the manteion back. "Up there, driver, with the shingled roof. See it?" He gripped the stick and made sure its tip would not slide on the floor of the floater; it was almost time to go.

The floater hovered, "Here, Patera?"

"No. One, two, three doors farther."

"Are you the augur everybody's talking about, Patera? The one that got enlightened? That's what somebody told me back at the estate."

Silk nodded. "I suppose so, unless there were two of us."

"You're going to bring back the caldé—that's what they say. I didn't want to ask you about it, you know? I hoped it would sort of come up by itself. Are you?"

"Am I going to restore the caldé? Is that what you're asking? No, that wasn't in my instructions at all."

"Instructions from a god." The floater settled to the roadway and its canopy parted and slid into its sides.

Silk struggled to his feet. "Yes."

The driver got out, to open the door for him. "I never thought there were any gods, Patera. Not really."

"They believe in you, however." Aided by the driver, Silk stepped painfully onto the first worn shiprock step in front of the street entrance to the manteion. He was home. "You believe in devils, it seems, but you do not believe in the immortal gods. That's very foolish, my son. Indeed, it is the height of folly."

Suddenly the driver was on his knees. Leaning on his stick, Silk pronounced the shortest blessing in common use and traced the sign of addition over the driver's head.

The driver rose. "I could help you, Patera. You've got a—a house or something here, don't you? I could give you a hand that far."

"I'll be all right," Silk told him. "You had better go back and get to bed."

Courteously, the driver waited for Silk to leave before restarting his blowers. Silk found that his injured leg was stiff as he limped to the narrow garden gate and let himself in, locking the gate behind him. By the time he reached the arbor, he was wondering whether it had not been foolish to refuse the driver's offer of help. He wanted very badly to rest, to rest for only a minute or so, on one of the cozy benches beneath the vines, where he had sat almost every day to talk with Maytera Marble.

Hunger urged him forward; food and sleep were so near. Blood, he thought, might have shown him better hospitality by giving him something to eat. A strong drink was not the best welcome to offer a man with an empty stomach.

His head pounded, and he told himself that a little food would make him feel better. Then he would go up to bed and sleep. Sleep until—why, until someone woke him. That was the truth: *until someone woke him.* There was no power but in truth.

The familiar, musty smell of the manse was like a kiss. He dropped into a chair, pulled the azoth from his stocking, and pressed it to his lips, then stared at it. He had seen it in her hand, and if the doctor was to be believed, it was her parting gift. How preposterous that he should have such a thing, so lovely, so precious, and so lethal! So charged with the forgotten knowledge of the earlier world. It would have to be hidden, and hidden well, before he slept; he was by no means sure that he could climb the steep and crooked stair to the upper floor, less sure that he could descend it again to prepare food without falling, but utterly certain that he would not be able to sleep at all unless the azoth was at hand—unless he could assure himself, whenever he was assailed by doubts, that it had not been stolen.

With a grunt and a muttered prayer to Sphigx (it was certainly Sphigxday by now, Silk had decided, and Sphigx was the goddess of courage in the face of pain in any event), he made his way slowly up the stair, got the rusty and utterly barren cash box that was supposed to secure the manteion's surplus funds from beneath his bed, locked the azoth in it, and returned the key to its hiding place under the water jug on his nightstand.

Descending proved rather easier than he had expected. By putting most of his weight on the stick and the railing, and advancing his sound foot one step at a time, he was able to progress quite well with a minimum of pain.

Giddy with success he went into the kitchen, leaned the stick in a corner, and after a brief labor at the pump washed his hands. Shadeup was peeping in through every window, and although he always rose early it was an earlier and thus a fresher morning than he had seen in some time. He really was not, he discovered with delight, so very tired after all, or so very sleepy.

After a second session with the pump, he splashed water over his face and hair and felt better still. He was tired, yes; and he was ravenously hungry. Still, he could face this new day. It might even be a mistake to go to bed after he had eaten.

His green tomatoes waited on the windowsill, but surely there had been four? Perplexed, he searched his memory.

There were only three there now. Might someone have entered the garden, intent upon the theft of a single unripe tomato? Maytera Marble cooked for the sibyls. Briefly Silk visualized her bent above a smoking pan, stirring his tomato into a fine hash of bacon and onions. His mouth watered, but nothing could possibly be less like Maytera Marble than any such borrowing.

Wincing with every step and amused by his own grimaces, he limped to the window and looked more closely. The remains of the fourth tomato were there, a dozen seeds and flecks of skin. Furthermore, a hole had been eaten—bored, almost—in the third.

Rats, of course, although this did not really look like the work of a rat. He pared away the damaged portion, sliced the remainder and the remaining pair, then belatedly realized that cooking would require a fire in the stove.

The ashes of the last were lifeless gray dust without a single gleam, as it seemed to Silk they always were. Others spoke of starting a new fire from the embers of the previous one; his own fires never seemed to leave those rumored, long-lived embers. He laid a few scraps of hoarded wastepaper on top of the cold ashes and added kindling from the box beside the stove. Showers of white-hot sparks from the igniter soon produced a fine blaze.

As he started out to the woodpile, he sensed a furtive movement, stopped, and turned as quickly as he could manage to look behind him. Something black had moved swiftly and furtively at the top of the larder. Too vividly he recalled the white-headed one, perched at the top of a chimney; but it was only a rat. There had been rats in the manse ever since he had come here from the schola, and no doubt since Patera Pike had left the schola.

The crackling tinder would not wait, rats or no rats. Silk chose a few likely-looking splits, carried them (once nearly falling) inside, and positioned them carefully. No doubt the rat was gone by now, but he fetched Blood's stick from its place in the corner anyway, pausing by the Silver Street window to study the indistinct, battered head at the end of the sharply angled handle. It seemed to be a dog's, or perhaps . . .

He rotated the stick, holding it higher to catch the grayish daylight.

Or perhaps, just possibly, a lioness's. After a brief uncertainty, he decided to consider it the head of a lioness; lionesses symbolized Sphigx, this was her day, and the idea pleased him.

Lions were big cats, and big cats were needed for rats, vermin too large and strong themselves for cats of ordinary size to deal with. Without real hope of success, he rattled the stick along the top of the larder. There was a flutter, and a sound he did not at once identify as a squawk. Another rattle, and a single black feather floated down.

It occurred to Silk then that a rat might have carried the dead bird there to eat. Possibly there was a rat hole in the wainscotting up there, but the bird had been too large to be dragged through it.

He paused, listening. The sound he had heard had not been made by a rat, surely. After a moment he looked in the waste bin; the bird was no longer there.

If his ankle had been well, he would have climbed up on the stool; as things (and he himself) stood, that was out of the question. "Are you up there, bird?" he called. "Answer me!"

There was no reply. Blindly, he rattled Blood's stick across the top of the high larder again; and this time there was a quite unmistakable squawk. "Get down here," Silk said firmly.

The bird's hoarse voice replied, "No, no!"

"I thought you were dead."

Silence from the top of the larder.

"You stole my tomato, didn't you? And now you think I'll hurt you for that. I won't, I promise. I forgive you the theft." Silk tried to remember what night choughs were supposed to eat in the wild. Seeds? No, the bird had left the seeds. Carrion, no doubt.

"Cut me," the bird suggested throatily.

"Sacrifice you? I won't, I swear. The Writings warned me the sacrifice would be ineffectual, and I shouldn't have tried one after that. I've been punished very severely by one of your kind for it, believe me. I'm not such a fool as to try the same sacrifice again."

Silk waited motionless, listening. After a second or two, he felt certain that he could hear the bird's stealthy movements above the crack of whips and rumble of cartwheels that drifted through the window from Silver Street.

"Come down," he repeated.

The bird did not answer, and Silk turned away. The fire in the stove was burning well now, yellow flame leaping from the cook hole. He rescued his frying pan from the sink, wiped it out, poured the remaining oil into it—shaking the last lingering drop from the neck of the cruet—and put the pan on the stove.

His tomatoes would be greasy if he put them into the oil while it was still cold, unpleasantly flavored if he let the oil get too hot. Leaning Blood's stick against the door of the larder, he gathered up the stiff green slices, limped over to the stove with them, and distributed them with care over the surface of the pan, rewarded by a cloud of hissing, fragrant steam.

There was a soft cluck from the top of the larder.

"I can kill you whenever I want, just by banging around up there with my stick," Silk told the bird. "Show yourself, or I'll do it."

For a moment a long crimson bill and one bright black eye were visible at the top of the larder. "Me," the night chough said succinctly, and vanished at once.

"Good." The garden window was open already; Silk drew the heavy bolt of the Silver Street window and opened it as well. "It's shadeup now, and it will be much brighter soon. Your kind prefers the dark, I believe. You'd better leave at once."

"No fly."

"Yes, fly. I won't try to hurt you. You're free to go."

Silk watched for a moment, then decided that the bird was probably hoping that he would lay aside Blood's stick. He tossed it into a corner, got out a fork, and began turning the tomato slices; they sputtered and smoked, and he added a pinch of salt.

There was a knock at the garden door. Hurriedly, he snatched the pan from the fire. "Half a minute." Someone was dying, surely, and before death came desired to receive the Pardon of Pas.

The door opened before he could hobble over to it, and Maytera Rose looked in. "You're up very early, Patera. Is anything wrong?" Her gaze darted about the kitchen, her eyes not quite tracking. One was pupilless, and as far as Silk knew, blind; the other a prosthetic creation of crystal and fire.

"Good morning Maytera." Awkwardly, the fork and the smoking pan remained in Silk's hands; there was no place to put them down. "I suffered a little mishap last night, I'm afraid. I fell. It's still somewhat painful, and I haven't been able to sleep." He congratulated himself—it was all perfectly true.

"So you're making breakfast already. We haven't eaten yet, over in the cenoby." Maytera Rose sniffed hungrily, a dry, mechanical inhalation. "Marble's still fooling around in the kitchen. The littlest thing takes that girl forever."

"I'm quite certain Maytera Marble does the best she can," Silk said stiffly.

Maytera Rose ignored it. "If you want to give me that, I'll take it over to her. She can see to it for you till you come back."

"I'm sure that's not necessary." Sensing that he must eat his tomatoes now if he was to eat them at all, Silk cut the thinnest slice in two with his fork. "Must I leave this instant, Maytera? I can hardly walk."

"Her name's Teasel, and she's one of Marble's bunch." Maytera Rose sniffed again. "That's what her father says. I don't know her."

Silk (who did) froze, the half slice of tomato halfway to his mouth. "Teasel?"

"Her father came pounding on the door before we got up. The mother's sitting with her, he said. He knocked over here first, but you didn't answer."

"You should have come at once, Maytera."

"What would have been the use when he couldn't wake you up? I waited till I could see you were out of bed." Maytera Rose's good eye was upon the half slice. She licked her lips and wiped her mouth on her sleeve. "Know where she lives?"

Silk nodded miserably, and then with a sudden surge of wholly deplorable greed thrust the hot half slice into his mouth, chewed, and swallowed. He had never tasted anything quite so good. "It's not far. I suppose I can walk it if I must."

"I could send Marble after Patera Pard when she's done cooking. She could show him where to go."

Silk shook his head.

"You're going to go after all, are you?" A moment too late, Maytera Rose added, "Patera."

Silk nodded.

"Want me to take those?"

"No, thank you," Silk said, miserably aware that he was being selfish. "I'll have to get on a robe, a collar and so forth. You'd better get back to the cenoby, Maytera, before you miss breakfast." He scooped up one of the smaller slices with his fork.

"What happened to your tunic?"

"And a clean tunic. Thank you. You're right, Maytera. You're quite right." Silk closed the door, virtually in her face, shot the bolt, and popped the whole sizzling slice into his mouth. Maytera Rose would never forgive him for what he had just done, but he had previously done at least a hundred other things for which Maytera Rose would never forgive him either. The stain of evil might soil his spirit throughout all eternity, for which he was deeply and sincerely sorry; but as a practical matter it would make little difference.

He swallowed a good deal of the slice and chewed the rest energetically.

"Witch," croaked a muffled voice.

"Go," Silk mumbled. He swallowed again. "Fly home to the mountains. You're free."

He turned the rest of the slices, cooked them half a minute more, and ate them quickly (relishing their somewhat oily flavor almost as much as he had hoped), scraped the mold from the remaining bread and fried the bread in the leftover liquid, and ate that as he once more climbed the stair to his bedroom.

Behind and below him, the bird called, "Good-bye!" And then, "Bye! Bye!" from the top of the larder.

CHAPTER
9   OREB AND OTHERS

Teasel lay upon her back, with her mouth open and her eyes closed. Her black hair, spread over the pillow, accentuated the pallor of her face. Bent above her as he prayed, Silk was acutely conscious of the bones underlying her face, of her protruding cheekbones, her eye sockets, and her high and oddly square frontal. Despite the mounting heat of the day, her mother had covered her to the chin with a thick red wool blanket that glowed like a stove in the sun-bright room; her forehead was beaded with sweat, and it was only that sweat, which soon reappeared each time her mother sponged it away, that convinced him that Teasel was still alive.

When he had swung his beads and chanted the last of the prescribed prayers, her mother said, "I heard her cry out, Patera, as if she'd pricked her finger. It was the middle of the night, so I thought she was having a nightmare. I got out of bed and went in to see about her. The other children were all asleep, and she was still sleeping, too. I shook her shoulder, and she woke up a little bit and said she was thirsty. I ought to've told her to go get a drink herself."

Silk said, "No."

"Only I didn't, Patera. I went to the crock and got a cup of water, and she drank it and closed her eyes." After a moment Teasel's mother added, "The doctor won't come. Marten tried to get him."

Silk nodded. "I'll do what I can."

"If you'd talk to him again, Patera . . ."

"He wouldn't let me in last time, but I'll try."

Teasel's mother sighed as she looked at her daughter. "There was blood on her pillow, Patera. Not much. I didn't see it till shadeup. I thought it might have come out of her ear, but it didn't. She felt so cold."

Teasel's eyes opened, surprising them both. Weakly, she said, "The terrible old man."

Her mother leaned forward. "What's that?"

"Thirsty."

"Get her more water," Silk said, and Teasel's mother bustled out. "The old man hurt you?"

"Wings." Teasel's eyes rolled toward the window before closing.

They were four flights up, as Silk, who had climbed all four despite his painful right ankle, was very much aware. He rose, hobbled to the window, and looked out. There was a dirty little courtyard far below, a garret floor above them. The tapering walls were of unadorned, yellowish, sun-baked brick.

Legend had it that it was unlucky to converse with devils; Silk asked, "Did he speak to you, Teasel? Or you to him?"

She did not reply.

Her mother returned with the water. Silk helped her to raise Teasel to a half-sitting position; he had expected some difficulty in getting her to drink, but she drank thirstily, draining the clay cup as soon as it was put to her lips.

"Bring her more," he said, and as soon as Teasel's mother had gone, he rolled the unresisting girl onto her side.

When Teasel had drunk again, her mother asked, "Was it a devil, Patera?"

Silk settled himself once more on the stool she had provided for him. "I think so." He shook his head. "We have too much real disease already. It seems terrible . . ." He left the thought incomplete.

"What can we do?"

"Nurse her and feed her. See she gets as much water as she'll drink. She's lost blood, I believe." Silk took the voided cross from the chain around his neck and fingered its sharp steel edges. "Patera Pike told me about this sort of devil. That was—" Silk shut his eyes, reckoning. "About a month before he died. I didn't believe him, but I listened anyway, out of politeness. I'm glad, now, that I did."

Teasel's mother nodded eagerly. "Did he tell you how to drive it away?"

"It's away now," Silk told her absently. "The problem is to prevent it from returning. I can do what Patera Pike did. I don't know how he learned it, or whether it had any real efficacy; but he said that the child wasn't troubled a second time."

Assisted by Blood's stick, Silk limped to the window, seated himself on the sill, and leaned out, holding the side of the weathered old window frame with his free hand. The window was small, and he found he could reach the crumbling bricks above it easily. With the pointed corner of one of the four gammadions that made up the cross, he scratched the sign of addition on the bricks.

"I'll hold you, Patera."

Teasel's father was gripping his legs above the knees. Silk said, "Thank you." He scratched Patera Pike's name to the left of the tilted *X*. Patera Pike had signed his work; so he had said.

"I brought the cart for you, Patera. I told my jefe about you, and he said it would be all right."

After a moment's indecision, Silk added his own name on the other side of the *X*. "Thank you again." He ducked back into the room. "I want you both to pray to Phaea. Healing is hers, and it would appear that whatever happened to your daughter happened at the end of her day."

Teasel's parents nodded together.

"Also to Sphigx, because today's hers, and to Surging Scylla, not only because our city is hers, but because your daughter called for water. Lastly, I want you to pray with great devotion to the Outsider."

Teasel's mother asked, "Why, Patera?"

"Because I told you to," Silk replied testily. "I don't suppose you'll know any of the prescribed prayers to him, and there really aren't that many anyway. But make up your own. They'll be acceptable to him as long as they're sincere."

As he descended the stairs to the street, one steep and painful step at a time, Mucor spoke behind him. "That was interesting. What are you going to do next?"

He turned as quickly as he could. As if in a dream, he glimpsed the mad girl's death's-head grin, and eyes that had never belonged to Teasel's stooped, hard-handed father. She vanished as he looked, and the man who had been following him down the stairs shook himself.

"Are you well, Marten?" Silk asked.

"I went all queer there, Patera. Don't know what come over me."

Silk nodded, traced the sign of addition, and murmured a blessing.

"I'm good enough now, or think I am. Worryin' too much about Sel, maybe. Rabbit shit on my grave."

In the past, Silk had carried a basin of water up the stairs to his bedroom and washed himself in decent privacy; that was out of the question now. After closing and locking both, he covered the Silver Street window with the dishrag and a dish towel, and the garden window (which looked toward the cenoby) with a heavy gray blanket he had stored on the highest shelf of the sellaria closet against the return of winter.

Retreating to the darkest corner of the kitchen, almost to the stair, he removed all his clothing and gave himself the cold bath he had been longing for, lathering his whole body from the crown of his head to the top of his cast, then sponging the suds away with clean, cool water fresh from the well.

Dripping and somewhat refreshed, yet so fatigued that he seriously considered stretching himself on the kitchen floor, he examined his discarded clothing. The trousers, he decided, were still salvageable: with a bit of mending, they might be worn again, as he had worn them before, while he patched the manteion's roof or performed similar chores. He emptied their pockets, dropping his prayer beads, Blood's two cards, and the rest on the scarred old kitchen table. The tunic was ruined, but would supply useful rags after a good laundering; he tossed it into the wash basket on top of his trousers and undershorts, dried those parts of himself that had not been dried already by the baking heat of the kitchen with a clean dish towel, and made his way up to bed. If it had not been for the pain in his ankle, he would have been half asleep before he passed the bedroom door.

His donkey was lost in the yellow house. Shards of the tumbler Blood broke with Hyacinth's golden needler cracked under the donkey's hooves, and a horned owl as big as a Flier circled overhead awaiting the moment to pounce. Seeing the double punctures the owl had left half concealed in the hair at the back of Teasel's neck, he shuddered.

The donkey fastened its teeth in his ankle like a dog. Though he flailed at it with Sphigx's walking stick, it would not let go.

Mother was riding Auk's big gray donkey sidesaddle—he saw her across the skylit rooftops, but he could not cry out. When he reached the place, her old wooden bust of the caldé lay among the fallen leaves; he picked it up, and it became the ball. He thrust it into his pocket and woke.

His bedroom was hot and filled with sunlight, his naked body drenched with sweat. Sitting up, he drank deeply from the tepid water jug. The rusty cash-box key was still in its place and was of great importance. As he lay down again, he remembered that it was Hyacinth whom he had locked away.

A black-clad imp with a blood-red sword stood upon his chest to study him, its head cocked to one side. He stirred and it fled, fluttering like a little flag.

Hard dry rain blew through the window and rolled across the floor, bringing with it neither wind nor respite from the heat. Silk groaned and buried his perspiring face in the pillow.

It was Maytera Marble who woke him at last, calling his name through the open window. His mind still sluggish with sleep, he tried to guess how long he had slept, concluding only that it had not been long enough.

He staggered to his feet. The busy little clock beside his triptych declared that it was after eleven, nearly noon. He struggled to recall the positions of its hands when he had permitted himself to fall into bed. Eight, or after eight, or possibly eight-thirty. Teasel, poor little Teasel, had been bitten by an owl—or by a devil. A devil with wings, if it had come in through her window, and thus a devil twice impossible. Silk blinked and yawned and rubbed his eyes.

"*Patera? Are you up there?*"

She might see him if he went near the window. Fumbling in a drawer for clean underclothes, he called, "What is it, Maytera?"

"*A doctor! He says he's come to treat you! Are you hurt, Patera?*"

"Wait a moment." Silk pulled on his best trousers, the only pair that remained, and crossed the room to the window, twice stepping painfully on pebbles.

Maytera Marble waited in the little path, her upturned face flashing in the hot sunshine. Doctor Crane stood beside her, a shabby brown medical bag in one hand.

"May every god favor you both this morning," Silk called down politely.

Crane waved his free hand in response. "Sphigxday and Hieraxday, remember? That's when I'm in this part of town! Today's Sphigxday. Let me in!"

"As soon as I get dressed," Silk promised.

With the help of Blood's lioness-headed walking stick, he hobbled downstairs. His arm and ankle seemed more painful than ever; he told himself firmly that it was only because the palliating effects of the drug Crane had given him the night before—and of the potent drinks he had imprudently sampled—had worn off.

Limping and wincing, he hurried into the kitchen. The heterogeneous collection of items he had left on the table there was rapidly transferred to his clean trousers, with only momentary hesitation over Hyacinth's gleaming needler.

"*Patera?*"

His blanket still covered the garden window; resisting the temptation to pull it down, he lurched painfully into the sellaria, flung open the door, and began introductions. "Maytera, this is Doctor Crane—"

Maytera Marble nodded demurely, and the physician said, "We've already met. I was tossing gravel through your window—I was pretty sure it was yours, since I could hear you snoring up there—when Marble discovered me and introduced herself."

Maytera Marble asked, "Did you send for him, Patera? He must be new to our quarter."

"I don't live here," Crane explained. "I only make a few calls here, two days a week. My other patients are all late sleepers," he winked at Silk, "but I hoped that Silk would be up."

Silk looked rueful. "I was a late sleeper myself, I'm afraid, today at least."

"Sorry I had to wake you, but I thought I might give you a ride when we're through—it's not good for you to walk too much on that ankle." By a gesture Crane indicated the sellaria. "I'd like to have you sitting down. Can we go inside?"

Maytera Marble ventured, "If I might watch you, Patera? Through the doorway . . . ?"

"Yes," Silk said. There should be ample opportunity to speak with Crane in private on the way to the yellow house. "Certainly, Maytera, if you wish."

"I hadn't known. Maytera Rose told Maytera Mint and me at breakfast, though she didn't seem to know a lot about it. You—you were testy with her, I think."

"Yes, very much so." Silk nodded sadly as he retreated into the sellaria, guilt overlaying the pain from his ankle. Maytera Rose had been hungry, beyond question, and he had turned her away. She had been inquisitive too, of course; but she could not help that. No doubt her intentions had been good—or at least no doubt she had told herself they were, and had believed it. How selflessly she had served the manteion for sixty years! Yet only this morning he had refused her.

He dropped into the nearest of the stiff old chairs, then stood again and shifted it two cubits so that Maytera Marble could watch from the doorway.

"All right if I put my bag on this little table here?" Crane stepped to his left, away from the doorway. There was no table there, but he opened his bag, held up a shapeless dark bundle so that Silk could see it (though Maytera Marble could not), dropped it on the floor, and set his bag beside it. "Now then, Silk. The arm first, I think."

Silk pushed up his sleeve and held out his injured arm.

Bright scissors Silk recalled from the previous night snipped away the bandages. "You probably think your ankle's worse, and in a way it is. But there's an excellent chance of blood-poisoning here, and that's no joke. Your ankle's not going to kill you—not unless we're playing in the worst sort of luck, anyway." Crane scrutinized the wounds under a tiny, brilliant light, muttered to himself, and bent to sniff them. "All right so far, but I'm going to give you a booster."

To keep his mind from the ampule, Silk said, "I'm very sorry I missed our prayers this morning. What time is it, Maytera?"

"Nearly noon. Maytera Rose said you had to—is that a bird, Patera?"

Crane snapped, "Don't jerk like that!"

"I was thinking of—of the bird that did this," Silk finished weakly.

"You could have broken off the needle. How'd you like me fishing around in your arm for that?"

"It *is* a bird!" Maytera Marble pointed. "It hopped back that way. Into your kitchen, I suppose, Patera."

"That's the stairwell, actually," Silk told her. "I'm surprised it's still here."

"It was a big black bird, and I think one of its wings must be broken. It wasn't exactly dragging it but it wasn't holding it right either, if you know what I mean. Is that the bird—? The one that—?"

"Just sit quietly," Crane said. He was putting a fresh bandage on Silk's arm.

Silk said, "No wonder it didn't fly," and Maytera Marble looked at him inquiringly.

"It's the one that I'd intended to sacrifice, Maytera. It had only fainted or something—had a fit, or whatever birds do. I opened the kitchen window for it this morning so it could fly away, but I suppose I must have broken its wing when I was poking around on top of the larder with my walking stick."

He held it up to show her. It reminded him of Blood, and Blood reminded him that he was going to have to explain to Maytera Marble— and if he was not extremely lucky, to Maytera Rose and Maytera Mint as well—exactly how he had received his injuries.

"On top of the larder, Patera?"

"Yes. The bird was up there then." Still thinking of the explanation the sibyls would expect, he added, "It had flown up there, I suppose."

Crane pulled a footstool into place and sat on it. "Up with your tunic now. Good. Shove your waistband down just a bit."

Maytera Marble turned her head delicately away.

Silk asked, "If I'm able to catch that bird, will you set its wing for me?"

"I don't know much horse-physic, but I can try. I've seen to Musk's hawks once or twice."

Silk cleared his throat, resolved to deceive Maytera Marble as little as possible without revealing the nature of his visit to the villa. "You see, Maytera, after I saw—saw Maytera Mint's friend, you know who I mean, I thought it might be wise to call on Blood. Do you remember Blood? You showed him around yesterday afternoon."

Maytera Marble nodded. "Of course, Patera. How could I forget?"

"And you had spoken afterward, when we talked under the arbor, about our buildings being torn down—or perhaps not torn down, but our having to leave. So I thought it might be wise for me to have a heart-to-heart talk with the new owner. He lives in the country, so it took me a good deal longer than I had anticipated, I'm afraid."

Crane said, "Lean back a little more." He was swabbing Silk's chest and abdomen with a blue solution.

Maytera Marble nodded dubiously. "That was very good of you, Patera. Wonderful, really, though I didn't get the impression that he—"

Silk leaned back as much as he could, pushing his hips forward. "But he did, Maytera. He's going to give me—to give us, I ought to say—another month here at least. And it's possible that we may never have to go."

"Oh, Patera!" Maytera Marble forgot herself so far as to look at him.

Silk hurried on. "But what I wanted to explain is that a man who works for Blood keeps several large birds as pets. I suppose there are several, at least, from the way that he and Blood talked about them."

Crane nodded absently.

"And he'd given this one to Blood," Silk continued. "It was dark, of course, and I'm afraid I got too close. Blood very graciously suggested that Doctor Crane come by today to see to my injuries."

"Why, Patera, how wonderful of him!" Maytera Marble's eyes positively shone with admiration for Silk's diplomatic skills, and he felt himself blush.

"All part of my job," Crane said modestly, replacing the stopper in the blue bottle.

Silk swallowed and took a deep breath, hoping that this was the proper moment. "Before we leave, Doctor, there's something I must bring up. A moment ago you said you would treat that injured bird if I was able to catch it. You were gracious about it, in fact."

Crane nodded warily as he rose. "Excuse me. Have to get my cutter."

"This morning," Silk continued, "I was called to bring the forgiveness of the gods to a little girl named Teasel."

Maytera Marble stiffened.

"She's close to death, but I believe—I dare to hope that she may recover, provided she receives the most basic medical attention. Her parents are poor and have many other children."

"Hold your leg out." Crane sat down on the footstool again and took Silk's foot in his lap. The cutter buzzed.

"They can't possibly pay you," Silk continued doggedly. "Neither can I, except with prayers. But without your help, Teasel may die. Her parents actually expect her to die—otherwise her father wouldn't have come here before shadeup looking for me. There are only two doctors in this quarter, and neither will treat anyone unless he's paid in advance. I promised Teasel's mother I'd do what I could to get her a doctor, and you're the only real hope I have."

Crane looked up. There was something in his eyes, a gleam of calculation and distant speculation, that Silk did not understand. "You were there this morning?"

Silk nodded. "That was why I got to bed so late. Her father had come to the cenoby before I returned from my talk with Blood, and when Maytera Rose saw that I had come home, she came and told me. I went at once." The memory of green tomatoes stung like a hornet. "Or almost at once," he added weakly.

Maytera Marble said, "You must see her, Doctor. Really you *must.*"

Crane ignored her, fingering his beard. "And you told them you'd try to get a doctor for whatshername?"

Hope blossomed in Silk. "Yes, I did. I'd be in your debt till Pas ends the whorl, and I'd be delighted to show you where she lives. We could stop there on the way."

Maytera Marble gasped. "Patera! All those steps!"

Crane bent over the cast again; his cutter whined and half of it fell away. "You're not going to climb a lot of stairs if I have anything to say about it. Not with this ankle. Marble here can show me—"

"Oh, yes!" Maytera Marble was dancing with impatience. "I've got to see her. She's one of mine."

"Or you can just give me the address," Crane finished. "My bearers will know where it is. I'll see to her and come back here for you." He removed the rest of the cast. "This hurt you much?"

"Not nearly as much as worrying about Teasel did," Silk told him. "But you've taken care of that, or at least taken care of the worst aspect of it. I'll never be able to thank you enough."

"I don't want your thanks," Crane said. He rose again, dusting particles of the cast from his trousers legs. "What I want is for you to follow my instructions. I'm going to give you a remedial wrapping. It's valuable and reusable, so I want it back when your ankle's healed. And I want you to use it exactly as I tell you."

Silk nodded. "I will, I promise."

"As for you, Marble," Crane turned to look at her, "you might as well ride along with me. It'll save you the walk. I want you to tell this girl's parents that I'm not doing this out of the goodness of my heart, because I don't want to be pestered night and day by beggars. It's a favor to Silk—Patera Silk, is that what you call him? And it's a one-time thing."

Maytera Marble nodded humbly.

The little physician went to his bag again and produced what looked like a wide strip of thin yellow chamois. "Ever see one of these?"

Silk shook his head.

"You kick them." Crane punted the wrapping, which flew against the wall on the other side of the room. "Or you can just throw it a couple of times, or beat something smooth, like that footstool." He retrieved the wrapping, juggling it. "When you do, they get hot. You woke it up by banging it around. You follow me? Here, feel."

Silk did. The wrapping was almost too hot to touch, and seemed to tingle.

"The heat'll make your ankle feel better, and the sonic—you can't hear it, but it's there—will get the healing process going. What's more, it'll sense the break in your medial malleolus and tighten itself enough to keep it from shifting." Crane hesitated. "You can't get them any more, but I've got this one. Usually I don't tell people about it."

"I'll take good care of it," Silk promised, "and return it whenever you ask."

Maytera Marble ventured, "Shouldn't we be going?"

"In a minute. Wrap it around your ankle Patera. Get it fairly tight. You don't have to tie it or anything—it'll hold on as long as it senses the broken bone."

The wrapping seemed almost to coil itself about Silk's leg, its heat intense but pleasant. The pain in his ankle faded.

"You'll know when its stopped working. As soon as it does, I want you to take it off and throw it against the wall like I showed you, or beat a carpet with it." The physician tugged at his beard. "Let's see. Today's

Sphigxday. I'll come back on Hieraxday, and we'll see. Regardless, you ought to be walking almost normally a week from now. If I don't take it Hieraxday, I'll pick it up then. But until I do, I want you to stay off that ankle as much as you can. Get a crutch if you need one. And absolutely no running and no jumping. You hear me?"

Silk nodded. "Yes, of course. But you told Blood it would be five—"

"It's not as bad as I figured, that's all. A simple misdiagnosis. Your head augur . . . What do they call him, the Prolocutor? Haven't you noticed that when he gets sick I'm not the one he sends for? Well, that's why. Now and then I make a mistake. The sort of doctors he has in never do. Just ask them."

Maytera Marble inquired, "How does it feel, Patera?"

"Marvelous! I'm tempted to say as though my ankle had never been injured, but it's actually better than that. As if I'd been given a new ankle, a lot better than the one I broke."

"I could give you dozens of things that would make you *feel* better," Crane told him, "starting with a shot of pure and a sniff of rust. This will really make you better, and that's a lot harder. Now, what about this bird of yours? If I'm going to have to doctor it, I'd like to do it before we go. What kind of bird is it?"

"A night chough," Silk told him.

"Can it talk?"

Silk nodded.

"Then maybe I can catch it myself. Maytera, would you tell my bearers to come around to Sun Street? They're on Silver. Tell them you'll be coming with me, and we'll leave in a minute or two."

Maytera Marble trotted away.

The physician shook his finger at Silk. "You sit easy, young man. I'll find him."

He vanished into the stairwell. Soon, Silk heard his voice from the kitchen, though he could not make out what was being said. Silk called, "You told Blood that it would take so long to heal so that I'd get more time, didn't you? Thank you, Doctor."

There was no response. The wrapping was still hot, and oddly comforting. Under his breath Silk began the afternoon prayer to Sphigx the Brave. A fat, blue-backed fly sizzled through the open doorway, looked around for food, and bumped the glass of the nearer Sun Street window.

Crane called from the kitchen, "You want to come here a minute, Silk?"

"All right." Silk stood and walked almost normally to the kitchen door, his right foot bare and the wrapping heavy about his ankle.

"He's hiding up there." Crane pointed to the top of the larder. "I got him to talk a little, but he won't come down and let me see his wing unless you promise he won't be hurt again."

"Really?" Silk asked.

The night chough croaked from the top of the larder, and Crane nodded and winked.

"Then I promise. May Great Pas judge me if I harm him or permit others to do so."

"No cut?" croaked the bird. "No stick?"

"Correct," Silk declared. "I will not sacrifice you, or hurt you in any other fashion whatsoever."

"Pet bird?"

"Until your wing is well enough for you to fly. Then you may go free."

"No cage?"

Crane nudged Silk's arm to get his attention, and shook his head.

"Correct. No cage." Silk took the cage from the table and raised it over his head, high enough for the bird to see it. "Now watch this." With both hands, he dashed it to the floor, and slender twigs snapped like squibs. He stepped on it with his good foot, then picked up the ruined remnant and tossed it into the kindling box.

Crane shook his head. "You're going to regret that, I imagine. It's bound to be inconvenient at times."

With its sound wing flapping furiously, the black bird fluttered from the top of the larder to the table.

"Good bird!" Crane told it. He sat down on the kitchen stool. "I'm going to pick you up, and I want you to hold still for a minute. I'm not going to hurt you any more than I have to."

"I was a prisoner myself for a while last night," Silk remarked, more than half to himself. "Even though there was no actual cage, I didn't like it."

Crane caught the unresisting bird expertly, his hands gentle yet firm. "Get my bag for me, will you?"

Silk nodded and returned to the sellaria. He closed the garden door, then picked up the dark bundle that Crane had displayed to him. As he had guessed, it was his second-best robe, with his old pen case still in its pocket; it had been wrapped around his missing shoe. Although he had no stocking for his right foot, he put on both, shut the brown medical bag, and carried it into the kitchen.

The bird squawked and fluttered as Crane stretched out its injured wing. "Dislocated," he said. "Exactly like a dislocated elbow on you. I've pushed it back into place, but I want to splint it so he won't pop it out again before it heals. Meanwhile he'd better stay inside, or a cat will get him."

"Then he must stay in on his own," Silk said.

"Stay in," the bird repeated.

"Your cage is broken," Silk continued severely, "and I certainly don't intend to bake in here with all the windows shut, merely to keep you from getting out."

"No out," the bird assured him. Crane was rummaging in his bag.

"I hope not." Silk pulled the blanket from the garden window, threw it open, and refolded the blanket.

"What time are you supposed to meet Blood at the yellow house?"

"One o'clock, sharp." Silk carried the blanket into the sellaria; when he returned, he added, "I'm going to be late, I imagine; I doubt that he'll do anything worse than complain about it."

"That's the spirit. He'll be late himself, if I know him. He likes to have everybody on hand when he shows up. I doubt if that'll be before two."

Stepping across to the Silver Street window, Silk took down the dish-rag and the dish towel and opened it as well. It was barred against thieves, and it occurred to him that he was caged in literal fact, here in this old, four-room manse he had taught himself to call home. He pushed away the thought. If Crane's litter had been on Silver Street, it was gone now; no doubt Maytera Marble had performed her errand and it was waiting on Sun Street.

"This should do it." Crane was fiddling with a small slip of some stiff blue synthetic. "You'll be ready to go when I get back?"

Silk nodded, then felt his jaw. "I'll have to shave. I'll be ready then."

"Good. I'll be running late, and the girls get cranky if they can't go out and shop." Crane applied a final strip of almost invisible tape to keep the little splint in place. "This will fall right off after a few days. When it does, let him fly if he wants to. If he's like the hawks, you'll find that he's a pretty good judge of what he can and can't do."

"No fly," the bird announced.

"Not now, that's for sure. If I were you, I wouldn't even move that wing any more today."

Silk's mind was elsewhere. "It's diabolic possession, isn't it? At the yellow house?"

Crane turned to face him. "I don't know. Whatever it is, I hope you have better luck with it than I've had."

"What's been happening there? My driver and I heard a scream last night, but we didn't go inside."

The little physician laid a finger to his nose. "There are a thousand reasons why a girl might scream, especially one of those girls. Might have been a stain on her favorite gown, a bad dream, or a spider."

A tiny needle of pain penetrated the protection of the wrapping; Silk opened the cabinet that closed the kitchen's pointed north corner and got out the stool Patera Pike had used at meals. "I doubt that Blood wants me to exorcise his women's dreams."

Crane snapped his medical bag shut. "No one except the woman herself is really occupying the consciousness of what people like you choose to call a 'possessed' woman, Silk. Consciousness itself is a mere abstraction—a convenient fiction, actually. When I say that a man's unconscious, I mean no more than that certain mental processes have been suspended. When I say that he's regained consciousness, I mean that they've resumed. You can't occupy an abstraction as if it were a conquered city."

"A moment ago you said the woman herself occupied it," Silk pointed out.

With a last look at the injured bird, Crane rose. "So they really do teach you people something besides all that garbage."

Silk nodded. "It's called logic."

"So it is." Crane smiled, and Silk discovered to his own surprise that he liked him. "Well, if I'm going to look in on this sick girl of yours, I'd better scoot. What's the matter with her? Fever?"

"Her skin felt cold to me, but you're a better judge of diseases than I."

"I should hope so." Crane picked up his bag. "Let's see—through the front room there for Sun Street, isn't it? Maybe we can talk a little more on our way to Orchid's place."

"Look at the back of her neck," Silk said.

Crane paused in the doorway, shot him a questioning glance, then hurried out.

Murmuring a prayer for Teasel under his breath, Silk went into the sellaria and shut and bolted the Sun Street door, which Crane had left standing open. As he passed a window, he caught sight of Crane's litter. Maytera Marble reclined beside the bearded physician, her intent metal face straining ahead as though she alone were urging the litter forward by sheer force of thought. While Silk watched, its bearers broke into a trot and it vanished behind the window frame.

He tried to recall whether there was a rule prohibiting a sibyl from riding in a man's litter; it seemed likely that there was, but he could not bring a particular stricture to mind; as a practical matter, he could see little reason to object as long as the curtains were up.

The lioness-headed walking stick lay beside the chair in which he had sat for Crane's examination. Absently, he picked it up and flourished it. For as long as the wrapping functioned he would not need it, or at least would need it very little. He decided that he would keep it near at hand anyway; it might be useful, particularly when the wrapping required restoration. He leaned it against the Sun Street door, so that he could not forget it when he and Crane left for the yellow house.

A few experimental steps demonstrated once again that with Crane's wrapping in place he could walk almost as well as ever. There seemed to be no good reason for him not to carry a basin of warm water upstairs and shave as he usually did. He re-entered the kitchen.

Still on the table, the night chough cocked its head at him inquiringly. "Pet hungry," it said.

"So am I," he told it. "But I won't eat again until after midday."

"Noon now."

"I suppose it is." Silk lifted a stove lid and peered into the firebox; for once a few embers still glowed there. He breathed upon them gently and added a handful of broken twigs from the ruined cage, reflecting that the night chough was clearly more intelligent than he had imagined.

"Bird hungry."

Flames were flickering above the twigs. He debated the need for real firewood and decided against it. "Do you like cheese?"

"Like cheese."

Silk found his washbasin and put it under the nozzle of the pump. "It's hard, I warn you. If you're expecting nice, soft cheese, you're going to be disappointed."

"Like cheese!"

"All right, you can have it." A great many vigorous strokes of the pump handle were required before the first trickle of water appeared; but Silk half filled his basin and set it on the stove, and as an afterthought replenished the night chough's cup.

"Cheese now?" the night chough inquired. "Fish heads?"

"No fish heads—I haven't got any." He got out the cheese, which was mostly rind, and set it next to the cup. "You'd better watch out for rats while I'm away. They like cheese too."

"Like rats." The night chough clacked its crimson beak and pecked experimentally at the cheese.

"Then you won't be lonely." The water on the stove was scarcely warm, the twigs beneath it nearly out. Silk picked up the basin and started for the stair.

"Where rats?"

He paused and turned to look back at the night chough. "Do you mean you like them to eat?"

"Yes, yes!"

"I see. I suppose you might kill a rat at that, if it wasn't too big. What's your name?"

"No name." The night chough returned its attention to the cheese.

"That was supposed to be my lunch, you know. Now I'll have to find lunch somewhere or go hungry."

"You Silk?"

"Yes, that's my name. You heard Doctor Crane use it, I suppose. But we need a name for you." He considered the matter. "I believe I'll call you Oreb—that's a raven in the Writings, and you seem to be some sort of raven. How do you like that name?"

"Oreb."

"That's right. Musk named his bird after a god, which was very wrong of him, but I don't believe that there could be any objection to a name from the Writings if it weren't a divine name, particularly when it's a bird's name there. So Oreb it is."

At his washstand upstairs, he stropped the big, bone-handled razor that had waited in his mother's bureau until he was old enough to shave, lathered his face, and scraped away his reddish-blond beard. As he wiped the blade clean, it occurred to him, as it did at least once a week, that the razor had almost certainly been his father's. As he had so many times before, he carried it to the window to look for some trace of ownership. There was no owner's name and no monogram, not even a maker's mark.

As often in this weather, Maytera Rose and Maytera Mint were enjoying their lunch at a table carried from the cenoby and set in the shade of the fig tree. When he had dried his face, Silk carried the basin back to the kitchen, poured out his shaving water, and joined the two sibyls in the garden.

By a gesture, Maytera Rose offered him the chair that would normally have been Maytera Marble's. "Won't you join us, Patera? We've more than enough here for three."

It stung, as she had no doubt intended. Silk said, "No, but I ought to speak with you for a moment."

"And I with you, Patera. I with you." Maytera Rose began elaborate preparations for rising.

He sat down hurriedly. "What is it, Maytera?"

"I had hoped to tell you about it last night, Patera, but you were gone."

A napkin-draped basket at Silk's elbow exuded the very perfume of Mainframe. Maytera Marble had clearly baked that morning, leaving the fruit of her labor in the cenoby's oven for Maytera Mint to remove after she herself had left with Crane. Silk swallowed his saliva, muttered, "Yes," and left it at that.

"And this morning it had quite escaped my mind. All that I could think of was that awful man, the little girl's father. I will be sending Horn to you this afternoon for correction, Patera. I have punished him already, you may be sure. Now he must acknowledge his fault to you—that is the final penalty of his punishment." Maytera Rose paused to render her closing words more effective, her head cocked like the night chough's as she fixed Silk with her good eye. "And if you should decide to punish him further, I will not object. That might have a salutary effect."

"What did he do?"

The synthetic part of Maytera Rose's mouth bent sharply downward in disgust; as he had on several similar occasions, Silk wondered whether the aged, disease-ridden woman who had once been Maytera Rose was still conscious. "He made fun of you, Patera, imitating your voice and gestures, and talking foolishness."

"Is that all?"

Maytera Rose sniffed as she extracted a fresh roll from the basket. "I would say it was more than enough."

Maytera Mint began, "If Patera himself—"

"Before Patera was born, I endeavored to inculcate a decent respect for the holy calling of augur, a calling—like that of we sibyls—established by Our Sacred Scylla herself. I continue that effort to this day. I try, as I have always tried, to teach every student entrusted to my care to respect the cloth, regardless of the man or woman who wears it."

"A lesson to us all." Silk sighed. "Very well, I'll talk to him when I can. But I'm leaving in a few minutes, and I may not be back until late. That was what I wanted to tell you—to tell Maytera Mint particularly."

She look up, a question in her melting brown eyes.

"I'll be engaged, and I can't say how long it may take. You remember Auk, Maytera. You must. You taught him, and you told Maytera Marble about him yesterday, I know."

"Oh, Patera, I do indeed." Maytera Mint's small, not uncomely face glowed.

Maytera Rose sniffed, and Maytera Mint dropped her eyes again.

"I spoke to him last night, Maytera, very late."

"You did, Patera?"

Silk nodded. "But I'm forgetting something I should tell you. I'd seen him earlier that evening, and shriven him. He's trying, quite sincerely I believe, to amend his life."

Maytera Mint looked up again, her glance bright with praise. "That's truly wonderful, Patera!"

"It is indeed; and it's far more your doing, and Patera Pike's, than it is mine. What I wanted to say, Maytera, is that when I last spoke with him, he indicated that he might come here today. If he does, I'm sure he'll want to pay his respects to you."

He waited for her to confirm it. She did not, sitting with folded hands and downcast eyes.

"Please tell him that I'm anxious to see him. Ask him to wait, if he can. I doubt that he'll come before supper. If I haven't returned, tell him that I'll be back as soon as possible."

Spreading rich yellow butter on another golden roll, Maytera Rose said, "Last night you had gone already by the time Horn had finished working for his father. I'll tell him that he'll have to wait, too."

"I'm certain you will, Maytera. Thank you both." Silk stood up, wincing when he put too much weight on his injured ankle. For a formal exorcism he would need the Chrasmologic Writings from the manteion, and images of the gods—of Pas and Scylla particularly. And of Sphigx the patroness of the day. The thought reminded him that he had never completed her prayers; hardly the way to gain favor.

He would take the triptych his mother had given him; her prayers might follow it. As he tramped upstairs again, more conscious of his ankle than he had been since before Crane's visit, he reflected that he had been trained only in dealing with devils who did not exist. He recalled how startled he had been when he had realized that Patera Pike credited them, and even spoke with gruff pride of personal efforts to frustrate them.

Before he reached the top of the stair, he regretted leaving Blood's walking stick in the sellaria. Sitting on his bed, he unwound the wrapping; it was distinctly cool to the touch. He dashed it against the wall as violently as he could and replaced it, then removed his shoe and put on a clean stocking.

Blood would meet him at the yellow house on Lamp Street. Musk, or someone as bad as Musk, might come with Blood. Silk folded up the triptych, laid it in its baize-lined teak case, buckled the straps, and pulled out its folding handle. This and the Writings, which he would have to get before he left; Pas's gammadion was about his neck already, his beads in his pocket. It might be prudent to take a holy lamp, oil, and other things as well. After considering and rejecting half a dozen possibilities, he got the key from beneath his water jug.

With the young eagle on his gauntleted left arm, Musk stood on the spattered white pavement by Scylla's fountain and looked about him, his head as proudly poised, and his back as straight, as any Guardsman's. They were watching from the deep shade of the portico: Blood, Councillor Lemur and his cousin Councillor Loris, Commissioner Simuliid, and half a dozen others. Mentally, Musk shook the dice cup.

The eagle had been trained to wrist and to the lure. It knew his voice and had learned to associate it with food. When he removed its hood, it would see the fountain, flowing water in a countryside in which water of any kind was now a rarity. The time had come for it to learn to fly—and he could not teach it that. It would return for the lure and the hackboard. Or it would not. Time to throw the dice.

Blood's voice came to him faintly through the plashing of the fountain. "Don't rush him."

Someone had asked what he was waiting for. He sighed, knowing he could not delay much longer. To hold on to this moment, in which the bird that he might never see again was still his.

The sky was empty or seemed so, the skylands invisible behind the endless, straight glare of the sun. Fliers, if there were any, were invisible too. Above the tops of the trees on the other side of the wall, distant fields curved upward, vanishing in a blue haze as they mounted the air. Lake Limna seemed a fragment of mirror set into the whorl, like a gaud into a cheap picture frame.

Time to throw.

As though it knew what was about to happen, the young eagle stirred. Musk nodded to himself. "Come back to me," he whispered. "Come back to me."

And then, as if somebody else (an interfering god or Blood's mad daughter) controlled it, his right arm went up. Self-willed, his hand grasped the scarlet-plumed hood and snatched it away.

The young eagle lifted its wings as though to fly, then folded them again. He should have worn a mask, perhaps. If the eagle struck at his face now, he would be scarred for life if he was not killed; but his pride had not permitted it.

"Away, Hawk!" He lifted his arm, tilting it to tip the bird into the air. For a split second he thought it was not going to fly at all.

The great wings seemed to blow him back. Slowly and clumsily it flew, its wingtips actually brushing the lush grass at every downstroke—out to the wall and left, past the gate and left again up the grassway. For a moment he thought it was returning to him.

Into the portico, scattering the watchers there like quail. If it turned right at the end of the wing, mistook the cat pen for the mews—

Higher now, as high as the top of the wall, and left again. Left until it passed overhead, its wings a distant thunder. Higher now, and higher still, still circling and climbing, riding the updraft from the baking lawn and the scorching roofs. Higher the young eagle rose and higher, black against the glare, until it, like the fields, was lost in the vastness of the sky.

When the rest had gone Musk remained, shading his eyes against the pitiless sun. After a long while, Hare brought him binoculars. He used them but saw nothing.

10 THE CAT WITH THE RED-HOT TAIL

Lamp Street was familiar and safe once more, stripped of the mystery of night. Silk, who had walked it often, found that he recognized several shops, and even the broad and freshly varnished door of the yellow house.

The corpulent woman who opened it in response to Crane's knock seemed surprised by his presence. "It's awfully early, Patera. Just got up myself." She yawned as if to prove it, only tardily concealing her mouth. Her pink peignoir gaped in sympathy, its vibrant heat leaving the bulging flesh between its parted lips a deathly white.

The air of the place poured past her, hot and freighted with a hundred stale perfumes and the vinegar reek of wasted wine. "I was to meet Blood here at one o'clock," Silk told her. "What time is it?"

Crane slipped past them into the reception room beyond.

The woman ignored him. "Blood's always late," she said vaguely. She led Silk through a low archway curtained with clattering wooden beads and into a small office. A door and a window opened onto the courtyard he had imagined the night before, and both stood open; despite them, the office seemed hotter even than the street outside.

"We've had exorcists before." The corpulent woman took the only comfortable-looking chair, leaving Silk an armless one of varnished wood. He accepted it gratefully, dropping his bag to the floor, laying the cased triptych across his thighs, and holding Blood's lioness-headed stick between his knees.

"I'll have somebody fetch you a pillow, Patera. This is where I talk to my girls, and a hard chair's better. It keeps them awake, and the narrow seat makes them think that they're getting fat, which is generally the case."

The memory of his fried tomatoes brought Silk a fresh pang of guilt, well salted with hunger. Could it be that some god spoke through this blowsy woman? "Leave it as it is," he told her. "I, too, need to learn to love my belly less, and my bed."

"You want to talk to all the girls together? One of the others did. Or I can just tell you."

Silk waved the question aside. "What these particular devils may have done here is no concern of mine, and paying attention to their malicious tricks would risk encouraging them. They are devils, and unwelcome in this house; that is all I know, and if you and—and everyone else living here are willing to cooperate with me, it is all I need to know."

"All right." The corpulent woman adjusted her own chair's ample cushions and leaned back. "You believe in them, huh?"

Here it was. "Yes," Silk told her firmly.

"One of the others didn't. He said lots of prayers and had the parade and all the rest of it anyway, but he thought we were crazy. He was about your age."

"Doctor Crane thinks the same," Silk told her, "and his beard is gray. He doesn't phrase it quite as rudely as that, but that's what he thinks. He thinks that I'm crazy too, of course."

The corpulent woman smiled bitterly. "Uh-huh, I can guess. I'm Orchid, by the way." She offered her hand as though she expected him to kiss it.

He clasped it. "Patera Silk, from the manteion on Sun Street."

"That old place? Is it still open?"

"Yes, very much so." The question reminded Silk that it soon might not be, although it was better not to mention that.

"We're not now," Orchid told him. "Not until nine, so you've got plenty of time. But tonight's our biggest night, usually, so I'd appreciate it if you were finished by then." At last noticing his averted eyes, she tugged ineffectually at the edges of the pink peignoir.

"It should take me no more than two hours to perform the initial rites and the ceremony proper, provided I have everyone's cooperation. But it may be best to wait until Blood arrives. He told me last night that he would meet me here, and I feel sure that he will wish to take part."

Orchid was eyeing him narrowly. "He's paying you?"

"No. I'm performing this exorcism as a favor to him—I owe him much more, really. Did he pay the other exorcists you spoke of?"

"He did or I did, depending."

Silk relaxed a little. "In that case, it's not to be wondered at that their exorcisms were ineffectual. Exorcism is a sacred ceremony, and no such ceremony can be bought or sold." Seeing that she did not understand, he added. "They cannot be sold—my statement is true in the most literal sense of its words—because once sold the ceremony loses all its sacred character. What is sold is then no more than a profane mummery. That is not what we will carry out here today."

"But Blood could give you something, couldn't he?"

"Yes, if he wished. No gift affects the nature of the ceremony. A gift is given freely—if one is given at all. The point upon which the efficacy of the ceremony turns is that there must be no bargain between us; and there is none. I would have no right to complaint if a promised gift were not forthcoming. Am I making this clear?"

Orchid nodded reluctantly.

"In point of fact, I expect no gift at all from Blood. I owe him several favors, as I said. When he asked me to do this, I was—as I remain—eager to oblige."

Orchid leaned toward him, the peignoir yawning worse than ever. "Suppose this time it works, Patera. I could give you something, couldn't I?"

"Of course, if you choose. However, you will owe me nothing."

"All right." She hesitated, considering. "Sphigxday's our big night, like I said—that's why Blood comes around, usually, today. To check up on us before we open up. We're closed Hieraxday, so not then either. But come in any other day and I'll give you a pass. How's that?"

Silk was stunned.

"You know what I mean, right, Patera? Not me. I mean with any of the girls, whoever you want. If you'd like to give her a little something for herself, that's all right. But you don't have to, and there won't be anything to the house." Orchid considered again. "Well, a card in a cart, huh? All right, that's a lay a month for a year." Seeing his expression she added, "Or I can get you a boy if you'd rather have that, but let me know in advance."

Silk shook his head.

"Because if you do, you don't get to see the gods? Isn't that what they say?"

"Yes." Silk nodded. "Echidna forbids it. One may see the gods when they appear in our Sacred Windows. Or one may be blessed by children of the body. But not both."

"Nobody's talking about sprats, Patera."

"I know what we're talking about."

"The gods don't come any more anyhow. Not to Viron, so why not? That last time was when I was—wasn't even born yet."

Silk nodded. "Nor I."

"Then what do you care? You're never going to see one anyway."

Silk smiled ruefully. "We're getting very far from the subject, aren't we?"

"I don't know." Orchid scratched her head and examined her nails. "Maybe. Or maybe not. Did you know that this place used to be a manteion?"

Stunned again, Silk shook his head.

"It did. Or anyhow, some of it did, the back part on Music Street. Only the gods didn't come around very much any more, even if they still did it once in a while back then. So they closed it down, and the ones that owned this house then bought it and tore down the back wall and joined the two together. Maybe that's why, huh? I'll get Orpine to show you around. Some of the old stuff's still back there, and you can have it if there's anything you want."

"That's very kind of you," Silk said.

"I'm a nice person. Ask anybody." Orchid whistled shrilly. "Orpine'll be along in a minute. Anything you want to know, just ask her."

"Thank you, I will. May I leave my sacra here until I require them?" The prospect of separation from his triptych made Silk uneasy. "Will they be safe?"

"Your sack? Better than the fisc. You could leave that box thing, too. Only I've been wondering, you know about the old manteion in back. We call it the playhouse. Could that be why it's happening?"

"I don't know."

"I asked one of the others and he said not. But I kind of wonder. Maybe the gods don't like some of the stuff we do here."

"They do not," Silk told her.

"You haven't even seen anything, Patera. We're not as bad as you think."

Silk shook his head. "I don't think you bad at all, Orchid, and neither do the gods. If they thought you bad, nothing that you could do would dismay them. They detest all the evil that you do—and all that I do—because they see in us the potential to do good."

"Well, I've been thinking maybe they sent this devil to get even with us." Orchid whistled again. "What's keeping that girl!"

"The gods do not send us devils," Silk told her, "and indeed, they destroy them wherever they meet them, deleting them from Mainframe. That, at least, is the legend. It's in the Writings, and I have them here in my bag. Would you like me to read the passage?" He reached for his glasses.

"No. Just tell me so I can understand it."

"All right." Silk squared his shoulders. "Pas made the whorl, as you know. When it was complete, he invited his queen, their five daughters and their two sons, and a few friends to share it with him. However—"

From the other side of the sun-bright doorway, someone screamed in terror.

Orchid lunged out of her chair with praiseworthy speed. Limping a little and repeating to himself Crane's injunction against running, Silk trailed after her, walking as quickly as he could.

The courtyard was lined with doorways on both floors. As he searched for the source of the disturbance, it seemed to him that whole companies of young women in every possible stage of undress were popping in and out of them, though he paid them little attention.

The dead woman lay halfway up a flight of rickety steps thrown down like a ladder by the sagging gallery above; she was naked, and the fingers of her left hand curled about the hilt of a dagger jutting from her ribs below her left breast. Her head was angled so sharply in Silk's direction that it almost appeared that her neck was broken. He found her oddly contorted face at once horrible and familiar.

Against all his training, he covered that face with his handkerchief before beginning to swing his beads.

It quieted the women somewhat, although the dagger, the wound it had made, and the blood that had so briefly spurted from that wound were still visible.

Orchid shouted, "Who did this? Who stabbed her?" and a puffy-eyed brunette, nearly as naked as the woman sprawled on the steps, drawled, "She did, Orchid—she killed herself. Use your head. Or if you won't, use your eyes."

Kneeling on a blood-spattered step just below the dead woman's head, Silk swung his beads, first forward-and-back, then side-to-side, thus describing the sign of addition. "I convey to you, my daughter, the forgiveness of all the gods. Recall now the words of Pas, who said, 'Do my will, live in peace, multiply, and do not disturb my seal. Thus you shall escape my wrath. Go willingly, and any wrong that you have ever done shall be forgiven.' O my daughter, know that this Pas and all the lesser gods have empowered me to forgive you in their names. And I do forgive you, remitting every crime and wrong. They are expunged." With his

beads, Silk traced the sign of subtraction. "You are blessed." Bobbing his
head nine times, as the ritual demanded, he traced the sign of addition.

A female voice breathed curses somewhere to his right, blasphemy
following obscenity. "Hornbuss Pas shag you Pas whoremaster Pas horn-
swallow Chidna sick-licker Pas . . ." It sounded to Silk as though the
speaker did not know what she was saying, and might well be unaware
that she was speaking at all.

"I pray you to forgive us, the living," he continued, and once again
formed the sign of addition with his beads above the dead woman's
handkerchief-shrouded head. "I and many another have wronged you
often, my daughter, committing terrible crimes and numerous offenses
against you. Do not hold them in your heart, but begin the life that
follows life in innocence, all these wrongs forgiven." He made the sign of
subtraction again.

A statuesque girl spat; her tightly curled hair was the color of ripe
raspberries. "What are you doing that for? Can't you see she's stiff?
She's dead, and she can't hear a shaggy word you're saying." At the final
phrase her voice cracked, and Silk realized that it was she whom he had
heard swearing.

He gripped his beads more tightly and bent lower as he reached the
effectual point in the liturgy of pardon. The sun beating down upon his
neck might have been the burning iron hand of Twice-Headed Pas himself, crushing him to earth while ceaselessly demanding that he perfectly
enunciate each hallowed word and execute every sacred rubric fault-
lessly. "In the name of all the gods, you are forgiven forever, my daughter. I speak here for Great Pas, for Divine Echidna, for Scalding
Scylla . . ." Here it was allowable to halt and take a fresh breath, and
Silk did so. "For Marvelous Molpe, for Tenebrous Tartaros, for Highest
Hierax, for Thoughtful Thelxiepeia, for Fierce Phaea, and for Strong
Sphigx. Also for all lesser gods."

Briefly and inexplicably, the glaring sun might almost have been the
swinging, smoking lampion in the Cock. Silk whispered, "The Outsider
likewise forgives you, my daughter, for I speak here for him, too."

After tracing one final sign of addition, he stood and turned toward
the statuesque young woman with the raspberry hair; to his considerable
relief, she was clothed. "Bring me something to cover her with, please.
Her time in this place is over."

Orchid was questioning the puffy-eyed brunette. "Is this her knife?"

"You ought to know." Fearlessly, the brunette reached beneath the

railing to pull the long dagger from the wound. "I don't think so. She'd
have showed it to me, most likely, and I've never seen it before."

Crane came down the steps, stooped over the dead woman, and
pressed his fingers to her wrist. After a second or two, he squatted and
laid an ausculator to her side.

(We acknowledge this state we call death with so much reluctance, Silk
thought, not for the first time. Surely it can't be natural to us.)

Withdrawing the dagger had increased the seepage from the wound;
under all the shrill hubbub, Silk could hear the dead woman's blood
dripping from the steps to the crumbling brick pavement of the courtyard, like the unsteady ticking of a broken clock.

Orchid was peering nearsightedly at the dagger. "It's a man's. A man
called Cat." Turning to face the courtyard, she shouted, "Shut up, all of
you! Listen to me! Do any of you know a cull named Cat?"

A small, dark girl in a torn chemise edged closer. "I do. He comes here
sometimes."

"Was he here last night? How long since you've seen him?"

The girl shook her head. "I'm not sure, Orchid. A month, maybe."

The corpulent woman waddled toward her, holding out the dagger, the
younger women parting before her like so many ducklings before a duck.
"You know where he lives? Who's he get, usually?"

"No. Me. Orpine sometimes, if I'm busy."

Crane stood up, glanced at Silk and shook his head, and put away his
ausculator.

Blood's bellow surprised them all. "What's going on here?" Thick-
bodied and a full head taller than most of the women, he strode into the
courtyard with something of the air of a general coming onto a battle-
field.

When Orchid did not answer, the raspberry-haired girl said wearily,
"Orpine's dead. She just killed herself." She had a clean sheet under her
arm, neatly folded.

"What for?" Blood demanded.

No one replied. The raspberry-haired girl shook out her sheet and
passed a corner up to Crane. Together, they spread the sheet over the
dead woman.

Silk put away his beads and went down the steps to the courtyard. Half
to himself he muttered, "She didn't—not forever. Not even as long as I."

Orchid turned to look at him. "No, she didn't. Now shut up."

Musk had taken the dagger from her. After scrutinizing it himself, he
held it out for Blood's inspection. Orchid explained, "A cully they call

Cat comes here sometimes. He must've given it to her, or left it behind in her room."

Blood sneered. "Or she stole it from him."

"My girls don't steal!" As a tower long subverted by a hidden spring collapses, Orchid burst into tears; there was something terrible, Silk felt, in seeing that fat, indurated face contorted like a heartsick child's. Blood slapped her twice, forehand and backhand, without effect, though both blows echoed from the walls of the courtyard.

"Don't do that again," Silk told him. "It won't help her, and it may harm you."

Ignoring him, Blood pointed to the still form beneath the sheet. "Somebody get that out of sight. You there. Chenille. You're plenty big enough. Pick her up and carry her to her room."

The raspberry-haired woman backed away, trembling, the rouged spots on each high cheekbone glaring and unreal.

"May I see that, please?" Deftly, Silk took the dagger from Musk. Its hilt was bleached bone; burned into the bone with a needle and hand-dyed, a scarlet cat strutted with a tiny black mouse in its jaws. The cat's fiery tail circled the hilt. Following the puffy-eyed brunette's example, Silk reached under the railing and retrieved his handkerchief from beneath the sheet. The slender, tapering blade was highly polished, but not engraved. "Nearly new," he muttered. "Not terribly expensive, but not cheap either."

Musk said, "Any fool can see that," and took back the dagger.

"Patera." Blood cleared his throat. "You were here. Probably you saw her do it."

Silk's mind was still on the dagger. "Do what?" he asked.

"Kill herself. Let's get out of this sun." With a hand on Silk's elbow, Blood guided him into the spotted shade of the gallery, displacing a chattering circle of nearly naked women.

"No, I didn't see it," Silk said slowly. "I was inside, talking to Orchid."

"That's too bad. Maybe you want to think about it a little more. Maybe you saw it after all, through a window or something."

Silk shook his head.

"You agree that this was a suicide, though, don't you, Patera? Even if you didn't see it yourself?" Blood's tone made his threat obvious.

Silk leaned back against the spalled shiprock, sparing his broken ankle. "Her hand was still on the knife when I first saw her body."

Blood smiled. "I like that. In that case, Patera, you agree that there's no reason to report this."

"I certainly wouldn't want to if I were in your place." To himself, Silk reluctantly admitted that he felt sure the dead woman had been no suicide, that the law required that her death by violence be reported to the authorities (though he had no illusions about the effort they would expend upon the death of such a woman), and that if he were somehow to find himself in Blood's place he would leave it as rapidly as possible— though neither honor nor morality required him to say any of these things, since saying them would be futile and would unquestionably endanger the manteion. It was all perfectly reasonable and nicely reasoned; but as he surveyed it, he felt a surge of self-contempt.

"I think we understand each other, Patera. There are three or four witnesses I could produce if I needed them—people who saw her do it. But you know how that is."

Silk forced himself to nod his agreement; he had never realized that even passive assent to crime required so much resolution. "I believe so. Three or four of these unhappy young women, you mean. Their testimony would not carry much weight, however; and they would be apt to presume upon your obligation afterward."

Under Musk's direction, a burly man with less hair even than Blood had picked up the dead woman's body, wrapping it in the sheet. Silk saw him carry it to the door beyond the entrance to Orchid's office, which Musk opened for him.

"That's right. I couldn't have put it better myself." Blood lowered his voice. "We've been having way too much trouble here as it is. The Guards have been in here three times in the past month, and they're starting to talk about closing us down. Tonight I'll have to come up with some way to get rid of it."

"To dispose of that poor woman's body, you mean. You know, I've been terribly slow about this, I suppose because these aren't the sort of people I'm accustomed to. She was Orpine, wasn't she? One of these women mentioned it. She must have had the room next to Orchid's office. Musk and another man have taken her body there, at any rate."

"Yeah, that was Orpine. She used to help out Orchid now and then, running the place." Blood turned away.

Silk watched him stride across the courtyard. Blood had called himself a thief the night before; it struck Silk now that he had been wrong—had been lying, in fact, in order to romanticize what he really did, though he would steal, no doubt, if given an opportunity to do so without risk; he was the sort of person who would consider theft clever, and would be inclined to boast of it.

But the fact was that Blood was simply a tradesman—a tradesman whose trades happened to be forbidden by law, and were inescapably colored by that. That he himself, Patera Silk, did not like such men probably meant only that he did not understand them as well as his own vocation required.

He strove to reorder his thoughts, shifting Blood (and himself as well) out of the criminal category. Blood was a tradesman, or a merchant of sorts; and one of his employees had been killed, almost certainly not by him or even under his direction. Silk recalled the pictured cat on the dagger; it reminded him of the engraving on the little needler, and he took it out to re-examine. There were golden hyacinths on each ivory grip because it had been made for a woman called Hyacinth.

He dropped it back into his pocket.

Blood's name . . . If the dagger had been made for him, the picture on its hilt would have shown blood, presumably: a bloody dagger of the same design, perhaps, or something of that sort. The cat had held a mouse in its jaws, and mice thus caught by cats bled, of course; but he could recall no blood in the picture, and the captive mouse had been quite small. He was no artist, but after putting himself in the place of the one who had drawn and tinted that picture, he decided that the mouse had been included mostly to indicate that the cat was in fact a cat, and not some other cat-like animal, a panther for example. The mouse had been a kind of badge, in other words.

The cat itself had been scarlet, but hardly with blood; even a large mouse would not have bled as much as that, and the cat had presumably been tinted to indicate that it was somehow burning. Its upright tail had actually been tipped with fire.

He took a step away from the wall and was punished by a flash of pain. On one knee, he pulled down his stocking and unwound Crane's wrapping, then flogged the guiltless wall he had just deserted.

When the wrapping was back in place, he went into the room next to Orchid's cramped office. It was larger than he had expected, and its furnishings were by no means devoid of taste. After glancing at a shattered hand mirror and a blue dressing gown he picked up from the floor, he uncovered the dead woman's face.

He found Blood in a private supper room with Musk and the burly man who had carried Orpine's body, discussing the advisability of keeping the yellow house closed that night.

Uninvited, Silk pulled up a chair and sat down. "May I interrupt? I have a question and a suggestion. Neither one should take long."

Musk gave him an icy stare.

Blood said, "They'd better not."

"The question first. What's become of Doctor Crane? He was out there with us a moment ago, but when I looked for him after you left I couldn't find him."

When Blood did not answer, the burly man said, "He's checking out the girls so they don't give anybody anything he hasn't got already. You know what I mean, Patera?"

Silk nodded. "I do indeed. But where does he do it? Is there some sort of infirmary—"

"He goes to their rooms. They got to undress and wait in their rooms until he gets there. When he's through with them, they can go out if they want to."

"I see." Silk stroked his cheek, his eyes thoughtful.

"If you're looking for him, he's probably upstairs. He always does the upstairs first."

"Fine," Blood said impatiently. "Crane's gone back to work. Why shouldn't he? You'd better do the same, Patera. I still want this place exorcised, and in fact it needs it now more than ever. Get busy."

"I am about my work," Silk told him. "This is it, you see, or at least it's a part of it, and I believe that I can help you. You spoke of disposing of that poor girl's—of Orpine's—body. I suggest that we bury it."

Blood shrugged. "I'll see about doing something—she won't be found, and she won't be missed. Don't worry about it."

"I mean that we should inter it as other women's bodies are interred," Silk explained patiently. "There must be a memorial sacrifice for her at my manteion first, of course. Tomorrow's Scylsday, and I can combine the memorial service with our weekly Scylsday sacrifice. We've a man in the neighborhood who has a decent wagon. We've used him before. If none of these women are willing to wash and dress their friend's body, I can provide one who will take care of that as well."

Grinning, Blood thumped Silk on the arm. "And if some shaggy hoppy sticks his nose in, why we didn't do anything irregular. We had an augur and a funeral, and buried the poor girl in respectable fashion—he's intruding on our grief. You're a real help, Patera. When can you get your man here?"

"As soon as I return to my manteion, I suppose, which will be as soon as I've exorcised this house."

Blood shook his head. "I want to get her out of here. What about that sibyl I talked to yesterday? Couldn't she get him?"

Silk nodded.

"Good." Blood turned to the handsome young man beside him. "Musk, go down to the manteion on Sun Street and ask for Maytera Marble—"

Silk interrupted. "She'll probably be in the cenoby. The front door's on Silver Street, or you could go through the garden and knock at the back."

"And tell her there's going to be a funeral tomorrow. Have her get this man with the wagon for you. What's his name, Patera?"

"Loach."

"Get Loach and his wagon, or if he's not available, get somebody else. You don't know what happened to Orpine. A doctor's looked at her, and she's dead, and Patera here is going to take care of the funeral for us, and that's all you know. Get the woman, too. I don't think any of these sluts could face up to it."

"Moorgrass," Silk put in.

"Get her. You and the woman ride in the wagon so you can show this cully Loach where it is. If the woman has to have anything to work with, see that she brings it with her. Now get going."

Musk nodded and hurried away.

"Meantime you can get back to your exorcism, Patera. Have you started yet?"

"No. I'd hardly arrived when this happened, and I want to find out a great deal more about the manifestations they have experienced here." Silk paused, stroking his cheek. "I said that I'd just arrived, and that is true; but I've had time enough to make one mistake already. I told Orchid that I didn't care what the devils—or perhaps I should say *the devil*, because she spoke as though there were only one—had been up to. I said it because it was what they taught us to say in the schola, but I believe it may be an error in this case. I should speak with Orchid again."

The burly man grunted. "I can tell you. Mostly it's breakin' mirrors."

"Really?" Silk leaned forward. "I would never have guessed it. What else?"

"Rippin' up the girls' clothes."

The burly man looked toward Blood, who said, "Sometimes they're not as friendly as we'd like them to be to the bucks. The girls aren't, I mean. A couple times one's talked crazy, and naturally the buck didn't like it. Maybe it was just nerves, but the girls got hurt."

"And we don't like that," the burly man said. "I got both those culls pretty good, but it's bad for business."

"You have no idea what may be doing this?"

"Devils. That's what everybody says." The burly man looked toward Blood again. "Jefe?"

"Ask Orchid," Blood told Silk. "She'll know. I only know what she tells me, and if an exorcism makes everybody feel better . . ." He shrugged.

Silk rose. "I'll speak to Orchid if I can. I realize she's upset, but I may be able to console her. That, too, is a part of my work. Eventually, I'd like a talk with Chenille as well. That's the tall woman with the fiery hair, isn't it? Chenille?"

Blood nodded. "She's probably gone by now, but she'll be back around dinner. Orchid's got a walk-up upstairs over the big room out front."

Chenille opened the door to Orchid's rooms and showed Silk in. Still wearing the pink peignoir, Orchid was sitting on a wide green-velvet couch in the big sellaria, her hard, heavy face as composed as it had been when they had talked in the cramped office downstairs.

Chenille waved toward a chair. "Have a seat, Patera." She herself sat down next to Orchid and put her arm around her shoulders. "He says Blood sent him up to talk to us. I said all right, but he'll probably come back later if you'd rather."

"I'm fine," Orchid told her.

Looking at her, Silk could believe it; Chenille herself seemed more in need of solace.

"What do you want, Patera?" Orchid's voice was harsher than he remembered. "If you're here to tell me how she's gone to Mainframe and all that, save it till later. If you still want somebody to show you around my place, Chenille can do it."

There was a glass on the wall to the left of the couch. Silk was watching it nervously, but no floating face had yet appeared. "I'd like to speak with you in private for a few minutes, that's all."

To Chenille he added, "I was going to say that it would give you a chance to get dressed—so many of you here are not—but I see that you're dressed already."

"Go out," Orchid said. And then, "It was nice of you to worry about me, Chenille. I won't forget this."

The tall girl rose, smoothing her skirt. "I was going to look for a new gown, before this happened."

"I have to speak to you, too," Silk told her, "and this should only take a few minutes. You can wait for me, if you prefer. Otherwise, I would appreciate it very much if you came to my manteion this evening."

"I'll be in my room."

Silk nodded. "That will be better. Please pardon me for not rising; I injured my ankle last night." He watched Chenille as she went out, waiting until she had closed the door behind her.

"Nice-looking, isn't she?" Orchid said. "Only she'd bring in more if she wasn't so tall. Maybe you like them that way. Or is it the hips?"

"What I like hardly matters."

"Good hips, nice waist for a girl as big as she is, and the biggest boobs in the place. Sure you won't change your mind?"

Silk shook his head. "I'm surprised you didn't mention her kind disposition. There must be a great deal of good in her, or she wouldn't have come here to comfort you."

Orchid stood up. "You want a drink, Patera? I've got wine and whatnot in the cabinet here."

"No, thank you."

"I do." Orchid opened the cabinet and filled a small goblet with straw-colored brandy.

"She seemed quite depressed," Silk ventured. "She must have been a close friend of Orpine's."

"Chenille's a real rust bucket, to hand you the lily, Patera, and they're always pretty far down anytime they're straight."

Silk snapped his fingers. "I knew I'd heard that name before."

Orchid resumed her seat, swirled her brandy, inhaled its aroma, and balanced the goblet precariously on the arm of the couch. "Somebody told you about her, huh?"

"A man I know happened to mention her, that's all. It doesn't matter." He waved the question away. "Aren't you going to drink that?" After he had spoken, he realized that Blood had asked the same question of him the previous night.

Orchid shook her head. "I don't drink until the last buck's gone. That's my rule, and I'm going to stick to it, even today. I just want to know it's there. Did you come here to talk about Chen, Patera?"

"No. Can we be overheard here? I ask for your sake, Orchid, not for my own."

She shook her head again.

"I've heard that houses like this often have listening devices."

"Not this one. And if it did, I wouldn't have any in here."

Silk indicated the glass. "The monitor doesn't have to appear to overhear what is said in a room, or so one's given me to understand. Does the monitor of that glass report to you alone?"

Orchid had the brandy goblet again, swirling the straw-colored fluid until it climbed the goblet to the rim. "That glass has never worked for as long as I've owned this house, Patera. I wish it did."

"I see." Silk limped across the room to the glass and clapped his hands loudly. The room's lights brightened, but no monitor answered his summons. "We have a glass like this in Patera Pike's bedroom—I mean in the room that he once occupied. I should try to sell it. I would think that even an inoperable glass must be worth something."

"What is it you want with me, Patera?"

Silk returned to his chair. "What I really want is to find some more tactful way of saying this. I haven't found it. Orpine was your daughter, wasn't she?"

Orchid shook her head.

"Are you going to deny her even in death?"

He had not known what to expect: tears, or hysteria, or nothing—and had felt himself ready for them all. But now Orchid's face appeared to be coming apart, to be losing all cohesion, as if her mouth and her bruised and swollen cheeks and her hard hazel eyes no longer obeyed a common will. He wanted her to hide that terrible face in her hands; she did not, and he turned his own away.

There was a window on the other side of the couch. He went to it, parted its heavy drapes, and threw it open. It overlooked Lamp Street, and though he would have called the day hot, the breeze that entered Orchid's sellaria seemed cool and fresh.

"How did you know?" Orchid asked.

He limped back to his chair. "That's what's wrong with this place, not enough open windows. Or one thing, anyhow." Wanting to blow his nose, he took out his handkerchief, saw Orpine's blood on it just in time, and put it away hastily.

"How did you know, Patera?"

"Don't any of the others know? Or at least guess?"

Orchid's face was still out of control, afflicted with odd, almost spastic twitchings. "Some of them have probably thought about it. I don't think she ever told anybody, and I didn't treat her any better than the rest." Orchid gulped air. "Worse, whenever there was any difference. I made her help me, and I was always yelling at her."

"I'm not going to ask you how this happened; it's none of my affair."

"Thanks, Patera." Orchid sounded as though she meant it. "Her father took her. I couldn't have, not then. But he said—he said—"

"You don't have to tell me," Silk repeated.

She had not heard. "Then I found her on the street, you know? She was thirteen, only she said fifteen and I believed her. I didn't know it was her." Orchid laughed, and her laughter was worse than tears.

"There's really no need for you to torment yourself like this."

"I'm not. I've been wanting to tell somebody about it ever since Sphigx was a cub. You already know, so it can't do any harm. Besides, she's—she's—"

"Gone," Silk supplied.

Orchid shook her head. "Dead. The only one alive, and I'll never have any more now. You know how places like this work, Patera?"

"No, and I suppose I should."

"It's pretty much like a boarding house. Some places, the girls are pretty much like in the Alambrera. They don't hardly ever let them out, and they take all their money. I was in a place like that once for almost two years."

"I'm glad that you escaped."

Orchid shook her head again. "I didn't. I got sick and they kicked me out—it was the best thing that ever happened to me. What I wanted to say, Patera, is I'm not like that here. My girls rent their rooms, and they can go anytime. About the only thing they can't do is bring in a buck without his paying. Are you with me?"

"I'm not sure I am," Silk admitted.

"Like if they meet him outside. If they bring him back here, he has to pay the house. So do those that come here looking. Tonight, we'll have maybe fifty or a hundred come. They pay the house, and then we show them all the girls that aren't busy, downstairs in the big room."

"Suppose that I were to come," Silk said slowly. "Not dressed as I am now, but in ordinary clothes. And I wanted a particular woman."

"Chenille."

Silk shook his head. "Another one."

"How about Poppy? Little girl, pretty dark."

"All right," Silk said. "Suppose I wanted Poppy, but she didn't want to take me to her room?"

"Then she wouldn't have to," Orchid said virtuously, "and you'd have to pick somebody else. Only if she did that very often, I'd kick her out."

"I see."

"Only she wouldn't, Patera. Not to you. She'd jump at you. Any of these girls would."

Orchid smiled, and Silk, confronted by the effect of her bruises, wanted to strike Blood. Hyacinth's azoth was under his tunic—he thrust the thought away.

Orchid had seen and misinterpreted his expression; her smile vanished. "I didn't get to finish telling you about Orpine, Patera. All right if I go on about her?"

Silk said, "Certainly, if you wish."

"I found her on the street, like I told you. That's something I do sometimes, go around looking for somebody if I've got an empty room. She said her name was Pine—you don't hardly ever get a straight name out of them—and she was fifteen, and it never hit me. It just didn't."

"I understand," Silk said.

"Somebody dusted her dial, you know what I mean? So I said, listen, lots of girls live with me, and nobody lays a finger on them. You come along, and we'll give you a good hot meal, free, and you'll see. So she said she didn't have the rent money, like they always do, and I said I'd trust her for the first month. That's what I always say.

"After she'd been here nearly a year, she ducked out of the big room. I said what's wrong, and she said her father had come in and he'd made her do certain things for him when she was little, and that was why she'd run out on him. You know what I mean, Patera?"

Silk nodded, his fists clenched.

"She told me his name, and I went out and looked at him again, and it was him. So then I knew who she was, and by and by I told her all about it." Orchid smiled; it seemed strange to Silk that the identical word should indicate her earlier expression as well.

"I'm glad I did it now. Real glad. I told her not to expect any favors, and I didn't give her any. Or at least, not very often. What I did, though —what I did—"

Silk waited patiently, his eyes averted.

"What I did was start having cake on the birthdays, so we could have it on hers. And I called her Orpine instead of Pine, and pretty soon everybody did." Orchid daubed at her eyes with the hem of the pink peignoir. "All right, that's it. Who told you?"

"Your faces, to begin with."

Orchid nodded. "She was beautiful. Everybody said so."

"Not when I saw her, because there was something in her face that didn't belong there. Still it struck me that her face was a younger version of your own, although that could have been coincidence or my imagination. A moment later I heard her name—Orpine. It sounds a great deal like yours, and it seemed to me that it was such a name as a woman named Orchid might choose, especially if she had lost an earlier daughter. Did you? You don't have to tell me about it."

Orchid nodded.

"Because orpines, which only sound like orchids, have another name. Country people call them live-forevers; and when I thought of that other name, I said, more or less to myself, that she had not; and you agreed. Then when Blood suggested that she might have stolen the dagger that killed her, you burst into tears and I knew. But to tell you the truth, I was already nearly certain."

Orchid nodded slowly. "Thanks, Patera. Is that all? I'd like to be alone for a little while."

Silk rose. "I understand. I wouldn't have disturbed you if I hadn't wanted to let you know that Blood's agreed that your daughter should be buried with the rites of the Chapter. Her body will be washed and dressed—laid out, as the people who do it say—and carried to my manteion, on Sun Street. We'll hold her service in the morning."

Orchid stared at him incredulously. "Blood's paying for this?"

"No." Silk actually had not considered the matter of expenses, though he knew only too well that some of those connected with the final offices of the dead could not be avoided. His mind whirled before he recalled Blood's two cards, which he had set aside for the Scylsday sacrifice in any event. "Or rather, yes. Blood gave me—gave my manteion, I should say, a generous gift earlier. We'll use that."

"No, not Blood." Orchid rose heavily. "*I'll* pay it, Patera. How much?"

Silk compelled himself to be scrupulously honest. "I should tell you that we often bury the poor, and sometimes they have no money at all. The generous gods have always seen to it—"

"I'm not poor!" Orchid flushed an angry red. "I been pretty flat sometimes, sure. Hasn't everybody? But I'm not flat now, and this's my sprat. The other girl, I had to—Oh, shag you, you shaggy butcher! How much for a good one?"

Here was opportunity. Not merely to save the manteion the cost of Orpine's burial, but to pay for earlier graves bought but never paid for; Silk jettisoned his scruples to seize the moment. "If it's really not inconvenient, twenty cards?"

"Let's go into the bedroom, Patera. That's where the book is. Come on."

She had opened the door and vanished into the next room before he could protest. Through the doorway he could see a rumpled bed, a cluttered vanity table, and a chaise longue half buried in gowns.

"Come on in." Orchid laughed, and this time there was real merriment in the sound. "I bet you've never been in a woman's bedroom before, have you?"

"Once or twice." Hesitantly, Silk stepped through the doorway, looking twice at the bed to assure himself that no one lay dying there. Presumably Orchid thought of it as a place for rest and lust, and possibly even for love. Silk could only too easily imagine his next visit, in ten years or twenty. All beds became deathbeds at last.

"Your mama's. You've gone into your mama's bedroom, I bet." Orchid plumped herself down before the vanity table, swept a dozen colored bottles and jars aside, and elevated an ormolu inkstand to the place of honor before her.

"Oh, yes. Many times."

"And looked through her things when she was out of the house. I know how you young bucks do." There were twenty bedraggled peacock quills at least wilting in the rings of the ormolu inkstand. Orchid selected one, then wrinkled her nose at it.

"I can sharpen that for you, if you like." Silk got out his pen case.

"Would you? Thanks." Revolving on the vanity stool, she handed the peacock quill to him. "Did you ever try on her underwear?"

Silk looked up from the quill, surprised. "No, I never even thought of it. I did open a drawer once and peep into it, though. I felt so bad about it that I told her the next day. Do you have something to catch the shavings?"

"Don't worry about them. You had a nice mama, huh? Is she still alive?"

Silk shook his head. "Would you prefer a broad nib?" Orchid did not reply, and he, contemplating the splayed and frowzy one before him, decided to give her one anyway. A broad nib used more ink, but she would not mind that; and broad nibs lasted longer.

"Mine died when I was little. I guess she was nice, but I really don't remember her very well. When somebody's dead, Patera, can they come back and see people they care about, if they want to?"

"It depends on what is meant by *see.*" With the slender blade of the long-handled penknife, Silk sliced yet another whitish sliver from the nib. He was accustomed to goose and crow quills; this was larger than either.

"Talk to them. Visit with them a while, or just let them see you."

"No," Silk said.

"Just no? Why not?"

"Hierax forbids it." He returned the quill to her and snapped his pen case shut. "If he did not, the living would live at the direction of the dead, repeating their mistakes again and again."

"I used to wonder why she never came to see me," Orchid said. "You know, I haven't thought about that in years, and now I'll think about Orpine, hoping that Hierax will let her out once or twice so I can see her again. Have a seat there on the bed, Patera. You're making me jittery."

Reluctantly, Silk smoothed the canary-colored sheet and sat down.

"A minute ago, you said twenty cards. That's about as cheap as they come, I bet."

"It would be modest," Silk admitted, "but certainly not contemptible."

"All right, what about fifty? What would she get for that much?"

"Gods!" He considered. "I can't be absolutely sure. A better sacrifice and a much better casket. Flowers. A formal bier with draperies. Perhaps a—"

"I'll make it a hundred," Orchid announced. "It will make me feel better. A hundred cards, and everything the best." Orchid plunged her quill into the inkwell.

Silk opened his mouth, closed it again, and put his pen case away.

"And you can say that I was her mother. I want you to say it. What do you call that thing where they stand up and talk in the manteion?"

"The ambion," Silk said.

"Right. I never told them here, because I knew—we both knew—what sort of things the other girls would say about her, and me too, behind our backs. You tell them tomorrow. From the ambion. And put it on her stone."

Silk nodded. "I will."

With florid sweeps of her quill, Orchid was writing the draft. "Tomorrow, right? When'll it be?"

"I had thought at eleven."

"I'll be there, Patera." Orchid's face hardened. "We all will."

Silk was still shaking his head as he closed Orchid's door behind him. Chenille was waiting in the hall outside; he wondered whether she had been eavesdropping, and if so how much she had heard.

She said, "You wanted to talk to me?"

"Not here."

"I waited in my room. You never came, so I came over here to see what was up."

"Of course." Orchid's draft for a hundred cards was still in his hand; he folded it once and thrust it into the pocket of his robe. "I told you I'd be there in a few minutes, didn't I? We were a great deal longer than that, I'm afraid. I can only apologize."

"You still want to talk in my room?"

Silk hesitated, then nodded. "We must speak privately, and I'd like to see where it is."

CHAPTER
11   SUMMONED

"What Orchid's got used to be for the owner and his wife," Chenille explained. "Then their sprats had rooms close to theirs, then upper servants, then maids, I guess. I'm about halfway on the inside. That's not so bad."

Turning left, Silk followed her down the musty hallway.

"Half look out on the court like mine does. That's not as good as it sounds, because they have big parties in there sometimes and it gets pretty noisy unless you stay till the end, and usually I don't. You take those drunks up to your room and they get sick—then you never get the smell out. Maybe you think it's gone, but wait for a rainy night."

They turned the corner.

"Sometimes they chase the girls along the gangways and make lots of noise. But the outside rooms on this side have windows on the alley. There's not much light, and it smells bad."

"I see," Silk said.

"So that's not so good either, and they have to have bars on their windows. I'd rather hang on to what I've got." Chenille halted, pulled a key on a string from between ample breasts, and opened a door.

"Are the rooms beyond yours vacant?"

"Huh-uh. I don't think there's an empty room in the place. She's been turning them away for the last month or so. I've got a girlfriend that would like to move in, and I've got to tell her as soon as somebody goes."

"Perhaps she might occupy Orpine's room." Chenille's was less than half the size of Orchid's bedroom, with most of its floorspace taken up by an oversized bed. There were chests along the wall, and an old wardrobe to which a hasp and padlock had been added.

"Yeah. Maybe. I'll tell her. You want me to leave the door open?"

"I doubt that it would be wise."

"All right." She closed it. "I won't lock us in. I don't lock when there's a man in here, it's not a good idea. You want to sit on the bed with me?"

Silk shook his head.

"Suit yourself." She sat down, and he lowered himself gratefully onto one of the chests, the lioness-headed stick clamped between his knees.

"All right, what is it?"

Silk glanced toward the open window. "I should imagine it would be easy for someone to stand there on the gallery, just out of sight. It would be prudent for you to make sure no one is."

"Look here." She aimed a finger at him. "I don't owe you one single thing, and you're not paying me, not even a couple bits. Orpine was kind of a friend of mine, we didn't fight much, anyhow, and I thought it was nice, what you did for her, so when you said you wanted to talk to me, I said fine. But I've got things to do, and I'll have to come back here tonight and sweat it like a sow. So talk, and I better like what you're going to say."

"What would you do if you didn't, Chenille?" Silk asked mildly. "Stab me? I don't think so; you've no dagger now."

Her brightly painted mouth fell open then clamped shut again.

Silk leaned back against the wall. "It wasn't terribly obscure. If the Civil Guard had been notified, as I suppose it should have been, I'm certain they would have understood what happened at once. It took me a minute or two, but then I know very little about such things."

Her eyes blazed. "She did it herself! You saw it. She stabbed herself." Chenille gestured toward her own waist.

"I saw her hand on the hilt of your dagger, certainly. Did you put it there? Or was it only that she was trying to pull it out when she died?"

"You can't prove anything!"

Silk sighed. "Please don't be foolish. How old are you? Honestly now."

"What does that have to do with anything?"

"Nothing, I suppose. It's only that you make me feel very old and wise, just as the children at our palaestra do. You're not much older than some of them, I believe."

For several seconds Chenille gnawed her lip. At last she said, "Nineteen. That's the lily word, too, or anyhow I think it is. As well as I can figure, I'm about nineteen. I'm older than a lot of the girls here."

"I'm twenty-three," Silk told her. "By the way, may I ask you to call me Patera? It will help me to remember who I am. What I am, if you prefer."

Chenille shook her head. "You think I'm some cank chit you can get to suck any pap you want to, don't you? Well, listen, I know a lot you never even dream about. I didn't stick Orpine. By Sphigx, I didn't! And you can't prove I did, either. What're you after, anyhow?"

"Fundamentally I'm after you. I want to help you, if I can. All the gods —the Outsider knows that someone should have, long ago."

"Some help!"

Silk raised his shoulders and let them drop. "Little help so far, indeed; but we've hardly begun. You say that you know much more than I. Can you read?"

Chenille shook her head, her lips tight.

"You see, although you know a great deal that I do not—I'm not denying that at all—what it comes down to is that we know different things. You are wise enough to swear falsely by Sphigx, for example; you know that nothing will happen to you if you do that, and I'm beginning to feel it's something I should learn, too. Yesterday morning I wouldn't have dared to do it. Indeed, I would hardly dare now."

"I wasn't lying!"

"Of course you were." Silk laid Blood's stick across his knees and studied the lioness's head for a moment. "You said that I couldn't prove what I say. In one sense, you're quite correct. I couldn't prove my accusation in a court of law, assuming that you were a woman of wealth and position. You're not, but then I have no intention of making my case in any such court. I could convict you to Orchid or Blood easily, however. I'd add that you've admitted your guilt to me, as in fact you have now. Orchid would have the bald man who seems to live here beat you, I suppose, and force you to leave. I won't try to guess what Blood might do. Nothing, perhaps."

The raspberry-haired girl, still seated on the bed, would not meet his eyes.

"I could convince the Civil Guard, also, if I had to. It would be easy, Chenille, because no one cares about you. Very likely no one ever has, and that's why you're here now, living as you do in this house."

"I'm here because the money's good," she said.

"It wouldn't be. Not any longer. The big, bald man—I never learned his name—would knock out a tooth or two, I imagine. What Musk might do if Blood allowed him a free hand I prefer not to speculate on. I don't like him, and it may be that I'm prejudiced. You know him much better, I'm sure."

The girl on the bed made a slight, almost inaudible sound.

"You don't cry easily, do you?"

She shook her head.

"I do." Silk smiled and shrugged again. "Another of my all too numerous faults. I've been close to tears since I first set foot in this place, and the pain in my ankle is no help, I'm afraid. Will you excuse me?"

He pushed down his black stocking and took off Crane's wrapping. It was warm still to his touch, but he lashed the floor with it and replaced it. "Shall I explain to you what happened, or would you prefer to tell me?"

"I'm not going to tell you anything."

"I hope to change your mind about that. It's necessary that you tell me a great deal, eventually." Silk paused to collect his thoughts. "Very well, then. This unhappy house has been plagued by a certain devil. We'll call her that for the present at least, though I believe that I could name her. As I understand it, several people have been possessed at one time or another. Did they all live here, by the way? Or were patrons involved as well? Nobody's talked about that, if some were."

"Only girls."

"I see. What about Orchid? Has she been possessed? She didn't mention it."

Chenille shook her head again.

"Orpine? Was she one of them?"

There was no reply. Silk asked again, with slightly more emphasis, *"Orpine?"*

The door opened, and Crane looked in. "There you are! They said you were still around somewhere. How's your ankle?"

"Quite painful," Silk told him. "The wrapping you lent me helped a great deal at first, but—"

Crane had crouched to touch it. "Good and hot. You're walking too much. Didn't I tell you to stay off your feet?"

"I have," Silk said stiffly, "insofar as possible."

"Well, try harder. As the pain gets worse you will anyhow. How's the exorcism coming?"

"I haven't begun. I'm going to shrive Chenille, and that's far more important."

Looking at Crane, Chenille shook her head.

"She doesn't know it yet, but I am," Silk declared.

"I see. Well, I'd better leave you alone and let you do it." The little physician left, closing the door behind him.

"You were asking about Orpine," Chenille said. "No, she was never possessed that I know of."

"Let's not change the subject so quickly," Silk said. "Will you tell me why that doctor takes such an interest in you?"

"He doesn't."

Silk made a derisive noise. "Come now. He obviously does. Do you think I believe he came here to inquire about my leg? He came here looking for you. No one but Orchid could have told him I was here, and I left her only a few moments ago; almost the last thing she said to me was that she wanted to be alone. I just hope that Crane's interest is a friendly one. You need friends."

"He's my doctor, that's all."

"No," Silk said. "He is indeed your doctor, but that's not all. When Orchid and I heard someone scream and went out into the courtyard, you were fully dressed. It was very noticeable, because you were the only woman present who was."

"I was going out!"

"Yes, precisely. You were going out, and thus dressed, which I found a great relief—sneer if you like. I didn't begin, of course, by asking myself why you were dressed, but why the others weren't; and the answers were harmless and straightforward enough. They'd been up late the previous night. Furthermore, they expected to be examined by Crane, who would make them disrobe in any event, so there was no reason for them to dress until he'd left.

"Crane and I had arrived together just a few minutes earlier, yet you were fully dressed, which was why I noticed you and asked you to bring something to cover poor Orpine's body. The obvious inference is that you had been examined already; and if so, you must certainly have been first. It seemed possible that Crane had begun at the far end of the corridor, but he didn't—this room is only halfway to the old manteion at the back of the house. Why did he take you first?"

"I don't know," Chenille said. "I didn't even know I was. I was waiting for him, and he came in. If nothing's wrong, it only takes a second or two."

"He sells you rust, doesn't he?"

Surprised, Chenille laughed.

"I see I'm wrong—so much for logic. But Crane has rust; he mentioned it to me this morning as something that he could have given me to make me feel better. Orchid and a friend who knows you have both told me you use it, and neither has reason to lie. Furthermore, your behavior when you encountered Orpine confirms it."

Chenille appeared about to speak, and Silk waited for her to do so while silence collected in the stuffy room. At last she said, "I'll level with you, Patera. If I give you the lily word, will you believe me?"

"If you tell me the truth? Yes, certainly."

"All right. Crane doesn't sell me, or anybody, rust. Blood would have his tripes if he did. If you want it, you're supposed to buy it from Orchid. But some girls buy it outside sometimes. I do myself, once in a while. Don't tell them."

"I won't," Silk assured her.

"Only you're dead right, Crane's got it, and sometimes he gives me some, like today. We're friends, you know what I mean? I've done him a few favors and I don't charge him. So he looks at me first, and sometimes he gives me a little present."

"Thank you," Silk said. "And thank you for calling me Patera. I noticed and appreciated that, believe me. Do you want to tell me about Orpine now?"

Chenille shook her head stubbornly.

"Very well, then. You said that Orpine had never been possessed, but that was mendacious—she was possessed at the time of her death, in fact." The moment had come, Silk felt, to stretch the truth in a good cause. "Did you really think that I, an anointed augur, could view her body and not realize that? When Crane had gone you took some of the rust he'd given you, dressed, and left your room by that other door, stepping out onto the gallery, which you call the gangway." Silk paused, inviting contradiction.

"I don't know where you had your dagger, but last year we found that one of the girls at our school had a dagger strapped to her thigh. At any rate, while you were coming down those wooden steps, you came face-to-face with Orpine, possessed. If you hadn't taken the rust Crane gave you, you would probably have screamed and fled; but rust makes people bold and violent. That was how I hurt my ankle last night, as it happens; I encountered a woman who used rust.

"In spite of the rust, Orpine's appearance must have horrified you; you realized you were confronting the devil all of you have come to fear, and your only thought was to kill her. You drew your dagger and stabbed her once, just below the ribs with the blade angled up."

"She said I was beautiful," Chenille whispered. "She tried to touch me, to stroke my face. It wasn't Orpine— I might have knifed Orpine, but not for that. I backed away. She kept coming, and I knifed her. I knifed the devil, and then it was Orpine lying there dead."

Silk nodded. "I understand."

"You figured out my dagger, didn't you? I didn't think of it until it was too late."

"The picture representing your name, you mean. Yes, I did. I had been thinking about Orpine's name ever since I'd heard it. There's no point in going into that here, but I had. Crane gave you the dagger, isn't that right? You said a moment ago that he occasionally makes you a present. Your dagger must have been one of them."

"You think he gave it to me to get me into trouble," Chenille said. "It wasn't like that at all."

"What was it like?"

"One of the other girls had one. She has, most of us have—do you really care about all this?"

"Yes," Silk told her. "I do."

"So she went out that night. She was going to meet him someplace to eat, I guess, only a couple of culls jumped her and tried to pull her down. She plucked, and cut them both. That's what she says. Then she beat the hoof, only she'd got blood on her.

"So I wanted to get one for when I go out, but I don't know much about them, so I asked Crane where I could get a good one, where they wouldn't cheat me. He said he didn't know either, but he'd find out from Musk, because Musk knows all about knives and the rest of it, so next time he brought me that one. He'd got it specially made for me, or anyhow the picture put on."

"I see."

"Do you know, Patera, I'd never even seen chenille, not to know it was my flower anyway, till he brought me a bouquet for my room last spring? And I love it—that's when I did my hair this color. He said sometimes they call it burning cattail. We laugh about it, so when I asked he gave me the dagger. Bucks buy dells things like that pretty often, to show they trust her not to do anything."

"Is Doctor Crane the friend you mentioned?"

"No. That's somebody younger. Don't make me tell you who, unless you want to get me hurt." Chenille fell silent, tight-lipped. "That's abram. This's going to hurt me a lot more, isn't it? But if I don't tell, he might help me if he can."

"Then I won't ask you again," Silk said. "And I'm not going to tell Orchid or Blood, unless I must to save someone else. If the Guard were investigating, I suppose I'd have to tell the officer in charge, but I believe it might be a far worse injustice to turn you over to Blood than to permit you to go unpunished. Since that's the case, I'll let you go unpunished, or almost unpunished, if you'll do as I ask. Orpine's service will take place at eleven tomorrow, at my manteion on Sun Street. Orchid's going to

demand that all of you attend it, and doubtless many of you will. I want
you to be among those who do."

Chenille nodded. "Yeah. Sure, Patera."

"And while the service is in progress, I want you to pray for Orpine
and Orchid, as well as for yourself. Will you do that as well?"

"To Hierax? All right, Patera, if you'll tell me what to say."

Silk gripped Blood's walking stick, flexing it absently between his
hands. "Hierax is indeed the god of death and the caldé of the dead, and
as such is the most appropriate object of worship at any such service. It
will be Scylsday, however, and thus our sacrifice cannot be his alone."

"Uh-huh. That's about the only prayer I know—what they call her
short litany. Will that be all right?"

Silk laid aside the stick and leaned toward Chenille, his decision made.
"There is one more god to whom I wish you to pray—a very powerful
one who may be able to help you, as well as Orchid and poor Orpine. He
is called the Outsider. Do you know anything about him?"

She shook her head. "Except for Pas and Echidna, and the days and
months, I don't even know their names."

"Then you must open your heart to him tomorrow," Silk told her,
"praying as you've never prayed before. Praise him for his kindness
toward me, and tell him how badly you—how badly all of us in this
quarter need his help. If you do that, and your prayers are heartfelt and
truthful, it won't matter what you say."

"The Outsider. All right."

"Now I'm going to shrive you, removing your guilt in the matter of
Orpine's death and any other wrongs that you have done. Kneel here.
You don't have to look at me."

Half the abandoned manteion had been converted into a small theater.
"The old Window's still back there," Chenille explained, pointing. "It's
the back of the stage, sort of, only we always keep a drop in front of it.
There's four or five drops, I think. Anyhow, we go in back of the Window
to towel off and powder, and there's a lot of hoses on the floor and
hanging down back there."

Silk was momentarily puzzled until he realized that the "hoses" were
in actuality sacred cables. "I understand," he said, "but what you describe could be dangerous. Has anyone been hurt?"

"A dell fell off the stage and broke her arm once, but she was pretty
full."

"The powers of Pas must indeed have departed from this place. And no wonder. Very well." He put his bag and the triptych on seats. "Thank you, Chenille. You may go out now if you wish, although I would prefer that you remain to take part in the exorcism."

"If you want me I'll stay, Patera. All right if I grab something to eat?"

"Certainly."

He watched her go, then shut the door to the courtyard behind her. Her mention of food had reminded him not only that he had given the cheese he had intended for his lunch to the bird, but of his fried tomatoes. No doubt Chenille would go to the pastry shop across the street. He shrugged and opened his bag, resolved to divert his mind from food.

There seemed to be a kitchen in the house, however; if Blood had not yet eaten, it was quite possible that he would invite him to lunch when the exorcism had been concluded. How long had it been since he had sat beneath the fig tree, watching Maytera Rose consume fresh rolls? Several hours, surely, but he had failed to share his breakfast with her; he was justly punished.

"I will not eat," he muttered to himself as he unpacked the glass lamps and the little flask of oil, "until someone invites me to a meal; then and only then shall I be free of this vow. Strong Sphigx, hardship is yours! Hear me now."

Perhaps Orchid would wish to speak to him again about the arrangements for tomorrow; judging from her appearance (and thus, as he reminded himself, very possibly unfairly) Orchid ate often and well. She might easily fancy a bowl of grapes or a platter of peach fritters . . .

Largely to take his mind off food, he called, "Are you here, Mucor? Can you hear me?"

There was no reply.

"I know it was you, you see. You've been following me, as you said you would last night. I recognized your face in Teasel's father's face this morning. Was it you that drank her blood? This afternoon I saw your face again, in poor Orpine's."

He waited but there was no whisper at his ear, no voice except his own echoing from the bare shiprock walls.

"Say something!"

A gravid silence filled the deserted manteion.

"That woman screaming in this house last night while I was outside in the floater—it was too apposite for mere chance. The devil was there because I was, and you're that devil, Mucor. I don't understand how you do the things you do, but I know it's you that do them."

He had packed the glass lamps in rags. As he unwrapped one, he caught sight of what might almost have been Mucor's death's-head grin. Carrying a lamp in each hand, he limped to the stage to look more closely at the painted canvas—it was presumably what Chenille had called a drop—behind it.

The scene was a crude mockery of Campion's celebrated painting of Pas enthroned. As depicted here, Pas had two erections as well as two heads; he nursed one in each hand. Before him, worshipful humanity engaged in every perversion that Silk had ever heard of, and several that were entirely new to him. In the original painting, two of Pas's taluses, mighty machines of a peculiarly lovely butter yellow, were still at work upon the whorl, planting a sacred goldenshower in back of Pas's throne. Here the taluses were furnished with obscene war rams, while Pas's blossom-freighted holy tree had been replaced by a gigantic phallus. Overhead the vast, dim faces of the spiritual Pas leered and slavered.

After carefully setting the blue lamps on the edge of the stage, Silk extracted Hyacinth's azoth from beneath his tunic. He wanted to slash the hateful thing before him to ribbons, but to do so would certainly destroy whatever might remain of the Window behind it. He pressed the demon, and with one surgical stroke slit the top of the painted canvas from side to side. The detestable painting vanished with a thump, in a cloud of dust.

Blood came in while he was setting up his triptych in front of the blank, dark face of the Window. Votive lamps burned again before that abandoned Window now, their bright flames stabbing upward from the blue glass as straight as swords; thuribles lifted slender pale columns of sweet smoke from the four corners of the stage.

"What did you do that for?" Blood demanded.

Silk glanced up. "Do what?"

"Destroy the scenery." Blood mounted the three steps at one side of the stage. "Don't you know what that stuff costs?"

"No," Silk told him. "And I don't care. You're going to make a profit of thirteen thousand cards on my manteion. You can use a fraction of it to replace what I've destroyed, if you choose. I don't advise it."

Blood kicked the pile of canvas. "None of the others did anything like this."

"Nor were their exorcisms effective. Mine will be—or so I have reason to believe." With the triptych centered between the lamps to his satisfaction, Silk turned to face Blood. "You are afflicted by devils, or one devil at least. I won't bother to explain just who that devil is now, but do you

know how a place or a person—any person—falls into the power of
devils?"

"Pah! I don't believe in them, Patera. No more than I do in your
gods."

"Are you serious?" Silk bent to retrieve the walking stick Blood had
given him. "You said something of the sort yesterday morning, but you
have a fine effigy of Scylla in front of your villa. I saw it."

"It was there when I acquired the property. But if it hadn't been, I
might have put up something like that anyway, I admit. I'm a loyal son of
Viron, Patera, and I like to show it." Blood stooped to examine the
triptych. "Where's Pas?"

Silk pointed.

"That whirlwind? I thought he was an old man with two heads."

"Any representation of a god is ultimately a lie," Silk explained. "It
may be a convenient lie, and it may even be a reverent one; but it's
ultimately false. Great Pas might choose to appear as your old man, or as
the spiraling storm which is his eldest representation. Neither image
would be more nearly true than the other, or more true than any other—
merely more appropriate."

Blood straightened up. "You were going to tell me about devils."

"But I won't, not at present at least. It would take some time, and you
wouldn't believe me in any case. You've saved me a decidedly unwelcome
walk, however. I want you to assemble every living person in this house in
this theater. Yourself, Musk if he's come back, Crane, Orchid, Chenille,
the bald man, all the young women, and anyone else who may be present.
By the time you get them in here, I will have completed my preparations."

Blood mopped his sweating face with a handkerchief. "I don't take
orders from you, Patera."

"Then I will tell you this much about devils." Silk freed his imagination
and felt it soar. "They are here, and one person has died already. Once
they have tasted blood, they grow fond of it. I might add that it is by no
means unusual to find them acting upon merely verbal resemblances,
notions that you or I might consider only puns. It's apt to occur to them
that if ordinary blood is good, the blood of Blood should be much better.
You'd be wise to keep that in mind."

The women arrived by twos and threes, curious and more or less willingly
driven by Musk and the muscular bald man, whose name seemed to be
Bass; soon they were joined by Loach and Moorgrass from Silk's own

manteion, both frightened and very glad to see him. Eventually Crane and a dry-eyed, grim Orchid took seats in the last row. Silk waited for Blood, Bass, and Musk to join them before he began.

"Let me describe—"

His words were drowned by the chattering of the women.

"Quiet!" Orchid had risen. "Shut up, you sluts!"

"Let me describe," Silk began again, "what has happened here and what we will be trying to accomplish. The entire whorl was originally under the protection of Great Pas, the Father of the Gods. Otherwise it could never have existed."

He paused, studying the faces of the twenty-odd young women before him intently, and feeling rather as if he were addressing Maytera Mint's class in the palaestra. "Great Pas planned every part of it, and it was constructed by his slaves under his direction. In that way were the courses of all our rivers charted, and Lake Limna itself dug deep. In that way were the oldest trees planted, and the manteions through which we are to know him built. You are sitting, of course, in one such manteion. When the whorl was complete, Pas blessed it."

Silk paused again, counting silently to three, as he so often had at the ambion, while he searched the faces of his audience for one that had come to resemble the mad girl's, however subtly. "Even if you're inclined to dispute what I've said, I require that you accept it for the present, for the sake of this exorcism. Is there anyone here who *cannot* accept it? If so, please stand." He stared hard at Blood, but Blood did not rise.

"Very well," Silk continued. "Please understand that it was not merely the whorl as a whole that received Pas's blessing and with it his protection. Each individual part received it as well, and most have it still.

"At times, however, and for good reasons, Pas withdraws his protection from certain parts of this whorl he created. It may be a tree, a field, an animal, a person, or even an entire city. In this instance, it is surely a building—the one we are in now, the one that has since become a part of this house, so that Pas's protection has departed from the entire house."

He let that sink in while his eyes roved from face to face. All of Orchid's women were relatively young, and one or two were strikingly beautiful; many if not most were more than ordinarily good-looking. None resembled Mucor in the least.

"What, you may ask, does that mean? Does it mean that the tree dies or the city burns? No, it does not. Suppose that one of you owned a cat, one that bit and scratched you until at last, in disgust, you thrust your cat out into the street and shut your door. That cat, which once was yours, would not die—or at least, it would not die immediately. But when dogs attacked it, there would be no one to defend it, and any passerby who wished to stone it or lay claim to it could do so with impunity.

"So it is with those of us from whom Pas's blessing has been taken. Some of you, I know, have suffered possession here, and in a few moments I am going to ask one of you who has been possessed to describe it."

A small dark woman at one end of the first row grinned, and though little in her face had changed, it seemed to Silk that he could see the skull that underlay it. He relaxed, and realized that his palms were running with sweat, that the carved handle of Blood's walking stick was slippery with it, his forehead beaded with perspiration that threatened to run into his eyes. He wiped it away with the sleeve of his robe.

"This object behind me was once a Sacred Window—I doubt that there is anyone present who is so ignorant that she does not know that. Through the Window that this once was, Lord Pas spoke to mankind. So it is with the gods, as every one of you must know—they speak to us by means of the Windows that Great Pas built for them and us. They have other ways as well, of course, of which augury is but one. That doesn't alter the fact that the Windows are the primary means. Is it any wonder, then, that when we permitted this one to fall into disrepair, Pas withdrew his blessing? I say we, because I include myself; we, every man and every woman in Viron, let this devilish thing happen.

"In preparation for this exorcism, I did everything that I could to repair your Window. I cleaned and tightened its connections, spliced and reconnected its broken cables, and attempted certain other more difficult repairs. As you see, I failed. Your Window remains lightless and lifeless. It remains closed to Pas, and we can only hope that he will take the will for the deed and restore his blessing to this house, as we pray."

Several of the young women traced the sign of addition in the air.

Silk nodded approvingly, then looked straight at the dark woman. "Now I am going to speak directly to the devil who has come among us, for I know that it is here, and that it hears me.

"That very great god the Outsider has placed you in my power. You, also, have a window, as we both know. I can close it, and lock it against you, if I choose. Depart from this house forever, or I will so choose." Silk struck the stage with Blood's stick. *"Be gone!"*

The young women started and gasped, and the dark one's grin faded. It was (Silk told himself) as though she'd had a fever; the fever was draining away as he watched, and her delirium with it.

"Now I have spoken enough for the present. Orchid, I asked Chenille a while ago whether you'd been possessed, and she said you hadn't. Is that correct?"

Orchid nodded.

"Stand up, please, and speak loudly enough for all of us to hear you."

Orchid rose and cleared her throat. "No, Patera. It's never happened to me. And I don't want it to."

Several of the young women tittered.

"It will never happen to any of you again. I believe that I can promise you that, and I do. Orchid, you know to whom it has already happened. Who are they?"

"Violet and Crassula."

Silk gestured with the walking stick. "Will they stand up, please?"

Reluctantly, they did so, Violet taller than most, with sleek black hair and flashing eyes; Crassula thin and almost plain.

Silk said, "This isn't all. I know that there's one more at least. If you've been possessed, please stand up, even if Orchid did not name you."

Blood was smiling in the back row; he nudged Musk, who smiled in return as he cleaned his nails with a long-bladed knife. The women stared at one another; a few whispered. Slowly, the small, dark woman rose.

"Thank you, my daughter," Silk said. "Yes, you're the one. Has the devil gone now?"

"I think so."

"So do I. What's your name, my daughter?"

"Poppy, Patera. Only I still don't feel quite like I did before."

"I see. You know, Poppy, Orchid mentioned you to me when we were talking earlier, I suppose—" He was on the point of saying that it had probably been because she was Chenille's opposite physically; at the last possible moment he substituted, "because you're very attractive. That may have had something to do with your possession, although I can't be certain. When were you possessed, Poppy?"

"Just now."

"Speak louder, please. I don't believe everyone can hear you."

Poppy raised her voice. "Just now, until you said be gone, Patera."

"And how did it feel, Poppy?"

The small, dark girl began to tremble.

"If it frightens you too much, you don't have to tell us. Would you rather sit back down?"

"I felt like I was dead. I didn't care any more about anything, and I was right here but far away. I was seeing all the same things, but they meant different things, and I can't explain. People were hollow, like clothes nobody was wearing, all of them except you."

Violet said, "I had my best pins in my hair, and I laid one on the washstand. I didn't want to, but I did, and the drain sort of reached up and ate it, a real good pin with a turquoise head, and I thought it was funny."

Silk nodded. "And for you, Crassula?"

"I wanted to fly, and I did. I stood up in the bed and jumped off and sort of flew around the room. He hit me, but I didn't care."

"Was this last night? One of you was possessed last night. Was it you, Crassula?"

The thin woman nodded wordlessly.

"Was it you who screamed last night? I was here then—outside the house, on Lamp Street, and I heard someone scream."

"That was Orpine. It had come back and I was throwing things. The flying was the first time, last month."

Silk nodded, looking thoughtful. "Thank you, Crassula. I should also thank Poppy and Violet, and I do. I've never had the opportunity to speak with anyone who's been possessed before now, and what you've told me may be helpful to me."

Mucor was gone, or at least he could no longer see her in any of the faces before him. When they had met in Sun Street, Blood had told him that there were human beings who could possess others; he wondered whether Blood did not at least suspect that the devil who had troubled this house was his daughter. Silk decided that it might be best not to give him more time in which to think of it.

"Now we're going to sing the song that we will sing in the course of the ceremony. Stand up, all of you, and join hands. Blood, you and Musk and the rest must sing with us. Come to the front and join hands."

Most of them did not know the *Hymn to Every God*, but Silk taught them the chorus and the first three verses, and eventually achieved a creditable performance, to which Musk, who so seldom spoke, supplied a more than adequate tenor.

"Good! That was our rehearsal, and in a moment we'll begin the ceremony. We'll start outside. This little jar of paint and this brush—" Silk displayed them, "have been blessed and consecrated already. Five of you, chosen from among those who live in this house, will participate in the restoration of the voided cross over the Music Street door, while the rest of us sing. It would be best if the three who have been possessed were among that five. After that, we'll circle the house three times in procession, and then assemble in here once more for the final casting out."

Outside, while surprised urchins stared and pointed at the women, many of whom were still only half dressed, Silk chose the additional representatives, selecting two who were slight of build from among those who seemed to be taking the proceedings most seriously. The *Hymn to Every God* sounded faint and thin in the open air of Music Street, but a score of watching loungers removed their hats as Blood and Bass gravely lifted each of the five in turn on their shoulders. Gammadion by gammadion the nearly effaced voided cross was restored to prominence. When the base line had been added beneath it, Silk burned the brush and the remainder of the paint in the largest thurible.

"Aren't you going to sacrifice?" Orchid asked. "The others did."

"I've just done so," Silk told her. "A sacrifice need not be of a living beast, and you've just witnessed one that wasn't. Should a second exorcism be required, we will offer a beast, and retrace the sacred design in its blood. Do you understand the sacrifice, and why we're doing all this? I'm assuming that the evil being entered your house through this Music Street door, since it is the only outside entrance to the profaned manteion."

Orchid nodded hesitantly.

"Good." Silk smiled. "As the second part proper of this exorcism, we will march in solemn procession, making a threefold circuit of the entire structure, while I read from the Chrasmologic Writings. It might be best if you were to walk behind me, and for the four men to take positions from which they can maintain order."

He raised his voice for the benefit of the listening women. "It will not be necessary for you to keep in step like troopers. It *will* be necessary that you remain in a single file and pay attention to what I read."

He got out his glasses, wiped them on his sleeve, and put them on. One of the young women tittered nervously.

Would Hyacinth laugh so, if she were to see him with these small and always somewhat smeared lenses before his eyes? Surely she would—she had laughed at less ridiculous things when they had been together. For the first time it struck him that she might have laughed as she had because she had been happy. He himself had been happy then, though for no good reason.

As he cleared his throat, he sought to recollect those emotions. No, not happy—joyful.

Joyous. Silk endeavored to imagine his mother offering Hyacinth the pale, greenish limeade that they had drunk each year during the hottest weather, and failed utterly.

" 'A devil does violence to itself, first of all, when it becomes an abscess and, as it were, a cancer in the whorl, as far as it can; for to be enraged at anything in the whorl is to separate oneself from that whorl, and its ultimately semi-divine nature, in some part of which the various natures of all other things whatsoever are contained. Secondly, a devil does violence to itself when it turns away from any good man, and moves against him with the intention of doing harm.' "

Silk risked a glance behind him. Orchid's hands were clasped in prayer, and the younger women were following in decent order, though a few seemed to be straining to hear. He elevated his voice.

" 'Thirdly, a devil does violence to itself whenever it succumbs to the pleasure of pain. Fourthly, when it plays a part, whether acting or speaking insincerely or untruthfully. Fifthly, when it acts or moves, always aimlessly . . .' "

They had completed half of the third and final circuit when a window shattered above their heads, subjecting Crane, near the end of their straggling line, to a shower of glass. "Just the devil departing," he assured the women around him. "Don't start yelling."

Orchid had stopped to stare up at the broken window. "That's one of my rooms!"

A feminine voice from the window, vibrant and firm, spoke like thunder. "Send up your augur to me!"

CHAPTER

12   DINNER ON AUK

Hers was the most beautiful face that Silk had ever seen. It hovered behind the glass in Orchid's sellaria, above a suggestion of neck and shoulders; and its smile was at once innocent, inviting, and sensual, the three intermingling to form a new quality, unknown and unknowable, desirable and terrifying.

"I've been watching you . . . Watching for you. Silk? Silk. What a lovely name! I've always, always loved silk, Silk. Come to me and sit down. You're limping, I've seen you. Draw up a chair to the glass. You mended our broken Window, mended it a little bit, anyway, and that's part of this house now, you said, Silk."

He had knelt, head bowed.

"Sit down, please. I want to see your face. Aren't you paying me honor? You should do what I ask."

"Yes, O Great Goddess," he said, and rose. This wasn't Echidna, surely; this goddess was too beautiful, and seemed almost too kind. Scylla had eight, or ten, or twelve arms; but he could not see her arms. Sphigx—it was Sphigxday—

"Sit down. There's a little chair behind you, Silk. I can see it. It was very nice of you to mend our terminal."

Her eyes were of a color he had never seen before, a blue so deep that it was almost black, without being truly black or even dark, their lids so heavy that she seemed blind.

"I would have revealed myself to you then, if I could. I could see and hear you, but not that. There's no power for the beam, I think. It still won't light. So disappointing. Perhaps you can do something more?"

He nodded, speechless.

"Thank you. I know you'll try. In mending that, you mended this, I think. It's dusty." She laughed, and her laughter was the chiming of bells far away, bells cast of a metal more precious than any gold. "Isn't it funny? I could break that window. By making the right sound. And holding it until the glass broke. Because I could hear you outside reading something. You didn't stop the first time I called. I suppose you didn't hear me?"

He wanted to run but shook his head instead. "No, Great Goddess. I'm terribly sorry."

"But I can't wipe the glass. Wipe this glass for me, Silk. And I'll forgive you."

"If you'll— My handkerchief has blood on it, Great Goddess. Perhaps in there—"

"I won't mind. Unless it's still wet. Do as I asked. Won't you, please?"

Silk got out his handkerchief, stained with Orpine's blood. At each step he took toward the glass, he felt that he was about to burst into flames or dissolve into the air like smoke.

"I watched him kill a thousand once. Men, mostly. It was in the square. I watched from my balcony. They made them kneel facing him, and some still knelt when they were dead."

It seemed the depth of blasphemy to whisk his ragged, bloodstained handkerchief up and down those lovely features, which when the dust was gone seemed more real than he. Not Molpe; Molpe's hair fell across her face. Not—

"I wanted to faint. But he was watching me from his balcony. Much higher up, with a flag over the thing there. The little wall. I was staying at his friend's house then. I saw so much then. It doesn't bother me any more. Have you sacrificed to me today? Or yesterday? Some of those big white bunnies, or a white bird?"

The victims identified her. "No, Kypris," Silk said. "The fault is mine; and I will, as soon as I can."

She laughed again, more thrilling than before. "Don't bother. Or let those women do it. I want other services from you. You're lame. Won't you sit down now? For me? There's a chair behind you."

Silk nodded and gulped, finding it very difficult to think of words in the presence of a goddess, harder still when his eyes strayed to her face. He struggled to recall her attributes. "I hurt my ankle, O Great Goddess Kypris. Last night."

"Bouncing out of Hyacinth's window." Her smile grew minutely wider. "You looked like a big black rabbit. You really shouldn't have. You know, Silk? Hy wouldn't have hurt you. Not with that big sword or any other way. She liked you, Silk. I was in her, so I know."

He took a deep breath. "I had to, Gentle Kypris, in order to preserve the anipotence by which I behold you."

"Because Echidna lets you see us in our Sacred Windows, then. Like a child."

"Yes, Gentle Kypris; by her very great kindness to us, she does."

"And am I the first, Silk? Have you never seen a god before?"

"No, Gentle Kypris. Not like this. I had hoped to, perhaps when I was old, like Patera Pike. Then yesterday in the ball court— And last night. I went into that woman's dressing room without knocking and saw colors in the glass there, colors that looked like the Holy Hues. I've still never seen them, but they told us—we had to memorize the descriptions, actually, and recite them." Silk paused for breath. "And it seemed to me—it has always seemed to me, ever since I used the glass at the schola, that a god might use a glass. May I tell them about this at the schola?"

Kypris was silent for a moment, her face pensive. "I don't think . . . No. No, Silk. Don't tell anybody."

He made a seated bow.

"I was there last night. Yes. But not for you. Only because I play with Hy sometimes. Now she reminds me of the way I used to be, but all that will be over soon. She's twenty-three. And you, Silk? How old are you?"

"Twenty-three, Gentle Kypris."

"There. You see. I prompted you. I know I did." She shook her head almost imperceptibly. "All that abstinence! And now you've seen a goddess. Me. Was it worth it?"

"Yes, Loving Kypris."

She laughed again, delighted. "Why?"

The question hung in the silence of the baking sellaria while Silk tried to kick his intellect awake. At length he said haltingly, "We are so much like beasts, Kypris. We eat and we breed; then we spawn and die. The most humble share in a higher existence is worth any sacrifice."

He waited for her to speak, but she did not.

"What Echidna asks isn't actually much of a sacrifice, even for men. I've always thought of it as a token, a small sacrifice to show her—to show all of you—that we are serious. We're spared a thousand quarrels and humiliations, and because we have no children of our own, all children are ours."

The smile faded from her lovely face, and the sorrow that displaced it made his heart sink. "I won't talk to you again, Silk. Or at least not very soon. No, soon. I am hunted . . . ." Her perfect features faded to dancing colors.

He rose and found that he was cold in his sweat-soaked tunic and robe, despite the heat of the room. Vacantly, he stared at the shattered window; it was the one he had opened when he had spoken with Orchid. The gods—Kypris herself—had prompted him to throw it open, perhaps; but Orchid had closed it again as soon as he left, as he should have known she would.

He trembled, and felt that he was waking from a dream.

An awful silence seemed to fill the empty house, and he remembered vaguely that it was said that haunted houses were the quietest of all, until the ghost walked. Everyone was outside, of course, waiting on Lamp Street where he had left them, and he would be able to tell them nothing.

He visualized them standing in their silent, straggling line and looking at one another, or at no one. How much had they overheard through the window? Quite possibly they had heard nothing.

He wanted to jump and shout, to throw Orchid's untasted goblet of brandy out the window or at the empty glass. He knelt instead, traced the sign of addition, and rose with the help of Blood's stick.

Outside, Blood demanded to know who had summoned him. Silk shook his head.

"You won't tell me?"

"You don't believe in the gods, or in devils, either. Why should I tell you something at which you would only scoff?"

A woman whose hair had been bleached until it was as yellow as Silk's own, exclaimed, "That was no devil!"

"You must keep silent about anything you heard," Silk told her. "You should have heard nothing."

Blood said, "Musk and Bass were supposed to have found every woman in the place and made them come to this ceremony of yours. If they missed any of them, I want to know about it." He turned to Orchid. "You know your girls. Are they all here?"

She nodded, her face set. "All but Orpine."

Musk was staring at Silk as though he wanted to murder him; Silk met his eyes, then turned away. Speaking loudly to the group at large, he said, "We've never completed our third circuit. It is necessary that we do so. Return to your places, please." He tapped Blood's shoulder. "Go back to your place in the procession."

Orchid had kept the Writings for him, her finger at the point at which he had stopped reading. He opened the heavy volume there and began to pace and read again, a step for each word, as the ritual prescribed: "Man, himself, creates the conditions necessary for advance by struggling with and yielding to his animal desires; yet nature, the experiences of the spirit, and materiality need never be. His torment depends upon himself, yet the effects of that torment are always sufficient. You must consider this."

The words signified nothing; the preternaturally lovely face of Kypris interposed itself. She had seemed completely different from the Outsider, and yet he felt that they were one, that the Outsider, who had spoken in so many voices, had now spoken in another. The Outsider had cautioned him to expect no help, Silk reminded himself as he had so many times since that infinite instant in the ball court; he felt that he had received it nevertheless, and was about to receive more. His hands shook, and his voice broke like a boy's.

". . . has of all merely whorlly intellectual ambition and aspiration."

Here was the door of the derelict manteion, with Pas's voided cross fresh and bright above it in black paint that had not yet dried. He closed the Writings with a bang and opened the door, led the way in and limped up the steps to the stage that had once been a sanctuary.

"Sit down, please. It doesn't matter whom you sit with, because we won't be long. We're almost finished."

Leaning on Blood's walking stick, he waited for them to get settled.

"I am about to order the devil forth. I see that the last person in our procession—Bass, I suppose—shut the door behind him. For this part of the ceremony it should be open." Providentially, he remembered the thin woman's name. "Crassula, you're sitting closest. Will you open it for us, please?

"Thank you. Since you were one of the possessed, it might be well to begin this final act of exorcism with you. Do you have a good memory?"

Crassula shook her head emphatically.

"All right. Who does?"

Chenille stood up. "I do, Patera. Pretty good, and I haven't had a drop since last night."

Silk hesitated.

"Please?"

Slowly, Silk nodded. This was to be a meritorious act, of course; he could only hope that she was capable. "Here's the formula all of us will use: *'Go, in the names of these gods, never to return.'* Perhaps you'd better repeat it."

"Go, in the names of these gods, never to return."

"Very good. I hope that everyone heard you. When I've finished, I'll point to you. Pronounce your own name loudly, then recite the formula

—'Go in the names of these gods, never to return.' Then I'll point out the next person, the woman beside you, and she is to say her own name and repeat the formula she'll have just heard you use. Is there anyone who doesn't understand?"

He scanned their faces as he had earlier, but found no trace of Mucor. "Very well."

Silk forced himself to stand very straight. "If there is anything in this house that does not come in the name of the gods, may it be gone. I speak here for Great Pas, for Strong Sphigx, for Scalding Scylla . . ." The sounding names seemed mere words, empty and futile as the sighings of the hot wind that had blown intermittently since spring; and he had not been able to make himself pronounce that of Echidna. "For the Outsider, and for Gentle Kypris. I, Silk, say it! *Go, in the names of these gods, never to return.*"

He pointed toward the woman with the raspberry-colored hair, and she said loudly, "Chenille! Go, in the names of these gods, never to return!"

"Mezereon. Go, in the names of these gods, never to return."

Orchid spoke after the younger women, in a firm, clear voice. After her, Blood positively thundered—there was, Silk decided, a broad streak of actor in the man. Musk was inaudible; Silk could not help but feel that he was calling to devils, rather than casting them out.

Silk waited on the uppermost of the three steps as he pointed to Bass, who stammered as he pronounced his own name and rumbled out the formula.

Silk started down the steps, hurrying despite his pain.

Doctor Crane, the final speaker, said, "Crane. Go, in the names of these gods, never to return. And now—"

Silk slammed shut the door to Music Street and shot the bolt.

"—I've got to go myself. I'm late already. Stay off that ankle!"

"Good-bye," Silk told him, "and thank you for the ride and your treatment." He raised his voice. "All of you may leave. The exorcism is complete."

Suddenly very weary, he sat down on the second step and unwound the wrapping. All the young women had begun to talk at once. He flailed the dull red tiles of the floor with the wrapping, and then, recalling Crane, flung it as hard as he could against the nearest wall.

A hush fell as the chattering women streamed out into the courtyard; by the time he had replaced the wrapping, he thought himself alone; he looked up, and Musk stood before him, as silent as ever, his hands at his sides.

"Yes, my son. What is it?"

"You ever see how a hawk kills a rabbit?"

"No. I spent all but one year of my boyhood here in the city, I'm afraid. Did you wish to speak to me?"

Musk shook his head. "I wanted to show you how a hawk kills a rabbit."

"Very well," Silk said. "I'm watching."

Musk did not respond; after half a minute or more Silk rose, gripping Blood's stick. The long-bladed knife seemed to come from nowhere—to appear in Musk's hand as though called forth by a nod from Pas. Musk thrust, and Silk felt an explosion of pain in his chest. He staggered and dropped the walking stick; one heel struck the step behind him, and he fell.

By the time that he was able to pull himself up, Musk was gone. Hyacinth's azoth was in Silk's hand, though he could not recall drawing it. He stared at it, dropped it clattering to the floor, clutched his chest, then opened his robe.

His tunic showed no tear, no blood. He pulled it up and touched the spot gingerly; it was inflamed and very painful. A single drop of darkly crimson blood appeared on the surface and trickled away.

He let his tunic fall again, and picked up the azoth to examine its pommel, running his fingers across the faceted gem there. That was it, and there had been no miracle. Musk had reversed his knife with a motion too swift to be seen as he had thrust, striking hard with its pommel, which must itself be in some fashion pointed or sharply angled.

And he himself, Patera Silk, the Outsider's servant, had been ready to kill Musk, believing that Musk had killed him. He had not known that he could come so easily to murder. He would have to watch his temper, around Musk particularly.

The gem, which he had supposed colorless, caught a ray of sunlight from the god-gate in the roof and flashed a watery green. For some reason, it reminded him of her eyes. He put it to his lips, his thoughts full of things that could never be.

To spare his broken ankle, he had waited until Moorgrass had finished washing and dressing the body, so that he might ride back to the manteion in Loach's wagon.

They would need a coffin, and ice. Ice was very costly, but having accepted a hundred cards from Orchid, he could not refuse her daughter ice. Mutes could be engaged easily and cheaply. On the other hand—

Loach's wagon lurched to a stop, and Silk looked up in surprise at the weather-stained façade of his own manteion. Loach inquired, "Lay her on the altar for now, Patera?"

He nodded; it was what they always did.

"Let me help you down, Patera. About my pay—"

The fisc was closed, of course, and would not open at all on Scylsday. "See me after sacrifice tomorrow," Silk said. "No, on Molpsday. Not before then." The icemongers might cash Orchid's draft for him if he bought enough ice, but there was no point in relying on that.

Auk came out of the manteion, waved, and wedged the door open; the sight of him snapped Silk out of his calculations. "I'm sorry I'm late," he called. "There was a death."

Auk's heavy, brutal face took on what seemed intended as an expression of concern. "Friend of yours, Patera?"

"No," Silk said. "I didn't know her."

Auk smiled. He helped Loach carry Orpine's shrouded body inside, where a new coffin, plain but sturdy-looking, waited on a catafalque.

Maytera Marble rose from the shadows, the silver gleam of her face almost ghostly. "I arranged for these, Patera. The man you sent said that we'd require them. They can be returned, if they're not suitable."

"We'll need a better casket tomorrow." Silk fumbled in his pockets, and at length produced Orchid's draft. "Take this, please. It's payable to bearer. Get ice, half a load of ice, and see if they'll cash it for you. Flowers, too. Arrange for a grave, if it's not too late."

A tiny, but abrupt and uncoordinated, movement of her head as she glanced at the draft betrayed Maytera Marble's surprise.

"You're right." Silk nodded as she looked up at him. "It's a great deal. I'll get the victims in the morning, a white heifer if I can find one, and a rabbit for Kypris—several, I ought to say. And a black lamb and a black cock for Tartaros; I pledged those last night. But we must have the ice tonight, and if you could take care of it, Maytera, I would be exceedingly grateful."

"For Kypris the—? All right, Patera. I'll try." She hurried away, the rapid taps of her footfalls like the soft rattle of a snare drum. Silk shook his head and looked about for Loach, but Loach had already left, unobserved.

Auk said, "If there's ice left in Viron, she'll find it. She teach you, Patera?"

"No. I wish now that she had—she and Maytera Mint. But I should have asked her to arrange for mutes. Well, it can be taken care of tomorrow. Can we talk here, Auk, or would you prefer to go to the manse?"

"Have you eaten yet, Patera? I was hoping you'd have a bite of supper with me while you told me what happened last night."

"I couldn't pay my share, I'm afraid."

"I asked you, Patera. I wouldn't let you pay if you wanted to. But you listen here." Auk's voice dropped to a whisper. "I'm in this as much as you are. It was me that helped you. I got a right to know."

"Of course. Of course." Silk sank wearily into a seat near the catafalque. "Sit down, please. It hurts my ankle to stand. I'll tell you whatever you want to know. To tell the truth, I need to tell someone—to talk all of it over, and other things, too. Everything that happened today. And I'd like very much to go to dinner with you. I'm beginning to like you, and I'm terribly hungry; but I can't walk far. Much as I appreciate your generosity, perhaps we should dine together some other night."

"We don't have to leg it over to the Orilla. There's a nice place right down the street. They got the tenderest, juiciest roasts you ever cut on the side of your flipper." Auk grinned, showing square, yellow teeth that looked fully capable of severing a human hand at the wrist. "Suppose I was to buy an augur—one that really needed it—a dimber uphill dinner. Whatever he wanted. That'd be a meritorious act, wouldn't it?"

"I suppose so. Nevertheless, you must consider that he may not deserve one."

"I'll keep it in mind." Auk strolled to the coffin and pulled down the shroud. "Who is she?"

"Orchid's daughter Orpine. That was nicely done, but you knew her, I'm sure."

"Her *daughter?*" Leaving Orpine's body, Auk took Silk's arm. "Come on, Patera. If we don't get over there, we'll have to eat in the public room."

Musk had caught sight of his eagle before he stepped out of the floater. She was at the top of a blasted pine, silhouetted against the brightening skylands.

She was looking at the hackboard, Musk knew. She could see the hackboard more clearly from half a league away than he had ever seen the palms of his own hands. She would be ravenous by now; like a falcon (as Musk reminded himself) an eagle would have to learn to fly before it could learn to hunt. Apparently, she had not yet gone after lambs, though she might tomorrow—it was his greatest fear.

He circled the villa. The meat bound to the hackboard had been there all day; it was nearly dry now, and blanketed with flies. He kicked the board to dislodge them before he brought out the lure and a bag of cracked maize.

The lure whistled as he spun it on its five-cubit line.

"Ho, hawk! Ho, hawk!"

Once he imagined that he heard the faint jingle of her bells, though he knew it was impossible. He scattered maize nearly to the wall, then returned to the hackboard and swung the lure again while he waited. It was late—perhaps too late. It would be dark very soon, and when it was she would not fly.

"Ho! Ho, hawk!"

As well as Musk could judge, the eagle on the remote snag had not stirred so much as a feather; but a plump brown wood weaver was settling on the cropped grass near the wall to peck at the maize.

He dropped the lure and crouched, his needler gripped with both hands and his left elbow braced on his left knee. It would be a long shot, in poor light.

The wood weaver fell, fluttered up, cannoned into the wall, and fell again. Before it could fly a second time, he had it. Back at the hackboard, he loosened the noose in the lure line and let the red-and-white lure fall to the ground. With the noose tight about the wood weaver's right leg, he twirled it, producing a fine and almost invisible shower of blood.

"Ha, hawk!"

The wide wings spread. For a moment Musk, watching the eagle, still twirling the dying wood weaver in its ten-cubit circle, felt that he more than possessed it.

Felt that he himself was the great bird, and was happy.

"You seen what they wrote on that wall, Patera." Auk sat down, having chosen a chair from which he could watch the door. "Some sprat from the palaestra, like you say. But I'd talk to them about it, if I was you. Could be trouble."

"I'm not responsible for every boy who finds a piece of chalk." This eating house had seemed remote indeed to Silk, though it was almost in sight of his manteion. He lowered himself into the capacious armchair the host was holding for him and looked around him at the white-washed shiprock walls. Their private dining room was smaller even than his bed-

room in the manse, still crowded after a waiter had removed two super-
fluous chairs.

"All of them good and thick," Auk said, answering the question Silk
had not asked, "and so's the door. This was the Alambrera back in the
old days. What do you like?"

Silk scanned the neatly lettered slate. "I'll have the chops, I think." At
eighteen cardbits, the chops were the least expensive meal; and even if
there were in fact only a single chop, this dinner would be his most
bountiful meal of the week.

"How'd you get over the wall?" Auk asked when the host had gone.
"Have any trouble?"

And so Silk told the whole story, from the cutting of his horsehair rope
by a spike to his ride back to the city in Blood's floater. Auk was roaring
with laughter when the waiter brought their dinners, but he had grown
very serious by the time Silk reached his interview with Blood.

"You didn't happen to mention me any time while you were talking to
him?"

Silk swallowed a luscious mouthful of chop. "No. But I very foolishly
tried to speak with you through the glass in Hyacinth's boudoir, as I told
you."

"He may not find out about that." Auk scratched his chin thoughtfully.
"The monitors lose track after a while."

"But he may," Silk said. "You'll have to be on guard."

"Not as much as you will, Patera. He'll want to know what you wanted
to talk to me about, and since you didn't, he can't get it from me. What
are you going to tell him?"

"If I tell him anything at all, I'll tell him the truth."

Auk laid down his fork. "That I helped you?"

"That I knew you were concerned about my safety. That you had
warned me about going out so late at night, and that I wanted to let you
know I had not come to harm."

Auk considered the matter while Silk ate. "It might go, Patera, if he
thinks you're crazy enough."

"If he thinks I'm honest enough, you mean. The best way to be
thought honest is to be honest—or at any rate that's the best that I've
ever found. I try to be."

"But you're going to try to steal twenty-six thousand for him, too."

"If that's what I must do to save our manteion, and I can get it in no
other way, yes. I'll be forced to choose between evils, exactly as I was last

night. I'll try to see that no one is hurt, of course, and to take the money only from those who can well afford to lose it."

"Blood will take your money, Patera. And have a good laugh over it."

"I won't let him take it until he furnishes safeguards. But there's something else I ought to tell you about. Did I mention that Blood wanted me to exorcise the yellow house?"

"Orchid's place? Sure. That's where that girl Orpine lived, only I never knew she was Orchid's daughter."

"She was." There was butter and soft, fresh bread in the middle of the table; Silk took a slice and buttered it, wishing that he might take the whole loaf home to the manse. "I'm going to tell you about that, too. And about Orpine, who died possessed."

Auk grunted. "That's your lay, Patera, not mine."

"Possession? It's really no one's now. Perhaps there was a time when most augurs believed in devils, as Patera Pike certainly did. But I may be the only augur alive who believes in them now, and even now I'm not certain that I believe in them in the same sense he did—as spirits who crept into the whorl without Pas's permission and seek to destroy it."

"What about Orpine? Was she really Orchid's daughter?"

"Yes," Silk said. "I spoke to Orchid about her and she admitted it. Practically boasted of it, in fact. What was Orpine like?"

"Good-looking." Auk hesitated. "I don't feel right talking about this stuff to you, Patera. She could be a lot of fun, because she didn't care what she did or what anybody thought about it. You know what I mean? She would've made more money if she'd been better at making people think she liked them."

Silk chewed and swallowed. "I understand. I wanted to know because I've been wondering about personalities, and so on—whether there's a particular type of person who's more prone to be possessed than another —and I never saw Orpine alive. I had been talking to her mother; we heard a scream and hurried outside, and found her lying there on the stair. She had been stabbed. Someone suggested that she might have stabbed herself. Her face— Have you ever seen a possessed person?"

Auk shook his head.

"Neither had I until this morning, shortly before I saw Orpine's body." Silk patted his lips with his napkin. "At any rate, she was dead; but even in death it seemed that her face was not quite her own. I remember thinking that there was something horrible about it, and a good deal that was familiar, as well. At first, the familiar part seemed quite easy. After I'd thought about it for a moment—the eyes and the shape of her nose and lips and so on—I realized that she looked rather like Orchid, the woman I'd just been speaking to. I asked her about it afterward, and she told me that Orpine had been her daughter, as I said."

"Maybe I should've known, too," Auk said, "but I never guessed. Orpine was a lot younger."

Silk shrugged. "You know a great deal more about women than I do, I'm sure. Perhaps I saw as much as I did mostly because I know so little about them. When one knows little about a subject, what one sees are apt to be the most basic things, if one sees anything at all. What I wanted to say, however, was that even the horrible element in her face was familiar."

"Go on." Auk refilled his wineglass. "Let's hear it."

"I'm hesitating because I'm fairly certain you won't believe me. Orpine reminded me of someone else I had been talking with not long before— of Mucor, the mad girl in Blood's villa."

Auk laid aside his fork, the steaming beef on its tines still untasted. "You mean the same devil had taken 'em both over, Patera?"

Silk shook his head. "I don't know, but I felt that I ought to tell you. I believe that Mucor has been following me in spirit. And I am coming to believe that she can, in some fashion, possess others, just as devils—and the gods, for that matter—are said to do at times. This morning I felt sure that I had glimpsed her in the face of an honest working man; and I think that she was possessing Orpine when Orpine died. Later I recognized her in another woman.

"If I'm correct, if she can really do such things and if she has been following me, you're running a substantial risk just by sitting with me at this table. I'm very grateful for this truly remarkable dinner, and even more grateful for your help last night. Furthermore, I'm hoping to ask you a few questions before we separate; and all of that puts me heavily in debt to you. I was too tired—and too hungry, I suppose—to consider the danger to which I was subjecting you when we spoke in the manteion. Now that I have, I feel obliged to warn you that you too may suffer possession if you remain in my company."

Auk grinned. "You're an augur, Patera. If she was to grab hold of me while we're sitting here, couldn't you make her beat the hoof?"

"I could try; but I have only one threat to use against her, and I've used it. You're not leaving?"

"Not me. I think I'll have another dumpling instead, maybe with a little of this gravy on it."

"Thank you. I hope you won't regret it. You haven't yet commented on my somewhat uneven performance last night. If you're afraid I might be insulted, I assure you that you could not be more severe with me than I've already been with myself."

"All right, I'll comment." Auk sipped his wine. "In the first place, I think if you can raise even a thousand, you'd better make sure Blood signs the manteion over to you before you cough up your goldboys. You were going on about safeguards a minute ago. I don't think you ought to trust in any safeguards except the deed, signed and witnessed by a couple dimber bucks who got nothing to do with Blood."

"You're right, I'm sure. I've been thinking much the same thing."

"You better. Don't trust him, even if something that he does makes you think you can."

"I'll be very careful." Silk's chops were bathed in a piquant, almost black sauce he found unspeakably delicious; he wiped some from his plate with another slice of bread.

"And I think you've probably found your true calling." Auk grinned. "I don't think I could've done much better, and I might not've done as good. This was your first time, too. By number ten I'll be begging to come along, just to watch you work."

Silk sighed. "I hope there won't be a tenth, for both our sakes."

"Sure there will. You're a real son of Tartaros. You just don't know it yet. Third or fourth, or whatever it is, I want to see what it is a dimber bucko like you needs a hand from me on. You want to go back to Blood's tonight and get your hatchet?"

Silk shook his head ruefully. "I won't be able to work on the roof until my ankle's healed, and it's more than half finished anyway. Do you recall what I said about Hyacinth's needler?"

"Sure. And the azoth. A nice azoth ought to bring a couple thousand cards, Patera. Maybe more. If you want to sell it, I can steer you to somebody who'll give you a lily price."

"I can't, because it isn't mine. Hyacinth intended to lend it to me, I'm sure. As I told you, I had told her that I was borrowing those weapons, and I promised that I would return them when I no longer required them. I feel certain she would not have sent the azoth to me by Doctor Crane if I had not said that earlier."

When Auk did not reply, Silk continued miserably, "Two thousand cards, if I actually received that much, would be an appreciable fraction of the twenty-six thousand that we require. More than five percent, in fact. You'll laugh at me—"

"I ain't laughing, Patera."

"You should. A thief who can't bring himself to steal! But Hyacinth trusted me. I cannot believe that the—that any god would wish me to betray a friendless woman's trust."

"If she lent it to you, I wouldn't sell it either," Auk told him. "Just to start out, she's there in Blood's house, and if you've got yourself a friend on the inside, that's not anything you want to fight clear of. You got any notion why this doctor would take on something as risky as that for her?"

"Perhaps he's in love with her."

"Uh-huh. It could be, but I'll bet he's got some kind of lock. It'd be worth your while to find out what it is, and I'd like to hear about it when you do. I'd like to see this azoth you got from her, too. Suppose I come around tomorrow night. Would you let me see it?"

"You may look at it now, if you like." Silk pulled the azoth from beneath his tunic and passed it across the table to Auk. "I brought it to Orchid's today because I feared I might require some sort of weapon."

Auk whistled softly, then held the azoth up, admiring the play of light along its gleaming grip. "Twenty-eight hundred easy. Might bring three thousand. Whoever gave it to her probably paid five or six for it."

Silk nodded. "I believe I may have some idea who that was, although I don't know where he could have gotten that much money." Auk regarded him quizzically, but Silk shook his head. "I'll tell you later, if it appears that I may be correct."

He held out his hand for the azoth, which Auk returned with a final grunt of admiration.

"I want to ask you about Hyacinth's needler. Blood took out the needles before he gave it back to me. Can you tell me where I might buy more without a brevet?"

"Sure, Patera. No problem at all. Have you got that with you, too?"

Silk took Hyacinth's engraved needler from his pocket and passed it to Auk.

"The smallest they make. I know 'em." He returned the needler and rose. "Listen, can you get by without me for a minute? I got to—you know."

"Of course." Silk directed his attention to his chops; there had been three, and hungry though he was, he had thus far eaten only the first. He attacked the second without neglecting the tender dumplings, buttered squash with basil, and shallots in oil and vinegar that the eating house had provided (apparently at no additional charge) to accompany them.

Mere worry, mere concern, would not save the manteion. It would be necessary to devise a plan, and that plan need not necessarily involve stealing twenty-six thousand cards. Enlisting the sympathy of some magnate might do as well, for example, or . . .

Silk was discovering that he had devoured his third and final chop without realizing he had finished the second when Auk returned.

CHAPTER

13 SILK FOR CALDÉ

Doctor Crane shut and bolted the door of his infirmary. It had been a hard day; he was glad to be back again, very glad that Blood (who had put in a grueling day as well) would not entertain tonight. With luck, Crane thought, he might get a good night's sleep, an uninterrupted night's sleep, a night in which the cats clawed no one, Musk's hawks refrained from footing Musk and his helper—most of all, a night in which none of the fools that Viron called women decided that some previously unnoticed mole was in fact the first symptom of a fatal disease.

Shuffling into his bedroom, which had no door to the hall, he closed the door to the infirmary and bolted it as well. Let them call him through the glass, if they wanted him. He removed his shoes and flung his stockings onto the pile of soiled clothing in a corner, reminding himself again that he must take those clothes to the laundry in the other wing.

Had he put the black stocking he'd cut off that fellow Silk in there? No, he'd thrown it away.

In bare feet, he padded to the window and stood staring out through the grille at the shadowy grounds. The weather had been fine all summer, glowing with the hot, dry heat of home; but it would be autumn soon. The sun would dim, and the winds bring chill, drenching rains. The calendar called it autumn already. He hated rain and cold, snow, and coughs and runny noses. For a month or more, the thermometer would fluctuate between ten and ten below, as if chained to the freezing point. Human beings were never intended for such a climate.

When he had pulled down the shade, he glanced at the calendar, his eyes following his thought. Tomorrow would be Scylsday; the market would be closed, officially at least, and nearly empty. That was the best time for turning in a report, and the trader would be leaving on Hieraxday. There were still five of the little carved Sphigxes left.

He squared his shoulders, reminding himself that he too was a trooper of a sort, brought out his pen case, the black ink, and several sheets of very thin paper. As always, it would be necessary to write in a way that would not reveal his identity, should his report be intercepted.

And to report sufficient progress to prevent his being withdrawn. Tonight that would not be difficult.

Not that he would not like to go home, he told himself, and particularly to go home before the rains arrived, though they said that home had once been as wet as this place. Or rather, as wet as this place normally was.

He chose a crow quill and meticulously touched up its point. "There is a movement to restore the Charter. It is centered upon one Silk, a young augur of no family. He is said to have been the object of miracles, attributed to Pas or Scylla. Thus far it seems confined to the lower orders. The watchword 'Silk for caldé' is written on walls, although not" (it was a guess, but Crane felt confident of his ground) "on the Palatine. I am in contact with him and am gaining his trust. I have seen to it that he has an azoth. This can be reported if it proves necessary to destroy him."

Crane grinned to himself; that had been pure luck, but it would open their eyes.

"The Civil Guard is being expanded again. All units are at or over full strength. There is talk of forming a reserve brigade, officered by veterans."

For nearly half a minute, he sat staring at what he had written; better to say too little than too much. He dipped the crow quill for the twentieth time. "The bird has been freed. Its trainer says this is necessary. He will try to lure it back within the next few days. Lemur and Loris are reported to have observed its release."

And to have emerged from the subcellar, as upon several previous occasions, Crane reminded himself. Unquestionably the Ayuntamiento was making extensive use of the half-flooded construction tunnels, though its headquarters was not there.

Or could not be located if it was, although so many had perished there searching for it. Besides Viron's dormant army, there were Vironese soldiers in those tunnels, as well as several taluses.

Crane shook his head, then smiled at the thought of the Rani's reward. Turning to his glass, he clapped his hands. "Monitor!"

The floating face appeared.

"Code. Snakeroot. What have you got for me?"

Blood's fleshy features filled the glass. "Councillor Lemur ought to hear this."

Blood's face was replaced by the deceptively cheerful-looking visage of
Potto. "You can give me the message."

"I'd rather—"

Crane smiled at Blood's reluctance.

"That doesn't matter. What is it?"

Crane edged nearer the glass.

When Blood had faded and the monitor reappeared to tell him there
were no further exchanges of interest, Crane dipped his quill again.
"Later. The bird has come back of its own volition. It is said to be in
good condition."

He wiped the quill carefully and returned it to his pen case, blew on
the paper, and folded and refolded it until it was scarcely larger than his
thumbnail. When he pressed it into Sphigx's swordless left hand, the
hand closed upon it.

Crane smiled, put away his pen case and the remaining paper, and
considered the advisability of a long soak in the tub before bed. There
was a good light in the bathroom—he had installed it himself—and if he
read for an hour, the tightly folded sheet would have taken on the brown
hue of the elaborately carved wood before he retired. He always liked
seeing that, enjoyed making sure. He was, as he had to be, a very careful
man.

"Thanks," Auk said as he resumed his seat. "I feel better now. Listen,
Patera, do you know how to use that thing?"

"The needler?" Silk shrugged. "I fired it, as I told you. Not other than
that."

Auk refilled his goblet. "I meant the azoth. No, naturally you don't,
but I'll tell you about the needler anyhow."

He drew his own needler, twice the size of the engraved and gold-
plated weapon in Silk's pocket. "Notice I got the safety on? There's a
lever like this on both sides."

"Yes," Silk said. "So it won't shoot. I know about that."

"Fine." Auk pointed with his table knife. "This pin here, sticking out?
You call this the status pin. If it's pushed out like that, you've got needles
left."

Silk took Hyacinth's needler from his pocket again. "You're right, it's
flush with the side."

"Now watch. I can empty mine by pulling this loading knob back."

A silver fountain of needles sprang from the breach of Auk's needler
and scattered over the table. Silk picked one up.

"There's not much to see," Auk said. "Just little rods of solid alloy—some kind of stuff that a lodestone pulls a lot better than steel."

Silk tested the tip with his finger. "I thought they'd be sharper."

"Huh-uh. They wouldn't work as good. If a thing as little as that went straight through somebody, it probably wouldn't do much damage. You want it to slew around so it cuts sidewise. The point's rounded just a shade to make it feed into the barrel, but not much."

Silk put down the needle. "What makes the noise?"

"The air." Auk smiled at Silk's surprise. "When you were a sprat, didn't some other sprat ever sling a rock at you and almost hit you? So you heard the rock go past your ear?"

Silk nodded.

"All right, there wasn't a bang like with a slug gun, was there? It was just a rock, and the other sprat threw it with his sling. What you heard was the rock going through the air, just like you might hear the wind in the chimney. The bigger the rock was, and the faster it was going, the more noise it would make."

"I see," Silk murmured, and with the words the entire scene returned, glowing with the vivid colors and hot shame of youth: the whizzing stones, his futile defense and final flight, the blood that had streamed from his face down his best white tunic to dye its embroidered flowers.

"All right, a needle's just a tiny little thing, but when it's shot out it goes so fast that the rock might just as well be traveling backwards. So it makes that noise you heard. If it had got slewed around before it hit that jug you shot, it would have screeched like a tomcat." Auk swept his needles into a pile with his hands. "They drop down inside the handle. See? All right. Right under my finger is a little washer with a hole in the middle and a lot of sparks in it."

Silk raised his eyebrows, more than ready to grasp at any distraction. "Sparks?"

"Just like you see if you pet a cat in the dark. They got put into the washer when this needler was made, and they chase each other around and around the hole in that washer till you need them. When I close the breech, that'll stick the first needle into the barrel, see?" Auk flicked on the safety. "If I'd have pulled the trigger, that would tap off some sparks for the coil. And as long as it's got sparks, that coil works like a big lodestone. It's up front here looped around the barrel, and it sucks the needle to it real fast. You'd think it would stay right there after it gets there, wouldn't you?"

Silk nodded again. "Or be drawn back to the coil, if it overshot."

"Right. Only it don't happen, because the last spark is through the coil before the needle ever gets there. Are you finished, Patera? I've told you just about everything I know."

"Yes, and the entire meal was delightful. Superb, in fact. I'm extremely grateful to you, Auk. However, I do have one more question before we go, though no doubt it will seem a very silly one to you. Why is your needler so much bigger than this one? What advantages are secured by the increase in size?"

Auk weighed his weapon in his hand before thrusting it away. "Well, Patera, for one thing mine holds a lot more needles. Full up, there's a hundred and twenty-five. I'd say your little one there most likely only holds fifty or sixty. Mine are longer, too, which is why I can't give you some of mine to use in yours. Longer needles mean a wider cut when they slew around, and a wider cut takes your cull out of the fight quicker. My barrel's longer, too, and the needles are a hair thicker. All that gives 'em half a dog's cheek more speed, so they'll go in deeper."

"I understand." Silk had drawn back the loading knob of Hyacinth's needler and was peering at the rather simple-looking mechanism revealed by the open breech.

"A needler like yours is all right inside a house or a place like this, but outside you'd better be up close before you pull the trigger. If you're not, your needle's going to start slewing around in the air before it ever gets to your cull, and once it starts doing that, don't even Pas's sprats—your pardon, Patera—know where it's going to end up."

Looking thoughtful, Silk got out one of Blood's cards. "If you would allow me, Auk. I'm heavily indebted to you."

"I already paid, Patera." Auk rose, pushing back his chair until it thumped the wall. "Some other time, maybe." He grinned. "Now then. You remember I said don't even the gods know where your needles are going?"

"Of course." Silk rose as well, finding his ankle less painful than he had anticipated.

"Well, maybe they don't. But I do, and I'll tell you soon as we get outside. I know where you and me are going to go, too."

"I should return to my manteion." By an effort of will, Silk was able to walk almost normally.

"This won't take more than a couple hours, and I got two or three surprises I want to show you."

The first was a litter for one, with a pair of bearers. Silk climbed into it with some trepidation, wondering whether there would be any such conveyance to carry him to the manse when the business of the evening was done. The shade had risen until no sliver of gold remained, and a dulcet breeze whispered soothingly that the dust and heat of vanquished day had been but empty lies. It fanned Silk's flushed cheeks, and the sensual pleasure it gave him told him he had drunk one goblet of wine too many. Sadly, he resolved to watch himself more strictly in the future.

Auk strode along beside the litter, his grin flashing in the semidarkness. Silk felt something small, squarish, and heavy thrust into his hand.

"What we was talking about, Patera. Put 'em in your pocket."

By that time, Silk's fingers had told him that it was a paper-wrapped packet, tightly tied with string. "How . . . ?"

"The waiter. I had a word with him when I stepped out, see? They ought to fit, but don't try them here."

Silk dropped the packet of needles into the pocket of his robe. "I— Thank you again, Auk. I don't know what to say."

"I had him whistle out this trot-about for you, and he sent a pot boy off after those. If they don't fit, tell me tomorrow. Only I think they will."

The litter halted much sooner than Silk had expected, before a tall house whose lower and third stories were dark, though the windows between them blazed with light. When Auk knocked, the door was opened by a lean old man with a small, untidy beard and white hair more disordered even than Silk's own.

"Aha! Good! Good!" The old man exclaimed. "Inside! Inside! Just shut the door. Shut the door, and follow me." He went up the stair two steps at a time, with a speed that Silk would have found astonishing in someone half his age.

"His name's Xiphias," Auk told him when he had finished paying the bearers. "He's going to be your teacher."

"Teacher of what?"

"Hacking. Thirty years ago, he was best. The best in Viron, anyhow." Turning, Auk led Silk inside and closed the door. "He says he's better now, but the younger men won't accept his challenges. They say they don't want to show him up, but I don't know." Auk chuckled. "Think how they'd feel if the old goat beat them."

Nodding and content to wonder for a few minutes longer what "hacking" might be, Silk seated himself on the second step and removed Crane's wrapping; it was cold, and though he could not be certain in the dimness of the hallway, he thought that he could feel actual ice crystals in the nap of its cloth covering. He struck the floor with it. "Do you know about these?"

Auk stooped to look more closely. "I don't know. What you got?"

"A truly wonderful bandage for my ankle." Silk lashed the floor again. "It winds itself around the broken bone almost like a serpent. Doctor Crane lent it to me. You're supposed to kick it or something until it gets hot."

"Can I see it for a minute? I can do that better, standing up."

Silk handed him the wrapping.

"I heard of them, and I saw one once, only I didn't get to touch it. Thirty cards they wanted for it." Auk slapped the wall with the wrapping; when he squatted to help Silk replace it, it felt hot enough to smoke.

The stair was as steep and narrow as the house itself, covered with torn carpeting so threadbare as to be actually slick in spots; but helped manfully by Auk and urged forward by curiosity, jaw set and putting as much weight as possible on Blood's lioness-headed stick, Silk climbed it almost as quickly as he might have with two sound legs.

The door at the top opened upon a single bare room that occupied the entire second story; its floor was covered with worn sailcloth mats, its walls decorated with swords, many of them of shapes that Silk had never seen or never noticed, and long cane foils with basketwork hilts.

"You're lame!" Xiphias called. "Limping!" He danced toward them, thrusting and parrying.

"I injured my ankle," Silk told him. "It should be better in a few weeks."

Xiphias pushed his foil into Silk's hands. "But you must start now! Begin your lessons this very evening! Do you know how to hold that? You're left-handed? Good! Very good! I'll teach you the right, too, eventually. Keep your stick in your right, eh? You may parry, but not thrust or cut with it. Is that understood? May I have a stick too? You agree that's fair? No objection? Where— Over there!" An astonishing bound carried him to the nearest wall, from which he snatched two more foils and a yellow walking stick so slender that it was scarcely more than a wand; like the foils it was of varnished bamboo.

Silk told him, "I can't engage you with this bad ankle, sir, and the Chapter frowns upon all such activities—not that I'd be an even match or anything like a match for you. Besides, I have no funds to pay for a lesson."

"Aha! Auk's your friend? Your word on his score, Auk? It's not just to get him killed, is it?"

Auk shook his head.

"He's my friend, and I'm his." As soon as Silk spoke, he realized that it was no more than the truth. He added, "Because I am, I won't let him pay."

Xiphias's voice dropped to a whisper. "You won't fight, you say, with your cloth and gimp leg. But what if you were attacked? You'd have to. Have to . . . And since Auk's your friend, he'd fight too, wouldn't he? Fight for you? You say you don't want him to pay. Don't you think he feels the same way?"

He tossed Auk a foil. "Not made of money are you, Auk? A good thief but a poor man, isn't that what they say about you? Wouldn't you— wouldn't you both like to save Auk all that money? Yes! Oh, yes! I know you would."

Auk unbuckled his hanger and laid it against the wall. "If we beat him, he won't charge me."

"That's right!" Xiphias sprang away. "Will you excuse me, Patera, while I remove my trousers?"

They fell as he spoke; one spindle-thin leg was black synthetic and gleaming steel. At the touch of the old man's fingers, it too fell away, leaving him swaying on a single, natural, knotted, blue-veined leg. "What do you think of my secret? Five it took!" He hopped toward them, balancing himself precariously with his foil and the yellow walking stick. "Five I found!"

Almost too late, Silk blocked a wide, whistling cut at his head.

"Too many parts? Scarcely enough!" Another swinging slash. "Don't cringe!"

Auk lunged at the old man. His parry was too swift for the eye to follow; the crack of his foil against Auk's skull sounded louder than Auk's shot in the Cock. Auk sprawled on the sailcloth mat.

"Now, Patera! Guard yourself!"

For the space of a brief prayer that seemed half the night, that was all Silk did, frantically fending off cut after cut, forehand, backhand, to the head, to the neck, to the arms, the shoulders, the waist. There was no time to think, no time to do anything but react. Almost in spite of himself, he began to sense a certain pattern, a rhythm that governed the old man's slashing attack. Despite his ankle, he could move faster, turn faster, than the old man on his one leg.

"Good! Good! After me! Good!"

Xiphias was on the defensive now, parrying the murderous cuts Silk launched at his head and shoulders.

"Use the point! Watch this!" The old man lunged, his slender stick the leg he lacked, the end of his foil between Silk's legs, then under his left arm. Silk himself thrust desperately. Xiphias's parry sent his point awry. Silk cut at his head and lunged when he backed away.

"Where'd you study, lad?"

Auk was on his feet once more, grinning and rubbing his head. Feeling that he had been betrayed, Silk thrust and parried, cut, and parried the old man's cuts. There was no time to speak, no time to think, no time to do anything but fight. He had dropped the lioness-headed stick, but it did not matter—the pain in his ankle was remote, the pain of somebody else far off, of some body that he hardly knew.

"Good! Oh, very nice!"

The *clack, clack, clack* of the foils was the beating of the Sphigxdrum that called men to war, the rattle of crotala that led the dance, a dance in which every movement had to be as quick as possible.

"I'll take him, Auk! I'll teach him! He's mine!"

Hopping and half falling, propped by his slender stick, the old man met each attack with careless ease, his mad eyes burning with joy.

Maddened too, Silk thrust at them. His bamboo blade flew wide, and the slender walking stick struck a single, paralyzing blow to his wrist. His foil dropped to the mat, and Xiphias's point thumped his breastbone. "You're dead, Patera!"

Silk stared at him, rubbed his wrist, and at last spat at the old man's feet. "You cheated. You said I couldn't hit with my stick, but you hit me with yours."

"I did! Oh, yes!" The old man flung it into the air and parried it as it fell. "But aren't I sorry? Isn't my heart torn? Overflowing with remorse? Oh, it is, it is! I weep! Where would you like to be buried?"

Auk said quietly, "There ain't any rules, Patera, not when we fight. Somebody lives, somebody dies. That's all there is."

Silk started to speak, thought better of it, swallowed, and said, "I understand. If I'd considered something that happened this afternoon more seriously—as I should have before now—I would have understood sooner. You're right, of course, sir. You're both right."

"Where did you study?" Xiphias asked. "Who's your old master?"

"No one," Silk told him truthfully. "We used to fence with laths when I was a boy, sometimes; but I'd never held a real foil before."

Xiphias cocked a bushy eyebrow at him. "Like that, eh? Or perhaps you're still angry because I tricked you?" He hopped over to Blood's fallen walking stick, snatched it up (practically falling himself) and tossed it to Silk. "Want to hit me back? Punish me for trying to save you? Do your worst!"

"Of course not. I'd rather thank you, Xiphias, and I do." Silk rubbed the crusted bruise Musk had left on his ribs. "It was a lesson I needed. When may I come for my next?"

While the old man was considering, Auk said, "He'll be a good contact for you, Patera. He's a master-of-arms, not just of the sword. He was the one that sold the boy your needles, see?"

"Mornings, afternoons, or evenings?" Xiphias inquired. "Would evenings be all right? Good! Can we say Hieraxday, then?"

Silk nodded again. "Hieraxday after shadelow, Master Xiphias."

Auk brought the old man his prosthetic leg and helped him keep his balance while he closed its socket about his stump.

"You see," Xiphias asked, tapping it with his foil, "that I've earned the right to do what I did? That I was cheated once myself? That I paid the price when I was as young and strong as you are today?"

Outside, in the hot, silent street, Auk said, "We'll find you a litter before long, Patera. I'll pay 'em, but then I'll have to get going."

Silk smiled. "If I can fight with that marvelous old madman on this ankle, I can certainly walk home on it. You may leave me now, Auk, and Pas's peace go with you. I won't try to thank you for everything you've done for me tonight. I couldn't, even if I talked until morning. But I'll repay you whenever I get the chance."

Auk grinned and clapped him on the back. "No hurry, Patera."

"Down this little street—it's String Street, I know it—and I'll be on Sun Street. A few steps east, and I'll be at the manteion. You have business of your own to attend to, I'm certain. And so good night."

He took care to stride along normally until Auk was out of sight, then permitted himself to limp, leaning on Blood's stick. His bout with Master Xiphias had left him drenched with sweat; fortunately the night wind had no edge to it.

Autumn was nearly over. Was it only yesterday that it had rained? Silk assured himself that it was. Winter was almost upon them, though there was only that shower to prove it. The crops were in—meager crops, most peasants said, hardly worth the work of harvest; the parched dead of summer seemed to last longer each year, and this year the heat had been terrible. As it still was, for that matter.

Here was Sun Street; wide though it was, he had almost missed the turning. The funeral tomorrow—Orpine's final rites, and very likely her first as well. He recalled what Auk had said about her and wished that he had known her, as perhaps Hyacinth had. Had Maytera been able to cash

Orchid's draft? He would have to find out—perhaps she had left him a note. He wouldn't have to tell her to sweep the manteion. Could rue still be had cheaply in the market? No, could rue be had at any price? Almost certainly, yes. And . . .

And there was the manse, with the manteion beyond it; but he had barred the Sun Street door.

He hobbled diagonally across Sun Street to the garden gate, unlocked and opened it, and locked it again carefully behind him. As he went along the narrow path to the manse, where no one slept or ate or lived except himself, voices floated into the garden through the open window. One was harsh, rising almost to a shout, then sinking to a mutter. The other, speaking of Pas and Echidna, of Hierax and Molpe and all the gods, was in some odd fashion familiar.

He paused for a moment to listen, then sat down on the old worn step. It was—surely it was—his own.

". . . who makes the crops to shoot forth from dirt," said this second voice. "You sprats have all seen it, and you'd think it wonderfully wonderful if you hadn't."

It was his talk at manteion from Molpsday, or rather a parody of it. But perhaps he had really sounded like that, had sounded that foolish. No doubt he sounded that foolish still.

"Thus when we see the trees dancing in the breeze we are to think of her, but not only of her, of her mother, too, for we would not have her without her mother, or the trees, or even the dance."

He had said that, surely. Those had been his precise words—that babble. The Outsider had not only spoken to him, but had somehow split him in two: the Patera Silk who lived here and was speaking now in the musty sellaria, and he himself, Silk the failed thief—Silk the foe and tool of Blood, Silk who was Auk's friend, who had in his waistband an azoth lent him by a whore and her trumpery needler in his pocket.

Silk who longed to see her again.

The harsh voice: "Silk good!"

Perhaps. But was it that Silk or this one, himself? Was it this one, with Hyacinth's azoth in its hand, drawn unconsciously? This Silk who feared and hated Musk, and ached to kill him?

Of whom was he afraid? That other Silk would not have harmed a mouse, had postponed getting the ratsnake he needed again and again, visualizing the suffering of—rats. And yet it would be a fearful thing to meet that Silk whom he had been, and was a fearful thing to meet him now, in voice and memory. Had he truly become someone else?

He tore open the heavy, paper-wrapped packet Auk had put into his hand, dropping several needles. More filled the open breech of the needler like water; he released the loading knob and the breech closed. The needler would fire now if he needed it.

Or perhaps would not.

Patera Silk, and Silk nightside. He found that he, the latter, was contemptuous of the former, though envious, too.

His own voice echoed from the manse. "In the names of all the immortal gods, who give us all we have."

Strange gifts, at times. He had saved this manteion, or had at least postponed its destruction; now, hearing the voice of its augur, he knew that it had never really been worth saving—though he had been sent to save it. Grim-faced, he rose, thrust the azoth back into his waistband and dropped the needler into his pocket again with what remained of the packet of needles, and dusted the back of his robe.

Everything had changed because he himself was changed. How had it happened? When he climbed Blood's wall? When he had entered the manteion to get the hatchet? Long ago, when he had helped force the window, with the other boys? Or had Mucor laid some spell on him, there in her filthy, lightless room? Mucor was one who might lay spells, if any did; Mucor was a devil, in so far as devils were. Was it she who had drunk poor Teasel's blood?

"Mucor," Silk whispered. "Are you here? Are you still following me?" For a moment he seemed to hear an answering whisper, as the night wind stirred the dry leaves of the fig tree.

Gabbling now, his voice from the window: "Here hear what the Writings here have to Say-ilk. Here hear the high hopes of Horrible Hierax."

"Here axe," repeated the harsh voice, as though mocking his finding the hatchet, and Silk recognized it.

No, it had not been Mucor, or his deciding to take the hatchet or any such thing. All gods were good, but might not the unfathomable Outsider be good in a dark way? As Auk was, or as Auk might be? Suddenly Silk remembered the whorl outside the whorl, the Outsider's immeasurable whorl beneath his feet. So dark.

Yet lit by scattered motes.

With one hand on the needler in his pocket, he opened the door of the manse and stepped inside.

LAKE
OF THE
LONG
SUN

For Dan Knight,
who will understand more than most

CHAPTER
1   THEY HAD SCIENTISTS

Silence fell, abrupt as a shouted command, when Patera Silk opened the door of the old, three-sided manse at the slanted intersection where Sun Street met Silver. Horn, the tallest boy in the palaestra, was sitting bolt upright in the least comfortable chair in the musty little sellaria; Silk felt sure he had dropped into it hastily when he heard the rattle of the latch.

The night chough (Silk had stepped inside and shut the door behind him before he remembered that he had named the night chough Oreb) was perched on the high, tapestried back of the stiff "visitor's" chair.

" 'Lo, Silk," Oreb croaked. "Good Silk!"

"And good evening to you. A good evening to you both. Tartaros bless you."

Horn had risen as Silk entered; Silk motioned for him to sit again. "I apologize. I'm terribly sorry, Horn. I truly am. Maytera Rose told me she meant to send you to talk to me this evening, but I forgot all about it. So much has been—O Sphigx! Stabbing Sphigx, have pity on me!"

This last had been in response to sudden, lancing pain in his ankle. As he limped to the room's sole comfortable chair, the one in which he sat to read, it occurred to him that its seat was probably still warm; he considered feeling the cushion to make sure, rejected the idea as embarrassing to Horn, then (propping himself with Blood's lioness-headed walking stick) laid his free hand on the seat anyway out of sheer curiosity. It was.

"I sat down there for a minute, Patera. I could see your bird better from there."

"Of course." Silk sat, lifting his injured ankle onto the hassock. "You've been here half the night, no doubt."

"Only a couple hours, Patera. I sweep out for my father while he empties the till and—and—locks the money up."

Silk nodded approvingly. "That's right. You shouldn't tell me where he keeps it." He paused, recalling that he had intended to steal this very manteion from Blood. "I wouldn't steal it, because I'd never steal anything from you or your family; but you never know who may be listening."

Horn grinned. "Your bird might tell, Patera. Sometimes they take shiny things, that's what I've heard. Maybe a ring or a spoon."

"No steal!" Oreb protested.

"I was thinking of a human eavesdropper, actually. I shrove an unhappy young woman today, and I believe there was someone listening outside her window the whole time. There was a gallery out there, and once I felt certain I heard the boards creak when he shifted his weight. I was tempted to get up and look, but crippled as I am at present, he would've been gone before I could have put my head out of the window —and back again, no doubt, the moment I sat down." Silk sighed. "Fortunately she kept her voice quite low."

"Isn't listening like that a major offense against the gods, Patera?"

"Yes. Not that he cares, I'm afraid. The worst part of the whole affair is that I know the man—or at least, I'm beginning to know him—and I've liked what I've seen of him. There's a great deal of good in him, I feel certain, though he tries so hard to conceal it."

Oreb fluttered his sound wing. "Good Crane!"

"I didn't mention his name," Silk told Horn, "nor did you hear any name."

"No, Patera. Half the time I can't make out what that bird's saying."

"Fine. Perhaps it would be even better if you had as much difficulty understanding me."

Horn colored. "I'm sorry, Patera. I didn't want to—It wasn't because—"

"I didn't mean that," Silk explained hastily. "Not at all. We haven't even begun to talk about that yet, though we will. We must. I merely meant that I shouldn't even have mentioned shriving that woman. I'm much too tired to keep a proper watch on my tongue. And now that Patera Pike has left us—well, I still have Maytera Marble to confide in. I'd go mad, I think, if it weren't for her."

He leaned forward in the soft old chair, struggling to concentrate his surging thoughts. "I was going to say that though he's a good man, or at least a man who might be good, he has no faith in the gods; yet I'm going to have to get him to admit he listened, so I can shrive him of the guilt. It's sure to be difficult, but I've been examining the matter from all sides, Horn, and I can see no way to evade my duty."

"Yes, Patera."

"I don't mean this evening. I've been entirely too busy this evening, and this afternoon, too. I saw . . . something I can't tell you about, unfortunately. But I've been thinking about this particular man and the problem he presents ever since I came in. Seeing that blue thing on the bird's wing reminded me."

"I was wondering what that was, Patera."

"A splint, I suppose you'd call it." Silk glanced at the clock. "Your mother and father will be frantic."

Horn shook his head. "The rest of the sprats'll tell them where I went, Patera. I told them before I left."

"By Sphigx, I hope so." Silk leaned forward and drew up his injured leg, pushed down his stocking, and unwound the chamois-like wrapping. "Have you seen one of these, Horn?"

"A strip of leather, Patera?"

"It's much more than that." Silk tossed it to him. "I want you to do something for me, if you will. Kick it hard, so that it flies against the wall."

Horn gawked.

"If you're afraid you'll break something, throw it down hard three or four times. Not here on the carpet, I think. Over there on the bare boards. Hard, mind."

Horn did as he was told, then returned the wrapping to Silk. "It's getting hot."

"Yes, I thought it would." Silk rewound it about his aching ankle and smiled with satisfaction as it tightened. "It isn't just a strip of leather, you see, although it may be that its exterior actually is leather. Inside there's a mechanism, something as thin as the gold labyrinth in a card. When that mechanism is agitated, it must take up energy. At rest, it excretes a part of it as heat. The remainder emerges as sound, or so I was told. It makes a noise we can't hear, I suppose because it's too soft or perhaps because it's pitched too high. Can you hear it now?"

Horn shook his head.

"Neither can I, yet I could hear sounds that Patera Pike could not—the squeaking of the hinges on the garden gate, for example, until I oiled them."

Silk relaxed, soothed by the wrapping and the softness of his chair. "These wonderful wrappings were made in the Short-Sun Whorl, I imagine, like glasses and Sacred Windows, and so many other things that we have but can't replace."

"They had scientists there, Patera. That's what Maytera Rose says."

Oreb croaked, "Good Crane!"

Silk laughed. "Did he teach you to say that while he was treating your wing, you silly bird? Very well, Doctor Crane's a scientist of sorts, I suppose; he knows medicine at least, which is more science than most of us know, and he let me borrow this, though I must return it in a few days."

"A thing like that must be worth twenty or thirty cards, Patera."

"More than that. Do you know Auk? A big man who comes to sacrifice on Scylsdays?"

"I think so, Patera."

"Heavy jaw, wide shoulders, big ears. He wears a hanger and boots."

"I don't know him to talk to, Patera, but I know who you mean." Horn paused, his handsome young face serious. "He's trouble, that's what everybody says, the kind who knocks down people who get in his way. He did that to Teasel's father."

Silk had taken out his beads; he drew them through his fingers absently as he spoke. "I'm sorry to hear it. I'll try to speak to him about it."

"You'd better keep away from him, Patera."

Silk shook his head. "I can't, Horn. Not if I'm to do my duty. In fact, Auk's precisely the sort of person I must get close to. I don't believe that even the Outsider— And it's too late for that in any case. I was going to tell you that I showed this wrapping to Auk, and he indicated that it was worth a great deal more. That isn't important, however. Have you ever wondered why so much knowledge was left behind in the Short-Sun Whorl?"

"I guess the ones that knew about those things didn't come to our whorl, Patera."

"Clearly they did not. Or if they did, they can't have settled here in Viron. Yet they knew many things that would be very valuable to us, and certainly they would have had to come if Pas had instructed them to."

"The Fliers know how to fly, Patera, and we don't. We saw one yesterday, remember? Just after the ball game. He was pretty low. That's what I'd like to know. How to fly like they do, like a bird."

"No fly!" Oreb announced.

Silk studied the voided cross dangling from his beads for a moment, then let the beads fall into his lap. "This evening I was introduced to an elderly man who has a really extraordinary artificial leg, Horn. He had to buy up five broken or worn-out legs to build it, but it's an artificial leg such as the first settlers had—a leg that might have been brought from the Short-Sun Whorl. When he showed it to me, I thought how marvelous it would be if we could only make things like that now for Maytera

Rose and Maytera Marble, and for all the beggars who are blind or crippled. It would be marvelous to fly, too, of course. I've always wanted to do it myself, and it may be that they are the same secret. If we could build wonderful legs like that for the people who need them, perhaps we could build wonderful wings as well for everyone who wanted to have them."

"That would be great, Patera."

"It may come to pass. It may yet come to pass, Horn. If people in the Short-Sun Whorl could teach themselves to do such things . . ." Silk shook himself and yawned, then rose with the help of Blood's stick. "Well, thank you for coming by. It's been a pleasure, but I'd better go up to bed."

"I was supposed—Maytera said—"

"That's right." Silk put away his beads. "I'm supposed to punish you. Or lecture you, or something. What was it you did that made Maytera Rose so angry?"

Horn swallowed. "I was just trying to talk like you do, Patera. Like in manteion. It wasn't even today, and I won't do it again."

"Of course." Silk settled back into his chair. "But it *was* today, Horn. Or at least, today was one of several such days. I heard you before I opened the door. I sat down on the step for a minute to listen, in fact. You imitated me so well that for a while I actually thought that your voice was my own; it was like hearing myself. You're very good at it."

"Good boy," Oreb croaked. "No hit."

"I won't," Silk told the bird, and it lurched through the air to his lap, then hopped from his lap to the arm of the chair, and from the arm to his shoulder.

"Maytera Rose hits us sometimes, Patera."

"Yes, I know. It's very courageous of her, but I'm not at all certain it's wise. Let's hear you again, Horn. Out on the step, I couldn't hear everything you said."

Horn muttered, and Silk laughed. "I couldn't hear you that time, either. Surely I don't sound like that. When I'm at the ambion, I can hear my bray echo from the walls."

"No, Patera."

"Then say it again, just as I would. I won't be angry, I promise you."

"I was only . . . You know. Like the things you say."

"No talk?" Oreb inquired.

Silk ignored him. "Fine. Let me hear it. That's what you came to talk about, and I feel sure it will be a valuable corrective for me. I tend to get above myself, I'm afraid."

Horn shook his head and stared at the carpet.

"Oh, come now! What sorts of things do I say?"

"To always live with the gods, and you do it any time you're happy with the life they've given you. Think about who's wise and act like he does."

"That was well said, Horn, but you didn't sound in the least like me. It's my own voice I want to hear, just as I heard it on the step. Won't you do that?"

"I guess I've got to stand up, Patera."

"Then stand, by all means."

"Don't look at me. All right?"

Silk shut his eyes.

For half a minute or more there was silence. Through his eyelids, Silk could detect the fading of the light (the best in the manse) behind his chair. He welcomed it. His right forearm, torn by the hooked beak of the white-headed one the night before, felt hot and swollen now; and he was so tired that his entire body ached.

"Live with the gods," his own voice directed, "and he does live with the gods who consistently shows them that his spirit is satisfied with what has been assigned to him, and that it obeys all that the gods will—the spirit that Pas has given every man as his guardian and guide, the best part of himself, his understanding and his reason. As you intend to live hereafter, it is in your power to live here. But if men do not permit you, . . ."

Silk stepped on something that slid beneath his foot, and fell with a start to the red clay tiles.

". . . think of wisdom only as great wisdom, the wisdom of a prolocutor or a councillor. That itself is unwise. If you could talk this very day with a councillor or His Cognizance, either would tell you that wisdom may be small, a thing quite suited to the smallest children here, as well as great. What is a wise child? It is a child who seeks out wise teachers, and hears them."

Silk opened his eyes. "What you said first was from the Writings, Horn. Did you know it?"

"No, Patera. It's just something I've heard you say."

"I was quoting. It's good that you've got that passage by heart, even if you learned it only to make fun of me. Sit down. You were talking about wisdom. Well, no doubt I must have spouted all that foolishness, but you deserve to learn better. Who are the wise, Horn? Have you really considered that question? If not, do so now. Who are they?"

"Well . . . you, Patera."

"NO!" Silk rose so abruptly that the bird squawked. He strode to the window and stood staring out through the bars at the ruts of Sun Street, black now under a flood of uncanny skylight. "No, I'm not wise, Horn. Or at least, I've been wise for a moment only—one moment out of my whole life."

He limped across the room to Horn's chair and crouched before it, one knee on the carpet. "Allow me to tell you how foolish I have been. Do you know what I believed when I was your age? That nothing but thought, nothing except wisdom, mattered. You're good at games, Horn. You can run and jump, and you can climb. So was I and so did I, but I had nothing but contempt for those abilities. Climbing was nothing to boast of, when I couldn't climb nearly as well as a monkey. But I could think better than a monkey—better than anyone else in my class, in fact." He smiled bitterly, shaking his head. "And that was how I thought! Pride in nonsense."

"Isn't thinking good, Patera?"

Silk stood. "Only when we think rightly. Action, you see, is the end that thought achieves. Action is its only purpose. What else is it good for? If we don't act, it's worthless. If we can't act, useless."

He returned to his chair, but did not sit down. "How many times have you heard me talk about enlightenment, Horn? Twenty or thirty times, surely, and you remember very well. Tell me what I said."

Horn glanced miserably at Oreb as though for guidance, but the bird merely cocked his head and fidgeted on Silk's shoulder as if eager to hear what Horn had to say. At last he managed, "It—it's wisdom a god sort of pours into you. That doesn't come from a book or anything. And— and—"

"Perhaps you'd do better if you employed my voice," Silk suggested. "Stand up again and try it. I won't watch you if it makes you nervous."

Horn rose, lifting his head, rolling his eyes toward the ceiling, and drawing down the corners of his mouth. "Divine enlightenment means you know without thinking, and that isn't because thinking's bad but because enlightenment is better. Enlightenment is sharing in the thinking of the god."

He added in his normal voice, "That's as close as I can come, Patera, without more time to remember."

"Your choice of words might be improved upon," Silk told him judiciously, "but your intonation is excellent, and you have my speech mannerisms almost pat. What is of much, much more importance, nothing that you said was untrue. But who gets it, Horn? Who receives enlightenment?"

"People who've tried to live good lives for a long time. Sometimes they do."

"Not always?"

"No, Patera. Not always."

"Would you believe me, Horn—credit me fully without reservation—if I told you that I myself have received it? Yes or no."

"Yes, Patera. If you say so."

"That I received it only yesterday?"

Oreb whistled softly.

"Yes, Patera."

Silk nodded, mostly to himself it seemed. "I did, Horn, and not through any merit of mine. I was about to say that you were with me, but it wouldn't be true. Not really."

"Was it before manteion, Patera? Yesterday you said you wanted to make a private sacrifice. Was it for that?"

"Yes. I've never made it, and perhaps I never will—"

"No cut!"

"If I do, it won't be you," Silk told Oreb. "Probably it won't be a live animal at all, although I'm going to have to sacrifice a lot of them tomorrow, and buy them as well."

"Pet bird?"

"Yes, indeed." Silk lifted Blood's lioness-headed stick to shoulder height; Oreb hopped onto it, turning his head to watch Silk from each eye.

Horn said, "He wouldn't let me touch him, Patera."

"You had no reason to touch him, and he didn't know you. All animals hate the touch of a stranger. Have you ever kept a bird?"

"No, Patera. I had a dog, but she died."

"I was hoping to get some advice. I wouldn't want Oreb to die—although I'd imagine that night choughs are hardy creatures. Hold out your wrist."

Horn did, and Oreb hopped onto it. "Good boy!"

"I wouldn't try to hold him," Silk said. "Let him hold you. You can't have had many toys as a child, Horn."

"Not many. We were—" Suddenly, Horn smiled. "There was one. My grandfather made it, a wooden man with a blue coat. It had strings, and if you did them right, you could make him walk and bow."

"Yes!" Silk's eyes flashed, and the tip of the lioness-headed stick thumped the floor. "That's exactly the sort of toy I mean. May I tell you about one of mine? You may think I'm straying from the topic, but I won't be, I promise you."

"Sure, Patera. Go ahead."

"There were two dancers, a man and a woman, very neatly painted. They danced on a little stage, and when I wound it up, music played. And they danced, the little woman quite gracefully, and the little man somer-saulting and spinning and cutting all sort of capers. There were three tunes—you moved a lever to choose the one you wanted—and I used to play with it for hours, singing songs I'd made up for myself and imagining things for him to say to her, and for her to say to him. Silly things, most of them, I'm afraid."

"I understand, Patera."

"My mother died during my last year at the schola, Horn. Possibly I've already told you that. I'd been cramming for an examination, but the Prelate called me into his chambers again and told me that after her last sacrifice I would have to go home and remove my personal belongings. Our house—her whole estate, but it was mostly the house—went to the Chapter, you understand. One signs an agreement before one enters the schola."

"Poor Silk!"

He smiled at the bird. "Perhaps, though I didn't think so at the time. I was miserable on account of my mother's death, but I don't believe that I ever felt sorry for myself. I had books to read, and friends, and enough to eat. But now I really am wandering from the subject.

"To hurry back to it, I found that toy in the back of my closet. I had been at the schola for six years, and I doubt that I'd so much as laid eyes on the toy for years before I left. Now here it was again! I wound it up, and the dancers danced once more, and the music played exactly as it had when I was a little boy. The tune was 'First Romance,' and I'll never forget that song now."

Horn coughed. "Nettle and me talk about that sometimes, Patera. You know, when we're older."

"Nettle and I," Silk corrected him absently. "That's good, Horn. It's very good, and you'll both be older much sooner than you imagine. I'll pray for you both.

"But I had intended to say that I cried then. I hadn't at her rites; I hadn't been able to, not even when her casket was put into the ground. But I did then, because it seemed to me that for the dancers no time at all had passed. That they couldn't know that the man who wound them now was the boy who had wound them the last time, or that the woman who had bought them on Clock Street was dead. Do you follow what I'm saying, Horn?"

"I think so, Patera."

"Enlightenment is like that for the whole whorl. Time has stopped for everyone else. For you, there is something outside it—a peritime in which the god speaks to you. For me, that god was the Outsider. I don't think I've said much about him when I've talked to the palaestra, but I will be saying a great deal about him in the future. Maytera Mint said something to me this afternoon that has remained with me ever since. She said that he was unlike the other gods, who take council with one another in Mainframe; that no one save himself knew his mind. Maytera Mint has great humility, but she has wisdom, too. I must remember not to let the first blind me to the second."

"Good girl!"

"Yes, and great goodness, too. Humility and purity."

Horn said, "About enlightenment, Patera. Yours, I mean. Is that why somebody's writing things about you getting to be caldé?"

Silk snapped his fingers. "I'm glad you mentioned that—I had intended to ask you about it. I knew I'd forgotten something. Someone had chalked, 'Silk for caldé,' on a wall; I saw it on the way home. Did you do that?"

Horn shook his head.

"Or one of the other boys?"

"I don't think it was one of us sprats at all, Patera. It's on two places. There on the slop shop, and then over on Hat Street, on that building Gosseyplum lives in. I've looked at them both, and they're pretty high up. I could do it without standing on anything and I think maybe Locust could, but he says he didn't."

Silk nodded to himself. "Then I believe you're correct, Horn. It was because I've been enlightened. Or rather it's happened because I told someone about it, and was overheard. I've told several persons now, yourself included, and perhaps I shouldn't have."

"What was it like, Patera? Besides everything stopped, like you said?"

For several tickings of the clock on the mantel, Silk sat silent, contemplating for the hundredth time the experience he had by this time revolved in his mind so often that it was like a water-smoothed stone, polished and opaque. At last he said, "In that moment I understood all that I'll ever truly need to know. It's erroneous, really, for me to call it a moment, when it was actually outside time. But I, Horn,"—he smiled—"I am inside time, just as you are. And I find that it takes time for me to comprehend everything that I was told in that moment that was not a moment. It takes time for me to assimilate it. Am I making myself clear?"

Poor Horn nodded hesitantly. "I think so, Patera."

"That may be good enough." Silk paused again, lost in thought. "One of the things I learned was that I'm to be a teacher. There's only one thing that the Outsider wishes me to do—I am to save our manteion. But it is as a teacher that he wishes me to do it.

"There are many callings, Horn, the highest being pure worship. That isn't mine; mine is to teach, and a teacher has to act as well as think. The old man I met this evening—the man with the wonderful leg—was a teacher, too; and yet he's all action, all activity, as old as he is, and one-legged, too. He teaches swordfighting. Why do you think he is as he is? All action?"

Horn's eyes shone. "I don't know, Patera. Why?"

"Because a fight with swords—still more, with azoths—affords no time for reflection; thus to be all action is a part of what he has to teach. Listen carefully now. *He has thought about that.* Do you understand? Even though fighting with a sword must be all action, teaching others that kind of fighting requires thought. The old man had to think not only about what he was to teach, but about how he could best teach it."

Horn nodded. "I think I understand, Patera."

"In the same way, Horn, you must think about imitating me. Not merely about how I can be imitated, but about what to imitate. And when to do it. Now go home."

Oreb flapped his sound wing. "Wise man!"

"Thank you. Go, Horn. If Oreb wishes to go with you, you may keep him."

"Patera?"

Silk rose as Horn did. "Yes. What is it?"

"Are you going to study swordfighting?"

For a moment Silk considered his reply. "There are more important things to learn than swordfighting, Horn. Whom to fight, for example. One of them is to keep secrets. Someone who holds in confidence only those secrets he has been told not to reveal can never be trusted. Surely you understand that."

"Yes, Patera."

"And there is more to be learned from any good teacher than the subject taught. Tell your father and mother that I didn't keep you so late in order to punish you, but through carelessness, for which I apologize."

"No go!" Fluttering frenziedly, Oreb half flew and half fell from Horn's shoulder to the lofty back of the tapestried chair. "Bird stay!"

Horn's hand was already on the latch. "I'll tell them we were just talking, Patera. I'll say you were teaching me about the Outsider and a lot of other things. It'll be the truth."

Oreb croaked, "Good-bye! Bye, boy!"

"You foolish bird," Silk said as the door closed behind Horn, "what have you learned from all this? A few new words, perhaps, which you will misapply."

"Gods' ways!"

"Oh, yes. You're very wise now." Although it was still warm, Silk unwound the wrapping. After beating the hassock with it, he wrapped it around his forearm over the bandage.

"Man god. My god."

"Shut up," his god told him wearily.

He had thrust his arm into the glass, where Kypris was kissing it. Her lips were as chill as death, but it was a death he welcomed at first. In time he grew frightened and struggled to withdraw it, but Kypris would not release it. When he shouted for Horn, no sound issued from his mouth. Orchid's sellaria was in the manse, which did not seem odd at all; a wild wind moaned in the chimney. He remembered that Auk had foretold such a wind, and tried to recall what Auk had said would happen when it blew.

Without relinquishing her grip on his arm, the goddess revolved, her own arms upraised; she wore a clinging gown of liquid spring. He was acutely conscious of the roundness of her thighs, the double globosity of her hips. As he stared, Blood's orchestra played "First Romance" and Kypris became Hyacinth (though Kypris still) and lovelier than ever. He kicked and tumbled, his feet above his head, but his hand clasped hers and would not be torn from it.

He woke gasping for breath. The lights had extinguished themselves. In the faint skylight from a curtained window, he saw Oreb hop out and flap away. Mucor stood beside his bed, naked in the darkness and skeletally thin; he blinked; she faded to mist and was gone.

He rubbed his eyes.

A warm wind moaned as it had in his dream, dancing with his ragged, pale curtains. The wrapping on his arm was pale too, white with frost that melted at a touch. He unwound it and whipped the damp sheet with it, then wound it about his newly painful ankle, telling himself that he should not have climbed the stairs without it. What would Doctor Crane say when he told him?

The whipping had evoked a spectral glow from the lights, enough for him to distinguish the hands of the busy little clock beside his triptych. It was after midnight.

Leaving his bed, he lowered the sash. Not until it was down did he realize that he could not have seen Oreb fly out—Oreb had a dislocated wing.

Downstairs, he found Oreb poking about the kitchen in search of something to eat. He put out the last slice of bread and refilled the bird's cup with clean water.

"Meat?" Oreb cocked his head and clacked his beak.

"You'll have to find some for yourself if you want it," Silk told him. "I haven't any." After a moment's thought he added, "Perhaps I'll buy a little tomorrow, if Maytera cashed Orchid's draft, or I can myself. Or at least a fish—a live one I could keep in the washtub until whatever's left over from the sacrifices runs out, and then share with Maytera Rose. And Maytera Mint, of course. Wouldn't you like some nice, fresh fish, Oreb?"

"Like fish!"

"All right, I'll see what I can do. But you have to be forthcoming with me now. No fish if you're not. Were you in my bedroom?"

"No steal!"

"I didn't say that you stole," Silk explained patiently. "Were you there?"

"Where?"

"Up there." Silk pointed. "I know you were. I woke up and saw you."

"No, no!"

"Of course you were, Oreb. I saw you myself. I watched you fly out the window."

"No fly!"

"I'm not going to punish you. I simply want to know one thing. Listen carefully now. When you were upstairs, did you see a woman? Or a girl? A thin young woman, unclothed, in my bedroom?"

"No fly," the bird repeated stubbornly. "Wing hurt."

Silk ran his fingers through his strawstack hair. "All right, you can't fly. I concede that. Were you upstairs?"

"No steal." Oreb clacked his beak again.

"Nor did you steal. That is understood as well."

"Fish heads?"

Silk threw caution to the wind. "Yes, several. Big ones, I promise you."

Oreb hopped onto the window ledge. "No see."

"Look at me, please. Did you see her?"

"No see."

"You were frightened by something," Silk mused, "though it may have been my waking. Perhaps you were afraid that I'd punish you for looking around my bedroom. Was that it?"

"No, no!"

"This window is just below that one. I *thought* I saw you fly, but I really saw you hop out the window and drop down into the blackberries. From there it would have been easy for you to get back here into the kitchen through the window. Isn't that what happened?"

"No hop!"

"I don't believe you, because—" Silk paused. Faintly, he had heard the creak of Patera Pike's bed; he felt a pang of guilt at having awakened the old man, who always labored so hard and slept so badly—although he had dreamed (only dreamed, he told himself firmly) that Pike was dead, as he had dreamed, also, that Hyacinth had kissed his arm, that he had talked to Kypris in an old yellow house on Lamp Street: to Lady Kypris, the Goddess of Love, the whores' goddess.

Shaken by doubt, he went back to the pump and worked its handle again until clear icy water gushed into the stoppered sink, splashed his sweating face again and again, and soaked and resoaked his untidy hair until he was actually shivering despite the heat of the night.

"Patera Pike is dead," he told Oreb, who cocked his head sympathetically.

Silk filled the kettle and set it on the stove, starting the fire with an extravagant expenditure of wastepaper; when flames licked the sides of the kettle, he seated himself in the unsteady wooden chair in which he sat to eat and pointed a finger at Oreb. "Patera Pike left us last spring; that's practically a year ago. I performed his rites myself, and even without a headstone, his grave cost more than we could scrape together. So what I heard was the wind or something of that sort. Rats, perhaps. Am I making myself clear?"

"Eat now?"

"No." Silk shook his head. "There's nothing left but a little maté and a very small lump of sugar. I plan to brew myself a cup of maté and drink it, and go back to bed. If you can sleep too, I advise it."

Overhead (above the sellaria, Silk felt quite certain) Patera Pike's old bed creaked again.

He rose. Hyacinth's engraved needler was still in his pocket, and before he had entered the manse that evening he had charged it with needles from the packet Auk had bought for him. He pulled back the loading knob to assure himself that there was a needle ready to fire, and pressed down the safety catch. Crossing the kitchen to the stair, he called, "Mucor? Is that you?"

There was no reply.

"If it is, cover yourself. I'm coming up to talk to you."

The first step brought a twinge of pain from his ankle. He wished for Blood's stick, but it was leaning against the head of his bed.

Another step, and the floor above creaked. He mounted three more steps, then stopped to listen. The night wind still sighed about the manse, moaning in the chimney as it had in his dream. It had been that wind, surely, that had made the old structure groan, that had caused him—fool that he was—to think that he had heard the old augur's bed creak, squeak, and readjust its old sticks and straps as Patera rolled his old body, sitting up for a moment to pray or peer out through the empty, open windows before lying down again on his back, on his side.

A door shut softly upstairs.

It had been his own, surely—the door to his bedroom. He had paid it no attention when he had put on his trousers and hurried downstairs to look for Oreb. All the doors in the manse swung of their own accord unless they were kept latched, opening or shutting in walls that were no longer plumb, cracked old doors in warped frames that had perhaps never been quite right, and certainly were not square now.

His finger was closing on the trigger of the needler; recalling Auk's warning, he put his fingertip on the trigger guard. "Mucor? I don't want to hurt you. I just want to talk to you. Are you up there?"

No voice, no footfall, from the upper floor. He went up a few more steps. He had shown Auk the azoth, and that had been most imprudent; an azoth was worth thousands of cards. Auk broke into larger and better defended houses than this whenever he chose. Now Auk had come for the azoth or sent an accomplice, seen his opportunity when the kitchen lights kindled.

"Auk? It's me, Patera Silk."

There came no answering voice.

"I've got a needler, but I don't want to have to shoot. If you raise your hands and offer no resistance, I won't. I won't turn you over to the Guard, either."

His voice had energized the single dim light above the landing. Ten steps remained, and Silk climbed them slowly, his progress retarded by fear as much as pain, seeing first the black-clad legs in the doorway of his bedroom, then the hem of the black robe, and at last the aged augur's smiling face.

Patera Pike waved and melted into silver mist; his blue-trimmed black calot dropping softly onto the uneven boards of the landing.

CHAPTER

2   LADY KYPRIS

Neither Silk nor Maytera Marble had remembered mutes, yet mutes appeared an hour before Orpine's rites were to begin, alerted by the vendor who had supplied the rue. Promised two cards, they had already gashed their arms, chests, and cheeks with flints by the time the first worshipers arrived, and were the very skiagraph of misery, their long hair fluttering in the wind as they rent their sooty garments, howled aloud, or knelt to smear their bleeding faces with dust.

Five long benches had been set aside in the front of the manteion for the mourners, who began to arrive by twos and threes some while after the unrestricted portion of the old manteion on Sun Street was full. For the most part they were the young women whom Silk had seen the previous afternoon at Orchid's yellow house on Lamp Street, though there were a few tradesmen as well (dragooned, Silk did not doubt, by Orchid), and a leaven of rough-looking men who could easily have been friends of Auk's.

Auk himself was there as well, and he had brought the ram he had pledged. Maytera Mint had seated him among the mourners, her face aglow with happiness; Silk assumed that Auk had explained to her that he had been a friend of the deceased. Silk accepted the ram's tether, thanked Auk with formal courtesy (receiving an abashed smile in return), and led the ram out the side door into the garden, where Maytera Marble presided over what was very nearly a menagerie.

"That heifer's stolen several mouthfuls of my parsley," she told Silk, "and trampled my grass a bit. But she's left me a present, too, so that I'll have a much nicer garden next year. And those rabbits—oh, Patera, isn't it grand! Just look at all of them!"

Silk did, stroking his right cheek while he deliberated the sacred sequence of sacrifice. Some augurs preferred to take the largest beast first, some to begin with a general sacrifice to the entire Nine; that would be the white heifer in either case today. On the other hand, . . .

"The wood hasn't arrived yet. Maytera insisted on going herself. I wanted to send some of the boys. If she doesn't ride back on the cart . . ."

That was Maytera Rose, of course, and Maytera Rose could scarcely walk. "People are still coming," Silk told Maytera Marble absently, "and I can stand up there and talk awhile, if necessary." He would (as he admitted after a moment of merciless self-scrutiny) have welcomed an excuse to begin Orpine's rites without Maytera Rose—and to complete them without her, for that matter. But until the cedar came and the sacred fire had been laid, there could be no sacrifices.

He reentered the manteion just in time to witness the arrival of Orchid, overdressed in puce velvet and sable in spite of the heat, and somewhat drunk. Tears streamed down her cheeks as he conducted her to the aisle seat in the first row that had been marked off for her; and though he felt that he ought to be amused by her unsteady gait and clattering jet beads, he discovered that he pitied her with all his heart. Her daughter, shielded by a nearly invisible polymer sheet from the dampness of her sparkling couch of ice, appeared by comparison contented and composed.

"The black ewe first," Silk found himself muttering, and could not have explained how he had reached his decision. He informed Maytera Marble, then stepped through the garden gate and out into Sun Street to look for Maytera Rose's cartload of cedar.

Worshipers were still trickling in, faces familiar from scores of Scylsdays, and unfamiliar ones who were presumably connected in some fashion to Orpine or Orchid, or had merely heard (as the whole quarter appeared to have heard) that rich and plentiful sacrifices would be offered to the gods today on Sun Street, in what was perhaps the poorest manteion in all Viron.

"Can't I get in, Patera?" inquired a voice at his elbow. "They won't let me."

Startled, Silk looked down into the almost circular face of Scleroderma, the butcher's wife, nearly as wide as she was high. "Of course you can," he said.

"There's some men at the door."

Silk nodded. "I know. I put them there. If I hadn't, there would have been no places for the mourners, and a riot before the first sacrifice, as likely as not. We'll let some of them stand in the side aisles once the wood arrives."

He took her through the garden gate and locked it behind them.

"I come every Scylsday."

"I know you do," Silk told her.

"And I put something in whenever I can. Pretty often, too. I almost always put in at least a bit."

Silk nodded. "I know that, too. That's why I'm going to take you in through the side door, quietly. We'll pretend that you brought a sacrifice. Hurriedly he added, "Although we won't say that."

"And I'm sorry about the cats' meat, that time. Dumping it all over you like that. It was a terrible thing to do. I was just mad." She had waddled ahead of him, perhaps because she did not want to meet his eyes; now she stopped to admire the white heifer. "Look at the meat on her!"

He could not help smiling. "I wish I had some of your cats' meat now. I'd give it to my bird."

"Have you got a bird? Lots of people buy my meat for their dogs. I'll bring you some."

He took her in through the side door as he had promised, and turned her over to Horn.

By the time that he had mounted the steps to the ambion, the first shoulderload of cedar was coming down the center aisle. Maytera Rose seemed to materialize beside the altar to supervise the laying of the fire, and the trope restored Patera Pike—almost forgotten in the bustle of preparations that morning—to the forefront of Silk's mind.

Or rather, as Silk told himself firmly, Patera's ghost. There was nothing to be gained by denial, by not calling the thing by its proper name. He had championed the spiritual and the supernatural since boyhood. Was he to fly in terror now from the mere mention of a supernatural spirit?

The Charismatic Writings lay on the ambion, placed there by Maytera Marble over an hour ago. On Phaesday he had told the children from the palaestra that they could always find guidance there. He would begin with a reading, then; perhaps there would be something there for him as well, as there had been on that afternoon two days ago. He opened the book at random and silenced the assembled worshipers with his eyes.

"We know that death is the door to life—even as the life we know is the door to death. Let us discover what counsel the wisdom of the past will provide to our departed sibling, and to us."

Silk paused. Chenille (her fiery hair, illuminated from behind by the hot sunshine of the entrance, identified her at once) had just stepped inside the manteion. He had told her to attend, he recalled—had demanded that she attend, in fact. Very well, here she was. He smiled at her, but her eyes, larger and darker than he remembered them, were fixed on Orpine's body.

"Let us hope that they will not only prepare us to face death, but better fit us to amend our lives." After another solemn pause, he scanned the page. " 'Everyone who is grieved at anything, or discontented, is like a pig for sacrifice, kicking and squealing. Like a dove for sacrifice is he who laments in silence. Our one distinction is that it is given us to consent, if we will, to the necessity imposed upon us all.' "

A wisp of fragrant cedar smoke drifted past the ambion. The fire was lit; the sacrifices might proceed. In a moment Maytera Marble, in the garden, would see smoke rising through the god gate in the roof and lead the black ewe out onto Sun Street and into the manteion through the main entrance. Silk gestured to the brawny laymen he had stationed there, and the side aisles began to fill.

"Here, truly, is the counsel we sought. Soon I will ask the gods to speak to us directly, should they so choose. But what could they tell us that would be of better service to us than the wisdom that they have just provided to us? Nothing, surely. Consider then. What is the necessity laid upon us? Our own deaths? That is beyond dispute. But much, much more as well. We are every one of us subject to fear, to disease, and to numerous other evils. What is worse, we suffer this: the loss of our friend, the loss of our lover, the loss of our child."

He waited apprehensively, hoping that Orchid would not burst into tears.

"All of these things," he continued, "are conditions of our existence. Let us submit to them with good will."

Chenille was seated now, next to the small, dark Poppy. Studying her blank, brutally attractive face and empty eyes, Silk recalled that she was addicted to the ocher drug called rust. It had stimulated Hyacinth, he remembered; presumably different people reacted differently, and it seemed likely that Hyacinth had not taken as much.

"Orpine lies here before us, yet we know that she is not here. We will not see her again in this life. She was kind, beautiful, and generous. Her happiness she shared with us. What her sorrows were we cannot now learn, for she did not trouble others with them but bore their burden alone. That she was favored by Molpe we know, for she died in youth. If you wonder why a goddess should favor her, consider what I have just said. Riches cannot buy the favor of the gods—everything in the whorl is already theirs. Nor can authority command it; we are subject to them, not they to us, and so it shall forever be. We of this sacred city of Viron did not greatly value Orpine, perhaps; certainly we did not value her as her merits deserved. But in the eyes of the all-knowing gods, our valuations mean nothing. In the eyes of the all-knowing gods she was precious."

Silk turned to address the grayish glow of the Sacred Window behind him. "Accept, all you gods, the sacrifice of this fair young woman. Though our hearts are torn, we—her mother" (there was a sudden hum of whispered questions among the mourners) "and her friends—consent."

The mutes, who had remained silent while Silk spoke, shrieked in chorus.

"But speak to us, we beg, of the times to come. Of hers as well as ours. What are we to do? Your lightest word will be treasured. Should you, however, choose otherwise . . ." He waited silently, his arms out-stretched. As always, there was no sound from the window, no flicker of color.

He let his arms fall to his sides. "We consent still. Speak to us, we beg, through our other sacrifices."

Maytera Marble, who had been waiting just inside the Sun Street door, entered leading the black ewe.

"This fine black ewe is presented to High Hierax, Lord of Death and Orpine's lord hereafter, by Orchid, her mother." Silk drew his sacrificial gauntlets and accepted the bone-hilted knife of sacrifice from Maytera Rose.

Maytera Marble whispered, "The lamb?" and he nodded.

A stab and slash almost too quick to be seen dispatched the ewe. Maytera Mint knelt to catch some of the blood in an earthenware chalice. A moment later she splashed it upon the fire, producing an impressive hiss and a plume of steam. The point of Silk's knife found the joint between two vertebrae, and the black ewe's head came off cleanly, still streaming blood. He held it up, then laid it on the fire. All four of the hoofs followed in quick succession.

Knife in hand, he turned again toward the Sacred Window. "Accept, O High Hierax, the sacrifice of this fine ewe. And speak to us, we beg, of the times that are to come. What are we to do? Your lightest word will be treasured. Should you, however, choose otherwise . . ."

He let his arms fall to his sides. "We consent. Speak to us, we beg, through this sacrifice."

Lifting the ewe's carcass to the edge of the altar, he opened the paunch. The science of augury proceeded from certain fixed rules, though there was room for individual interpretation as well. Studying the tight convolutions of the ewe's entrails and the bloodred liver, Silk shuddered. Maytera Mint, who knew something of augury too, as all the sibyls did, had turned her face away.

"Hierax warns us that many more are to walk the path that Orpine has walked." Silk struggled to keep his voice expressionless. "Plague, war, or famine await us. Let us not say that the immortal gods have permitted these evils to strike us without warning." There was an uneasy stir among the worshipers. "That being so, let us be doubly thankful to the gods, who graciously share their meal with us.

"Orchid, you have presented this gift, and so have first claim upon the sacred meal it provides. Do you want it? Or a part of it?"

Orchid shook her head.

"In that case, the sacred meal will be shared among us. Let all those among us who wish to do so come forward and claim a portion." Silk pitched his voice to the laymen at the Sun Street entrance, although their continued presence went far to answer his question. "Are there more outside? Many more?"

A man replied, "Hundreds, Patera!"

"Then I must ask those who share in the sacred meal to leave at once. One additional person will be admitted for each who leaves."

At every sacrifice that Silk had previously performed, those who came to the altar had gotten no more than a single thin slice. This was his chance to indulge his charitable nature, and he did—an entire leg to one, half the loin to another, and the whole breast to a third; the neck he passed to one of the women who cooked for the palaestra, a rack to an elderly widow whose house was not fifty strides from the manse. The twinges in his ankle were a small price to pay for the smiles and thanks of the recipients.

"This black lamb I myself offer to Tenebrous Tartaros, in fulfillment of a vow."

The lamb dispatched, Silk addressed the Sacred Window. "Accept, O Tenebrous Tartaros, the sacrifice of this lamb. And speak to us, we beg, of the times that are to come. What are we to do? Your lightest word will be treasured. Should you, however, choose otherwise . . ."

He let his arms fall to his sides. "We consent. Speak to us, we beg, through this sacrifice."

The black lamb's entrails were somewhat more favorable. "Tartaros, Lord of Darkness, warns us that many of us must soon go into a realm he rules, though we shall emerge again into the light. Those of you who will are welcome to come forward and claim a portion of this sacred meal."

The black cock struggled in Maytera Marble's grasp, freeing and flapping its wings, always a bad sign. Silk offered it entire, filling the manteion with the stink of burning feathers.

"This gray ram is offered by Auk. Since it is neither black nor white, it cannot be offered to the Nine, singly or collectively. It can, however, be offered to all the gods or to some specific minor god. To whom are we to offer it, Auk? You'll have to speak loudly, I'm afraid."

Auk rose. "To that one you're always talking about, Patera."

"To the Outsider. May he speak to us through augury!" Suddenly and inexplicably Silk was overjoyed. At his signal, Maytera Rose and Maytera Mint heaped the altar with fragrant cedar until its flames reached beyond the god gate and leaped above the roof.

"Accept, O Obscure Outsider, the sacrifice of this fine ram. And speak to us, we beg, of the times that are to come. What are we to do? Your lightest word will be treasured. Should you, however, choose otherwise . . ."

He let his arms fall to his sides. "We consent. Speak to us, we beg, through this sacrifice."

The ram's head burst in the fire as he knelt to examine the entrails. "This god speaks to us freely," he announced after a protracted study. "I do not believe I have ever seen so much written in a single beast. There is a message here for you personally, Auk, by which I mean that it carries the sign of the giver. May I pronounce it now? Or would you prefer that I impart it to you in private? I would call it good news."

From his place on a front bench, Auk rumbled, "Whatever you think best, Patera."

"Very well then. The Outsider indicates that in the past you have acted alone, but that time is nearly over. You will stand at the head of a host of brave men. They and you will triumph."

Auk's mouth pursed in a silent whistle.

"There is a message here for me as well. Since Auk has been so forthright, I can do no less. I am to do the will of the god who speaks, and the will of Pas as well. Certainly I will strive to do both, and from the manner in which they are written here, I believe that they are one." Silk hesitated, his teeth scraping his lower lip; the joy that he had felt a moment before had melted like the ice around Orpine's body. "There is a weapon here as well, a weapon aimed at my heart. I will try to prepare." He drew a deep breath, fearful, yet ashamed of his fear.

"Lastly, there is a message for all of us: When danger threatens, we are to find safety between narrow walls. Does anyone know what that may mean?"

Though his legs felt weak, Silk rose and scanned the sea of faces before him. "The man sitting near Tartaros's image. Have you a suggestion, my son?"

The man in question spoke, inaudibly to Silk.

"Would you stand, please? Let us hear you."

"There's old tunnels underneath of the city, Patera. Fallin' down in places, an' some's full of water. My bunch hit one last week, diggin' for the new fisc. Only they had us to fill it in so nobody'd get hurt. Pretty narrow down there, an' everything shiprock."

Silk nodded. "I've heard of them before. They could be a place of refuge, I suppose, and they may well be what is meant."

A woman said, "In our houses. There's nobody here that has a big house."

Orchid turned in her seat to glare at her.

"In a boat," suggested a man on the other side of the aisle.

"Those are all possibilities as well. Let us keep the Outsider's message in mind. I feel certain that its meaning will be made apparent to us when the time comes."

Maytera Marble was standing at the back of the manteion with a pair of doves. Silk said, "Auk has first claim on the sacred meal. Auk? Do you wish to claim all or a portion of it, my son?"

Auk shook his head, and Silk swiftly divided the ram's carcass, casting its heart, lungs and intestines into the altar fire when everything else was gone.

Maytera Marble held one dove while Silk presented the other to the Sacred Window. "Accept, O Comely Kypris, the sacrifice of these fine white doves. And speak to us, we beg, of the times that are to come. What are we to do? Your lightest word will be treasured. Should you, however, choose otherwise . . ."

He let his arms fall to his sides. "We consent. Speak to us, we beg, through this sacrifice."

A single deft motion severed the head of the first dove. Silk consigned it to the flames, then held the fluttering, crimson and white body so that the blazing cedar was sprayed with blood. At first he thought the staring eyes and open mouths of the mourners and the throng who had come to worship or in hope of sharing Orpine's mortuary sacrifices no more than a reaction to something that had happened at the altar. Perhaps his gauntlets or his robe had taken fire, or old Maytera Rose had fallen.

* * *

Maytera Marble saw the Sacred Window blaze with color, and heard an
indistinct voice. A god spoke, as Pas had in Patera Pike's time. She fell to
her knees, and in so doing involuntarily freed the dove she had been
holding. It shot toward the roof, and then, seeming almost to ride the
sacred flames, rose through the god gate and was gone. An unshaven
man in the second row, seeing her upon her knees, knelt too. In a moment more, the bespangled, brilliantly dressed young women who had
come with Orchid were kneeling, too, nudging one another and tugging
at the skirts of those who still sat transfixed. When Maytera Marble
raised her head at last to see, for what would almost certainly be the final
time in her life, the swirling colors of present divinity, Patera Silk was
beside her, his hands lifted in supplication.

"Come back!" Silk implored the dancing colors and that gentle thunder. "Oh, come back!"

> *Maytera Mint saw the goddess's face clearly and heard her voice, and
> even Maytera Mint, who knew so little of the world and wished to
> know less, knew that both exceeded in beauty any mortal woman's.
> They were also very much like her own, and seemed to become more
> so as she looked, until at last, moved by reverence and superabundant
> modesty, she closed her eyes. It was the greatest sacrifice that she had
> ever made, though she had made thousands, of which five at least had
> been very great indeed.*

Maytera Rose was the last of the three sibyls to kneel, out of no lack of
reverence, but because kneeling involved certain body parts with which
she had been born—parts that were now in a strict sense dead, though
they still functioned and would continue to function for years to come.
Echidna had blinded her to the gods, the goddess's just punishment, and
so she saw and heard nothing, though the holy hues danced again and
again across and down the Sacred Window. In the deep tones of the
divine voice, tones that she found herself comparing to those of a cello,
she occasionally caught a word or a phrase. Young Patera Silk (who was
always so careless, and never more careless than when dealing with matters of the greatest importance) had dropped the knife of sacrifice, the
knife that Maytera Rose had cleaned and oiled and sharpened now for
almost a century, still dyed with the dove's blood. Stretching, Maytera
Rose retrieved it. Its bone handle had not cracked; its blade did not even
seem to have been soiled by its brief contact with the floor, though she

wiped it on her sleeve as a precaution. Absently, she tested the point against the tip of her thumb as she listened and sometimes made out, or nearly made out, a short sentence played by an orchestra too wonderful for this poor whorl, this whorl which was, like Maytera Rose herself, worn out and worn away, past its time which had never come, too old, though it was not even as old as Maytera Marble and though it was so much nearer to death. Cellos of the woods of Mainframe, flutes of diamond. Maytera herself, old Maytera Rose who was so tired that she no longer knew that she was tired, had once played the flute. She had not thought of her flute since the shame of blood. Pain's eaten it away, she thought, tortured it to silence, though once it sounded sweetly, oh, so sweetly, at evening.

Somehow old Maytera Rose sensed that this goddess was not Echidna. Thelxiepeia, maybe, or even Scalding Scylla. Scylla was another favorite of hers, and this was Scylsday, after all.

The voice was stilled. Slowly, the colors faded like the beautiful and complex tinctures of river-washed stones, which fade to nothing as the stones dry in the sunshine. Still on his knees, Silk bowed, his forehead touching the floor of the sanctuary. A murmur rose from the mourners and worshipers and soared until it was like the roaring of a storm. Silk glanced over his shoulder at them. One of the rough-looking men sitting with Orchid appeared to be shouting as he shook his fist at the Sacred Window, his eyes bulging and his face purple with some emotion at which Silk could only guess. A lovely young woman with curls as black as Orchid's beads was dancing in the center aisle to a music played for her alone.

Silk stood and limped slowly to the ambion. "All of you are entitled to hear—"

His voice seemed nonexistent. His tongue and lips had moved, and air had passed them, but no trumpeter could have made himself heard above the din.

Silk raised his hands and looked at the Sacred Window again. It was a shimmering gray, as empty as if no goddess had ever spoken through it. Yesterday in the yellow house on Lamp Street, the goddess had told him that she would speak to him again soon, repeating *soon.*

She kept her word, he thought.

Almost idly it occurred to him that the registers behind the Sacred Window would no longer be empty, as he had always seen them. One would show a single one, now; the other would display the length of the goddess's theophany, in units that no living person understood. He wanted to look at them, to verify the reality of what he had just seen and heard.

"All of you are entitled to hear—" His voice sounded weak and reedy, but at least he could hear it.

All of you are entitled to hear yourselves speaking when you could not hear yourselves at all, he thought. All of you are entitled to know how you felt and what you said to the goddess, or wanted to say—though most of us never will.

The tumult was subsiding now, falling like a wave on the lake. Strongly, Silk told himself, from the diaphragm. They had praised him for this at the schola.

"You are entitled to know what the goddess said, and the name that she gave. It was Kypris; and that is not a name from the Nine, as you know." Before he could stop himself, he added, "You are entitled to know as well, that Kypris has previously appeared to me in a private revelation."

She had told him not to speak of that, and now he had; he felt sure that she would never forgive him, as he would never forgive himself.

"Kypris is mentioned seven times in the Writings, where it is said that she always takes an interest in—in—in young women. Women of marriageable age, who are young. No doubt she took an interest in Orpine. I feel sure she must have."

They were almost quiet now, many listening intently; but his mind was still whelmed by the wonder of the goddess, and barren of cohesive thought.

"Comely Kypris, who has so favored us, is mentioned upon seven occasions in the Chrasmologic Writings. I think I said that before, though some of you may not have heard it. White doves and white rabbits are to be offered her, which was why we had those doves. The doves were supplied by her mother—I mean by Orpine's mother, by Orchid."

Providentially, he remembered something more. "In the Writings she is honored as the most favored companion of Pas among the minor gods."

Silk paused and swallowed. "I said you were entitled to hear everything that she said. That is what is called for by the canon. Unfortunately, I cannot adhere to that canon as I would wish. A part of her message was directed to the chief mourner alone. I must deliver that in private, and I'll try to arrange to do that as soon as I am finished here."

The sea of faces stirred. Even the mutes were listening with wide eyes and open mouths.

"She—I mean Comely Kypris—said three things. One was the private message that I must deliver. She said also that she would prophecy, in order that you would believe. I don't think there's anyone here who does not, not now. But possibly some of us might question her theophany later. Or possibly she intended our whole city, all of us in Viron.

"Her prophecy was this: there will be a great crime, a successful one, here in Viron. She spreads her mantle above the—the criminals, and because of it they will succeed."

Shaken and trying frantically to collect his wits, Silk fell silent. He was rescued by a man sitting near Auk, who shouted, *"When?* When'll it be?"

"Tonight." Silk cleared his throat. "She said it would be tonight."

The man's jaw snapped shut, and he stared about him.

"The third was this: that she would come again to this Sacred Window, soon. I asked her—you must have heard me, some of you. I implored her to come back, and she said she would, and soon. That—that's everything I can tell you now."

He saw Maytera Marble's bowed head, and sensed that she was praying for him, praying that he would somehow receive the strength and presence of mind that he so clearly needed. The knowledge itself strengthened him.

"And now I must request that the chief mourner come up here. Orchid, my daughter, please join me. We must retire to—to a private place, in order that I can deliver the goddess's message to you."

He would take her out the side door and into the garden, and thinking of the garden reminded him of the heifer and the other victims. "Please remain where you are, all of you. Or leave if you like, and let others join in the sacred meal. That would be a meritorious act. As soon as I have conveyed the goddess's message, we will proceed with Orpine's rites."

He had left Blood's lioness-headed walking stick behind the Sacred Window; he retrieved it before they started down the stair to the side door. "There are seats in the arbor, outside. I have to take off this thing around my leg and—and beat it against something. I hope you won't mind."

Orchid did not reply.

It was not until he stepped out into the garden that Silk realized how hot it had been in the manteion, near the altar fire. The whole place seemed to glow; the rabbits lay on their sides gasping for breath, and Maytera Marble's herbs were wilting almost visibly; but to him the hot, dry wind felt cool, and the burning bar that was the midday sun, which should have struck him like a blow, seemed without force.

"I ought to have something to drink," he said. "Water, I mean. Water's all we have. No doubt you should, too."

Orchid said, "All right," and he led her to the arbor and limped into the kitchen of the manse, pumped and pumped until the water came, then doused his head in the gushing stream.

Outside again, he handed Orchid a tumbler of water, sat down, and filled another for himself from the carafe he had brought. "It's cold, at least. I'm sorry I don't have wine to offer you. I'll have some in a day or two, thanks to you; but there wasn't time this morning."

"I have a headache," Orchid said. "This's what I need." And then, "She was beautiful, wasn't she?"

"The goddess? Oh, yes! She was—she's lovely. No artist—"

"I meant Orpine." Orchid had emptied her tumbler; as she spoke she held it out to be refilled, and Silk nodded as he tilted the carafe.

"Don't you think that was one reason why this goddess came? I'd like to think so anyhow, Patera. And it might be true."

Silk said, "I had better give you the goddess's message now—I've already waited too long. She said that I was to tell you that no one who loves something outside herself can be wholly bad. That Orpine had saved you for a while, but that you must find something else to save you now. That you must find something new to love."

Orchid sat silent for what seemed to Silk a long while. The white heifer, lying beneath the dying fig tree, moved to a more comfortable position and began to chew her cud. The people waiting in Sun Street, on the other side of the garden wall, were chattering excitedly among themselves. Silk could not understand, though he could easily guess, what they were saying.

At last she murmured, "Does love really mean more than life, Patera? Is it more important?"

"I don't know. I think it may be."

"I would've said I loved a lot of other things." Her mouth twisted in a bitter grin. "Money, just for starters. Only I gave you a hundred cards for this, didn't I? Maybe that shows I don't love it as much as I thought."

Silk groped for words. "The gods have to speak to us in our own language, a language that we are always corrupting, because it's the only one we understand. They, perhaps, have a thousand words for a thousand different kinds of love, or ten thousand words for ten thousand; but when they talk to us, they must say 'love,' as we do. I think that at times it must blur their meaning."

"It won't be easy, Patera."

Silk shook his head. "I never imagined it would be, nor do I think that Kypris believed it would. If it were going to be easy, she wouldn't have sent her message, I feel sure."

Orchid fingered her jet beads. "I've been wondering why somebody—Kypris or Pas or whatever—didn't save her. I think I've got it now."

"Then tell me," Silk said. "I don't, and I would like to very much."

"They didn't because they did. It sounds funny, doesn't it? I don't think Orpine loved anybody except me, and if I'd died before she did . . ." Orchid shrugged. "So they let her go first. She was beautiful, better looking than I ever was. But she wasn't as tough. I don't think so, anyhow. What do you love, Patera?"

"I'm not certain," Silk admitted. "The last time that we talked, I would have said this manteion. I know better now, or at least I think I do. I try to love the Outsider—I'm always talking about him, just as Auk said—but sometimes I almost hate him, because he has given me responsibility, as well as so much honor."

"You were enlightened. That's what somebody told me on the way here. You're going to bring back the Charter and be caldé yourself."

Silk shook his head and rose. "We'd better go inside. We're keeping five hundred people waiting in that heat."

She patted his shoulder when they parted, surprising him.

When the last sacrifice had been completed and the last morsel of the sacred meal that it had provided parceled out, he cleared the manteion. "We will lay Orpine in her casket now," he explained, "and close the casket. Those who wish to make a final farewell may do so on the way out, but everyone must leave. Those of you who will accompany the casket to the cemetery should wait outside on the steps."

Maytera Rose had left already, to wash his gauntlets and the sacrificial knife. Maytera Mint whispered, "I'd rather not watch, Patera. May I . . . ?"

He nodded, and she hurried off to the cenoby.

The mourners were filing past, Orchid waiting so as to be last in line. Maytera Marble said, "Those men will carry it, Patera. That's why they were here. Yesterday I happened to think that there would have to be someone, and the address was on the draft. I sent a boy with a note to Orchid."

"Thank you, Maytera. As I've said a thousand times, I don't know what I'd do without you. Have them wait at the entrance, please."

Chenille was still in her seat. "You should go, too," he told her, but she appeared not to have heard him.

When Maytera Marble returned, they lifted Orpine's body from its bed of ice and laid it in the waiting casket. "I'll help you with the lid, too, Patera."

He shook his head. "Chenille wishes to speak with me, I believe, and she won't as long as you're here. Go to the entrance, please, Maytera, where you won't overhear us if we keep our voices down." To Chenille he added, "I'm going to fasten the lid now. You can talk to me while I do it, if you like."

Her eyes flickered toward him, but she did not speak.

"Maytera must remain, you see. There must be two of us, so that each can testify that the other did not rob the body or molest it." Grunting, he lifted the heavy lid into place. "If you stayed to ask whether I've confided anything that you told me in your shriving to anyone else, I have not. You probably won't believe this, but I've actually forgotten most of it already. We make an effort to, you see. Once you've been forgiven, you're forgiven; that part of your life is over, and there's no point in our retaining it."

Chenille remained as before, staring straight ahead. Her wide, rounded forehead gleamed with perspiration; while Silk studied her, a single droplet trickled into her left eye and out again, as though reborn as a tear.

The casket builder had provided six long brass screws, one for each corner. They were hidden, with the screwdriver from the palaestra's broom closet, under the black cloth that draped the catafalque. Holes had been bored to receive each screw. As Silk got them out, he heard Chenille's slow steps in the aisle and glanced up. She was looking toward him now, but her motions seemed almost mechanical.

He told her, "If you'd like to say good-bye to Orpine, I can remove the lid. I haven't started the first screw yet."

She made an inarticulate noise and shook her head.

"Very well, then." He forced himself to look down at his work. He had not realized she was so beautiful—no, not even when they had sat talking in her room at Orchid's. In the garden, he had begun to say that no artist could paint a face half so lovely as Kypris's. Now it seemed to him that the same thing might almost be said of Chenille, and for a moment he imagined himself a sculptor or a painter. He would pose her beside a stream, he thought, her face uptilted as though she were watching a meadowlark. . . .

He sensed her proximity before he had tightened the first screw. Her cheek, he felt certain, was within a span of his ear. Her perfume filled his nostrils; and though it was in no way different from any other woman's, and stronger than it ought to have been, though it was mingled with perspiration, the inferior scents of face and body powders, and even the miasma of a woolen gown that had been stored for most of this protracted summer in one of the battered old trunks he had seen in her room, he found it intoxicating.

As he drove the third screw, her hand came to rest on his own. "Perhaps you'd better sit down," he told her. "You're not supposed to be in here, actually."

She laughed softly.

He straightened up and turned to face her. "Maytera's watching. Have you forgotten? Go and sit down, please. I have no desire to exert my authority, but I will if I must."

When she spoke, it was with mingled wonder and amusement. She said, *"This woman's a spy!"*

CHAPTER 3   COMPANY

Though he had been in the old cemetery often, Silk had never ridden the deadcoach before—or rather, as he told himself sharply, the deadcoach had been Loach's wagon. They always walked behind it in procession, as custom demanded, on the way there; and Loach nearly always invited him to ride back to the quarter, sitting beside Loach on the weathered gray board that was the driver's seat.

This was a real deadcoach, however, all glass and black lacquered wood, with black plumes and a pair of black horses, the whole rented for a staggering three cards from the maker of Orpine's casket. Silk, who had scarcely been able to limp along by the time they reached the cemetery, had been relieved when the liveried driver had offered him a ride, and utterly astonished to find that the deadcoach seat had a back, both seat and back stylishly upholstered in shiny black leather, like a costly chair. The seat was very high as well, which afforded him a fresh perspective on the streets through which they passed.

The driver cleared his throat and spat expertly between his horses. "Who was she, Patera? Friend of yours?"

"I wish I could say she was," Silk replied. "I never met her. Her mother's a friend, however, or so I hope. She paid for this fine coach of yours, as well as a great many other things, so I owe her a great deal."

The driver nodded companionably.

"This is a new experience for me," Silk continued, "my second in three days. I'd never ridden in a floater; but I did the day before yesterday, when a gentleman very kindly had one of his take me home. And now this! Do you know, I almost like this better. One sees so much more from up here, and one feels—I really can't say. Like a councillor, perhaps. Is this what you do every day? Driving like this?"

The driver chuckled. "An' curry the horses, an' feed an' water, an' muck out an' so on an' such like, an' takin' care of the coach. Waxin' an' polishin', an' keepin' everythin' clean, an' greasin' the wheels. Them that rides in back don't complain more'n once. Mebbe less. But their relations does, sayin' it sounds so dismal an' all. So I keeps 'em greased, which ain't nearly so hard as all the waxin' an' washin'."

"I envy you," Silk said sincerely.

"Oh, it's not no bad life, long as you rides up front. You get the rest of the day off, do you, Patera?"

Silk nodded. "Provided that no one requires the Pardon of Pas."

The driver extracted a toothpick from an inner pocket. "But if somebody does, you got to go, don't you?"

"Certainly."

"An' before we ever loaded her in, you'd done for how many pigeons an' goats and such like?"

Silk paused, counting. "Altogether, fourteen including the birds. No, fifteen in all, because Auk brought the ram he'd pledged. I had forgotten it for a moment, although its entrails indicated that I—never mind."

"Fifteen, an' one a ram. An' you done for the lot, an' read 'em, an' cut 'em up, I bet."

Silk nodded again.

"An' marched out to the country on that bad leg, readin' prayers an' so forth the whole way. Only now you get to pull your boots off, unless somebody's decided to leave. Then you don't. Have a easy time of it, don't you, you augurs? 'Bout like us, huh?"

"It isn't such a bad life," Silk said, "as long as one gets to ride back." They both laughed.

"Somethin' happen in there? In your manteion?"

Silk nodded. "I'm surprised that you heard about it so quickly."

"They were talkin' 'bout it when I got there, Patera. I ain't religious. Don't know nothin' 'bout gods an' don't want to, but it sounded interestin'."

"I see." Silk stroked his cheek. "In that case, what you know is fully as important as what I know. I know only what actually transpired, while you know what people are saying about it, which may be at least as important."

"What I was wonderin' was why she come after nobody for so long. Did she say?"

"No. And of course I could not ask her. One does not cross-examine the gods. Now tell me what the people outside the manteion were saying. All of it."

It was practically dark by the time the driver reined up in front of the garden gate. Kit and Villus, who had been playing in the street, were full of questions: "Did a goddess really come, Patera?" "A real goddess?" "What'd she look like?" "Could you see her really good?" "To talk to?" "Did she tell things, Patera?" "Could you tell what she said?" "What'd she say?"

Silk raised his hand for silence. "You could have seen her, too, if you'd come to our sacrifice as you should have."

"They wouldn't let us." "We couldn't get in."

"I'm very sorry to hear that," Silk told them sincerely. "You would have seen Comely Kypris just as I did, and most of the people who attended—there must have been five hundred, if not more—could not. Now listen. I know you're anxious to have your questions answered, just as I would be in your place. But I'm going to have to talk a great deal about the theophany in the next few days, and I don't want to go stale. Besides, I'll have to tell all of you in the palaestra, in a lot of detail, and you'll be bored if you have to listen to all of it twice."

Silk crouched to bring his own face to the level of the quite dirty face of the smaller boy. "But, Kit, there's a lesson in this, for you especially. Only two days ago, you asked me whether a god would actually come to our Window. Do you remember that?"

"You said it would be a long time, but it wasn't."

"I said it might be, Kit, not that it would be. You're fundamentally quite right, however. I did think it would be a long time, probably decades, and I was badly mistaken; but the thing I wanted to point out was that when you asked your question all the other students laughed. They thought it was very funny. Remember?"

Kit nodded solemnly.

"They laughed as though you'd asked a foolish question, because they thought it a foolish question. They were even more mistaken than I, however; and that must be plain even to them now. Yours was a serious and an important question, and you erred only in asking of someone who knew very little more than you did. You must never let yourself be turned aside from life's serious and important questions by ridicule. Try not to forget that."

Silk fumbled in his pocket. "I want you boys to run an errand for me. I'd go myself, but I can hardly walk, much less run. I'm going to give you, Villus, five bits. Here they are. And you, Kit, three. You, Kit, are to go to the greengrocer's. Tell him the vegetables are for me, and ask him to give you whatever is best and freshest, to the amount of three bits. You, Villus, are to go to the butcher. Tell him I want five bits worth of nice chops. I'll give each of you," Silk paused, ruminating, "a half bit when you bring me your purchases."

Villus inquired, "What kind of chops, Patera? Mutton or pork?"

"We will let him decide that."

Silk watched as the two dashed off, then unlocked the garden gate and stepped inside. The grass had been sadly trampled, just as Maytera Marble had said; even in the last dying gleam of day that was apparent, as was the damage to Maytera's little garden. He reflected philosophically that in a normal year the last produce from the garden would have come weeks before in any event.

"Patera!"

It was Maytera Rose, leaning from a window of the cenoby and waving, an offense for which she would have reprimanded Maytera Marble or Maytera Mint endlessly.

"Yes," Silk said. "What is it, Maytera?"

"Did they come back with you?"

He hobbled to the window. "Your sibs? No. They were going to walk back together, so they said. They should be here soon."

"It's past time for supper," Maytera Rose asserted. (The assertion was manifestly untrue.)

Silk smiled. "Your supper should be here shortly, too, and may Scylla bless your feast." He turned away, still smiling, before she could question him further.

There was a package wrapped in white paper and tied with white string on the kitchen doorstep of the manse. He picked it up and turned it over in his hands before opening the door.

Oreb, who from the scattered drops had been drinking from his cup, was on the kitchen table. " 'Lo, Silk."

"Hello, yourself." Silk got out the paring knife.

"Cut bird?"

"No, I'm going to open this. I'm too tired—or too lazy—to pick apart these knots, but if I cut them I should be able to save most of the string anyway. Did you kill that rat I threw away, Oreb?"

"Big fight!"

"I suppose I ought to congratulate you, and thank you as well. All right, I do." Unwrapping the white paper exposed a collection of odorous meat scraps. "This is cat's meat, Oreb. Having had a bucket of it dumped on my head once, I'd know it anywhere. Scleroderma promised us some, and she's made good her promise already."

"Eat now?"

"You may, if you wish. Not me. But you ate a good deal of that rat you killed. Don't tell me you're still hungry!"

Oreb only fluttered his wings and cocked his head inquiringly.

"I'm not at all sure that so much meat is good for you."

"Good meat!"

"As a matter of fact it isn't." Silk pushed it toward the bird. "But if I keep it, it will only get worse, and we have no means of preserving it. So go ahead, if you like."

Oreb snatched a piece of meat and managed to carry it, half flying and half jumping, to the top of the larder.

"Scylla bless your feast, too." For the two thousandth time it occurred to Silk that a feast blessed by Scylla ought logically to be of fish, as the Chrasmologic Writings hinted it had originally been. Sighing, he took off his robe and hung it over the back of what had been Patera Pike's chair. Eventually he would have to carry the robe upstairs to his bedroom, brush it, and hang it up properly; and eventually he would have to re-move the manteion's copy of the Writings themselves from the robe's big front pocket and restore it to its proper place.

But both could wait, and he preferred that they should. He started a fire in the stove, washed his hands, and got out the pan in which he had fried tomatoes the day before, then filled the old pot Patera Pike had favored with water from the pump and set it on the stove. He was con-templating the kettle and the possibility of maté or coffee when there was a tap at the Silver Street door.

Unbarring it, he took from Villus a package similar to the one he had found on the step, though much larger, and fumbled in his pocket for the promised half bit.

"Patera . . ." Villus's small face was screwed into an agony of effort.

"Yes, what is it?"

"I don't want nothing." Villus extended a grimy hand, displaying five shining bits, small squares sheared from so many cards.

"Are those mine?"

Villus nodded. "He wouldn't take 'em."

"I see. But the butcher gave you these chops anyway; you certainly didn't wrap this package. And now, since he would not accept money from me—I shouldn't have told you to tell him the meat was for me—you feel that you should not either, as a boy of honor and piety."

Villus nodded solemnly.

"Very well, I certainly won't make you take it. I owe your mother a bit, however; so give four back to me and give the fifth to her. Will you do that?"

Villus nodded again, handed over four bits, and vanished into the twilight.

"These chops are neither yours nor mine," Silk told the bird on the larder as he closed the Silver Street door and lifted the heavy bar back into place, "so leave them alone."

Large as his pan was, the chops filled it. He sprinkled them with a minute pinch of precious salt and set the pan on the stove. "We are made plutocrats of the supernatural," he informed Oreb conversationally, "and that to a degree that's almost embarrassing. Others have money, as Blood does, for example. Or power, like Councillor Lemur. Or strength and courage, like Auk. We have gods and ghosts."

From the top of the larder, Oreb croaked, "Silk good!"

"If that means you understand, you understand a great deal more than I. But I try to understand, just the same. Plutocrats of the supernatural do not need money, as we've seen—though they get it, as we've also seen. Strength and courage hasten to assist them." Silk dropped into his chair, the cooking fork in one hand and his chin in the other. "What they require is wisdom. No one understands gods or ghosts, yet we have to understand them: Lady Kypris today, Patera at the top of the stairs last night, and all the rest of it."

Oreb peered over the edge of the larder. "Bad man?"

Silk shook his head. "You may perhaps object that I've omitted Mucor, who is not dead and thus cannot be a ghost, and certainly is not a god. She behaves almost exactly like a devil, in fact. Which reminds me that we have those too, or one at any rate—that is to say, poor Teasel has or had one. Doctor Crane thinks she was bitten by some sort of bat, but she herself said it was an old man with wings."

The chops were beginning to sputter. Silk got up and prodded one experimentally with his fork, then lifted another to study its browning underside. "Speaking of wings, what do you say we begin with the simplest puzzle? I mean yourself, Oreb."

"Good bird!"

"I dare say. But not so good that you can fly with that bad wing, though I saw you do it last night just before I saw Mucor, and watched her vanish. That is suggestive—"

"Patera?" Steel knuckles rapped the door to the garden.

"Just a moment, Maytera, I have to turn your chops." To Oreb, Silk added, "I didn't include Mucor because I won't call what she does supernatural. I freely admit that it appears to be. I may be the only man in Viron who would scruple to call it that."

With the fork still in his hand, he threw wide the door.

"Good evening, Maytera. Good evening, Kit. May all the gods be with you both. Are those my vegetables?"

Kit nodded, and Silk accepted the big sack and laid it on the kitchen table. "This seems like a great deal to get for three bits, Kit, as high as prices are now. And there are bananas in there, too—I smell them. They're always very dear."

Kit remained speechless. Maytera Marble said, "He was standing in the street, Patera, afraid to knock. Or rather, I think he may have knocked very softly, and you failed to hear him. I took him into the garden, but he wouldn't give up that huge bag."

"Very properly," Silk said. "But, Kit, I wouldn't bite you for bringing me vegetables, particularly when I asked you to do it."

Kit extended a grubby fist.

"I see. Or at least, I think I may. He wouldn't take the money?"

Kit shook his head.

"And you were afraid that I'd be angry about that—as to tell the truth I am, somewhat. Here, give it to me."

Maytera Marble inquired, "Who wouldn't take your money, Patera? Marrow, up the street?"

Silk nodded. "Here, Kit. Here's the half bit that I promised you. Take it, close the gate after you, remember what I told you, and don't be afraid."

"I'm afraid," Maytera Marble announced when the boy was gone. "Not for myself, but for you, Patera. They don't like anyone to be too popular. Did Kind Kypris promise to protect you? What will you do if they send the Guard for you?"

Silk shook his head. "Go with them, I suppose. What else could I do?"

"You might not come back."

"I'll explain that I have no political ambitions, which is the simple truth." Silk drew his chair nearer the doorway and sat down. "I wish I could invite you in, Maytera. Will you let me bring the other chair out for you?"

"I'm fine," Maytera Marble said, "but your ankle must be very painful. You walked a long way today."

"It's not really as bad as it was yesterday," Silk said, feeling the wrapping. "Or perhaps I'm getting a second wind, so to speak. A great many things happened Phaesday, and they took place very fast. First there was the very great thing I told you about while we were sitting in the arbor during the rain, then Blood's coming here, then meeting Auk and riding out to Blood's villa, hurting my ankle, and talking to Blood. Then on Sphixday, bringing the Pardon of Pas to poor little Teasel, Orpine's death and an exorcism, and Orchid's wanting to have Orpine's final sacrifice here. I wasn't accustomed to so much happening so rapidly."

Maytera Marble looked solicitous. "No one could expect you to be, Patera."

"Last night I was just beginning to find my feet, if I may put it like that, when several other things took place. And today, Kypris favored us—the first manteion in Viron to be so favored in over twenty years. If—"

Maytera Marble interrupted him. "That was wonderful. I'm still trying to come to terms with it, if you know what I mean, trying to integrate it into my operating parameters. But it just—you know, Patera, this business with Marrow, for instance. I saw 'Back to the Charter!' painted on the side of a building. And then this, at our manteion. Do be careful!"

"I will," Silk promised. "As I was trying to explain, I've gotten my mental equilibrium back. I've done what you said you were trying to do—gotten all of it worked into my operating whateveryoucallums, my way of thinking. While we were following the deadcoach, I had time to sort things out. It gave me an opportunity to weigh my own impressions against the Writings as I read them. Do you recall the passage that begins, 'Sovereign nature, which governs the whole, will soon change all the things you see, and from their substance make other things, and again still other things from the substance of them, in order that the whorl may be ever new'?

"In the context of her last sacrifice, it meant no more than that Orpine would grow up again as grass and flowers, of course. And yet, that passage struck home to me particularly, as though it had been put there for me, specifically, to read today. I wish I could learn to say things to other people that would affect them half as much as that passage affected me. I realized as I read it that the peaceful life here that I'd imagined I had, the life that I'd hoped would continue without interruption and almost without incident until I was old, had been nothing of the sort—that it had been no more than the current state of things in an endless flux of states. My final year in the schola, for example—"

"Did you say something about those chops being for me when I knocked, Patera? You meant that they would save me all the work of preparing the main course, and I appreciate it very much. They smell delicious. I feel certain Maytera Rose and Maytera Mint will enjoy them immensely."

Silk sighed. "You're telling me it's time to turn them again, aren't you?"

"No, Patera. Time to take them up—to put them on a platter. You've turned them once already."

He hobbled off to the stove. Oreb had been at the cat's meat while he had been talking with Kit and Maytera Marble; it was scattered over the table, with addenda on the floor. The undersides of the chops were a deep, golden brown. Silk piled them on the largest plate in the cupboard, draped them with a clean cloth, and carried them to Maytera Marble on the other side of the threshold.

"Thank you very, very much, Patera." She peeped beneath the cloth. "Oh, my! Aren't they marvelous! You've saved at least three for yourself, I hope."

Silk shook his head. "I had chops last night when Auk bought my dinner, and I really don't care for meat."

She made him a tiny bow. "I must hurry off before they get cold."

"Maytera?" He hobbled after her, down the graveled path toward the cenoby. The burning line of the sun was completely obscured by the shade now; the night air hung still and dry and hot, like one driven by fever to the border of death.

"What is it, Patera?"

"You said those chops smelled delicious. Do things—does food really smell good to you, Maytera? You can't eat it."

"But I can cook it, and I do," she reminded him gently, "so naturally I know when something smells good."

"I was thinking only of Maytera Rose, and that was wrong of me. I should have gotten something all three of you could enjoy." Silk paused, groping futilely for words that would not be inadequate. "I'm really terribly sorry, and I'll try to find a way to make up for it."

"I *do* enjoy this, Patera. It gives me great pleasure to be the one to take this good food to my sibs. Now please go back to the manse, where you can sit down. I hate seeing you in pain."

He hesitated, wanting to say more, nodded, and turned back. Turning seemed to twist his ankle inside the rapidly loosening wrapping, bringing pain so sharp he nearly cried out. Wincing, he grasped the arbor, then a convenient limb of the little pear tree.

There was a distant knock.

He would have halted to listen if he had not been halted already. Another knock, a trifle louder, and beyond question from his left, from Sun Street. The front door of the manse was on Sun Street—the cenoby had no door on Sun Street at all.

He meant to shout for the visitor to wait, but he did not shout, immobilized with surprise. A shadow (very faint because the lights there had darkened almost to extinction) had flitted across the curtains of his bedroom. Someone up there was going to answer that knock—someone, so at least it seemed, who had watched him limp down the path in pursuit of Maytera Marble.

All of the manse's windows facing the garden were wide open. Through them he heard the swift rattle of feet on the crooked stairs; and then, unmistakably, the bar being lifted from the door on Sun Street and the creaking of the hinges as that door opened; there was an indistinct murmur of voices—not friendly voices, or so they sounded.

It was strange how little pain his ankle gave him now. He opened the sellaria door as quietly as he could, but both turned to face him at once, one smiling, one glaring.

"Here he is," Chenille announced. "You can tell him yourself, whatever it is."

Musk snarled and shoved her aside. Catlike, he stalked across the sellaria to seat himself in Silk's reading chair.

Silk cleared his throat. "Although I have no desire to appear inhospitable, I must ask both of you what you're doing here."

Musk sneered; Chenille endeavored to look demure, almost successfully. "I wasn't—really I wasn't—up to walking that far behind the deadcoach. Not in these sham shoes. And Orchid hadn't said we had to go to the grave. She just said for us to come to Orpine's rites, and I'd done it. Some of the others didn't even come."

Silk said, "Go on."

"That was all that you said I had to do, too. I mean, to come and pray, and I'd done it."

"Women are not to set foot in this manse," Silk told her harshly. Musk was sitting in his chair, and he refused as a matter of principle to take one of the others. "Excuse me for a moment."

In the kitchen, his pot of water was boiling vigorously; he added a good-sized split to the firebox and found Blood's walking stick in a corner.

When he stepped back into the sellaria, Chenille said, "You say that

I'm not supposed to be in here, but I didn't know that. I wanted to talk to you back in your manteion, when you were fastening down the lid of the coffin, but it didn't seem like the best time or the best place, with that chem woman watching us. I was going to wait for you there, but you never came back. After a couple hours, I went into your garden looking for a drink of water and found this cute little house. I played with your pet bird for a while, and then . . . Well, I'm afraid I lay down and went to sleep."

Silk nodded, half to himself. "I know you use rust, and you must drink heavily sometimes, too. When you were telling me you had a good memory yesterday during the exorcism, you said that you hadn't had a drop that day. Were you drinking here?"

"I wouldn't bring a bottle to Orpine's funeral!"

Musk snickered. He had drawn his knife and was scraping his fingernails.

"Perhaps not," Silk conceded. "And if you had, I would have seen it, unless it was a very small one. But you would have brought money, and there are a dozen places within an easy walk that would sell you beer or brandy, or anything else you wanted."

Musk said, "How much did Orchid give you?"

"Ask her. She knows you, and no doubt she's afraid of you—most women seem to be. I'm sure she'll tell you."

"A lot, that's what I heard. Lots of flowers and enough livestock to keep every god in Mainframe fed for a week. That much. This whore's in your bed and you're scratching to pump what she's there for, you putt."

Chenille ran her hands down her gown. "Look at me, I'm dressed. Would I be dressed?"

Silk rapped the floor with Blood's walking stick. "This is senseless! Be quiet, both of you. Chenille, you say you wish to talk with me. I tried to talk to you this afternoon in the manteion, but you would not reply."

She had a trick of staring down at his feet with a half smile, as if she found his scuffed black shoes amusing; he had a sudden presentiment that he could come to know it only too well. "Explain yourself," he said, "or leave at once."

"I couldn't talk with you just then, Patera. I had so much thinking to do! That was why I waited. You know, to make amends, kind of like Musk said. Only I want to talk to you too, when we're alone."

"I see. And what about you, Musk? Have you come for a private talk, as well? I warn you, I have some sharp things to say to you."

Musk's face showed a flicker of surprise; for an instant the point of his knife paused in its patrol of his nails. "I can tell you now. Blood sent me."

Silk nodded. "So I had assumed."

"He gave you how long? Four weeks? Some dog puke like that?"

Silk nodded. "Four weeks, at the end of which I was to produce a substantial sum; when I did so, we were to confer again."

Musk rose as lithely as one of the beasts Mucor called lynxes. He held his knife level, its blade flat and its point aimed at Silk's chest, reminding Silk forcibly of the warning he had read in the entrails of Auk's ram. "That doesn't go, not anymore. You get a week for everything. One week!"

From the top of the dusty cabinet of curios beside the stair, Oreb croaked, "Poor Silk?"

"We had an agreement," Silk said.

"You want to see what your shaggy agreement's worth?" Musk spat at Silk's feet. "You got a week for everything. Maybe. Then we come."

"Bad man!"

The long knife flashed the length of the sellaria, to stick quivering in the wainscotting over the cabinet. Oreb gave a terrified squawk, and one black feather drifted toward the floor.

"You got yourself a turd bird," Musk whispered, "to make us dimber hornboys, didn't you? Well, up lamp! There's not a hawk I'd feed your turd bird to, and if you're warm to keep it you'd better teach it to shut its flap."

Chenille grinned. "If you're going to throw knives at him, you'd better be good enough to hit him. Missing's not so impressive."

Musk swung at her, but Silk caught his wrist before the blow landed. "Don't be childish!"

Musk spat in his face, and the carved hardwood handle of the walking stick caught Musk beneath the jaw with the hard, incisive rap of a mason's maul. Musk's head snapped back; he staggered backward, smashing a small table as he fell.

"Ah!" It was Chenille, her eyes bright with excitement, and her face intent.

Musk lay still for a second or two that seemed a great deal longer; his eyes opened, gazing for a protracted moment at nothing. He sat up.

Silk raised the stick. "If you've a needler, this is the time to pluck it."

Musk glowered at him, then shook his head.

"All right. Was that your message? That I have a week in which to pay Blood his twenty-six thousand?" With his free hand, Silk got his handkerchief and wiped Musk's spittle from his face.

Scarcely parting his lips, Musk rasped, "Or less."

Silk lowered the walking stick until he could lean on it. "Was there anything else?"

"No." Laboriously, Musk got to his feet, a hand braced against the wall.

"Then I have something to say to you. Orpine's rites were held today. You knew her, clearly, and both of you were working for Blood, directly or indirectly. You knew that she had died. You did not attend her rites, nor did you provide a beast for sacrifice. When her grave was closed, I asked Orchid whether she had received any expression of regret from you or Blood. She said very forcibly that she had not. Do you dispute that?"

Musk said nothing, though his eyes flickered toward the Sun Street door.

"Did you send anything or say anything? Don't try to go just yet. I don't advise it."

Musk met Silk's stare with his own.

"Possibly you believed that Blood had said something or done something in both your names. Was that it?"

Musk shook his head, the faded lights of the sellaria gleaming on his oiled hair.

"Very well then. You are a member of our human race. You have shirked your human duty, and it is mine to remind you of it—to teach you how a man acts, if you don't know it already. The lesson won't be quite so easy next time, I warn you." Silk strode past him to the Sun Street door and opened it. "Go in peace."

Musk left without a word or a backward glance, and Silk closed the door behind him. As he was fitting the bar into place, he felt Chenille's swift kiss on the nape of his neck. "Don't do that!" he protested.

"I wanted to do it, and I knew you wouldn't let me kiss your face. He did have a needler, you know."

"I surmised it. So do I. Won't you please sit down? Anywhere. My ankle hurts, and I can't sit until you do."

She took the stiff wooden chair in which Horn had sat the night before, and Silk dropped gratefully into his usual seat. Crane's wrapping was noticeably cold now; he unwound it and flogged the hassock with it.

"I've tried doing this more often," he remarked, "but it doesn't seem to have much effect. I suppose this thing's got to cool before it will heat up again."

Chenille nodded.

"You said that you wished to speak with me. May I ask you a question first?"

"You can ask," Chenille told him. "I don't know if I'll be able to answer it. What is it?"

"When we were in the manteion—when I was securing the lid of Orpine's casket—you indicated that she had been a spy, and refused to speak again when I asked what you meant. A few minutes ago, I was warned by one of our sibyls that I was at risk because a few people in our quarter seem to be trying to thrust me into politics. If I have performed the funeral rites of a spy, and when it becomes known, my risk will be substantially increased, and thus—"

"I didn't, Patera! Orpine wasn't a spy. I was talking about myself—talking like I was somebody else. It's a bad habit I have."

"About *yourself?*"

She nodded vigorously. "You see, Patera, until then I hadn't really realized what was happening—what I'd been doing. Then while I was sitting through the funeral it was like I'd been struck by lightning. It's really awfully hard to explain."

Silk rewrapped his ankle. "You've been spying on our city? On Viron? Don't try to evade or prevaricate, please, my daughter. This is an extremely serious matter."

Chenille stared at his shoes.

After a long moment had passed, Oreb poked his head over the edge of the curio cabinet. "Man go?"

"Yes, he's gone," Chenille said. "But he may come back, so you have to be careful."

The night chough bobbed his head and began to wrestle with Musk's knife, tugging the pommel with his beak, then perching on the handle and pushing against the wainscotting with one scarlet foot. Chenille watched, apparently amused—though perhaps, Silk thought, merely glad of any distraction.

He cleared his throat. "I said that I wanted to ask you just one question, and have already asked several, for which I apologize. You indicated that you wanted my advice, and I said, or at least I implied, that you might have it. What is it you wish to discuss?"

"That's it," she said, turning from the busy bird to Silk. "I'm in trouble, just like you said. I'm not sure how much you're in, Patera, but I'm in one shaggy lot more. If the Guard ever finds out what I've been doing, I'll most likely be shot. I've got to have a place to stay where he can't find me, to start with, because if he does I'll be in that much deeper. I don't know where I can stay, but I'm not going back to Orchid's tonight."

"He?" For an instant Silk shut his eyes; when he opened them again, he asked, "Doctor Crane?"

Chenille's eyes widened. "Yes. How did you know?"

"I didn't. It was nothing more than a guess, and now I suppose I should be gratified because I was right. But I'm not."

"Was it because he came to my room yesterday while you and I were talking?"

Silk nodded. "For that and other reasons. Because he gave you a dagger, as you told me yesterday. Because he saw you first, out of all the women at Orchid's, and sometimes gave you rust. He might have examined you before the others simply as a favor to you, so that you could go out sooner, as you implied when I asked about it yesterday. But it seemed clear that it could also have been because he expected to get something of value from you; and information of some sort was one possibility."

Silk paused, rubbing his cheek. "Then too, you had that dagger concealed on your person when you encountered Orpine. Most women who carry weapons carry them at night, or so I've been told; but Blood, at least, expected you back at Orchid's for dinner. Later you yourself told me that you expected to work very hard at Orchid's in the evening."

"Women like me that have to go out nightside need some kind of weapon, Patera, believe me."

"I do. But you weren't going to be out after dark, so you were going into some other danger, or thought you were. That the man who had given you your dagger was the man who was sending you into danger seemed a reasonable guess. Do you want to tell me where you were going?"

"To take a— No. Not yet, anyhow." She leaned forward, sincere and deeply troubled, and at that moment he would have sworn she was ignorant of her own beauty. "All this is wrong. I mean it's right—all the facts are right—but it doesn't seem like it really was. It makes it seem like I'm really from another city. I'm as Vironese as you are. I was born right here, and I used to sell watercress around the market when I wasn't much bigger than that stool you got your foot up on."

Silk nodded, wondering whether she realized how much he wanted to touch her. "I believe you, my daughter. If you wish me to know the truth, however, you must tell me. How did it appear to you at the time?"

"Crane was a friend, just like I said yesterday. He was nice, and he brought me things, when he didn't have to. You remember about the bouquet of chenille? Little stuff like that, but nice. Most of the girls like him, and sometimes I gave him a free one. He's got a thing for big girls. He sort of laughs about it."

Silk said, "He's sensitive about his height; he told me so the first time we met. It may be that a tall woman makes him feel taller. Go on."

"So that's how it's been with us ever since I moved into Orchid's place. He didn't say, I want you to do some spying, so promise to sell out your city and I'll give you a uniform. We were talking a couple months ago, four or five of us in the big room when Crane was there. There were jokes about what he does when he looks us over. About the checkups. You know the kind of thing?"

"I don't," Silk admitted wearily, "though I can readily imagine."

"Somebody let it drop that a commissioner had been in, and Crane kind of whistled and asked who hooked him. I said it was me, and he wanted to know if he gave me much of a tip. Then later, when he was looking me over, he wanted to know if this commissioner happened to mention the caldé."

Silk's eyebrows shot up. "The caldé?"

"That's the way I felt, Patera. I said no, he didn't, and I thought the caldé was dead. Crane said, yeah, sure, he is. But when we were done and I was getting dressed, he said that if this commissioner or anybody else ever said anything about the caldé or the Charter, he'd like for me to tell him about it, or if he said anything about a councillor. Well, he had said something about councillors—"

"What was it?" Silk asked.

"Just that he'd gone out to the lake to see a couple of them, Tarsier and Loris. I went oh! and ah! the way you're supposed to, but I didn't think it sounded like it was very important. Crane just sort of stopped when I told it. You know what I mean?"

"Certainly."

"Then when I was dressed and going out, he was coming out of Violet's room and he passed me this folded up paper. He stuck it—you know, Patera—right down here. When I was alone I pulled it out and looked, and it was a bearer draft for five cards, signed by some cull I never even heard of. I thought probably it was no good, but I was going up that way anyhow, so I took it to the fisc and they gave me five cards for it, no who are you or how'd you get hold of this at all. Just like that, five cards slap on the counter." Chenille paused, waiting for his reaction. "How often do you think I snaffle a dimber five-card tip like that, Patera?"

He shrugged. "Since you've entertained a commissioner, once a month, perhaps."

"Not counting that one, I've got two in my whole life and that's lily. At Orchid's the cully's forked ten bits to get in and look at the dells, and then he's got to pay me a card—I've got to split with Orchid—unless it's somebody like that commissioner. He gets in free and gets it free, because nobody wants trouble. The best of everything and keep telling him how good he is, and usually he don't tip, either. From the ones that pay, I gct a card like I said. That's for all night if they want it. So if the first one does and he won't tip, I clear half a card for the whole night."

Silk said, "I know people who don't get half a card for a week's hard work."

"Sure you do. Why do you think we do it? But what I'm saying is that in a good week, with tips, I might clear four or five. Maybe six. Only if it is, next week'll be two or three every time. So here I've got as much as I'd make in a good week, just for telling Cranc something this commissioner said. Real candy! You're going to tell me I should've known, but I didn't think much about it back then, and that's lily." Chenille paused again, as if anticipating an accusation.

Silk murmured, "So that was how it began. What about the rest, my daughter?"

"Since then I've passed along maybe six or eight other things and taken things to a couple people for him dayside. Then if a commissioner or maybe a colonel—somebody like that, you know?—comes in, I'm really nice to them and I don't work them for tips and presents or anything like the other dells would. It's got to where they ask for me when I'm not around."

The night chough stirred uneasily on top of the curio cabinet, his head cocked inquiringly and his long, crimson beak half open.

"So ever since I saw Orpine on ice, I've been thinking." Chenille drew her chair nearer Silk's and lowered her voice. "You've got to fork twenty-six thousand to Blood if you want to hang onto this place? That's what Musk said."

Silk's head inclined less than a finger's width.

"All right, then. Why don't you—why don't you and me get it from Crane, Patera?"

"Man here," Oreb warned them. "Out there."

Chenille glanced up at him apprehensively.

"There now," Oreb insisted. "No knock."

CHAPTER

4   The Prochein Ami

Silk rose as silently as he could, irresistibly reminded of his failure to surprise Musk and Chenille earlier. Leaving Blood's walking stick beside his chair, he crossed the room to the Sun Street door, snatched the heavy bar out of its fittings and (retaining the bar in his left hand for use as a weapon if necessary) jerked the door open.

The tall, black-robed man waiting in the street beyond the step did not appear in the least surprised. "Did my presence here—ah—disturb you, Patera?" he inquired in a reverberant, nasal voice. "I strove to be discreet and—um—unobtrusive. Do you follow me? Subdued, eh? Not so skillful about it, perhaps. I'd reached your door before I heard the—ah—lady's voice."

Silk leaned the bar against the wall. "I know that it's somewhat irregular, Your Eminence—"

"Oh, no, no, no! You have your reasons, I'm certain, Patera." The black-robed man bowed from the waist. "Good evening, my dear. Good evening, and may every god be with you this night." He favored Silk with a toothy smile that gleamed even in the glimmering light from the skylands. "I took great care to stand well out of the—ah—zone of—um—listening, Patera. Audibility? Earreach. Beyond the—ah—carry of the lady's voice. I could hear voices, I confess, save when a cart passed, if you follow me. But not one word you said. Couldn't make out a single thing, hey?" He smiled again. "Sweet Scylla, bear witness!"

Silk left the manse to stand upon its doorstep. "I'm exceedingly sorry that I was so abrupt, Your Eminence. We heard—I should say we were told—"

"Perfectly proper, Patera." One hand flipped up in a gesture of dismissal. "Quite, quite correct."

"—that there was someone outside, but not who—" Silk took a deep breath. "Your business must be urgent, or it wouldn't have brought you out so late, Your Eminence. Won't you come in?"

He held the door, then barred it again when the black-robed man had entered. "This is our sellaria, I'm afraid. The best room we have. I can

offer you water and—and bananas, if you'd like some." He recalled that
he had not yet explored Kit's sack. "Perhaps some other sort of fruit, as
well."

The black-robed man waved Silk's fruit away. "You were advising this
young lady, weren't you, Patera? Not shriving her, I hope. Not yet at
least, though I didn't understand a word. I'd recognize the—ah—cadence
of the Pardon of Pas, or so I fancy, having performed it so many, many
times myself. The litany of Sacred Names, hey? Speak here for Great
Pas, for Divine Echidna, for Scalding Scylla, and the rest. And I heard
nothing like that. Nothing at all."

Chenille, who had followed Silk to the door and stood behind him in
the doorway, inquired, "You're an augur, too, Patera?"

The black-robed man bowed again, then held up the voided cross he
wore; its gold chain gleamed like the Aureate Path itself in the dingy
little sellaria. "I am indeed, my dear. One quite, quite capable of discretion, or I should not be where I am today, eh? So you've nothing to fear,
not that I overheard a single word you said."

"I'm confident that I can trust you implicitly, Patera. I was about to say
that Patera Silk and I are liable to be quite some time. I can go somewhere else and come back in an hour or two—however much time you
estimate that you may require."

Silk stared at her, astonished.

"Such a lady as you, my dear? In *this* quarter? I would not—ah—will
not hear of it. Not for a single instant! But perhaps I might have a word
with Patera now, eh? Then I'll be on my way."

"Of course," Chenille told him. "Please disregard me completely, Your
Eminence."

He was more than half a head taller than Silk (though Silk was nearly
as tall as Auk) and at least fifteen years his elder. Thin, coal-black hair
spilled down his forehead; he tossed his head to keep it out of his eyes as
he spoke. "It is Patera Silk, hey? I don't believe I've had the—ah—
pleasure, Patera. I'm a perfect stranger, eh? Or nearly. Near as makes no
matter. I wish it weren't so. Wish that—ah—that we met now as old
acquaintances, eh? Though I did you a bad turn, eh? Couple of years
ago. I admit it. I acknowledge it. No question about it, but I've got to do
what's best for the Chapter, eh? The Chapter's our mother, after all, and
bigger than any man. I'm Remora."

He turned his smile on Chenille. "This young beauty may prefer to
maintain an—ah—ah—discreet anonymity, eh? That might be the prudent course, hey? However she prefers, and no offense taken."

Chenille nodded. "If you don't object, Patera."

"No, no, indeed not." Remora's hand waved negligently. "Indeed not. Why I—ah—advise it myself."

Silk said, "You attended my graduation, Your Eminence. You were on the dais, to the right of our Prelate. I don't expect you to remember me."

"Oh, but I do! I do! Won't you sit, my dear? I do indeed, Silk. You received honors, after all, eh? Never forget the sprats that get those. You were quite the huskiest cub the old place could show that year. I recall remarking to Quetzal—the Prolocutor, my dear, and I ought to have said His Cognizance. Remarking afterward that you ought to have gone into the arena, eh? So we—ah—ah—sent you there. Yes, we did! Merely a jest, to be sure. I was—um—I am responsible. My fault, all of it. That you were sent here, I mean. To this quarter, this manteion. I suggested it." With a sidelong glance at the wreckage of the table upon which Musk had fallen, Remora lowered his lanky body into Silk's reading chair. "I urged it—sit down, Patera—and dear Quetzal quite agreed."

"Thank you, Your Eminence." Silk sat. "Thank you very much. I couldn't have gone to a better place."

"Oh, you don't mean it. I can't blame you. Not at all, eh? Not at all. You've had a miserable time of it. I—ah—we know that, Quetzal and I. We realize it. But poor old—um—your predecessor. What was his name?"

"Pike, Your Eminence. Patera Pike."

"Quite right. Patera Pike. What if we'd sent poor old Pike one of those rabbity little boys, eh? Killed and eaten him on the first day, in this quarter, eh? You know it now, Patera, and I knew it then. So I suggested to Quetzal that we send you, and he saw the logic of it straight off. Now here you are, hey? All alone. Since Pike left for—ah—purer climes? You've done a fine, fine job of it, too, Patera. An—ah—exceptional job. I don't think that's too strong an expression."

Silk forced himself to speak. "I would like to agree, Your Eminence." The words came singly and widely spaced, as heavy as waystones. "But this manteion has been sold. You must know about that. We couldn't even pay taxes. The city seized the property; I assume that the Chapter was notified, though I was not. The new owner will certainly close the manteion and the palaestra, and he may well tear them both down."

"He's worked hard, my dear," Remora told Chenille. "You don't live in the quarter, eh? So you can't know. But he has. He has."

Silk said, "Thank you, Your Eminence. You're very kind. I wish, though, that there were no need for your kindness. I wish I had made a success of this manteion, somehow. When I thanked you for assigning me here, I wasn't being polite. I don't really love this place—these cramped old, run-down buildings and so forth, though I used to try to make myself believe I did. But the people— We have a great many bad people here. That's what everyone says, and it's true. But the good ones have been tried by fire and remained good in spite of everything that the whorl could throw against them, and there's nothing else like them in the whorl. And even the bad ones, you'd be surprised—"

At that moment, Oreb fluttered into Chenille's lap with Musk's knife in his beak.

"Hey? Extraordinary! What's this?"

"Oreb has a dislocated wing," Silk explained. "I did it by accident, Your Eminence. A physician put the bone back in the socket yesterday, but it hasn't healed yet."

Remora waved Oreb's woes aside. "But this dagger, hey? Is it yours, my dear?"

Chenille nodded without a trace of a smile. "I threw it to illustrate a point that I was making to Patera Silk, Your Eminence. Now Oreb's kindly returned it to me. He likes me, I think."

Oreb whistled.

"*You* threw it? I don't want—ah—intend to appear skeptical, my dear—"

Chenille's hand flicked in the direction of the cabinet, and the wainscotting above its top boomed like a kettledrum. With its blade half buried in oak, Musk's knife did not even vibrate.

"Oh! O you gods!" Remora rose and went to examine the knife. "Why, I'd never— This is really most—ah—um—most . . ." He grasped the hilt and tried to pull the knife out, but was forced to work it back and forth. "There's only the single scar here, one—um—hole in the wood."

"I thought Patera Silk would prefer that I mark his wall as little as possible," Chenille told him demurely.

"Hah!" Remora gave a snort of triumph as he succeeded in freeing the knife; he returned it with a profound bow. "Your weapon, my dear. I knew that this quarter is said to be—ah—rough? Tough. Lawless. And I observed the broken table. But I hadn't realized . . . Patera, my—ah—our admiration for you was already very great. But it's—um—mine's now, well . . ." He seated himself again. "That's what I was about to remark, Patera. You may possibly imagine that we—um—Quetzal and I—"

His attention shifted to Chenille. "As this good augur knows, I am His

Cognizance's—ah—prochein ami, my dear. Doubtless you are already familiar with the—ah—um—locution. His adjutant, as they would say it in the Guard. His coadjutor, hey? That's the—ah—formal official phraseology, the most correct usage. And I was about to say that we have been following Patera's progress with attention and admiration. He has had difficulties. Oh, indeed! He has encountered obstacles, eh? His has been no easy field to plow, no—um—quiet pasture, this manteion, poor yet dear to the immortal gods."

Chenille nodded. "So I understand, Your Eminence."

"He ought to have come to us for—ah—assistance, eh? He ought to have appealed, frankly and forthrightly, to His Cognizance and to me. Ought to have laid his case before us, so to speak. Do you follow me? But we, still more, hey? We still more ought to have proffered our assistance without any of that. Yes, indeed! Proffered the ready assistance of the Chapter, and—ah—more. Much more. And much sooner than this."

"I couldn't get in to see you," Silk explained somewhat dryly. "Your prothonotary kindly informed me that a crisis was occupying all your attention."

Remora wheezed. "Doubtless one was, Patera. Frequently it seems that my sole task, my—ah—entire duty consists of wrestling with an unending—um—onrushing and—ah—remorseless torrent of continually worsening crises."

Blowers roared to the west, louder and louder as an armed Civil Guard floater roared along Sun Street. Remora paused to listen.

"It's our—ah—invariable policy with young augurs, Patera, as you must understand, to—ah—permit them to try their wings. To observe their first flights, as it were, from a distance. To thrust them rudely from the nest, if I may say it. You follow me? It is an examination you have passed very—um—creditably indeed."

Silk inclined his head. "I'm gratified, Your Eminence, although thoroughly conscious that I'm not entitled to such praise. This may be the best opportunity I'll have, however, to report—I mean informally—the very great honor that was accorded to our troubled manteion today by the—"

"Troubled did you say, Patera? This manteion?" Remora smiled all difficulties away. "It has been—ah—um—well, sold, as you say. But the sale is only a legality, eh? You follow me? A mere contrivance or—ah—stratagem of old Quetzal's, actually. The new owners—ah. The name is—the name . . ."

"Blood," Silk supplied.

"No, that's not it. Something more common, hey?"

Chenille murmured, "Musk?"

"Quite, quite correct. Musk, indeed. Rather a foolish name, hey? If I may put it so. Infants do not, as a rule, smell half so—ah—sweet. But this Musk has paid your taxes. That's how he got it. You follow me? For the taxes and some trifling amount over. These buildings are in need of—ah—refurbishing, eh? As you pointed out yourself, Patera. We'll let him do it, hey? Why not? Let him bear the expense, and not the burse, eh? Eventually he'll donate everything to us again. Give it all back to the Chapter, eh? A meritorious act."

Chenille shook her head. "I doubt—"

"We have ways, my dear, as you'll see. Dear old Quetzal has, most particularly. He's very good at it. His—ah—um—consequence as the Prolocutor of the Chapter. And his influence with the Ayuntamiento, eh? He has plenteous—ah—standing there even yet, never doubt it. An arsenal of pressures that he—ah—that we can, and will, exert in any such an eventuality as—ah—this present instance. As yours here on Sun Street, Patera."

Silk said, "Musk is no more than the owner of record, Your Eminence. Blood controls this property, and Blood is threatening to tear down everything."

"Doesn't matter. Doesn't matter. You'll see, Patera." Remora flashed his toothy smile again. "It will not occur—ah—come to pass. No fear. No fear at all. Or if it should, the old structures will be replaced with better ones. That would be the best way, eh? Rebuilt in a better style, and upon a more—ah—commodious scale. I must remember to speak to Quetzal about it tomorrow when he has had his beef tea."

Remora inclined his head toward Chenille. "He's quite fond of beef tea, is old Quetzal. Doubtless Patera knows. These things get bandied about, you know, among us. Like a bunch of—um—washerwomen, eh? Gossip, gossip. But dear old Quetzal should eat more, hey? I'm forever after him about it. A man can't live on beef tea and air, hey? But Quetzal does. Feeble, though."

He glanced at the clock above the sellaria's diminutive fireplace. "What I—ah—ventured out to inform you of, Patera Silk— You see, my dear, I'm terribly selfish. Yes, even after half a lifetime spent in the pursuit of—ah—sacrosanctity. I wished to inform him myself. Patera, you shall no longer labor alone. I said—um—earlier, eh? I assured you that your struggles had not gone unnoticed, hey? But now I can say more, as I —ah—most certainly shall. As I do. An acolyte, a youthful augur who

only in the springtide of this very year completed his studies with honors
—um. As you yourself did, Patera. I—ah—we are very aware of that.
With a prize, I was about to say, for hierologics will arrive in the morning. You yourself shall know the joy of leading this promising neophyte
down the very paths that you yourself have traversed with so much credit.
You have two bedrooms, I believe, upstairs here? Please have the less—
ah—vantaged prepared to receive Patera Gulo."

Remora rose and extended his hand. "It has been a great pleasure,
Patera. A pleasure and an honor much, much too long delayed. And
denied. Self-denial, indeed, and self-denial must have an end, hey?"

Silk rose with the assistance of Blood's walking stick, and they shook
hands solemnly.

"My dear, I'm sorry to have disrupted your own interview with your—
ah—spiritual guide. With this devout young augur. I do apologize. Our
little tête-à-tête cannot have been of much interest to you, yet—"

"Oh, but it was!" Chenille's smile might well have been sincere.

"Yet it was brief at least. Ah—succinct. And now my blessing upon
you, whatever your troubles may be." Remora traced the sign of addition
in the air. "Blessed be you in the Most Sacred Name of Pas, Father of the
Gods, in that of Gracious Echidna, His Consort, in those of their Sons
and their Daughters alike, this day and forever, in the name of their
eldest child, Scylla, Patroness of this, Our Holy City of Viron."

"The new owner," Silk informed Remora with some urgency, "insists
that any moneys above the operating expenses of the manteion must be
turned over to him. In light of what transpired today at sacrifice—Your
Eminence simply cannot have remained unaware of it—"

Remora grunted as he set aside the heavy bar. "You have a good deal
here in need of repair, Patera. Or replacement. Or—ah—augmentation.
Items which this Musk will not—um—exert himself to rehabilitate. Your
own—ah—um—wardrobe, eh? That would be a fair beginning. You
might do—um—much. Many things. As for the rest, you tote up your
own accounts, I take it? Doubtless you can discover many good uses for
this—ah—merely presumptive surplus. And you have borrowed various
sums, I believe. So I'm—ah—we, His Cognizance and I, have been given
to understand."

The door clicked shut behind him.

Oreb whistled. "Bad man."

Chenille put out her arm, and the bird hopped onto it. "Not really,
Oreb. Only a man deeply in love with his own cleverness."

A slight smile played about the corners of her mouth as she spoke to

Silk. "All that for a single manifestation by a merely minor goddess. For one not numbered among the Nine—didn't you say something like that in the manteion? I think I remember that."

Silk dropped the bar into place and turned to reply, but she raised a hand. "I know what you intend to say, Patera. Don't say it. My name is Chenille. That is to be a given, not subject to debate or qualification. You're to call me Chenille, even when we're alone. And you're to treat me as Chenille."

"But—"

"*Because I am Chenille.* You don't really grasp these things, no matter how much you may have studied. Now sit down. Your leg hurts, I know."

Silk dropped into his chair.

"There was something else you wanted to say—not that other, which isn't really true. What is it?"

"I'm afraid that it may offend you, but it isn't intended to offend." He hesitated and swallowed. "Chenille, you . . . you talk very differently at different times. Yesterday at Orchid's, you spoke like a young woman who had grown up in the streets, who couldn't read but who had picked up a few phrases and some sense of grammatical principles from better-educated people. Tonight, before His Eminence came, you used a great deal of thieves' cant, as Auk does. As soon as His Eminence arrived, you became a young woman of culture and education."

Her smile widened. "Do you want me to justify the way I speak to you, Patera? Hardly the request of a gentleman, much less a man of the cloth."

Silk sat in silence for a time, stroking his cheek. Oreb hopped from Chenille's wrist to her shoulder, then to the top of the battered library table next to Silk's chair.

At length Silk said, "If you had spoken to His Eminence as you spoke to me, he would have assumed that I had hired you for the evening or something of that kind. To save me from embarrassment, you betrayed your real nature to me. I wish I knew how to thank you properly for that, Chenille."

"You pronounce my name as though it were a polite lie. I assure you, it's the truth."

Silk asked, "But if I were to use another name—we both know which —wouldn't that be the truth as well?"

"Not really. Far less than you believe, and it would lead to endless difficulties."

"You're more beautiful tonight than you were in Orchid's house. May I say that?"

She nodded. "I wasn't trying then. Or not much. Not well. Men think it's all bones and makeup. But a lot is . . . Certain things I do. My eyes and my lips. The way I move. The right gestures. You do it too, unconsciously. Silk. I like to watch you. When you don't know I'm watching." She yawned and stretched until it seemed that her full breasts would split her gown. "There. That wasn't very beautiful, was it? Though he used to love it when I yawned, and kiss my hand. I did it sometimes. Just to give him pleasure. Such delight. Silk, I'm going to have to have a place to sleep tonight. I love your name, Silk. I've been wanting to say it all night. Most names are ugly. Will you help me?"

"Of course," he said. "I am your slave."

"Chenille."

He swallowed again. "I'll help you all I can, Chenille. You can't sleep here, but I feel sure we can find something better."

Suddenly she was again the woman he had met at Orchid's. "We've got to talk about that, but there are other things to talk about first. You do realize why that awful man came? Why you're getting an acolyte? Why that awful man and this Prolocutor are going to try to take your manteion back from Blood?"

Silk nodded gloomily. "I'm naive at times, I admit; but not that naive. Once I was on the point of suggesting that he drop the pretense."

"He would have turned nasty, I'm sure."

"So am I." Silk drew a deep breath and exhaled with mingled relief and disgust. "That acolyte's being sent to keep an eye on me. I'd like to find out how he's spent the summer."

"You think he may be a protégé of Remora's? Something of that kind?"

Silk nodded. "He's probably been an assistant to his prothonotary. Not the prothonotary himself, because I've met him and his name isn't Gulo. If I can talk with some other augurs who were in the same class, they may be able to tell me."

"So you intend to spy on the spy." Chenille smiled. "At least your manteion's safe."

"I doubt that. In the first place, I don't have a great deal of confidence in His Cognizance's ability to manipulate Blood. Less, anyway, than His Eminence has, or says that he has. Everyone knows the Chapter doesn't have the influence in the Ayuntamiento that it once had, although Lady Kypris's theophany today may help considerably. And . . ."

"Yes? What is it now?" Chenille was stroking Oreb's back. Stretching out his neck, the bird rubbed her arm with his crimson beak.

"In the second, if they can manipulate Blood I won't be here much longer. I'll be transferred, most likely to some administrative position, and this Patera Gulo will take over everything."

"Um-hum. I'm proud of you." Chenille was still looking at the bird. "Then my little suggestion is still of interest to you?"

"Spying on Viron?" Silk gripped Blood's lioness-headed stick with both hands as if he intended to break it. "No! Not unless you order me to do it. And, Chenille—you really are Chenille? Now?"

She nodded, her face serious.

"Then, Chenille, I can't allow you to continue to do it either. All questions of loyalty aside, I can't let you risk your life like that."

"You're angry. I don't blame you, Silk. Though it's better to be cold. He . . . You call him Pas. Someone said once that he was always in a cold fury. Not always, Silk."

She licked her lips. "It wasn't true. But almost. And he came to rule the whole—whorl. Our whorl, bigger than this. So fast. All in a few years. No one could believe it."

Silk said, "I don't think I'm very good at cold furies, but I'll try. I was going to ask what will happen if we succeed? Suppose that we get twenty-six thousand cards from Doctor Crane to hand over to Blood. I doubt that it's even possible, but suppose we do. What good would it do anybody except Blood?"

Silk fell silent for a time, his face in his hands. "I should want to do good to Blood, of course, as I should want to do good to everyone. Even when I broke into his house to try to make him give my manteion back, I did it in part to keep him from staining his spirit by converting the property to a bad purpose. But getting money for him that he doesn't need isn't going to do him any good, and it may even do him harm."

Oreb dropped onto Silk's shoulder, startling him into looking up; as he did, Oreb caught a lock of his straying hair and tugged at it.

"He knows what you're feeling," Chenille said quietly. "He would like to make you laugh, if he can."

"He's a good bird—a very good bird. This isn't the first time he's come to me of his own accord."

"You would take him with you, wouldn't you? Even if you were sent to that administrative position? Silk. It isn't against some rule for augurs to keep pets?"

"No. They're permitted."

"So everything wouldn't be lost, even then." Chenille floated from her chair to slip behind his own. "I could . . . Supply some trifling comfort, too. Now, Silk. If you wish it."

"No," he repeated.

Silence refilled the little sellaria. After two minutes or more had passed, he added, "But thank you anyway. Thank you very much. What you said shouldn't make me feel better; but it does, and I'll always be grateful to you."

"I'll take advantage of your gratitude, you know."

He nodded soberly. "I hope you do. I want you to."

"You don't like girls like me."

"That isn't so." He fell silent for a moment to think about it. "I don't like what you do—the kinds of things that go on every night at Orchid's —because I know they do everyone involved more harm than good, and injure all of us eventually. I don't dislike you or Poppy or the others; in fact, I like you. I even like Orchid, and every god"—He would have stopped, but it was already too late—"knows I felt sorry for her this afternoon."

She laughed softly. "All the gods don't know. Silk. . . . One does. Two. You think those men don't marry because they have us. Most are married already, and shouldn't be."

He nodded reluctantly.

"You've seen how young most of us are. What do you think happens to us?"

"I've never considered it." He wanted to say that many probably perished like Orpine; but she had stabbed Orpine.

"You think we all turn into Orchids, or use too much rust and die in convulsions. Most of us marry, that's all. You don't believe me, but it's the truth. We marry some buck who always asks for us. Silk."

She was stroking his hair. Inexplicably he felt that if he were to turn around he would not see her; that these were the fingers of a phantom.

"You said you wouldn't. Silk. Because you wanted to see a god. To someone. Yesterday? And now?"

"Now I don't know," he admitted.

"You're afraid I'll laugh. You'll be clumsy. All men are. Silk. Patera. You're frightened of my laughter."

"Yes, I am."

"Would you kill me? Silk? For fear that I might laugh? Men do that."

He did not reply at once. Her hands were where Musk's had been, yet he knew they would bring no pain. He waited for her to speak again, but

heard only the distant crackle of the dying fire in the kitchen stove and
the rapid tick of the clock on the mantel. At last he said, "Is that why
some men strike women, in love? So they won't laugh?"

"Sometimes."

"Does Pas strike you?"

She laughed again, a silver flood, whether at Pas or at him he could not
have told. "No. Silk. He never strikes anyone. He kills . . . or nothing."

"But not you. He hasn't killed you." He was conscious again of her
mingled perfumes, the mustiness of her gown.

"I don't know." Her tone was serious, and he did not understand.

Oreb whistled abruptly, hopping from Silk's shoulder to the tabletop.
"She here! Come back." He hoppcd to the shade of the broken reading
lamp, fluttering from there to the top of the curio cabinet. "Iron girl!"

Silk nodded and rose, limping to the garden door.

Chenille murmured, "I didn't mean, by the way, that we should spy on
Viron *for* Crane. I don't think I'll be doing it anymore myself. What I
meant to suggest was that we get your money from Crane."

She yawned again, covering her mouth with a hand larger than most
women's. "He seems to have a lot. To control a lot, at least. So why
shouldn't we take it? If you were the owner of this manteion, it would be
awkward to transfer you, I'd think."

Silk gawked at her.

"Now you expect me to have an elaborate plan. I don't. I'm not good
at them, and I'm too tired to think anymore tonight anyway. Since you
won't sleep with me, you think about it. And I will, too, when I get up."

"Chenille—"

Maytera Marble's steel knuckles tapped the door.

"It's that mechanical woman of yours, like Oreb said. What is it they
called them? Robota? Robotniks? There used to be a lot more."

"Chems," he whispered as Maytera Marble knocked again.

"Whatever. Open the door so she can see me, Silk."

He did so, and Maytera Marble regarded the tall, fiery-haired Chenille
with considerable surprise.

"Patera has been shriving me," she told the sibyl, "and now I need
someplace to stay. I don't think he wants me to sleep here."

"You . . . ? No, no!" Although it was impossible, Maytera Marble's
eyes appeared to have widened.

Silk interposed, "I thought that you—and Maytera Rose and Maytera
Mint—might put her up in the cenoby tonight. You have vacant rooms, I

know. I was about to come over and ask. You must have read my mind, Maytera."

"Oh, no. I was just bringing back your plate, Patera." She held it out. "But—but . . ."

"You'd be doing me an enormous favor." He accepted the plate. "I promise that Chenille won't give you any trouble, and perhaps you, and Maytera Rose and Maytera Mint, may be able to advise her in ways that I, a man, cannot—though if Maytera Rose is not willing, Chenille will have to stay elsewhere, of course. It's getting late, but I'll try to find a family that will open its home to her."

Maytera Marble nodded meekly. "I'll try, Patera. I'll do my best. Really, I will."

"I know," he assured her, smiling.

Leaning against the doorjamb with the plate in his hand, he watched the two women, Maytera Marble in her black habit and Chenille in her black gown, alike yet so very unlike as they walked slowly along the little path. When they had nearly reached the door of the cenoby, the second, lagging behind, turned to wave.

And it seemed to Silk at that moment that the face he glimpsed was not Chenille's, and not a conventionally good-looking face at all but one of breathtaking loveliness.

Hare was waiting outside the floater shed. "Well, it's finished," Hare said.

"Will it fly?"

Hare shrugged. He had noticed the bruise on Musk's jaw, but was too wise to mention it.

"Will it *fly?*" Musk repeated.

"How'd I know? I don't know anything about them."

Musk, a head shorter, advanced a step. "Will it fly? This's the last time."

"Sure." Hare nodded, tentatively at first, then more vigorously. "Sure it will."

"How the shag do you know, putt?"

"He says it will. He says it'll lift a lot, and he's been making them for fifty years. He ought to know."

Musk waited, not speaking, his face intent, his hands hovering near his waist.

"It looks good, too." Hare took a half step backward. "It looks real. I'll show you."

Musk nodded almost reluctantly and motioned toward the side door. Hare hurried to open it.

The shed was too new to have the creeping greenish sound-activated lights that the first settlers had brought with them or, just possibly, had themselves known how to make. Beeswax candles and half a dozen lamps burning fish oil illuminated its cavernous interior now; there was a faint, heavy odor from the hot wax, a fishy reek, and dominating both a stronger and more pungent smell of ripe bananas. The kite builder was bent above his creation, adjusting the tension of the almost invisible thread that linked its ten-cubit wings.

Musk said, "I thought you said it was finished. All finished, you said."

The kite builder looked up. He was smaller even than Musk; but his beard was gray-white, and he had the shaggy brows that mark the penultimate season in man's life. "It is," he said. His voice was soft and a trifle husky. "I was trimming."

"You could fly it now? Tonight?"

The kite builder nodded. "With a wind."

Hare protested, "She won't fly at night, Musk."

"But this. This'll fly now?"

The kite builder nodded again.

"With a rabbit? It'll carry that much?"

"A small rabbit, yes. Domestic rabbits get very large. It wouldn't carry a rabbit that big. I told you."

Musk nodded absently and turned to Hare. "Go get one of the white ones. Not the littlest one, the next to littlest, maybe. About like that."

"There's no wind."

"A white one," Musk repeated. "Meet us on the roof." He motioned to the kite builder. "Bring it and the wire. Anything you're going to need."

"I'll have to disassemble it again, then reassemble it up there. That's going to take at least an hour. Could be more."

"Give me the wire," Musk told him. "I'll go up first. You stay down here and hook it up. I'll pull it up. Hare can show you how to get up there."

"You haven't let out the cats?"

Musk shook his head, went to the bench, and got the reel. "Come on."

Outside, the night hung hot and still. No leaf stirred in the forest beyond the wall.

Musk pointed. "Stand right over there, see? Where it's three floors. I'll be up on that roof."

The kite builder nodded and went back to the floater shed to crank open the main door, three floaters wide. When he picked it up, the new kite felt heavy in his hands; he had not weighed it, and now he tried to guess its weight: as much as the big fighting kite he'd built when he was just starting, with the big black bull on it.

And that wouldn't fly in any wind under a gale.

He carried the new kite along the white stone path, then across the rolling lawn to the spot that Musk had pointed out. There was no sign of Hare and no dangling wire. Craning his neck, the kite builder peered up at the ornamental battlement, black as the bull against the mosaic gaiety of the skylands. There was no one there.

Some distance behind him, the cats were pacing nervously in their pen, eager for their time of freedom. He could not hear them, yet he was acutely conscious of them, their claws and amber eyes, their hunger and their frustration. Suppose that the talus were to free them without waiting for Musk's order? Suppose that they were free already, slinking through the shrubbery, ready to pounce?

Something touched his cheek.

"Wake up down there!" It was Musk's husky, almost feminine voice, calling from the roof.

The kite builder caught the wire and fastened the tiny snap hook at its end to the kite's yoke, then stepped back to admire his work as his kite swiftly mounted the dressed stone, his kite like a man smaller and slighter than almost any actual man, with a dragonfly's gossamer wings.

Hare was coming over the lawn with something pale in his arms. The kite builder called, "Let me see that," and trotted to meet him, taking the white rabbit from him and holding it up by its ears. "It's too heavy!"

"This is the one he said to bring," Hare told him. He retrieved the rabbit.

"It can't lift one that big."

"There's no wind anyhow. You coming up?"

The kite builder nodded.

"Come on, then."

Entering the original villa by a rear door, they climbed two flights of stairs and clattered up the iron spiral that Silk had descended two nights before; Hare threw open the trap door. "We had a big buzzard up here," Hare said. "We called him Hierax, but he's dead."

Somewhat out of breath, the kite builder felt obliged to chuckle nonetheless.

They crossed the tiles and scrambled up onto the roof of the wing, the

kite builder holding the docile rabbit again and passing it to Hare when
Hare had attained the higher roof, accepting a hand as he himself scrambled up.

Musk was sitting on the battlement, practically hidden by the kite.
"Show a little life. I've been waiting for an hour. Are you going to have to
run with it?"

"I'll hold the spool," the kite builder said. "Hare can run with it. But it
won't fly without a wind."

"There's wind," Musk told him.

The kite builder moistened his forefinger and held it up; there was
indeed some slight stir here, fifty cubits above the ground. "Not enough,"
he said.

"I could feel it," Musk told him. "Feel it trying to go up."

"Naturally it wants to." The kite builder could not and would not
conceal his pride in his craft. "Mine all do, but there's not enough wind."

Hare asked, "You want me to tie the rabbit on?"

"Let me see him." Musk, too, lifted the rabbit by its ears, and it
squealed in protest. "This is the little one. You putt, you brought the
little one."

"I weighed 'em. There's two lighter than this, I swear."

"I ought to drop it off. Maybe I ought to drop you off, too."

"You want me to get them? I'll show them to you. It'll only take a
minute."

"What if it gets threshed and goes off? We haven't got any more this
little. What'll we use in the morning?" Musk returned the rabbit to Hare.

"Two of them, by Scylla's slime. By any shaggy gods you want to name.
I wouldn't lie to you."

"That's not a rabbit, it's a shaggy rat."

A passing breeze ruffled the kite builder's hair, like the fingers of an
unseen goddess. He felt that if he were to turn quickly he might glimpse
her: Molpe, goddess of the winds and all light things, Molpe, whose
suitor he had been all his life. *Molpe, make your winds blow for me. Don't
shame me, Molpe, who have always honored you. A brace of finches for
you, I swear.*

Musk snapped, "Tie it on," and Hare knelt on the sun-soft tar, whipping the first cord around the unfortunate rabbit and tying it cruelly tight.

"Split along!"

"Cooler. I can't see a shaggy thing I'm doing here. We should've
brought a lantern."

"So it can't fall out."

Hare rose. "All right. It won't." He took the kite from Musk. "Should I hold it over my head?"

The kite builder nodded. He had picked up the reel of wire; now he moistened his finger again.

"Want me to run down that way?"

"No. Listen to me. You have to run toward me, into the wind—into whatever wind there is, anyway. You're running so that the wind will feel stronger to the kite than it really is. If we're lucky, that false wind will lift it enough to get it up to where the wind really is stronger. Go down that way, all the way to the corner. I'll reel out as you walk down, and reel in as you run back. Any time the kite wants to lift out of your hands, toss it up. If it starts to fall, catch it."

"He's from the city," Musk explained. "They don't fly them there."

The kite builder nodded absently, watching Hare. "Hold it by the feet, as high as you can get it. Don't run until I tell you to."

"It looks real now," Musk said, "but I don't know if it looks real enough. It'll be daylight and sunshine, and they can see a shaggy scut better than we can. Only they don't always know real from fake. They don't think about it like we do."

"All right," the kite builder called. "Now!"

Hare ran, long-legged and fast, the kite's wings moving, stroking the air a trifle at every stride as though it would fly like a bird if it could. Halfway along the long roof he released it, and it rose.

Molpe! O Molpe!

At twice Hare's height it stalled, hung motionless for an instant, dipped until it nearly touched the roof, lifted again to head height, and fell lifeless to the tar.

"Catch it!" Musk screamed. "You're supposed to catch it! You want to bust its shaggy neck?"

"You're worried about your rabbit," the kite builder told him, "but you've got more, and you could buy a dozen tomorrow morning. I'm worried about the kite. If it's broken it could take two days to mend it. If it's broken badly, I'll have to start over."

Hare had picked up the kite. "The rabbit's all right," he called across the roof. "Want to try again?"

The kite builder shook his head. "That bowstring's not tight enough. Bring it here."

Hare did.

"Hold it up." The kite builder knelt. "I don't want to put it down on this tar."

"Maybe we could tow it behind one of the floaters," Hare suggested.

"That would be riskier even than this. If it went down, it would be dragged to rags before we could stop." By touch alone, he loosened the knot. "I wanted to put a turnbuckle in this," he told Musk. "Maybe I should have."

"We'll try it again when you've got it right," Musk said.

"There might be a wind in the morning."

"I'm going to fly Aquila in the morning. I don't want to be wondering about this."

"All right." The kite builder stood, wet his forefinger again, and nodded to Hare, pointing.

This time the enormous kite lifted confidently, though it seemed to the kite builder that there was no wind at all. Fifteen, twenty, thirty cubits it soared—then dipped—swooped abruptly with a terrified squeal from its passenger, and struggled to climb again, nearly stalling.

"If it gets down below the roof, the house'll kill the wind."

"Exactly right." The kite builder nodded patiently. "The very same thought had occurred to me earlier."

"You're pulling it down! What are you doing that for? It was going to fly that time."

"I need to slack off the lower bridle line," the kite builder explained. "That's the string going from the feet to the yoke."

To Hare he called, "Coming down! Catch it!"

"All right, that's enough!" Musk's needler was in his hand. "We'll try again in the morning. We'll try it again when there's more wind, and it had better fly and fly good when we do. *Are you listening to me, old man?*"

Hare had the kite now; the kite builder released the reel crank. "About that much." He indicated the distance with his fingers. "Didn't you see it dive? If it dove like that into this roof, or into the ground, it could be completely wrecked."

While Hare held the kite up, the kite builder loosened the lower bridle string and let it out the distance he had indicated. "I thought that I might have to do this," he explained, "so I left a little extra here."

Musk told Hare, "We won't risk it again tonight."

"Be quiet." The kite builder's fingers had stopped, the bridle string half-retied. Far away he had heard the murmur of the dry forest, the shaking of raddled old leaves and the rubbing a million dry twigs upon a million more. He turned his head blindly, questing.

"What is it?" Hare wanted to know.

The kite builder straightened up. "Go to the other corner this time," he said.

"It had better not break." Musk slipped his needler beneath his tunic.

"If it breaks, I'll be safe," the kite builder remarked. "You couldn't repair it, and neither could he."

"If it flies you'll be safer," Musk told him grimly.

Two chains and more away, Hare could hear their voices. "All right?"

Automatically the kite builder glanced down at his reel. The trees had fallen silent now, but he felt Molpe's phantom fingers in his hair. His beard stirred. *"NOW!"*

Hare held onto the huge kite until he was halfway across the roof, and loosed it with an upward toss. Immediately it shot up fifty, then sixty cubits; there it paused, as though gathering strength.

"Up," Musk muttered. "Away hawk!"

For a full two minutes, the kite soared no higher, its transparent wings almost invisible against the skylands, its human body as black as the shade, the rabbit a writhing dot upon its chest. At last the kite builder smiled and let out more wire. It climbed confidently, higher and higher, until it seemed that it would be lost among tessellated fields and sparkling rivers on the other side of the whorl. "Is that enough?" the kite builder asked. "Shall I bring it down?"

Musk shook his head.

Hare, who had joined them to watch the kite, said, "Looks good, don't it? Looks like the lily thing."

"I want my money," the kite builder told Musk. "This is what we agreed upon. I've built it, you've approved it, and it will carry a rabbit."

"Half now," Musk whispered, still watching the kite. "I don't approve until Aquila goes for it. I'm still not sure it's going to look right to her."

Hare chuckled. "Poor little bunny! I bet it don't even know where it's got to. I bet it's lonesome way up there."

Musk contemplated the distant rabbit with a bitter smile. "It'll get some company in the morning." The mounting wind fluttered his embroidered tunic and pushed a long strand of curling hair across his handsome forehead.

The kite builder said, "If you don't think that it will deceive your eagle, tell me what changes you'd like me to make. I'll try to have them finished by morning."

"It looks good now," Musk conceded. "It looks exactly like a real flier holding a rabbit."

* * *

In bed, tossing and turning, Silk drove the deadcoach through a dark and
ruined dreamscape, the land of the dead still a land of the living. The
wind was blowing and blowing, fluttering all the yellow-white curtains of
all the bedroom windows, fluttering the velvet hangings of the deadcoach
like so many black flags; like the slashed poster on Sun Street with old
Councillor Lemur's eyes gouged out, his nose and his mouth dancing,
dancing in the wind; like the kind face of old Councillor Loris cut away
and blowing down the gutter; like Maytera Rose's wide black habit,
heavy with hemweights and death but fluttering anyway while the tall
black plumes bent and swayed, while the wind caught the black lash of
Silk's dancing whip, so that when he intended to whip one black horse he
whipped the other. The unwhipped black horse lagged and lagged, dogged and dogged it, snorted at the billowing yellow dust but was never
whipped. He should have been for cheating his brother who sweated and
lunged at the harness though his flanks were crusted with yellow dust
that the white foam had already dyed black.

   In the deadcoach Orpine writhed naked and white, Silk's old torn
cotton handkerchief falling from her face, always falling but never fallen,
always slipping but never slipped, though the wind whistled against the
glass and carried dust through every crack. While whipping the wrong
horse, always the wrong horse, Silk watched her clawing Chenille's dagger, saw her claw and pull at it though it was wedged between her ribs,
saw her clawing like a cat at the red cat with the fiery tail, at the fine
brass guard all faceted with file work. Her face beneath the slipping
handkerchief was stained with her blood, forever the face of Mucor, of
Blood's crazed daughter. There were sutures in her scalp and her brown
hair was shaved away, her black hair shaved by Moorgrass, who had
washed her body and shaved half her head so that the stitches showed
and a drop of blood at each stitch though her full breasts leaked milk
onto the black velvet. The grave awaited her, only the grave, one more
grave in a whorl of graves where so many lay already watched over by
Hierax, God of Death and Caldé of the Dead, High Hierax the White-
Headed One with her white spirit in his claws because the second one
had been a brain surgeon, for whom if not for her?

   Nor did Silk, alone in the padded black-leather driver's seat, know
what any of these things meant, but only that he was driving to the grave
and was late as usual. He always came to a grave too late and too soon,
driving nightside in a dark that was darker than the darkest night, on a
day that was hotter than the hottest day, so that it burned the billowing
dust as an artist's earths are burned in an artist's little furnace, glowing

gold in the heat, the black plumes billowing while he whipped the wrong horse, a sweating horse that would die at the grave if the other did not pull too. And where would Orpine lie, with the dead black horse in her grave?

"Hi-yup!" he shouted, but the horses did not heed him, for they were at the grave and the long sun gone out, burned out, dead forever until it kindled next time. "Too deep," Chenille told him standing by the grave. "Too deep," the frogs echoed her, frogs he had caught as a boy in the year that he and his mother had gone to the country for no reason and come back to a life no different, the frogs he had loved and killed with his love. *"Too deep!"* and the grave was too deep, though its bottom was lined with black velvet so that the sand and the cold clay would never touch her. The cold, sinking waters of underground streams that were sinking every year it seemed would never wash Orpine, would not rot her back to trees and flowers, never wash off Blood's blood nor wet the fiery cat with the black mouse in its jaws, nor the golden hyacinths. Never fill the golden pool in which the golden crane watched golden fish forever; for this was no good year for golden fish, nor even for silver ones.

"Too deep!"

And it was too deep, so that the yellow dust would never fill it and the velvet at the bottom was sprinkled with sparks that might flicker at last but hadn't flickered yet as Maytera Marble told him pointing, and by the light of that one there she was young again, with a face like Maytera Mint's and brown gloves like flesh covering her hard-working steel fingers.

"Too long!" he told the horses, and the one that never pulled at all lunged and plunged and put his back into it, pulling for all he was worth, though the wind was in his teeth and the night darker than any night could be, with never a patch of skylands showing. The long road underground was buried forever in the billowing dust and all this blowing brush.

"Too long!"

Hyacinth sat beside him on the padded leather seat; after a time he gave her his old, bloodstained handkerchief to cover her nose and mouth. Though the wind bayed like a thousand yellow hounds, it could not blow their creaking, shining, old deadcoach off of this road that was no road at all, and he was glad of her company.

CHAPTER
5   THE SLAVE OF SPHIGX

It was Molpsday, Silk reminded himself as he sat up in bed: the day for light-footed speed, and after work for singing and dancing. He did not feel particularly light-footed as he sat up, swung his legs over the side of his bed, and rubbed his eyes and his bristling jaw. He had slept—how long? Almost too long, but he could still join the sibyls in their morning prayers if he hurried. It had been the first good night's sleep he had gotten since. . . .

Since Thelxday.

He stretched, telling himself he would have to hurry. Breakfast later or not at all, though there was still fruit left and vegetables enough for half the quarter.

He stood, resolved to hurry, received a flash of pain in his right ankle for his effort, and sat down again abruptly.

Blood's lioness-headed stick was leaning against the head of the bed, with Crane's wrapping on the floor beside it. He picked up the wrapping and lashed the floor with it.

"Sphigx will be the goddess for me today," he muttered, "my prop and my support." He traced the sign of addition in the air. "Thou Sabered, Stabbing, Roaring Sphigx, Lioness and Amazon, be with me to the end. Give me courage in this, my hour of hardship."

Crane's wrapping was burning hot; it squeezed his ankle like a vise and felt perfectly wonderful as he trotted down the stairs to fill his washbasin at the kitchen pump.

Oreb was asleep on top of the larder, standing on one leg, his head tucked beneath his sound wing. Silk called, "Wake up, old bird. Food? Fresh water? This is the time to ask."

Oreb croaked in protest without showing his face.

There was still some of his old cage left, and a large, live ember from the fire that had cooked no vegetables last night. Silk laid half a dozen twigs across it, puffed, and actually rubbed his hands at the sight of the young flame. He would not have to use any precious paper at all!

"It's morning," he told the bird. "The shade's up, and you should be too."

There was no reply.

Oreb, Silk decided, was openly ignoring him. "I have a broken ankle," he told the bird happily. "And a stiff arm—Master Xiphias thought I was left-handed, did I tell you about that? And a sore belly, and a fine big black-and-blue mark on my chest where Musk hit me with the pommel of his knife." He arranged three small splits on top of the blazing, snapping twigs. "But I don't care one bit. It's Molpsday, marvelous Molpsday, and I feel marvelous. If you're going to be my pet, so must you, Oreb." He clanged shut the firebox and set his shaving water on the stove.

"Fish heads?"

"No fish heads. There hasn't been time for fish heads, but I believe there might be a nice pear left. Do you like pears?"

"Like pears."

"So do I, so it's share and share alike." Fishing out of the sink the knife he had used to slice his tomatoes, he wiped the blade (noticing with a pang of guilt that it was beginning to rust) and whacked the pear in half, then bit into his share, drained the sink, pumped more water, and splashed his face, neck, and hair. "Wouldn't you like to join us for morning prayers, Oreb? You don't have to, but I have the feeling it might be good for you." Picturing Maytera Rose's reaction to the bird he laughed. "It would be good for me, too, in all likelihood."

"Bird sleep."

"Not until you've finished your pear, I trust. If it's still here when I get back, I'll eat it myself."

Oreb fluttered down to the tabletop. "Eat now."

"Very wise," Silk commended him, and took another bite from his half, thinking first of his dream—it had been a remarkable dream, from what he remembered of it—then of the yellowish surgical catgut lacing Mucor's scalp. Had he seen that, or merely dreamed it? And then of Crane who was a doctor too, and had almost certainly implanted the horned cats in the mad girl's womb, doubtless two or even three at a time.

Upstairs, while he lathered and scraped, he remembered what Chenille had said about getting enough money from Crane to save the manteion. Ordinarily he would have discarded any suggestion as wild as that summarily, but Chenille was not Chenille—or at least, not Chenille solely—and no matter what she might say, there was no point in deceiving himself about that, though politeness, apparently, demanded a pretense. He had begged Comely Kypris to return, but she had done him one better: she had never left—or rather, merely left the Sacred Window to possess Chenille.

It was a great honor for Chenille, to be sure. For a moment he envied her. He himself had been enlightened by the Outsider, however, and that was a greater honor still. After that, he should never envy anyone else anything at all. Kypris was the whores' goddess. Had Chenille been a good whore? And was she being rewarded for it? She—or rather, the goddess—or perhaps both—had said she would not go back to Orchid's.

He wiped and dried his razor and inspected his face in the mirror.

Did that mean, perhaps, that Kypris loved them without loving what they did? It was an inspiring thought, and very possibly a correct one. He did not know nearly as much as he urgently needed to know about Kypris, just as he remained lamentably ignorant of the Outsider, though the Outsider had showed him so very much and Kypris had revealed something of herself last night—her relations with Pas, particularly.

Silk toweled his face and turned to the wardrobe for a clean tunic, recalling as he did that Patera Remora had as much as ordered him to buy himself new clothes. With the cards left from Orpine's rites, there should be no trouble about that.

Hyacinth had held his tunic for him, had helped him put it back on despite his injured arm. He found that instead of running downstairs to join the sibyls in the manteion he was sitting on his bed again with his head in his hands, his head swimming with thoughts of Hyacinth. How beautiful she had been, and how kind! How wonderful, sitting beside him as they drove to the grave. He would have to die—all men died—and so would she; but they need not die alone. With a slight shock he realized that his dream had been no idle phantom of the night but had been sent by a god, no doubt by Hierax, who had figured in it (that in itself was a nearly determinative signature) with Orpine's white spirit in his hands.

Filled with joy again, Silk stood and snatched a clean tunic from the wardrobe. Blood had called his bird Hierax, a deliberate blasphemy. He, Silk, had killed that bird, or at least had fought against it and caused its death. Hierax therefore had favored him—indeed, Hierax had been favoring him ever since, not only by sending him a dream filled with the god's symbols, but by giving him Orpine's very profitable rites. No one could say Hierax had been ungrateful!

The robe he had worn the day before was soiled now, and badly spotted with dried blood; but there was no clean robe with which to replace it. He got out his clothes brush and whaled away, making the dust fly.

Men and women, made of mud (originally by the Outsider, according to one somewhat doubtful passage in the Writings) turned to dust at last. Fell to dust only too quickly, in all truth. The same sober thought had crossed his mind toward the close of Orpine's rites, as he had been driving the screws to fasten the lid of Orpine's casket.

And Chenille had interrupted him, rising like—like . . . The comparison slipped away. He tried to recreate the scene in his mind. Chenille, taller than many men, with tightly curled fiery hair, big bones, flat cheeks, and large breasts, wooden yet twitching in her plain blue gown.

No. It had been a black gown, as was proper. Had she been wearing blue when he had seen her first, at Orpine's? No, green. Almost certainly green.

Horn's toy! That was it. He had never seen it. (He brushed harder than ever.) But he had seen toys like it, jointed figures worked with four strings on a wooden cross. Horn's had worn a painted blue coat, and Chenille had, at first, moved like such a toy, as if the goddess had not yet learned to work her strings well. She had talked no better than Oreb.

Was it possible that even a goddess had to learn to do new things? That was a fresh thought indeed.

But goddesses learned quickly, it seemed; by the time Patera Remora had arrived she had been able to throw Musk's knife better than Musk himself. Musk, who last night had given him a scant week in which to redeem the manteion. The manteion might not be worth preserving, but the Outsider had told him to save it, so save it he must.

Now here was the pinch at last. What was he going to do today? Because there was no time to waste, none at all. He must get more time from Blood today—somehow—or acquire most or all of that enormous sum.

He slapped his trousers pocket. Hyacinth's needler was still there. Kneeling, he pulled the cashbox from beneath his bed, unlocked it, and took out the azoth; with the azoth under his tunic he relocked the cashbox, replaced the key, and returned the empty box to its hiding place.

"Sabered Sphigx," he murmured, "remember your servants, who live or die by the sword." It was a Guardsman's prayer, but it seemed to him that it suited him at least as well.

Chenille was waiting in the garden when Silk, preceded by Maytera Rose and followed by Maytera Marble and little Maytera Mint, emerged from the side door of the manteion. Oreb called, "Good Silk!" from her shoulder and hopped over to perch on his; but Maytera Rose's back was to him, so that he missed her expression—if in fact she had noticed the living bird.

Maytera Marble said, "I thought of inviting you to join us, Chenille, but you were sleeping so soundly. . . ."

Chenille smiled. "I'm glad you didn't, Maytera. I was terribly tired. I peeked in on you later, though. I hope you didn't see me."

"Did you really?" Maytera Marble smiled in return, her face lifted and her head cocked slightly to the right. "You should have joined us then. It would have been all right."

"I had Oreb, and he was frightened. You had reached the anamnesis, anyway."

Silk nodded to himself. There was nothing of Kypris in Chenille's face now, and the already-hot sunshine was cruel to it; but Chenille would not know that term. He said, "I hope that Chenille wasn't too much of a bother to you last night, Maytera?"

"No, no. None at all. None. But you'll have to excuse me now. The children will be arriving before long. I have to unlock, and look over the lesson."

As they watched her hurry away, Chenille said, "I make her nervous, I'm afraid. She'd like to like me, but she's afraid I've corrupted you."

"You make me nervous, too, Chenille," Silk admitted. As he spoke, both of them noticed Maytera Mint, waiting with downcast eyes in the diffused shade of the arbor. Softening his voice, Silk inquired, "Was there something you wished to speak to me about, Maytera?"

She shook her head without looking up.

"Perhaps you wanted to say farewell to your guest; but to tell the truth, I'm not sure she won't have to stay with you and your sibs tonight, as well."

For the first time since Silk had met her, Maytera Mint actually startled him, stepping out of the shadows to stare up into Chenille's face with a longing he could not quite fathom. "You don't make me nervous," she said, "and that's what I wanted to say to you. You're the only grownup who doesn't. I feel drawn to you."

"I like you, too," Chenille said quietly. "I like you very much, Maytera."

Maytera Mint nodded, a nod (Silk thought) of acceptance and understanding. "I must be fifteen years older than you are. More, perhaps—I'll be thirty-seven next year. And yet I feel that— Perhaps it's only because you're so much taller . . . ."

"Yes?" Chenille inquired gently.

"That you're really my older sister. I've never had an older sister, really. I love you." And with that, Maytera Mint whirled with a swirl of black bombazine and hurried off toward the cenoby, swerved suddenly halfway down the path, and cut across the dry, brown lawn toward the palaestra, on the other side of the playground.

"Bye-bye!" Oreb called. "Bye, girl!"

Silk shook his head. "I would never have expected that. The whorl holds possibilities beyond my imagining."

"Too bad." Chenille sighed. "I have to tell you. To explain. Silk. Patera. We ought to be talking about the other thing. Getting money from Crane. But I . . . We've a problem. There with poor Maytera Mint. It's my doing. In a way."

Silk said, "I hope it's not a serious problem. I like her, and I feel responsible for her."

"So do I. Still, we may. We do, I know. Perhaps we could go back to your little house? And talk?"

Silk shook his head. "Women aren't supposed to enter a manse, although there are a whole string of exceptions—when an augur's ill, a woman may come in to nurse him, for example. When I want to talk with Maytera Marble, we do it here in the arbor, or in her room in the palaestra."

"All right." Chenille ducked beneath the drooping grape vines. "What about Maytera Mint? And the old one, Maytera Rose? Where do you talk to them?"

"Oh, in the same places." With a slight pang of guilt, Silk took the old wooden seat across from Chenille's; it was the one in which Maytera Marble normally sat. "But to tell you the truth, I seldom talk very long with either of them. Maytera Mint is generally too shy to reply, and Maytera Rose lectures me." He shook his head. "I should listen to her much more closely than I do, I'm afraid; but after five or ten minutes I can't think of anything except getting away. I don't intend to imply that either isn't a very good woman. They are."

"Maytera Mint is." Chenille licked her lips. "That's why I feel bad. As I do. Silk. It was . . . Well, not *me*. Not Chenille."

"Of course!" Silk nodded vigorously. "She senses the goddess in you! I should've understood at once. You don't want her to tell—"

"No, no. She does, but it's not that. And she won't tell anybody. She doesn't know herself. Not consciously."

Silk cleared his throat. "If you feel that there may be some physical attraction—I'm aware that these things take place among women as they do among men—it would certainly be better if you slept elsewhere tonight."

Chenille waved the subject away. "It wouldn't matter. But it's not that. She doesn't want . . . She doesn't want anything. Anything from me. She wants to help. Give me things. I understand it. It's not . . . discreditable. Is that what you'd say? Discreditable?"

"I suppose it is."

"But all this . . . It doesn't matter. None of it. I'm going to have to tell you. More. I won't lie." Her eyes flashed. "I *won't!*"

"I wouldn't want you to," Silk assured her.

"Yes. Yes, you do, Silk. Silk. Possession, you . . . We talked about it last night. You think a god . . . Me? I mean Kypris. Or another one. That horrible woman with the snakes. You think we go into people. Like fevers?"

"I certainly would not have put it like that."

Chenille studied him hungrily through heavy-lidded eyes that seemed larger than they had been outside the arbor, dark eyes that glowed with their own light. "But you think it. I know. We . . . It goes in through the eyes. We gods aren't . . . Something you see? We're patterns. We change. Learning and growing. But still patterns? And I'm not Kypris. I told you that. . . . You thought I lied."

Oreb whistled. "Poor girl!"

And Silk, who had turned away from the frightful power and craving of those dark eyes, saw that they had begun to weep. He offered his handkerchief, recalling that Maytera Marble had given him hers, here under the arbor, before he had gone to Blood's villa.

"I didn't. I don't. Not much. Not unless I've got to. And I'm not. But what you call possession— Kypris copied a part, just a little part of herself." Chenille blew her nose softly. "I haven't had one little sniff. Not since before Orpine's . . . This's what it does, Patera. Not getting it, I mean. Everything you look at you think, that's not rust, and everything's so sad."

"It will be over very quickly," Silk said, hoping that he was right.

"A week. Maybe two. I did it, one other time. Only . . . Never mind. I wouldn't. I won't now. If you had a whole cup full of rust and held it out for me to take as much as I wanted right now, I wouldn't take any."

"That's wonderful," he said, and meant it.

"And that's because of the pattern. The little piece of Kypris that she's put inside of me, through my eyes, in your manteion yesterday. You don't understand, do you? I know you don't."

"I don't understand about the patterns," Silk said. "I understand the rest, or at least I believe I do."

"Like your heart. Patterns of beats. Yes, yes, no, no, no, yes, yes. There's this thing behind everybody's eyes. I don't understand everything myself. The mechanical woman? Marble? Somebody too clever learned he could do it to them. Change programs in little ways. People made machines. Just to do that. So that people like Maytera Marble would work for them instead of for the State. Steal for them. He . . . Pas, you call him. He had people study it. And they found out that you could do something like it with people. It was harder. The frequency was much higher. But you could, and so we do. That was how it all began. Silk. Through the terminals, through their eyes."

"Now I am lost," Silk admitted.

"It doesn't matter. But it's flashes of light. Light no one else can see. The thuds, the pulses, making up the program, the god that runs in Mainframe. Kypris is the god, that program. But she closed her eyes. Mint did. Maytera Mint. And I wasn't through, it wasn't finished."

Silk shook his head. "I know this must be important, and I'm trying to understand it; but to tell you the truth, I have no idea of what you mean."

"Then I'll lie." Chenille edged toward him until her knees touched his. "I'll lie, so that you can understand, Patera. Listen to me now. I . . . Kypris wanted to possess Maytera Mint—never mind why."

"You're Chenille now."

"I'm always Chenille. No, that's not right. Lying, I'm Kypris. All right, then. I'm Kypris now, talking the way Chenille used to. Say yes."

Silk nodded, "Yes, Great Goddess."

"Fine. I wanted to possess Maytera Mint by sending my divine person flowing into her, through her eyes, from the Sacred Window. See?"

Silk nodded again. "Certainly."

"I knew you'd understand. If it was wrong. All right. It feels good, really good, so practically nobody ever shuts their eyes. They want it. They want more. They don't even blink, drinking it in."

Silk said, "It's wholly natural for human beings to want some share of your divine life, Great Goddess. It's one of our deepest instincts."

"Only she did, and that's what you've got to understand. She only got a piece of me—of the goddess. I can't even guess what it may do to her."

Silk slumped, stroking his cheek.

Oreb, who had deserted Silk's shoulder to explore the vines, muttered, "Good girl."

"Yes, she is, Oreb. That's one of the reasons this worries me so much."

"Good now!"

After half a minute of anxious silence, Silk threw up his hands. "I wouldn't have believed that a god could be divided into parts."

Chenille nodded. "Me either."

"But you said—"

"I said it happened." She put her hand upon his knee. "I wouldn't have thought it could. But it did, and it may make her different. I think it already has. I'm Chenille, but I feel like there's somebody else in here with me now, a way of thinking about things and doing things that wasn't here till yesterday. She doesn't. She has a part of Kypris, like you might have a dream."

"This is a terrible thing to say, I suppose, Chenille. But can it be undone?"

She shook her head, her fiery curls bouncing. "Kypris could do it, but we can't. She'd have to be in front of a terminal—a Sacred Window or a glass, it wouldn't matter—when Kypris appeared. Even then, there'd be something left behind. There always is. Some of Maytera Mint's own . . . spirit would go into Kypris, too."

"But you're Kypris," Silk said. "I know that, and I keep wanting to kneel."

"Only in the lie, Patera. If I were a real goddess, you couldn't resist me. Could you? Really I'm Chenille, with something extra. Listen, here's another lie that may help. When somebody's drunk, haven't you ever heard somebody else say it was the brandy talking? Or the beer, or whatever?"

"Yes, that's a very common saying. I don't believe that anyone intends it seriously."

"All right, it's kind of like that. Not exactly, maybe, but pretty close, except that it won't ever die in her the way brandy does. Maytera Mint will be like she is now for the rest of her life, unless Kypris takes herself back—copies the part that went into her, with all of the changes, and erases what was in her."

"Then the only thing that we can do is watch her closely and be, ah," (Silk felt a sudden rush of sympathy for Patera Remora) "try to be tolerant of the unexpected."

"I'm afraid so."

"I'll tell Maytera Marble. I don't mean that I'll tell her what you told me, but I'll warn her. Maytera Rose would be worthless for this. Worse, if anything. Maytera Marble will be wonderful, although she can't be in her own room at the palaestra and in Maytera's at the same time, of course. Thank you, Chenille."

"I had to say something," Chenille dabbed at her nose and eyes. "Now, about the money. I was thinking about that while you were in the manteion, because I'm going to need it. I'm going to have to find a new way to live. A shop? Something . . . And I'll help you all I can, Silk. If you'll go halves?"

He shook his head. "I must have twenty-six thousand for Blood, so that I can buy this manteion from him; so that has to come first. But you can have anything above that amount. Say that we somehow obtain one hundred thousand—though I realize that's an absurd figure. You could keep seventy-four thousand of it. But if we obtain only twenty-six, the entire sum must go to Blood." He paused to look at her more closely. "You're shivering. Would it help if I brought out a blanket from the manse?"

"It will be over in a minute or two, Patera. Then I'll be fine. I've got a lot more control of this than she did. I'm taking you up. On your offer? Have I said that? Your generous offer. That's what I ought to call it. . . . Have you thought of a plan? I'm good at . . . certain things? But I'm not a very good planner. Not really, Silk. Silk? And neither was she. Am I talking right now?"

"I would say so, although I don't know her well. I was hoping you had devised a plan, however. As Chenille, you're much more familiar with Crane than I, and you should have a much clearer conception of the espionage operation that you tell me he's conducting."

"I've tried to think of something. Last night, and then again this morning. The easiest thing would be to threaten to reveal what he's doing, and I've got this." She took an image of Sphigx carved of hard, dark wood from a pocket of her gown. "I was supposed to give it to a woman who has a stall in the market? That's where I was going when I—you know. It was why I got dressed so fast? Then it happened, and I stayed at Orchid's. You know why. And then there was the exorcism. Your exorcism, Silk? So by the time I got to the market it was closing? There was hardly anybody left, except the ones who stay all night. To watch whatever they sell? She'd already gone."

Silk accepted the devotional image. "Sphigx is holding a sword," he murmured, "as she nearly always does in these representations. She also has something square, a tablet, perhaps, or a sheaf of papers; perhaps they represent Pas's instructions, but I don't think I've ever seen them before." He returned the carving to Chenille.

"You would have if you'd seen this woman's stall. She always had three or four of them? Most of them were bigger than this. I'd give mine to her, and she'd say something like are you sure you don't want it? Very pretty and very cheap. And I'd shake my head and go away, and she'd put it on the board with the rest, just like I'd only been looking at it for a minute."

"I see. That stall might be worth a visit." Uncertain how far he could presume upon the goddess's patronage, he hesitated before casting the dice. "It's a shame you're not actually Kypris. If you were, you might be able to tell me the significance of—"

"Man come!" announced Oreb from the top of the arbor, and a moment later they heard a loud knock at the door of the manse.

Silk rose and stepped from under the vines. "Over here, Auk. Won't you join us? I'm glad to see you, and there's someone else here whom you may be glad to see."

Chenille called, "Auk? Is that you? It's me. We need your help."

For a moment, Auk gaped. "Chenille?"

"Yes! In here. Come sit with me."

Silk parted the vines so that Auk could enter the arbor more easily; by the time that he himself had ducked inside, Auk was seated next to Chenille. Silk said, "You know each other, clearly."

Chenille dimpled, and suddenly seemed no older than the nineteen years she claimed. "Remember day before yesterday, Patera? When I said there was somebody? Somebody younger than Crane? And I said I thought he might help me . . . us? With Crane?"

Auk grinned and put his arm around her shoulders. "You know, I don't think I ever saw you in the daytime, Chenille. You're a lot better looking than I expected."

"I've always known how . . . handsome? You are, Auk." She kissed him, quickly and lightly, on the cheek.

Silk said, "Chenille's going to help me get the money that I need to save this manteion, Auk. That's what we've been talking about, and we'd like your advice."

He turned his attention to her. "I should tell you that Auk has already helped me—with advice, at least. I don't think he'll mind my saying that to you."

Auk nodded.

"And now both you and I require it. I'm sure he'll be as generous with us as he has been with me."

"Auk has always been . . . very good to me. Patera? He always asked for me. Since . . . spring?"

She clasped Auk's free hand in her own. "I won't be at Orchid's anymore, Auk. I want to live someplace else, and not . . . You know. Always asking men for money. And no more rust. It was . . . nice. Sometimes when I was afraid. But it makes girls too brave? After a while it owns you. With no rust, you're always so down. Always so scared. So you take it, take more, and get pregnant. Or get killed. I've been too brave. Not pregnant. I don't mean that. Patera will tell you. Auk?"

Auk said, "This sounds good. I like it. I guess you two got together after the funeral, huh?"

"That's right." Chenille kissed him again. "I started thinking. About dying, and everything, you know? There was Orpine and she was so young and healthy and all that? Am I talking better now, Patera Silk? Tell me, and please don't spare my feelings."

Oreb poked his brightly colored head from the half-dead grape leaves to declare, "Talk good!"

Silk nodded, hoping that his face betrayed nothing. "That's fine, Chenille."

"Patera's helping me sound more . . . You know. Uphill? Auk. And I thought Orpine could be me. So I waited. We had a big talk last night, didn't we, Silk? And I stayed with the sibyls." She giggled. "A hard bed and no dinner, not a bit like Orchid's. But they gave me breakfast. Have you eaten breakfast, Auk?"

Auk grinned and shook his head. "I haven't been to bed. You heard what the goddess said yesterday, didn't you, Jugs? Well, look here."

Taking his arm from her shoulders and half standing, Auk groped in his pocket. When his hand emerged, it coruscated with white fire. "Here you go, Patera. Take it. It's not any shaggy twenty-six thousand, but it ought to bring three or four, if you're careful where you sell it. I'll tell you about some people I know." When Silk did not reach for the proffered object, Auk tossed it into his lap.

It was a woman's diamond anklet, three fingers wide. "I really can't—" Silk swallowed. "Yes, I suppose I can. I will because I must. But, Auk—"

Auk slapped his thigh. "You got to! You were the one that could understand Lady Kypris, weren't you? Sure you were, and you told us. No fooling around about having to get the word from somebody else first. All right, she said it and I believed it, and now I got to let her know

I'm the pure keg, too. They're all real. You look at them all you want to. Get some nice sacrifices for her, and don't forget to tell her where they come from."

Silk nodded. "I will, though she will know already, I'm sure."

"Tell her Auk's a dimber cull. Treat him brick and he treats you stone." Taking Chenille's hand, Auk slipped a ring onto her finger. "I didn't know you were going to be here, but this's for you, Jugs. Twig that big red flare? That's what they call a real blood ruby. Maybe you scavy you seen 'em before, but I lay five you didn't. You going to sell it or keep it?"

"I couldn't ever sell this, Hackum." She kissed him on the lips, so passionately that Silk was forced to avert his eyes, and so violently that they both nearly fell from the little wooden bench. When they parted, she added, "You gave it to me, and I'm going to keep it forever."

Auk grinned and wiped his mouth and grinned again, wider than ever. "Sharp now. If you change your mind don't do it without me with you."

He turned back to Silk. "Patera, you got any idea what shook last night? I'd bet there was a dozen houses solved up on the Palatine. I haven't heard yet what else went on. The hoppies are falling all over themselves this morning." He lowered his voice. "What I wanted to talk to you about, Patera—what'd she say to you exactly? About coming back here?"

"Only that she would," Silk told him.

Auk leaned toward him, his big jaw outthrust and his eyes narrowed. "What words?"

Silk stroked his cheek, recalling his brief conversation with the goddess in the Sacred Window. "You're quite right. I'm going to have to report everything she said to the Chapter, verbatim, and in fact I should be writing that report now. I pleaded with her to return. I can't give you the precise words, and they aren't important anyway; but she replied, 'I will. Soon.' "

"She meant this manteion here? Your manteion?"

"I can't be absolutely—"

Chenille interrupted him. "You know she did. That's just what she meant. She meant that she was going to come right back to the same Window."

Silk nodded reluctantly. "She didn't actually say that, as I told you; but I feel—now, at least—that it must have been what she intended."

"Right . . . ." Chenille had found a patch of sunlight that drew red fire from the ring; she watched it as she spoke, turning her hand from side to side. "But we've got to tell you about Crane, Auk. Do you know Crane? He's Blood's pet doctor."

"Patera might've said something last night."

Auk looked his question to Silk, who said, "I did not actually tell Auk, although I may have hinted or implied that I believe that Doctor Crane may have presented an azoth to a certain young woman called Hyacinth. Those cost five thousand cards or more, as you probably know; and thus I was quite ready to believe you when you suggested that it might be possible to extort a very large sum from him. If he did give such a thing to Hyacinth—and I'm inclined to think he did—he must control substantial discretionary funds." Compelled by an inner need, Silk added, "Do you know her, by the way?"

"Uh-huh. She does what I used to do, but she's working for Blood direct now, instead of Orchid. She left Orchid's a couple weeks, maybe, after I moved in."

Reluctantly, Silk dropped the gleaming anklet into the pocket of his robe. "Tell me everything you know about her, please."

"Some of the other dells know her better than I do. I like her, though. She's—I'm not quite sure how to put it. She's not always saying, well, this one's good but that one's bad. She takes people the way they come, and she'll help you if she can, even if you haven't always been as nice to her as you ought to be. Her father's a head clerk in the Juzgado. Are you sure you want to hear this, Silk?"

"Yes, indeed."

"And one of the commissioners saw her when she was maybe fourteen and said, 'Listen, I need a maid. Send her up and she can live at my house'—they had eight or nine sprats, I guess—'and she can make a little money, too, and you'll get a nice promotion.' Hy's father was just a regular clerk then, probably.

"So he said all right and sent Hy up on the Palatine, and you know what happened then. She didn't have to work much—no hard work, just serve meals and dust, and she started to get quite a bit of money. Only after a while the commissioner's wife got really nasty. She lived for a while with a captain, but there was some sort of trouble. . . . Then she came to Orchid's."

Chenille blew her nose into Silk's handkerchief. "I'm sorry, Patera. It's always like this if you haven't had any for a day or so. My nose will run and my hands will shake until Tarsday, probably. After that everything ought to be all right."

For Auk's sake as well as his own, Silk asked, "You're not going to use rust anymore? No matter how severe your symptoms become?"

"Not if we're going to do this. It makes you too brave. I guess I said that. Didn't I? It's great to have a sniff or a lipful. . . . Some people do that too, but it takes more when you're scared practically to death. But after a while you find out that it was what you ought to have been scared of. It's worse than Bass or even Musk, and a lot worse than the cull that looked so bad out in the big room. Only by that time it's got you. It has me, and it has Hy, too, I think. Silk?"

He nodded, and Auk patted Chenille's arm.

"I know her, but now that I think about her, there's not a whole lot I know, and I've already told you most of it. Have you seen her?"

"Yes," Silk said. "Phaesday night."

"Then you know how good-looking she is. I'm too tall for most bucks. They like dells tall, but not taller than they are, or even the same. Hy's just right. But even if I was this much shorter, they'd still run after her instead of me. She's getting really famous, and that's why she works for Blood direct. He won't split with Orchid or any of the others on somebody that brings in as much as she does."

Silk nodded to himself. "He has other places, besides the yellow house on Lamp Street?"

"Oh, sure. Half a dozen, most likely. But Orchid's is one of the best." Chenille paused, her face pensive. "Hy was kind of flat-chested when I met her at Orchid's. . . . I guess that's something else Crane's given her, huh? Two big things."

Auk chuckled.

"From what you've said, she was born here in Viron."

"Sure, Patera. Over on the east side someplace? Or at least that's what I heard. There's another girl at Orchid's from the same quarter."

Auk said, "Patera thinks she might be an informant. For you and him, now, I guess."

"And he'll want to pay her from my share," Chenille said bitterly. "Nothing doing unless I give the nod."

"That isn't what I meant at all. As Auk just told you, I believe that Hyacinth might help me against Blood; but I have no reason to believe that she would willingly help us against Crane, which is what we need at present. I ought to explain, Auk, that Chenille feels quite sure that Crane is spying on Viron, although we don't know for what city. Do we, Chenille?"

"No. He never said he was a spy at all, and I hope that I never said he did. But he is . . . he was hot to find out about all sorts of gammon, Auk. Especially about the Guard. He just about always wanted to know if any of the colonels had been in, and what did they say? And I still think the little statues are messages, Patera, or they've got messages inside them."

Sensing Auk's disapproval, she added, "I didn't know, Hackum. He was nice to me, so I helped him now and then. I didn't get flash till yesterday."

Auk said, "I wish I'd met this Crane. He must be quite a buck. You're going to wash him down, or try to, Patera? You and Jugs?"

"Yes, if washing someone down means what I suppose it does."

"It means you deal him out and keep the cards. You're going to try to bleed your twenty-six out of him?"

Chenille nodded, and Silk said, "Much more, if we can, Auk. Chenille would like to buy a shop."

"The easy out for him would be to lay you both on ice. You scavy that?"

"To murder us, you mean, or to have someone else do it. Yes, of course. If Crane is a spy, he won't hesitate to do that; and if he controls money enough to present Hyacinth with an azoth, he could readily employ someone else to do it, I imagine. We will have to be circumspect."

"I'll say. I could name you twenty bucks who'd do it for a hundred, and some of 'em good. If this cull Crane's been working for Blood long—"

"For the past four years," Silk put in, "or so he told me that night."

"Then he'll know who to get about as good as I do. This Hy—" Auk scratched his head. "You remember when we had dinner? You told me about the azoth, and I told you I bet Crane's got a lock. Well, if he was after Jugs to tell him about colonels, this Hy would be a lot better from what you said about her. So that's the lock. She was staying out at Blood's place in the country, right? Does she ever come into town?"

"She seemed to be. She had a suite of rooms there, and the monitor in her glass referred to her as its mistress." Silk recalled Hyacinth's wardrobes, in which the monitor had suggested he hide. "She had a great deal of clothing there, too."

Chenille said, "She gets to the city pretty often, but I'm not sure where she goes . . . or when. When she does, there'll be somebody with her to watch her, unless Blood's gone abram."

Auk straightened up, his left hand on the hilt of the big, brass-

mounted hanger he wore. "All right. You wanted my advice, Patera. I'll
give it to you, but I don't think you're going to get it down easy."

"I'd like to have it, nevertheless."

"I thought you would. You run wide of this Hy, for now anyhow. Just
finding her's liable to be dicey, and more than likely she'll squeak to this
Crane buck straight off. Jugs says she didn't know she was spying. Maybe
so. But if this Crane stood this Hy an azoth, you can bet the basket this
Hy knows, and is trotting behind. If she was the only handle you had, I'd
say go to it. But that's not the lay. If this Crane had Jugs telling him all
about colonels and what they said, and this Hy doing the same, and that's
what it sounds like, wouldn't he have maybe four or five others, too?
Most likely at some of Blood's other kens. And when Jugs is gone—
'cause she says she's going—won't he line up somebody else at
Orchid's?"

Chenille suggested, "The best thing might be for me to go back to
Orchid's after all. If I'd talk against Viron a little, he might let me help
more. Maybe I could find out who the woman in the market is."

Silk explained, "There's a stallkeeper there who seems to be a contact
of Crane's, Auk. Crane had Chenille carry images of Sphigx to her. Was
it always Sphigx, Chenille?"

She nodded, her fiery curls trembling. "They always looked just like
that one I showed you, as near as I can remember."

"Then see what happens to them," Auk suggested. "When the market
closes, where does this mort go?"

"Good Silk!" Oreb dropped from the vines to light in his lap. "Fish
heads?"

"Possibly," Silk told the bird, as it hopped onto his shoulder. "In fact, I
think it likely."

He returned his attention to Auk. "You're quite right, of course. I've
been thinking too much about Hyacinth. I'd hate to see Chenille return
to Orchid's, but either of the courses that you suggest—and they're by no
means mutually exclusive—would be preferable to approaching Hyacinth, I'm afraid, without some hold on her. When we learn a bit more,
however, we should have such a hold. We'll be able to warn her that we
know Crane's an agent of another city, that we have evidence that's at
least highly suggestive, and that we're aware that she's been assisting
him. We'll offer to protect her, provided that she'll assist us."

Chenille asked, "You don't think Crane's Vironese? He talks like one
of us."

"No. Mostly because he seems to control so much money, but also because of something he once said to me. I know nothing of spies or spying, however. Nor do you, I think. What about you, Auk?"

The big man shrugged. "You hear this and that. Mostly it's traders, from what they say."

"I suppose that practically every city must question its traders when they return home, and no doubt some traders are actually trained agents. I would imagine that an agent well supplied with money would be like them—that is to say, a citizen in the service of his native city—and probably thoroughly schooled in the ways of the place to which he was to be sent. An agent willing to betray his own city might betray yours as well, surely; particularly if he were given a chance to make off with a fortune."

Chenille asked, "What was it Crane said to you, Patera?"

Silk leaned toward her. "What color are my eyes?"

"Blue. I wish mine were."

"Suppose that a patron at Orchid's requested a companion with blue eyes. Would Orchid be able to oblige him?"

"Arolla. No, she's gone now. But Bellflower's still there. She has blue eyes, too."

Silk leaned back. "You see, blue eyes are unusual—here in Viron, at any rate; but they're by no means really rare. Collect a hundred people, and it's quite likely that at least one will have blue eyes. I notice them because I used to be teased about mine. Crane noticed them, too; but he, a much older man than I, said that mine were only the third he'd seen. That suggests that he has spent most of his life in another city, where people are somewhat darker and blue eyes rarer than they are here."

Auk grinned. "They got tails in Gens. That's what they say."

Silk nodded. "Yes, one hears all sorts of stories, most quite false, I'm sure. Nevertheless, you have only to look at the traders in the market to see that there are contrasts as well as similarities."

He paused to collect his thoughts. "I've let myself be drawn off the subject, however. I was going to say, Auk, that although both the courses you suggested are promising, there is a third that seems more promising still to me. You're not at fault for failing to point it out, since you weren't here when Chenille provided the intimation.

"Chenille, you told me that a commissioner had been to Orchid's, remember? And that Crane was intensely interested when you told him that this commissioner had told you he had gone to Limna—you said to the lake, but I assume that's what was intended—to confer with two councillors."

Chenille nodded.

"That started me thinking. There are five councillors in the Ayuntamiento. Where do they live?"

She shrugged. "On the hill, I guess."

"That's what I'd always supposed myself. Auk, you must be far more familiar with the residents of the Palatine than either Chenille or I am. Where does, say, Councillor Galago make his home?"

"I always figured in the Juzgado. I hear there's flats in there, besides some cells."

"The councillors have offices in the Juzgado, I'm sure. But don't they have mansions on the Palatine as well? Or their own country villas like Blood's?"

"What they say is nobody's supposed to know, Patera. If they did, people would always be wanting to talk to them or throw rocks. But I know who's in every one of those houses on the hill, and it isn't them. All the commissioners have big places up there, though."

Silk's voice sank to a murmur. "But when a commissioner was to speak with several councillors, he did not go home to the Palatine. Nor did he merely ascend a floor or two in the Juzgado. From what Chenille says, he went to Limna—to the lake, as he told her. When one man is to speak with several, he normally goes to them rather than having them come to him, and that is particularly so when they're his superiors. Now if Crane is in fact a spy, he must surely be concerned to discover where every member of the Ayuntamiento lives, I'd think. All sorts of things might be learned from their servants, for example." He fell silent.

"Go on, Patera," Chenille urged.

He smiled at her. "I was merely thinking that since you told Crane about the commissioner's boast some months ago, he's apt to have been there several times by now. I want to go there myself today and try to find out who he's talked to and what he's said to them. If the gods are with me—as I've reason to believe—that alone may provide all the evidence we require."

She said, "I'm coming with you. How about you, Auk?"

The big man shook his head. "I've been up all night, like I told you. But I'll tell you what. Let me get a little sleep, and I'll meet you in Limna where the wagons stop. Say about four o'clock."

"You needn't put yourself out like that, Auk."

"I want to. If you've got something by then, I might be able to help you get more. Or maybe I can turn up something myself. There's good fish places there, and I'll spring for dinner and ride back to the city with you."

Chenille hugged him. "I always knew how handsome you were,

Hackum, but I never knew how sweet you are. You're a real dimberdamber!"

Auk grinned. "To make a start, this's my city, Jugs. It's not all gilt, but it's all I got. And there's a few friends in the Guard. When you two have washed down this buck Crane, what do you plan to do with him?"

Silk said, "Report him, I'd think."

Chenille shook her head. "He'd tell about the money, and they'd want it. We might have to kill him ourselves. Didn't you augurs send sprats to Scylla in the old days?"

"That could get him tried for murder, Jugs," Auk told her. "No, what you want to do is roll this Crane over to Hoppy. Only if you're going to queer it, you'd be better off doing him, They'll beat it out of you, grab the deck and send you with him. It'd be a lily grab on you, Jugs, 'cause you helped him. As for the Patera here, Crane saw to his hoof and rode him to Orchid's in his own dilly, so it'd be candy to smoke up something."

He waited for them to contradict him, but neither did.

"Only if you go flash, if you roll him over to some bob culls with somebody like me to say Pas for you, we'll all be stanch cits and heroes too. Hoppy'll grab the glory while we buy him rope. That way he'll hand us a smoke smile and a warm and friendly shake, hoping we'll have something else to roll another time. I've got to have pals like that to lodge and dodge. So do you two, you just don't know it. You scavy I never turned up the bloody rags, riffling some cardcase's ken? You scavy I covered 'em up and left him be? Buy it, I washed him if he'd stand still. And if he wouldn't, why, I rolled him over."

Silk nodded. "I see. I felt that your guidance would be of value, and I don't believe that Chenille could call me wrong. Could you, Chenille?"

She shook her head, her eyes sparkling.

"That's rum, 'cause I'm not finished yet. What's this hotpot's name, Jugs?"

"Simuliid."

"I'm flash. Big cully, ox weight, with a mustache?"

She nodded.

"Patera and me ought to pay a call, maybe, when we get back from the lake. How's your hoof, Patera?"

"Much better today," Silk said, "but what have we to gain from seeing the commissioner?"

Oreb cocked his head attentively and hopped up into the grapevines again.

"I hope we won't. I want a look around, 'specially if you and Jugs go empty at the lake. Maybe those councillors live way out there like you say, Patera. But maybe, too, there's something out there that they wanted to show off to him, or that he had to show off to them. You hear kink talk about the lake, and if you and Jugs plan to fish for this Crane cull, you might want bait. So we'll pay this Simuliid a call, up on the hill tonight. Plate to me, bait to you, and split the overs."

Oreb hopped onto the back of the old wooden seat. "Man come!"

Nodding, Silk rose and parted the vines. A thick-bodied young man in an augur's black robe was nudging shut the side door of the manteion; he appeared to be staring at something in his hands.

"Over here," Silk called. "Patera Gulo?" He stepped out of the arbor and limped across the dry, brown grass to the newcomer. "May every god favor you this day. I'm very pleased to see you, Patera."

"A man in the street, Patera"—Gulo held up a dangling, narrow object sparkling with yellow and green—"he simply—we—he wouldn't—"

Auk had followed Silk. "Mostly topaz, but that looks like a pretty fair emerald." Reaching past him, he relieved Gulo of the bracelet and held it up to admire.

"This lady's Chenille, Patera Gulo." By a gesture, Silk indicated the arbor, "and this gentleman is Auk. Both are prominent laypersons of our quarter, exceedingly devout and cherished by all of the gods, I feel sure. I'll be leaving with them in a few minutes, and I rely on you to deal with the affairs of our manteion during my absence. You'll find Maytera Marble—in the cenoby there—a perfect fisc of valuable information and sound advice."

"A man gave it to me!" Gulo blurted. "Just a minute ago, Patera. He simply pressed it into my hand!"

"I see." Silk nodded matter-of-factly as he reassured himself that the azoth beneath his tunic was indeed there. "Return that to Patera Gulo, please, Auk.

"You'll find our cashbox under my bed, Patera. The key is underneath the carafe on the nightstand. Wait a moment." He took the diamond anklet from his pocket and handed it to Gulo. "Put them in there and lock them up safely, if you will, Patera. It might be best for you to keep the key in your pocket. I should return about the time that the market closes, or a little after."

"Bad man!" Oreb proclaimed from the top of the arbor. "Bad man!"

"It's your black robe, Patera," Silk explained. "He's afraid he may be sacrificed. Come here, Oreb! We're off to the lake. Fish heads, you silly bird."

In a frantic flurry of wings, the injured night chough landed heavily on Silk's own black-robed shoulder.

CHAPTER 6   LAKE LIMNA

"What was it you said, my son?" Silk dropped to one knee to bring his face to the height of the small boy's own.

"Ma says ask a blessing." His attention seemed equally divided between Silk and Oreb.

"And why do you wish it?"

The small boy did not reply.

"Isn't it because you want the immortal gods to view you with favor, my son? Didn't they teach you something about that at the palaestra? I'm sure they must have."

Reluctantly, the small boy nodded.

Silk traced the sign of addition over the boy's head and recited the shortest blessing in common use, ending it with, "In the name of their eldest child, Scylla, Patroness of this, Our Holy City of Viron, and in that of the Outsider, of all gods the eldest."

"Are you really Patera Silk?"

None of the half dozen persons waiting for the holobit wagon to Limna turned to look, yet Silk was painfully aware of a sudden stiffening of postures; Lake Street, although it was far from quiet, seemed somehow quieter.

"Yes, he is," Chenille announced proudly.

One of the waiting men stepped toward Silk and knelt, his head bowed. Before Silk could trace the sign of addition, two more had knelt beside the first.

He was saved by the arrival of the wagon—long-bodied, gaily painted, surmounted by a jiggling old patterned canvas canopy, and drawn by two weary horses. "One bit," boomed the driver, vaulting from his post. "A bit to Limna. No credit no trade, everybody sits in the shade."

"I've got it," Chenille said.

"So do I," Silk told her in his most inflexible tone, and hushed several passengers who tried say that Patera Silk ought to ride free. When he pocketed Silk's bits, the driver said, "You'll have to get off if anybody complains about the bird," and was startled by a chorus of protests.

"I don't like this," Silk told Chenille as they found places on one of the long, outward-facing benches. "People have been writing things on walls, and I don't like that, either."

The driver cracked his whip, and the wagon lurched ahead.

" 'Silk for Caldé . . . ?' Is that what you mean, Silk? A good idea."

"That's right." He extracted his beads from his pocket. "Or rather, it's wrong. Wrong as concerns me, and wrong as it concerns the office of caldé. I'm not a politician, and no inducement that you could name would ever persuade me to become one. As for the caldéship, it's become nothing more than a popular superstition, a purely historical curiosity. My mother knew the last caldé, but he died shortly after I was born."

"I remember him. I think?"

Without looking at her, Silk told her miserably, "If you meant half what you've said, you can't possibly recall him, Comely Kypris. Chenille's four years younger than I am."

"Then I'm thinking about . . . someone else. Aren't you worried? Silk? Traveling with somebody like me? All of these people know who you are."

"I hope that they do, Great Goddess, and that they're thoroughly disillusioned now—that without dishonoring my sacred calling I save my life."

A particularly vicious jolt threw Silk against the woman on his right, who apologized profusely. When he had begged her pardon instead, he began the prayer of the voided cross. "Great Pas, designer and creator of the whorl, lord guardian and keeper of the Aureate Path—" The path across the sky that was the spiritual equivalent of the sun, he reminded himself. Sacrifices rose to it, and so were brought in the end to Mainframe, where both the sun and the Path began, at the east pole. The spirits of the dead walked that glorious road, too, if not weighted with evil, and it was asserted in the Chrasmologic Writings that the spirits of certain holy theodidacts had at times abandoned the shapen mud of their corporeal bodies and—joining the crowding, lowing beasts and the penitent dead—journeyed to Mainframe to confer for a time with the god who had enlightened them. He himself was a theodidact, Silk reminded himself, having been enlightened by the Outsider.

He had finished the voided cross and (he counted them by touch) four beads already. Murmuring the prescribed prayers and adding the name of the Outsider to them all, he willed himself to leave his body and this crowded street and unite with the hastening traffic of the Aureate Path.

For an instant it seemed that he had succeeded, though it was not the sun's golden road that he saw, but the frigid black emptiness beyond the whorl, dotted here and there with gleaming sparks.

"Talking of writing on walls, Silk. Silk? Look there. Open your eyes."

He did. It was a poster, badly but boldly printed in red and black, so new that no one had yet torn it or scrawled an obscene drawing over it, which in this quarter probably meant that it had been up less than an hour.

STRONG YOUNG MEN
WILL BE WELCOMED IN
THE NEW PROVISIONAL RESERVE BRIGADE
Have YOU Wished to Become a GUARDSMAN?
The Reserve Brigade Will Drill Twice Weekly
Will Receive PAY and UNIFORMS
Will Receive FIRST CONSIDERATION
for
TRANSFER TO THE REGULAR FORMATIONS
Apply
THIRD BRIGADE HEADQUARTERS
Colonel Oosik, Commanding

"You don't think the kite tired him too much?"

It was not the first time Blood had asked the question, and Musk had tired of saying no. This time he said, "I told you. Aquila's a female." The huge hooded bird on his wrist baited as he spoke, whether at the sound of her name, or at that of his voice, or by mere coincidence. Musk waited for her to slake before he finished the thought. "Males don't get this big. For Molpe's sake listen sometime."

"All right—all right. Maybe a smaller one could fly higher."

"She can do it. The bigger they are, the higher they fly. You ever see a sparrow fly any higher than that bald head of yours?" Musk spoke without looking at the fleshy, red-faced man to whom he spoke, his eyes upon his eagle or on the sky. "I still think we should've let Hoppy in."

"If they bring it back, in a week they'll have done it themselves."

"They fly high, way up close to the sun. If we get one, he could come down anywhere."

"We've got three floaters with three men in each floater. We've got five on highriders."

With his free hand, Musk lifted his binoculars. Though he knew there was nothing there, he scanned the clear vacancy overhead.

"Don't point those things at the sun. You could blind yourself." It was not the first time Blood had said that, either.

"He could come down anywhere in the whorl. You heard where the kite came down, and it was on a shaggy string, for Molpe's sake. You think that it's got to be close to a road because you travel on them." It was a long speech for Musk. "If you'd hunted with my hawks a couple of times, you'd know different. Most of the whorl's not anywhere near any shaggy road. Most of the whorl's twenty, thirty, fifty stades from a shaggy road."

"That's good," Blood said. "What I'm afraid of is some farmer peeping to Hoppy." He waited for Musk to speak again; when Musk did not, he added, "They can't really get up near the sun. The sun's a lot hotter than any fire. They'd be burned to death."

"Maybe they don't burn." Musk lowered his binoculars. "Maybe they're not even people."

"They're people. Just like us."

"Then maybe they got needlers."

Blood said, "They won't carry anything they don't have to carry."

"I'm shaggy glad you know. I'm shaggy glad you asked them."

Aquila adjusted the position of one huge talon with a minute jingle of hawk bells as Musk lifted his binoculars again.

"There's one!" Blood said unnecessarily. "Are you going to fly her?"

"I don't know," Musk admitted. "He's a long ways off, the yard."

Blood trained his own binoculars on the flier. "He's coming closer. He's headed this way!"

"I know. That's why I'm watching him."

"He's high."

Musk struggled to speak in the bored and bitter tones he had affected since childhood. "I've seen them higher." The thrill of the hunt was upon him, as sudden as a fever and as welcome as spring.

"I told you about that big gun they built. They shot at them for a month, but shells don't go straight up there, and they couldn't get them high enough anyway."

Musk let his binoculars drop to his chest. He could see the flier clearly now, silhouetted against the silver mirror that was Lake Limna, mounting into the sky on the other side of the city.

"Wait for him to get closer," Blood said urgently.

"If we wait much longer, he'll be farther by the time she gets up there."

"What if—"

"Stand back. If she goes for you, you're dead." With his free hand Musk grasped the crown of scarlet plumes and snatched the hood. *"Away, hawk!"*

This time there was no hesitation. The eagle's immense wings spread, and she sprang into the air with a whirlwind roar that for a moment frightened even Musk, flying hard at first, laboring to gain the thermal from the roof, then lifting, rising, and soaring, a jet black, heraldic bird against the sun-blind blue of the open sky.

"Maybe the rabbit filled her up."

Musk laughed. "That baby bunny? It was the littlest we had. That only made her strong." For the second time since they had met, he took Blood's hand.

And Blood, desperately happy but pretending that nothing had occurred, inquired as calmly as he could, "You think she sees him?"

"Shag yes, she sees him. She sees everything. If she went straight for him she'd spook him. She'll get above him and come down at him out of the sun." Unconsciously Musk rose upon his toes, so as to be, by the thickness of three fingers, nearer his bird. "Just like a goose. Just like he was a big goose. They're born knowing it. You watch." His pale, handsome face was wreathed in smiles; his devil's eyes glittered like black ice. "You just watch her, old cully shagger."

Iolar saw the eagle far below him to the north, and put on speed. The front, marked by a line of towering clouds, was interesting and might even be important; but the front was two hundred leagues off, if not more, and might never reach this parched and overheated region. The index was a hundred fifteen here, a hundred nine over much of the sun's length; with the seasonal adjustment—he checked the date mentally—a hundred and eighteen here.

He had forgotten the eagle already.

He was a small man by any standard, and as thin as his own main struts; his eyes were better than average, and most of those who knew him thought him introverted and perhaps a trifle cold-blooded. He seldom spoke; when he did, his talk was of air masses and prevailing winds, of landmarks by day and landmarks by night, of named solar reaches unrecognized (or only grudgingly recognized) by science, and of course of wings and flightsuits and instruments and propulsion modules. But then the talk of all fliers was like that. Because he was so near the ideal, both physically and mentally, he had been permitted three wives, but the second had left him after something less than a year. The first had borne him three nimble, light-boned children, however, and the third, five as cheerful and active as crickets, of whom the younger girl was his favorite, tiny, laughing-eyed Dreoilin. "I can see the wings of her," he sometimes told her mother; and her mother, who could not, always happily agreed. He had been flying for eighteen years.

His increased speed had cost him altitude. He upped the thrust again and tried to climb, but the temperature of the air was falling a bit, and the air with it in the daylight downdraft of the big lake. There would be a corresponding updraft once he got over land again, and he resolved to take it as high as it would take him. He would need every cubit of altitude he could scrape up when he reached those distant thunderheads.

He did not see the eagle again until it was almost upon him, flying straight down, the enormous thrust of its wings driving it toward the land below far faster than any falling stone until, at the last possible split second, it folded its wings, spun in the air, and struck him with its talons, double blows like those of a giant's mailed fists.

Perhaps it stunned him for a moment. Certainly the wild whirl of earth and sky did not disorient him; he knew that his left wing was whole and sound, that the other was not, and that his PM did not respond. He suspected that he had half a dozen broken ribs and perhaps a broken spine as well, but he gave little attention to those. With a superb skill that would have left his peers openmouthed, could they have witnessed it, he turned his furious tumble into a controlled dive, jettisoned the PM and his instruments, and had halved his rate of descent before he hit the water.

"Did you see that splash!" Chenille rose from her seat in the holobit wagon as she spoke, shading her eyes against the sunglare from the water. "There are some monster fish in the lake. Really huge. I remember—I haven't been out here since I was a little girl. . . . Or anyhow, I don't think I have."

Nodding, Silk ducked from under the canopy to glance at the sun. Unveiled by clouds moving from east to west, that golden blaze streaking the sky was—he reminded himself again—the visible symbol of the Aureate Path, the course of moral probity and fitting worship that led Man to the gods. Had he strayed? He had felt no willingness in himself to offer Crane in sacrifice, though a goddess had suggested it.

And that, surely, was not what the gods expected from an anointed augur.

"Fish heads?" Oreb tugged at Silk's hair.

"Fish heads indeed," he told the bird, "and that is a solemn promise."

Tonight he would help Auk rob Chenille's commissioner. Commissioners were rich and oppressive, battening upon the blood and sweat of the poor; no doubt this one could spare a few jewels and his silver service. Yet robbery was wrong at base, even when it served a greater good.

Though this was Molpsday, he murmured a final prayer to Sphigx as he returned his beads to his pocket. Sphigx above all would understand; Sphigx was half lioness, and lions had to kill innocent creatures in order to eat—such was the inflexible decree of Pas, who had given to every creature save Man its proper food. As he completed the prayer, Silk bowed very slightly to the ferocious, benevolent face on the handle of Blood's walking stick.

"We used to come here to pick watercress," Chenille said. "Way over on that side of the lake. We'd start out before shadeup and walk here, Patera. I don't know how many times I've watched for the water at the first lifting. If I couldn't see it, I'd know we had a long way to go yet. We'd have paper, any kind of paper we could find, and we'd wet it good and wrap our watercress in it, then hurry back to the city to sell it before it wilted. Sometimes it did, and that was all we had to eat. I still won't eat it. I buy it, though, pretty often, from little girls in the market. Little girls like I was."

"That's very good of you," Silk told her, though he was already planning.

"Only there isn't much these days, because so many of the best cress creeks have gone dry. I never eat it anyway. Sometimes I feed it to the goats, you know? And sometimes I just throw it away. I wonder how many of the ladies that used to buy it from me did the same thing."

The woman next to Silk said, "I make sandwiches. Watercress and white cheese on rye bread. I wash it thoroughly first, though."

Silk nodded and smiled.

"It makes a fine hot weather lunch."

Speaking across Silk, Chenille asked her, "Do you have friends here in Limna?"

"Relations," the woman said. "My husband's mother lives out here. She thinks the pure air off the lake is good for her. Wouldn't it be wonderful if our relations could be our friends, too?"

"Oh, wouldn't it, though! We're looking for a friend. Doctor Crane? A small man, around fifty, rather dark? He has a little gray beard . . . ?"

"I don't know him," the woman said grimly, "but if he's a doctor and he lives in Limna, my mother-in-law does. I'll ask her."

"He just bought a cottage here. So that he can get away from his practice, you know? My husband's helping him move in, and Patera's promised to bless it for him. Only I can't remember where it is."

The man on her left said, "You can ask at the Juzgado, on Shore Street. He'll have had to register the transfer of deed."

"Is there a Juzgado here, too?" Chenille asked him. "I thought that was just in the city."

"Just a small one," the man told her. "Some local cases are tried there, and they hold a handful of petty prisoners. There's no Alambrera here—those with long sentences are sent back to Viron. And they take care of the tax rolls and property records."

By this time the holobit wagon they rode was trundling along a narrow, crooked, cobbled street lined with tottering two- and three-storied wooden houses, all with high, peaked roofs and many a weathered silver-gray from lack of paint. Silk and Chenille, with the man who knew about the Juzgado and the woman who made watercress sandwiches, were on the landward side of the long wagon; but Silk, looking over his shoulder, could catch occasional glimpses of dirty water and high-pooped, single-masted fishing boats between the houses.

"I haven't been here since I was just a sprat myself," he told Chenille. "It's odd to think now that I fished here fifteen years ago. They don't use shiprock like we do, do they? Or mud brick, either."

The man on Chenille's left said, "It's too easy to cut trees on the banks and float the logs to Limna."

"I see. I hadn't considered that—although I should have, of course."

"Not many people would," the man said; he had opened his card case, and he extracted a pasteboard visiting card as he talked. "May I give you this, Patera? Vulpes is my name. I'm an advocate, and I've got chambers here on Shore Street. Do you understand the procedure if you're arrested?"

Silk's eyebrows shot up. "Arrested? Molpe defend us! I hope not."

"So do I." Vulpes lowered his voice until Silk could barely hear him above the street noises and the squeaking of the wagon's axels. "So do we all, I think. But do you understand the procedure?"

Silk shook his head.

"If you give them the name and location of an advocate, they have to send for him—that's the law. If you can't give them a name and the location, however, you don't get one until your family finds out what's happened and engages somebody."

"I see."

"And," Vulpes leaned in front of Chenille and tapped Silk's knee to emphasize his point, "if you're here in Limna, somebody with chambers in Viron won't do. It has to be somebody local. I've known them to wait, when they knew someone might be coming here soon, so as to make the arrest here for exactly that reason. I want you to put that in your pocket, Patera, so that you can show it to them if you have to. Vulpes, on Shore Street, right here in Limna, at the sign of the red fox."

At the word *fox,* the wagon creaked to a stop, and the driver bawled, "Everybody off! Rides back to Viron at four, six, and eight. You get 'em right here, but don't dare be late."

Silk caught him by the sleeve as he was about to enter the barn. "Will you tell me something about Limna, Driver? I'm not at all familiar with it."

"The layout, you mean?" The driver pinched his nostrils thoughtfully. "That's simple enough, Patera. It's not no great big place like Viron. The main thing you got to hang on to is where we are now, so you'll know where to go to catch your ride back. This here's Water Street, see? And right here's pretty close to the middle o' town. There's only three streets that amount to much—Dock, Water, and Shore. The whole town curls around the bay. It's shaped kind o' like a horseshoe, only not bent so much. You know what I'm tellin' you? The inside's Dock Street—that's where the market is. The outside's Shore Street. If you want to go out on a boat, Dock Street's the place, and I can give you a couple good names. If you want to eat, try the Catfish or the Full Sail. The Rusty Lantern's pretty good, too, if you got deep pockets. Stayin' overnight?"

Silk shook his head. "We'd like to get back to the city before dark, if we can."

"You'll want the six o'clock wagon, then," the driver said as he turned away.

When he had gone, Chenille said, "You didn't ask him where the councillors live."

"If neither you nor I nor Auk knew, it can't be common knowledge," Silk told her. "Crane will have had to discover that for himself, and the best thing for us to learn today may well be whom he asked. I doubt that he'll have ridden down on one of the wagons as we did. On Scylsday he had a hired litter."

She nodded. "It might be better if we split up, Patera. You high, and me low."

"I'm not sure what you mean by that."

"You talk to the respectable people in the respectable places. I'll ask around in the drinking kens. When did . . . Auk? Say he'd meet us here?"

"Four o'clock," Silk told her.

"Then I'll meet you right here at four. We can have a bite to eat. With Auk? And tell each other whatever we've learned."

"You were very skillful with that woman on the wagon," Silk said. "I hope that I can do half as well."

"But it didn't get us anything? Stick with the truth, Patera. Silk? Or close to it. . . . I don't think you'll be terribly good with the . . . other thing? What're you going to say?"

Silk stroked his cheek. "I was thinking about that on the wagon, and it seemed to me that it will have to depend upon the circumstances. I might say, for example, that such a man witnessed an exorcism I performed, and since I haven't returned to the house that had been afflicted, I was hoping he could tell me whether it had been effective."

Chenille nodded. "Perfectly true. . . . Every bit of it. You're going to be all right. I can see that. Silk?" She had been standing close to him already, forced there by the press of traffic in the street; she stepped closer still, so that the nipples of her jutting breasts pressed the front of his tunic. "You don't love me, Patera. You wouldn't, even if you didn't think I belonged to . . . Auk? But you love Hy? Don't you? Tell me. . . ."

He said miserably, "I shouldn't. It isn't right, and a man in my position —an augur—has so little to offer any woman. No money. No real home. It's just that she's like the— There are things I can't seem to stop thinking about, no matter how hard I try. Hyacinth is one of them."

"Well, I'm her, too." Swift and burning, Chenille's lips touched his. By the time he had recovered, she was lost among porters and vendors, hurrying visitors and strolling, rolling fishermen.

"Bye, girl!" With his uninjured wing, Oreb was waving farewell. "Watch out! Good luck!"

Silk took a deep breath and looked around. Here at the end nearest Viron, Lake Limna had nurtured a town of its own, subject to the city while curiously detached from it.

Or rather (his first two fingers inscribed slow circles on his cheek), Lake Limna, in its retreat, had drawn a fleck of Viron with it. Once the

Orilla had been the lakeshore—or Dock Street, as it was called here. To judge from its name, Shore Street had been the same in its day, a paved prelude to wharves, with buildings on its landward side that overlooked the water. As the lake had continued to shrink, Water Street, on which he stood, had come into being. Still later, twenty or thirty years ago, possibly, Water Street had been left behind like the rest.

And yet the lake was still immense. He tried to imagine it as it must have been when the first settlers occupied the empty city built for them at what was then its northern end, and concluded that the lake must have been twice its present size. Would there come a time, in another three centuries or so, when there was no lake at all? It seemed more likely that the lake would then be half its present size—and yet the time must surely come, whether in six hundred years or a thousand, when it would vanish altogether.

He began to walk, wondering vaguely what the respectable places the goddess wished him to visit were. Or at least which such places would be most apt to yield information of value.

Drawn by boyhood recollections of cool water and endless vistas, he followed a block-long alley to Dock Street. Here half a dozen fishing boats landed silver floods of trout, shad, pike, and bass; here cookshops supplied fish as fresh as the finest eating houses in the city at a tenth the price; and top-lofty inns with gaily painted shutters displayed signboards for those anxious to exchange the conveniences of Viron for zephyrs at the height of summer, and those who, in whatever season, delighted in swimming, fishing, or sailing.

Here, too, as Silk soon discovered, was the fresh poster that he and Chenille had seen before their holobit wagon had left the city, offering "strong young men" an opportunity to become part-time Guardsmen and holding out the promise of eventual full-time employment. As he read it through again, Silk recalled the darkly threatening entrails of the ewe. No one spoke as yet of war—except the gods. Or rather, he reflected, only the gods and this poster spoke of war to those who would listen.

The next-to-final line of the poster had been crossed out with black ink, and the phrase *at the Juzgado in Limna* had been substituted; the new reserve brigade would station a company or two here at the lake, presumably—perhaps an entire battalion, if enough fishermen could be persuaded to enlist.

For the first time it struck him that Limna would make an excellent base or staging area for an army moving against the city, offering shelter for many if not all of the enemy troops, assurance against surprise from the south, a ready source of food, and unlimited water for men and animals. No wonder, then, that Crane had been interested to learn that the councillors were here, and that a commissioner had come to confer with them.

"Fish heads!" Oreb fluttered from Silk's shoulder to the ground, then ran with unexpected speed three-quarters the length of a nearby jetty to peck at them.

"Yes," Silk murmured to himself, "fish heads at last, and fish guts, too."

As he strolled down the jetty, admiring the broad blue purity of the lake and the scores of bobbing, heeling craft whose snowy sails dotted it, he meditated upon Oreb's meal.

Those fish belonged to Scylla, just as serpents belonged to her mother, Echidna, and cats of all kinds to her younger sister, Sphigx. Surging Scylla, the patroness of the city, graciously permitted her worshipers to catch such fish as they required, subject to certain age-old restrictions and prohibitions. Yet the fish—even those scraps that Oreb ate—were hers, and the lake her palace. If devotion to Scylla was still strong in the Viron, as it was though two generations had passed since she had manifested her divinity in a Sacred Window, what must it be here?

Joining Oreb, he sat down upon the head of a convenient piling, removed Crane's almost miraculous wrapping from his fractured ankle, and whipped the warped planks of the jetty with it.

What if Crane wished to erect a shrine to Scylla on the lakeshore in fulfillment of some vow? If Crane could hand out azoths as gifts to favored informers, he could certainly afford a shrine. Silk knew little of building, but he felt certain that a modest yet appropriate and wholly acceptable shrine could be built at the edge of the lake for a thousand cards or less. Crane might well have asked his spiritual advisor—himself —to select a suitable site.

Better still, suppose that Chenille's commissioner were the grateful builder—no one would question the ability of a commissioner to underwrite the entire cost of even a very elaborate structure. It would not be a manteion, since it could have no Sacred Window, but sacrifice might take place there. Fostered by a commissioner, it might well support a resident augur—someone like himself.

And Crane would have gone where Chenille's commissioner had gone, assuming that he had learned where that was.

"Good! Good!" Oreb had completed his repast; balanced upon one splayed crimson foot, he was scraping his bill with the other.

"Don't soil my robe," Silk told him. "I warn you, I'll be angry."

As he replaced Crane's wrapping, Silk tried to imagine himself the commissioner. Two councillors had summoned him to the lake for a conference, presumably a confidential one, possibly concerned with military matters. He would (Silk decided) almost certainly travel to Limna by floater; but he would—again, almost certainly—leave his floater and its driver there in favor of a mode of transportation less likely to attract attention.

To focus his thoughts as he often did in the palaestra, Silk pointed his forefinger at his pet. "He might hire a donkey, for example, like Auk and I did the other night."

A small boat was gliding toward the lakeward end of the jetty, a gray-haired man minding its tiller while a couple of boys hastily furled its single sail.

"That's it!"

The night chough eyed him quizzically.

"He would hire a boat, Oreb. Perhaps with a reliable man or two to do the sailing. A boat would be much faster than a donkey or even a horse. It would carry a secretary or a confidential clerk as well as the commissioner, and he could go straight to whatever point on the lake—"

"Silk good?" Oreb stopped preening the tuft of scarlet feathers on his breast to cock his sleek head at Silk. "All right?"

"No. Slightly wrong. He wouldn't hire a boat. That would cost him money of his own, and he might not feel that he could trust the men who sailed it for him. But the town must have boats—to keep the fishermen from fighting among themselves, for example—and whoever's governing it would fall all over himself hurrying to help a commissioner. So climb aboard, you silly bird. We're going to the Juzgado." After looking in several pockets, Silk found the advocate's visiting card. "On Shore Street. His chambers were on the same street as the Juzgado. Remember, Oreb? No doubt it's convenient when he has to hurry off to court."

As the door of the big shed opened, the old kite builder looked up in some surprise.

The small, gray-bearded man in the doorway said, "Excuse me. I didn't know you were in here."

"Just packing up to leave," the kite builder explained. For an instant he wondered whether Musk had thought that he might steal, and had sent this man to watch him.

"I heard about the kite. You built it? Everyone says it was a beautiful job."

"It certainly wasn't pretty." The kite builder tied a string around a sheaf of slender sticks. "But it was what they wanted, and it was one of the biggest I've ever done. The bigger they are, the higher they fly. To get up high, they have to lift a lot of wire, you know."

"I'm Doctor Crane," the bearded man said. "I should have introduced myself earlier." He picked up one of the fish-oil lamps and shook it gently. "Nearly full. Have you been paid yet?"

"Musk paid me, the full amount." The kite builder patted his pocket. "Not cards, a draft on the fisc. I suppose Blood sent you to see me out."

"That's right, before they left. They're all gone now, I think. Blood and Musk are, at any rate, the guards, and a few of the servants."

The kite builder nodded. "They took all the floaters. There were a couple in here. All the highriders, too. Am I supposed to talk to Blood before I leave? Musk didn't say anything about it."

"Not as far as I know." Crane smiled. "The front gate's open and the talus got fired, so you can go whenever you like. You're welcome to stay, though, if you want to. When they get back from wherever they've gone, Blood might have a driver run you home. Where did they go, anyhow? Nobody told me."

Scrabbling around for his favorite spokeshave, the kite discovered it under a scape of cloth. "To the lake. That's what some of them said."

Crane nodded and smiled again. "Then they'll be gone quite a while, I'm afraid. But you're welcome to wait if you want to." He closed the door behind him and hurried back to the villa. If he did not look now, he asked himself, when would he? He'd never have a better chance. The pantry door stood open, and the door to the cellar stair was unlocked.

The cellar was deep and very dark, and from what he had gathered during friendly chats with the footmen, there should be a wine cellar deeper yet. That might or might not be the same as the subcellar a maid had mentioned. Halfway down the stairs, Crane stopped to raise his lamp.

Emptiness. Rusted, dust-shrouded machinery that could not, almost certainly, ever be set in motion again. And—

He descended the remaining steps and trotted across the dirty, uneven floor to look. Jars of preserves: peaches in brandy, and pickles. No doubt they'd come with the house.

Would they post a sentry at the entrance to the tunnels? He had decided some time ago that they would not. The door (if it was a door) would be locked, however, or barred from below. Possibly hidden as well —located in a secret room or something of that kind. Here, behind the ranks of shelves, was another stair with, yes, footprints leading to it still visible in the dust.

A short flight of steps this time, with a locked door at the bottom. His pick explored the lock for half a minute that seemed like five before the handle would turn to draw back the bolt.

The creak of the hinges activated a light whose perpetual crawl had brought it near the peak of the low vault overhead. By its foggy light, he saw wine racks holding five hundred bottles at least; stacks of cases of brandy, agardente, rum, and cordials; and kegs of what was presumably strong beer. He moved several of the last and studied the floor beneath them, then scanned the floor everywhere, and at last tapped the walls.

Nothing.

"Well, well, well, a well," he murmured, "and a drink for the plowman." Opening a squat, black bottle that had clearly been sampled previously, he took a long swallow of pallid, fiery arrack, recorked the bottle, and made a last inspection.

Nothing.

He closed the wine cellar door silently behind him and twisted its handle clockwise, the muted squeal of the bolt recalling unpleasantly a small dog he had once watched Musk torment.

For a moment he considered leaving the door unlocked; it would save time and almost certainly be blamed—if in fact Blood's sommelier or anyone else ever discovered it—upon a careless servant. Caution, however, as well as extensive training, urged him to leave everything precisely as he had found it.

Sighing, he took out his picks, twisted the one that he had used to enter in the lock, and was rewarded by a faint click.

"You're very good at it, aren't you?"

Crane spun around. Someone—in the thick twilight of the cellar it appeared to be a tall, handsome, white-haired man—stood at the top of the short flight of steps looking down at him.

"You recognize me, I hope?"

Crane dropped his picks, drew, and fired in one single blur of motion, the rapid *crack, crack, crack* of his needler unnaturally loud in the confined space.

"You can't hurt me with that," Councillor Lemur informed him. "Now come up here and give it to me, and I'll take you where you've been trying to go."

"You had a commissioner come in this spring," Silk told the plump, middle-aged woman behind the heaped worktable. "You very kindly provided him with a small sailing vessel of some type." He gave her his most understanding smile. "I'm not about to ask you to provide me with a boat as well. I realize that I'm no commissioner."

"Last spring, Patera? A commissioner from the city?" The woman looked baffled.

At the precise moment that Silk became certain that he had forgotten the commissioner's name, he recalled it; he leaned closer to the woman, wishing he had asked Chenille for a more detailed description. "Commissioner Simuliid. He's an extremely important official. A large and" (Silk struggled to capture the prochein ami's perpetual note of prudence and confidentiality) "—an—um—portly man. He wears a mustache."

When the woman's expression remained blank, he added desperately, "a most becoming mustache, now, I would say, although perhaps—"

"Commissioner Simuliid, Patera?"

Silk nodded eagerly.

"It wasn't that long ago. Not spring. Two months ago, maybe. Not more than three. It was terribly hot already, I remember, and he had on a big straw hat. You know the sort of thing, Patera?"

Silk nodded encouragement. "Perfectly. I used to have one myself."

"And he had a stick, too. Bigger than yours. But he didn't want a boat. We'd have been glad to lend him one, if he had, so it wasn't that." The woman nibbled at her pen. "He asked for something else, and we didn't have it, but I can't remember what it was."

Oreb cocked his head. "Poor girl!"

"Yes, indeed," Silk said, "if she was unable to assist Commissioner Simuliid."

"I did help him," the woman insisted. "I know I did. He was quite satisfied when he left."

Silk strove to appear an augur who moved frequently in the company of commissioners. "Certainly he didn't complain about you to me."

"Don't you know what he wanted, Patera?"

"Not what he wanted from you," he told the plump woman, "because I had been under the impression that he wanted a boat. There are some perfectly marvelous vistas all along the lakeshore, I understand; and I have been thinking that it would be a meritorious act for Commissioner

Simuliid—or anyone—to erect an appropriate shrine to our Patroness on such a spot. Something tasteful, and not too small. The Commissioner may quite possibly have been thinking the same thing, from all that I know of him."

"Are you sure he wasn't offering to repair it, Patera? Or build an addition? Something like that? Scylla's got a beautiful shrine near here already, and some very important people from the city often go out there to, you know, think things over."

Silk snapped his fingers. "An addition! An attached aedicule for the practice of hydromancy. Why, of course! Even I ought to have realized—"

Oreb croaked, "No cut?"

"Not you, in any event," Silk told him. "Where is this shrine, my daughter?"

"Where—?" Suddenly the woman's face was wreathed in smiles. "Why, that's what Commissioner Simuliid wanted, I remember now. A map. How to get there, really. We don't have any maps that show the shrine, there's some sort of a regulation, but you don't need one. All you have to do is follow the Pilgrims' Way, I told him. West around the bay, then south up onto the promontory. It's quite a climb, but if you just go from one white stone to the next, you can't possibly miss it." The woman got out a map. "It's not on here, but I can show you. The blue is the lake, and these black lines are for Limna. Do you see Shore Street? The shrine's right where I'm pointing, see? And this is where the Pilgrims' Way goes up the cliffs. Are you going to go up there yourself, Patera?"

"At the first opportunity," Silk told her. Simuliid had made the pilgrimage; that seemed practically certain. The question was whether Crane had followed him.

"And I thank you very much indeed, my daughter. You've been extremely helpful. Did you say that even councillors go there to meditate sometimes? An acquaintance of mine, Doctor Crane—you may know him; I believe he must spend a good deal of time out here at the lake—"

The woman shook her head. "Oh, no, Patera. They're too old, I think."

"Doctor Crane may have misinformed me, then. I thought he had gotten his information here, most likely from you. A small man with a short gray beard?"

She shook her head. "I don't think he's been in here, Patera. But I don't think the councillors really come. He was probably thinking of commissioners. We've had several of them, and judges and so on, and sometimes they want to go in a boat, only we have to tell them they can't.

It's up on a cliff, and there's no path up from the water. You have to follow the Pilgrims' Way. You can't even ride, because of where there's steps cut into the rock. I suppose that must be why the councillors don't come, too. I've never seen a councillor."

Neither had he, Silk reflected as he left the Juzgado. Had anyone? He had seen their pictures—there had been a group portrait in the Juzgado, in fact—and Silk had seen the pictures so often that until he had actually considered it he had supposed that he had at some time or other seen the councillors themselves. But he had not, and could not recall having met anyone who had.

Simuliid had, however; or at least he had told Chenille he had. Not, presumably, at the shrine of Scylla, since the councillors never went there. In one of the eating places, perhaps, or on a boat.

"No cut?" Oreb wanted more reassurance.

"Absolutely not. A shrine isn't really the best place for sacrifice, anyway, although it's often done. A properly instructed person, such as myself, is more apt to visit a shrine to meditate or do a little religious reading."

Various political figures from the city often went to this lake shrine of Scylla's, according to the woman in the Juzgado. It seemed odd—politicians might make a show of belief, but he had never heard of one who seemed to have any genuine depth of religious feeling. The Prolocutor had little influence in the governance of the city these days, according to everyone except Remora.

Yet either Auk or Chenille—it had been Auk, surely—had called Simuliid, whom he had known by sight, oxweight or something of that sort. Had implied, at any rate, that he was a large and very heavy man. Yet Simuliid had made a pilgrimage to this shrine of Scylla's (or so it appeared) on foot, after the hot weather had begun. It seemed improbable in the extreme, particularly since he could not have met the councillors there.

Silk massaged his cheek as he walked, gazing idly into shop windows. It was quite conceivable that Commissioner Simuliid's boast to Chenille had been nothing more than a vainglorious lie, in which case Chenille had not earned her five cards, and any time that Crane might have spent here had been wasted.

But whether Crane had wasted his time or not, he did not appear to have traced Simuliid through Limna's Juzgado, as he himself had. It might even be that Crane had not traced him at all.

"Something's very wrong here, Oreb. We've a rat in the wainscotting, if you know what I mean."

"No boat?"

"No boat, no doctor, and no councillors. No money. No manteion. No ability, either—not a speck of whatever it was that the Outsider thought he saw in me." Although the immortal gods, as reason taught and the Writings confirmed, did not "think" that they saw things. Not really. Gods knew.

With no special purpose in mind, he had been strolling west along Shore Street. Now he found it obstructed by a sizable boulder, painted white and crudely carved with the many-tentacled image of Scylla.

He crossed to the center of the street to examine the image more closely and discovered a rhyming prayer beneath it. Tracing the sign of addition in the air, he appealed to Scylla for help (citing her city's need for the manteion and apologizing for his impetuosity in rushing off to the lake with so little reason to believe that there was anything to be gained) before reciting the prayer, somewhat amused to find that the great goddess's features, as depicted on the boulder, bore a chance resemblance to those of the helpful woman in the Juzgado.

Members of the Ayuntamiento never visited the shrine, she had said, though commissioners came quite often. Did she herself visit the shrine with any frequency, and thus see who came and who did not? Almost certainly not, Silk decided.

With a start, he realized that half a dozen passersby stood watching him as he prayed with head bowed before the image; when he turned away, a stocky man about his own age excused himself and asked whether he intended to make the pilgrimage to the shrine.

"That was one of the points on which I begged for the goddess's guidance," Silk explained. "I told a good woman only a few minutes ago that I would go as soon as I had the opportunity. It was a rash promise, of course, because it can be very difficult to judge what 'opportunity' signifies. I have business here today, and so may be said to have none; but there is a remote chance that a pilgrimage to the shrine would further it. If that is so, I am clearly bound."

A woman of about the same age said, "You shouldn't even think of it, Patera. Not when it's this hot."

"Good girl!" Oreb muttered.

"This is my wife, Chervil," the stocky man told Silk. "My name's Coypu, and we've made the pilgrimage twice." Silk started to speak, but Coypu waved it away. "That place over there has cold drinks. If you hike up to the shrine today, you'll need all the wet stuff you can hold, and we'd like to buy you something. But if you'll let us, and listen to us, you probably won't go at all."

"Thirsty!"

Chervil laughed, and Silk said, "Be quiet, Oreb. So am I for that matter."

It was mercifully cool inside, and to Silk, stepping in from the sunlight, it seemed very dark. "They have beer, fruit juices—even coconut milk, if you haven't tried that—and spring water," Coypu told him. "Order whatever you like."

To the waiter who appeared as soon as they sat down, he said, "My wife will have the bitter orange, and I'll take whatever kind of beer's been in your cistern the longest."

He turned to Silk. "And you, Patera? Anything that you want."

"Spring water, please. Two glasses would be nice."

"We saw your picture on a fence," Chervil told him. "It can't have been more than five minutes ago—an augur with a bird on his shoulder, quite artistically rendered in chalk and charcoal. Over your head the artist had written, 'Silk is here!' And yesterday, back in the city, we saw 'Silk for Caldé.' "

He nodded grimly. "I haven't seen the picture with the bird you mentioned, but I believe that I can guess who drew it. If so, I must have a word with her."

The waiter set three moisture-beaded bottles—yellow, brown, and clear—on their table, with four glasses, and marked their score on a small slate.

Coypu fingered the brown bottle and smiled. "There's always a crowd on Scylsday, and everything's pretty warm. These were probably let down then."

Silk nodded. "It's always cold underground. I suppose that the night that surrounds the whorl must be a winter's night."

Coypu shot him a startled glance as he opened his wife's orange juice. "Haven't you ever thought of what lies beyond the whorl, my son?"

"You mean if you keep digging down? Isn't it just dirt, no matter how far down you go?"

Silk shook his head as he opened his own bottle. "The most ignorant miner knows better than that, my son. Even a grave digger—I talked with several of them yesterday, and they were by no means unintelligent— would tell you that the soil our plows till is scarcely thicker than the height of a man. Clay and gravel lie beneath it, and below them, stone or shiprock."

Silk poured cool water into a glass for Oreb while he collected his thoughts. "Beneath that stone and shiprock, which is not as thick as you might imagine, the whorl spins in emptiness—in a night that extends in every direction without limit." He paused, remembering, as he filled his own glass. "It is spangled everywhere with colored sparks, however. I was told what they were, though at the moment I cannot recall it."

"I thought it was just that the heat didn't reach down there."

"It does," Silk told him. "It reaches beyond the depths of this cistern, and deeper than the wells at my manteion, which always yield cold water with sufficient pumping. It extends, in fact, to the outermost stone of the whorl, and there it is lost in the frigid night. If it weren't for the sun, the first as well as the greatest gift Pas gave to the whorl, we would all freeze." For a moment Silk watched Oreb drinking from his glass, then he drank deeply from his own. "Thank you both. It's very good."

Chervil said, "I wouldn't argue with Pas or you about the value of the sun, Patera, but it can be dangerous, too. If you really want to see the shrine, I wish you'd consider making your pilgrimage in the evening, when it's not so hot. Remember last time, Coypu?"

Her husband nodded. "We'd gone out last fall, Patera. We enjoyed the hike, and there's a magnificent view from the shrine, so we decided we'd do it again this year. When we finally got around to it the figs were getting ripe, but it wasn't as hot as it is now."

"Not nearly," Chervil put in.

"So off we went, and it got hotter and hotter. You tell him, sweetheart."

"He left the path," Chervil told Silk. "The Pilgrims' Way, or whatever you call it. I could see the next couple of stones ahead of us, but he was veering off to the right down this little—I don't know what they call it. This rocky little valley between two hills."

"Ravine?" Silk suggested.

"Yes, that's it. This ravine. And I said, 'Where are you going? That's not the way.' And he said, 'Come on, come along or we'll never get there.' So I ran after him and caught up with him."

They'll have a child in another year, Silk thought. He pictured the three of them at supper in a little courtyard, talking and laughing; Chervil was neither as beautiful nor as charming as Hyacinth, yet he found that he envied Coypu with all his heart.

"And it ended. The ravine. It just stopped at a slope too steep to climb, and he didn't know what to do. Finally I said, 'Where do you think you're going?' And he said, 'To my aunt's.'"

"I see." Silk had drained his glass; he poured the rest of the bottle into it.

"It took me a long time to get him back to the path, but when I did I saw this man coming toward us, coming back from the shrine. I screamed for him to help me, and he stopped and asked what the matter was and made Coypu go along a little bit farther to where there was some shade, and we got him to lie down."

"It was the heat, of course," Silk said.

"Yes! Exactly."

Coypu nodded. "I was all mixed up, and somehow I got the idea we were in the city, walking to my aunt's house. I kept wondering what had happened to the street. Why it had changed so much."

"Anyway, this man stayed there with us until Coypu felt better. He said it was the early stages of heat stroke, and that the thing to do was to get out of the sun and lie down, and eat salty food and drink cold water, if you could. Only we couldn't because we hadn't brought anything, and it was way too high up for us to climb down to the lake. He was a doctor."

Silk stared at her. "Oh, you gods!"

"What's the matter, Patera?"

"And yet some people will not believe." He finished his water. "I—even I, who ought to know better if anyone does—often behave as though there were no forces in the whorl beyond my own feeble strength. I suppose I ought to ask you this doctor's name, for form's sake; but I don't have to. I know it."

"I've forgotten it," Coypu admitted, "although he stayed there talking to us for a couple of hours, I guess."

Chervil said, "He had a beard, and he was only a little taller than I am."

"His name is Crane," Silk told them, and signaled to the waiter.

Chervil nodded. "That was it. Is he a friend of yours, Patera?"

"Not exactly. An acquaintance. Would you like another, both of you? I'm going to get one."

They nodded, and Silk told the waiter, "I'm paying for everything—for our first drinks and these, too."

"Five bits if you want to pay now, Patera. You know anything about this Patera Silk, in the city?"

"A little," Silk told him. "Not as much as I should, certainly."

"Had a goddess in his Window? Supposed to be some sort of wonder worker?"

"The first is true," Silk said, "the second is not." He turned back to Coypu and Chervil. "You said Doctor Crane talked with you for some time. If I'm not presuming on our brief acquaintance, may I ask what he talked about?"

"He *is* Patera Silk," Chervil told the waiter. "Don't you see his bird?"

Silk laid six cardbits on the table.

Coypu said, "He wanted to know if my mother and father were in good health, and he kept feeling my skin. And what my grandmother'd died of. I remember that."

"He asked a lot of questions," Chervil said. "And he made me keep fanning him—fanning Coypu, I mean."

Oreb, who had been listening intently, demonstrated with his sound wing.

"That's right, birdie. Exactly like that, only I used my hat."

"I must get one," Silk muttered. "Get another, I should say. Fortunately I have funds."

"A hat?" Coypu asked.

"Yes. Even the commissioner was wearing—it doesn't matter. I don't know the man, and I don't wish to make you believe I do. I've done enough of that. What I should say is that before I start for the shrine, I want to buy a straw hat with a broad brim. I saw some in a shop window here, I know."

The waiter brought three more sweating bottles and three clean glasses.

Coypu told Silk, "Half the shops here sell them. You can get an ugly sunburn out on a boat on the lake."

"Or even swimming, because people mostly just sit on the rocks." Chervil laughed; she had an attractive laugh, and Silk sensed that she knew it. "They come here from the city because the lake's nice and cold, and they think they want that. But once they get into it they jump out pretty fast, most of them."

Silk nodded and smiled. "I'll have to try it myself one of these days. Do you remember any of Doctor Crane's other questions?"

"Who built the shrine," Coypu said. "It was Councillor Lemur, about twenty-five years ago. There's a bronze plate on it that says so, but the doctor must not have noticed it when he was out there."

Chervil said, "He wanted to know if Coypu was related. I don't think he knew what a coypu is. And whether we knew him, or any of them, and about how old they were. He said most of them became our councillors more than forty years ago, so they must have been pretty young then."

"I'm not sure that's right," Coypu told her.

"And if we knew how badly off some of the other cities were, and didn't we think we ought to help. I said that the first thing we ought to do was make sure everyone there got a fair share of their own food, because a lot of the trouble was because of people there buying up corn and waiting for higher prices. I said prices in Viron were high enough for me already without our sending rice to Palustria."

She laughed again, and Silk laughed with her as he put his unopened bottle of spring water into the front pocket of his robe; but his thoughts were already following the trail of white stones, the Pilgrims' Way stretching from Limna to Scylla's shrine—the holy place that both Doctor Crane and Commissioner Simuliid had visited—on the cliffs above the lake.

When he set off nearly an hour later, the sun seemed a living enemy, a serpent of fire across the sky, powerful, poisonous, and malign. The Pilgrims' Way shimmered in the heat, and the third white stone, upon which he sat in order to re-energize Crane's wrapping, felt as hot as the lid of a kettle on the stove.

As he wiped his forehead with his sleeve, he tried to recall whether it had been equally hot two or three months before, when Simuliid has made his pilgrimage, and decided that it had not. It had been hot—indeed it had been so hot that everyone had complained incessantly. But not as hot as it was now.

"This is the peak," he told Oreb. "This is the hottest that it will get all day. It might have been wiser to wait until evening, as Chervil suggested; but we're supposed to meet Auk this evening for dinner. We can comfort ourselves with the thought that if we can stand this—and we can—we can stand the worst that this sun can do and that from this moment on things can only get better. Not only will the way back be downhill, but it will be cooler then."

Oreb clacked his bill nervously but said nothing.

"Did you see the look on Coypu's face when I limped away from our table?" Silk slapped the wrapping against the side of the white-painted boulder one final time. "When I told him I had a broken ankle, I was afraid he might try to keep me in Limna by main force."

As Silk stood up, he reflected that Simuliid's age and weight had probably been handicaps as great or greater than his ankle. Had he, like

Crane, encountered pilgrims on the path? And if so, what had he told them?

For that matter, what should he himself, Patera Silk, from Sun Street, tell those he met; and what should he ask them? As he walked, he tried to contrive some reasonably truthful account that would permit him to ask whether they, too, had ever talked with Crane on the Pilgrims' Way, and what Crane had said to them, all without revealing his own purpose.

There was no occasion for it. Though well marked (as the woman in the Juzgado had said), the path was deserted, steep, and stony, its loneliness and blazing heat relieved only by a succession of views of the steel blue lake that were increasingly breathtaking, breathtaken, and hazardous.

"If an augur were to make this pilgrimage every day of his life," Silk asked Oreb, "in all weathers and whether he was well or ill, don't you believe that eventually, perhaps on the final day of his whorldly existence, Surging Scylla would reveal herself to him, rising from the lake? I do, and if I didn't have the manteion to take care of—if the people of our quarter didn't have need of me and it, and if the Outsider hadn't ordered me to save it—I'd be tempted to try the experiment. Even if it failed, one might live a far worse life."

Oreb croaked and muttered in reply, peering this way and that.

"It's Scylla, Pas's eldest child, who selects us to be augurs, after all. Each year arrives like a flotilla laden with young men and women—this is what they tell you at the schola, you understand."

A beetling rock provided a few square cubits of shade; Silk squatted in it, fanning his dripping face with the wide hat he had bought in Limna.

"Some, drawn to the ideal of holiness, sail very near Scylla indeed; and from those she plucks a number that is neither great nor small, but the necessary number for that year. Others, repelled by the augurial ideals of simplicity and chastity, sail as far from her as they dare; from them, also, she takes a number that is neither great nor small but the necessary number for the year. That is why artists show her with many long arms like whips. She snatched me up with one, you see. It may even be that she snatched you as well, Oreb."

"No see!"

"Nor I," Silk confessed. "I didn't see her either. But I felt her pull. Do you know, I believe all this walking's doing my ankle good? It must've reached the stage at which it needs exercise more than rest. We're coming to another point. What do you say, shall I sacrifice Blood's stick to Lady Scylla?"

"No hit?"

"No hit, I swear."

"Keep it."

"Because someone else might find it and hit you? Don't worry. I'll stand out there and throw it as far as I can."

Silk rose and walked to the point, advancing ever more cautiously until he stood at the very edge of the projecting rock, above a drop of five hundred cubits, jumbled slabs of stone, and breaking waves. "How about it, Oreb? Should we make the offering? An informal sacrifice to Surging Scylla? It must surely have been Scylla who sent that nice couple to us. They told me where they live quite willingly, and some of the questions Doctor Crane had asked them were certainly suggestive."

He paused. Like a gift from the goddess, a sudden gust of cool wind from the lake set his black robe flapping behind him, and dried the sweat that had soaked his tunic.

"Auk and Chenille—and I, too—talked about turning him over to the Guard, Oreb, after we'd taken his money; it bothered me at the time, and it's been bothering me more and more ever since. I'd almost prefer failing the Outsider to doing that."

"Good man."

"Yes." Silk lowered the walking stick, discovered that he had nowhere to rest its ferrule, and took a step backward. "That's precisely the trouble. If I were to find out that someone I knew had gone to a foreign city to spy for Viron, I'd consider him a brave man and a patriot. Doctor Crane is clearly a spy for some other city—his home, whether it's Ur, Urbs, Trivigaunte, Sedes, or Palustria. Well, isn't he a brave man and a patriot, too?"

"Walk now?"

"You're right, I suppose. We ought to be on about our business." Silk remained where he was, nevertheless, gazing down at the lake. "I could say, I suppose, that if Scylla accepted my sacrifice—that is to say, if this stick fell into the water—it would be all right to let Crane go free once the manteion had been saved; he'd have to leave Viron, of course; but we wouldn't hand him and our evidence over to the Guard—roll him over to Hoppy, as Auk would say." He tapped the rock with the tip of the stick. "But it would be pure superstition, unworthy of an augur. What we need is a regular sacrifice, preferably on a Scylsday, with all of the forms strictly observed, before a Sacred Window."

"No cut!"

"Not you. How many times do I have to say that? A ram or something.

You know, Oreb, there really is—or was—a science of hydromancy, by which the officiating augur read Scylla's will in the patterns of waves. I suggested it to that nice woman in the Juzgado by purest chance—seeing the lake before we went in probably brought it to mind—but I wouldn't be surprised if that's what Councillor Lemur had in mind when he built this shrine we're going to. It was practiced up until about a hundred years ago, so when the shrine was built there must still have been thousands of people who remembered it. Perhaps Councillor Lemur hoped to revive it."

The bird did not reply. For another two minutes or more Silk stood staring at the surging waters below him before shifting his attention to the rugged cliffs on his right. "Look, you can see the shrine from here." He pointed with the walking stick. "I believe they've actually shaped the pillars that support the dome like Scylla's arms. See how wavy they are?"

"Man there."

A dim figure moved back and forth in the bluish twilight beneath Scylla's airy chalcedony shell, then vanished as he (presumably) knelt.

"You're quite right," Silk told the bird, "so there is. Someone must have been on the path ahead of us all that time. I wish we'd caught up with him."

He contemplated the otherwhorldly purity of the distant shrine for some time longer, then turned away. "I suppose we'll meet him on the path. But if we don't, we probably ought to wait until he's completed his own devotions. Now what about the stick? Should I go back and throw it?"

"No throw." Oreb unfolded his wings and seemed minded to fly. "Keep it."

"All right. I suppose my leg may be worse before we get back, so you're probably wise."

"Silk fight."

"With this, Oreb?" He twirled it. "I've got Hyacinth's azoth and her little needler, and either would be a much more effective weapon."

"Fight!" the night chough repeated.

"Fight who? There's no one here."

Oreb whistled, a low note followed by a slightly higher one.

"Is that bird speech for 'who knows?' Well, I certainly don't. And neither do you, Oreb, if you ask me. I'm glad I brought the weapons, because my having them here means that Patera Gulo can't find them, and I'd be willing to bet that by now he's searched my room; but if they were mine instead of Hyacinth's, I'd be inclined to pitch them to the goddess after the stick. Gulo'd never find them then."

"Bad man?"

"Yes, I believe he is." Silk returned to the Pilgrims' Way. "I'm guessing, of course. But if I must guess—and it seems that I must—then my guess is that he's the sort of man who thinks himself good, and that's by far the most dangerous sort of man there is."

"Watch out."

"I'll try," Silk promised, though he was not sure whether the bird was referring to Patera Gulo or the path, which wound along the edge of the cliff here. "So—if I'm right—this Patera Gulo's the exact reverse of Auk, who's a good man who believes himself to be a bad one. You've noticed that, I take it."

"Take it."

"I felt sure you had. Auk's helped in a dozen different ways, without even counting that diamond trinket. Patera Gulo was scandalized sufficiently by that, and the bracelet some other thief gave him. I can't imagine what he'd have done, or said, if he'd found the azoth."

"Man go."

"Do you mean Patera Gulo? Well, I wish I had some means of arranging that, I really do; but for the moment it seems to be beyond my reach."

"Man go," Oreb repeated testily. "No pray."

"Gone from the shrine now, is that what you mean?" Silk pointed with the walking stick. "He can't have gone, unless he jumped. I didn't see him come out, and it's in full view from here."

Rather to Silk's surprise, Oreb launched himself from his shoulder and managed to struggle up to half again his height before settling again. "No see."

"I'm perfectly willing to believe that you can't see him from here," Silk told the bird, "but he has to be there just the same. Possibly there's a chapel below the shrine, cut into the cliff. The path turns inland again up ahead, but even so we should find out in half an hour or less."

CHAPTER
7   THE ARMS OF SCYLLA

"May every god be with you this, er, noon, Patera," Remora said as soon as his prothonotary had closed the door behind Gulo. It was extraordinary condescension.

"Even so, may they be with Your Eminence." Gulo bowed nearly to the floor. The bow and conventional phrases gave him time for a final review of the principal items he had come to report. "May Maidenly Molpe, patroness of the day, Great Pas, patron of the whorl, to whom we owe all that we possess, and Scalding Scylla, patroness of this our Sacred City of Viron, be with you always, Your Eminence, every day of your life." In the course of his bow, Gulo had contrived to pat the pocket containing the bracelet and the letter.

Straightening up, he added, "I trust that Your Eminence enjoys the best of good health? That I have not come at an inconvenient moment?"

"No, no," Remora told him. "Um—not at all. I'm—ah—delighted, really quite delighted to see you, Patera. Please sit down. What do you—ah—make of young Silk, eh?"

Gulo lowered his pudgy body to the black velvet seat of the armchair beside Remora's escritoire. "I've had little opportunity to observe his person thus far, Your Eminence. Very little. He left our manteion a moment or two after my arrival, and he had not yet returned when I myself left it in order to make this report to Your Eminence. He will not return before evening, or so he said, so it would seem less than likely that he is there now."

Remora nodded.

"He made an impression on me, however, even though I saw him so briefly, Your Eminence. A distinct one."

"I—ah—see." Remora leaned back in his chair, his long fingers tip to tip. "Would it be—um—convenient for you to describe this, um, momentary interview in detail, hey?"

"As Your Eminence desires. Shortly after I entered the quarter a man had given me this." Patera Gulo pulled the bracelet from his pocket and held it up; Remora pursed his lips.

"I must add, Your Eminence, that several other such men have come to the door of the manse since then. It was my impression—my marked impression, Your Eminence—that they had come to proffer similar gifts. They declined to do so when they learned Patera Silk was not present, however."

"You—ah—pressed them, Patera?"

"As much as I dared, Your Eminence. They weren't men of a kind one would care to press too far."

Remora grunted.

"I was about to say, Your Eminence, that when I showed this to Patera Silk he gave me a similar piece and told me to lock both of them in his cashbox. It was a diamond anklet, Your Eminence. There were two other persons with him at the time, a man and a woman. All three were going to the lake, I think. Something was said to that effect." Gulo gave an apologetic cough. "Possibly, Your Eminence, only Patera and the woman."

"You would appear to feel that Patera ought to have been more discreet." Remora seemed to sink deeper into his chair. "Yet unless you have—um—ascertained the identities of these two, you cannot very well, um, gauge how indiscreet he may have been. Have you, eh?"

Gulo fidgeted. "He called them Auk and Chenille, Your Eminence. He introduced them to me."

"Let me see that—ah—bangle." Remora held out his hand for the bracelet. "It ought scarcely to be—ah—needful for me to say that you yourself, Patera, should have been, er, very much more discreet than you were. Ah—by discreet in—ah—this instance, Patera I, um, intend *forceful.* The word will bear that—ah—interpretation, I am confident. To be discreet, Patera, is to, er, exercise good judgment, hey? In this present—ah—matter, good judgment would have—ah—prompted a forcible—um—strategy? Approach. Or attitude."

"Yes, Your Eminence."

"You ought to have gracefully and—ah—graciously received any offerings from the faithful, Patera." Remora held up the bracelet so that it caught the light from the bull's-eye window behind him, and swung it from side to side. "I will not—ah—um—desire excuses on that—ah—score, Patera. Do you follow me? None at all, eh?"

Gulo nodded humbly.

"These—ah—gentlemen may return, hey? Perhaps when Patera is absent, as he was in the—um—occasion. You will be—ah—vouchsafed an—um—golden opportunity, when that—ah—hour strikes, with which you may—ah—um—redeem your credit, eh? Not impossibly. See that you do, Patera."

Gulo squirmed. "I shall try, Your Eminence. I will be forceful, I assure you."

"Now then. Your—ah—observations of Silk himself? You needn't—ah —vex yourself with physical description. I've seen him."

"Yes, Your Eminence." Gulo hesitated, his mouth open, his protuberant eyes vague. "He seemed determined."

"Determined, hum?" Remora laid the bracelet on a stack of papers. "To do which?"

"I don't know, Your Eminence. But his jaw was firm, I thought. His manner was decisive. There was—if I may say it, Your Eminence—a glint as of steel in his eyes, I thought. Perhaps that simile is something overblown, Your Eminence—"

"Perhaps it is," Remora told him severely.

"And yet it at least expresses what I sensed in him. At the schola, Your Eminence, Patera was two years before me."

Remora nodded.

"I noticed him there as anyone would, Your Eminence. I thought him good-looking and studious, but rather slow, if anything. Now, however—"

Remora waved the present aside. "You implied, I think, Patera, that Patera—ah—decamped, eh? With a couple. A married couple? Were they—um—ah—wed, so far as you could judge?"

"I believe they may have been, Your Eminence. The woman had a fine ring."

Remora's long fingers toyed with the jeweled gammadion he wore. "Describe them, eh? Their—ah—appearance."

"The man was tough-looking, Your Eminence, and somewhat older than I, I should say. He had not shaved, yet he was decently dressed and wore a hanger. Straight brown hair, Your Eminence. A reddish beard, and dark and piercing eyes. Quite tall. I took note of his hands, particularly, when he took that," Gulo indicated the bracelet, "from me. And when he returned it to me, Your Eminence. He had unusually large and powerful ones, Your Eminence. A brawler, I should say. Your Eminence finds me fanciful, I fear."

Remora grunted again. "Go ahead, Patera. Let me hear it. I'll tell you afterward, eh?"

"His hanger, Your Eminence. It was brass-fitted, with a large guard, and to judge from the scabbard it had a longer, broader blade than most, rather sharply curved. It seemed to me that the weapon was like to the man, Your Eminence, if you understand what I mean."

"I—ah—misdoubt that you do yourself, Patera. Yet these details may not be, um, wholly valueless. What of the woman, eh? This Chenille? Be as fanciful as you please."

"Remarkably attractive, Your Eminence. About twenty, tall though not stately. And yet there was an air—"

Remora's uplifted palm halted the younger augur in mid-thought. "Cherry-colored hair?"

"Why, yes, Your Eminence."

"I know her, Patera. I have had a—ah—achates or, um, three out looking for her since last night. So this—ah—fiery vixen was back at Silk's manteion this morning, eh? I will have this and that to say to my, um, adherents, Patera. Let's see that gaud again."

He picked the bracelet up. "I don't suppose you know what this is worth? The green stone, eh? Particularly?"

"Fifty cards, Your Eminence?"

"I have no idea. You haven't had it—um—valuated? No, no, don't. Return it to Silk's box, eh? Tell him—ah—nothing. I'll tell him myself. Tell Incus on your way out that I want to speak with Patera on Tarsday. Have Incus send a note with you, but it's not to mention that you were here, hey? Have him mark the time on my regimen."

Gulo nodded forcefully. "I will, Your Eminence."

"This—ah—woman. Precisely what did she say and do while she was in your presence? Every word, eh?"

"Why nothing, Your Eminence. I don't believe she ever spoke. Let me think."

Remora waved permission. "Take as long as you—ah—consider best. No, um, circumstance too trivial to mention, hey?"

Gulo shut his eyes and bent his head, a hand pressed to his temple. Silence descended upon the large and airy room from which Patera Remora, as coadjutor, conducted the often-tangled affairs of the Chapter. Through four blazing eyes, Twice-headed Pas regarded Gulo's bowed back from a priceless painting by Campion; a Guardsman's restless mount nickered in the street below.

After a minute or two had passed, Remora rose and walked to the bull's-eye window behind his chair. It stood open, and through its circular aperture (whose diameter exceeded his own very considerable height), he could see the gabled roofs and massive towers of the Juzgado at the foot of this, the western and least precipitous slope of the Palatine. High above the tallest, flying from a pole some trick of the glaring sunlight rendered nearly invisible, floated the bright green banner of Viron. Upon it, fitfully animated by the hot and dilatory wind, Scylla's long, white arms appeared to beckon, just as the papillae of certain invertebrates of her lake waved in evident imitation of its surface, searching the clear waters blindly and ceaselessly for bits of carrion and living fish alike.

"Your Eminence? I believe I can tell you everything I saw now."

Remora turned back to Gulo. "Excellent. Ah—capital! Proceed, Patera."

"It was brief, as I said, Your Eminence. If it had been longer I would be less confident. Is Your Eminence familiar with the small garden attached to our manteion?"

Remora shook his head.

"There is such a place, Your Eminence. One can enter it from the manteion proper—that's how I entered it upon my arrival. I had looked in the manteion first, thinking that I might find Patera Silk at prayer."

"The woman, please, Patera. This—ah—Chenille, eh?"

"There's a grape arbor near the center, Your Eminence, with seats under the vines. She was sitting there, almost completely concealed by the dependent foliage. Patera and the layman, Auk, had been talking there with her, I believe. They came to meet me, but she remained seated."

"She—ah—emerged, eventually?"

"Yes, Your Eminence. We spoke for a minute or so, and Patera gave me their names, as I've reported them. Then he said that he was leaving, and his bird—is Your Eminence familiar with his bird?"

Remora nodded again. "The woman, Patera."

"Patera said they would leave, and she left the arbor. He said—these are his precise words, I believe—'This is Patera Gulo, Chenille. We were speaking of him earlier.' She nodded and smiled."

"And then, Patera? What—ah—next transpired, hey?"

"They left together, Your Eminence. The three of them. Patera had said, 'We're off to the lake, you silly bird.' And as they went out of the gate—there's a gate to Sun Street from the garden, Your Eminence—the layman said, 'Hope you get something, only don't go down in the chops if you don't.' But the woman said nothing at all."

"Her dress, Patera?"

"Black, Your Eminence. I remember that for a moment I thought it was a sibyl's habit, but it was actually just a black wool gown, such as fashionable women wear in winter."

"Jewelry? You said she wore a ring, eh?"

"Yes, Your Eminence. And a necklace and earrings, both jade. I noticed her ring particularly because it sparkled as she pushed the grapevines to one side. There was a dark red gem like a carbuncle, quite large, I believe in a simple setting of yellow gold. If Your Eminence would only confide in me . . . . ?"

"Tell you why she's—um—central? She may not be." Sighing, Remora pushed his chair away from the escritoire and returned to the window. With his back to Gulo and his hands clasped behind it, he repeated, "She may not be."

Moved by an excess of mannerliness, Gulo stood, too.

"Or yet, she—um—may. You're anxious to minister to the gods, Patera. Or so you declare, eh?"

"Oh, yes, Your Eminence. Extremely anxious."

"And also to risc in the—ah—books of an—er—um—remarkably extensive family, hey? That I have—ah—made note of as well. You have considered that in, um, due course you might eventually become Prolocutor, hey?"

Gulo blushed like a girl. "Oh, no, Your Eminence. That—that is—I—"

"No, no, you have, eh? Every young augur does; I did it myself. Has it struck home yet that by the time you get so much as—um—a whiff of mulberry, those whom you hope to—ah—impress? Overawe. That they will be dead? Gone, eh? Forgotten by everyone except the gods, Patera Gulo my boy. And you, eh? Forgotten by everyone save the gods and yourself. And who can vouch for the gods, eh? Such is the—ah—fact of the matter, I, er, warrant you."

No doubt wisely, Gulo swallowed and remained silent.

"You cannot do it by any stretch, Patera. Eh? By none. Assume the office. If you ever do. Not till I myself have gone, eh? And my successor, likewise. You are—ah—too young at present. Not even if I live long, hey? You know it, eh? Take an idiot not to, hey?"

Poor Gulo nodded, desperately wishing that he might flee instead.

The coadjutor turned to face him. "I cannot—um—speak for him, eh? My successor. Only for myself. Ah—yes. For myself, I—ah—um—meditate a reign longer than old Quetzal's, hey?"

"I would never wish you less, Your Eminence."

"His chambers are over there, Patera." Remora waved his left hand vaguely. "On this very floor of the palace, hey? South side. Faces our garden." He chuckled. "Bigger than Patera Silk's. Much more—ah—

extensive, er, doubtless. Fountains—ah—statuary, and big trees. All that."

Gulo nodded. "They're lovely, I know, Your Eminence."

"He's held the office for thirty-three years already, hey? Old Quetzal. There are one hundred and—ah—odd of your generation, Patera. Many better—um—connected. I—ah—proffer a nearer target, an—ah—straighter road for your ambition."

Remora resumed his chair and motioned for Gulo to sit. "An—ah—little game now, eh? A sport, to while away this, um, overheated hour. Choose yourself a city, Patera. Any city you care to name, so long as it is not Viron. I'm perfectly serious. Within the—um—hedge of the game. Consider. Large? Fair? Rich? Which city will you have, eh, Patera?"

"Palustria, Your Eminence?"

"Down amongst the pollywogs, hey? Good enough. Then conceive yourself at the head of the Chapter in Palustria. Perhaps—ah—a decade hence. You will tithe, I should think, to the parent Chapter, here in Viron. You continue subject to the Prolocutor, eh? Whomever he may be. To old Quetzal, or to—ah—myself, as is more probable in ten years time. Do you find it a—um—attractive prospect, Patera?" Remora raised a hand as he had before. "Needn't say so, if it—ah—troubles you."

"Your Eminence—?"

"I have no idea, Patera. None whatsoever, eh? But the drought. You're aware of that, hey? Can't escape it. How fairs your—ah—choice, Patera? How fares Palustria in the drought?"

Gulo swallowed. "I've heard that the rice crop failed, Your Eminence. I know there's no rice in the market here, though traders usually bring it."

Remora nodded. "There is rioting, Patera. There is—um—no starvation. None as yet. But there is the specter of starvation. Soldiers trying to, er, check the—ah—mob. Practically—ah—worn out, some of those soldiers. Uncle a military man, eh?"

Bewildered by the sudden shift in topic, Gulo managed, "Wh—why I —one is, Your Eminence."

"Major in the Second Brigade. Ask him where our army is, Patera. Or perhaps you can tell me now? Heard his—um—table talk? Where is it, eh?"

"In storage, Your Eminence. Underground. Here in Viron the Civil Guard is all we need."

"Precisely. Not so elsewhere though, Patera. We die, eh? Grow old like

—ah—His Cognizance. And tread the path to Mainframe. Chems last longer, though. Forever?"

"I hadn't considered the matter, Your Eminence. But I would think—"

A corner of Remora's mouth twitched upward. "But you will, eh? To be sure you will, Patera. Now, eh? Good to know that the—ah—arms of Scylla are good as new, eh? Or—ah—very nearly so. Not like—ah—um —Palustria's, hey? And many others. Soldiers and their—ah—weapons like new or nearly. Think about it, Patera."

Remora straightened up in his chair, resting his elbows on the escritoire. "What—um—more have you to report concerning Patera, Patera?"

"Your Eminence mentioned weapons. I found a paper packet of needles, Your Eminence. Opened."

"A paper of needles, Patera? I fail—"

"Not sewing needles," Gulo added hastily. "Projectiles for a needler, Your Eminence. In one of Patera's drawers, under clothing."

"I—ah—must consider that," Remora said slowly. "I—um—it is of— um—concern. No question. Anything—ah—further?"

"My final item, Your Eminence. One that I would much rather not have to report. This letter." Gulo extracted it from the pocket of his robe. "It's from—"

"You have, er, opened it." Remora favored him with a gentle smile.

"It's in a feminine hand, Your Eminence, and is heavily perfumed. Under the circumstances I think that what I did was justified. I hoped, very sincerely, Your Eminence, that it would prove to have emanated from a sister or some other female relation, Your Eminence. However—"

"You are—ah—bold, Patera. That's well, or so I am—ah—disposed to conclude. Sphigx favors the bold, eh?" Remora peered at the superscription. "Not from this—um—lady Chenille, hey? Or you would've said so previously, hum?"

"No, Your Eminence. From another woman."

"Read it to me, Patera. You must have—ah—puzzled out that—um— contorted scribble. I should, er, choose not to."

"I fear that you will find, Your Eminence, that Patera Silk has compromised himself. I wish—"

"I'll be the—ah—judge, eh? Read it, Patera."

Gulo cleared his throat and unfolded the letter. " 'O My Darling Wee Flea: I call you so not only because of the way you sprang from my window, but because of the way you hopped into my bed! How your lonely bloss has longed for a note from you!!!' "

"Bloss, Patera?"

"A pretended wife, I believe, Your Eminence."

"I—ah—very well. Proceed, Patera. Is there—ah further revelation?"

"I'm afraid so, Your Eminence. 'You might have sent one by the kind friend who brought you my gift, you know!' "

"Let me—ah—examine that, Patera." Remora extended his hand, and Gulo passed him the much-creased paper.

"Ah—hum."

"Yes, Your Eminence."

"She really does—ah—write like that, hey? Doesn't she? Yes—ah—does she not. I would not have—ah—conceded, er, previously, that a human being could."

Brows knit, Remora bent over the paper. " 'Now you have to tender me your,'—ah—um—'thanks,' I suppose that must be, eh? 'And so much more, when,'—ah—um—'next we meet,' with yet another screamer. 'Don't you know that little,'—um—'place up on the Palatine—' Well, well, well!"

"Yes, Your Eminence."

" 'That little place up on the Palatine where Thelx,' I suppose she—ah—intends Thelxiepeia but doesn't—ah—apprehend the spelling. 'Where Thelx holds up a mirror? *Hieraxday.*' That last—um—underscored. Heavily, eh? Signature, 'Hy.' "

Remora tapped the paper with a long fingernail. "Well—ah—do you, Patera? Where is it, eh? A picture, I—ah—if I may guess at hazard. Not in one of the manteions, hey? I know them all."

Gulo shook his head. "I've never seen a picture like that, Your Eminence."

"In a—ah—house, most likely, Patera. A private—um—residence, I would—um—opine." Remora bawled, *"Incus!"* over Gulo's shoulder, and a small, sly-looking augur with buckteeth looked in so quickly as to suggest that he had been eavesdropping.

"Whereabouts might we—ah—descry Thelxiepeia and a mirror, here on the hill, eh, Incus? You don't know. Make—um—inquiries. I shall expect their result tomorrow at, um, no later than luncheon. Should be a simple matter, eh?" Remora glanced down at the letter's broken seal. "And fetch a seal with a—um—heart or kiss or some such for this." He tossed Hyacinth's letter across the room to Incus.

"Immediately, Your Eminence."

Remora turned back to Gulo. "It won't—um—signify if Patera has seen this one, Patera. She's the sort who'll have a round dozen at fewest, eh? You don't know how to—um—preserve the seal? Incus can show you. A useful art, eh?"

As the latch clicked behind his bowing prothonotary, Remora rose once more. "You take that back to Sun Street with you, eh? When he's through with it. If Patera isn't back, put it on the mantel. If he is, say it was—ah—handed to you as you went out, eh? You haven't glanced at it, hey?"

Gulo nodded glumly. "Naturally, Your Eminence."

Remora leaned closer to peer at him. "Something—um—troubling you, Patera. Out with it."

"Your Eminence, how could an anointed augur, a man of Patera's high promise, compromise himself so? I mean this absurd, filthy woman. And yet a goddess—! I understand now, only too well, why Your Eminence believes Patera must be watched, but—but a theophany!"

Remora sucked his teeth. "It's an—ah—habitual observation of old Quetzal's that the gods don't have laws, Patera. Only preferences."

"I myself can see, Your Eminence—but when the augur in question—"

Remora silenced him with a gesture. "Possibly we will, er, be made privy to the secret, Patera. In due time, eh? Possibly there's none. You've considered Palustria?"

Afraid to trust his voice, Gulo merely nodded.

"Capital." Remora regarded him narrowly. "Now then. What do you know about the—ah—history of the caldés, Patera?"

"The caldés, Your Eminence? Only that the last one died before I was born, and the Ayuntamiento decided that nobody could replace him."

"And replaced him—um—themselves, hey? In effect. You realize that, Patera?"

"I suppose so, Your Eminence."

Remora stalked across the room to a tall bookcase. "I knew him, eh? The last. A loud, tyrannical, tumultuous sort of man. The mob—um—doted upon him, hey? They always love that kind." He extracted a thin volume bound in russet leather and recrossed the room to drop it into Gulo's lap. "The Charter, eh? Written in—ah—deity by Scylla and corrected by Pas. So it—um—asserts. Have a look at clause seven. Quickly, hey? Then tell me what you find—um—outré in it."

Silence settled over the spacious, somberly furnished room once more as the young augur bent over the book. In the street, litter bearers fought like sparrows with much shouting and a few blows; as the minutes ticked by, Remora watched their dispute through the open window.

Gulo looked up. "It provides for the election of new councillors, Your Eminence. Every three years. I assume that this provision has been suspended?"

"Delicately—um—phrased, Patera. You may—ah—attain Palustria yet. What else?"

"And it says the caldé is to hold office for life, and may appoint his successor."

Remora nodded. "Reshelve it, will you? Not done now, eh? No caldé at all. Yet it's still law. You know of the frozen embryo trade, Patera? New breeds of cattle, exotic pets, slaves, too, in places like Trivigaunte, eh? Where do they come from, hey?"

Gulo hurried to the bookcase. "From other cities, Your Eminence?"

"Which say the same, Patera. Seeds and cuttings that grow plants of—um—bizarre form. They die, hey? Or most do. Or, um, thrive beyond nature."

"I've heard of them, Your Eminence."

"Most of the beasts, and men, are—ah—commonplace. Or nearly, eh? A few—um—monstrosities, eh? Pitiful. Or fearful. Extraordinary prices for those. Give ear now, Patera."

"I'm listening, Your Eminence."

Remora stood beside him, a hand on his shoulder, nearly whispering. "This was common knowledge, eh? Fifteen years ago. The caldé's folly, we called it. Forgotten now, hum? And you're not to speak about it to anyone, Patera. Not to stir it up, hey?"

Craning his neck to meet the eyes of the coadjutor, Gulo declared, "Your Eminence can rely upon me absolutely."

"Capital. Before he—ah—collected his reward from the gods, Patera, the caldé paid out a sum of that—um—magnitude, hey? Bought a human embryo. Something—ah—extraordinary."

"I see." Gulo moistened his lips. "I appreciate your confidence in me, Your Eminence."

"A successor, eh? Or an—ah—weapon. Nobody knows, Patera. The Ayuntamiento's no—ah—wiser than yourself, Patera, now that I've told you."

"If I may inquire, Your Eminence . . . ?"

"What became of it? That is the—ah—crux, Patera. And what could it do? Extraordinary strength, perhaps. Or hear your thoughts, eh? Move

things without touching them? There are rumors of such people. Ayuntamiento searched, eh? Never stopped, never gave up."

"Had it been implanted, Your Eminence?"

"No one knew. Still don't, eh?" Remora returned to his escritoire and
sat down. "A year passed. Then two, five—ah—ten. They came to us.
Wanted us to test every child in every palaestra in the city, and we did it.
Memory, eh? Dexterity. All sorts of things. There were a few we—ah—
took an interest in. No good, hey? The harder we, er, scrutinized them,
the less—ah—outlandish they looked. Early development, eh? A few
years and the rest caught up."

Remora shook his head. "Not—ah—um—unforeseen, we said, and the
—ah—Lemur, Loris, and the rest likewise. They're not always what
they're cracked up to be, these frozen embryos. Die in the womb, more
often than not. Everybody forgot it. You follow me?"

Though Gulo was seldom subject to flashes of insight, he had one at
that moment. "Y-y-your Eminence has located this person! It's this
woman Chenille!"

Remora pursed his lips. "I did not—ah—asseverate anything of the
kind, Patera."

"Indeed not, Your Eminence."

"Patera has become an—ah—popular figure, Patera, as I, er, implied
to you yesterday. This theophany, to be sure. 'Silk for caldé' daubed upon
walls forest-to-lake. Bound to attract all sorts, eh? He must be watched
over by an acolyte of—um—sagacity. And large discretion. His associates
must be watched likewise. A weighty—um—obligation for one so young.
But for the future coadjutor for Palustria, a fitting devoir."

Sensing his dismissal, Gulo rose and bowed. "I will do my best, Your
Eminence."

"Capital. See Incus about that letter, and my note to Patera."

Greatly daring, Gulo inquired, "Do you think that Patera himself may
have guessed, Your Eminence? Or that this woman may have told him
outright?"

Remora nodded gloomily.

Here, at its loftiest point, the cliff jutted into the lake like the prow of a
giant's boat. Here, according to a modest bronze plaque let into its side
next to the entrance, Lacustral Scylla's most humble petitioner Lemur,
Presiding Officer of the Ayuntamiento, had erected to her glory this
chaste hemispherical dome of milky, translucent, blue stone, supported
on the wavering tips of these (Silk counted them) ten tapering, fragile-

looking pillars, themselves resting upon a squat balustrade. There were fine-lined drawings of her exploits, both factual and legendary, traced in bronze on the balustrade. Most impressive of all, there was her representation, with floating hair and bare breasts, inlaid in bronze in the stone floor, with ten coiling arms extended toward the ten pillars.

And there was nothing else.

"There's no one here, Oreb," Silk said. "Yet I know we saw somebody."

The bird only muttered.

Still shaking his head in perplexity, Silk stepped into the deep shadow of the dome. As his dusty black shoe made contact with the floor, he thought he heard a faint groan from the solid rock beneath him.

And very much to Silk's surprise, Oreb flew. He did not fly well or far, merely out between two pillars to alight heavily upon a spur of naked rock eight or ten cubits from the shrine; but fly he did, Crane's little splint a bright blue against his sable plumage.

"What are you afraid of, silly bird? Falling?"

Oreb cocked his sleek head in the direction of Limna. "Fish heads?"

"Yes," Silk promised. "More fish heads just as soon as we get back."

"Watch out!"

Fanning himself with his wide straw hat, Silk turned to admire the lake. A few friendly sails shone here and there, minute triangles of white against the prevailing cobalt. It was cooler here than it had been among the rocks, and would be cooler still, no doubt, in a boat like those he watched. If he preserved the manteion as the Outsider wished, perhaps he might some summer bring a party from the palaestra here, children who had never seen the lake or ridden in a boat or caught a fish. It would be an experience that they would never forget, surely; an adventure they would treasure for the whole length of their lives.

"Watch arm!"

Oreb's voice came on the land breeze, faint but shrill. Silk glanced up automatically at his own left hand, lifted nearly to the low dome as he leaned against one of the bent pillars; it was perfectly safe, of course.

He looked around for Oreb, but the bird seemed to have vanished in the jumble of naked rock inland.

Oreb was returning to the wild now, Silk told himself—to freedom, exactly as he himself had invited him to do on that first night. To think of the once-caged bird happy and free should not have been painful, yet it was.

Scanning the rocks for Oreb, he saw, from the corner of one eye, the delicately curved pillars nearest the entrance drop from the dome. One barred the entrance with a double *S*. The other reached for him, its sinuous motion seemingly casual and almost careless. He dodged and struck at it with Blood's walking stick.

Effortlessly, the pillar looped about his waist, a noose of stone. Blood's stick shattered at the third blow.

In the floor, Scylla opened stony lips; irresistibly the tentacle carried him toward her gaping mouth, and as he hung struggling above the dark orifice, dropped him into it.

The initial fall was not great; but it was onto carpeted steps, and he tumbled down them, rolling in wild confusion until he sprawled at last on a floor twenty or thirty cubits below the shrine, with sore knees and elbows and a bruised cheek.

"Oh, you gods!"

The sound of his voice brought light; there were large, comfortable-looking armchairs here, upholstered in brown and burnt orange, and a sizable table; but Silk gave them small attention, gripping his injured ankle in one hand while the other lashed the carpet with Crane's wrapping.

As though by a miracle, the circular panel of deep blue that was the farther end of the room irised wide, revealing a towering talus; its ogre's face was of black metal, and the slender black barrels of buzz guns flanked its gleaming fangs. *"You again!"* it roared.

The memory of Blood's blade-crowned wall returned—the still and sweltering night, the gate of thick-set bars, and this shouting giant of brass and steel. Silk shook his head as he replaced the wrapping; though it required an effort to keep his voice steady, he said loudly, "I've never been here before."

"I knew you!" Swiftly, the talus's left arm lengthened, reaching for him.

He scrambled up the carpeted stair. "I didn't want to come here! I wasn't trying to get in."

"I know you!"

A metal hand as large as a shovel closed on Silk's right forearm, clamping the injuries inflicted by the white-headed one; Silk screamed.

"Does this hurt you!"

"Yes," he gasped. "It hurts. Terribly. Please let me go. I'll do whatever you say."

The steel hand shook him. *"You don't care!"*

Silk screamed again, writhing in the grasp of fingers as thick as pipes. *"Musk punished me! Humiliated me!"*

The shaking stopped. The enormous mechanical arm lifted Silk, and, as he dangled puppylike in midair, contracted. Through chattering teeth, he gasped, "You're Blood's talus. You stopped me at his gate."

The steel hand opened, and he fell heavily to the floor. *"I was right!"*

The azoth he had carried from the city to the lake was no longer in his waistband. Striving to keep his voice from breaking, he said, "May I stand up?" hoping to feel it slip down his trouser leg.

"Musk sent me away!" the talus roared; grotesquely, its vertical upper body angled forward as it addressed him.

Silk stood, but the azoth was gone; it had been in place when he had admired the lake from the shrine, certainly; so it had presumably been lost in his fall, and might still be near the top of the stair.

He risked a cautious step backward. "I'm terribly sorry—really, I am. I don't have any influence with Musk, who dislikes me much more than he could ever dislike you. But I may have some small amount with Blood, and I'll do whatever I can to get you reinstated."

"No! You won't!"

"I will." Silk essayed another small backward step. "I will, I assure you."

"You soft things!" Noiselessly, and apparently without effort, the talus glided over the carpet on twin dark belts, the crest of its brazen helmet almost scraping the ceiling. *"You look the same because you are the same! Easy to break! No repair! Full of filth!"*

Still edging backward, Silk asked, "Were you in the shrine? Up there?"

"Yes! My processor by interface!"

Both the talus's steel hands reached for him this time, extended so swiftly that he escaped them by no more than the width of a finger. He stumbled backward, desperately pushed a heavy armchair into the path of one hand, and dove beneath the table.

It was lifted, rotated in the air, and slammed down flat to kill him as a man swats a fly; he rolled frantically to one side and felt the edge of its massive top brush the wide sleeve of his robe, the sudden gust as it crashed down.

Something lay on the floor, not a cubit from his face, a green crystal in a silver setting. He snatched it up as the talus snatched him up, holding him this time by the back of his robe, so that he dangled from its hand like a black moth caught by its sooty wings.

"Musk hurt me!" the talus roared. *"Hurt me and made me go! I returned to Potto! He was not pleased!"*

"I had nothing to do with that." Silk's voice was as soothing as he could make it. "I'll help you if I can—I swear it."

"You got inside! I was on guard!" It shook him. *"In the tunnel the red water won't matter!"*

It was backing through the irised wall with him, moving slowly but steadily, its arms retracting to bring him ever closer to its fearsome face.

"I don't want to hurt you," Silk told it. "It's evil—that means very wrong—to destroy chems, as wrong as it is to destroy bios, and you're very nearly a chem."

That halted it momentarily. *"Chems are junk!"*

"Chems are wonderful constructions, a race that we bios created long ago, our own image in metal and synthetics."

"Bios are fish guts!" The backward glide resumed.

Silk held the azoth firmly in his left hand, his thumb on the demon. "Please say that you won't kill me."

"No!"

"Let me return to the surface."

"No!"

"I'll do you no more harm, I swear; and I'll help you if I can."

"I will drop you and crush you!" the talus roared. *"One blow!"* The wall irised closed behind them, leaving them in a long, dim passageway, a little more than twice the talus's width, bored through the solid stone of the cliff.

"Don't you fear the immortal gods, my son?" Silk asked in desperation. "I'm the servant of one god and the friend of another."

"I serve Scylla!"

"As an augur, I receive the protection of all the gods, including hers."

The steel fingers shook him more violently than before, then released his robe; he fell, nearly losing his grip on the azoth as he struck the dark and dirty stone floor. Sprawling, half-blind with pain, he looked up into that ogre's mask of a metal face and glimpsed the steel fist lifted higher than its owner's head.

The wings of Hierax roared in his ears; without time to think, reason, threaten, or equivocate, he pressed the demon.

Stabbing out from the hilt, the azoth blade of universal discontinuity caught the talus below the right eye; jagged scraps of incandescent slag burst from the point it struck. The steel fist smashed down but appeared to lose direction as it descended, hammering the stone floor to his left.

Black smoke and crackling orange flames erupted from the mass of wreckage that had been the talus's head, and with them a deafening roar of rage and anguish. The great steel fists swung wildly, pounding flying chips as sharp as flints from the stone sides of the passageway. Eyeless and ablaze, the talus lurched toward him.

A single slash from the azoth severed both the wide dark belts on which it had moved; they lashed the floor, the walls, and the dying talus itself like whips, then fell limp. There was a muffled explosion; flames shot up from the wagonlike body behind the vertical torso.

Scrambling away from the heat and smoke, Silk released the demon, stood, thrust the azoth back into his waistband, dusted off his black robe, and got out his beads. Swinging their voided cross toward the burning talus, he traced the sign of addition again and again. "I convey to you, my son, the forgiveness of all the gods."

His chant was flat and almost mechanical at first, but as the wonder and magnanimity of divine amnesty filled his mind, his voice grew louder and shook with fervor. "Recall now the words of Pas, who said, 'Do my will, live in peace, multiply, and do not disturb my seal. Thus you shall escape my wrath. Go willingly, and any wrong that you have ever done shall be forgiven you. . . .' "

Incus returned Hyacinth's letter to Gulo with a smirk. Its new seal, similar though not identical to the original one, displayed a leaping flame between cupped hands. "Her full name would be *Hymenocallis,* I expect," Incus remarked. "Very pretty. I've used it a time or two myself."

"I didn't write it," Gulo told him sullenly. "But you're supposed to write to Patera Silk now, telling him to wait upon His Eminence Tarsday. You're to set the hour and mark it on His Eminence's regimen."

The buck-toothed prothonotary nodded. "You'll deliver it for us? I'd rather not have to whistle up another boy just now so old Remora can whip your randy cur to kennel."

Pudgy Patera Gulo advanced on him with clenched fists and reddening cheeks. "Patera Silk's a real man, you manse-wife. Whatever he may've done with this woman, he's worth a dozen of you and three of me. Remember that, and the proportion."

Incus grinned up at him. "Why Gully! You're in *love!*"

CHAPTER
8   FOOD FOR THE GODS

Patera Silk took two long steps back from the still tightly closed door and eyed it with the disgust he felt for himself and his failure. It opened in some fashion—the talus had opened it, after all. Open, it would give him access to the stair that led up to the floor of the cliff-top shrine, and from there it might be possible (might even be easy) to open the mouth of the image of Scylla graven in the floor above and so climb out into the shrine and return to Limna.

Commissioners, Silk told himself, and—what else had the woman said?—judges and the like came here, clearly to confer with the Ayuntamiento. Before he had killed it with the azoth—

(He had to force himself to face those words, although he had told himself repeatedly and with perfect truth that he had killed only to save his own life.)

Before he had killed it, the talus had said that having been discharged by Musk it had returned here to Potto; and by "Potto" it had intended Councillor Potto, surely.

Thus the figure who had entered the shrine and vanished had no doubt been a commissioner, a judge, or something of the sort. Nor was his disappearance at all mysterious: He had entered and been seen, presumably by the talus; possibly he had shown some sort of tessera; Scylla's mouth had opened for him, and he had descended the stair and been conducted to a location that could not be remote, since the talus had been back at its post a half hour later.

It was all perfectly logical and showed clearly that the Ayuntamiento had offices nearby. The realization bowed Silk's shoulders like a burden. How could he, a citizen and an augur, withhold all that he had learned about Crane's activities, even to save the manteion?

Heartsick, he turned back to the door that had opened so smoothly for the talus, but would not open at all for him. It appeared to have no lock, no handle, and in fact no mechanism of any kind to open it. Its irising plates were so tightly fitted that he could scarcely make out the curving lines between them. He had shouted *open* and a hundred other plausible words at it, without result.

Hoarse and discouraged, he had hewed and stabbed it with the shimmering discontinuity that was the blade of the azoth, scarring and fusing the plates until it was doubtful that even one who knew their secret could cause them to iris as they had for the talus. It had made an earsplitting racket, causing stones enough to drop from the walls and ceiling of the tunnel to have killed him ten times over, and at length it rendered the hilt of the azoth almost too hot to hold—all without opening the door or piercing even a single small hole in one plate.

And now there was, Silk told himself, no alternative but to set off, weary and hungry and bruised though he was, down the tunnel in the faint hope of finding some other place of egress. Ready almost to rage against the Outsider and every other god from sheer frustration, he sat down on the naked rock of the floor and removed Crane's wrapping. Crane, Silk recalled with some bitterness, had instructed him to beat only smooth surfaces with it, instancing his hassock or a carpet. No doubt Crane's recommendation had been intended to preserve the wrapping's soft, leather-like surface from needless wear; the rough floor hardly qualified, and he owed something to Crane, not least because he intended to extort the money Blood demanded from Crane if he could, though Crane had befriended him more than once.

Sighing, Silk took off his robe, folded it, laid it on the floor, and lashed the folded cloth until the wrapping felt hotter than the hilt of the azoth. When it was back in place, he climbed laboriously to his feet, put on his robe again (its warmth was welcome in the cool and ever-soughing air) and set out resolutely, choosing the direction that seemed most likely to bring him nearer Limna.

He began with the idea of counting his steps, so as to know how far he had traveled underground; he counted silently at first, moving his lips and extending a finger from his clenched fist at each hundred. Soon he found that he was counting aloud, comforted by the faint echo of his voice, and that he was no longer certain whether he had reclosed his fist once for five hundred steps or twice for a thousand.

The tunnel, which had appeared so unchanging, altered in minor ways as he progressed, and these soon became of such interest that he forgot his count in his hurry to examine them. In places the native freestone gave way to shiprock, graduated like a cubit stick by seams at intervals of twenty-three steps. Here and there the creeping sound-kindled lights failed entirely, so that he was forced to advance in the dark; and though he realized how foolish such fears were, he could not entirely dispel the thought that he might fall into a pit, or that another talus or something more fearsome still might await him in the dark. Twice he passed irising doors much like the one that had excluded him from the room beneath Scylla's shrine, both tightly closed; once the tunnel divided, and he followed the left at random; three times side tunnels, dark and somehow menacing, opened from the one he followed.

And always it seemed to him that it descended ever so slightly, and that its air grew cooler and its walls damper.

He prayed his beads as he walked, then tried to reconcile the distance covered during three recitals with his subsequent count of steps, eventually concluding that he had taken ten thousand, three hundred and seventy—or the equivalent of five complete recitals of his beads and an odd decade. To this, add the original five hundred (or possibly one thousand) making . . .

By that time his ankle was acutely painful; he renewed the wrapping as before and hobbled off down the tunnel again, which oppressed him more with each halting stride.

Frequently he was tormented by an almost uncontrollable urge to turn back. If he had allowed the azoth to cool and attacked the door again, it seemed to him almost certain that it would have given way easily; by now he would have been back in Limna. Auk had recommended eating places there; he tried to recall their names, and those of the ones he had passed while looking for the Juzgado.

No, it had been the driver of the wagon who had recommended eating places. One, he had said, was quite good but expensive; that had been the Rusty Lantern. He had no fewer than seven cards in his pocket, five from Orpine's rites, plus two of the three that Blood had surrendered to him on Phaesday. His dinner with Auk in an uphill eating house had cost Auk eighteen bits. It had seemed an extravagant sum then, but it was a small one compared to seven cards. A sumptuous dinner in Limna at one of the better inns, a comfortable bed, and a fine breakfast would leave him change from a single card. It seemed foolish not to turn back, when all these things were (or might so easily be made) so near. Half a dozen words that might open the door, all untried, occurred to him in quick succession: *free, disengage, separate, loose, dissolve,* and *cleave.*

Far worse was the unfounded feeling that he had already turned back, that he was walking not north toward Limna but south again, that at any minute, around any slight curve or turning, he would catch sight of the dead talus.

Of the talus he had killed; but the talus had, or so it seemed, sent him
to the grave. It was dead, he buried. Soon, he felt, he would encounter
Orpine, old Patera Pike, and his mother, each in the appropriate state of
decay. He and they would lie down together on the floor of the tunnel,
perhaps, one place being as good as another here, and they would tell
him the many things he would need to know among the dead, just as
Patera Pike had instructed him (when he had arrived at Sun Street)
concerning the shops and people of the quarter, the necessity of buying
one's tunics and turnips from those few shopkeepers who attended sacrifice with some regularity, and the need to beware of certain notorious
liars and swindlers. Once he heard a distant tittering, a lunatic laughter
without humor or merriment or even humanity: the laughter of a devil
devouring its own flesh in the dark.

After what seemed half a day or more of weary, frightened walking, he
reached a point at which the floor of the tunnel was covered with water
for as far as he could see, the dim reflections of the bleared lights that
crept along the ceiling showing plainly that the extent of the flood was by
no means inconsiderable. Irresolute at the brink of that clear, still pool,
he was forced to admit that it was even possible that the tunnel he had
followed so long was, within the next league or two, entirely filled.

He knelt and drank, discovering that he was very thirsty indeed. When
he tried to stand, his right ankle protested so vehemently that he sat
instead, no longer able to hide from himself how tired he was. He would
rest here for an hour; he felt certain that it was dark on the surface.
Patera Gulo would no doubt be wondering what had become of him,
eager to begin spying in earnest. Maytera Marble might be wondering
too; but Auk and Chenille would have gone back to the city some time
ago, after having left word for him at the wagon stop.

Silk took off his shoes and rubbed his feet (finding it a delightful
exercise), and at last lay down. The rough floor of the tunnel ought
certainly to have been uncomfortable, but somehow was not. He had
been wise, clearly, to take this opportunity to nap on the seat of Blood's
floater. He would be more alert, better able to grasp every advantage
that their peculiar relationship conferred, thanks to this brief rest. "Can't
float too fast," the driver told him, "not going *this* way!" But quite soon
now, as the swift floater sailed over a landscape grown liquid, his mother
would come to kiss him good-night; he liked to be awake for it, to say
distinctly, "Good night to you, too, Mama," when she left.

He resolved not to sleep until she came.

* * *

Weaving and more than half-drunk, Chenille emerged from the door of
the Full Sail, caught sight of Auk, and waved. "You there! You, Bucko.
Don't I know you?" When he smiled and waved in return, she crossed
the street and caught his arm. "You've been to Orchid's place. Sure you
have, lots, and I oughta know your name. It'll come to me in a minute.
Listen, Buck, I'm not queering a lay for you, am I?"

Auk had learned early in childhood to cooperate in such instances.
"Dimber with me. Stand you a glass?" He jerked his thumb toward the
Full Sail. "I bet there's a nice quiet corner in there?"

"Oh, Bucko, would you?" Chenille leaned upon his arm, walking so
close that her thigh brushed his. "Wha's your name? Mine's Chenille. I
oughta know yours too, course I should, only I got this queer head an'
we're at the lake, aren't we?" She blew her nose in her fingers. "All that
water, I seen it down one of these streets, Bucko, only I ought to get back
to Orchid's for dinner an' the big room after that, you know? She'll get
Bass to winnow me out if I'm not lucky."

Auk had been watching her eyes from the corner of his own; as they
entered the Full Sail, he said, "That's the lily word, ain't it, Jugs? You
don't remember."

She nodded dolefully as she sat down, her fiery curls trembling. "An'
I'm reedy, too—real reedy. You got a pinch for me?"

Auk shook his head.

"Just a pinch an' all night free?"

"I'd give it to you if I had it," Auk told her, "but I don't."

A frowning barmaid stopped beside their table. "Take her someplace
else."

"Red ribbon and water," Chenille told the barmaid, "and don't mix
them."

The barmaid shook her head emphatically. "I gave you more than I
should've already."

"An' I gave you all my money!"

He laid a card on the table. "You start a tab for me, darling. My
name's Auk."

The barmaid's frown vanished. "Yes, sir."

"And I'll have a beer, the best. Nothing for her."

Chenille protested.

"I said I'd buy you one in the street. We're not in the street." Auk
waved the barmaid away.

"That's your name!" Chenille was triumphant. "Auk. I told you I'd
think of it."

He leaned toward her. "Where's Patera?"

She wiped her nose on her forearm.

"Patera Silk. You come out here with him. What'd you do with him?"

"Oh, I remember him. He was at Orchid's when—when Auk, I need a pinch bad. You've got money. Please?"

"In a minute, maybe. I ain't got my beer. Now you pay attention to what I say. You sat in here awhile lapping up red ribbon, didn't you?"

Chenille nodded. "I felt so—"

"Up your flue." He caught her hand and squeezed hard enough to hurt. "Where were you before that?"

She belched softly. "I'll tell you the truth, the whole thing. Only it isn't going to make any sense. If I tell you, will you buy me one?"

His eyes narrowed. "Talk fast. I'll decide after I hear it."

The barmaid set a sweating glass of dark beer in front of him. "The best and the coldest. Anything else, sir?"

He shook his head impatiently.

"I got up shaggy late," Chenille began, " 'cause we'd had a big one last night, you know? Real big. Only you weren't there, Hackum. See, I remember you now. I wished you would have been."

Auk tightened his grip on her hand again. "I know I wasn't. Get naked."

"An' I had to dress up 'cause it was the funeral today an' Orchid wanted everybody to go. 'Sides, I'd told that long augur I would." She belched again. "Wha's his name, Hackum?"

"Silk," Auk said.

"Yeah, that's him. So I got out my good black dress, this one, see? An', you know, fixed up. There was a lot going together, only they'd already gone so I had to go by myself. Can't I have just one li'l sippy of that, Hackum? Please?"

"All right."

Auk pushed the sweating glass across the table to her, and she drank and wiped her mouth on her forearm. "You're not s'posed to mix them, are you? I better be careful."

He took back the glass. "You went to Orpine's funeral. Go on from that."

"That's right. Only I had a big pinch first, the last I had. Really sucked it up. I wish I had it back now."

Auk drank.

"Well, I got to the manteion, an' Orchid and everybody was already there an' they'd started, but I got a place an' sat down, an', an'—"

"And what?" Auk demanded.

"An' then I got up, but they were all gone. I was just looking at the Window, you know? But it was just a Window, and there wasn't anybody else in there hardly at all, only a couple old ladies, an' nobody or nothing anymore." She had started to cry, hot tears spilling down the broad flat cheeks. Auk pulled out a not-very-clean handkerchief and gave it to her. "Thanks." She wiped her eyes. "I was so scared, an' I still am. You think I'm scared of you, but it's just so nice to be with somebody an' have somebody to talk to. You don't know."

Auk scratched his head.

"An' I went outside, see? An' I wasn't in the city at all, not on Sun Street or any other place. I was way down here where we used to go when I was little, an' everybody gone. I found this place where they had awnings an' tables under them an' I had maybe three or four, and then this big black bird came, it kept hopping around and talking almost like a person till I threw this one little glass at it an' they made me get out."

Auk stood. "You hit it with that glass? Shag, no, you didn't. Come on. Show me where this place with the awnings is."

A steep hillside covered with brush barred Silk from the cenoby. He scrambled down it, scratching his hands and face and tearing his clothes on thorns and broken twigs, and went inside. Maytera Mint was in bed, sick, and he was briefly glad of it, having forgotten that no male was supposed to enter the cenoby save an augur to bring the pardon of the gods. He murmured their names again and again, each time sure that he had forgotten one, until a short plump student he never remembered from the schola arrived to tell him that they were all going down the street to call on the Prelate, who was also ill. Maytera Mint got out of bed, saying she would come too, but she was naked under her pink peignoir, her sleek metal body gleaming through it like silver. The peignoir carried the cloying perfume of the blue-glass lamp, and he told her she would have to dress before she could go.

He and the short, plump student left the cenoby. It was raining, a hard, cold, pounding rain that chilled him to the bone. A litter with six bearers was waiting in the street, and they discussed its ownership though he felt certain that it was Maytera Marble's. The bearers were all old, one was blind, and the dripping canopy was old, faded, and torn. He was ashamed to ask the old men to carry them, so they went up the street to a large white structure without walls whose roof was of thin white slats set on edge a hand's breadth apart; in it there was so much white furniture that there was scarcely room to walk. They chose chairs and sat down to wait. When the Prelate came, he was Mucor, Blood's mad daughter.

They sat in the rain with her, shivering, discussing the affairs of the schola. She spoke about a difficulty she could not resolve, blaming him for it.

He sat up cold and stiff, and crossed his arms to put his freezing fingers in his armpits. Mucor told him, "It's drier farther on. Meet me where the bios sleep." She was sitting cross-legged on the water, and like the water, transparent. He wanted to ask her to guide him to the surface; at the sound of his voice she vanished with the rest of his dream, leaving only a shimmer of greenish light like slime on the water.

If that still, clear water had receded while he slept, the change was not apparent. He took off his stockings, tied his shoes together by their laces and hung them around his neck, and stuffed the wrapping into the pocket of his robe. He knotted the corners of his robe about his waist and rolled his trousers legs as high as he could while promising himself that exercise would soon warm him, that he would actually be more comfortable once he entered the water and began to walk.

It was as cold as he had feared, but shallow. It seemed to him that its very frigidity, its icy slapping against his injured ankle, should numb it; each time he put his weight on it, a needle stabbed deep into the bone nevertheless.

The faint splashings of his bare feet woke more lights, enabling him to see a considerable distance down the tunnel, which was flooded as far as the light reached. He did not actually know that water would harm the wrapping, and in fact he did not really believe it likely—people clever enough to build such a device would surely be able to protect it from an occasional wetting. But the wrapping was Crane's and not his, and though he would steal Crane's money if he had to in order to preserve the manteion, he would not risk ruining Crane's wrapping to save himself a little pain.

He had walked some distance when it occurred to him that he could warm himself somewhat by re-energizing the wrapping and returning it to his pocket. He tried the experiment, slapping the wrapping against the wall of the tunnel. The result was eminently satisfactory.

He thought of Blood's lioness-headed walking stick with nostalgia; if he had it now, it would take some weight off his injured ankle. Half a day ago (or a little more, perhaps) he had been ready to throw it away, calling his act of contempt a sacrifice to Scylla. Oreb had been frightened by that, and Oreb had been right; the goddess had engaged and defeated that walking stick (and thus her sister Sphigx) when he had brought it into her shrine.

His feet disturbed a clump of shining riparial worms, which scattered in all directions flashing tidings of fear in pale, luminous yellow. The water was deeper here, the gray shiprock walls dark with damp.

On the other hand, the talus he had killed had professed to serve Scylla; but that boast presumably meant no more than that it served Viron, Scylla's sacred city—as did he, for that matter, since he hoped to end Crane's activities. More realistically, the talus had unquestionably been a servant of the Ayuntamiento. It had been Councillor Lemur who had built the shrine; and thus, almost certainly, it was the councillors who met with commissioners and judges in the room below it. This though they must surely come to the Juzgado (the real one in Viron, as Silk thought of it) from time to time. He had seen a picture of Councillor Loris addressing a crowd from the balcony not long ago.

And the talus had said that it had returned to Potto.

Silk halted, balancing himself on his sound foot, and slapped the wrapping against the wall of the tunnel again.

If, however, the talus served the Ayuntamiento (and so by a permissible exaggeration Scylla), what had it been doing at Blood's villa? Mucor had indicated not only that it was his employee, but that it might be corrupted.

This time Silk wound the wrapping around his chest under his tunic, finding that it did not constrict sufficiently to make it difficult for him to breathe.

At first Silk thought the flashes of pain from his ankle had somehow affected his hearing. The roar increased, and a pinpoint of light appeared far down the tunnel. There was no place to run, even if he had been capable of running, no place to hide. He flattened himself as much as he could against the wall, Hyacinth's azoth in his hand.

The point of light became a glare. The machine racing toward him held its head low, like that of an angry dog. It roared past, drenching him with icy water, and vanished in the direction from which he had come.

He fled, splashing through water that grew deeper and deeper, and saw the steeply rising side tunnel at the same moment that he heard a roar and clatter behind him.

A hundred long and exquisitely painful strides carried him clear of the water; but he did not sit down to rewrap his ankle and resume his shoes and stockings until distance had taken him out of sight of the tunnel he had left. He heard something—he assumed it was the same machine— roar along it once more and listened fearfully, half-convinced that it would turn down this new tunnel. It did not, and soon its clamor faded away.

Now, he told himself, his luck had changed. Or rather, some gracious god had decided to favor him. Perhaps Scylla had forgiven him for bringing her sister's walking stick into her shrine and for proposing to cast it into the lake as a sacrifice to herself. This tunnel could not go far, rising as it did, before it must necessarily reach the surface; and it seemed certain to do so near Limna, if not actually within the village itself. Furthermore, it was above the level of the water, and seemed likely to remain so.

Having put the azoth back into his waistband, he rolled down his trousers legs and untied his robe.

He was no longer counting steps, but he had not gone far before his nose detected the unmistakable tang of wood smoke. It couldn't really be (he told himself) the odor of sacrifice, the fragrant smoke of cedar blended with the pungent smells of burning flesh, fat, and hair. And yet —he sniffed again—it was uncannily like it, so much so that for a moment or two he wondered whether there might not be an actual sacrifice in progress here in these ancient tunnels.

As he approached the next bleared and greenish light, he noticed footprints on the tunnel floor. The tracks of a man, shod as he was, left in a faint, gray deposit that his fingers easily wiped away.

Was it possible that he had been walking in a circle? He shook his head. This tunnel had been climbing steeply from its beginning; and as he scanned the footprints and compared them to his own, he saw that it could not be true: the steps were shorter than his, this walker had not limped, and the shoes that had made them had been somewhat smaller; nor were their heels badly worn at the outside like his own.

The light by which he studied them appeared to be the last for some distance—the tunnel ahead looked as black as pitch. He searched his mind, then each pocket in turn, for some means of creating light, coughed, and found none. He had Hyacinth's azoth and her needler, the seven cards and a quantity of bits he had never counted, his beads, his old pen case (containing several quills, a small bottle of ink, and two folded sheets of paper) his glasses, his keys, and the gammadion his mother had given him, hanging from his neck on a silver chain.

He sneezed.

The reek of smoke had increased, and now his feet were sinking into some soft, dry substance; moreover he saw, not more than a few steps ahead, a fleck of dull red such as he had only too seldom observed in the firebox of the kitchen stove. It was an ember, he felt sure; when he reached it, went to his knees in the dark invisible softness, and blew gently, he knew that he had been correct. He twisted one of the sheets from his pen case into a spill and applied its end to the brightened ember.

Ashes.

Ashes everywhere. He stood upon the lowest slope of a great gray drift that blocked the tunnel entirely on one side, and on the other rose so high that he would be forced to stoop if he was not to knock his head against the ceiling.

He hurried forward, anxious to pass that narrow opening (as the earlier walker, who had left tracks there, had done) before the feeble yellow flame from the spill flickered out. It was difficult going; he sank in ash nearly to his knees at every step, and the fine haze that his hurrying feet stirred up clutched at his throat.

He sneezed again, and this time his sneeze was answered by an odd, low stridulation, louder and deeper than the noise of even a very large broken clock, yet something akin to it.

The flame of the spill was almost touching his fingers; he shifted his hold on the spill and puffed its flame higher, then dropped it, having seen its glow reflected in four eyes.

He shouted as he sometimes shouted at rats in the manse, snatched the azoth from his waistband, waved its deadly blade in the direction of the eyes, and was rewarded by a shriek of pain. It was quickly followed by the boom of a slug gun and a soft avalanche of ash that left him half buried.

The slug gun spoke again, its hollow report evoking a half-human screech. A strong light pierced swirling clouds of ash, and a creature that seemed half dog and half devil fled past him, stirring up more ash. As soon as he could catch his breath he shouted for help; minutes passed before two soldiers, thick-limbed chems two full heads taller than he, found him and jerked him unceremoniously out of the ash.

"You're under arrest," the first told him, shining his light in Silk's face. It was not a lantern or a candle, or any other portable lighting device with which Silk was familiar; he stared at it, much too interested to be frightened.

"Who are you?" asked the second.

"Patera Silk, from the manteion on Sun Street." Silk sneezed yet again while trying hopelessly to brush the ash from his clothes.

"You come down the chute, Patera? Put your hands where I can see them. Both hands."

He did so, displaying their palms to show that both were empty.

"This is a restricted area. A military area. What are you doing here, Patera?"

"I'm lost. I hoped to speak to the Ayuntamiento about a spy some foreign city has sent into Viron, but I got lost in these tunnels. And then—" Silk paused, at a loss for words. "Then all this."

The first soldier said, "They send for you?" And the second, "Are you armed?"

"They didn't send for me. Yes, I've got a needler in my trousers pocket." Inanely he added, "A very small one."

"You planning to shoot us with it?" The first soldier sounded amused.

"No. I was concerned about the spy I told you about. I believe he may have confederates."

The first soldier said, "Pull out that needler, Patera. We want to see it."

Reluctantly, Silk displayed it.

The soldier turned his light upon his own mottled steel chest. "Shoot me."

"I'm a loyal citizen," Silk protested. "I wouldn't want to shoot one of our soldiers."

The soldier thrust the gaping muzzle of his slug gun at Silk's face. "You see this? It shoots a slug of depleted uranium as long as my thumb and just about as big around. If you won't shoot me, I'm going to shoot you, and mine will blow your head apart like a powder can. Now shoot."

Silk fired; the crack of the needler seemed loud in the tunnel. A bright scratch appeared on the soldier's massive chest.

"Again."

"What would be the point?" Silk dropped the needler back into his pocket.

"I was giving you another chance, that's all." The first soldier handed his light to the second. "All right, you've had your turn. Give it to me."

"So that you can shoot me with it? It would kill me."

"Maybe not. Hand it over, and we'll see."

Silk shook his head. "You said I was under arrest. If I am, you have to send for an advocate, provided I wish to engage one. I do. His name is

Vulpes, and he has chambers on Shore Street in Limna, which can't be far from here."

The second soldier chuckled, a curiously inhuman sound like a steel rule run along the teeth of a rack. "Leave him alone, corporal. I'm Sergeant Sand, Patera. Who's this spy you were talking about?"

"I prefer to reserve that unless asked by a member of the Ayuntamiento."

Sand leveled his slug gun. "Bios like you die all the time down here, Patera. They wander in and most of them never get out. I'll show you one in a minute, if you're not dead yourself. They die and they're eaten, even the bones. Maybe there's scraps of clothes, maybe not. That's the truth, and for your sake you'd better believe me."

"I do." Silk rubbed his palms on his thighs to get off as much ash as he could.

"Our standing orders are to kill anybody who endangers Viron. If you know about a spy and won't tell us, that's you, and you're no better than a spy yourself. Do you understand what I'm telling you?"

Silk nodded reluctantly.

"Corporal Hammerstone was playing with you. He wouldn't really have shot you, just roughed you up a little. I'm not playing." Sand pushed off the safety of his slug gun with an audible click. "Name the spy!"

It was difficult for Silk to make himself speak: another moral capitulation in what seemed to be an endless series of such capitulations. "His name is Crane. Doctor Crane."

Hammerstone said, "Maybe he heard it too."

"I doubt it. What time did you come down here, Patera? Any idea?"

Doctor Crane would be arrested, and eventually shot or sent to the pits; Silk recalled how Crane had winked, pointing to the ceiling as he said, "Somebody up there likes you, some infatuated goddess, I should imagine." At which he, Silk, had known that Hyacinth had provided the object Crane had passed to him, and guessed that it was her azoth.

Sand said, "Make a guess if you can't be sure, Patera. This's Molpsday, pretty late. About when was it?"

"Shortly before noon, I believe—perhaps about eleven. I'd ridden the first wagon from Viron, and I must have spent at least an hour in Limna before I started up the Pilgrims' Way to Scylla's shrine."

Hammerstone asked, "Did you use the glass there?"

"No. Is there one? If there is, I didn't see it."

"Under the plaque that tells who built it. You lift it up and there's a glass."

Sand said, "What he's getting at, Patera, is that some news came over our glass at Division Headquarters before we jumped off tonight. It seems like Councillor Lemur caught himself a spy, in person. A doctor called Crane."

"Why, that's wonderful!"

Sand cocked his head. "What is? Finding out that you came down here for nothing?"

"No, no! It's not that." For the first time since Oreb had left him, Silk smiled. "That it won't be my fault. That it isn't. I felt it was my duty to tell somebody everything I'd learned—someone in authority, who could take action. I knew Crane would suffer as a result. That he'd probably die, in fact."

Sand said almost gently, "He's just a bio, Patera. You get built inside each other, so there's millions of you. One more or less doesn't matter." He started back up the hill of ash, sinking deeply at every step but making steady progress in spite of it. "Fetch him along, Corporal."

Hammerstone prodded Silk with the barrel of his slug gun. "Get moving."

One of the doglike creatures lay bleeding in the ash less than a chain from the point at which the soldiers had found Silk, too weak to stand but not too weak to snarl. Silk asked, "What is that?"

"A god. The things that eat you bios down here."

Staring down at the dying animal, Silk shook his head. "The impious harm no one but themselves, my son."

"Get going, Patera. You're an augur, don't you sacrifice to the gods every week?"

"More often, if I can." The ash made it increasingly difficult to walk.

"Uh-huh. What about the leftovers? What do you do with them?"

Silk glanced back at him. "If the victim is edible—as most are—its flesh is distributed to those who have attended the ceremony. Surely you've been to at least one sacrifice, my son."

"Yeah, they made us go." Shifting his slug gun to his left hand, Hammerstone offered Silk his right arm. "Here, hang on. What about the other stuff, Patera? The hide and head and so forth, and the ones you won't eat?"

"They are consumed by the altar fire," Silk told him.

"And that sends them to the gods, right?"

"Symbolically, yes."

Another doglike animal lay dead in the ash; Hammerstone kicked it as he passed. "Your little fires aren't really up to it, Patera. They're not big enough or hot enough to burn up the bones of a big animal. Sometimes they don't even burn up all the meat. All that stuff gets dumped down here with the ashes. When they build a manteion, they try to put it on top of one of these old tunnels, so there's a place to get rid of the ashes. There's a manteion in Limna, see? We're right under it. Up around the city, there's a lot more places like this, and a lot more gods."

Silk swallowed. "I see."

"Remember those we chased off? They'll be back as soon as we're out of here. We'll hear them laughing and fighting over the good parts."

Sand had halted some distance ahead. He called, "Hurry it up, Corporal."

Silk, who was already walking as fast as he could, tried to go faster still; Hammerstone murmured, "Don't worry about that, he does it all day. That's how you get stripes."

They had almost reached Sand before Silk realized that the shapeless gray bundle at Sand's feet was a human being. Sand pointed with his slug gun. "Have a look, Patera. Maybe you knew him."

Silk knelt beside the body and lifted one mangled hand, then tried to scrape the caked ash away from the place where a face should have been; there were only shreds of flesh and splinters of bone beneath it. "It's gone!" he exclaimed.

"Gods can do that. They tear the whole thing off with one bite, the way I'd pull off my faceplate, or maybe you'd bite into a . . . What do you call those things?"

Silk rose, rubbing his hands in a desperate effort to get them clean. "I'm afraid I don't know what you mean."

"The round red things from the trees. Apples, that's it. Aren't you going to bless him or something?"

"Bring him the Pardon of Pas, you mean. We can do that only before death is complete—before the last cells of the body die, technically. Did you kill him?"

Sand shook his head. "I won't lie to you, Patera. If we'd seen him and yelled for him to halt, and he had run, we would've shot him. But we didn't. He had a lantern, it's over there someplace. And a needler. I've got that now. So he probably figured he'd be all right. But there must have been gods hanging around here like there always are. It's always pretty dark here, too, because ash gets on the lights. Maybe his lantern blew out, or maybe the gods got extra hungry and rushed him."

Hammerstone grunted his assent. "This isn't a good place for bios, Patera, like the sergeant said."

"He should be buried at least," Silk told them. "I'll do it, if you'll let me."

"If you were to bury him in these ashes, the gods would dig him up as soon as we were gone," Sand said.

"You could carry him. I've heard that you soldiers are a great deal stronger than we are."

"I could make you carry him, too," Sand told Silk, "but I'm not going to do that, either." He turned and strode away.

Hammerstone followed him, calling over his shoulder, "Get going, Patera. You can't help her now, and neither can we."

Suddenly fearful of being left behind, Silk broke into a limping trot. "Didn't you say it was a man?"

"The sergeant did, maybe. I went through her pockets, and she seemed like a woman in man's clothes."

Half to himself, Silk said, "There was someone in front of me on the Pilgrims' Way, only about half an hour ahead of me then. I stopped and slept awhile—I really can't say how long. She didn't, I suppose."

Hammerstone threw back his head in a grin. "My last nap was seventy-four years, they tell me. Back at Division, I could show you a couple hundred replacements that haven't ever been awake. Some of you bios, too."

Recalling the words Mucor had spoken in his dream, Silk said, "Please do. I'd like very much to see them, my son."

"Get a move on, then. The major may want to lock you up. We'll see."

Silk nodded, but stopped for a moment to look behind him. The name-less corpse was merely a shapeless bundle again, its identity—even its identity as the mortal remains of a human being—lost in the darkness that had rushed back even faster than the misshapen animals the soldiers called gods. Silk thought of Patera Pike's death, alone in the bedroom next to his own, an old man's peaceful death, a silent and uncontested cessation of breath. Even that had seemed terrible; how much worse, how unspeakably horrible, to die in this buried maze of darkness and decay, these wormholes in the whorl.

CHAPTER 9 IN DREAMS LIKE DEATH

"Patera Silk went this way?" Auk asked the night chough on his shoulder.

"Yes, yes!" Oreb fluttered urgently. "From here! Go shrine!"

"Well, I'm not going," Chenille told them.

An old woman who happened to be passing the first white stone that marked the Pilgrims' Way ventured timidly, "Hardly anyone goes out there after dark, dear, and it will be dark soon."

"Dark good," Oreb announced with unshakable conviction. "Day bad. Sleep."

The old woman tittered.

"A friend of ours went out to the shrine earlier," Auk explained. "He hasn't come back."

"Oh, my!"

Chenille asked, "Is there something out there that eats people? This crazy bird says the shrine ate him."

The old woman smiled, her face breaking into a thousand cheerful creases. "Oh, no, dear. But you can fall. People do almost every year."

"See?" Chenille shrilled. "You can hike half to shaggy Hierax through those godforsaken rocks if you want to. I'm going back to Orchid's."

Auk caught her wrist and twisted her arm until she fell to her knees.

Awed, Silk stared up at the banked racks of gray steel. Half, perhaps, were empty; the remainder held soldiers, each lying on his back with his arms at his sides, as if sleeping or dead.

"Back when this place was built, it was under the lake," Corporal Hammerstone told Silk conversationally. "No going straight down if somebody wanted to take it, see? And pretty tough to figure out exactly where it was. They'd have to come quite a ways through the tunnels, and there's places where twenty tinpots could stand off an army."

Silk nodded absently, still mesmerized by the recumbent soldiers.

"You'd think the water'd leak inside here, but it didn't. There's lots of solid rock up there. We got four big pumps to send it back if it did, and three of them haven't ever run. I was pretty surprised to find out the lake had gone over the hill on us when I woke up, but it'd still be a dirty job to take this place. I wouldn't want to be one of them."

"You slept here like this for seventy-five years?" Silk asked him.

"Seventy-four, the last time. All these been awake some time, like me. But if you want to keep going, I'll show you some that never was yet. Come on."

Silk followed him. "There must be thousands."

"About seven thousand of us left now. The way he set it up, see, when we come here from the Short Sun, was for all the cities to be independent. Pas figured that if somebody had too much territory, he'd try to take over Mainframe, the superbrain that astrogates and runs the ship."

Somewhat confused, Silk asked, "Do you mean the whole whorl?"

"Yeah, right. The *Whorl*. So what he did, see—if you ask me, this was pretty smart—was to give every city a heavy infantry division, twelve thousand tinpots. For a big offensive you want armor and air and armored infantry and all that junk. But for defense, heavy infantry and lots of it. Bust the *Whorl* up into a couple of hundred cities, give each of them a division to defend it, and the whole thing ought to stay put, no matter what some crazy caldé someplace tries to do. So far it's held for three hundred years, and like I said, we've still got over half our strength fit for duty."

Silk was happy to be able to contribute some information of his own. "Viron doesn't have a caldé anymore."

"Yeah, right." Hammerstone sounded uneasy. "I heard. It's kind of a shag-up, because standing orders say that's who we're supposed to get our orders from. The major says we got to obey the Ayuntamiento for now, but nobody really likes it much. You know about standing orders, Patera?"

"Not really." Silk had lagged behind him to count the levels in a rack: twenty. "Sand said something about them, I think."

"You've got them too," Hammerstone told him. "Watch this."

He aimed a vicious left cross at Silk's face. Silk's hands flew up to protect it, but the oversized steel fist stopped a finger's width short of them.

"See that? Your standing orders say your hands got to protect your clock, just like ours say we've got to protect Viron. You can't change them or get rid of them, even if maybe somebody else could do it by messing around inside of your head."

"A need to worship is another of those standing orders," Silk told the soldier slowly. "It is innate in man that he cannot help wanting to thank the immortal gods, who give him all that he possesses, even life. You and your sergeant saw fit to disparage our sacrifices, and I will very willingly grant that they're pitifully inadequate. Yet they satisfy, to a considerable degree, that otherwise unmet need, for the community as well as for many individuals."

Hammerstone shook his head. "It's pretty hard for me to picture Pas biting into a dead goat, Patera."

"But is it hard for you to picture him being made happy, in a very minor fashion, by that concrete evidence that we have not forgotten him? That we—even the people of my own quarter, who are so poor—are eager to share such food as we have with him?"

"No, I can see that all right."

"Then we have nothing to argue about," Silk told him, "because that is what I see, too, applied not only to Pas but to all the other gods, the remaining gods of the Nine, the Outsider, and all the minor deities."

Hammerstone stopped and turned to face Silk, his massive body practically blocking the aisle. "You know what I think you're doing now, Patera?"

Silk, who had finished speaking before he fully realized what he had said—that he had just refused to number the Outsider among the minor gods—felt certain he was about to be charged with heresy. He could only mumble, "No. I've no idea."

"I think you're practicing what you're going to tell the brass on me. How you're going to try to get them to let you go. Maybe you don't know it, but I think that's what it is."

"Perhaps I was trying to justify myself," Silk conceded with an immense sense of relief, "but that doesn't show what I said to be false, nor does it prove me insincere in saying it."

"I guess not."

"Do you believe that they will?"

"I dunno, Patera. Neither does Sand." Hammerstone threw back his head in a grin. "That's why he's letting me show you around like this, see? If he'd of been sure the brass would turn you loose, he'd of turned you loose himself and not said nothing. Or if he was sure they'd lock you up, he'd have you locked up right now, sitting in the dark in a certain room we got, with maybe a swell bottle of water 'cause he likes you. But you were talking about how we had to send for your advocate, and Sand's not sure what the major's going to say, so he let you clean up a little and he's treating you nice while I keep an eye on you."

"He allowed me to keep my needler as well—or rather, the one a kind friend lent me, which was very good of him." Silk hesitated, and when he spoke again did so only because his conscience demanded it. "Perhaps I shouldn't say this, my son, but haven't you told me a great deal that a spy would wish to know? I'm not a spy but a loyal citizen, as I said earlier; and because I am, it disturbs me that an actual spy could learn some of the things I have. That our army numbers seven thousand, for example."

Hammerstone leaned against a rack. "Don't overheat. If I was just some dummy, you think I'd be awake pulling C.Q.? All that I've told you is that taking this place would be holy corrosion. Let the spies go back home and tell their bosses that. Viron don't care. And I've not just told you, I'm flat *showing* you, that Viron's got seven thousand tinpots it can call on any day of the week. No other city in this part of the *Whorl*'s got more than half that, from what we hear. So they better leave Viron alone, and if Viron says spit oil, they better spit far."

"Then the things you've told me should not endanger me further?" Silk asked.

"Not a drip. Still want to see the replacements?"

"Certainly, if you're still willing to show them to me. May I ask why you're concerned about spies at all, when you don't object to someone who might be a spy—I repeat that I am not—touring this facility?"

"Because this isn't what the spies are looking for. If it was, we'd just trot them around and send them back. What they want to know is where our government's got to."

Silk looked at him inquiringly. "Where the Ayuntamiento meets?"

"For now, yeah."

"It would seem to me that it would be even more heavily defended than this headquarters is. If so, what would be the point?"

"It is," Hammerstone told him, "only not the same way. If it was, that would make it easy to spot. You've seen me and you've seen the sergeant. You figure we're real tough metal, Patera?"

"Very much so."

Hammerstone lifted a most impressive fist. "Think you might whip me?"

"Of course not. I'm well aware that you could kill me very quickly, if you wished."

"Maybe you know a bio that you think could do it?"

Silk shook his head. "The most formidable bio I know is my friend Auk. Auk's somewhat taller than I am, and a good deal more strongly built. He's an experienced fighter, too; but you would defeat him with ease, I'm sure."

"In a fistfight? You bet I would. I'd break his jaw with my first punch. And you remember this." Hammerstone pointed to the bright scratch left by Hyacinth's needler on his camouflaged chest. "But what about if we both had slug guns?"

Diplomatically, Silk ventured, "I don't believe that Auk owns one."

"Supposing Viron hands him one with a box of ammo."

"In that case, I would imagine that it would be largely a matter of luck."

"Does this Auk that you know have many friends besides you, Patera?"

"I'm sure he must. There's a man named Gib—a larger man even than Auk, now that I come to think of it. And one of our sibyls is certainly Auk's friend."

"We'll leave her out. Suppose I had to fight you and Auk and this other bio Gib, and all three of you had slug guns."

Still anxious not to offend, Silk said, "I would think that any outcome would be possible."

Hammerstone straightened up and took a step toward Silk, looming above him. "You're right. Maybe I'd kill all three of you, or maybe you'd kill me and never get a scratch doing it. But what would you say's most likely? I'm telling you right now that if you lie to me, I'm not going to be as nice to you as I been up till now, and you best think some about that before you answer. So what about it? The three of you against me, and we've all got guns."

Silk shrugged. "If you wish. I certainly don't know a great deal about fighting, but it would seem to me probable that you would kill one or two of us, but that you would be killed yourself—in the process, so to speak."

Hammerstone threw back his head in another grin. "You don't scare easy, do you, Patera?"

"On the contrary, I'm a rather timid man. I was quite frightened when I said that—as I still am—but it was what you had asked me for, the truth."

"How many bios in Viron, Patera?"

"I don't know." Silk paused, stroking his cheek. "What an interesting question! I've never actually thought about it."

"You're a smart man, I've seen that already, and it's been a long time since I spent much time in the city. How many would you say?"

Silk continued to stroke his cheek. "Ideally we—the Chapter, I mean

—would like to have a manteion for each five thousand residents, and these days nearly all of those residents would be bios—there are a few chems left, of course, but the number is probably less than one in twenty. I believe that there are a hundred and seventeen manteions in current operation. That was the figure, at least, when I was at the schola."

"Five hundred and fifty-five thousand, seven hundred and fifty," Hammerstone told him.

"But the actual ratio is much higher. Certainly over six thousand, and perhaps as high as eight or nine."

"All right, let's say six thousand bios," Hammerstone decided, "since you sound pretty sure it's more than that. That's seven hundred and two thousand bios. Suppose that half are sprats, all right? And half the rest are females, and not enough of them will fight to make much difference. That leaves a hundred and seventy-five thousand five hundred males. Say half those are too old or too sick, or they run off. That's eighty-seven thousand seven hundred and fifty. You see what I'm getting at, Patera?"

Bewildered by the deluge of figures, Silk shook his head.

"You and me said three to one would probably end up with me dead. All right, eighty-seven thousand seven hundred and fifty against thirty-five hundred tinpots, which is about what we think Wick's got, just to grab a for instance, makes it about twenty-five to one."

"I believe I'm beginning to understand," Silk said.

Hammerstone aimed a finger as thick as a crowbar at his face. "That's everybody that'll fight. Take just the Guard. Five brigades?"

"They're forming a new one," Silk told him, "a reserve brigade, which will make six."

"Six brigades, with four or maybe five thousand troopers in each of them. So what matters if there's a new war soon, Patera? Us tinpots, or the Ayuntamiento, that gives the Guard its orders and could pass out slug guns to half the bios in Viron if it wanted to?"

Lost in thought, Silk did not reply.

"You know now, Patera, and so do we. These days we're an elite corps, where we used to be the whole show. Come on, I want to show you those replacements."

At the back of that wide and lofty arsenal, in the racks nearest the rear wall, lay soldiers swaddled in dirty sheets of polymer, their limbs smeared with some glutinous brownish black preservative. Full of wonder, Silk stooped to examine the nearest, blowing at the dust and cobwebs, and (when that proved insufficient) wiping them away with his sleeve.

"One company," Hammerstone announced with casual pride, "still exactly like they came out of Final Assembly."

"He's never spoken a word, or . . . or sat up and looked around? Not in three hundred years?"

"A little longer than that. They were stockpiling us for maybe twenty years before we ever went on board."

This man had come into being at about the same time as Maytera Marble, Silk reflected—had come to be at the same time that Hammerstone himself had, for that matter. Now she was old and worn and not far from death; but Hammerstone was still young and strong, and this man still unborn.

"We could wake him up right now," Hammerstone explained, "just yell in his ear a little and beat on his chest. Don't do it though."

"I won't." Silk straightened up. "That would start his mental processes?"

"They're started already, Patera. They had to do that at Final Assembly to make sure everything worked. So they just left them on. Only turned way down, if you know what I mean, so there's practically no reduction in parts life at all. He knows we're here, kind of. He's listening to us talking, but it doesn't mean a lot to him and he won't think about it. The good thing is that if there's ever an emergency like a fire in here, he'd wake up, and he'd have his Standing Orders."

"There's a question about all those things you told me earlier that I'm anxious to ask you," Silk said. "Several questions, really, and I hope very much that you won't be angry, although you may consider them impolite; but before I do, is it the same for all these other soldiers sleeping in these racks?"

"Not exactly." Hammerstone sounded troubled, reminding Silk of his dissatisfaction with the Ayuntamiento. "When you've been awake for a while it's harder to shut down. I guess because there's so much more that's got started up. You know what I mean?"

Silk nodded. "I think so."

"At first it just seems to you like you're just lying there. You think something's wrong and you're not going to sleep at all and you might as well get up. You never quite do, but that's how you think. So then you think, well, I got nothing better to do, so I'll just go over some the best stuff that happened, like the time Schist got the shell in backwards. And it goes on like that, except that after a while it's not quite the way it really happened, and maybe you're somebody else." Hammerstone made an odd, unfinished gesture. "I can't really explain it."

"On the contrary," Silk told him, "I would say you've explained it very well indeed."

"And it keeps getting darker. There's something else I wanted to show you, Patera. Come on, we got to follow this back wall a ways to see it."

"Just a moment, please, my son." Silk put his right foot on the lowest transverse bar of the rack and unwound Crane's wrapping. "May I ask those questions I mentioned while I take care of this?"

"Sure. Shoot."

"Some time ago, you mentioned a major who would decide whether to put me under arrest. I assume that he's the highest-ranking officer awake?"

Hammerstone nodded. "He's the real C.Q., the Officer in Charge of Quarters. The sergeant and me and all the rest of us are really the O.C.Q.'s detail. But we say we're on C.Q. It's just the way everybody talks about it."

"I understand. My question is why is this major—or any officer—an officer, while you're a corporal? Why is Sand a sergeant, for that matter? It seems to me that all of you soldiers should be interchangeable."

Hammerstone stood silent and motionless for so long that Silk became embarrassed. "I apologize, my son. I was afraid that was going to sound insulting, although it wasn't intended to be, and it emerged worse even than I had feared. I withdraw the question."

"It isn't that, Patera. It's just that I was thinking everything over before I shot off my mouth. It's not like there was only the one answer."

"I don't even require one," Silk assured him. "It was an idle and ill-advised question, one that I should never have asked."

"To start with, you're right. Just about all the basic hardware's the same, but the software's different. There's a lot that a corporal has to know that a major doesn't need, and probably the other way 'round, too. You ever notice the way I talk? I don't sound exactly like you do, do I? But we're both of us speaking the same shaggy language, begging your pardon, Patera."

Silk said carefully, "I haven't noticed your diction as being in any way odd or unusual, but now that you've called my attention to it, you're undoubtedly correct."

"See? You talk kind of like an officer, and they don't talk as good as privates and corporals do, or even as good as sergeants. They use a lot more words, and longer words, and nothing's ever said as clear as a corporal would say it. Why is that? All right, next time there's a war, Sand and me are going to be doing this and that with Guards, privates, corporals, and sergeants, won't we? Maybe showing them where we want their buzz guns set up and things like that. So we got to talk like they do, so they'll understand and so we'll both be fighting the enemy and not each other. For the major, it's the same thing with officers, so he has to talk like them. And he does. You ever tried to talk like I do, Patera?"

Silk nodded, shamefaced. "It was a lamentable failure, I'm afraid."

"Right. Well, the major can't talk like me either, and I can't talk like him. For either of us to do it, we'd have to have software for both speech patterns. Trouble is, our heads won't hold all the crap that's floating around, see? We only got so much room up there, just like you do, so we can't spare the extra space. Out where the iron flies, that means the major wouldn't make as good a corporal as me, and I wouldn't make as good a major as him."

Silk nodded. "Thank you. I feel better now about the way I speak."

"Why's that?"

"It's troubled me up until now that the people of our quarter don't speak as I do, and that I can't speak as they do. After hearing you, I realize that all is as it should be. They live—if I may put it so—where the iron flies. They cannot afford to waste a moment, and though they need not deal with the complexities of abstract thought, they dare not be misunderstood. I, however, am their legate—their envoy to the wealthier levels of our society, where lives are more leisured, but where the need to deal with complexities and abstractions is far more frequent and the penalties for being misunderstood are not nearly so great. Thus I speak as I must if I am to serve the people that I represent."

Hammerstone nodded. "I think I get you, Patera. And I think you get me. All right, there's other stuff, too, like A.I. You know about that? What it means?"

"I'm afraid I've never heard the term." Silk had been slapping Crane's wrapping against one of the rack's upright members. He put his foot on the transverse beam again and rewound the wrapping.

"It's just fancy talk for learning stuff. Everything I do, I learn a little better from doing it. Suppose I take a shot at one of those gods. If I miss it, I learn something from missing. If I hit it, I learn from that, too. So my shooting gets better all the time, and I don't waste shells firing at stuff I'm not going to hit except from dumb luck. You do the same thing."

"Of course."

"Nope! That's where you're wrong, Patera." Hammerstone waggled his big steel forefinger in Silk's face. "There's a lot that don't. Take a floater. It knows about not going too fast south, but it never does learn what it can float over and what it can't. The driver's got to learn about that for it. Or take a cat now. You ever try to teach a cat anything?"

"No," Silk admitted. "However I have—I ought to say I had—a bird that certainly appeared to learn. He learned my name and his own, for example."

"I'm talking cats particularly. Back in the second year against Urbs, I found this kitty in a knocked-out farmhouse, and I kept her awhile just so's to have something to talk to and scrounge for. It was kind of nice, sometimes."

"I know precisely what you mean, my son."

"Well, we had a big toss gun sighted in up on a hilltop that summer, and when the battle got going we were firing it as fast as you ever seen anything like that done in your life, and the lieutenant hollering all the time for us to go faster. A couple times we had eight or nine rounds in the air at once. You ever man a toss gun, Patera?"

Silk shook his head.

"All right, suppose you just go up to one and open up the breech, cold, and shove a H.E. round in there, and shoot it off. Then you open the breech again and out comes the casing, see? And it'll be pretty hot."

"I should imagine."

"But when you're keeping six, seven, eight rounds in the air all at once, that breech'll get so hot itself that it'll practically cook off a fresh round before you can pull the lanyard. And when that casing pops out, well, you could see it in the dark."

"So we're shooting and shooting and shooting, and hiking up more ammo and tossing it around and shooting some more till we were about ready to light up ourselves, and we got a pile of empty casings about so high off to the side, and here comes that poor little kitty and decides to sit down someplace where she can watch us, and she picks out that pile of casings and jumps right up. Naturally the ones at the top of the pile was hot enough to solder with."

Silk nodded sympathetically.

"She gives a whoop and off she scoots, and I didn't see her again for two-three days."

"She did return, though?" Silk felt somewhat heartened by the implication that Oreb might return as well.

"She did, but she wouldn't get anywheres near to one of those casings after that. I could show it to her, and maybe push a paw or her nose up against it to prove it was stone-cold, and it wouldn't make one m.o.a.'s difference. She'd learned those casings were hot, see, Patera? After that, she couldn't ever learn that one wasn't, no matter how plain I showed it. She didn't have A.I., and there's people that's the same way, too, plenty of them."

Silk nodded again. "A theodidact once wrote that the wise learn from the experiences of others. Fools, he said, could learn only from experiences of their own, while the great mass of men never learn at all. By which I imagine that he meant that the great mass had no A.I."

"You're right on target, Patera. But if you've got it, then the more experience somebody's got, the higher up you want him. So Sand's a sergeant, I'm a corporal, and Schist is a private. You said you had a couple questions. What's the other one?"

"Since we have a walk ahead of us, perhaps we'd better begin it now," Silk suggested; and they set off together, walking side-by-side down the wide aisle between the wall and the rearmost row of racks. "I wanted to ask you about Pas's provision to keep the cities independent. When you described it to me, it seemed eminently sound; I felt sure that it would function precisely as Pas intended."

"It has," Hammerstone confirmed. "I said I thought it was pretty smart, and I still do."

"But afterward, we spoke of a soldier such as yourself engaging three bios with slug guns like his own, and about the Civil Guard, and so forth. And it struck me that the arrangement you'd described, admirable as it may once have been, can hardly prevail now. If Wick has three thousand five hundred soldiers and our own city seven thousand, our city is twice as strong only if soldiers are the only men of value in war. If Guardsmen to the number of ten or twenty thousand are to fight as well—to say nothing of hundreds of thousands of ordinary citizens—then may Wick not be as strong, overall, as Viron? Or stronger? What becomes of Pas's arrangement under such circumstances as these?"

Hammerstone nodded. "That's something that's worrying everybody quite a bit. The way I see it, Pas was thinking mostly about the first two hundred years. Maybe the first two hundred and fifty. I think maybe he figured after that we'd have learned to live with each other or kill each other off, which isn't so dumb either. See, Patera, there weren't anywheres near so many bios at first, and they weren't big on making stuff. The cities were all there when they come, paved streets and shiprock buildings, mostly. Growing food was the big thing. So when they made stuff, it was mostly tools and clothes, and mud bricks so they could put up more buildings where Pas hadn't put any but they felt like they needed some.

"Stop right here, Patera, and I'll show you in a minute."

Hammerstone halted before a pair of wide double doors, standing with his broad body in front of the line at which they met, clearly to block Silk's view of some object.

"Like I was saying, back three hundred years ago there wasn't all that many bios. A lot of the work was done by chems. Us soldiers did some, but mostly it was civilians. Maybe you know some. They don't have armor and they've got different software."

"They're largely gone now, I'm sorry to say," Silk told him.

"Yeah, and that's one place where I feel like old Pas sort of slipped up. Me and a fem-chem could make a sprat. You know about that?"

"Certainly."

"Each of us is hardwired with half the plans. But the thing is, it might take us a year or so if we're lucky, maybe twenty if we weren't, where you bios can do the main business any night after work."

"Believe me," Silk told him, "I wish with all my heart that you were more like us, and we more like you. I have never been more sincere in my life."

"Thanks. Well, anyhow, after a while there got to be more bios and the tools were better, mostly 'cause there was still a lot of chems around to make them. Also, there was quite a few slug guns floating around in all the cities that'd had wars, 'cause the soldiers that had owned them were dead. A slug gun isn't all that tough to make, really. You got to have some bar stock and a lathe for the barrel, and a milling machine's nice. But there's nothing a milling machine can do that somebody careful can't do about as good with a set of files and a hand drill, if he's got the time."

Hammerstone included the entire armory in a gesture. "So here we are. Not near as steady as we used to be, and all set to lay the blame on poor old Pas the first time we lose."

"It seems a pity," Silk said pensively.

"Chin up, Patera. Right here's the best thing I got to show you, you being a augur, so I saved it for the last, or almost the last, anyway. Have you ever heard of what they call Pas's seal?"

Silk's eyes went wide with astonishment. "Certainly I have. It's mentioned in the Pardon. 'Do my will, live in peace, multiply, and do not disturb my seal. Thus you shall escape my wrath.' "

Hammerstone threw back his head in another grin. "Have you ever seen it?"

"Why no. Pas's seal is—to the best of my knowledge at any rate—largely a metaphor. If I were to shrive you, for example, anything I learned during your shriving would be under the seal of Pas, never to be divulged to a third party without your express permission."

"Well, have a look," Hammerstone said, and stepped to one side.

Waist-high on the line where the double doors met, they were joined by a broad daub of dark synthetic. Silk dropped to one knee to read the letters and numbers pressed into it.

5553   8783   4223   9700   34
2221   0401   1101   7276   56
SEALED FOR THE MONARCH

"There it is," Hammerstone told Silk. "It's been there ever since we came on board, and whenever people talk about Pas's seal, that thing you're looking at's what they're talking about. There used to be a lot more of them."

"If this imprint is truly what is intended by the seal of Pas," Silk whispered, "it is a priceless relic." Bowing reverently, he traced the sign of addition in the air before the seal and murmured a prayer.

"If we could take it off and carry it up to one of those big manteions it would be, maybe. The thing is, you can't. If you were to try to get it off of those doors, that black stuff would bust into a million pieces. We broke a bunch after we got here, and what's left isn't a whole lot bigger than H-Six Powder."

"And no one knows what lies beyond it?" Silk inquired. "In the next room?"

"Oh, no. We know what's in there all right. It's pretty much like this one, a whole lot of people in the rack. Only in there it's bios. Want to see them?"

"Bios?" Silk repeated. At the word, his dream of a few hours earlier returned to the forefront of his mind with an urgency and immediacy that were wholly new: the bramble-covered hillside, Maytera Marble (absurdly) sick in bed, the oversweet scent of Maytera Rose's blue-glass lamp, and Mucor seated upon the still water when the dream in which she had played her part had vanished. *"It's drier farther on. Meet me where the bios sleep."*

"Sure," Hammerstone confirmed, "bios just like you. See, this one we're in right now had extra soldiers, and this next one, with the seal still on the doors, has extra bios. Old Pas must of been scared there might be some kind of a disease, or maybe a famine, and Viron would have to have more bios to get started again. They don't get to lie down like us, though. They're all standing up. Want to see them?"

"Certainly," Silk told him, "if it can be done without breaking Pas's seal."

"Don't worry. I've done this probably a couple dozen times." Hammerstone's steel knuckles rang against one of the doors. "That's not so somebody'll come and let us in, see. I got to stir up the lights inside, or you won't be able to see anything."

Silk nodded.

"I doubt your hands are strong enough, so I'll have to do it for you." He wedged chisel-like fingernails into the crevice between the doors. "There's a button underneath of the seal and it's got them latched shut. That's the way a lot of them were when we first come aboard. So Pas's seal won't break even when I pull as hard as I can. But I can get this top part far enough apart for you to peek inside if you put your eye to the crack. Have a look."

There was a faint thrumming from Hammerstone's thorax as he spoke, and the dark line where the edges of the doors met became a thread of greenish light. "You'll have to sort of wiggle between me and the door to see in, but you got to get your eye up close to see anything anyhow."

With his body pressed against the hard, smooth surfaces of the doors, Silk managed to peer through the crevice. He was looking at a thin section of what appeared to be a wide and brilliantly illuminated hall. Here, too, stood racks of gray-painted steel; but the motionless bios in the row nearest the floor (in line with the crevice through which he peered) were nearly upright. Each was contained in what appeared to be a cylinder of the thinnest glass, glass rendered visible only by a coating of dust. With his vision constricted by the narrow opening between the doors, he could make out only three of these sleepers clearly: a woman and two men. All three were naked and were (in appearance at least) of approximately his own age. All three stared straight ahead, with open eyes in empty, untroubled faces.

"Lights on enough?" Hammerstone asked; he leaned forward to peer through the crevice himself, the tip of his chin well above the top of Silk's head.

"Someone's in there," Silk informed him. "Someone who's not asleep."

"Inside?" There was a metallic clang as Hammerstone's forehead struck the doors.

"Look at how bright it is. Every light in the room must be blazing. A few taps on the door cannot possibly have done that."

"There can't be anybody in there!"

"Of course there can," Silk told him. "There's another way in, that's all."

Slowly—so slowly that at first Silk was not sure he was seeing them move at all—the woman in the lowest row lifted her hands to press against the crystalline wall that confined her.

"Corporal of the guard!" Hammerstone blared. "Back of Personnel Storage!" Faintly, a distant sentry took up the cry.

Before Silk could protest, Hammerstone had slammed the butt of his slug gun against the seal, which shattered into coarse black dust. As Silk recoiled in horror, Hammerstone jerked open both doors and charged into the enormous hall beyond them.

Silk knelt, collected as much of the black dust as he could, and, lacking any more suitable receptacle, folded it into his remaining sheet of paper and deposited it in his pen case.

By the time that he had closed the case and returned it to the pocket of his robe, the imprisoned woman's hands were clutching her throat and her eyes starting from her head. He scrambled to his feet, hobbled into the brilliantly lit hall, and wasted precious seconds trying to discover some means of broaching the transparent cylinder that confined her before snatching Hyacinth's needler from his pocket and striking the almost invisible crystal with its butt.

It shattered at the first blow. At once the atmosphere within it darkened to the blue-black of ripe grapes, swirling and spiraling as it mixed with air, then vanished as abruptly as Mucor in the aftermath of his dream. With somnambulistic slowness the naked woman's hands returned to her sides.

She gasped for breath.

Silk averted his eyes and untied the bands of his robe. "Will you put this on, please?"

"We'll be lovers," the woman told him loudly, her voice breaking at the penultimate syllable. Her hair was as black as Hyacinth's, her eyes a startling blue deeper than Silk's own.

"Do you know this place?" Silk asked her urgently. "Is there another way out?"

"Everything." Moving almost normally, she stepped from the rack.

"I must get away." Silk spoke as quickly as he could, wondering whether she would understand him even if he had spoken as slowly as he would have to a child. "There must be another way out, because there was someone in here who hadn't come through these doors. Show me, please."

"That way."

He risked a glance at her face, careful not to let his gaze stray below her long and graceful neck; there was something familiar—something horrible that he struggled to deny—in her smile. With cautious hands, he draped his robe about her shoulders. "You'll have to hold it closed in front."

"Tie it for me?"

He hesitated. "It would be better . . ."

"I don't know how."

She stepped toward him. "Please?" Her voice was under better control now, and almost familiar.

He fumbled the bands; it seemed unfair that something he did automatically each morning should be so difficult to do for someone else.

"Now I can fly!" With outstretched arms she spread the robe wide, running slowly and clumsily down the aisle until she nearly disappeared from view at the distant wall. There she turned and dashed back, sprinting without wasted motion. "I—really—can!" She gulped for air, breasts heaving. "But—you—can't—see—me—then." Still gasping, she smiled proudly, her head thrown back like Hammerstone's; and in her smile, the grinning rictus of a corpse, Silk knew her.

"You have no right to this woman, Mucor!" He traced the sign of addition. "In the name of Pas, Master of the Whorl, be gone!"

"I—am—a—woman. Oh—yes!"

"In the name of Lady Echidna, be gone!"

"I—know—her. She—likes—me."

"In the names of Scylla and Sphigx! In the most sacred name of the Outsider!"

She was no longer paying attention. "Do you—know why this—place is —so high?" She gestured toward the domed ceiling. "So that fliers— could fly—over it without—having to—walk." She pointed to a jumbled heap of bones, hair, and blackened flesh at the bottom of a cylinder on the second level. "I was her—once. She—remembered."

"To me you're the devil who possessed that poor woman's daughter," Silk told her angrily. "The devil who possessed Orpine." He saw a flash of fear in her eyes. "I am a bad man, granted—a lawless man, and often less than pious. Yet I am a holy augur, consecrated and blessed. Is there no name that you respect?"

"I will not be afraid, Silk." She backed away from him as she spoke. "In the name of Phaea, go! In the name of Thelxiepeia, go! In the name of Molpe, whose day this is, and in those of Scylla and Sphigx. Be gone in the names of these gods!"

"I wanted to help. . . ."

"Be gone in the names of Tartaros and Hierax!"

She raised her hands, as he had to ward off Hammerstone's blow; and Silk, seeing her fear, remembered that *Hierax* had been the name that Musk had given the white-headed one, the griffon vulture on Blood's roof. With that memory, Phaesday night returned: his frantic dash across Blood's lawn in the shadow of a racing cloud; the thump of his forked branch on the roof of the conservatory; and the blade of his hatchet wedged between the casement of Mucor's window and its frame, the window that had supplied the threat he had used the next day to banish her from Orchid's.

Almost kindly he told her, "I will close your window, Mucor, so that it can never be opened again, if you don't leave me alone. Go."

As though she had never been present, she abandoned the tall, raven-haired woman who faced him; he had seen nothing and heard nothing, but he knew it as surely as if there had been a flash of fire or a gale of wind.

The woman blinked twice, her eyes unfocused and without comprehension. "Go? Where?" She drew his robe about her.

"Praise Great Hierax, the Son of Death, the New Death, whose mercy is terminal and infinite," Silk said feelingly. "Are you all right, my daughter?"

She stared at him, a hand between her breasts. "My—heart?"

"It's still racing from Mucor's exertions, I'm sure; but your pulse should slow in a few minutes."

She trembled, saying nothing. In the silence he heard the pounding of steel feet.

He closed the double doors that Hammerstone had opened, reflecting that Hammerstone had specified the back of the armory. It might be some time before the hurrying soldiers realized that he had actually meant to summon them to this vast hall beyond it. "Perhaps if we walk a little," he suggested. "We may be able to find a place of comfort, where you can sit down. Do you know a way out?"

The woman said nothing but offered no objection as Silk led her along an aisle he chose at random. The bases of the crystal cylinders, as he now saw, were black with print. By rising on his toes, he was able to examine one on the second tier, reading the name (Olive) of the woman in the cylinder, her age (twenty-four), and what he took to be a précis of her education.

"I ought to have read yours." He spoke to her as he had to Oreb, to give form to his thoughts. "But we'd better not go back. If I had when I had the opportunity, I'd know your name, at least."

"Mamelta."

He looked at her curiously. "Is that your name?" It was one that he had never heard.

"I think so. I can't . . . ."

"Remember?" he suggested gently.

She nodded.

"It's certainly not a common name." The greenish lights overhead were dimming now; in the twilight that remained, he glimpsed Hammerstone running down an intersecting aisle half the hall away and asked, "Can you walk just a little faster, Mamelta?"

She did not reply.

"I'd like to avoid him," he explained, "for reasons of my own. You don't have to be afraid of him, however—he won't hurt you or me."

Mamelta nodded, although he could not be sure that she understood.

"He won't find what he's searching for, I'm afraid, poor fellow. He wants to find the person who energized all these lights, but I'm reasonably sure that it was Mucor, and she's gone."

"Mucor?" Mamelta indicated herself, both hands at her face.

"No," Silk told her, "you are not Mucor, although Mucor possessed you for a short time. It woke you, I think, while you were still in your glass tube. I don't believe that was supposed to happen. Can we walk a bit faster now?"

"All right."

"It wouldn't do to run. He might hear, and it would make him suspicious, I'm sure; but if we walk, we may be able to get away from him. If we don't, and he finds us, he'll think you energized the lights, no doubt. That should satisfy him, and we'll have lost nothing." Under his breath Silk added, "I hope."

"Who is Mucor?"

He looked at Mamelta in some surprise. "You're feeling better now, aren't you?"

She stared straight ahead, her gaze fixed on the distant wall, and did not appear to have heard his question.

"I suppose—no, I know—that you're morally entitled to an answer, the best I can provide; but I'm afraid I can't provide a very good one. I don't know nearly as much about her as I'd like, and at least two of the things I think I know are conjectural. She is a young woman who can leave her body—or to put it another way, send forth her spirit. She's not well mentally, or at least I felt that she wasn't on the one occasion when I met her face-to-face. Now that I've had time to think about her, I believe she may be less disturbed than I assumed. She must see the whorl very differently from the way that most of us see it."

"I feel I am Mucor. . . ."

He nodded. "This morning—though I suppose it may be yesterday morning by now—I conferred with—" Words failed him. "With someone I'll call an extraordinary woman. We were talking about possession, and she said something that I didn't give as much attention as I should have. But I was thinking about our conversation as I walked out to the shrine— I'll tell you about that later, perhaps—and I realized that it might be extremely important. She had said, 'Even then, there would be something left behind, as there always is.' Or words to that effect. If I understood her, Mucor must leave a part of her spirit behind when she leaves a person, and must take a small part of that person's spirit with her when she goes. We usually think of spirits as indivisible, I'm afraid; but the Writings compare them to winds again and again. Winds aren't indivisible. Winds are air in motion, and air is divided each time we shut a door or draw a breath."

Mamelta whispered, "So many dead." She was looking at a crystalline cylinder that held only bones, what appeared to be black soil, and a few strands of hair.

"Some of that must be Mucor's doing, I'm afraid." Silk fell silent for a moment, tortured by conscience. "I said I'd tell you about her, but I haven't told you one of the most important things—to me, at any rate. It is that I betrayed her. She's the daughter of a man named Blood, a powerful man who treats her abominably. When I talked with her, I told her that whenever I had a chance to see her father I'd remonstrate with him. Later I had a lengthy conversation with him, but I never brought up his treatment of his daughter. I was afraid he'd punish her if he knew she'd spoken to me; but now I feel it was a betrayal nonetheless. If she were shown that others value her, she might—"

"Patera!" It was Hammerstone's voice.

Silk looked around for him. "Yes, my son?"

"Over this way. Couple rows, maybe. You all right?"

"Oh, yes, I'm fine," Silk told him. "I've been, well, more or less touring this fascinating warehouse or whatever you call it, and looking at some of the people."

"Who were you talking to?"

"To tell you the truth, to one of these women. I've been lecturing her, I'm afraid."

Hammerstone chuckled, the same dry, inhuman sound Silk had heard from Sergeant Sand in the tunnel. "You see anybody?"

"Intruders? No, no one."

"All right. The guard detail ought to be here now, but they haven't showed. I'm going to find out what's keeping them. Meet me over at the door where we came in." Without waiting for Silk's reply, Hammerstone clattered away.

"I must get back into the tunnels," Silk told Mamelta. "I left something valuable there; it isn't mine, and even if that soldier's officer allows me to leave, he's sure to see that I'm escorted back to Limna."

"This way," she said, and pointed, though Silk was not sure at what.

He nodded and set off. "I can't run, I'm afraid. Not like you. I'd run now, if I could."

For the first time, she seemed to see him. "You have a bruise on your face, and you're lame."

He nodded. "I've had various accidents. I was dropped down a flight of stairs, for one thing. My bruises will heal though, quite quickly. I was going to tell you about Mucor, who I'm afraid will not. Are you sure we're going the right way? If we go back—"

Mamelta pointed again, and this time he saw that she was indicating a green line in the floor. "We follow that."

He smiled. "I should have realized that there must be a system of some kind."

The green line ended before a cubical structure faced with a panel of many small plates. Mamelta pressed its center, and the plates shuddered and squealed, turned pale, and eventually creaked into motion, first reminding Silk of the irising door that had defied his efforts, then of the unfolding of a blush rose. "It's beautiful," he told Mamelta. "But this can't be the way out. It looks like . . . a toolshed, perhaps."

The square room, revealed as the rose door opened, was dim and dirty; there were bits of broken glass on its floor, and its corners held heaps of the gray-painted steel. Mamelta sat on one, educing a minute puff of dust. "Will this take us to the lifter?"

Although she had looked at him as she spoke, Silk felt it was not his face that she had seen. "This won't take us anywhere, I'm afraid," he told her as the door folded again. "But I suppose that we might hide here for a time. If the soldiers have gone when we come out, I may be able to find my way back to the tunnels."

"We want to go back. Sit down."

He sat, feeling unaccountably that the stacked steel—that the whole storeroom in fact—was sinking beneath him. "What is the lifter, Mamelta?"

"The *Loganstone,* the ship that will take us up to the starcrosser *Whorl.*"

"I think—" Silk wrestled briefly with the unfamiliar term. "I mean, don't you—haven't you considered—that, that perhaps this boat that was to take you wherever it was, that it may have been a long time ago? A very long time?"

She was staring straight ahead; he was conscious of the tightness of her jaw.

"I was going to tell you about Mucor. Perhaps I ought to finish that; then we can go on to other things. I realize all this must be very unsettling to you."

Mamelta nodded almost imperceptibly.

"I was going to say that it has bothered me a great deal that her father appears to be unaware of what she does. She goes forth in spirit, as I told you. She possesses people, as she possessed you. She appeared to me, bodiless, in my manse, and later—today, actually—in the tunnels after I dreamed of her. Furthermore, the ghost of a very dear friend—of my teacher and advisor, I should have said—appeared to me at almost the same time that she did. I believe her appearance must have made his possible in some fashion, though I really know much less than I should about such matters."

"Am I a ghost?"

"No, certainly not. You're very much alive—a living woman, and a very attractive one. Nor was Mucor a ghost when she appeared to me. It was a spirit of the living that I saw, in other words, and not that of someone who had died. When she spoke, what I heard was actual sound, I feel certain, and she must have shouted or broken something in the room outside to make the lights so bright." Silk bit his lips; some sixth sense told him (though clearly falsely) that he was falling, falling forever, the stack of gray steel and the glass-strewn floor itself dropping perpetually from under him and pulling him down with them.

"I was going to say that when Mucor possessed some women at a house in our city, her father never appeared to suspect that the devil they complained of was his own daughter; that puzzled me all day. I believe I've hit upon the answer, and I'd like you to tell me, if you can, whether I'm correct. If Mucor left a small part of her spirit with you, it's possible you know. Has she ever undergone a surgical procedure? An operation on her head?"

There was a long pause. "I'm not sure."

"Because her father and I talked about physicians, among many other things. He has a resident physician, and he told me that an earlier one had been a brain surgeon." Silk waited for Mamelta's reaction, but there was none.

"That seemed strange to me until it occurred to me that the brain surgeon might have been employed to meet a specific need. Suppose that Mucor had been a normal child in every respect except for her ability to possess others. She would have possessed those closest to her, or so I'd think, and they can hardly have enjoyed it. Blood probably consulted several physicians—treating her phenomenal ability as a disease, since he is by no means religious. Eventually he must have found one who told him that he could 'cure' her by removing a tumor or something of that kind from her brain. Or perhaps even by removing a part of the brain itself, though that is such a horrible thought that I wish there were some way to avoid it."

Mamelta nodded.

Encouraged, Silk continued, "Blood must have believed that the operation had been a complete success. He didn't suspect it was his own daughter who was possessing the women because he firmly believed, as he presumably had for years, that she was no longer able to possess anyone. I think it's probable that the operation did in fact interfere with her ability until she was older, just as it seems to have damaged her thought processes. But in time, as that part of her brain regenerated, her ability returned; and having been granted a second chance, she was prudent enough to go farther afield, and in general to conceal her restored ability; although it would seem that she followed her father or some other member of the household to the place where the women lived, as she undoubtedly followed me later. Does any of this sound at all familiar to you, Mamelta? Can you tell me anything about it?"

"The operation was before I went on the ship."

"I see," Silk said, although he did not. "And then . . . ?"

"It came. I remember now. They strapped us in."

"Was it a slave boat? We don't have them in Viron, but I know that some other cities do, and that there are slave boats on the Amnis that raid the fishing villages. I would be sorry to learn that there are slave boats beyond the whorl as well."

"Yes," Mamelta said.

Silk rose and pressed the center of the door as Mamelta had, but the door did not open.

"Not yet. It will open automatically, soon."

He sat down again, feeling unaccountably that the whole room was slipping left and falling too. "The boat came?"

"We had to volunteer. They were—you couldn't say no."

"Do you recall being outside, Mamelta? Grass and trees and sky and so on?"

"Yes." A smile lifted the corners of her mouth. "Yes, with my brothers." Her face became animated. "Playing ball in the patio. Mama wouldn't let me go out in the street the way they did. There was a fountain, and we'd throw the ball through the water so that whoever caught it would get wet."

"Could you see the sun? Was it long or short?"

"I don't understand."

Silk searched his memory for everything Maytera Marble had ever said relating to the Short Sun. "Here," he began carefully, "our sun is long and straight, a line of burning gold fencing our lands from the skylands. Was it like that for you? Or was it a disk in the center of the sky?"

Her face crumpled, while tears overflowed her eyes. "And never come back. Hold me. Oh, hold me!"

He did so, awkward as a boy and acutely conscious of the soft, warm flesh beneath the worn black twill of the robe he had lent her.

CHAPTER

10   ON THE BELLY OF THE

WHORL

Auk leaned across the squat balustrade of Scylla's shrine to study the jagged slabs of gray rock at the foot of the cliff. Their disordered, acutely angled surfaces gleamed ghostly pale in the skylight, but the clefts and fissures between them were as black as pitch.

"Here, here!" Oreb pecked enthusiastically at Scylla's lips. "Shrine eat!"

"I'm not going back with you," Chenille told Auk. "You made me walk all the way out here in my good wool dress for nothing. All right. You hit me and kicked me—all right, too. But if you want me to go back with you, you're going to have to carry me. Try it. Smack me a couple more times and give me a good hard kick. See if I get up."

"You can't stay here all night," Auk growled.

"I can't? Watch me."

Oreb pecked again. "Here Auk!"

"Here yourself." Auk caught him. "Now you listen up. I'm going to pitch you over like I pitched you off the path back there. You look for Patera Silk like you did before. If you find him, sing out."

With weary indifference, Chenille warned, "He won't come back this time."

"Sure he will. Get set, bird. Here you go." He tossed Oreb over the balustrade and watched as he glided down.

Chenille said, "There's a hundred places where that long butcher could have fallen."

"Eight or ten, maybe. I was looking."

She stretched out on the stone floor. "Oh, Molpe, I'm so tired!"

Auk turned to face her. "You really going to stay here all night?"

If she nodded, it was too dark beneath the dome of the shrine for him to see her.

"Somebody could come out here."

"Somebody worse than you?"

He grunted.

"That's so funny. I'd bet everything I've got that if you checked out every last cull in that godforsaken little town you couldn't find a single—"

"Shut up!"

For a time she did, whether from fear or sheer fatigue she could not herself have said. In the silence, she could hear the lapping of the waves at the foot of the cliff, the sob of the wind through the strangely twisted pillars of the shrine, the surge of blood in her own ears, and the rhythmic thumping of her heart.

Rust would have made everything all right. Recalling the empty vial she had left on her bed at Orchid's, she imagined one twenty times larger, a vial bigger than a bottle, filled with rust. She would sniff a pinch, and drop a big one in her lip, and walk back with Auk till they reached that bit where you felt like you were hanging in air, then push him off, down and down, until he fell into the lake below.

But there was no such vial, there never would be, and the half bottle of red she had drunk had died in her long ago; she pressed her fingers to her throbbing temples.

Auk bawled, "*Bird!* You down there? Sing out!"

If Oreb heard him, he did not reply.

Argumentatively, Auk inquired, "Why would he come way out here?"

Chenille rolled her head from side to side. "You asked me that before I don't know. I remember us riding in some kind of cart or something, all right? Horses. Only somebody else was in charge then, and I wish she'd come back." She bit her knuckle, herself astonished by what she had said. Wearily she added, "She did a better job of it than I do. A better job than you're doing, too."

"Shut up. Listen, I'm going to climb down a ways. As far as I can go without falling. You rest. I should be back pretty soon."

"We'll have a parade," Chenille told him. Some minutes afterward she added, "A big one, right up the Alameda. With bands."

Then she slept and entered a great, shining room full of men in black-and-white and jeweled women. A three-sun admiral in full dress walked beside her holding her arm and did not count in the least. She walked proudly, smiling, and her wide collar was entirely of diamonds, and diamonds cascaded from her ears and flashed like the lights in the night sky from her wrists; and every eye was on her.

Then Auk was shaking her shoulder. "I'm going. You want to come or not?"

"No."

"There's good places to eat in Limna. I'll buy dinner and rent a room, and we can head back to the city tomorrow. You want to come?"

By now she was awake enough to say, "You don't listen, do you? No. Go away."

"All right. If some cull gets to you out here, don't blame me. I did the best I could for you."

She closed her eyes again. "If some cully wants to rape me, that's dimber with me, just as long as he's not you and he doesn't want me to wiggle around while he's doing it. If he'd like to vent my pipe, that'll be dimber, too." She sighed. "Long as he doesn't want me to help."

Distinctly, she heard the scraping of Auk's boots as he left the shrine, and after what seemed to her a very short time she struggled to her feet. The night was clear; eerie skylight glimmered on the rolling lake and illuminated every harsh, bare point of rock. On the horizon, distant cities wrapped with Viron in the night appeared as tiny smears of fox fire, not half so desirable as the icy sparkles that had deserted her wrists.

"Hackum?" she called, lifting her voice. "Hackum?"

Almost at once he emerged from the shadows of the rocks to stand upon that very outthrust point of rock from which Silk had watched the spy vanish from the shrine, and from which she had imagined herself pushing him. "Jugs? Are you all right?"

Something invisible tightened around her throat. "No. But I will be. Hackum?"

"What is it?" The flooding skylight that rendered every bush and outcrop far and fey prevented her from reading his posture (she was good at that, although she was unaware of it), even while it revealed it; and his tone was flat and devoid of emotion, though perhaps it was only made to sound so by distance.

"I'd like to start over. I thought maybe you'd like to start over, too."

He was silent while she counted seven thuddings of her pulse. At last: "You want me to come back?"

"No," she called, and he seemed to have become minutely smaller. "What I mean is . . . I want you to come to Orchid's some night. All right?"

"All right." It was not the echo.

"Maybe next week. And I don't know you. And you don't know me. Start over."

"All right," he called again. And then, "Sometime I'd like to meet you."

She intended to say *we will,* but the words stuck in her throat; she waved instead, and then, realizing that he could not see her, stepped from under the dome so that she too was in the clear, soft skylight and waved again, and watched him disappear where the Pilgrims' Way bent inland.

That was it, she thought.

She was tired and her feet hurt, and for some reason she did not want to step back under the dome again; she sat down on the smooth, flat rock outside the entrance to the shrine instead, kicked off her shoes, and comforted her blisters.

It was funny how you knew. That was it, and this's him, and I never knew till he said that: *Someday I'd like to meet you.*

He'd want her to leave Orchid's, and quite unexpectedly she realized she'd be glad to leave shaggy Orchid's to live anywhere, even under a bridge, with him.

Funny.

There was a brass plate thing let into the smooth stone of the shrine; she fingered its letters idly, naming the ones she knew. The plate seemed to move, ever so slightly, as if it was not solidly fastened but hinged at the top. She got her nails under it, lifted it, and saw swirling colors: reds and blues and pinks and yellows and golden browns and greens and greenish blacks and others for which she had no names.

"Immediately, Your Eminence," Incus said, bowing again. "I understand entirely, Your Eminence, and I shall be on the scene within the hour. You can trust in me absolutely, Your Eminence. As always."

He shut the door slowly and almost noiselessly, bowing all the while, and made certain that the latchbar had dropped before he spat. The Circle was to convene after a dinner at Fulmar's, and Bittersweet had promised to show everyone the wonders she claimed to have achieved with an old porter, who would—as she reportedly had confided to Patera Tussah—adore her as Echidna, Scylla, Molpe, Thelxiepeia, Phaea, or Sphigx on command, all of it supposedly executed in compiler. Incus had wanted (never more than now) to see that. He had wanted very much to see the porter with his skullplate and faceplate removed. He had been (as he told himself angrily) more than merely anxious to witness at first hand an actual demonstration of Bittersweet's technique in order that he might compare it to his own.

Was it actually possible for anyone to download—or was the whole thing, perhaps, a great deal simpler than he had imagined? Ideally, one subverted the art of the Short Sun programmers, utilizing it to one's own advantage, as an expert wrestler threw an opponent too heavy to lift by enlisting his opponent's strength in his own cause.

Clenching his teeth and slamming his small fist into his palm, Incus sought to convince himself that there would be a raid tonight and that some well-disposed god had maddened old Remora so that he might be spared; but it was nonsense, and he knew it. He was *entitled* to go tonight. The Circle would not meet again until next month, and no one had toiled harder at black mechanics than he—no one had shared all that he had learned more willingly, earning this night a dozen times over. There was no fairness, no justice in the whorl. The gods did not care—or rather, were inimical. Beyond question, they were inimical to him.

Dropping angrily into his chair, he jammed the nearest quill into the inkwell.

My Dear Friend Fulmar:
    It is with deep regret that I must tell you that the old fool has cooked up another perfectly ridiculous piece of busywork for me. I am to go to Limna tonight, and no other night will do. I am to consort with fishermen in search of a woman (yes, I write a woman) I have never seen, who may not be there at all, all because his worthless spies have failed him again.
    So grieve, my dear friend, for your poor coworker Myself who would be with you this night if he could.

Myself standing for *I*, as even that fool Fulmar could not help but understand. Briefly but satisfyingly, Incus reread, admired, amended mentally, and at last approved the note before ripping it in two, wadding it up, and flinging the wad into the incineratium. The chances that old Remora would ever see what he had written and identify him as the writer were slight, but not so slight that prudence did not forbid him to write his mind in any such fashion. A fresh sheet, in that case, and more ink—with the quill grasped wrongly.

My Dear Friend,
    Pressing duties constrain me to forebear the pleasant social meal to which you were so very kind as to invite me tonight.

His characteristic spiky *M* had been replaced by a new character remarkably like a double *E* upside down. Good—good!

You know, my friend, yet it might more thoughtfully be said that you cannot know, how much I have been looking forward to a <u>plain</u> <u>firsthand account</u> of the marvelous adventures of our mutual acquaintance Bee. Bee himself

No, it would not do. Fulmar would be utterly thrown off the scent by the male pronoun; it would be necessary to stop at his house and leave a clear, straightforward message with his valet. Nor would the trouble and loss of time go entirely unrecompensed; he, Incus, would at least have the satisfaction of inquiring just how long it had been since the unfortunate valet had received his wages, and observing the chem's baffled incomprehension. The valet had been a most creditable little project, and one Fulmar could never have brought to its wholly successful conclusion without his help.

Rising from his chair, Incus whistled shrilly and told the fat and worried-looking boy who answered his summons, "I need a *fast* litter with eight bearers to take me to the lake. Some fool woman— Never mind. His Eminence won't authorize renting a floater, although he insists upon speed. Tell the men that there will be only one passenger, myself. You might well describe me, I'm not weighty. They'll receive *double pay* at Limna and be dismissed there. Do the best you can, but hurry. Meanwhile I've got a hundred urgencies that must— Go, I say! Hurry! Is your bottom still sore? I'll make it sorer if you don't fly."

"Yes, Patera. At once, Patera. Immediately." Bowing, the fat boy shut the door, made sure the latchbar had dropped, and spat expertly into a corner.

Fascinated, Silk watched as the door opened in a swirl of petals, seeming to create the lofty green corridor beyond it. "It took me a while to identify the sensation," he confided to Mamelta, "but I placed it eventually. It was the feeling I'd had as a small boy when my mother had been holding me and put me down." He paused, musing.

"And now we're in another place altogether, much deeper underground. Truly extraordinary! Is there a way to prevent Hammerstone's following us down in this thing?"

Mamelta shook her head, whether in negation or merely to clear it, Silk could not have said. "So strange . . . Is this another dream?"

"No," he assured her. He rose from his seat. "No, it isn't. Put that thought from your mind entirely. Did you dream much, up there?"

"I don't know how long it was. Suppose I dreamed once each hundred years . . . ?"

Silk stepped out into the corridor. There was a well in it not far from the petaled door: a twilit shaft descended by spiraling steps. He set off down the corridor to examine it, felt something through the worn sole of one shoe, and stopped to pick it up.

It was a card.

"Look at this, Mamelta!" He held it up. "Money! My luck's certainly changed since I met you. Some god smiles on you, and smiles on me, too, because I'm with you."

"That is not money."

"Yes, it is," he told her. "Did you have money of some other kind on the Short Sun Whorl? This is the sort we use in Viron, and traders from foreign cities accept it, so I suppose they must use cards, too. This would buy a nice goat for Pas, for example—even a white ewe, if the market were depressed. Chop it into a hundred pieces, and every piece is one bit. A bit will buy two large cabbages or half a dozen eggs. Aren't you going to come out? I don't believe that the moving room is going to sink any farther."

She rose and followed him into the corridor.

"Maytera Marble remembers the Short Sun. I'll try to introduce you to her. You'll have a great deal in common, I'm sure."

When Mamelta did not reply, he asked, "Do you want to tell me about your dreams? That might help. What did you dream about?"

"People like you."

Silk leaned over the coping of the shaft to peer down. The first six steps bore six words:

HE WHO DESCENDS SERVES PAS BEST

"Look at this," he said; she did not, and he asked, "Who were these people in your dreams?"

She was silent so long that he thought she was not going to reply; he went through a gap in the coping and down to the first step. "There's writing on all of these," he told her. "The next series says, 'I will teach my children how I carried out the Plan of Pas.' There must be a shrine of Pas's at the bottom. Would you care to see it?"

"I am trying to . . . think of a way to tell you. We did not speak. Words. I have to remember to speak words now. I say something. But you do not hear me unless I move my lips. To move my lips and my tongue . . . while I make this noise in my throat."

"You're doing very well," Silk told her warmly. "Soon we'll have to go back up again, but not in that same little room since I'd assume it would take us to the place we left. I have to get back into the tunnels under Limna, however, and find the ashes from the manteion there. I'm not at all sure that we ought to take the time to look around this shrine and recite prayers and so forth. What do you think?"

"I . . ." Mamelta fell silent, staring.

"Patera Pike—my predecessor, and a most devout man—used to call out in dreams," Silk told her. "Sometimes he'd wake me in the next room. I think you may be afraid to speak, believing that this, too, is a dream; and that you might wake other sleepers. It isn't, so you will not."

She nodded, the movement of her head barely perceptible. "I may have called out in the beginning. One was small, the Monarch's second daughter. The one you used to see dance."

"Molpe?" Silk suggested.

"I remember seeing her often at home, dancing through my dreams. She was a wonderful dancer, but we cheered because we were afraid. You saw the hunger in her face for the kind of cheers the others got."

"It may be Pas who favors you," Silk decided. "Indeed it probably is, since the moving room carried us straight to this shrine of his. If so, he'll certainly be offended if we don't visit it, after all that he's done for us. Won't you come with me?"

She joined him on the uppermost step, and side-by-side they descended the spiral, seeing the footprints of those who had preceded them in the thin dust on the treads, and shivering in the cool air of the shaft, which narrowed and grew darker as they descended.

They were less than halfway down when a faint odor of decay set Silk's nostrils twitching; it was as though an altar had not been properly cleansed and purified, and he (assuming that the shrine he anticipated included such an altar) resolved to purify it himself if need be.

Mamelta, who had lagged behind him by a few steps, now touched his arm. "Is that a hammerstone?"

Silk looked back at her. "Hammerstone? Where?"

"Down there." She indicated the bottom of the shaft by a vague gesture. "Moaning? Something is moaning."

Silk stopped to listen; the sound was so faint that he could not be certain he did not imagine it, an eerie keening, rising and falling, always at the edge of his hearing, and often threatening to fade away altogether.

It was no louder at the bottom, where the soldier lay. Silk gripped the dead man's left arm and rolled him over, in the process discovering that he was no longer as strong as he had been. There was a ragged hole the size of his thumb in the dead man's blue-painted chest.

When he had recovered breath he said, "You'd better stand back, Mamelta. Chems seldom explode once the moment of death is past, but there's always a risk." Squatting, he employed one of the steel gammas forming the voided cross he wore to remove the dead man's faceplate. When bridging connections with the gamma produced no arc, he shook his head.

"How . . . ? Mamelta is my name, and I told you. Have you told me yours?"

"Patera Silk." He straightened up. "Call me Patera, please. Were you about to ask how this man died?"

"He is a machine." She was looking at the dead man's wound. "A robot?"

"A soldier," Silk told her, "though I've never seen a blue one before. Ours are mottled—green, brown, and black—so I suppose he must have come from another city. In any case he's been dead a long time, while someone in the shrine is alive and in pain."

A massive door in the side of the shaft stood ajar. Silk opened it and stepped into the shrine, finding himself (to his astonishment) in a circular room a full thirty cubits high, with padded divans and glasses and multicolored readouts on its ceiling, its floor, and its curving wall. Every glass was energized, and in them all bobbed a tattered, skull-like thing that was no longer a face, wailing.

He clapped his hands. "Monitor!"

Gabbling sounds issued from the face. An irregular hole opened and closed; the sounds rose to a piercing shriek and a trapdoor in the center of the room flew back.

"It wants you to go into the nose," Mamelta said.

Silk crossed to the opening in the floor and stared down. At its bottom, fifty cubits away, swam three bright pinpricks that moved as one; irresistibly reminded of similar lights at the bottom of a grave he had dreamed was Orpine's, he watched until they vanished, replaced by a single spark. "I'm going down there."

"Yes. That is what it wants."

"The monitor? Could you understand him?"

She shook her head, a minute motion. "I have seen this. Going to the ship that would lift us off the *Whorl.*"

"This can't be any sort of boat," Silk protested. "This entire shrine must be embedded in solid rock."

"That is its berth," she murmured, but he had dropped to the floor already and swung his legs into the circular opening revealed by the trapdoor. Rungs set in the wall permitted him to climb down to a lucent bubble through which he looked across a benighted plain of naked rock. As he stared at it, a nameless mental mechanism adjusted, and the sparks swarming under the concave crystal floor were not merely distant but infinitely remote, the lamps and fires of new skylands.

"Great Pas . . ."

The divine name sounded empty and foolish here, though he had employed it with no doubts of its validity all his life; Great Pas was not so great as this, nor was Pas a god here, outside.

Silk swallowed, dry-mouthed and swallowing nothing, then traced the sign of addition with the gammadion he wore about his neck. "This is what you showed me, isn't it? The same thing I saw in the ball court, the black velvet and colored sparks below my feet."

There was, or so it seemed to him, an assent that was not a spoken word.

It steadied him as nothing else could have. One at a time, he removed his sweating hands from the icy rungs of the ladder and wiped them on his tunic.

"If you wish for me to die, then I'll die, I know; and I wouldn't have it otherwise. But after you showed me this in the ball court, you asked me to save our manteion, so please let me go back to—to the whorl I know. I'll offer you a white bull, I swear, as soon as I can afford it."

This time there was no response.

He stared about him; some of the pinpricks of light were red, some yellow as topaz, some violet, many like diamonds. Here and there he saw what appeared to be mists or clouds of light—whole cities, surely. The somber plain was pitted like the cheeks of a child who had survived the pox, and far more barren than the sheer cliffs of the Pilgrims' Way; no tree, no flower, no least weed or dot of moss sprouted from its rock.

Silk remained where he was, staring down at the gleaming dark, until Mamelta, from a higher rung, touched the top of his head to get his attention; then he started, peered up at her in surprise, and looked away, dismayed by his glimpse of her unclothed loins.

"What you found? I have found where it belongs. Give it to me."

"I'll bring it," he told her. When he tried to climb, he discovered that his hands were cold and stiff. "You mean the card?"

She did not reply.

All the rooms were small, though the widest was lined with innumerable divans and was higher than the principal tower of the Grand Manteion, facing the Prolocutor's palace on the Palatine. In a room above that very tall cylindrical room, Silk's heel slipped on a small white rotted thing, and he learned where the pervasive odor of decay originated. A dozen such flecks of dead flesh were scattered over the floor. He asked Mamelta what they were, and she bent to examine one and said, "Human."

Crouching to look at another, he recognized the coarse black dust in which it lay; the polished metal cabinet that had presumably held thousands or tens of thousands originally had, like the room in which Mamelta and so many other bios had stood sleeping, been sealed with the Seal of Pas; that seal had been broken, and the embryos flung wantonly about. At the schola, Silk had been taught to regard the mere misuse of any divine name as blasphemous. If that was true, what was this? Shuddering, he hurried after Mamelta.

In a compartment so small that he could not help brushing against her, she pointed to a frame and dangling wires. "This is the place. You won't know how to tag it. Let me."

Curious, and still half-stunned by the looting of Pas's treasures, he gave her a card. She attached three clips, then studied a glass overhead. "This is a different kind," she said. Stooping, she inserted it in the frame at ankle height. "Let me see them all."

He did; and she tested each as she had the first, working slowly and appearing unsure of her decisions at times, but always making the correct one. As she worked, a broken gray face took shape in the glass. "Is it time?" the face inquired—and again: "Is it time?" Silk shook his head, but the face continued to inquire.

Mamelta told Silk, "If you have more, you must give them to me."

"I don't. There were seven left after Orpine's rites, two left from Blood's sacrifice, and the one that you saw me find. I've given them all to you to repair this poor monitor. I never knew that money . . ."

"We must have more," Mamelta said.

He nodded. "More if I'm to save my manteion, certainly. Far more than ten. Yet if I take back those ten cards, he'll be as he was when we arrived." Exhausted, Silk leaned against the wall, and would have sat if he could.

"Have you eaten? There is food on board."

"I must go back down." He sternly repressed the sudden pleasure her concern gave him. "I have to see it again. The monitor— Is this really a kind of boat?"

"Not like the *Loganstone*. This is smaller."

"Its monitor was correct, in any event—what I saw from the bow was something I was meant to see. But you're correct as well. I should eat first. I haven't eaten since—since the morning of the day we went to the lake; I suppose that was yesterday now. I ate half a pear then, very quickly before we said our morning prayers. No wonder I'm so tired."

Small dishes swathed in a clouded film that Mamelta ate with obvious enjoyment grew almost too hot to hold as soon as the film was peeled away, and proved to be pressed from hard, crisp biscuit. Still shivering and grateful for the warmth, they devoured the dishes themselves as well as their contents, sitting side-by-side on one of the many divans; all the while, the monitor inquired, "Is it time? Is it time?" until Silk, at least, ceased to hear it. Mamelta presented him with a deep green twining vegetable whose taste reminded him of the gray goose he had offered to all the gods on the day he had come to Sun Street; he gave her a little dusky-gold cake in return, though she appeared to feel that it was too much.

"Now I'm going to go down into the bow again," he told her. "I may never return to this place, and I couldn't bear it if I hadn't gone again to prove to myself forever that I saw what I saw."

"The belly of the *Whorl?*"

He nodded. "If that's what you wish to call it, yes—and what lies beyond the belly. You can rest up here if you need to, or leave if you'd rather not wait for me. You're welcome to my robe, but please leave my pen case here if you go. It's in the pocket."

A little food remained, with some of the crisp dish; but he found that he did not want either. He stood up, brushing crumbs from his ash-smeared tunic. "When I come back, we—I alone, if you don't want to come—will have to return to the tunnels to recover the azoth I left there when I met the soldiers. It will be very dangerous, I warn you. There are terrible animals."

Mamelta said, "If you have no more cards, there may be other repairs I can make." He turned to go, but she had not finished speaking. "This is my work, or at least a part of my work."

The ladder was the same, the pinpricks of unimaginably distant light the same, yet new. This otherwhorldly boat was a shrine after all, Silk decided, and smiled to himself. Or rather, it was the doorway to a shrine bigger than the whole whorl, the shrine of a god greater even than Great Pas.

There were four divans in the bubble below the end of the ladder. While eating with Mamelta, he had noticed thick woven straps dangling from the divan on which they sat; these divans had identical straps; seeing them, he thought again of slaves, and of the slavers said to ply the rivers that fed Lake Limna.

Reflecting that straps stout enough to hold slaves would hold him as well, he dropped to the upper end of the nearest divan and buckled its uppermost strap so that he could stand on it, virtually at the center of the bubble, while grasping the last rung.

By the time he looked out again, something wholly new was happening. The plain of rock had blanched unwatched, and was streaked with sable. Craning his neck to look behind him, he saw a thin crescent of blinding light at the utmost reach of the plain. At that moment it seemed to him that the Outsider had grasped the entire whorl as a man might grasp a stick—grasped it in a hand immensely greater, of which no more than the tip of the nail on a single finger had appeared.

Terrified, he fled up the ladder.

CHAPTER

11   SOME SUMMATIONS

"Auk? Have you forgotten me?"

He had thought himself utterly alone on the windswept Pilgrims' Way, trudging back to Limna. Twice before he had stopped to rest, sitting on white stones to scan the skylands. Auk was frequently outdoors and alone nightside, and it was something he enjoyed doing when he had the time: tracing the silver threads of rivers from which he would never drink, and exploring mentally the innumerable unknown cities in which the pickings were (as he liked to imagine) considerably better. Despite Chenille's insistence, he had not believed that she would actually remain in Scylla's shrine all night; but he had never supposed that she might overtake him. He pictured her as she had been when they reached it, footsore and exhausted, her face shining with sweat, her raspberry curls a mass of sodden tangles, her voluptuous body drooping like a bouquet on a grave.

Yet he felt sure it had been her voice that had sounded behind him. "Chenille!" he called. "Is that you?"

"No."

He rose, nonplussed, and shouted, "Chenille?"

The syllables of her name echoed from the rocks.

"I won't wait for you, Chenille."

Much nearer: *"Then I'll wait for you at the next stone."*

The faint pattering might have been rain; he glanced up at the cloudless sky again. The sound grew louder—running feet on the Pilgrims' Way behind him. As his eyes had traced the rivers, they followed its winding path across the barren, jutting cliff.

The clear skylight revealed her almost at once, nearer than he had supposed, her skirt hiked to her thighs and her arms and legs pumping. Abruptly she vanished in the shadow of a beetling rock, only to emerge like a stone from a sling and shoot toward him. For an instant he felt that she was running faster and faster with every stride, and would never slow or stop, or even stop gaining speed. Gaping, he stood aside.

She passed like a whirlwind, mouth wide, teeth gleaming, eyes starting from their sockets. A moment more and she was lost among stunted trees.

He drew his needler, checked the breech and pushed off the safety, and advanced cautiously, the needler in his hand ready to fire. The moaning wind brought the sound of tearing cloth, and her hoarse respirations.

"Chenille?"

Again, there was no reply.

"Chenille, I'm sorry."

He felt that some monstrous beast awaited him among the shadows; and although he called himself a fool, he could not free himself from the presentiment.

"I'm sorry," he repeated. "It was a rotten thing to do. I should have stayed there with you."

Half a chain farther, and the shadows closed about him. The beast still waited, nearer now. He mopped his sweating face with his bandanna; and as he wadded it into his pocket, he caught sight of her, quite naked, sitting on one of the white stones in a patch of skylight. Her black dress and pale undergarments were heaped at her feet, and her tongue lolled from her mouth so far that she appeared to lick her breasts.

He halted, tightening his grip on the needler.

She stood and strode toward him. He backed into deeper shadow and leveled the needler; she passed him without a word, stalking through the leafless spinney straight to the edge of the cliff. For a second or two she paused there, her arms above her head.

She dove, and after what seemed too long an interval he heard the faint splash.

He was halfway to the edge before he pushed the safety back up and restored the needler to his waistband. Heights held no fear for him; still, he knew fear as he stood at the brink of the cliff and stared down, a hundred cubits or more, into the skylit water.

She was not there. Wind-driven combers charged at the tumbled rocks like a herd of white-maned horses, but she was not among them.

"Chenille?"

He was about to turn away when her head burst through from a wave. *"I'll meet you,"* she called, *"there."* An arm that for an instant seemed but one of many pointed down the rocky beach toward the scattered lights of Limna.

"Arms?"

The question was Oreb's, and had come from a clump of straggling bushes to Auk's right.

He sighed, glad of any company and ashamed to be glad. "Yeah. Too many arms." He mopped his sweating face again. "No, that's gammon. It was like in a mirror, see? Chenille held her arms up out of the water, and it reflected 'em so it looked like there was more underneath, that's all. You find Patera?"

"Shrine eat."

"Sure. Come over and I'll give you a lift to Limna."

"Like bird?"

"I guess. I won't hurt you if that's what you mean, but you're Patera's, and I'm going to give you back to him if we ever find him."

Oreb fluttered up from the bushes to a landing on Auk's shoulder. "Girl like? Now like?"

"Chenille? Sure." Auk paused. "You're right. That's not her, is it?"

"No, no!"

"Yeah, right." Auk nodded to himself. "It's some kind of devil that only looks like Chenille. Shag, I don't know whether it likes birds or not. If I had to guess, I'd say it probably likes 'em for breakfast and lunch, but maybe it'd like something a little more solid for dinner. Anyhow, we'll dodge it if we can."

Worn out though he was, it seemed to him that his lagging feet flew over the next hill and all the rest, when he would have preferred that entire months be consumed in climbing and descending each. An hour passed in weary walking seemed less than a minute to him; and though Oreb kept him company on his shoulder, he had seldom felt so alone.

"I've found it!" Chenille's voice sounded practically at his ear; he jumped and Oreb squawked. "Can you swim? Are you carrying valuables that would be damaged by water?"

"A little," Auk admitted. He had stopped in his tracks to look for her; it was difficult to keep his hand away from his needler. When he spoke again, he was afraid that he might stammer. "Yeah, I am. Couple things."

"Then we must have a boat." Like mist from the lake, she rose between him and the rocky beach—he had been looking in the wrong direction. "You don't comprehend the littlest part of this, do you? I'm Scylla."

It was, to Auk's mind, an assertion of such preeminent significance that no being of which he could conceive would have the audacity to make it falsely. He fell to his knees and mumbled a prayer.

"It's 'lovely Scylla,' " his deity told him, " 'wonderful of waters', not 'woman of the water.' If you must mouth that nonsense, do it correctly."

"Yes, Scylla."

She caught him by the hair. "Straighten up! And stop whining. You're a burglar and a thug, so you may be useful. But only if you do precisely as I direct." For a moment she glared at him, her eyes burning into his. "You still don't understand. Where can we find a boat? Around that village, I suppose. Do you know?"

Standing, he was a head taller than she, and felt that he ought to cower. "There's boats there for rent, lovely Scylla. I've got some money."

"Don't try to make me laugh. It will do you no good, I warn you. Follow me."

"Yes, Scylla."

"I don't care for birds." She did not trouble to look back at Oreb as she spoke. "They belonged to Daddy, and now to Molpe and ones like that to little Hierax. I don't even like having my people named for them. You know I'm oldest?"

"Yes, I sure do, lovely Scylla." Auk's voice had been an octave too high; he cleared his throat and made an effort to regain his self-possession. "That's the way Patera Pike always told it at the palaestra."

"Pike?" She glanced back at him. "That's good. Is he particularly devoted to me?"

"Yes, lovely Scylla. Or anyhow he was. He's dead."

"It doesn't matter."

Already they had reached the beginning of the Pilgrims' Way; the glowing windows of cookshops and taverns illuminated the street; late diners bound for rented beds stared rudely at Chenille's nakedness, or resolutely did not stare.

"Six children after me! Daddy had this thing about a male heir, and this other thing about not dying." A drunken carter tried to tweak her nipple; she gouged his eyes with both thumbs and left him keening in the gutter. "Molpe was just another girl, but you would have thought Tartaros would do it. Oh, no. So along came little Hierax, but even Hierax wasn't enough. So then three more girls, and after that—I suppose you already knew we could take you over like this?"

Oreb croaked, "Girl?" But if she heard him she gave no sign of it.

Auk muttered, "I didn't know it could still happen now, lovely Scylla."

"It's our right, but most of us have to have a glass or a Window. That's what you call them. A terminal. But this whole lake's my terminal, which gives me lots of power around here."

She was not looking at him, but Auk nodded.

"I haven't been here for a while, though. This woman's a whore. No wonder Kypris went for her."

Auk nodded again, weakly.

"In the beginning we chose up, with Daddy to be the god of everything —that's what his name meant—and boss over everybody. You see? Where are the boats?"

"If we turn the next corner and go down a ways we might find some, lovely Scylla."

"He's dead now, though. We wiped him out of core thirty years ago. Anyway, Mama got to pick next, and she grabbed the whole inner surface. I knew she'd stay on land, mostly, so I took the water. I was doing lots of diving back then. Molpe took the arts, like you'd expect." As Chenille rounded the corner, she caught sight of a fishing boat moored at the end of the alley; she pointed. "That one's already got a man on it. Two, and one's an augur. Perfect! Can you sail? I can."

Pas was dead! Auk could think of nothing else.

"No? Then don't kill them. I was going to say that we took new names that would fit. Daddy was Typhon the First, back home. What none of us knew was that he'd let *her* choose, too. So she picked love, what a surprise. And got sex and everything dirty with it. She didn't meddle very much in the beginning, knowing that—"

Hearing her voice, Patera Incus had looked up.

"You! Augur! Prepare to cast off." Chenille herself was off like a sprinter, disappearing in the dense shadow of a salting shed. A moment later Auk saw her leap—flying in a way that he knew would have been impossible had she not been possessed—to land with a roll upon the deck of the fishing boat.

"I said prepare to cast off. Are you deaf?"

She struck the augur with her left hand and the fisherman with her right, and the sounds of the blows might almost have been the slamming of double doors. Auk drew his needler and hurried after her.

Another hot—another scorching—morning. Maytera Marble fanned herself with a pamphlet. There were coils in her cheeks; their plan no longer appeared at her call, but she was almost sure of it. Her main coils were in her legs, with an auxiliary coil in each cheek; there the fluid that carried such strength as she still possessed was brought (or at least ought to have been brought) into intimate contact with her titanium faceplate, which was in turn in intimate contact with the air of the kitchen.

And the air was supposed to be cooler.

But no, that couldn't be right. She had once looked—she was almost sure she had looked—distinctly like a bio. Her cheeks had been overlaid with . . . with some material that would very likely have impeded the transfer of heat. What had she told dear Patera Silk the other day? Three centuries? Three hundred years? The decimal had slipped, must certainly have slipped to the left.

It had to have. She had looked like a bio then—like a bio girl, with black hair and red cheeks. Like a somewhat older Dahlia in fact, and Dahlia had always been so bad at arithmetic, forever mixing up her decimals, multiplying two decimal numbers and getting one with two decimal points, mere scrambled digits that meant not even His Cognizance could have said what.

With her free hand, Maytera Marble stirred the porridge. It was done, nearly overcooked. She lifted it from the stove and fanned herself again. In the refectory on the other side of the doorway, little Maytera Mint waited for her breakfast with exemplary patience. Maytera Marble told her, "Perhaps you'd better eat now, sib. Maytera Rose may be ill."

"All right, sib."

"That was obedience, wasn't it?" The pamphlet drifted past Maytera Marble's face; it bore a watery picture of Scylla frolicking with sunfish and sturgeon, but carried no cooling. Deep within Maytera Marble, an almost-forgotten sensor stirred dangerously. "You don't have to obey me, sib."

"You're senior, sib." Normally the words would have been nearly inaudible; this morning they were firm and clear.

Maytera Marble was too hot to notice. "I won't make you eat now if you don't want to, but I've got to take it off the stove."

"I want what you want, sib."

"I'm going to go upstairs. Maytera may require my help." Maytera Marble had an inspiration. "I'll take her bowl up on a tray." That would make it possible for Maytera Mint to eat her breakfast without waiting for the eldest sibyl. "First I'm going to give you porridge, and you must eat it all."

"If that's what you wish, sib."

Maytera Marble opened the cupboard and got Maytera Rose's bowl and the old, chipped bowl that Maytera Mint professed to prefer. Climbing the stair would overheat her; but she had not thought of that in time, so she would have to climb. She ladled out porridge until the ladle dissolved into a cloud of digits, then stared at it. She had always taught her classes that solid objects were composed of swarming atoms, but she had been wrong; every solid object, each solid thought, was swarming numbers. Shutting her eyes, she forced herself to dip up more porridge, to drop the pamphlet and find the lip of a bowl with her fingers and dump more porridge in.

The stair was not as onerous as she had feared, but the second story of the cenoby had vanished, replaced by neat rows of wilting herbs, by straggling vines. Someone had chalked up a message: SILK FOR CALDE!

"Sib?" It was Maytera Mint, her voice faint and far. "Are you all right, sib?"

The crude letters and the shiprock wall fell into digits.

"Sib?"

"Yes. Yes, I was going upstairs, wasn't I? To look in on Maytera Betel." It would not do to worry timorous little Maytera Mint. "I only stepped out here for a minute to cool down."

"I'm afraid Maytera Betel's left us, sib. To look in on Maytera Rose."

"Yes, sib. To be sure." These dancing bands of numbers were steps, she felt. But steps leading to the door or to an upper floor? "I must have become confused, Maytera. It's so hot."

"Be brave, sib." A hand touched her shoulder. "Perhaps you'd like to call me that? We're sisters, you and I."

Now and again she saw actual stairs, the strip of brown carpet with its pattern worn away that she had swept so often. Maytera Rose's door ended the short corridor: the corner room. Maytera Marble knocked and found that her knuckles had smashed the panel; through the splintered wood she glimpsed Maytera Rose still in bed, her mouth and eyes open and her face dotted with flies.

She entered, ripped Maytera Rose's threadbare nightgown from neck to hem, and opened Maytera Rose's chest; then she pulled off her habit, hung it neatly over a chair, and opened her own. Almost reluctantly, she began to exchange components with her dead sib, testing each as it went into place, and rejecting a few. This is Tarsday, she reminded herself, but Maytera's gone, so this can't be theft.

I won't need these any more.

The glass on the north wall showed a fishing boat under full sail; a naked woman standing beside the helmsman wore a flashing ring. Maytera, naked herself, averted her eyes.

Silk's head throbbed, and his eyes seemed glued shut. Short and fat yet somehow huge, Councillor Potto loomed over him, fists cocked, waiting for his eyes to open. Somewhere—somewhere there had been peace. Turn the key the other way, and the dancers would dance backward, the music play backward, vanished nights reappear . . . .

Darkness and a steady thudding, infinitely reassuring. Knees drawn up, arms bent in prayer. Wordless contemplation, free of the need to eat or drink or breathe.

The tunnel, dark and warm but ever colder. Anguished cries, Mamelta beside him, her hand in his and Hyacinth's tiny needler yapping like a terrier.

How much did they give you? Blows that rocked him.

Ashes, unseen but choking.

"This is the place."

How much did you tell Blood?

A shower of fire. Morning prayers in a manteion in Limna that was perhaps thirty cubits, yet a thousand leagues away.

"Behind you! Behind you!" Whirl and shoot.

The dead woman's lantern, its candle three-quarters consumed. Mamelta blowing on a glowing coal to light it.

"I am a loyal cit—"

"Councillor, I am a loyal cit—"

Spitting blood.

"Those who harm an augur—"

How much—

Silk's right eye opened, saw a wall as gray as ash, and closed again.

He tried to count his shots—and found himself in the eating house again. "Well, Patera, for one thing mine holds a lot more needles. . . . All of them good and thick, this was the Alambrera in the old days." The door opened and Potto came in with their dinners on a tray, Sergeant Sand behind him with the box and the terrible rods.

Back! Back!

Kneeling in the ashes, digging with his hands. A god who took five needles and still stood at the edge of the lantern light, snarling, blood and slaver running from its mouth. The boom of a slug gun, loud in the tunnel and very near.

. . . did you give him?

Metal rods jammed into his groin, Sand's arm spinning the crank, his expressionless face washed away by unbearable pain.

He bought your manteion.

"Yes. I'm a—"

Indefinitely? He let you stay indefinitely?

"Yes."

Indefinitely.

"Yes. I don't know . . ."

(Back, oh, back, but the current is too strong.)

Silk's left eye opened. Painted steel, gray as ash. He rubbed his eyes and sat up, his head aching and his stomach queasy. He was in a gray-walled room of modest size, without windows. He shivered. He had been lying on a low, hard, and very narrow cot.

A voice from the edge of memory said, "Ah, you're awake. I need somebody to talk to."

He gasped and blinked. It was Doctor Crane, one hand raised, eyes sparkling. "How many fingers?"

"You? I dreamed . . ."

"You got caught, Silk. So did I. How many fingers do you see?"

"Three."

"Good. What day is it?"

Silk had to consider; it was an effort to remember. At last he said, "Tarsday? Orpine's obsequies were on Scylsday; we went to the lake on Molpsday, and I went down . . ."

"Yes?"

"Into these tunnels. I've been down here a long time. It might even be Hieraxday by now."

"Good enough, but we're not in the tunnels."

"The Alambrera?"

Crane shook his head. "I'll tell you, but it'll take some explaining, and I ought to warn you first that they've probably locked us up together hoping we may say something useful. You may not want to oblige them."

Silk nodded and found it a mistake. "I wish I had some water."

"It's all around us. But you'll have to wait till they give us some, if they ever do."

"Councillor Potto hit me with his fist." Silk caressed the swelling on the side of his head gingerly. "That's the last thing that I remember. When you say *they,* do you mean our Ayuntamiento?"

"That's right." Crane sat down on the cot beside him. "I hope you don't mind. I was sitting on the floor while you were unconscious, and it's cold and hard on the buttocks. Why did you go out to the lake? Mind telling me?"

"I can't remember."

Crane nodded approvingly. "That's probably the best line to take."

"It isn't a line at all. I've—I've had very strange dreams." Silk pushed away terrifying memories of Potto and Sand. "One about a naked woman who had strange dreams too."

"Tch, tch!"

"I talked with a—it doesn't matter. And I vanquished a devil. You won't believe that, Doctor."

"I don't," Crane told him cheerfully.

"But I did. I called on the gods in turn. Only Hierax frightened her."

"A female devil. Did she look like this?" Crane bared his teeth.

"Yes, a little." Silk paused, rubbing his head. "And it wasn't a dream—it's not fading. You know her. You must."

Crane lifted an eyebrow. "I know the devil you drove away? My circle of acquaintances is wide, I admit, but—"

"She's Mucor, Blood's daughter. She can possess people, and she possessed the woman I was with."

Suddenly serious, Crane whistled softly.

"Was it you who operated on her?"

Crane shook his head. "Blood told you?"

"He told me he'd had a brain surgeon in the house before you. When I learned what Mucor could do, I understood—or at least, I think I do. Will you tell me about it?"

Crane fingered his beard, then shrugged. "Can't hurt, I suppose. The Ayuntamiento knows all the important points anyhow, and we've got to pass the time some way. If I do, will you answer a few questions of mine? Honest, complete answers, unless it's something that you don't want them to know?"

"I know nothing that I wouldn't want the Ayuntamiento to learn," Silk declared, "and I've already answered a great many questions for Councillor Potto. I'll tell you anything concerning myself, and anything I know about other people that wasn't learned under the seal."

Crane grinned. "In that case I'll start with the most basic one. Who are you working for?"

"I should have said that I'll answer after you answer my own questions about Mucor. That was the agreement, and I'd like to help her if I can."

The eyebrow went up again. "Including my first one?"

"Yes," Silk said. "Very much including that one. That one first of all. Is Mucor really Blood's daughter? That's what she told me."

"Legally. His adopted daughter. Unmarried men aren't usually allowed to adopt, but Blood's been working for the Ayuntamiento. Were you aware of that?"

Silk remembered in the nick of time not to shake his head. "No. Nor do I believe it now. He's a criminal."

"They don't pay him so many cards, you understand. They let him operate without interference as long as there's no serious trouble at any of his places, and do him favors. This seems to have been one of them. A word to the judge from any of the councillors would have been more than enough, and by adopting her he could control her up to the age of consent."

"I see. Who are her real parents?"

Crane shrugged again. "She doesn't have any. Not in our whorl, anyhow. And whoever they were, they probably met in a petri dish. She was a frozen embryo. Blood paid a good deal for it, I imagine. I know he paid a small fortune to get that brain man you mentioned."

Recalling the bare and filthy room in which he had first encountered Mucor, Silk said bitterly, "A fortune to destroy what he had given so much to get."

"Not really. It was supposed to make her pliable. She was a holy terror, from what I've heard. But when the brain man—he came from Palustria, by the way, which is how we found out what was going on. When he opened up her cranium, he got hit with a new organ." Crane chuckled. "I've read his report. It's in the medical file back at the villa."

"A new organ? What was it?"

"I didn't mean that it wasn't a brain. It was. But it wasn't like anything the brain man had worked on before. It wasn't a human brain for medical purposes, or an animal's brain, either. He had to go by guess and good gods, as they say. And in the end he made a botch of it. He as much as admitted it."

Silk wiped his eyes.

"Oh, come now. It was ten years ago, and we spies are supposed to be of sterner stuff."

"Has anybody ever cried for her, Doctor?" Silk asked. "You, or Blood, or Musk, or the brain surgeon? Anyone at all?"

"Not that I know of."

"Then let me cry for her. Let her have that at least."

"I wouldn't think of trying to stop you. You haven't asked why Blood didn't get rid of her."

"She's his daughter, according to what you just told me—his daughter legally, at least."

"That wouldn't stop him. It was because the brain man said her subrogative abilities could regenerate some time after she'd healed. It was only a guess, but judging from your story about a devil, they have. And the Ayuntamiento knows it now, thanks to you. It's going to make Viron more dangerous than ever."

Silk daubed at his eyes again with a corner of his robe and wiped his nose. "More formidable, you mean. That may trouble your government in Palustria, but it doesn't bother me."

"I see." Crane slid backward on the cot until he could prop his spine against the steel wall. "You promised you'd tell me who you were working for, if I told you about Mucor. Now you're going to say you're working for His Cognizance the Prolocutor, or something like that. Is that it? Hardly what I'd call fair play."

"No. Or perhaps, in a way, I am. It's a nice ethical point. Certainly I'm doing what His Cognizance would wish me to do, but I haven't told him —haven't informed the Chapter formally, I should say. I really haven't had time, the old excuse. Would you have believed me if I'd said I was a spy for His Cognizance?"

"I wouldn't and I don't. Your Prolocutor's got spies, plenty of them. But they aren't holy augurs. He's not so foolish as that. Who is it?"

"The Outsider."

"The god?"

"Yes." Silk sensed that Crane's eyebrow had been raised again, though he was not looking at Crane's face; he filled his lungs and expelled the air through his mouth. "No one believes me—except for Maytera Marble, a little—so I don't expect you to, either, Doctor. You least of all. But I've already told Councillor Potto, and I'll tell you. The Outsider spoke to me last Phaesday, on the ballcourt at our palaestra." He waited for Crane's snort of contempt.

"Now that's interesting. We ought to be able to talk about that for a long time. Did you see him?"

Silk considered the question. "Not in the way I see you now, and in fact I feel sure it's impossible to see him like that. All visual representations of the gods are ultimately false, as I told Blood a few days ago; they're more or less appropriate, not more or less like. But the Outsider showed himself to me—his spirit, if one can speak of the spirit of a god— by showing me innumerable things he had done and made, people and animals and plants and myriad other things that he cares very much about, not all of them beautiful or lovable things to you, Doctor, or to me. Huge fires outside the whorl, a beetle that looked like a piece of jewelry but laid its eggs in dung, and a boy who can't speak and lives—well, like a wild beast.

"There was a naked criminal on a scaffold, and we came back to that when he died, and again when his body was taken down. His mother was watching with a group of his friends, and when someone said he had incited sedition, she said that she didn't think he had ever been really bad, and that she would always love him. There was a dead woman who had been left in an alley, and Patera Pike, and it was all connected, as if they were pieces of something larger." Silk paused, remembering.

"Let's get back to the god. Could you hear his voice?"

"Voices," Silk said. "One spoke into each ear most of the time. One was very masculine—not falsely deep, but solid, as if a mountain of stone were speaking. The other was feminine, a sort of gentle cooing; yet both voices were his. When my enlightenment was over, I understood far, far better than I ever had before why artists show Pas with two heads, though I believe, too, that the Outsider had a great many more voices as well. I could hear them in back of me at times, although indistinctly. It was as if a crowd were waiting behind me while its leaders whispered in my ears; but as if the crowd was actually all one person, somehow: the Outsider. Do you want to comment?"

Crane shook his head. "When both voices spoke at once, could you understand what they said?"

"Oh, yes. Even when they were saying quite different things, as they usually did. The difficult thing for me to understand, even now—one of the difficult things, anyway—is that all of this took place in an instant. I think I told someone later that it seemed to last hundreds of years, but the truth is that it didn't occupy any amount of time at all. It took place during something else that wasn't time, something I've never known at any other time. That's badly expressed, but perhaps you understand what I mean."

Crane nodded.

"One of the boys—Horn, the best player we have—was reaching for a catch. He had his fingers almost on the ball, and then this took place outside of time. It was as if the Outsider had been standing in back of me all my life, but had never spoken until it was necessary. He showed me who he was and how he felt about everything he had made. Then how he felt about me, and what he wanted me to do. He warned me that he wouldn't help me. . . ." The words faded away; Silk pressed his palm to his forehead.

Crane chuckled. "That wasn't very nice of him."

"I don't believe it's a question of niceness," Silk said slowly. "It's a matter of logic. If I was to be his agent, as he asked—he never demanded anything. I ought to have emphasized that.

"But if I was to be his agent, then he was doing it; he was preserving our manteion, because that was what he wanted me to do. He is preserving it through me. I'm the help he sent, you see; and you don't rescue the rescuer, just as you don't scrub a bar of soap or buy plums to hang on your plum tree. I said I'd try to do it, of course. I said I'd try to do whatever he wanted me to."

"So then you sallied forth to save that run-down manteion on Sun Street? And that little house where you live, and the rest of it?"

"Yes." Silk nodded, wished he had not, and added, "Not necessarily the buildings that are there now. If they could be replaced with new and larger buildings—Patera Remora, the coadjutor, hinted at that the other night—it would be even better. But that answers your question. That tells you whom I'm working for. Spying for, if you like, because I was spying on you."

"For a minor god called the Outsider."

"Yes. Correct. We were going—I was going to tell you that I knew you were a spy, the next time you came to treat my ankle. That I'd talked to people who'd provided you with information without realizing why you wanted it, who'd carried messages for you and to you; and I'd seen a pattern in those things—I see it more clearly now, but I had seen it even then."

Crane smiled and shook his head in mock despair. "So did Councillor Lemur, unfortunately."

"I see other things, too," Silk told him. "Why you were at Blood's, for example; and why I encountered Blood's talus here in the tunnels."

"We're not in the tunnels," Crane said absently, "didn't you hear me say that there's water all around us? We're in a sunken ship in the lake. Or to be a little more exact, in a ship that was built to sink, and to float to the surface on the captain's order. To swim underwater like a fish, if you can believe that. This is the secret capital of Viron. I'd be a wealthy man as well as a hero, if only I could get that information to my superiors back home."

Silk slid from the cot and crossed the room to its steel door. It was locked, as he had expected, and there was no pane of glass or peephole through which he could look out. Suddenly conscious of the odor of his body and the smears of ash on his clothing, he asked, "Isn't there any way we can wash here?"

Crane shook his head again. "There's a slop jar under the cot, if you want that."

"No. Not now."

"Then tell me why you cared whether I was a spy or not, if you weren't going to hand me over to the Ayuntamiento."

"I was," Silk said simply, "if you wouldn't help me save our manteion from Blood. I was going to say that if you did that, I'd let you leave the city."

He sat down in the corner farthest from the cot, finding the steel floor as cold and as hard as Crane had said. "But if you wouldn't, I planned to roll you over to the hoppies. That's the way the people of our quarter would say it, and I was working for them as well as for the Outsider, who wanted to save our manteion because he cares so deeply about them."

He pulled off his shoes. "By 'hoppies' they mean the troopers of our Civil Guard. They say that the Guardsmen look like frogs, because of their green uniforms."

"I know. Why did you go into the tunnels? Because I'd asked some people about them?"

Silk was peeling off his stockings as he replied. "Not really. I didn't intend to enter the tunnels, although I'd heard of them vaguely—circles of black mechanics meeting there and so on, which they told us at the schola was a lot of nonsense. You and this wrapping you lent me had made it possible for me to walk out to Scylla's shrine on the lake. I went out there because Commissioner Simuliid had; and the person who told me that said you'd been interested to learn of it."

"Chenille."

"No." Silk shook his head, knowing that it would hurt, but eager to make his answer as negative as possible.

"You know it was. Not that it matters. I was listening outside while you shrove her, by the way. I couldn't hear a lot, but I wish I'd heard that."

"You couldn't have heard it, because it was never said. Chenille acknowledged her own transgressions, not yours." Silk removed the wrapping.

"Have it your way. Did Blood's talus turn you over to Potto?"

"It was more complicated than that," Silk hesitated. "I suppose it's imprudent for me to say it; but if Councillor Potto has someone listening to us, all the better—I want to get this off my conscience. I killed Blood's talus. I had to in order to preserve my own life; but I didn't like it, and I haven't come to like it any better since it happened."

"With . . . ?"

Silk nodded. "With an azoth I happened to have upon my person. It was later taken from me."

"I've got you. Maybe we'd better not say anything else about that."

"Then let's talk about this," Silk said, and held up the wrapping. "You very generously lent me this, and I've been as ungrateful as I could possibly be. You know my excuse, which is that I was hoping to do what the Outsider had asked—to justify his faith in me, who in twenty-three years had never paid him even trifling honors. It wouldn't be right for me to keep this, and I'm grateful for this opportunity to return it."

"I won't accept it. Is it cold now? It must be. Do you want me to recharge it for you?"

"I want you to take it, Doctor. I would have extorted the money I need from you if I could. I deserve no favors from you."

"You've never gotten any, either." Crane drew his legs onto the cot to sit cross-legged. "I didn't invent you, but I wish I had, because I'd like to take credit for you. You're exactly what we've needed. You're a rallying point for the underclass in Viron, and a city divided is a city too weak to attack its neighbors. Now recharge that thing and put it back on your ankle."

"I never wished to weaken Viron," Silk told him. "That was no part of my task."

"Don't blame yourself. The Ayuntamiento did the damage when they assassinated the caldé and governed in defiance of your Charter and their people—which won't save your life when Lemur's finished with you. He'll kill you just like he'll kill me."

Silk nodded ruefully. "Councillor Potto said something of the sort. I hoped—I still hope that it was no more than a threat. That he will no more kill me, despite his threat, than Blood would."

"The situation is entirely different. You'd gone out to Blood's, and it seemed likely that others knew about it. If his talus caught you and dragged you into the tunnels, it's not likely that anybody else knows the Ayuntamiento has you. Not even the talus, since you say you killed it."

"Only Mamelta, the woman who was captured with me."

"What's more," Crane said, "killing you would have made Blood much less secure. Killing you would make Lemur and the rest *more* secure. In fact, I'm surprised they haven't done it already. Who's Mamelta, by the way? One of those holy women?"

"One of the people whom Pas put into the whorl when he had finished it. Did you know that some of them are still alive, though sleeping?"

Crane shook his head. "Did he tell you that? Pas?"

"No, she did. I had been captured by soldiers—I left the azoth behind when that happened, because I knew I'd be searched. A drift of ashes almost filled that tunnel, and I left it buried in them when the soldiers pulled me out."

Crane grinned. "Shrewd enough."

"It wasn't. Not really. I was going to say that one of the soldiers showed me the sleeping people and told me they had been there since the time of the first settlers. Mucor woke one, Mamelta, and I exorcised Mucor, as I told you."

"Yes."

"Mamelta and I got away from the soldiers—Hammerstone will be punished for that, I'm afraid—but we were arrested again when we went back for the azoth. They locked me up in a place worse than this one, and after a while they brought me my robe. Mamelta had been wearing it, so they must have given her proper clothing; at least, I hope they did." Silk paused, gnawing his lower lip. "I could have resisted the soldiers with the azoth, I suppose; it's quite possible that I would have killed them both. But I couldn't bring myself to do it."

"Very creditable. But by the time you were rearrested Potto was there?"

"Yes."

"And he soon realized who you were."

"I told him," Silk admitted. "That is to say, he asked my name, and I gave it. I would do it again. I'm a loyal citizen, as I assured him repeatedly."

"I wonder if it's possible to be loyal while dead. But that's your bailiwick. The thing that interests me is that you escaped the first time, with this woman. Mind telling me how you reconciled that with your loyalty?"

"I had an urgent matter to attend to," Silk said. "I won't go into detail now, but I did; and because I had done nothing wrong, I was morally justified in leaving when the opportunity presented itself."

"But now you have? Are you a criminal deserving of death?"

"No. My conscience isn't entirely clear, but the worst thing on it is that I've failed the Outsider. If I could get away again in some fashion—though that appears impossible now—it's conceivable that I might succeed after all."

"Then you'd be willing to escape if we could?"

"From an iron room with a locked door?" Silk ran his fingers through his untidy thatch of yellow hair. "How do you propose to do it, Doctor?"

"We may not be here forever. Would you be willing?"

"Yes. Certainly."

"Then recharge your wrapping. We may have to run, and I hope we will. Go ahead, kick it or wallop the floor with it."

Silk did as he had been told, flailing the steel plates. "If there's even the slightest chance to fulfill my pledge to the Outsider, I must take it; and I will. He'll surely bless you, as I do, for your magnanimity."

"I won't bank on it." Crane smiled, and for a moment actually appeared cheerful. "You had a cerebral accident, that's all. Most likely a tiny vein burst as a result of your exertions during the game. When that happens in the right spot, delusions like yours aren't at all uncommon. Wernicke's area, it's called." He touched his own head to indicate the place.

CHAPTER 12 LEMUR

Silk knelt in silent prayer, his face to the gray-painted wall of the compartment.

Marvelous Molpe, be not angry with me, who have always honored you. Music is yours. Am I never to hear it again? Recall my music box, Molpe, how many hours I spent with it when I was a child. It is in my closet now, Molpe, and if only you will free me I will oil the dancers and its works as well, and play it each night. I have searched my conscience, Molpe, to discover that in which I have displeased you. I find this: that I dealt overharshly with Mucor when she possessed Mamelta. Those whose wits are disordered and those who, though grown, remain as children are, are yours, I know, Molpe, and for your sake I should have been more gentle with her. Nor should I have called her a devil, for she is none. I renounce my pride, and I will separate Mucor from Blood if I can, and treat her as I would my own child. This I swear. A singing bird to you, Molpe, if you will but—

Crane asked, "You don't think that stuff really helps, do you?"

A singing bird to you, Molpe, if you will but set us free.

Tenebrous Tartaros, be not angry with me, who have always honored you. Theft is yours, murder, and foul deeds done in darkness. Am I never again to walk freely the dark streets of my native city? Recall how I walked there with Auk, like me a thief. When I surmounted Blood's wall, you favored me, and I gladly paid the black lamb and the cock I swore. Recall that it was I who brought the Pardon of Pas to Kalan, and allow me to steal away now, Tartaros, and Doctor Crane with me. I will never forget, Tartaros, that thieves are yours and I am one. I have searched my conscience, Tartaros, to discover that in which I have displeased you. I find this: that I detested your darksome tunnels with all my heart, never thinking in my pride that you had sent me there, nor that they were a most proper place for such as I. I renounce my pride; if ever you send me there again, I will strive to be grateful, recalling your favors. This I swear. A score of black rats to you, Tartaros, if you will but set us free.

Highest Hierax, be not angry with me, who have always honored you. Death is yours. Am I never to comfort the dying again? Recall my kindnesses to Pricklythrift, Shrub, Flax, Orpine, Bharal, Kalan, and Exmoor, Hierax. Recall how Exmoor blessed me with his dying breath, and forget not that it was I who slew the bird to whom blasphemers had given your name. If only you will free us, I will bring pardon to the dying all my life, and burial to the dead. I have searched my conscience, Hierax, to discover that in which I have displeased you. I find this: that—

"I thought you fellows used beads."

"Potto took them, as I told you," Silk said dispiritedly. "He took everything, even my glasses."

"I didn't know you wore glasses."

That when I beheld those who had died in the sleep into which Pas had cast them, I did not propose their burial, or so much as offer a prayer for them; and when Mamelta and I found the bones of she who had carried a lantern, I in my pride took her lantern without interring her bones. I renounce my pride and will be ever mindful of the dead. This I swear. A black he-goat to you, Hierax, if you will but set us free.

Enchanting Thelxiepeia, be not angry with me, who have always honored you. Prophesy and magic are yours. Am I never to cast the Thelxday lots again, nor to descry in the entrails of sacrifice the records of days to come? Recall that of the many sacrifices I offered for Orpine, for Auk, and for myself on Scylsday past, I read all save the birds. I have searched my conscience, Thelxiepeia, to discover that in which I have displeased—

Abruptly the room was plunged in such darkness as Silk had never known, not even in the ash-choked tunnel, a darkness palpable and suffocating, without the smallest spark or hint of light.

Crane whispered urgently, "It's Lemur! Cover your head."

Despondent, not knowing why he should cover it or what he might cover it with, Silk did not.

I find this: that I sought no charm—

The door opened; Silk turned at the sound in time to see someone who nearly filled the doorway enter. The door closed again with a solid thud, but no snick from the bolt.

"Stand up, Patera." Councillor Lemur's voice was deep and rich, a resonant baritone. "I want both of you. Doctor, take this."

A thump.

"Pick it up."

Crane's voice: "This is my medical bag. How did you get it?"

Lemur laughed. (Silk, rising, felt an irrational longing to join in that laughter, so compellingly agreeable and good-natured was it.) "You think we're in the middle of the lake? We're still in the cave, but we'll be putting out shortly. I spoke to Blood and one of his drivers brought it, that's all.

"Patera, I have some little presents for you, too. Take them, they're yours."

Silk held out both hands and received his prayer beads and the gammadion and silver chain his mother had given him, the beads and chain in a single, tangled mass. "Thank you," he said.

"You're a bold man, Patera. An extremely bold man, for an augur. Do you consider that you and the doctor, acting in concert, might overpower me?"

"I don't know."

"But not so bold now that you've lost your god. Doctor, what about you? You and the augur, together?"

Crane's voice, from the direction of the cot, "No." As he spoke, Silk heard the soft snap of a catch.

"I have your needler in my waistband. And yours, Patera. It's in my sleeve. In a moment I'm going to give them back to you. With your needlers back in your possession, do you think you and your friend the doctor could kill me in the dark?"

Silk said, "May all the gods forbid that I should ever kill you, or anyone, or even wish to."

Lemur laughed again, softly. "You wanted to kill Potto, didn't you, Patera? He questioned you for hours, according to what he told me. I've known Potto all my life, and there is no more objectionable man in the whorl, even when he's trying to ingratiate himself."

"It is true that I could not like him." Silk chose his words. "Yet I respected him as a member of the Ayuntamiento, and thus one of the legitimate rulers of our city. Certainly I did not wish to harm him."

"He hit you repeatedly, and eventually so hard that you were in a coma for hours. The whorl would be well rid of my cousin Potto. Don't you want your needler back?"

"Yes. Very much." Silk extended his hand blindly.

"And you'll try to kill me?"

"Hammerstone challenged me in the same way," Silk said. "I told Councillor Potto about it, and he must have told you; but you're not a soldier."

"I'm not even a chem."

Crane's voice: "He's never seen you."

"In that case, look at me now, Patera."

A faint glow, a nebulous splotch of white phosphorescence near the

ceiling, appeared to relieve the utter darkness. As Silk stared in fascina-
tion, the closely shaven face of a man of sixty or thereabouts appeared. It
was a noble face, with a lofty brow surmounted by a mane of silver hair,
an aquiline nose, and a wide mobile-looking mouth; staring up at it, Silk
realized that Councillor Lemur had to be taller even than Gib.

The face spoke: "Aren't you going to ask how I do this? My skin is
self-luminescent. Even my eyes. Watch."

Two more faintly glowing splotches appeared and became Lemur's
hands. One held a needler as large as Auk's by the barrel. "Take it,
Doctor. It's your own."

Crane's voice, from the darkness beyond Lemur's hands: "Silk's not
impressed."

Leaving Lemur, the needler vanished.

"He's a man of the spirit." Crane chuckled.

"As am I, Patera. Very much so. You've lost your god. May I propose
another?"

"Tartaros? I was praying to him before you came in."

"Because of the dark, you mean." Lemur's face and hands faded, replaced by a blackness that now seemed blacker still.

"And because it's his day," Silk said. "At least, I'd assume that it's
Tarsday by now."

"Tartaros and the rest are only ghosts, Patera. They've never been
anything more, and ghosts fade. With the passing of three hundred years,
Pas, Echidna, Tartaros, Scylla, and the rest have faded almost to invisibil-
ity. The Prolocutor knows it, and since you're going to succeed him, you
should know it, too."

"Since I—" Silk fell silent, suddenly glad that the room was dark.

Lemur laughed again; and Silk—heartsick and terrified—nearly
laughed with him, and found that he was smiling. "If only you could see
yourself, Patera! Or have your likeness taken."

"You . . ."

"You're a trained augur, I'm told. You graduated from the schola with
honors. So tell me, can Tartaros see in the dark?"

Silk nodded, and by that automatic motion discovered that he had
already accepted the implication that Lemur could see in the dark as
well. "Certainly. All gods can, actually."

Crane's voice: "That's what you were taught, anyhow."

Lemur's baritone, so resonant that it made Crane sound thin and
scratchy in comparison. "I can, too, no less than they. By waves of energy
too long for your eyes, I'm seeing you now. And I hear and see in places

where I am not. When you woke, Doctor Crane held up his fingers and required you to count them. Now it's your turn. Any number you choose."

Silk raised his right hand.

"All five. Again."

Silk complied.

"Three. Crane held up three for you. Again."

"I believe you," Silk said.

"Six. You believed Crane as well, when he told you that I plan to kill you both. It's quite untrue, as you've heard. We mean to elevate and honor you both."

"Thank you," Silk said.

"First I shall tell you the story of the gods. Doctor Crane knows it already, or guesses if he does not know. A certain ruler, a man who had the strength to rule alone and so called himself the monarch, built our whorl, Patera. It was to be a message from himself to the universe. You have seen some of the people he put on board it, and in fact you have walked and talked with one."

Silk nodded, then (conscious of Crane) said, "Yes. Her name is Mamelta."

"You talked about Mucor. The monarch's doctors tinkered with the minds of the men and women he put into the whorl as Blood's surgeon did with hers. But more skillfully, erasing as much as they dared of their patients' personal lives."

Silk said, "Mamelta told me she had been operated upon before she was lifted up to this whorl."

"There you have it. The surgeons found, however, that their patients' memories of their ruler, his family, and some of his officials were too deeply entrenched to be eliminated altogether. To obscure the record, they renamed them. Their ruler, the man who called himself the monarch, became Pas, the shrew he had married Echidna, and so on. She had borne him seven children. We call them Scylla, Molpe, Tartaros, Hierax, Thelxiepeia, Phaea, and Sphigx."

In the darkness, Silk traced the sign of addition.

"The monarch had wanted a son to succeed him. Scylla was as strong-willed as the monarch himself, but female. It is a law of nature, as concerns our race, that females are subject to males. Her father allowed her to found our city, however, and many others. She founded your Chapter as well, a parody of the state religion of her own whorl. She was hardly more than a child, you understand, and the rest younger even than she."

Silk swallowed and said nothing.

"His queen bore the monarch another, but she was worse yet, a fine dancer and a skilled musician, but female, too, and subject to fits of insanity. We call her Molpe."

There was a soft click.

"Nothing useful in your bag, Doctor? We searched it, naturally.

"To continue. Their third child was male, but no better than the first two, because he was born blind. He became that Tartaros to whom you were recommending yourself, Patera. You believe he can see without light. The truth is that he cannot see by daylight. Am I boring you?"

"That wouldn't matter, but you're risking the displeasure of the gods, and endangering your own spirit."

Crane's dry chuckle came out of the darkness.

"I'll continue to do it. Echidna conceived again and bore another male, a boy who inherited his father's virile indifference to the physical sensations of others to the point of mania. You must know, Patera, as we all do, the exquisite pleasure of inflicting pain upon those we dislike. He allowed himself to be seduced by it, to the point that he came to care for nothing else and while still a child slaughtered thousands for his amusement. We call him Hierax now, the god of death.

"Shall I go on? There are three more, all girls, but you know them as well as I. Thelxiepeia with her spells and drugs and poisons, fat Phaea, and Sphigx, who combined her father's fortitude with her mother's vile temper. In a family such as hers, she would be forced to cultivate those qualities or die, unquestionably."

Silk coughed. "You indicated that you intended to return my needler, Councillor. I'd like very much to have it back."

This time the uncanny light wrapped Lemur's entire body, strong enough to glow faintly through his tunic and trousers. "Watch," he said, and held out his right arm. A dark smudge beneath the embroidered satin of his sleeve crept down his arm to the elbow, then down his forearm until Hyacinth's gold-plated needler slid into his open hand. "Here you are."

"How did you do that?" Silk inquired.

"There are thousands of minute circuits in my arms. By flexing certain muscles, I can create a magnetic field, and by tightening them in sequence while relaxing others, I can move the field. Watch."

Hyacinth's needler crept from Lemur's hand to his wrist, and disappeared into his sleeve. "You say you'd like to have it back?"

"Yes, very much."

"And you, Doctor Crane? I have already given you yours, and I plan to make use of your services. Will you count your needler as your fee, paid in advance?"

The light that streamed from Lemur was now so bright that Silk could make out Crane, seated on the cot, as he drew his needler and held it out. "You can have it back, if you want. But give Silk his, and I'll accept that."

"Doctor Crane has already tried to shoot me, you see." Lemur's shining face smiled. "He's playing a cruel trick on you, Patera."

"No, he's being the same kind friend he has been to me since we first met. There are men who are ashamed of their best impulses, because they have come to associate goodness with weakness. Give it to me, please."

It was not Hyacinth's needler but her azoth that crawled like a silver spider into Lemur's open hand. Silk reached for it, but the hand closed about it; Lemur laughed, and they were plunged in darkness again.

Crane's voice: "Silk tells me you captured a woman with him. If you've hurt her badly, I want to see her."

"I could squeeze this hard enough to crush it," Lemur told them. "That would be dangerous even for me."

Silk had succeeded in untangling the silver chain; he put it about his neck and adjusted the position of Pas's gammadion as he spoke. "Then I advise you not to do it."

"I won't. Before I told you the truth about your gods, Patera, I hinted that I'd propose a new god to you, a living god to whom the wisest might kneel. I meant myself, as you must have realized. Are you ready to worship me?"

"I'm afraid we lack an appropriate victim for sacrifice."

Lemur's eyes glowed. "You're wasting your tact, Patera. Don't you want to be Prolocutor? When I happened to mention it, I expected you to kiss my rump for the thought. Instead you're acting as if you didn't hear me."

"After the first moment or two, I assumed you intended a subtle torture. To speak frankly, I still do."

"Not at all. I'm completely serious. The doctor said he wished he'd invented you. So do I. If you're what he and his masters required, you suit my purposes even better."

Silk felt as though he were choking. "You want me to tell people that you're a god, Councillor? That you are to be paid divine honors?"

Warm and rich and friendly, Lemur's voice boomed out of the darkness. "More than that. The present Prolocutor could do that, and would in a moment if I told him to. Or I could replace him with any of a hundred augurs who would."

Silk shook his head. "I doubt it. But even if you're correct, they would not be believed."

"Precisely. But you would be. His Cognizance is old. His Cognizance will die, tomorrow perhaps. In a surprising but hugely popular development, it will be discovered that he has named you as his successor, and you will explain to the people that Pas has withheld his rains out of consideration for me. They need only pay me proper honors to be forgiven. Eventually they will come to understand that I am, as I am, a greater god than Pas. After all that I've told you, do you retain some loyalty to him? And Echidna and their brats?"

Silk sighed. "I realized as you spoke how little I have ever had. Your blasphemies ought to have outraged me. I was merely shocked instead, like a maiden aunt who overhears her cook swearing; but you see, I've encountered a real god, the Outsider—"

Crane whooped with laughter.

"And Kypris, a real goddess. Thus I know what divinity is, the look and the sound and the true texture of it. You said something else that I ignored, Councillor."

For the first time, Lemur sounded dangerous and even deadly. "Which was . . . ?"

"You said that you were not a chem. I'm not one of those ignorant and prejudiced bios who consider themselves superior to chems, but I know—"

"You lie!" Doubly terrifying in the darkness, the blade of the azoth tore the plane of existence like so much paper, shooting past Silk's ear, manifest to every cell in his body, and horrible as nothing the universe contained could be.

From the other side of the room, Crane shouted, "You'll sink us!" and the vessel lurched and shook as he spoke. Chips of burning paint and flakes of incandescent steel showered Silk with fire; he backed away in horror.

"One born a biological man did that, Patera. A man who has become more." Something rang in the darkness as a hammer rings against an anvil. "I *am* a biological man *and* a god." The harrowing discontinuity that had wounded the very fabric of the universe was gone.

"Thank you," Silk said. He gasped for breath. "Thank you very much. Please don't do that again."

As the violence of the vessel's motion abated to steady thrumming, Lemur's luminous arm reappeared; his hand opened, and the hilt of the azoth slid smoothly into its sleeve.

There was a thump as Crane dropped his medical bag. "Are you inside there?"

Lemur's voice was warm again. "Why do you ask?"

"Just curious. I was wondering if it might not be like conflict armor, but better."

"Which would be of some interest to your masters in the government of . . . ?"

"Palustria."

"No. Not Palustria. We have eliminated certain cities, and that is one of them. Like Patera Silk, you'll soon come to serve Viron, and when you do, you must be more forthright. Meanwhile, let it be enough for you that I am in another part of this boat. Perhaps I'll show you when we're done with the business at hand."

"Serve you, you mean."

"We gods have many names."

"Patera, you needn't concern yourself about your paramour from the past. She's nursing Doctor Crane's patient even as I speak, and worrying about you."

Crane's voice: "You use some old-fashioned words. How old are you, Councillor?"

"How old would you say I am?" Lemur extended his shining hand. "You doctors like to speak of pronounced tremors. Can you pronounce upon that one?"

"You've held office under two caldés, and for twenty-two years since the death of the last. Naturally we wondered."

"In Palustria. Yes, in Palustria, naturally you did. When you see me elsewhere you can formulate an estimate of your own, and I'll be interested to learn it."

"Patera, doesn't all this astound you?"

"I can understand how you could be a bio with prosthetic parts; our Maytera Rose is like that." Silk discovered that his own hands were trembling and pushed them into his pockets. "Not how you could be in another part of this boat."

"In the same way that a glass conveys to you the image of a room at the opposite end of the city. In the same way that your Sacred Window showed you the tricked-out image of a woman dead three hundred years and convinced you that you had spoken with a minor goddess." Lemur chuckled. "But I've wasted too much time already, while Doctor Crane's patient lies dying. I trust he'll forgive me, I was enjoying myself." The luminous hand held up Hyacinth's needler. "Here's Doctor Crane's fee, as specified by him. Doctor, I wish you to look at a patient. To earn this fee, you need only examine him and tell him the truth. Is it a violation of medical ethics to tell a patient the truth?"

"No."

"There have been times when I've thought that it must be. This fourth prisoner of mine's a spy, too. Will you do it? He's badly injured."

"After which you'll kill Silk and me." Crane snorted. "All right, I've lived as a quacksalver. Since I've got to die, I'll die as one, too."

"Both of you will live," Lemur told him, "because you will both become admirably cooperative. I could have you so now, if I wished, but for the present you serve me better as opponents. I will not say foes. You see, I have told this fourth prisoner that the doctor who will examine him and the augur who will shrive him are no friends of mine. That they have, in fact, seen fit to intrigue against the government I direct."

The luminosity of Lemur's hand and arm brightened, and Hyacinth's engraved, gold-plated, little needler slithered like a living animal into his open palm. "Your Cognizance? Here you are." He handed the needler to Silk. "Will you, as an anointed augur, administer the Pardon of Pas to Doctor Crane's patient, if Crane judges him in imminent danger of death?"

"Of course," Silk said.

"Then let's go. I know you'll find this interesting." Lemur threw open the door. Blinking and wiping their eyes, they followed him along a narrow corridor floored with steel grating, and down a flight of steel stairs almost as steep as a ladder.

"I'm taking you all the way down to the keel," Lemur told them. "I hope you weren't expecting this boat to rock, by the way. We've put out —I gave the order while we were playing with that azoth—and we're cruising beneath the surface now, where there's no wave action."

He led them to a heavy door set into the floor, spun two handwheels, and threw it back. "Down here. I'm about to show you the hole in our bottom."

Silk went first. The vibration that had shaken the boat since Lemur had threatened him with the azoth was stronger here, almost an audible sound; there was a cool freshness to the air, and the iron railing of the steps he descended felt damp beneath his hand. Green lights that seemed imitations of the ancient lights provided the first settlers by Pas, and an indefinable odor that might have been no more than the absence of any other, made him feel for the first time that he was actually beneath the waters of Lake Limna.

The flier's broken wings were the first things he saw. They had been laid out, with scraps of the nearly invisible fabric that had covered them, on the transparent canopy of a sizable yawl—shattered spars of a material that might have been polished bone, less thick than his forefinger.

"Wait there a moment, Your Cognizance," Lemur called. "I want to show you these. You and Doctor Crane both. It will be well worth your while."

"You got one after all," Crane said. "You've brought down a flier."

There was a note of defeat in his voice that made Silk turn to stare back at him.

"They'd all gone," Crane explained. "Blood and his thugs and most of the malc servants. I thought this might be it, but I hoped . . ." He left the sentence incomplete and shrugged.

Lemur had picked up an oddly curved, almost tear-drop-shaped grid of the cream-colored material. "We have, Doctor. And this is the secret. Simple, yet infinitely precious. Don't you want to examine it? Wouldn't you like to provide your masters with the secret of flight? The key that opens the sky? This is its shape. Pick it up if you wish. See how light it is. Run your fingers over it, Doctor."

Crane shook his head.

"Then you, Your Cognizance. When your followers have installed you as caldé, it could prove a most useful thing to know."

"I'll never be caldé," Silk told him, "and I have never wished to be." He accepted the almost weightless grid, and stared at its fluid lines. "This is what lets a flier fly? This shape?"

Lemur nodded. "With the material from which it's made. Tarsier's analyzing that. When you broke into Blood's villa Phaesday night—I know all about that, you see. When you broke in, didn't you wonder why Crane's city had sent him to watch Blood?"

"I didn't realize he was a spy then," Silk explained. He put down the grid and fingered the swelling that Potto's fist had left on the side of his head. He felt weak and a little dizzy.

"To keep his masters appraised of Blood's progress with the eagle," Lemur told him. "More than twenty-five years ago, I realized the possibilities of flight. I saw that if our troopers could fly as fliers did, enemy troop movements would be revealed at once, that picked bodies of men could land behind an enemy's lines to disrupt communications, and all the rest of it. As soon as I was free to act, I backed various experimenters whose work appeared promising. None developed a device capable of carrying a child, much less a trooper."

Recalling Hammerstone, Silk asked, "Why not a soldier?"

Crane grunted. "They're too heavy. Lemur there weighs four times as much as you and me together."

"Ah!" Lemur turned to Crane. "You've looked into the matter, I see."

Crane nodded. "Fliers are actually a bit smaller than most troopers. I'm small, as everybody keeps reminding me. But I'm bigger than most fliers."

"You sound as though you've seen some close up."

"Through a telescope," Crane said. "Want to object that I had nothing to compare them to?"

"To oblige you, yes."

"I didn't need anything. A small man isn't proportioned like a big one, and as a small physician I'm very much aware of that. A small man's head is bigger in proportion to his shoulders, for instance."

Silk fidgeted. "If someone may be dying . . ."

"That someone could be you, Your Cognizance." Lemur laid a heavy hand upon Silk's shoulder. "Purely as an hypothesis, let's say that I plan to pull your head off as soon as you've conveyed the Pardon of Pas to this unfortunate. If that were the case, shortening our discussion would materially shorten your life."

"As a citizen I'm entitled to a public trial, and to an advocate. As an augur—"

The pressure of Lemur's fingers increased. "It's too bad you're not an advocate yourself, Your Cognizance. If you were you'd realize that there's a further, unwritten provision. It is that the urgent needs of Viron must be served. As we speak a mendacious and malcontented radical faction is attempting to overthrow our lawfully constituted Ayuntamiento and substitute for it the rule of one inexperienced—but deep, and I admit that freely—augur, stirring up the populace by alleging a lot of superstitious taradiddle about enlightenment and the supposed favor of the gods. Am I crushing your shoulder?"

"It is certainly very painful."

"It can easily become more so. Did you really speak to a goddess in a house of ill repute? Say no, or I'll crush it."

"A goddess in the sense that the god who enlightened me is a god? Doctor Crane insists that there is no such being. Whether he's right or not, I'm inclined to doubt that there are any more such gods."

Lemur tightened his grip, so that Silk would have fallen to his knees if he could. "I want to tell you in some detail, Your Cognizance, how I hit upon the notion of using a bird of prey to bring down a flier for our examination. How I saw a hawk take a merganser at twilight and conceived the idea. How I combed Viron, with the utmost secrecy, for the right man to carry it out. And how I found him."

Silk moaned, and Crane said, "And so on and so forth. Let him go, and I'll tell you how we learned of it."

"Let him go!" It was Mamelta, dashing out of the dimness and throwing herself on Silk. *"You damned robot! You THING!"* She was naked save for a blood-smeared rag knotted about her waist, her full breasts and rounded thighs trembling, her bare skin the color of old ivory.

Lemur released Silk and cuffed her almost casually; white bone gleamed where his long nails had torn her forehead, until blood streamed forth to cover it.

Crane crouched beside her and snapped open his brown bag.

"Very good, Doctor," Lemur said. "Patch her up by all means. But not here." He threw her over his shoulder and stalked away.

"Come on." Agilely for a man of his age, Crane mounted the steps to the trapdoor Lemur had opened for them and tugged at one of its wheels.

"We can't leave her," Silk said. He moved his shoulder experimentally and decided no bones had been broken.

"We can't help her while we're prisoners ourselves."

Lemur's mocking voice echoed from the other end of the hold. "A man is dying, and this woman is bleeding like a stuck pig. Don't either of you care?"

"I do," Silk called, and hobbled in the direction of the voice.

Beyond the bow of the yawl, the flier lay on a blanket spread on the steel floor, his sun-browned face twisted in agony. Beside him stretched a second trapdoor, far larger than the one through which they had come— large enough, as Silk realized with some astonishment, to admit the yawl. An instrument panel stood against the bulkhead at the end of the compartment.

Lemur dropped Mamelta next to the flier. In a deafening roar that reminded Silk of the talus, he called, *"Rejoin us, Doctor. You can't open that hatch."* To Silk he added, "I tightened those locking screws, you see. And I'm a great deal stronger than both of you together, as well as a great deal heavier."

Silk had already knelt at the flier's head. "I convey to you, my son, the forgiveness of all the gods. Recall now the words of Pas, who—"

"That's enough." Lemur took him by the shoulder again. "We want the doctor first, I think. If he won't come, you must bring him."

"I'm here," Crane announced.

"This is our flier," Lemur said. "His name's Iolar. He has told us a little, you see, though nothing of value, not even the name of his city. I would have to agree that he's scarcely taller than you, and he may well be a trifle lighter. Yet he is flier enough, or almost enough."

Crane did not reply. After a moment he took scissors from his bag and began to cut away the flightsuit. Silk tore a strip from his robe, wound it twice about Mamelta's head, and tied it.

Lemur nodded approvingly. "She will live to be grateful for your efforts, I'm sure, Patera. So will Iolar, I hope. Are you listening, Doctor Crane?"

Crane nodded without looking up. "I'm going to have to roll you over. Put your arms above your head. Don't try to roll yourself. Let me do it."

"You see," Lemur continued conversationally, "Iolar came down right here, in the lake. In one way, that was extremely convenient for us. We sent our little boat to the surface and scooped up him and his wings without help from the Civil Guard. Or from Blood, I should add, and very much to the discomfiture of them both." Lemur chuckled.

"That was early yesterday morning. As it chanced, I was ashore at the time, so Loris directed the recovery. Whether I could've managed things better, I can't say. Loris is not Lemur, but then who is? In any event one vital part was not retrieved, although the flier himself was, with most of the wings and harness and so on that permitted him to fly. He calls it a propulsion module, or PM. Isn't that so, Iolar?"

Crane glanced up at Lemur, then looked quickly back to his patient.

"Precisely so, Doctor. Without the device, our troopers will still be able to fly in a manner of speaking. But only to glide, as a gull does when it rides the breeze without moving its wings. It should be possible for such a trooper to launch himself from a cliff or a tower and fly a great distance, given a strong and favoring wind. Only under the most extraordinary conditions, however, could he take off from a level field. Under no conceivable conditions could he fly into the eye of any wind, even the weakest. Is this too technical for you, Patera? Doctor Crane's following me, I believe."

Silk said, "So am I, I think."

"At first the deficiency appeared only temporary. Iolar had a propulsion module—he admitted as much. Presumably it was torn free by the impact when he struck the water. We could fish it up, which we tried to do all that day, or he could tell us how to make them. This last, I am sorry to say, he refuses to do."

Crane said, "You must have some sort of medical facility on this boat. Something better than this."

"Oh, we do," Lemur assured him. "In fact, we had him there for a while. But he didn't repay our kindness, so we brought him back here. Is he conscious?"

"Didn't you hear me talking to him a minute ago? Of course he is."

"Fine. Iolar, listen to me. I'm Councillor Lemur, and I am speaking to you. I may never do this again, and what I'm about to say will be more important to you than anything you've ever heard before, or that you're ever apt to hear. Do you hear me now? Say something or move your head."

The flier lay face down, his face turned toward the long steel hatch in the deck. His voice, when it came, was weak and strangely accented. "I hear."

Lemur smiled and nodded. "You've found me to be a man of my word, haven't you? Very well, I'm giving you my word that everything I'm about to say is true. I'm not going to try to trick you again, and I'm not inclined to be patient with you any longer. These are the men Potto and I told you about. This doctor is an admitted spy, just like you. Not a spy of ours, you may be sure. A spy from Palustria, or so he says. This augur is the leader of the faction that has been trying to seize control of our city. If Doctor Crane says you're going to die, you've won our argument. I'll let the augur bring you Pas's Pardon, and that's that. But if Doctor Crane says you'll live, you'll be surrendering your life if you continue to refuse. Have I made myself clear? I'm not going to waste any more of my time, or Potto's, in trying to force the facts we need from you. We're building new equipment to find your propulsion module on the bottom. We'll get it, and you'll have died for nothing. If we don't find it, we still have the eagle. She knows her business now, and all we'll have to do to get a propulsion module is send her after the next flier we see."

Lemur pointed a finger at Crane. "No threats, Doctor. No promises. Truth will cost you nothing, and a lie gain you nothing. Is he going to live?"

"I don't know," Crane said levelly. "He's got a couple of broken ribs— they haven't punctured the lung, or he might be dead already. At least four thoracic vertebrae are in pretty bad shape. There's damage to the spinal cord, but I don't think it's been severed, although I can't be sure. Given proper care and a first-rate surgeon, I'd say he might have a good chance."

Lemur looked sceptical. "A complete recovery?"

"I doubt it. He might be able to walk."

"Now then." Lemur's voice dropped to a whisper. "Which will it be? In two or three hours we could have you ashore. Those black canisters all of you wear—how do they work?"

Silence filled the hold. Silk, bent over Mamelta, saw her eyelids flutter, and clasped her hand. Crane shrugged and snapped his bag shut, the sound as abrupt and final as the report of Auk's needler in the Cock.

"I didn't think you would," Lemur told the flier almost conversationally. "That's why I put out. Patera, you can start your rigmarole, if you want to. I don't care. He'll be dead almost before you finish it."

"What are you going to do?" Crane asked.

"Put him off the boat." Lemur strode to the instrument panel. "As a man of science you might be interested in this, Doctor. This compartment is at the bottom of our boat, as I told you. It's tightly sealed, as you discovered a few minutes ago when you tried to open the hatch. At present," he glanced at one of the gauges, "we're seventy cubits below the surface. At this depth, the water pressure around our hull is roughly three atmospheres. Has anyone explained to you how we rise and sink?"

"No," Crane said. "I've wondered." He glanced at Silk as though to see whether he, too, was curious; but Silk was chanting and swinging his beads over the head of the injured flier.

"We do it with compressed air. If we want to go deeper, we open one of our ballast tanks. That lets lake water in, so we lose buoyancy and sink. When we want to surface, we valve compressed air into that tank to force the water out. The tank becomes a float, so we gain buoyancy. Simple but effective. When I open this valve, more air will flow into this compartment." Lemur turned it, producing a loud hiss.

"If I were to let it in fast, you'd find it painful, so I've only cracked the valve. Swallow if your ears hurt."

Silk, who had been giving Lemur some small fraction of his attention, paused in his chant to swallow. As he did, the injured flier whispered, "The sun . . ." His eyes, which had been half-shut, opened wide, and he struggled to turn his face toward Silk. "Tell your people!"

No audible response was permitted until the liturgy was complete, but Silk nodded, swinging his beads in the sign of subtraction. "You are blessed." While bobbing his head nine times, as the ritual demanded, he made the sign of addition.

"When the pressure here reaches three atmospheres, as it soon will, we can open that boat hole without flooding the compartment." Lemur chuckled. "I'll loosen up the fittings now."

Crane started to protest, then clamped his jaw.

"We're losing control," the flier whispered to Silk, and his eyes closed.

With his free hand, Silk stroked the flier's temple to indicate that he had heard. "I pray you to forgive us, the living." Another sign of addition. "I and many another have wronged you often, my son, committing terrible crimes and numerous offenses against you. Do not hold them in your heart, but begin the life that follows life in innocence, all these wrongs forgiven." With his beads, he traced the sign of subtraction again.

Mamelta's hand found Silk's again and closed upon it. "He . . . Am I dreaming?"

Silk shook his head. "I speak here for Great Pas, for Divine Echidna, for Scalding Scylla, for Marvelous Molpe, for Tenebrous Tartaros, for Highest Hierax, for Thoughtful Thelxiepeia, for Fierce Phaea, and for Strong Sphigx. Also for all lesser gods." Lowering his voice, Silk added, "The Outsider likewise forgives you, my son, for I speak here for him."

"He's going to die?"

Silk put a finger to his lips. In a surprisingly gentle tone, Crane said, "Lemur's going to kill him. He's opted for it. So would I."

"So do I." Mamelta touched the black cloth with which Silk had bandaged her head. "They said we were going to a wonderful world of peace and plenty, where it would be noon all day. We knew they lied. When I die, I'll go home. My mother and brothers . . . Chiquito on his perch in the patio."

Crane took out his scissors again. He was cutting away the cloth when Lemur threw open the hatch.

It was—to Silk the thought was irresistible—as if the Outsider himself had entered the hold. Where the dark steel hatch had been a moment before, there was a rectangle of liquid light, translucid and coolly lambent. The light of the Long Sun, penetrating the clear water of Lake Limna even to a depth of seventy cubits, was refracted and diffused, filling the opening that Lemur had so suddenly revealed and invading the hold with a supernal dawn of celestial blue. For a few seconds, Silk could scarcely believe that the ethereal substance was water. Leaning across the flier with his right hand (still grasping his beads) braced upon the coaming, he dipped his fingers into it.

Crane said, "A little air escaped. Did you feel it?"

Staring down into the crystal water, Silk shook his head. A school of slender silver fish materialized at one end of the hatchway, and in the space of a breath appeared to drift to the other, ten cubits or more beneath the steel plate on which he knelt.

Lemur said, "Move, Patera," and picked up the flier.

Crane shouted, "Watch out! Don't hold him like that!"

"Afraid I'll damage him further, Doctor?" Lemur smiled and lifted the flier effortlessly above his head. "It won't matter.

"What about it, Iolar? Anything to say? This is the last chance."

"Thank the woman," the flier gasped. "The men. Strong wings."

Lemur threw him down. The lambent water that filled the hatchway erupted in Silk's face, drenching and momentarily blinding him. By the time he could see again, the flier had nearly passed out of sight. A brief glimpse of his agonized face, his startled eyes and open mouth, from which bubbles like spheres of thin glass streamed, and he was gone.

Lemur slammed down the hatch with a deafening crash and tightened its fastenings. "When I open the one that we came through, the pressure here will equalize with the pressure in the rest of the ship. Keep your mouths open, or it may blow out your eardrums."

He led them up a different companionway this time, and along a broader corridor (in which they passed Councillors Galago and Potto deep in conversation), and at last through a doorway guarded by two soldiers. "This is what you were looking for, Doctor," he told Crane, "although you may not have known it. In this stateroom you will behold our true, biological selves. I'm over there."

He pointed toward a circle of gleaming machines; Crane hurried toward it. Silk, limping and supporting Mamelta, followed more slowly.

Councillor Lemur's bio body lay upon an immaculate white pallet, an equally immaculate white sheet drawn to his chin. His eyes were closed, his cheeks sunken; his chest rose and fell gently and slowly; the faint wheeze of his breath was barely audible. A wisp of white hair escaped the circlet of black synthetic and network of multicolored wires that bound his brows. Snakelike tubes from a dozen machines (clear, straw-yellow, and darkly crimson) ducked beneath the sheet.

"No treacherous bios in here," Lemur told them. "We're nursed by devoted chems, and the machines that maintain us in life are maintained by chems. They love us, and we love them. We promise them immortality, and we will deliver it: a never-ending supply of replacement parts. They repay us with infinite prolongation of our merely mortal lives."

Crane was inspecting one of the machines. "Your life-support equipment seems very impressive. I wish I had it."

"My kidneys and liver have failed. So we have devices to perform those functions. There's a booster on my heart that's capable of taking over its function completely whenever that becomes necessary. Pulses of oxygen, of course."

Crane sucked his teeth and shook his head.

Mamelta said softly, "This is the first time I haven't been cold."

"The air in here is completely reprocessed every seventy seconds. It is filtered, irradiated to destroy bacteria and viruses, and maintained at a relative humidity of thirty-five percent, within a quarter degree of the normal temperature of the bio body."

Looking down at the recumbent councillor, Silk told him, "I'd never have thought I'd feel sorry for you. But I do."

"I'm seldom conscious of lying here. This is me." Lemur struck his chest, and the sound was that of the ringing hammer Silk had heard in the dark. "Vigorous and alert, with perfect hearing and vision. All that I lack is good digestion. And at times," Lemur paused significantly, "patience."

Crane was bending over the recumbent figure; before Lemur could move to stop him, he pushed up one gray eyelid with his thumb. "This man is dead."

"Don't be absurd!" Lemur started toward him, but Silk, acting immediately upon an impulse of which he was scarcely aware, stepped into his path. And Lemur, perhaps responding to some childhood injunction to respect an augur's habit, stopped short.

"Look." Crane reached with thumb and forefinger into the empty socket and drew out a pinch of black detritus that might almost have been a mixture of earth and tar. After exhibiting it to Lemur, he dropped it on the pristine sheet, where it lay like so much filth, and wiped his fingers on the thin white pillow, leaving dingy, mephitic streaks.

Lemur made a sound, not loud, that Silk had never heard before (though Silk had already, young as he was, heard so much grief). It was a snuffling, and in it a whine like the cry of a small shaft driven faster and faster—the sound of a drill that has struck a nail, and, impelled by a madman, spins on harder and harder and faster and faster until it smokes, destroying itself by its own boundless, ungoverned energy. Some hours later, Silk would think of that sound and recall the clockwork universe the Outsider had shown him on the Phaesday before in the ballcourt; for it was the sound of that universe dying, or rather of a part of it dying, or rather (he would decide sleepily) of the whole of it dying for someone.

Lemur crouched, slowly and unsteadily, as he sounded the note that would stay with Silk until night; his hands moved haplessly, as though of their own volition, not pawing or clawing or indeed doing anything at all, but writhing as the dead flier's hands were moving (perhaps) even then, in the cold waters of the lake as they awaited the onset of that stiffening which follows death and endures for half a day. (Or a day, or a day and a half, depending upon a variety of circumstances, and always subject to some dispute.) As he crouched, Lemur's eyes never left the mummified councillor on the snowy pallet; and at length, when one knee was on the green-tiled floor, and it seemed that Lemur could not crouch further, his arms fell.

Then the silver azoth that Silk had taken from a drawer in Hyacinth's dressing table, on the night of the same day that the Outsider had revealed to Silk the essence of the universe in which he existed, fell from Lemur's tapestried sleeve and skittered across the floor.

And Crane dove for it, bumping hard against one of the medical machines that surrounded the dead councillor's bed and sending it crashing down on its side; but quickly and deftly, gray-bearded though he was, he snatched up the azoth.

Its terrible beam shot forth, and Lemur exploded in a ball of flame. Silk and Mamelta staggered back, covering their faces with their arms.

Crane dashed past them and was out the door by the time that Silk could see again.

Mamelta screamed.

Silk held her arm and dragged her behind him, conscious that he should silence her but conscious also that it would probably prove impossible and that there was not a second to waste in any event.

The soldiers at the door were firing when Silk opened it. Before he could draw back, they charged down the broad corridor, running at thrice the speed even a fleet boy like Horn could have managed and ten times the best that Silk, handicapped by his ankle and the shrieking Mamelta, could hope to achieve; the two of them had not covered half the distance when there was a flash from the companionway and a double explosion— horribly painful, though not loud to ears still shocked and ringing from Lemur's detonation.

"We must get there before he shuts the hatch," Silk told Mamelta, and then, when she still would not run, he (to his own later amazement) picked her up bodily, and throwing her over one shoulder like a rolled mattress or a sack of flour, ran himself, stumbling and staggering, once crashing into a bulkhead and nearly falling headlong down the companionway. Someone was shouting, *"Wait! Wait!"* and he had reached the hatch before he realized that it was himself.

It was shut, but he dropped Mamelta and wrenched around the handwheels. A roaring wind from below lifted it as he did.

"Doctor!"

"Help me!" Crane shouted. "We can get away in the boat."

Half a dozen slug guns boomed in the corridor as Silk and Mamelta stumbled down the short companionway into the boat hold, and a slug slammed the hatch like a sledgehammer as he retightened its fastenings.

When he reached Crane, the little physician was heaving at the longer hatch that covered the boat hole. The three of them threw it back, with chill lake water gushing in after it, helping to lift it as air pressure had opened the much smaller hatch above. For a moment Silk was conscious of floundering in rising water. He spat, managed to get his face clear, and gasped for breath.

The flood slacked, then held steady for a second or two that seemed a minute at least; he was conscious of the full-throated hoot of the air valve, and of someone (whether it was Mamelta or Crane he could not be sure) struggling and splashing nearby.

The flow reversed. Slowly at first, then swifter and swifter, sweeping him along, the flood that had practically filled the compartment rushed back to Lake Limna. Helpless as a doll in a maelstrom, he spun in a dizzy whorl of blue light, slowed (his lungs ready to burst), and caught sight of another figure suspended like himself with splayed limbs and drifting hair.

And then, dimly, of a monstrous mottled face—black, red, and gold—far larger than any wall of the manse, and a gaping mouth that closed upon the splayed figure he had seen. It passed below him as a floater rushing down some reeling mountain meadow might pass a floating thistle seed, and the turbulence of its wake sent him spinning.

CHAPTER
13   THE CALDÉ SURRENDERS

"Patera? Oh, Patera!"

Maytera Marble was waving from the front steps of the old manteion on Sun Street. Two troopers in armor stood beside her; their officer, in dress greens, indulgently exhibited his sword to little Maytera Mint. Gulo hurried forward.

The officer glanced up. "Patera Silk? You are under arrest." Gulo shook his head and explained.

Maytera Marble sniffed, a sniff of such devastating power and contempt that it burned to dust all the pleasure the young officer had enjoyed from Maytera Mint's wide-eyed admiration. "Take Patera Silk away? You can't! Such a holy—"

A soft snarl came from the crowd that had been clustered about Gulo. Gulo was not an imaginative man, yet it seemed to him that an unseen lion was awakening; and the prayers he had chanted each Sphigxday were not nonsensical after all.

"Don't fight!" Maytera Mint returned the officer's sword and raised her hands. "Please! There's no need."

A stone flew, striking the helmet of one of the troopers. A second whizzed past Maytera Marble's head to thump the door, and the trooper who had been hit fired, his shot followed by a scream. Maytera Mint dashed down the steps into the crowd.

The trooper fired again, and his officer slapped down the muzzle of his slug gun. "Open these," the officer told Gulo. "We had better go inside." More stones flew as they fled into the manteion. The trooper who had been hit fired twice more as Maytera Marble and the other trooper swung its heavy door shut, his shots so closely spaced that they might almost have been one. There was an answering rattle of stones.

"It is the heat." The officer spoke confidently and even smiled. "They will forget now that we are out of sight." He sheathed his sword. "This Patera Silk is popular."

Maytera Marble nodded. And then, *"Patera!"*

"I have to go." Gulo was sliding back the bolt. "I—I shouldn't have gone in here at all." He struggled to remember the other sibyl's name, failed, and concluded lamely, "She was right."

The officer snatched at his robe an instant too late as Gulo slipped out; angry yells invaded the manteion, then muted as the troopers shut the door and bolted it again. Faintly, the officer could hear Gulo shouting, *"People! People!"*

"They won't hurt him, Maytera." He paused to listen, his head cocked. "I do not like arresting . . ."

He let the apology trail away, having realized that he no longer had her attention. Her metal face mirrored faint hues: lemon, pink, and sorrel. Following the direction of her gaze, he saw the swirling color of the Sacred Window and knelt. The dancing hues created patterns he could not quite distinguish, glyphs, figures, and landscapes half formed, a face that swam, melted, and coalesced before the goddess spoke in a tongue he almost understood, a language that he too had known in a long-past life in an unimaginable place at an inconceivable time. In this, he was a maggot; her utterance proclaimed that he had once been a man, though the memories she woke were perhaps no more than the dead thoughts of the man he devoured.

I will, Great Goddess. I will. He will be safe with us.

Behind and above him he heard the chem talking to the fat augur. "A god came while you were outside, Patera. Honored us without a sacrifice. There was no one to interpret. I'm so terribly sorry you missed it—" And the augur, "I didn't, Maytera. Not all of it."

The officer willed them to be quiet. Her divine voice still strummed in his ears, far and sweet; and he knew what she desired him to do.

To breach the surface of the lake as Silk did, to rise from suffocation and see afresh the thin, bright streak of the sun and draw one's first breath, was to be reborn. He was not a strong swimmer, and indeed was hardly a swimmer at all; yet exhausted as he was, he managed to stay afloat on the long, slow swell, kicking spasmodically, dimly fearful that each kick might draw the attention of the huge fish.

There was a distant shout, followed by the clamor of a pan wildly beaten; he ignored both until the swell heaved him high enough to see the worn brown sails.

Three half-naked fishermen pulled him onto their boat. "There's someone else," he gasped. "We've got to find him."

"They already have!" And Crane was grinning at him.

The tallest and most grizzled of the fishermen slapped him on the back. "Gods look out for augurs. That's what my paw used to tell, Patera."

Crane nodded sagely. "Augurs and fools."

"Yes, sir. Them, too. Next time you go sailin', you take a sailor. Let's hope we can find your woman."

The thought of the great fish filled Silk's mind, and he shuddered. "It's good of you to look, but I'm afraid . . ."

"Couldn't reach her, Patera?"

"No, but— No."

"Well, we'll haul her out if we see her."

Silk stood; at once the rolling of the boat cost him his footing, and he found himself sitting on piled nets.

"Stay where you are and rest," Crane muttered. "You've been through a lot. So've I. But we've gotten a thorough washing, and that's good. Lots of isotopes released when a chem blows." He held up a gleaming card. "Captain, could you find us something to eat? Or a little wine?"

"Let me put her about, sir, and I'll see what's left."

"Money belt," Crane whispered, noticing Silk's puzzled look. "Lemur made me turn out my pockets but never patted me down. I promised them a card to take us back to Limna."

"That poor woman," Silk said to no one in particular, "three hundred years, for that." A black bird was perched in the rigging of a distant boat; seeing it, Silk recalled Oreb, smiled, and reproached himself for smiling.

Guiltily he glanced about him, hoping that his unseemly levity had passed unnoticed. Crane was watching the captain, and the captain, the largest sail. One sailor stood in the bow with a foot upon the bowsprit. The other, grasping a rope connected to the long stick (Silk could not recall its name, if he had ever known it) that spread the sail, appeared to be waiting for a signal from the captain—the back of his head seemed uncannily familiar. As Silk altered his position to get a better view of it, he realized that the nets on which he sat were dry.

Crane had brought Silk a red tunic, brown trousers, and brown shoes to replace the black ones he had kicked off in the lake. He changed in a deserted alley, throwing his robe, his torn tunic, and his old trousers behind a pile of refuse. "I got Hyacinth's needler back," he said, "and my gammadion and my beads; but not my glasses or any of my other possessions. Perhaps that's a sign."

Crane shrugged. "They were probably in Lemur's pocket." He had a new tunic and new trousers, too, and he had bought a razor. Glancing toward the mouth of the alley, he added, "Keep your voice down."

"What did you see?"

"Couple of Guardsmen."

"The Ayuntamiento will surely think we're dead," Silk objected. "Until they learn otherwise, we have no reason to fear the Guard."

Crane shook his head.

"If they thought we might have survived, they could have come to the surface and looked for us, couldn't they?"

"Not without telling everybody on the lake about their underwater boat. How do those fit?"

"They're a trifle large." Silk looked down at himself, wishing that he had a mirror. "Their boat must have come to the surface to collect poor Iolar."

"You're thin," Crane told him. "No, they sent up that little one we saw. They couldn't send it after us because that compartment down in the keel would've flooded again as soon as they undogged the hatch."

"It flooded when we opened the one in the floor," Silk murmured.

"That's right. I'd opened the air valve as far as it would go, but it hadn't had much time to build up pressure after you and the woman vented it coming down. Naturally a lot of water came in. It cut down the air space and pushed the pressure up to the water pressure, so the water flowed out again almost right away."

Silk hesitated, then nodded. "But if they open the upper hatch—the one in the corridor—the compartment will flood again, won't it?"

"Sure. Water would rise into the rest of the boat, too. Which is why they couldn't send their little boat after us. I can't imagine how they'll shut the boat door when they can't get into the compartment to do it, but no doubt they'll figure out something."

Silk leaned against a wall and removed Crane's wrapping from his ankle. "I'm not a sailor, but if it were up to me, I'd go far out in the lake, where there wasn't much chance of being seen—or perhaps into the cave Lemur mentioned when you asked how he had gotten your bag."

"I wish I hadn't lost that." Crane fingered his beard. "I'd had it twenty years."

Recalling his pen case, Silk said, "I know how you must feel, Doctor." He flogged the wall with the wrapping.

"Suppose they did go back into their cave. They'd still have the problem. That underwater boat's too big to drag up on shore."

"But they could tilt it," Silk said. "Shift everything to one side and

force all the water out of the floats on the other. They might even be able
to pull it over with a cable attached to the side of the cave."

Crane nodded, still watching the mouth of the alley. "I suppose so. Are
you ready?"

When Crane had gone, Silk opened the window. Their room was on the
third floor of the Rusty Lantern, and provided a magnificent view of the
lake, as well as a refreshing breeze. Leaning across the sill, Silk looked
down into Dock Street. Crane had wanted to get out of sight, or so he
had said; but he had called for pen and paper as soon as they had taken
this room, and gone out into the street again, leaving Silk behind, after
scribbling a not very lengthy note. Looking up and down Dock Street
now, Silk decided that if it did no harm for Crane to go out again, it
could surely do none for him to study the street from a window this high.

Limna was peaceful, the innkeeper had said; but there had been rioting in the city the night before, rioting put down harshly by the Guard.
"Silk's men," the innkeeper had told them wisely. "They're the ones
stirring it up, if you ask me."

Silk's men.

Who were they? Deep in thought, Silk stroked his cheek, feeling two
days' beard beneath his fingertips. The men who had chalked up his
name, no doubt. There were some in the quarter who would do that and
more, beyond doubt, and even assert that they were acting under his
direction. Not for the first time, it occurred to him that some of them
might be the men who had knelt in Sun Street for his blessing when he
had told Blood he had been enlightened—men so desperate that they
would accept any leader who appeared to have the favor of the gods.

Even himself.

Two Guardsmen in mottled green conflict armor were coming up Dock
Street with slug guns at the ready. They were showing themselves,
clearly, in the hope that the sight of them by day would prevent distur-
bances tonight—would prevent men with clubs and stones, and hangers
like Auk's and a few needlers, from fighting troopers in armor, armed
with slug guns. For a moment Silk considered calling out to them, telling
them that he was Patera Silk, and that he was ready to give himself up if
that would end the fighting. The Ayuntamiento could hardly kill him
without a trial if he surrendered publicly; it would have to try him, and
even if he could not prove his innocence he would have the satisfaction
of declaring it.

The manteion was not yet safe, however. He had promised to save it if he could, and it was in more danger than ever now. Musk had given him how long? A week? Yes, one week from Scylsday. But had Musk really been speaking for Blood as he had claimed, or for himself? Legally, the manteion was Musk's: to give himself up now would be to turn his manteion over to Musk.

Something deep in Silk's being recoiled at the thought. To Blood, perhaps, if it could not be helped. But never, surely never, to someone—to . . . Why, the very possibility had moved the Outsider to enlighten him in order to prevent it. He would kill Musk if—

If there was no other way, and he could bring himself to do it.

He turned away from the window and stretched himself on his bed, recalling Councillor Lemur and the way Lemur had died. As Presiding Officer of the Ayuntamiento, Lemur had been caldé, in fact if not in name; and Crane had killed him. It had been Crane's right to do that, perhaps, since Lemur had intended to execute Crane without a trial.

And yet a trial would have been a mere formality. Crane was a spy and had admitted it—a spy from Palustria. Had Crane then really had the right to kill Lemur? And did that matter?

Belatedly, it struck Silk that the note that Crane had written so hurriedly had almost certainly been a message to the government of his city —to the caldé of Palustria, or whatever they called him. To the prince-president. Crane would have described the Ayuntamiento's underwater boat (Crane had considered it extremely important) and the peculiar teardrop shape that was the cross section of a wing that could fly.

There were steps in the hall outside, and Silk held his breath. Crane had told him to unbar the door only to three quick taps, but it did not matter. The Guard would come, would search this inn and every other inn, beyond question, as soon as the Ayuntamiento chose a new Presiding Officer and that Presiding Officer decided there was a chance that he and Crane (and even poor Mamelta, for the new Presiding Officer could not be sure that Mamelta was dead either) might have survived. Crane had defended the cost of this room in the best inn in Limna by saying that the Guard would be less ready to disturb them if they appeared rich; but spurred by urgent orders from the Ayuntamiento, the Guard would not hesitate to disturb anyone, no matter how rich.

The steps faded away and were gone.

Silk had sat up and pulled off his new red tunic before he fully realized that he had resolved to shave. Rising, he jerked the bellpull vigorously and was rewarded by a distant drumroll on the stairs. Two days' beard might disguise him, but it would also mark him as someone requiring a disguise, and the Outsider could not reasonably object to his shaving, something that he did every day. If he were arrested, well and good. There would be no further rioting and loss of life; and he would be arrested as himself—as Silk, the man others called caldé, and not as some skulking fugitive.

"Soap, towels, and a basin of hot water," he told the deferential maid who answered his ring. "I'm going to get rid of all this right now." She had brought the aroma of the kitchen with her, and one whiff of it woke his hunger. "I'll have a sandwich or something, too. Whatever you can prepare quickly. Maté or tea. Put everything on our bill."

Crane had rung for more towels and fresh shaving water as soon as he bustled in. "I'll bet you thought I'd deserted you," he said as he arranged them on the washstand.

Silk shook his head and, finding the action practically painless, fingered the lump left by Potto's fist. "If you hadn't returned, I'd have known you were under arrest. Do you intend to shave off your beard? I hope you don't mind my borrowing your razor."

"No, not a bit." Crane eyed himself in the luxuriously large mirror. "I think I'd better whack away the best part of it, anyhow."

"Most men in your position would have shaved first and sent their report afterward. Do you think those fishermen who rescued us will tell the Guard, if they're questioned?"

"Uh-huh." Crane slipped out of his tunic.

"Then the Guard will know enough to look for us here, in Limna."

"They'd look here anyhow. This is the most likely spot, if we lived."

"I suppose so. You gave those fishermen a card? A card must be a great deal of money to a fisherman."

"They saved our lives. Besides, the captain will go to Viron to buy something, and his sailors will get drunk. If they're drunk enough, they won't be questioned."

Silk nodded again, knowing that Crane could see him in the mirror. "I can't tell you how surprised I was to find that the driver who had taken me home from Blood's was one of the crew. He's become a fisherman, it seems."

Crane turned to stare at Silk, his face lathered and the razor in his hand. "I keep underestimating you. Every time I do, I tell myself that's the last time." He waited for a reply, then turned back to the mirror. "Thanks for keeping it to yourself until we were alone."

"I thought he seemed familiar, but we were in the harbor before I placed him. He tried to keep his face turned away from me, and it gave me a good view of the back of his head; and that had been what I'd seen, mostly, when he took me to my manteion. I'd been sitting behind him."

Crane dabbed at one sideburn with the razor. "Then you knew."

"I didn't really understand until just now, when I was thinking about what a good spy you are—how valuable you must be to your city."

Crane chuckled. "We're soaping each other's beards, it seems."

"I didn't really understand about the fishing boat until we changed clothes in that alley," Silk told him. "Before that I was simply mystified; but someone aboard that fishing boat, the captain or more plausibly the driver who had taken me home, had given you several cards."

"You saw there was no money belt. I've been kicking myself ever since and hoping you hadn't noticed."

"When Chenille told you about that commissioner . . ."

"Simuliid."

"Yes, Simuliid. When Chenille told you he'd gone to the lake to meet with members of the Ayuntamiento, you came here yourself to investigate. I know you did, because I spoke to a young couple you befriended. If you didn't have somebody here already, you decided then that you should have someone all the time; and you hired the captain and his boat. I'd imagine they were to keep an eye on the Pilgrims' Way. The path runs along the edge of the cliffs in places, and anyone on it could be seen easily from a boat on that part of the lake. I won't inform on him or you now, of course; yet I'm curious. Is the captain Vironese?"

"Yes," Crane told him. "Not that it matters."

"You're not shaving. I didn't intend to interrupt you."

Crane turned to face him again. "I'd rather give you my complete attention. I hope you realize I've been working for you as well as for my city. Working to put you in power because it might head off a war."

"I don't want power," Silk told him, "but it would be iniquitous not to thank you for everything you've done—for saving my life, too, when it would have been safer for you to have left me in the water."

"If you really feel like that, are you willing to formalize our alliance? Viron's Ayuntamiento's going to kill us if it gets hold of us again. I'm a spy, and you've become a major threat to its power. You realize that, don't you?"

Reluctantly, Silk nodded.

"Then we'd better stand back to back, or we'll lie side by side. Tell me everything you know, and I'll tell you anything else you want to know. My word on it. You've got no particular reason to trust it, but it's better than you think. What do you say?"

"It's hardly fair to you, Doctor. The things that I've guessed will be of no particular value to you; but you may have information that will be extremely valuable to me."

"There's more. You do everything you can to see to it that my people and I aren't picked up, and to free us if we are. I promise we'll do nothing to injure your city. You realize, don't you, that you may have to run if you want to keep breathing? If we can't make you caldé, we'll at least give you a place to go. Not because we're overflowing with kindness, but because you'll be a focus for discontent as long as you're alive. You need us now, and you may need us a lot more in a few days."

"You'll answer all my questions openly and honestly?"

"I said so, didn't I? Yes. You've got my word on all of it. We'll put you in power if we can, and you'll keep the peace when we do and not go after us. Now I want your word. Have I got it?"

Slowly, Silk nodded. He extended his hand. Crane laid aside his razor, and he and Silk joined hands.

"Now tell me what you learned about my operation."

"Very little, really. Hyacinth's working for you, of course. Isn't she?"

Crane nodded.

"That's why I'm doing this." Silk had taken his beads from his pocket; he pulled them through his fingers as he spoke. "Turning against my city, I mean. That burst vein in my brain—I don't feel up to arguing with you about it, you see. Not yet, because it might make us enemies again. It wants me to save the manteion, and so I must if I can; but I myself want to save Hyacinth. You must think that's foolish, too."

"I'm trying to save her myself," Crane told him. "And the men on the fishing boat who saved us both from drowning. All of them are my people. I feel responsible for them. By Tartaros, I *am* responsible for them. If it wasn't for that, I'd have told you about the boat when we picked you up. But what if you were caught and talked? Those three men would be killed, and they're mine."

Silk nodded again. "I feel like that about the people who come to sacrifice at our manteion. You would probably say that they're only porters and thieves and washer-women, but they are our manteion, really. The buildings and even our Sacred Window could be replaced, just as I could; they can't." He stood and went to the window.

"As I said, Doctor, I was thinking about how important you were, and how silly I'd been not to realize it earlier. You must be fifty at least."

Crane turned back to the mirror and washed the dried foam from his beard. "Fifty-six."

"Thank you. So you've been a spy for a long time, and you're likely to be of high rank. Besides you're a doctor, and that in itself would make you important to your city's government. They wouldn't just send you off to Blood's by yourself. Hyacinth's Vironese. I know that because I've spoken with someone who knew her when she was younger. But my driver is from your own city, or so I would guess. Was he your second in command?"

"That's right." Crane was lathering his beard for the second time, plying the big boar's-hair brush with sweeping strokes.

"Blood told Musk to have a driver bring a floater around for me; but you had anticipated that, and when you left us you told your second in command to be ready. You'd brought me the azoth, of course, and there was a chance that whoever drove me might see it."

"You're right." Crane scraped a little hair from one cheek. "I also wanted him to get a look at you and become acquainted. I thought it might be useful later. I could say now that it has been."

"I suppose I ought to be flattered." Silk leaned out of the window, peering upward. "The important point, I'd say, is that in order to act as he did—I mean today—your second in command must have known not only that you had been captured, but that you had been taken to the lake. It would even appear that he knew precisely where the Ayuntamiento's underwater boat was when we were swept out of it, since he had your fishing boat so accurately positioned that he and the fishermen were able to pick you up as soon as you came to the surface. You can't have gotten out of the underwater boat much before I did; nor can you have reached the surface much faster. I wasn't in the water very long, yet you were already in the boat when I was rescued, and there had been time for your second in command to pass you some money. He would have been prepared for that, because he would've known that your possessions had been taken from you. Even if he was the person who brought your medical bag to Lemur—"

"He wasn't. He'd left Blood's earlier. In a way that was too bad. He might've been able to slip something useful past them."

"I was about to say that even if he had learned that you were at the lake because he brought your bag, or overheard the order that another driver do it, he had to have had some further means of locating you. I've been trying to imagine what that means might be, and the only things I can think of are that he can send forth his spirit like Mucor, or that you're carrying a very small glass, or at least some device of that kind. You promised to answer my questions. Will you tell me whether I'm correct, and how they failed to find it?"

"Because it's in here." Crane tapped his chest. "Eight years ago I had bypass surgery. We took the opportunity to implant a gadget that sends a half-second signal every two minutes. It tells anyone who's listening how my heart's doing, and the direction of the signal lets them find me. So if you're ever in need of rescue again, just kill me."

He grinned. "While I'm still among the living, can I ask why you're so interested in that window?"

"I've been wondering whether we could get out of here if we had to—if the Guard began breaking down the door, for example. I could reach the edge of the roof and pull myself up, I believe."

"I couldn't. When I was your age I might have." Crane went back to his shaving.

"Can't you fly?"

Crane chuckled. "I wish I could."

"But that's what you reported to the prince-president, isn't it? That shape Lemur showed us? How fliers fly?"

"You're wrong there. I didn't."

Silk turned away from the window. "A secret with so much military value? Why not?"

"I wish I could tell you, I really do. But I can't. It wasn't included in our agreement. I hope you realize that. I swore I'd tell you everything you wanted to know about my organization and our operation. I can tell you what *was* in my report. My report was a part of the operation, I admit."

"Go on."

"But it didn't go to the prince-president of Palustria. Did you really think I'd tell that maniac Lemur the truth? You did, I know. But I'm not you."

"I hope you're not about to say that you're not a spy at all, Doctor."

"No, I'm a spy all right. What do you think of this? Or should I shave it all off?"

"I'd remove it all."

"I was afraid you were going to say that." Reluctantly, Crane pared away another patch of beard. "Aren't you going to ask who I spy for? It's Trivigaunte."

"The women?"

Crane chuckled again. "In Trivigaunte they'd say, 'The *men?*' Viron's

dominated by men, like most other cities. Do you think the Ayuntamiento's got no female spies? It's got all it wants, I guarantee you."

"Naturally our women are loyal."

"Admirable." Crane turned to face Silk, gesturing with his razor. "So
are men in Trivigaunte. We're not slaves. If anything we're better off than
your women are here."

"Is this the truth?"

"Absolutely. The truth, and nothing over."

"Then tell me what was in your report."

"I will," Crane wiped his razor. "It was pretty short. You saw me write
it so you know that already, or you ought to. I reported that the Ayuntamiento was onto me, that I'd been picked up and had killed Councillor
Lemur while making my escape. That they'd brought down a flier but lost
the PM in the lake. That I'd found their headquarters, a boat in Lake
Limna that sails under the water. I claimed the reward our Rani's offered
for that."

Grinning more broadly than ever, Crane continued, "And I'll get it,
too. When I go back to Trivigaunte I'll be a rich man. But I said I wasn't
going to leave yet because I thought there was a good chance that Silk
might unseat the Ayuntamiento. I'd rescued him from them, he had
reason to be grateful to me, and I thought a change in government here
was worth any risk."

"I am grateful to you," Silk said. "Very much so, as I've told you
already. Was that all?"

Crane nodded. "That's the lot, pretty much exactly as I wrote it down.
Now I want you to explain to me how you knew Hyacinth was working
for me. Did she say so?"

"No. I looked at the engraving on this needler." Silk took it from his
pocket. "It has hyacinths all over it, but here on the top there's a tall bird
—a heron, I thought—standing in a pool; when I realized that it could be
a crane instead of a heron, I knew you must have had it engraved for
her." He opened the breech. "I hope that the water hasn't ruined it."

"Let it dry out before you try to shoot. Oil it first, and it should be all
right. But the fact that I presented Hy with a fancy needler can't have
been the only thing that tipped you off. Any old fool with a crush on a
beautiful woman might have given her something like that."

"That's true, of course; but she kept the azoth in the same drawer. Do
you still have it, by the way?"

Crane nodded.

"So it seemed likely that it had been given her by the same person, since she wouldn't want you to see it if you hadn't given it to her. An azoth's worth several thousand cards; thus if you'd given her one, you were clearly more than you seemed. Furthermore, you passed it to me while you were examining me in Blood's presence. I didn't believe the man you were pretending to be would have dared to do that."

Crane chuckled again. "You're so shrewd, I'm beginning to doubt your innocence. Sure you're not of my trade?"

"You're confusing innocence with ignorance, though I'm ignorant in many ways as well. Innocence is something one chooses, and something one chooses for the same reason one chooses any other thing—because it seems best."

"I'll have to think about that. Anyhow, you're wrong about me giving Hy the azoth. Somebody'd searched my room a couple of days before. They didn't find it, but I asked Hy to keep it for me to be on the safe side."

"When you put it in my waistband—"

"I said that there was a goddess up there who liked you, sure. She brought it to me and said we had to figure out a way of getting it to you, because she thought Blood was going to have Musk kill you. When she came in she thought she'd find me patching you up, but I'd finished with you and sent you in to Blood. Musk came to get me while we were talking it over, so I tipped Hy a wink and took the azoth with me, figuring I'd have a chance to slip it to you."

"But she came to you and asked you to do it?"

"That's right," Crane said, "and if that makes you feel good, I don't blame you. When I was your age, it would've had me swinging on the rafters."

"It does. I don't deny it." Silk gnawed his lip. "As a favor—a very great favor—may I see the azoth again, please? Just for a minute or two? I don't intend to harm you with it, or even project the blade, and I'll return it the moment you ask. I just want to look at it again, and hold it."

Crane took the azoth from his waistband and handed it to him.

"Thank you. While I had it, it bothered me that there were no hyacinths on it; but I understand that now. This demon, is it a bloodstone?"

"That's right. It was meant to be a present for Blood. Our Rani gave me a nice bit of money in case it looked like we ought to buy him, and one of our khanums threw in that azoth for an extra goodwill gift. He's got a couple already, but back then we hadn't found that out yet."

"Thank you." Silk revolved the azoth in his hands. "If I'd known that this was yours and not Hyacinth's, I wouldn't have returned with

Mamelta to search those devilish tunnels for it. She and I would not have been overtaken by Lemur's soldiers, and she wouldn't have died."

"If you hadn't gone back, you might have been picked up anyhow," Crane told him. "But Lemur wouldn't have had that azoth, and without it I couldn't have killed him. By this time you and I would both be dead. Your woman friend, too, most likely."

"I suppose so." For what he believed to be the final time, Silk pressed his lips to the gleaming silver hilt. "I feel that it's brought me only bad luck; yet if I hadn't had it, the talus would have killed me." With some reluctance, he handed it back to Crane.

That night, as Silk lay in his rented bed whispering to a strange ceiling, the tunnels involved themselves in all his thoughts, their dim, tangled strands looping underneath everything. Was that lofty chamber in which the sleepers waited in their fragile tubes beneath him now, as he waited for sleep? It seemed entirely possible, since that chamber had not been far from the ash-choked tunnel, and its ashes had fallen from the manteion here in Limna. No doubt his own manteion on Sun Street was above just such a tunnel, as Hammerstone had implied.

How horribly cramped those tunnels had seemed, always about to close in and crush him! The Ayuntamiento hadn't built them—could not have built them. The tunnels were far older, and workmen digging new foundations struck them now and then, and wisely reclosed the holes in tunnel walls that they had made by accident.

But who had made the tunnels, and what had been their purpose? Maytera Marble recalled the Short Sun. Did she remember the tunnels, the digging of the tunnels, and the uses of the tunnels as well?

Their room, which should have been cool, was over-warm—hotter than his bedroom in the manse, which was always too warm, always baking, though both its windows, the Silver Street window and the garden window, stood wide open, their thin white curtains flapping in a hot wind that did nothing to cool the room. All the while Doctor Crane waited outside with Maytera Marble, throwing chips of shiprock from the tunnels through his window to tell him that he must go back for Hyacinth's silver azoth.

Like smoke, he rose and drifted to the window. The dead flier floated there, his last breath bubbling from nose and mouth. Everyone drew a final breath eventually, not knowing it for the last. Was that what the flier had been trying to say?

The door burst open. It was Lemur. Behind him waited the monstrous black, red, and gold face of the fish that had devoured the woman who slept in the glass tube, the tube in which he himself now slept beside Chenille, who was Kypris, who was Hyacinth, who was Mamelta, with Hyacinth's jet-black hair, which the fish had and would devour, snap, snap, snap, snapping monstrous jaws. . . .

Silk sat up. The room was wide and dark and silent, its warm, humid air retaining the memory of the sound that had awakened him. Crane stirred in the other bed.

It came again, a faint tapping, a knock like the rapid ticking of the little clock in his room in the manse.

"The Guard." Silk could not have explained how he knew.

Crane muttered, "Probably just a maid wanting to change the beds."

"It's still dark. The middle of the night." Silk swung his legs to the floor.

The tapping resumed.

An armored Guardsman with a slug gun stood in the middle of Dock Street, scarcely visible in the cloud-dimmed sunlight. He waved as he caught sight of Silk at the window, then came to attention and saluted.

"It is the Guard," Silk said. By an effort of will, he kept his tone conversational. "I'm afraid they have us."

Crane sat up. "That's not a Guardsman's knock."

"There's one outside, watching our window." Silk slid back the bolt and swung the door wide. A uniformed captain of the Civil Guard saluted, the click of polished boot heels as sharp as the snap of the great fish's jaws. Behind the captain, another armored trooper saluted like the first, his flattened hand across the barrel of his slug gun.

"May every god favor you," Silk said, not knowing what else to say. He stood aside. "Would you like to come in?"

"Thank you, My Caldé."

Silk blinked.

They stepped over the threshold, the captain negligently elegant in his tailored uniform, the trooper immaculate in waxed green armor.

Crane yawned. "You haven't come to arrest us?"

"No, no!" the captain said. "By no means. I've come to warn you—to warn our caldé particularly—that there are others who *will* arrest him. Others who are searching for him even as we speak. I take it that you are Doctor Crane, sir? There are warrants for you both. You stand in urgent need of protection, and I have arrived. I am sorry to have disturbed your sleep, but delighted that I found you before the others did."

Silk said slowly, "This is happening because of an ill-considered remark of Councillor Lemur's, I believe."

"I know nothing of that, My Caldé."

"Some god overheard him—I believe I can guess which. What time is it, Captain?"

"Three forty-five, My Caldé."

"Too early to start back to the city, then. Sit—no, first bring the trooper who's watching our window inside. Then I want you to sit down, all three of you, and tell us what's been happening in Viron."

"It might be better to leave him where he is, My Caldé, if we wish the others to believe I am arresting you."

"And now you've made the arrest." Silk picked up his trousers and sat on the bed to put them on. "Doctor Crane and I have been subdued and disarmed, so the man outside is no longer needed. Bring him in."

The captain motioned to the trooper, who strode to the window and gestured; the captain himself took a chair.

Silk slapped Crane's wrapping against the bedpost. "You addressed me as caldé. Why did you do that?"

"Everyone knows, My Caldé, that there is supposed to be a caldé. The Charter, written by Our Patroness and Lord Pas himself, says so plainly —yet there has been no caldé in twenty years."

Crane said, "But everything's gone along pretty well, hasn't it? The city's quiet?"

The captain shook his head. "Not really, Doctor." He glanced toward his trooper, then shrugged. "There was more rioting last night, and houses and shops were burned. An entire brigade was scarcely enough to defend the Palatine. Unbelievable! It gets a little worse each year. The heat has made things very bad this year, and the high prices in the market . . ." He shrugged again. "If the Ayuntamiento had asked my opinion, I would have advised buying up staples—corn and beans, the foods of the poor—and reselling them below cost. They did not ask, and I shall write my opinion in their blood."

Unexpectedly, the trooper said, "A goddess spoke to us, Caldé."

The captain smoothed his thin mustache. "That is so, My Caldé. We were signally honored yesterday at your manteion, where now the gods speak again."

Silk wound the wrapping about his ankle. "One of you understood her?"

"We all did, My Caldé. Not in the way that I understand you, and not in the way that you yourself would beyond doubt have understood her.

Yet she told us plainly that what we had been ordered to do was blasphemy, that you are accounted sacred. By the favor of the goddess, your acolyte returned as she spoke. He can relate her message in her own words. The substance was that the immortal gods are displeased with our unhappy city, that they have chosen you to be our caldé, and that all who resist you must perish. My own men—"

As if on cue, there was a knock at the door; the trooper opened it to admit his comrade.

"These men," the captain continued, "were ready to kill me if I insisted we carry out our orders, My Caldé. I had no intention of doing so, however, you may be sure."

Silk received this in silence. When the captain had finished speaking, Silk pulled on his red tunic.

The trooper who had just come in glanced at his captain; he nodded, and the trooper said, "Everybody can see there's something wrong. Pas is holding back the rain, and there's all this heat. One crop after another's failing. My father had a good big pond, but we pumped it dry to water the corn. Now it's stayed dry all summer, and he was lucky to get ten quintals."

The captain cocked his head toward the trooper who had spoken as if to say *you see the difficulties with which I must deal.* "There is talk of digging canals from the lake, My Caldé, but it will take years. Meanwhile the skies are locked against us, and every manteion in the city is silent except yours. Long before the goddess spoke, it was clear that the gods are displeased with us. Many of us feel that it is equally obvious why. Are you aware, My Caldé, that people all over the city have been chalking 'Silk for Caldé' on walls?"

Silk nodded.

"Tonight my men and I have been doing a bit of chalking of our own. We write, 'Silk *is* Caldé.' "

Crane chuckled dryly. "They mean the same thing, don't they, Captain? 'Silk will be killed if caught.' "

"Let us be grateful that it has not occurred, Doctor."

"I'm grateful, I can tell you that." Crane threw aside his sweat-soaked sheet. "But gratitude won't get the caldé into the Juzgado. Can you suggest a place where we could hide until that's attended to?"

"I'm not going to hide," Silk told him. "I'm going back to my manteion."

Crane's eyebrow went up, and the captain stared.

"In the first place, because I want to consult the gods. In the second, because I have to tell everyone that we must overthrow the Ayuntamiento by peaceful means, if we can."

The captain stood up. "But you agree that it must be overthrown, don't you, My Caldé? Peacefully if it can be done peacefully, but by force if force is required?"

Silk hesitated.

"Remember Iolar," Crane muttered.

"All right," Silk said at last. "New councillors must replace those presently in the Ayuntamiento, but it's to be accomplished without bloodshed if possible. You three have indicated that you're ready to fight for me. Are you ready to accompany me to my manteion as well? If someone comes to arrest me, you can tell them I'm under arrest already, just as you were going to do here. You might say you returned me to my manteion so I could collect my belongings. A courtesy like that, extended to an augur, wouldn't be out of place, would it?"

"It will be very dangerous, My Caldé," the captain said grimly.

"Anything we do will be dangerous, Captain. What about you, Doctor?"

"Here I shaved my beard, and you're going to go back to the quarter where everybody knows you."

"You can begin on a new one today."

"Then how could I refuse?" Crane grinned. "There's no way to get rid of me, Caldé. You couldn't scrape me off of your shoes."

"I was hoping you'd say something like that. Captain, have you been searching for me all night? That's what it sounded like."

"Since the goddess favored us, My Caldé. First in the city, then here because your acolyte said you'd gone here."

"Then all three of you ought to have something to eat before we leave, and so should Doctor Crane and I. Could you send one of your troopers down to wake up the innkeeper? Tell him we'll pay for everything, but we must eat and go as soon as possible."

A look sent one of the troopers hurrying out.

Crane asked, "Do you have a floater?"

The captain's face fell. "Only horses. One must be a colonel at least to authorize a floater. My Caldé, it might be possible to commandeer a floater for you here. I will make the attempt."

Silk said, "Don't be ridiculous. A floater for your prisoner! I'll walk in front of your horse with my hands tied. Isn't that how you do it?"

Reluctantly, the captain nodded. "However—"

Crane sputtered, "He's lame! You must've noticed it. He has a broken
ankle. He can't possibly walk from here to Viron."

"There is a Guard post here, My Caldé. I could procure an additional
horse there, perhaps."

Recalling his ride to Blood's villa with Auk, Silk said, "Donkeys. It
must be possible to rent donkeys here, and I can have Horn or one of the
other boys bring them back. An augur and a man of the doctor's age
might be permitted to ride donkeys, I'd think."

The first gray light of shadeup had filled the streets of Limna before they
were ready to leave. Silk was still murmuring the morning prayer to High
Hierax as he mounted the young white donkey one of the troopers held
for him, and put his hands behind his back for the other to tie.

"I'll make this real loose, Caldé," the trooper told him apologetically.
"Loose enough so it won't hurt, and you can shake it off whenever you
want to."

Silk nodded without interrupting his prayer. It seemed strange to pray
now in a red tunic, though he had frequently prayed in colored clothes
before he entered the schola. He would change at the manse, he told
himself; he would put on a clean tunic and his best robe. He was a poor
speaker (in his own estimation), and people would make fun of him if he
wasn't habited like an augur.

There would have to be a lot of people, too. As many as he and the
three sibyls—and, yes, of course, the students from the palaestra—could
get together. When he spoke . . . In the manteion or outside? When he
spoke, he—

The captain had mounted his prancing charger. "If you are ready, My
Caldé?"

Silk nodded. "It's occurred to me that you might easily turn this pretended arrest into a real one, Captain. If you do, you'll have nothing to
fear from me—or from the gods, I believe."

"Hierax have my bones if I intend any such treachery, My Caldé. You
may take the reins whenever you wish."

Though Silk could not recall kicking it, his donkey was ambling forward. After a moment's reflection, he concluded that the trooper who
had tied his hands had probably prodded it from behind.

Crane was studying the black cloud banks rolling across the lake. "Going to be a dark day." He urged his donkey forward to keep up with
Silk's. "The first one in quite a while. At least we won't have to fry on
these things in the sun."

Silk asked how long he thought the ride would take.

"On these? Four hours, minimum. Don't donkeys ever run?"

"I saw one run across a meadow when I was a boy," Silk said. "Of course it had no man on its back."

"That fellow just finished tying my hands, and my nose itches already."

They trotted up Shore Street, past the Juzgado in which the helpful woman who had admired Oreb had mentioned Scylla's shrine and the Pilgrims' Way, past Advocate Vulpes's gaudy signboard with its scarlet fox. Vulpes would wonder why he had not given the captain his card, Silk thought—assuming that Vulpes saw him and recognized him in his new clothes. Vulpes would protest that criminals arrested in Limna should not be returned to the city to deprive them of his services.

Vulpes's card had been lost with so many other things when he had been searched—with his keys to the manteion, now that he came to think of them. Possibly Lemur, who had gotten Hyacinth's needler, the azoth, and his gammadion and beads from Councillor Potto, had taken Vulpes's card as well, though it would do Lemur no good in the court to which he had gone. . . .

Silk looked up, and Limna had vanished behind them. The road wound among low, sandy hills that must have been islets and shallows even when the lake was much larger. He turned in his saddle for a final glimpse of the village, but behind the captain and the two troopers on their horses saw only the steely blue waters of the lake.

"This must be about the time Chenille used to arrive as a child," he told Crane. "She used to look for the water at shadeup. Did she ever tell you about it?"

"That would have been earlier than this."

A falling drop of water darkened the hair of the white donkey's neck; another splashed Silk's own rather less tidy hair, wet but astonishingly warm.

"Good thing this didn't come a little earlier," Crane said, "not that I like it anytime."

Silk heard the rattle of shots an instant after he saw Crane stiffen. Behind him, the captain shouted, "Get down!" and something else, words drowned by the boom of a trooper's slug gun.

The rope about Silk's wrists, which had been about to fall off a moment before, seemed to tighten as soon as he tried to free his hands from it.

"Caldé! Get down!"

He dove from the saddle into the dust of the road. By a seeming miracle, one hand was free. The roar of a floater was followed by a longer coarse, dry rattle, the sound of an immense child hurrying a lath along the bars of a cage.

He scrambled to his feet. Crane's hands were free, too; he put them about Silk's neck as Silk helped him off his donkey. More shots. The captain's charger screamed—a horrible sound—reared and plunged into them, knocking them both into the ditch.

"My left lung," Crane muttered. Blood trickled from his mouth.

"All right." Silk pushed up Crane's tunic and tore it in a single motion. "Azoth."

The booms of slug guns were followed by the greater boom of thunder, as if the gods were firing and dying too. Pale drops the size of pigeons' eggs splattered the dust.

"I'm going to bandage you," Silk said. "I don't think it's fatal. You're going to be all right."

"No good." Crane spat blood. And then, "Pretend you're my father." A torrent of rain engulfed them like a wave.

"I *am* your father, Doctor." Silk pushed a wadded rag into the hot and pulsing cavity that was Crane's wound and tore a long strip from Crane's tunic to hold it in place.

"Caldé. Take the azoth." Crane put it into his hands, and died.

"All right."

Bent above him, the useless strip of rag in his hands, Silk watched him go, saw the shudder that convulsed him and the upward rolling of his eyes, felt the final stiffening of his limbs and the relaxation that followed, and knew that life had gone, that the great and invisible vulture that was Hierax at such moments had swooped through the driving rain to seize Crane's spirit and tear it free from Crane's body—that he himself, kneeling in the mud, knelt in the divine substance of the unseen god. As he watched, Crane's wound ceased to throb with blood; in a second or two, the rain had washed it white.

He put Crane's azoth into his own waistband and took out his beads. "I convey to you, Doctor Crane, the forgiveness of all the gods. Recall now the words of Pas, who said, 'Do my will, live in peace, multiply, and do not disturb my seal. Thus you shall escape my wrath.'"

Yet Pas's seal had been disturbed many times; he himself had scraped up the remains of one such seal. Embryos, mere flecks of rotten flesh, had lain among the remains of another. Was Pas's seal to be valued more than the things it had been intended to protect? (Thunder crashed.) Pas's wrath had been loosed upon the whorl.

" 'Go willingly,' " (Where?) " 'and any wrong that you have ever done shall be forgiven.' "

The floater was nearer, the roar of its blowers audible above the roaring of the storm.

"O Doctor Crane, my son, know that this Pas and all the lesser gods have empowered me to forgive you in their names. And I do forgive you, remitting every crime and wrong. They are expunged." Streaming water, Silk's beads traced the sign of subtraction. "You are blessed."

There was no more shooting. Presumably the captain and both troopers were dead. Would the Guard let him bring them the Pardon of Pas before he was taken away?

"I pray you to forgive us, the living." Silk spoke as quickly as he could, racing words his teachers at the schola would never have approved. "I and many another have wronged you often, Doctor, committing terrible crimes against you. Do not hold them in your heart, but begin the life that follows life in all innocence, all these wrongs forgiven."

A slug gun boomed three times in rapid succession, very near. The buzz gun rattled again, and mud erupted a hand's breadth from Crane's head.

The effectual point: "In the name of all the gods you are forgiven forever, Doctor Crane. I speak here for Great Pas—" So many in the Nine, each with an honorific. Silk was seized by the feeling that none of them really mattered, not even Hierax, though Hierax was surely present. "And for the Outsider and all lesser gods."

He stood.

A muddy figure crouching behind a dead horse shouted, "Run, My Caldé! Save yourself!" then turned to fire again at the Guard floater bearing down on them.

Silk raised his hands, the rope that had not bound him still dangling from one wrist. "I surrender!" The azoth in his waistband seemed a lump of lead. He limped forward as fast as he could, slipping and sliding in the mud while rain pelted his face. "I'm Caldé Silk!" Lightning flared across the sky, and for an instant the advancing floater seemed a talus with tusks and staring, painted eyes. "If you have to shoot someone, shoot me!"

The mud-smeared figure dropped its slug gun and raised its hands as well.

The floater halted, the air blasting from its blowers raising a secondary rain of muddy water.

"They fired upon us from ambush, My Caldé." As though by a trick, the muddy figure spoke with the captain's voice. "We die for you and for Viron."

A hatch below the turret opened, and an officer whose uniform was instantly soaked with rain vaulted out.

"I know," Silk said. "I'll never forget you." He tried to recall the captain's name, but if he had ever heard it, it was gone, like the name of the trooper with the long, serious brown face, the one whose father's pond had gone dry.

The officer strode toward them, halted, and drew his sword with a flourish. Heels together and head erect, he saluted with it as though upon the drill field, holding it vertically before his face. "Caldé! Thank Hierax and all the gods that I was able to rescue you!"

APPENDIX

APPENDIX

GODS, PERSONS, AND ANIMALS MENTIONED IN THE TEXT

N.B. In Viron, biochemical males are named for animals or animal products: Auk, Blood, Crane, Musk and Silk bear names of this type. Biochemical females are named for plants (most frequently flowers) or plant products: Chenille, Mint, Orchid, Rose. Chemical persons, both male and female, are named for metals or minerals: Hammerstone, Marble, Sand Schist.

Aquila, a young eagle being trained by Musk.

Arolla, a woman who has left Orchid's.

Auk, a housebreaker, a friend of Silk's, devoted to Mint, a large and powerful man with a heavy jaw and prominent ears. Called "Hackum" by Chenille

Bass, the bully who maintains order at Orchid's.

Bellfower, on of the women at Orchid's.

Maytera *Betel*, once one of the sibyls at the manteion on Sun Street, now deceased.

Bittersweet, a member of the Incus's circle of black mechanics.

Blood, a crime lord, the de facto owner of Silk's manteion and Orchid's yellow house. Tall, heavy, balding, and red-faced; about fifty-five.

Chenille, one of the women at Orchids. She is probably nineteen, is tall and athletic, and has dyed her hair the fiery shade of her name-flower. Called "Jugs" by Auk.

Chervil, a young middle-class woman from Viron, wife of Coypu.

Coypu, a young middle-class man from Viron, husband of Chervil.

Chiquito, a parrot once owned by Mamelta's parents.

Doctor *Crane*, Blood's private physician, a small, fussy man with an iron-gray beard.

Dreoilin, Iolar's favorite daughter.

Echidna, a major goddess, consort of Pas, mother of the gods, and chief goddess of fertility. Particularly associated with snakes, mice, and other crawling creatures.

Feather, a small boy at Silk's palaestra.

Fulmar, a member of Incus's circle of black mechanics.

Councillor *Galago*, a member of the Ayuntamiento and its expert on diplomacy and foreign affairs.

Gib, the big man who maintains order in the Cock. A friend of Auk's.

Patera *Gulo*, a young augur.

Corporal *Hammerstone*, a soldier in Viron's army.

Hare, Musk's assistant.

Hierax, a major god, the god of death, and patron of the fourth day of the week. Particularly associated with carrion birds, jackals, and (like Tartaros) with black animals of every kind.

Hoppy, a derogatory name for a Guardsman.

Horn, the leader of the older boys at Silk's palaestra.

Hyacinth, a beautiful courtesan controlled by Blood.

Patera *Incus*, Remora's prothonotary, a small, sly man with buck teeth. His hobby is black mechanics.

Iolar, a Flier.

Kalan, a thief killed by Auk.

Kit, a small boy who attends Silk's palaestra.

Kypris, a minor goddess, the goddess of love. Particularly associated with rabbits and doves.

Councillor *Lemur*, the Secretary of the Ayuntamiento and thus the de facto ruler of Viron.

Councillor *Loris*, a member of the Ayuntamiento, its presiding officer in Lemur's absence.

Mamelta, a sleeper wakened by Mucor and freed by Silk.

Maytera *Marble*, now a sibyl at Silk's manteion, junior to Rose but senior to Mint; she is over three hundred years old, and nearly worn out.

Marrow, a greengrocer.

Maytera *Mint,* the junior sibyl at Silk's manteion.

Molpe, a major goddess, the goddess of music, dancing, and art, of the winds and of all light things, patroness of the second day of the week. She is particularly associated with songbirds and butterflies.

Mucor, Blood's adopted daughter; she is about fifteen, capable of asomatous travel, and something akin to a devil.

Musk, Blood's steward and lover.

Nettle, Horn's sweetheart.

Olive, a sleeper.

Colonel *Oosik,* the commander of the Third Brigade of the Civil Guard of Viron.

Orchid, madame of the yellow house on Lamp Street. Orpine's mother.

Oreb, Silk's pet night chough, a large black bird with scarlet legs and a crimson beak.

Orpine, Orchid's daughter, stabbed by Chenille.

The *Outsider,* the minor god who enlightened Silk.

Pas, the father of the gods and ruler of the Whorl, which he built. The god of sun and rain, of mechanisms and much else, pictured with two heads. He is particularly associated with cattle and birds of prey.

Phaea, a major goddesss, the goddess of food and healing and patroness of the sixth day of the week. She is particularly associated with swine.

Patera *Pike,* an augur, Silk's predecessor at the manteion on Sun Street, now deceased.

Poppy, one of the women at Orchid's, small, dark, and pretty.

Councillor *Potto,* a member of the Ayuntamiento and its expert on law enforcement and espionage, round-faced and deceptively cheerful-looking.

Patera *Quetzal,* the Prolocutor of Viron and as such the head of the Chapter. Addressed as "Your Cognizance."

Patera *Remora,* coadjutor to Quetzal. Tall and thin, with a sallow face and lank black hair. Addressed as "Your Eminence."

Maytera *Rose,* the senior sibyl at Silk's manteion, largely a collection of prosthetic parts. Over ninety.

Sargeant *Sand,* a soldier in the army of Viron.

Private *Schist,* a soldier in the army of Viron.

Scleroderma, the butcher's wife. She sells meat scraps as food for pets and is sometimes called "the cats' meat woman." Short and very fat.

Scylla, a major goddess of lakes and rivers, and the patroness of the first day of the week and of Silk's native city of Viron; particularly associated with horses, camels, and fish; pictured with eight, ten or twelve arms.

Patera *Silk*, augur of the old manteion on Sun Street; he is twenty-three, tall and slender, with disorderly yellow hair.

Commissioner *Simuliid*, a key bureaucrat in the government of Viron, tall and very fat, with a thick black mustache.

***Sphigx*,** a major goddess, the goddess of war and courage, and the patroness of the seventh day of the week; particularly associated with lions and other felines.

Councillor *Tarsier*, a member of the Ayuntamiento and its expert on architecture and engineering.

***Tartaros*,** a major god, the god of night, crime, and commerce, and the patron of the third day of the week; particularly associated with owls, bats and moles, and (like Hierax) with black animals of every kind.

***Teasel*,** a girl at Silk's palaestra.

***Thelxiepeia*,** a major goddess, the goddess of magic, mysticism, and poisons, and the patroness of the fifth day of the week; particularly associated with poultry, deer, apes, and monkeys.

***Villus*,** a small boy at Silk's palaestra.

***Vulpes*,** an advocate of Limna.